1979
THE COMPLETE HANDBOOK OF
BASEBALL

More SIGNET Sports Books

1979
THE COMPLETE HANDBOOK OF
BASEBALL

EDITED BY ZANDER HOLLANDER

A SIGNET BOOK
NEW AMERICAN LIBRARY
TIMES MIRROR

ACKNOWLEDGMENTS

Is it possible that Pete Rose and Reuven Katz, his lawyer, haven't made arrangements for national theater and/or TV distribution of their historic 25-minute film? That's the one tracing Pete's career, shown to club owners during the Pete Rose Sweepstakes in December. It could be a candidate in the short subject category for an Oscar or an Emmy, as indeed Reuven Katz should be named Lawyer-Agent of the Year for his role in producing the richest player contract in history.

For achieving the fattest (384 pages) and fullest COMPLETE HANDBOOK OF BASEBALL in its nine-year history, we thank our bylined writers and associate editor Jim Poris, Eric Compton, Frank Kelly, Lee Stowbridge, Richie Sherwin, Susan Sherwin, Phyllis Hollander, Curt Nichols, Ray Wall, White Cloud, Dot Gordineer and Beri Greenwald of Libra Graphics, Seymour Siwoff, Bob Wirz, Bob Fishel, Blake Cullen, Katy Feeney and the publicity directors of the 26 major league teams.

Zander Hollander

PHOTO CREDITS: Cover—Rich Pilling; back cover—Rich Pilling. Inside photos—Nancy Hogue, Steve Jenner, Mitchell Reibel, Malcolm Emmons, George Gojkovich, Ronald Modra, ABC-TV and UPI.

SIGNET TRADEMARK REG. U.S. PAT. OFF. AND FOREIGN COUNTRIES
REGISTERED TRADEMARK—MARCA REGISTRADA
HECHO EN CHICAGO, U.S.A.

SIGNET, SIGNET CLASSICS, MENTOR, PLUME and MERIDIAN BOOKS
are published by The New American Library Inc. 1301 Avenue of the
Americas, New York, New York 10019

First Printing, March, 1979

1 2 3 4 5 6 7 8 9

PRINTED IN THE UNITED STATES OF AMERICA

CONTENTS

Editor's Note: The material herein includes trades and rosters up to final printing deadline.

RON GUIDRY
VS.
SANDY KOUFAX

By PHIL PEPE

Comparisons are inevitable in sports and so they abound, each generation begging a comparison with its predecessor.

Was Rube Marquard as good as Rube Waddell? Was Herb Pennock as good as Marquard? Was Lefty Grove as good as

Ragin' Cajun won his Cy Young with Louisiana lightning.

Sandy Koufax pitched four no-hit games for the Dodgers.

Pennock? Was Warren Spahn as good as Grove? Was Sandy Koufax as good as Spahn?

Is Ron Guidry as good as Koufax?

Somehow, the heroes of our time always seem bigger than life, their accomplishments more remarkable as the years pass, and the thought of anyone coming along to warrant comparison with them threatens not only the memory, but our own monument to ourselves.

Ron Guidry as good as Sandy Koufax?

Ridiculous, we say.

"Not yet," says Maury Wills, who played with Koufax and watches Guidry as a television commentator for NBC. "Maybe after another year like his last one you can begin to put him in a class with Koufax. Not now. Guidry is a super pitcher, a special kind of person, and the mere fact that we can stand here and discuss the possibility that he is as good as Koufax tells you how special he is."

Like Ron Guidry and Sandy Koufax, Phil Pepe has a Lafayette connection. He attended Lafayette High School in Brooklyn, Sandy's school. Phil, however, is a right-hander for the New York Daily News.

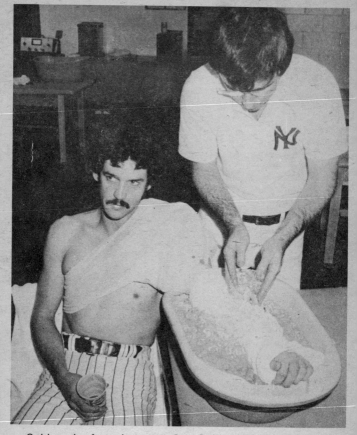

Cold packs for a hot arm: Can Guidry keep up the pace?

Even Paul Blair, who hit against Koufax and played behind Guidry, is unwilling to make the comparison just yet.

"Let Ron have a few more good years, then you can compare him with Koufax," says Blair, as astute a judge of baseball players as there is in the game. "I think Guidry will have those good years. He has become a pitcher, not just a thrower. He's a student of the game, who listens and learns. He proved that last season when he was able to win even when he didn't have his good fastball. But until he has a few more good years, it's too soon to make comparisons."

Arthritis cut short Sandy's brilliant career.

Is it, really? Does Ron Guidry suffer by such comparisons?

If you hold them under a microscope, the similarities between Guidry and Koufax are many, the differences between them very slight. Because they are so few, take the differences first.

Basically, the differences are accidents of birth, background and physical size. Sandy Koufax was a city kid off the streets of New York; Guidry a country boy, out of Louisiana Cajun Country.

Koufax was a strapping 6-2 and 210 pounds, accounting for his ability to start 40 or more games in three of his last four seasons, missing the fourth because of injury. Guidry, a skinny 5-11, 152 pounds, must conserve his energy by pitching every fifth day instead of every fourth. Consequently, his 35 starts in 1978 are as many as he can ever expect to make.

The similarities between the two, however, are so many and so close as to be startling. For example:

Both are, of course, left-handed power pitchers.

Neither pitched in high school, but earned reputations in other sports.

Both had one year of college.

Both floundered for six years before attaining major league success.

Both entertained thoughts of quitting the game.

Both had their super year at age 27.

And both came out of Lafayette—Guidry from Lafayette, La.; Koufax from Lafayette High School in Brooklyn.

At Lafayette High, Koufax was renowned as a basketball player. He played on the baseball team as a light-hitting first baseman, but it wasn't until the summer after his senior year that he began pitching in sandlot games and his powerful arm attracted major league scouts. He accepted a basketball scholarship to the University of Cincinnati, where he stayed one year, then signed a bonus contract with the Brooklyn Dodgers.

At Northside High in Lafayette, La., Guidry was a 9.7 sprinter. He played no baseball simply because Northside had no baseball team. But in American Legion ball, he pitched well enough to be given a scholarship to the University of Southwestern Louisiana, where he enjoyed only moderate success, but attracted the eye of Yankee scout, Atley Donald. On Donald's recommendation, the Yankees selected him on the third round of the June, 1971, free agent draft, the 65th selection in the nation.

Most pitchers mature late. Those who have success at a young age frequently burn out at a young age. The great ones often don't mature into successful pitchers until their late 20s.

Warren Spahn spent his early years in military service and did not win a major league game until he was 25.

Bob Lemon spent his early years as an outfielder-third baseman and did not win his first major league game until he was 26.

Ron Guidry spent his early years in the minor leagues and did not win his first major league game until he was 26.

Sandy Koufax spent his early years ruminating on the Dodger bench, his talent wasting away. He would have profited from spending those years in the minor leagues, but a major league rule in effect at the time decreed that any player signed for a bonus of at least $25,000 must spend at least two years on the major league roster.

It was a device aimed at preventing wealthy clubs from cornering the market on young talent. Instead, it retarded the progress of a lot of young talent. Koufax was almost one of them.

Used sparingly, he pitched in only 28 games those first two seasons, winning four and losing six. He had a strong arm, but was frustrated by his inability to throw strikes. In spring training, a Dodger coach would take Koufax behind a building, out of the sight of spectators, in an effort to help Sandy discover the general vicinity of the strike zone.

Koufax became so discouraged, he thought about quitting baseball and finding another career.

Guidry's frustration was over the Yankees' refusal to give him the opportunity to pitch in New York. He had risen up the team's farm system with moderate success. By the spring of 1976, after five minor league seasons, he felt he was ready to pitch in the big leagues. The Yankees had other ideas and returned him to Syracuse of the International League.

Guidry's reaction was a simple protestation: "Hell, no, I won't go."

"They said you're not pitching enough, you have to go down," Guidry recalls. "They don't pitch me for 45 days, then

Cy Young Award came as no surprise to Ronnie and Bonnie.

Guidry and the Hall-of-Famers

There are only 11 left-handed pitchers enshrined in the Baseball Hall of Fame in Cooperstown, N.Y. Taking the best year of their careers, here is how Ron Guidry's phenomenal 1978 season stacks up against each of the Hall of Famers:

	Year	Age	W-L	Pct.	ERA	GS	CG	IP	H	BB	SO	SHO
Whitey Ford	1961	32	25-4	.862	3.21	39	11	283	242	92	209	3
Lefty Gomez	1934	24	26-5	.839	2.33	33	25	281	223	96	158	6
Lefty Grove	1931	31	31-4	.886	2.06	30	27	288	249	62	175	3
Carl Hubbell	1936	33	26-6	.813	2.31	34	25	304	265	57	123	3
Sandy Koufax	1963	27	25-5	.833	1.88	40	20	311	214	58	306	11
Rube Marquard	1911	21	25-7	.781	2.50	33	22	277	221	106	237	5
Herb Pennock	1926	32	23-11	.676	3.62	33	19	266	294	43	78	1
Ed Plank	1912	36	25-6	.806	2.22	30	24	259	234	83	110	3
Eppa Rixey	1922	31	25-13	.658	3.53	38	26	313	337	45	80	2
Warren Spahn	1953	32	23-7	.767	2.10	32	24	265	211	70	148	5
Rube Waddell	1902	25	25-7	.781	2.05	27	26	251	249	75	172	0
Ron Guidry	1978	27	25-3	.893	1.74	35	16	273	187	72	248	9

they say I'm not pitching enough. I got fed up. I decided that was it, I had had it. I packed all my stuff in the car and was on Route 80, heading south, going home."

It was here that a cooler head—and a prettier one—prevailed.

"Do you really want to quit?" asked Bonnie Guidry, Ron's wife. "You know you won't be happy not playing ball. Don't do something you'll regret the rest of your life."

"Okay," said Ron. "If you don't mind going back to Syracuse, it's all right with me. I'll give it one more try."

His "one more try" in Syracuse produced sensational statistics, and the realization that he was a certain future star. But even that did not happen immediately. Ron barely made the Yankee pitching staff in 1977 and spent the early part of the season mostly sitting, pitching in games that were long gone.

But a series of injuries to Yankee pitchers gave Guidry his chance. And when opportunity knocked, Guidry answered its call. Once he got into the starting rotation, there was no removing him. He became the Yankees' most reliable pitcher, finishing with a 16-7 record and a 2.82 earned run average. He won 10 of his last 12 decisions and followed that by winning one game each in the American League playoffs and World Series.

All that waiting had paid off for Ron Guidry, just as it had for Sandy Koufax.

While Guidry had done his waiting in minor league towns, Koufax did his on the Dodger bench. For six seasons, Guidry ate in the greasy spoons and rode the bumpy buses of the minor leagues. For six seasons, Koufax was a struggling young pitcher with a 36-40 record.

In his seventh season, Guidry had a 16-7 record.

In his seventh season, Koufax posted a respectable 18-13 mark, leading the National League in strikeouts with 269.

Then, in their eighth years, both at age 27, Guidry and Koufax each had their super season, Koufax in 1963, Guidry in 1978.

Koufax led the National League in wins (25), ERA (1.88), strikeouts (306) and shutouts (11).

Guidry led the American League in wins (25), winning percentage (.893), ERA (1.74) and shutouts (9).

And that's not all:

His winning percentage was the highest in major league history for pitchers winning 20 games or more.

His ERA is the second lowest in AL history to Dutch Leonard's 1.01 in 1914.

He set a Yankee team record with 248 strikeouts, breaking

continued on page 378

David Hartman takes his cuts in spring training.

DAVID HARTMAN'S LOVE AFFAIR WITH BASEBALL

By PHIL PEPE

It is just a few minutes past 10 in the morning, a time when most people are drinking their second cup of coffee, hoping it will stimulate them and help them get through the early hours of a long work day.

But not David Hartman. At a few minutes past 10 in the morning, David Hartman is in the middle of his day, sitting at his desk, lunching on a grilled cheese sandwich and a can of diet soda.

David Hartman has been up for hours. He has awakened millions with a cheery "Good Morning, America." He has informed them, entertained them, charmed them with his warm smile and pleasant demeanor, made sure they have not missed their buses and commuter trains and sent them off to work.

Now he is in his office where he only has time for a hurried lunch while catching up with his correspondence and giving a quick interview before it is time to prepare for the next day's show. The office is small, but neatly crowded, the walls adorned with photographic mementoes that are a pictorial description of his career and his interests.

There are several pictures of baseball players, in action and posed, and Hartman lifts himself out of the chair behind his desk, stretches to his full six feet, five inches, removes one of the framed pictures from the wall and offers it proudly.

The picture shows two players, clearly outfielders, in the uniform of the San Francisco Giants. Their bodies have become entangled after a collision with a cyclone fence.

"That's Willie Mays and Bobby Bonds," David Hartman says. "It was opening day, either 1972 or 1973, one of the greatest catches I've ever seen. Buck caught the ball." He uses the nickname ballplayers call Mays. He says it unpretentiously, like one who has an intimate relationship with one of the game's greatest players.

Captain of Mt. Hermon nine in Massachusetts.

"After the game, I congratulated him on the catch," Hartman recalled. "Then, when the photographer who took this shot gave a copy to Mays, he turned it over to me and I got him and Bobby to sign it for me."

Hartman takes the picture back, handling it carefully as if it is some rare gem, and delicately places it back on the wall.

Baseball has been one of David Hartman's great loves for as long as he can remember, back to his boyhood days in suburban New York. His acting career took him away from New York for years, but he returned to host ABC's eye-opening morning show, "Good Morning, America," and his return brought back many pleasant memories.

"Different times of the year conjure up different boyhood memories," he said. "For instance, in the spring, when the snow begins to melt, that reminds me of a similar time of year when I was a kid. As soon as the snow melted and there were patches of brown grass showing through, soggy and wet, I remember thinking, 'It's OK to get my glove and go out and begin playing baseball.' "

His romance with baseball, Hartman says, goes back to "when I was a tiny kid, maybe two or three. I have a brother, three years older, and he used to get me out to play catch. One day, he threw a ball to me and I didn't catch it, so he whacked me on the head with a bat and I wound up with a concussion. Learning to play baseball was not a matter of love, it was a matter of survival."

There were frequent visits to the Polo Grounds, thanks to a father who indulged his passion, and there were also visits to Ebbets Field, although David was a Giant fan, his brother a St. Louis Cardinal fan.

"One day we went to Ebbets Field to see the Cardinals play," he recalled. "I remember we got off the subway and walked to the ballpark. There was a big iron gate in centerfield with about a six-inch opening at the bottom that you could peek under. We got on our bellies and looked under the fence to see if the ballplayers were there. Once we saw them, it was all right to go in."

Mel Ott was David Hartman's first baseball hero and later there was Bobby Thomson and Jackie Robinson, the hated enemy who was tolerated by a socially conscious teenage Giant fan. And, of course, Willie Mays. But there will always be a place in his heart for the St. Louis Cardinals because of one of those touching stories that might appear in the Readers Digest or wind up as a television drama.

"I'll probably start bawling when I tell this story," he began

Pick him out? David is fourth from left, front row.

tentatively. "It was 1942 and my parents learned that my brother had osteomyelitis, the same bone disease that Mickey Mantle had. He was only 12 and his weight dropped from about 90 pounds to 45. He was taken to Columbia Presbyterian Hospital, where they shot him full of penicillin. But doctors gave him very little hope."

He paused now to collect himself, then continued.

"My folks knew what a great Cardinal fan my brother was and my dad either wired or called the Cardinals to tell them about my brother. A few days later, a special delivery letter arrived. It was a personal, hand-written letter from Billy Southworth, the Cardinal manager. He sent a sheet with all the Cardinal statistics and in the letter he wrote, 'We'll win the World Series for you.'

"My brother didn't let go of that letter for 10 days. The Cardinals won the World Series and my brother got well and there was no doubt that the Cardinals and Billy Southworth's letter had a great deal to do with his recovery."

It is ironic, David Hartman said, that years later he played the title role in a television series, "Lucas Tanner," a former St. Louis Cardinal pitcher whose sore arm caused him to quit baseball and become a high school teacher.

Baseball continued to be an important part of David Hartman's life as he grew. He played all sports, but baseball was his favorite.

"I just happened to love baseball over football or basketball," he explains. "I played football, but maybe I was just chicken. You know, don't hurt the face. I didn't like the contact, although I never did mind slamming into a catcher. I grew to 6-5, but I never had the jumping ability in basketball. So I just gravitated to baseball by attrition. I was a catcher until I grew to 6-3, then they switched me to first base."

At Mt. Hermon Prep in Massachusetts, Hartman captained the baseball team and, upon graduation, some major league teams expressed interest in him. The legend grows that David Hartman might have become another Hank Greenberg or a Jimmy Foxx, and it keeps growing as Hartman's television career soars.

It is often that way with famous men who gave up athletic careers to follow other pursuits. I remember interviewing His Eminence Francis Cardinal Spellman of New York, who had played varsity baseball at Fordham University.

"Your Eminence," I said, "I understand you were a pretty good second baseman in your day."

"I became a better second baseman," he replied, "AFTER I

became Cardinal."

David Hartman is no less modest about his baseball ability.

"I always could hit," he says. "And, sure, I sometimes fantasize about hitting one into the left field seats in a World Series game. Who wouldn't like to have done that? When I was young, I would rather play baseball than eat. But I really don't know if I could ever have hit a big league curveball . . . and I will never know."

From Mt. Hermon, Hartman went to Duke University, where he could have played baseball, but chose not to.

"It was too time-consuming and I had too many other interests," he says.

Music was one, and theater, and academics. He was an honor student and a cadet commander in Duke's Air Force ROTC program and when he graduated, with a degree in economics, he had offers from 32 major U.S. firms. At Duke, he managed to keep his love for baseball alive, broadcasting the university's baseball games in 1952 and forming a friendship with a young Duke shortstop named Dick Groat.

"When Dick wanted to practice," Hartman recalls, "and there was nobody else around, I would hit him ground balls by the thousands."

After graduation, Hartman served in the Air Force and wound up playing baseball on a base team.

"We played in an Air Force tournament and there were a lot

Tough assignment: an interview with Yanks' Munson, Jackson.

A couple of knockouts: Cheryl Tiegs and Ali with the host.

of scouts around and I hit like crazy," he recalls. "I must have hit over .600. It was just one of those hot streaks. Everything they threw, I hit. A few scouts asked me if I was interested in a pro career, but I was 25 by then and I had other goals. It would have been fun to have been a big league ballplayer. It's something I would have liked in my early 20s. Despite my love for baseball, I guess I just never wanted it badly enough. If I did, I would have given it a try."

Years later, his actor-celebrity status gave David Hartman entree to baseball and he has enjoyed a close relationship with many ballplayers. He had played in a celebrity softball game in Los Angeles, became friendly with some of the Dodgers and was invited to work out with the club when time permitted. He even went to spring training with them one year and worked out daily.

One day, just as the Dodgers were to take pre-game infield practice, first baseman Wes Parker turned to Hartman. "Hey, David, take my infield for me, will you?"

Naturally, Hartman was delighted to fill in for the Dodger first baseman.

"But the next day," he recalls, "one of the coaches told me Al Campanis didn't want me taking pregame infield."

That ended Hartman's relationship with the Dodgers, but he missed the fun and camaraderie of spring training and when he

continued on page 379

"To all the pitchers who made it possible."

PETE ROSE's Pitching Pinups

From Zachary to Stallard to Downing to Zachry. This is not a triple play combination but the names of pitchers whom fate has cruelly hit. Zachary (Tom) served Babe Ruth his 60th home run in 1927. Stallard (Tracy) delivered Roger Maris his 61st four-sacker in 1961. Downing (Al) pitched Hank Aaron home run No. 715 in 1974. And Zachry (Pat) gave Pete Rose his 37th—not home run—consecutive game with at least one hit. That tied Rose with Tommy Holmes for the modern National League hitting streak record last summer.

Of course, the ex-Cincinnati Kid went on to pass Holmes by victimizing the Mets' Craig Swan in No. 38, and wound up tied with Wee Willie Keeler at 44 for second place on the all-time streak list.

Zachary, Stallard, Downing, Zachry and Swan all have a unique place—although not coveted—in streak history. But let's not overlook all the other reluctant contributors who enabled Charlie Hustle to come out smelling like a rose. Stand up and take a bow, gentlemen, and say cheese as the photographer clicks. If it be a consolation, know that forever you'll be in Pete Rose's Pitching Hall of Fame.

PETE'S PINUPS

Game 1
Dave Roberts
Chicago
2 Singles

Game 2
John Denny
St. Louis
1 Single, 1 Double

Game 3
Pete Vuckovich
St. Louis
1 Single

Game 3
Buddy Schultz
St. Louis
1 Single

Game 4
Silvio Martinez
St. Louis
1 Single

Game 5
John Montefusco
San Francisco
1 Double

Game 5
John Curtis
San Francisco
1 Single

Game 6
Ed Halicki
San Francisco
1 Single

Game 7
Charlie Williams
San Francisco
1 Single

Game 8
Burt Hooton
Los Angeles
1 Single

Game 9
Don Sutton
Los Angeles
2 Singles, 1 Double

Game 9
Bob Welch
Los Angeles
1 Single

PETE'S PINUPS

**Game 10
Tommy John
Los Angeles
2 Singles**

**Game 11
Mark Lemongello
Houston
1 Single**

**Game 12
Joe Niekro
Houston
1 Single**

**Game 13
Tom Dixon
Houston
1 Single**

**Game 14
Floyd Bannister
Houston
1 Double**

**Game 15
Lance Rautzhan
Los Angeles
1 Single**

Game 16
Bob Welch
Los Angeles
1 Single

Game 16
Terry Forster
Los Angeles
1 Single

Game 16
Charlie Hough
Los Angeles
1 Single

Game 17
Rick Rhoden
Los Angeles
1 Double

Game 18
Doug Rau
Los Angeles
1 Double

Game 19
Floyd Bannister
Houston
1 Double

PETE'S PINUPS

Game 19
Bo McLaughlin
Houston
2 Singles

Game 20
J.R. Richard
Houston
1 Single

Game 21
Joe Niekro
Houston
1 Single

Game 22
Vida Blue
San Francisco
2 Singles

Game 22
John Curtis
San Francisco
1 Single

Game 23
Jim Barr
San Francisco
1 Single

Game 24
John Montefusco
San Francisco
1 Single

Game 25
Ed Halicki
San Francisco
2 Singles

Game 25
Bob Knepper
San Francisco
1 Single

Game 26
Jerry Koosman
New York
1 Double

Game 26
Skip Lockwood
New York
1 Single

Game 27
Pat Zachry
New York
2 Singles

PETE'S PINUPS

Game 28
Craig Swan
New York
1 Single

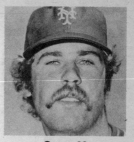

Game 29
Paul Siebert
New York
1 Double

Game 30
Ross Grimsley
Montreal
1 Single

Game 31
Hal Dues
Montreal
1 Single, 1 Double

Game 32
Ron Reed
Philadelphia
1 Single

Game 33
Jim Kaat
Philadelphia
1 Single

Game 34
Ross Grimsley
Montreal
1 Single

Game 35
Dan Schatzeder
Montreal
1 Single

Game 36
Steve Rogers
Montreal
1 Single

Game 36
Darold Knowles
Montreal
1 Double

Game 37
Pat Zachry
New York
1 Single

Game 37
Skip Lockwood
New York
1 Single

PETE'S PINUPS

Game 38
Craig Swan
New York
2 Singles, 1 Double

Game 39
Nino Espinosa
New York
1 Double

Game 40
Randy Lerch
Philadelphia
1 Double

Game 41
Steve Carlton
Philadelphia
1 Single

Game 42
Jim Lonborg
Philadelphia
2 Singles

Game 42
Jim Kaat
Philadelphia
1 Single

Game 43
Larry Christensen
Philadelphia
2 Singles

Game 44
Phil Niekro
Atlanta
1 Single

THE VILLIANS

Game 45
Larry McWilliams
Atlanta
1 Walk, 0-for-2

On Aug. 1, 1978, peppery Pete ran afoul of a couple of hard-slinging dudes in Atlanta. He drew 0-for-4 against Larry McWilliams and Gene Garber. And all winter long Pete threw darts at them in his pinup gallery.

Game 45
Gene Garber
Atlanta
0-for-2

STEVE GARVEY
and the
DODGER DILEMMA

By BILL LIBBY

Are the Dodgers a team divided? The late-season wrestling match between the team's top pitcher, Don Sutton, and heavies hitter, Steve Garvey, brought out into the open a degree o dissension which insiders knew existed behind closed doors And the team's second successive World Series defeat, in whicl Sutton and Garvey played dreadfully, made many wonder i manager Tommy Lasorda's "happy family" was heading towarc fratricide.

It is difficult to be sure of anything around the Dodgers thes days. For all their hugging and kissing, the arm wrappec around a teammate in enthusiastic embrace may have a dagge in its hand.

Following last season, the Dodgers faced a dilemma: Shoulc they make changes, and how many? Should they separate Sut ton and Garvey by trade, and should they separate others tha sided with one or the other? Should they keep intact a team which had won two consecutive pennants, or rebuild a team which had lost two straight World Series?

There was a lot at stake. The love affair between the Los Angeles and the Dodgers resulted in a six million attendance figure the last two seasons, including a major league record 3.3 million in 1978. The Dodgers are by far the biggest money-making machine in sports. Said to be the best-run franchise in the business, the front office hasn't dared to alienate the affec-tions of the faithful. But the brawl between Sutton and Garvey hurt the team's image.

Both players are religious sorts, but Garvey preaches the straight life more openly and gets a good press because he

Bill Libby is a West Coast freelance who has written more than 50 books, including John Roseboro's "Glory Days with the Dodgers."

American dream: All-Star Game MVP Garvey, wife Cyndy.

Happier days for Garvey and Sutton—Dodgers' '74 NL pennant

always is available. Handsome Steve, beautiful wife Cyndy, and their two children are regarded as the ideal family. Called "Mr. Clean," Steve even had a junior high school named for him because he set such a splendid example for youth. Sutton, his wife Patti, and their children have never attracted such attention. But Sutton has an impish sense of humor and has always been more popular with the players.

It is hard to explain why professional athletes resent clean-cut types, but they do. Most players lead carefree lives and resent those who do not go along with them. Revelations that some Dodgers thought Garvey too good to be true surfaced in an interview with an unidentified Dodger printed in a suburban newspaper a few years ago. Was it Sutton?

And last season when Sutton was accused of throwing doctored baseballs, an unidentified Dodger refused to defend him saying the charges were true. Was it Garvey?

Sutton then gave an interview in which he said, "All you hear about on our team is Steve Garvey, the All-American boy. Well, the best player on the team for the last two years—and we all know it—is Reggie Smith. Reggie doesn't go out and publicize himself. He doesn't smile at the right people or say the right things. He tells the truth. Reggie's not a facade or a Madison Avenue image. He's a real person."

Stars Walter Matthau and Jerry Lewis gag with Garvey.

The conflict came to head in New York when Garvey confronted Sutton in front of his locker. The pitcher not only denied the story, but said something about Garvey's wife. Suddenly, the two were wrestling on the floor, scratching one another's face "like a couple of girls," according to one of the players who broke up the fight.

Lasorda tried to shrug it off. "I love my brothers, but we have fights. There are fights on all teams, but they're forgotten. I'm sorry this happened between these two fine young men, but I'm sure they'll forget it. I'm sure it won't hurt the team."

"We're still a team. I like both guys and I'm just sorry they made me the man in the middle," said Smith.

Said Garvey: "I've dedicated myself to doing everything I could, on and off the field, to set a good example for young people and promote my sport. I've been knocked before about things I've done, but I think they're positive things. And I don't think they should be criticized to the press, but to my face.

"I'm only human and there comes a time when you have to

stand up for yourself, your family, and the things you believe in."

Sutton tried to laugh it off and wouldn't discuss the incident until it became clear public reaction was running strongly against him. Even Lasorda said, "Some people make fun of family men. They make fun of guys who like their wives."

Sutton, who once asked to be traded from the Dodgers, was visibly shaken by the incident. Less than a week after his fight with Garvey he called a press conference to apologize.

Tearfully, he said he regretted having fought except that it gave him a chance to ask God's help in setting his life straight. He thanked God for Garvey and apologized to anyone who had been embarrassed.

Some thought Garvey should have apologized for his part in the fight, but, after watching the scene, he simply said, "I will not be able to forget what happened, and neither will Don Sutton, but I accept his apology. Hopefully, he realizes now the things I do are positive and there will be a better understanding."

However, Garvey and Sutton, who live only three houses apart in the Los Angeles suburbs, did not start a round of friendly family gatherings. But their feud seemed to have a catalytic effect on the Dodgers, who swept to their second straight National League pennant with a strong stretch run.

The Dodgers have been a beloved team since their days in Brooklyn when they won nine pennants, but only one World Series (1955) from the hated New York Yankees. Since moving to Los Angeles in 1958, the Dodgers have won seven pennants and three World Series and have drawn over one-and-one half million fans for 21 straight seasons. However, the last World Series the Dodgers won was in 1965 and they now have lost their last four, including three in the last five years. This 13-year drought and recent failure deeply disturbs many of the faithful, but perhaps they have set their standards too high and are spoiled. The Boston Red Sox have not won a World Series since 1918, the Chicago White Sox since 1917, the Chicago Cubs since 1908. The Philadelphia Phillies, losers of the last three National League pennant playoffs, have never won a World Series.

The Dodgers won 102 games to outrun the Reds to the National League's Western Division title in 1974, and, after being beaten by the Reds in 1975 and 1976, won 98 games in 1977 and 95 in 1978 to end the Reds' dream of a dynasty. The Dodgers frustrated the Phillies in the last two pennant playoffs, only to lose to the Yankees in the last two World Series.

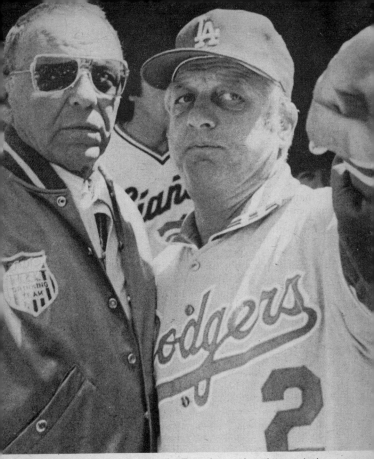

Frank Sinatra is a regular in Tom Lasorda's inner circle.

After 23 years of the introverted, calm, soft-spoken leadership of Walter Alston, the Dodgers turned to the extroverted, excited, loud leadership of Tommy Lasorda. With 30 years in the organization, Lasorda talked a lot about "The Great Dodger In the Sky" in his first season as manager, but after bleeding "Dodger blue blood" in the 1977 World Series setback, he talked a lot less about it this last season. Yet he continued to encourage his players enthusiastically, hugging and even kissing them after victories. Some feel this act is wearing thin.

Lasorda said: "I don't give a damn what they say. I hugged

continued on page 380

So You Want To Be An Official Scorer!

By JIM HAWKINS

He is not listed in the official program. He doesn't appear on the field, either. And he doesn't wear a uniform with his number and name sewn on the back of the shirt.

He is the official scorer, an integral part of every baseball game since the turn of the century.

So what does the official scorer do?

First, he gets into the ballpark for free, and sits in the comfort of the press box, munching a complimentary hot dog or two and sipping a Coke while watching the game.

And for that, major league baseball will gladly pay him 50 bucks a game (a total of $500 for the World Series).

Along the way he has to decide whether a particular ball is worth a base hit or whether a fielder deserves an error. But he has relatively few tough decisions. And when the game is over and he has finished his hot dogs and ice cream and soda pop —all free, of course—he has to fill out a statistical report to send to the league office, just so it knows he was really at the game.

On the surface, that's all there is to it. Talk about having fun and getting paid for it, too!

Sounds like a great job, doesn't it?

Unfortunately, as every official scorer soon finds out, there's much more to the job than meets the eye. None of it is particularly pleasant.

On any given day he may be booed by the fans, cursed, threatened or even physically assaulted by the ballplayers, and criticized by his colleagues in the press box.

He must be prepared to be questioned, second-guessed, and accused of ignorance, partiality and feeble eyesight, regardless of which way he rules.

Jim Hawkins is a baseball writer for the Detroit Free-Press *and the co-author of Ron LeFlore's autobiography, "Breakout."*

SCHLAMP

Johnny Vander Meer's two straight no-hitters made him a hero

According to baseball rule 10:01 (c): "The scorer is an official representative of the league and is entitled to the respect and dignity of his office."

However, that's not easy to tell a fuming, 6-foot-5, 225-pound outfielder who is convinced he was robbed of a base hit by a skinny, bespectacled sportswriter who probably had to sit on the bench in Little League.

Ballplayers are, by nature, a greedy lot. They want everything to go their way all of the time. It is not at all unusual to stroll into a clubhouse after a team has won and hear the players complaining about the official scorer's calls instead of celebrating a victory.

Players insist that as the home team they should be given the benefit of the doubt. Yet they groan loud and long when those same decisions go against them on the road.

If the scorer gives a batter a hit, the pitchers moan it should have been an error. If he charges the fielder with a fumble, the batter complains the scorer is taking bread off his table.

Some official scorers admit there have been times they felt genuine fear because of calls they made. Others insist they dread the job.

Howard Ehmke lost double no-hitter to scorer.

The majority, though, relish the prestige and power that g[o] with the position—not to mention the pay.

"Just remember," advised Jerome Holtzman of the *Chicag[o] Sun Times*, who has been scoring for 22 years, "when you're th[e] official scorer, you're never wrong."

Sometimes, though, you're the only one who feels that way

Former Oakland catcher Frank Fernandez once stunned th[e] fans, not to mention the sportswriters upstairs, when he hurle[d] his batting helmet up at the press box after he failed to ge[t] credit for what he thought was a base hit.

In addition to his shoddy fielding, former Pittsburgh firs[t] baseman Dick Stuart was famous for waving his middle finge[r] in the direction of the official scorer whenever a call displease[d] him.

But few people ever feel sorry for the official scorer.

Years ago, Joe Kuhel of the old Washington Senators, incensed at being charged with an error, took a swing at sportswriter Shirley Povich, when the latter entered the clubhouse after the game.

Povich protested that Kuhel had the wrong target, that Bob Considine had been the official scorer that day.

"If you've seen one lousy sportswriter, you've seen them all," growled Kuhel.

Senators' owner Clark Griffith fined Kuhel $100 for the incident, but when the player arrived at the park the next day he found a note from a fan in his locker. "Here's $50 to pay half your fine for taking a punch at Povich," the note read. "I'd have sent you the other half if you hadn't missed."

More often than not it is useless for the official scorer to try to rationally defend his calls. Most players don't understand the scoring rules anyway.

Although the rules are clearly prejudiced in favor of the hitters ("Always give the batter the benefit of the doubt"), the hitters complain more than anyone else. On the other hand, under the rules, all that is required of a fielder to avoid an error is "ordinary effort."

However, it is seldom that simple.

A scorer in Cleveland once called a ground ball by the Indians' Pedro Gonzales a base hit. But when the box score appeared in the newspaper the next day, the play was listed as an error.

Gonzales, who had a reputation as a very tough customer, confronted the scorer in the clubhouse and began ranting and raving in broken English.

"The paper made a mistake," the writer patiently explained.

Virgil Trucks got a no-hitter after scorer changed his mind.

"It was a typographical error."

"It wasn't no kind of error!" screamed Gonzales. "It was a hit!"

Ike Brown was playing third base for Detroit one day when the Tigers trapped an opponent in a rundown between second and third. Brown's throw hit the runner in the back and, in accordance with the rules, the official scorer, Ed Browalski, charged Ike with an error.

The next day, Brown sought out Browalski to protest. "How could you give me an error?" argued Ike. "It ain't my fault he got in the way of the ball."

At one time or another, nearly all players complain, including the best ones. Hank Aaron, with more than 3,000 hits and more than 715 home runs already to his credit, once called the press box to moan because he wasn't given a single on a routine ground ball that the shortstop threw away.

After giving up a colossal home run to Minnesota's Bobby Darwin and eventually being knocked out of the game, Texas pitcher Ferguson Jenkins called the press box to complain be-

continued on page 374

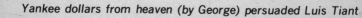

Yankee dollars from heaven (by George) persuaded Luis Tiant

The New Millionaires
III

The 1978 Class of Millionaires was not as large as those of 1977 or 1976, the year that Peter Seitz freed the slaves. But this year's graduates included some of baseball's oldest stars and its valedictorian, Pete Rose, became the highest-paid baseball player of all time.

The head of the first free agent Class of 1976 was Reggie Jackson, whom the New York Yankees signed for $2.93 million for five years. The Yankees made Rich Gossage the leader of the Class of 1977, giving the relief pitcher $3.6 million for six years. But Rose's contract with the Philadelphia Phillies makes both look like paupers—$3.2 million for four years, or $800,000 a year.

The Phillies' bid was the lowest of the five clubs seriously seeking Rose's services. After a week of shuttle negotiations in which he was offered $1 million (Atlanta), race horses (Pittsburgh), Budweiser commercials (St. Louis) and the benefits of a pharmaceutical fortune (Kansas City), Pete tolled the Liberty Bell his heart was really in Philadelphia.

It remains to be seen how extensively Rose has altered baseball's salary structure. But he and this year's other leading free agents have championed the cause of geriatrics—they have revised the market value of stars approaching their final baseball years. Rose, who will 38 on April 14, Luis Tiant, 38, and Tommy John, 35, both signed by the Yankees, and Mike Marshall, 36, who signed in January, indicate that clubs are willing to gamble big money on players whose talents could desert them at any time.

PLAYER	TEAM	YEARS	TOTAL
Pete Rose	Philadelphia	4	$3,200,000
Larry Gura	Kansas City	5	1,350,000
Tommy John	Yankees	3	1,200,000
Luis Tiant	Yankees	2	900,000
Mike Marshall	Minnesota	3	900,000

AMERICAN LEAGUE

By PHIL PEPE and **JIM HAWKINS**
New York News *Detroit Free Press*

	East	West
PREDICTED ORDER OF FINISH	New York Yankees	Kansas City Royals
	Milwaukee Brewers	California Angels
	Baltimore Orioles	Minnesota Twins
	Boston Red Sox	Texas Rangers
	Detroit Tigers	Seattle Mariners
	Cleveland Indians	Chicago White Sox
	Toronto Blue Jays	Oakland A's

Playoff Winner: New York

EAST DIVISION

		Owner		Morning Line Manager
1	**YANKEES** navy blue pin stripe Wins last three outs. Can repeat	George M. Steinbrenner	1978 W 100 L 63	**4-5** Bob Lemon
2	**BREWERS** white, blue & gold Improving rapidly, can challenge	Bud Selig	1978 W 93 L 69	**2-1** George Bamberger
3	**ORIOLES** black, white & orange Look for steady race in hands of top jockey.	Jerry Hoffberger	1978 W 90 L 71	**3-1** Earl Weaver
4	**RED SOX** navy blue, scarlet & white Needs a win to gain confidence.	Mrs. Thomas Yawkey	1978 W 99 L 64	**4-1** Don Zimmer
5	**TIGERS** white & navy blue Excellent potential, but in over head.	John Fetzer	1978 W 86 L 76	**10-1** Les Moss
6	**INDIANS** scarlet, white & blue Can improve over last, but still short.	Steve O'Neill	1978 W 69 L 90	**40-1** Jeff Torborg
7	**BLUE JAYS** blue, white & red Never in contention.	Don McDougall	1978 W 59 L 102	**200-1** Roy Hartsfield

After early foot, **RED SOX** will fade and give up lead at the turn with the **YANKEES** coming on strong in stretch to pass tired horses. **BREWERS** will head up for second, nipping **ORIOLES** at wire, **RED SOX** fading to fourth. **TIGERS** will show early speed, no staying power. **INDIANS** will lag badly from start and **BLUE JAYS** will never challenge.

THE BANKERS' HANDICAP

79th Running, American League Race. Distance, 162 games, plus playoff. Purse: $12,000 per winning player, division; $15,000 added, pennant; $6,000 added, World Championship. A field of 14 entered in two divisions.

Track Record 111 Wins—Cleveland 1954

WEST DIVISION	Owner		Morning Line Manager
1 ROYALS royal blue & white Class of field and has the winning habit.	Ewing Kauffman	1978 W 92 L 70	**6-5** Whitey Herzog
2 ANGELS navy blue, red, gold & white Strongest challenger, but no staying power.	Gene Autry	1978 W 87 L 75	**3-1** Jim Fregosi
3 TWINS scarlet, white & blue Best rider gets most out of entry.	Calvin Griffith	1978 W 73 L 89	**7-1** Gene Mauch
4 RANGERS red, blue & white Poor winter workouts, will not challenge.	Brad Corbett	1978 W 87 L 75	**10-1** Pat Corrales
5 MARINERS blue & gold Coming fast, but not primed for distance.	Danny Kaye-Lester Smith	1978 W 56 L 104	**50-1** Darrell Johnson
6 WHITE SOX black & white Last effort was poor.	Bill Veeck	1978 W 71 L 90	**100-1** Don Kessinger
7 A'S green, gold & white No chance.	Charles O. Finley	1978 W 69 L 93	**200-1**

ROYALS can win as they please, despite early challenge from **ANGELS**. **TWINS** will be surprise of race and could be in lead for a half, then passed by leaders, but will hold on to fight off **RANGERS** for third. **MARINERS**, **WHITE SOX** and **A's** will never contend.

NEW YORK YANKEES

TEAM DIRECTORY: Principal Owner: George Steinbrenner III; Pres.: Al Rosen; VP-GM: Cedric Tallis; VP-Player Development: Jack Butterfield; Dir. Pub. Rel.: Mickey Morabito; Trav. Sec.: Bill Kane; Mgr.: Bob Lemon. Home: Yankee Stadium (57,545). Field distances: 312, l.f. line; 387, l.f.; 430, l.c.; 417, c.f.; 385, r.c.; 353, r.f.; 310, r.f. line. Spring training: Ft. Lauderdale, Fla.

SCOUTING REPORT

HITTING: Offensive production was off all the way down the line for the Yankees, which makes one wonder if it was simply an off year or if age is getting to be a factor. Their top hitter was Lou Piniella, who will play at 36, but remains one of the league's top hitters. "There's nobody I'd rather see batting to keep a rally alive," says president Al Rosen.

Reggie Jackson, Thurman Munson, Graig Nettles, Chris Chambliss and Mickey Rivers all fell off at bat, but there is still plenty of quality and enough offense to make the champs' attack formidable. Jackson, Munson, Nettles and Chambliss were all plus 90 in RBIs, Jackson and Nettles combined for 54 homers and more of the same is expected. Rivers can get back

Will Reggie Jackson and Ron Guidry drink bubbly in 1979?

most of the 61 points he lost.

Attempts to pick up some bench strength were unsuccessful. But Rosen held firm to his belief that the Yankees could win again without another deal. "We have strengthened ourselves immeasurably," he said. "We don't have to do anything. When we talk deals, people act like we have no players. What did we finish, last?"

PITCHING: It must be etched in the minds and hearts of Yankee officials, the slogan "You never can have too much pitching." A year ago, they had pitchers coming out of their ears, but a succession of mishaps and trades left them with two reliable starters and one ace reliever. Somehow, the Yankees managed to patch it up and lead the league in pitching. Naturally, much of that came from Ron Guidry, whose 1.74 ERA, 25 wins and nine shutouts (the entire staff had 16) were tops. Ed Figueroa, a 20-game winner for the first time, and reliever Rich Gossage, tops with 27 saves, also contributed mightily. All three are expected to have big years, but just in case, the Yankees also have veteran Catfish Hunter and Jim Beattie and Ken Clay waiting in the wings, and have added free agents Tommy John and Luis Tiant, the ageless old Yankee killer.

Pitching in Yankee Stadium with the cavernous left field, his great sinker, natural grass and the Yankee defense, should suit John. "To hit a home run off him in our park," says Rosen, "you're going to need a five-iron."

Again, the Yankees seem overloaded with arms. But it is written on minds and heart of all Yankees, "You never can have too much pitching."

FIELDING: Gold Gloves populate the corners of the Yankee infield, worn by Graig Nettles and Chris Chambliss, whose fielding percentages last season were the highest in Yankee history. Among them, Nettles, Chambliss, shortstop Bucky Dent and second baseman Willie Randolph handled 3,168 chances with only 41 errors. The outfield defense lacks speed in some places, arms in others, but Juan Beniquez, acquired from Texas, is a good pickup.

OUTLOOK: The rich get richer. The addition of John and Tiant make the Yankees even stronger going into 1979 than they were going into 1978, especially since their chief opposition made no deals to strengthen themselves. The Yankees proved their class by coming back from a 14-game deficit, which will leave a lasting impression on AL rivals.

NEW YORK YANKEES 1979 ROSTER

MANAGER Bob Lemon
Coaches—Yogi Berra, Mike Ferraro, Jim Hegan, Elston Howard, Charley Lau, Tom Morgan

PITCHERS

No.	Name	1978 Club	W-L	IP	SO	ERA	B-T	Ht.	Wt.	Born
45	Beattie, Jim	Tacoma	3-0	23	15	1.57	R-R	6-6	210	7/4/54 Hampton, VA
		New York (AL)	6-9	128	65	3.73				
43	Clay, Ken	New York (AL)	3-4	76	32	4.28	R-R	6-2	194	4/6/54 Lynchburg, VA
—	Davis, Ron	Midland	3-3	68	45	6.35	R-R	6-4	205	8/6/55 Houston, TX
		West Haven	9-2	60	39	1.51				
		New York (AL)	0-0	2	0	13.50				
31	Figueroa, Ed	New York (AL)	20-9	253	92	2.99	R-R	6-0	191	10/14/48 Puerto Rico
54	Gossage, Rich	New York (AL)	10-11	134	122	2.01	R-R	6-3	190	7/5/51 Colorado Springs, CO
—	Griffin, Mike	Tulsa	6-19	169	112	6.06	R-R	6-4	195	6/26/57 Colusa, CA
49	Guidry, Ron	New York (AL)	25-3	274	248	1.74	L-L	5-11	153	8/28/50 Lafayette, LA
35	Gullett, Don	New York (AL)	4-2	45	28	3.60	R-L	6-0	187	1/5/51 Lynn, KY
29	Hunter, Catfish	New York (AL)	12-6	118	56	3.58	R-R	6-0	205	4/8/46 Hertford, NC
25	John, Tommy	Los Angeles	17-10	213	124	3.30	R-L	6-3	185	5/22/43 Terre Haute, IN
—	Lysgaard, Jim	Tacoma	10-8	157	61	3.61	R-R	6-1	180	6/11/54 Senal, Sask.
—	Mirabella, Paul	Tuscon	9-6	143	83	3.97	L-L	6-1	190	3/20/54 Bellville, NJ
		Texas	3-2	28	23	5.79				
—	Slagle, Roger	West Haven	1-0	9	7	0.00	R-R	6-3	190	11/4/53 Wichita, KS
		Tacoma	13-8	179	96	3.07				
23	Tiant, Luis	Boston	13-8	212	114	3.31	R-R	5-11	205	11/23/40 Cuba
19	Tidrow, Dick	New York (AL)	7-11	185	73	3.84	R-R	6-4	213	5/14/47 San Francisco, CA

CATCHERS

No.	Name	1978 Club	H	HR	RBI	Pct.	B-T	Ht.	Wt.	Born
41	Johnson, Cliff	New York (AL)	32	6	19	.184	R-R	6-4	217	2/22/47 San Antonio, TX
15	Munson, Thurman	New York (aL)	183	6	71	.297	R-R	5-11	195	6/7/47 Akron, OH
38	Narron, Jerry	Tacoma	121	15	84	.278	L-R	6-3	185	1/15/56 Goldsboro, NC

INFIELDERS

No.	Name	1978 Club	H	HR	RBI	Pct.	B-T	Ht.	Wt.	Born
10	Chambliss, Chris	New York (AL)	171	12	90	.274	L-R	6-1	209	2/22/47 Dayton, OH
20	Dent, Bucky	New York (AL)	92	5	40	.243	R-R	5-11	181	11/25/51 Savannah, GA
—	Doyle, Brian	Tacoma	38	2	16	.286	L-R	5-10	165	1/26/55 Glasgow, KY
		New York (AL)	10	0	0	.192				
—	Garcia, Damaso	Tacoma	103	1	53	.268	R-R	6-1	165	2/7/57 Dominican Republic
		New York (AL)	8	0	1	.195				
—	McDonald, Jim	West Haven	127	18	83	.286	L-L	6-2	190	10/20/57 Lynwood, CA
9	Nettles, Graig	New York (AL)	162	27	93	.276	L-R	6-0	186	8/20/44 San Diego, CA
30	Randolph, Willie	New York (AL)	139	3	42	.279	R-R	5-11	164	7/6/54 Holly Hill, SC
18	Sherrill, Dennis	West Haven	142	14	60	.293	R-R	6-0	165	3/3/56 Miami, FL
12	Spencer, Jim	New York (AL)	34	7	24	.227	L-L	6-2	195	7/30/47 Hanover, PA
—	Staiger, Roy	Tacoma	119	19	85	.283	R-R	6-0	195	1/6/50 Tulsa, OK
11	Stanley, Fred	New York (AL)	35	1	9	.219	R-R	5-10	166	8/13/47 Farhamville, OH

OUTFIELDERS

No.	Name	1978 Club	H	HR	RBI	Pct.	B-T	Ht.	Wt.	Born
—	Beniquez, Juan	Texas	123	11	50	.260	R-R	5-11	165	5/13/50 Puerto Rico
2	Blair, Paul	New York (AL)	22	2	13	.176	R-R	6-0	177	2/1/44 Cushing, OK
—	Cruz, Tommy	Tacoma	146	17	81	.319	L-L	5-8	170	1/15/51 Puerto Rico
44	Jackson, Reggie	New York (AL)	140	27	97	.274	L-L	6-0	205	5/18/46 Wyncote, PA
—	Jemison, Greg	Tulsa (AL)	109	3	44	.263	L-R	6-0	165	7/15/54 Coatesville, PA
27	Johnstone, Jay	Philadelphia	10	0	4	.179	L-R	6-1	185	11/20/46 Manchester, CT
		New York (AL)	17	1	6	.262				
14	Piniella, Lou	New York (AL)	148	6	69	.314	R-R	6-2	200	8/28/43 Tampa, FL
17	Rivers, Mickey	New York (AL)	148	11	48	.265	L-L	5-10	165	10/30/48 Miami, FL
—	Smith, Garry	Tacoma	138	13	73	.325	R-R	6-2	185	10/23/55 Jacksonville, NC
24	Thomasson, Gary	Oak.-N.Y. (AL)	63	8	36	.233	L-L	6-1	180	7/29/51 San Diego, CA
6	White, Roy	New York (AL)	93	8	43	.269	B-R	5-10	171	12/27/43 Los Angeles, CA

YANKEE PROFILES

REGGIE JACKSON 32 6-0 205   Bats L Throws L

The "straw that stirs the drink" . . . Mr. October . . . Sensitive man with a massive ego that is easily hurt . . . But can carry the club all by himself when he's hot . . . At his best under pressure . . . Only second player in history to have candy bar named after him . . . The other was Ty Cobb, not Babe Ruth . . . Drives a Rolls Royce . . . Homered again in final game of '78 World Series after hitting three dramatic HRs to climax '77 Series . . . Born May 18, 1946, in Wyncote, Pa. . . . Signed by Yanks for $3 million as a free agent before '77 . . . Suspended for five games by Billy Martin for refusing to bunt . . . His lack of contrition led to Martin's final outburst and subsequent resignation . . . Enjoyed peace under Bob Lemon . . . Finished year as DH.

Year	Club	Pos	G	AB	R	H	2B	3B	HR	RBI	SB	Avg.
1967	Kansas City	OF	35	118	13	21	4	4	1	6	1	.178
1968	Oakland	OF	154	553	82	138	13	6	29	74	14	.250
1969	Oakland	OF	152	549	123	151	36	3	47	118	13	.275
1970	Oakland	OF	149	426	57	101	21	2	23	66	26	.237
1971	Oakland	OF	150	567	87	157	29	3	32	80	16	.277
1972	Oakland	OF	135	499	72	132	25	2	25	75	9	.265
1973	Oakland	OF	151	539	99	158	28	2	32	117	22	.293
1974	Oakland	OF	148	506	90	146	25	1	29	93	25	.289
1975	Oakland	OF	157	593	91	150	39	3	36	104	17	.253
1976	Baltimore	OF	134	498	84	138	27	2	27	91	28	.277
1977	New York (AL)	OF	146	525	93	150	39	2	32	110	17	.286
1978	New York (AL)	OF	139	511	82	140	13	5	27	97	14	.274
	Totals		1650	5884	973	1582	299	35	340	1031	202	.269

THURMAN MUNSON 31 5-11 195   Bats R Throws R

Hobbled by injuries, aches and pains through much of '78 . . . Yet, in clutch, he's still one of players the Yankees all look to . . . Team captain and perhaps the most indispensable man on the club . . . "Thurman is the best I've ever had at handling pitchers," said Billy Martin . . . Born June 7, 1947, in Akron, Ohio . . . Has hit .300 five times . . . Among catchers, only Ernie Lombardi and Bill Dickey reached that plateau more often . . . Called "Little Fat Guy" or "Fatso" by his teammates . . . Would like to be traded to a team closer to his Canton, Ohio, home . . . "One of the greatest players I've seen in 50 years," says former Yankee president Gabe Paul.

Year	Club	Pos	G	AB	R	H	2B	3B	HR	RBI	SB	Avg.
1969	New York (AL)....	C	26	86	6	22	1	2	1	9	0	.256
1970	New York (AL)....	C	132	453	59	137	25	4	6	53	5	.302
1971	New York (AL)....	C-OF	125	451	71	113	15	4	10	42	6	.251
1972	New York (AL)....	C	140	511	54	143	16	3	7	46	6	.280
1973	New York (AL)....	C	147	519	80	156	29	4	20	74	4	.301
1974	New York (AL)....	C	144	517	64	135	19	2	13	60	2	.261
1975	New York (AL)....	C-OF-1B-3B	157	597	83	190	24	3	12	102	3	.318
1976	New York (AL)....	C-OF	152	616	79	186	27	1	17	105	14	.302
1977	New York (AL)....	C	149	595	85	183	28	5	18	100	5	.308
1978	New York (AL)....	C-OF	154	617	73	183	27	1	6	71	2	.297
	Totals..........		1326	4962	654	1448	201	29	110	662	47	.292

CATFISH HUNTER 32 6-0 205   Bats R Throws R

Overcame early season arm woes to help pitch Yanks to pennant and World Championship . . . Won final game of World Series . . . First of the free agents . . . Plans to retire at end of the season . . . "That's it. Nothing can make me change my mind." . . . Brought a touch of class to Yankees . . . Frustrated by injuries past two years and thought career was over when couldn't throw in '78 . . . Underwent special treatment and became 12-game winner when Yankees needed him most . . . Instrumental in their drive to catch Boston . . . Born April 8, 1946, in Hertford, N.C. . . . Still same quiet, unassuming farm boy he was when he began his career . . . Only fourth pitcher in history (Cy Young, Walter Johnson, Christy Mathewson) to win 200 games before 31st birthday.

Year	Club	G	IP	W	L	Pct.	SO	BB	H	ERA
1965	Kansas City..............	32	133	8	8	.500	82	46	124	4.26
1966	Kansas City..............	30	177	9	11	.450	103	64	158	4.02
1967	Kansas City..............	35	260	13	17	.433	196	84	209	2.80
1968	Oakland.................	36	234	13	13	.500	172	69	210	3.35
1969	Oakland.................	38	247	12	15	.444	150	85	210	3.35
1970	Oakland.................	40	262	18	14	.563	178	74	253	3.81
1971	Oakland.................	37	274	21	11	.656	181	80	225	2.96
1972	Oakland.................	38	295	21	7	.750	191	70	200	2.04
1973	Oakland.................	36	256	21	5	.808	124	69	222	3.34
1974	Oakland.................	41	318	25	12	.676	143	46	268	2.49
1975	New York (AL)..........	39	328	23	14	.622	177	83	248	2.58
1976	New York (AL)..........	36	299	17	15	.531	173	68	268	3.52
1977	New York (AL)..........	22	143	9	9	.500	52	47	137	4.72
1978	New York (AL)..........	21	118	12	6	.667	56	35	98	3.58
	Totals.................	481	3344	222	157	.586	1978	920	2730	3.19

GRAIG NETTLES 34 6-0 186   Bats L Throws R

Astounded national TV audience with his diving catches at third base in World Series, especially during third game . . . But his performance didn't surprise Graig . . . "I've been making plays like that for eight or nine years" . . . Never has received credit due him for all he's done . . . Came to Yankees in '73 from Cleveland where his efforts went unnoticed . . . Born Aug. 20, 1944, in San Diego . . . Always seems to have one hot month with bat . . . Clever quipster . . . Named the all-time Yankee third baseman . . . "I guess I'm not controversial enough," he says of lack of publicity.

Year	Club	Pos	G	AB	R	H	2B	3B	HR	RBI	SB	Avg.
1968	Minnesota	OF-3B-1B	22	76	13	17	2	1	5	8	0	.224
1969	Minnesota	OF-3B	96	225	27	50	9	2	7	26	1	.222
1970	Cleveland	3B-OF	157	549	81	129	13	1	26	62	3	.235
1971	Cleveland	3B	158	598	78	156	18	1	28	86	7	.261
1972	Cleveland	3B	150	557	65	141	28	0	17	70	2	.253
1973	New York (AL)	3B	160	552	65	129	18	0	22	81	0	.234
1974	New York (AL)	3B-SS	155	566	74	139	21	1	22	75	1	.246
1975	New York (AL)	3B	157	581	71	155	24	4	21	91	1	.267
1976	New York (AL)	3B	158	583	88	148	29	2	32	93	11	.254
1977	New York (AL)	3B	158	589	99	150	23	4	37	107	2	.255
1978	New York (AL)	3B	159	587	81	162	23	2	27	93	1	.276
	Totals		1533	5466	742	1377	209	18	244	792	29	.252

CHRIS CHAMBLISS 30 6-1 209   Bats L Throws L

The quiet Yankee . . . Hampered by hand injury that forced him to bench during World Series . . . Still one of the keys to club's hopes in '79 . . . Owner George Steinbrenner calls his two-run homer that tied sixth World Series game in '77 "perhaps the biggest hit of the year for us." . . . Born Dec. 26, 1948, in Dayton, Ohio . . . Obtained from Cleveland in 1974 . . . Consistent hitter in clutch situations.

Year	Club	Pos	G	AB	R	H	2B	3B	HR	RBI	SB	Avg.
1971	Cleveland	1B	111	415	49	114	20	4	9	48	2	.275
1972	Cleveland	1B	121	466	51	136	27	2	6	44	3	.292
1973	Cleveland	1B	155	572	70	156	30	2	11	53	4	.273
1974	Cleve.-N.Y. (AL)	1B	127	467	46	119	20	3	6	50	0	.255
1975	New York (AL)	1B	150	562	66	171	38	4	9	72	0	.304
1976	New York (AL)	1B	156	641	79	188	32	6	17	96	1	.293
1977	New York (AL)	1B	157	600	90	172	30	6	17	90	4	.287
1978	New York (AL)	1B	162	625	81	171	26	3	12	90	2	.274
	Totals		1139	4348	532	1227	235	30	87	543	16	.282

MICKEY RIVERS 30 5-10 165   Bats L Throws L

The little man who makes the Yankee offense go . . . In and out of trouble with management, though, because of his attitude . . . Very moody . . . Hobbled by ankle and hip injuries that reduced effectiveness during playoffs and World Series . . . Born Oct. 31, 1948, in Miami . . . Walks like a broken down old man, but runs like the wind . . . One of the many outspoken Yanks . . . Credits Paul Blair for his marked improvement in throwing from the outfield.

Year	Club	Pos	G	AB	R	H	2B	3B	HR	RBI	SB	Avg.
1970	California	OF	17	25	6	8	2	0	0	3	1	.320
1971	California	OF	78	268	31	71	12	2	1	12	13	.265
1972	California	OF	58	159	18	34	6	2	0	7	4	.214
1973	California	OF	30	129	26	45	6	4	0	16	8	.349
1974	California	OF	118	466	69	133	19	11	3	31	30	.285
1975	California	OF	155	615	70	175	17	13	1	53	70	.285
1976	New York (AL)	OF	137	590	95	184	31	8	8	67	43	.312
1977	New York (AL)	OF	138	565	79	184	18	5	12	69	22	.326
1978	New York (AL)	OF	141	559	78	148	25	8	11	48	25	.265
	Totals		872	3376	472	982	136	53	36	306	216	.291

RON GUIDRY 28 5-11 153   Bats L Throws L

Put together one of the greatest seasons of all time . . . Won AL Cy Young Award . . . Was 13-0 at one point when rest of Yankee pitchers were all losing . . . Led league in victories, winning percentage, ERA and shutouts . . . Won sudden-death showdown with Boston that put Yankees into playoffs . . . Was once being groomed to replace Sparky Lyle as left-handed reliever . . . "I have respect for no hitter in the league." . . . Born Aug. 28, 1950, in Lafayette, La. . . . Overpowers batters with blazing fastball . . . Throws incredibly hard for size . . . Also excellent fielding pitcher . . . Got chance in '77 because of injuries to Catfish Hunter and Ken Holtzman . . . The premier pitcher in AL.

Year	Club	G	IP	W	L	Pct.	SO	BB	H	ERA
1975	New York (AL)	10	16	0	1	.000	15	9	15	3.38
1976	New York (AL)	20	16	0	0	.000	12	4	20	5.63
1977	New York (AL)	31	211	16	7	.696	176	65	174	2.82
1978	New York (AL)	35	274	25	3	.893	248	72	187	1.74
	Totals	96	517	41	11	.788	451	150	396	2.35

WILLIE RANDOLPH 24 5-11 164 · Bats R Throws R

Displayed maturity to go with natural talent in 1978 . . . "The more I see him, the more I like him," says former coach Gene Michael. "Not only his great tools, but the way he takes charge and the way he plays the game. He's a winner." . . . Missed playoffs and World Series because of pulled hamstring muscle . . . Born July 6, 1954, in Holly Hills, S.C., but grew up in Brooklyn . . . May someday be remembered as one of best Yankee second basemen ever . . . Signed with Pirates, later traded to Yanks . . . Quick hands make him adept at turning double plays.

Year	Club	Pos	G	AB	R	H	2B	3B	HR	RBI	SB	Avg.
1975	Pittsburgh	2B-3B	30	61	9	10	1	0	0	3	1	.164
1976	New York (AL)	2B	125	430	59	115	15	4	1	40	37	.267
1977	New York (AL)	2B	147	551	91	151	28	11	4	40	13	.274
1978	New York (AL)	2B	134	499	87	139	18	6	3	42	36	.279
	Totals		436	1541	246	415	62	21	8	125	87	.269

LOU PINIELLA 35 6-2 200 Bats R Throws R

Found permanent place in lineup after Bob Lemon replaced Billy Martin . . . Boasted fourth best batting average in AL . . . One of the most serious, devoted students of hitting in the game . . . Extremely popular with Yankee fans . . . A fierce competitor whose temper tantrums are legendary . . . Yet charming off the field with the press and with the public . . . Born Aug. 28, 1943, in Tampa, Fla. . . . One of the best needlers around . . . Every hit has to be a solid one because he has little speed.

Year	Club	Pos	G	AB	R	H	2B	3B	HR	RBI	SB	Avg.
1964	Baltimore	PH	4	1	0	0	0	0	0	0	0	.000
1968	Cleveland	OF	6	5	1	0	0	0	0	1	0	.000
1969	Kansas City	OF	135	493	43	139	21	6	11	68	2	.282
1970	Kansas City	OF-1B	144	542	54	163	24	5	11	88	3	.301
1971	Kansas City	OF	126	448	43	125	21	5	3	51	5	.279
1972	Kansas City	OF	151	574	65	179	33	4	11	72	7	.312
1973	Kansas City	OF	144	513	53	128	28	1	9	69	5	.250
1974	New York (AL)	OF-1B	140	518	71	158	26	0	9	70	1	.305
1975	New York (AL)	OF	74	199	7	39	4	1	0	22	0	.196
1976	New York (AL)	OF	100	327	36	92	16	6	3	38	0	.281
1977	New York (AL)	OF-1B	103	339	47	112	19	3	12	45	2	.330
1978	New York (AL)	OF	130	472	67	148	34	5	6	69	3	.314
	Totals		1257	4431	487	1283	226	36	75	593	28	.290

RICH GOSSAGE 27 6-3 190   Bats R Throws R

Led league in saves with 27 . . . Throws bullets . . . "Seventy-five percent of relief pitching is mental." . . . Nicknamed "The Goose" . . . Found golden egg worth $3.6 million when signed as free agent with Yanks . . . Shoved Cy Young Award winner Sparky Lyle aside when he entered Yankee bullpen . . . Born July 5, 1951, in Colorado Springs . . . Was starting pitcher for White Sox in '76 but returned to bullpen with Pirates the following year . . . Was voted AL Fireman of the Year in '75 while with Sox.

Year	Club	G	IP	W	L	Pct.	SO	BB	H	ERA
1972	Chicago (AL)	36	80	7	1	.875	57	44	72	4.28
1973	Chicago (AL)	20	50	0	4	.000	33	37	57	7.38
1974	Chicago (AL)	39	89	4	6	.400	64	47	92	4.15
1975	Chicago (AL)	62	142	9	8	.529	130	70	99	1.84
1976	Chicago (AL)	31	224	9	17	.346	135	90	214	3.94
1977	Pittsburgh	72	133	11	9	.550	151	49	78	1.62
1978	New York (AL)	63	134	10	11	.476	122	59	87	2.01
	Totals	323	852	50	56	.472	692	296	699	3.18

BUCKY DENT 27 5-11 181   Bats R Throws R

Hero of Yankees' thrilling showdown victory over Red Sox in Eastern Division playoff and their World Series conquest of Dodgers . . . Won Series MVP Award for his four-for-four, three-RBI performance in decisive sixth game . . . Not bad for a guy who hits ninth in the batting order . . . "Where else would I bat on this team?" . . . Claims he likes hitting ninth because pitchers have tendency to relax and let up when they get to him . . . Born Nov. 25, 1951, in Savannah, Ga. . . . Came to the Yankees in trade from White Sox the day before the '77 season opened . . . One of the best defensive shortstops in the game . . . The first time he ever saw a major league game, he played in it.

Year	Club	Pos	G	AB	R	H	2B	3B	HR	RBI	SB	Avg.
1973	Chicago (AL)	2B-3B-SS	40	117	17	29	2	0	0	10	2	.248
1974	Chicago (AL)	SS	154	496	55	136	15	3	5	45	3	.274
1975	Chicago (AL)	SS	157	602	52	159	29	4	3	58	2	.264
1976	Chicago (AL)	SS	158	562	44	138	18	4	2	52	3	.246
1977	New York (AL)	SS	158	477	54	118	18	4	8	49	1	.247
1978	New York (AL)	SS	123	379	40	92	11	1	5	40	3	.243
	Totals		790	2633	262	672	93	16	23	254	14	.255

LUIS TIANT 38 5-11 190   Bats R Throws R

Refugee from Cuba now a Yankee . . . "El Tiante" of the herky-jerky motion, dark mustache and ever-present cigar joined George Steinbrenner's stable of thoroughbreds after Red Sox refused to sign him for two years . . . Yanks took him as a free agent for $900,000 for two years . . . Then "Looie" will become club's director of Latin Affairs, spreading George's gospel of capitalism to our underdeveloped neighbors to the south . . . Man of many motions, knows how to keep hitters off-balance and how to get them out . . . One of most popular Red Sox ever . . . Has won 204 games in 15 years . . . Born Nov. 23, 1940, in Havana, Cuba . . . "My mother told me I was born on Nov. 23, 1940," Tiant says to those who think he's older . . . Don't give up on him yet, no matter how old he is.

Year	Club	G	IP	W	L	Pct.	SO	BB	H	ERA
1964	Cleveland...............	19	127	10	4	.714	105	47	94	2.83
1965	Cleveland...............	41	196	11	11	.500	152	66	166	3.54
1966	Cleveland...............	46	155	12	11	.522	145	50	121	2.79
1967	Cleveland...............	33	214	12	9	.571	219	67	177	2.73
1968	Cleveland...............	34	258	21	9	.700	264	73	152	1.60
1969	Cleveland...............	38	250	9	20	.310	156	129	229	3.71
1970	Minnesota..............	18	93	7	3	.700	50	41	84	3.39
1971	Boston.................	21	72	1	7	.125	59	32	73	4.88
1972	Boston.................	43	179	15	6	.714	123	65	128	1.91
1973	Boston.................	35	272	20	13	.606	206	78	217	3.34
1974	Boston.................	38	311	22	13	.629	176	82	281	2.92
1975	Boston.................	35	260	18	14	.563	142	72	262	4.02
1976	Boston.................	3B	279	21	12	.636	131	64	274	3.06
1977	Boston.................	32	189	12	8	.600	124	51	210	4.52
1978	Boston.................	32	212	13	8	.619	114	57	185	3.31
	Totals..................	503	3067	204	148	.580	2166	974	2653	3.16

TOMMY JOHN 35 6-3 185   Bats R Throws L

Another rich Yankee, thanks to the free-agent draft . . . Takes unfair advantage of hitters because he uses both his left and right arms to pitch . . . In 1974, Dr. Frank Jobe used a tendon from his right forearm to reconstruct the ligament in his left elbow . . . Took a year of rehabilitation to turn his left hand from a shriveled hook to a usable hand . . . Sinker ball induces ground ball, and that should do him just fine in the caverns of Yankee Stadium . . . Lost to Yanks in '77 Series, but pitched a victory in Series opener last year . . . Born May 22, 1943, in Terre Haute, Ind. . . . His 17 victories in '78 for the Dodgers was his eighth consecutive season in double figures . . . Has won 47 games since returning to baseball in '76 from the surgery . . . Ambition is to race in the Baja California Off-Road race.

Year	Club	G	IP	W	L	Pct.	SO	BB	H	ERA
1963	Cleveland	6	20	0	2	.000	9	6	23	2.25
1964	Cleveland	25	94	2	9	.182	65	35	97	3.93
1965	Chicago (A.L.)	39	184	14	7	.667	126	58	162	3.03
1966	Chicago (A.L.)	34	223	14	11	.560	138	57	195	2.62
1967	Chicago (A.L.)	31	178	10	13	.435	110	47	143	2.48
1968	Chicago (A.L.)	25	177	10	5	.667	117	49	135	1.98
1969	Chicago (A.L.)	33	232	9	11	.450	128	90	230	3.26
1970	Chicago (A.L.)	37	269	12	17	.414	138	101	253	3.28
1971	Chicago (A.L.)	38	229	13	16	.448	131	58	244	3.62
1972	Los Angeles	29	187	11	5	.688	117	40	172	2.89
1973	Los Angeles	36	218	16	7	.696	116	50	202	3.10
1974	Los Angeles	22	153	13	3	.813	78	42	133	2.59
1975	Los Angeles			Did Not Play						
1976	Los Angeles	31	207	10	10	.500	91	61	207	3.09
1977	Los Angeles	31	220	20	7	.741	123	50	225	2.78
1978	Los Angeles	33	213	17	10	.630	124	53	230	3.30
	Totals	450	2804	171	133	.563	1611	797	2651	2.99

JUAN BENIQUEZ 28 5-11 165　　　　Bats R Throws R

The Magic Juan . . . A defensive genius . . . Can roam the outfield with anyone . . . Won Gold Glove in 1977 . . . He developed into a much better hitter in Texas than he was with Boston . . . Credits the fact that he's now playing regularly . . . "I don't like the bench." . . . Born May 13, 1950, in San Sabastian, P.R. . . . Traded to Texas in November, 1975 for Fergie Jenkins . . . Yanks got him for Sparky Lyle . . . Can also play the infield . . . Good-natured speedster stole 36 bases in past two years.

Year	Club	Pos	G	AB	R	H	2B	3B	HR	RBI	SB	Avg.
1971	Boston	SS	16	57	8	17	2	0	0	4	3	.298
1972	Boston	SS	33	99	10	24	4	1	1	8	2	.242
1974	Boston	OF	106	389	60	104	14	3	5	33	19	.267
1975	Boston	OF-3B	78	254	43	74	14	4	2	17	7	.291
1976	Texas	OF-2B	145	478	49	122	14	4	0	33	17	.255
1977	Texas	OF	123	424	56	114	19	6	10	50	26	.269
1978	Texas	OF	127	473	61	123	17	3	11	50	10	.260
	Totals		628	2174	287	578	84	21	29	195	84	.266

TOP PROSPECTS

PAUL MIRABELLA 25 6-1 190　　　　Bats L Throws L

Received a total of 18 runs in winning first two major league starts . . . Has potential to be outstanding . . . Born March 20, 1954, in Bellville, N.J. . . . Attended Montclair State University

. . . Began pro career at Ashville, N.C., in 1976 where he struck out 136 batters in 149 innings. Came to Yanks in Lyle deal.

DAMASO GARCIA 22 6-1 165   **Bats R Throws R**

Highly regarded infield prospect . . . Problem will be finding a place for him to play . . . Called up in 1978 when Willie Randolph was injured . . . Can also play short . . . Born Feb. 7, 1957, in Moca, Dominican Republic . . . Rod Carew was his boyhood idol . . . A soccer star in high school and college in the Dominican.

MANAGER BOB LEMON: Took over for Billy Martin on July 29 and guided the Yankees to the World Championship . . . The first manager ever to be fired by one club and lead another to the pennant and World Series triumph that same season . . . Fired by White Sox because he lacked flair . . . Brought peace and tranquility to previously troubled Yankee clubhouse . . . Born Sept. 22, 1920, in San Bernadino, Cal. . . . Low-keyed, easy-going guy . . . "I never take a game home with me. I leave it in the bar." . . . Was Manager of Year with White Sox in '77 . . . Hall of Fame pitcher with Cleveland Indians, although didn't begin pitching regularly until he was 27 . . . Supposed to move into front office next season when Martin returns as manager.

GREATEST PITCHER

They called him "Chairman of the Board" when he was in his prime and there was nothing phoney or contrived about that title. Because when Whitey Ford was on the mound, everyone in the ballpark knew he was in command.

By the time he retired, the gutsy, clever, 5-10, 180-pound left-hander won more games than any Yankee pitcher in history (236). And he compiled the best winning percentage (.690) of any pitcher ever.

His earned run average of 2.74 is unsurpassed by any south-paw who ever tried to throw a baseball. He appeared in more World Series games than anyone, and he strung together a record 33⅔ consecutive scoreless innings against the best competition the National League could muster.

But, above all else, Whitey Ford was a winner. And that attitude rubbed off on his Yankee teammates.

When he wasn't pitching, Ford was famous for his good humor. But, as friend and foe alike soon learned, when he stepped on the mound, it was no laughing matter.

Whitey Ford won record 10 World Series games for Yankees.

ALL-TIME YANKEE LEADERS

BATTING: Babe Ruth, .393, 1923
HRs: Roger Maris, 61, 1961
RBIs: Lou Gehrig, 184, 1931
STEALS: Fred Maisel, 74, 1914
WINS: Jack Chesbro, 41, 1904
STRIKEOUTS: Ron Guidry, 248, 1978

MILWAUKEE BREWERS

TEAM DIRECTORY: Chairman of the Board: Ed Fitzgerald; Pres.: Allan "Bud" Selig; Exec. VP-GM: Harry Dalton; VP-Marketing: Richard Hackett; VP-Stadium and Broadcast Operations: Gabe Paul Jr.; Farm Dir. and Admin. of Scouting: Tony Siegle; Pub. Rel.: Tom Skibosh; Mgr.: George Bamberger. Home: Milwaukee County Stadium (54,187). Field distances: 320, l.f. line; 402, c.f.; 315, r.f. line. Spring training: Sun City, Ariz.

SCOUTING REPORT

HITTING: Free agency can help. One man can make a difference. In the case of the Brewers, the one man is Larry Hisle, a $3.2 million baby who made a difference, his .290, 34-homer, 115-RBI bat working wonders for the Brews.

Paul Molitar hit .273, scored 73 runs as a Brewer rookie.

In one season, the Brewers went from 67 victories to 93, jumping three notches and 26½ games in the standings. They went from a .258 team average to .276, going from 10th in the league to first; they improved their home run production by 48, their RBI production by 164 to lead the AL in both departments. And they did all that with Sixto Lezcano missing 30 games, Cecil Cooper missing 55 and Robin Yount missing 35. That's 120 games from three key players, who can make a difference.

PITCHING: Found, a pitching leader for the young Brewers. He's lefty Mike Caldwell, whose six shutouts included two against the world champion Yankees and whose 22 victories represented an increase of 17 over 1977 and earned him "Comeback of the Year" honors. Speaking of comebacks, don't forget Jim Slaton, Bill Travers and Moose Haas. Slaton came back as a free agent from Detroit, where he won 17; Travers, 12-11 last year, hopes to continue his comeback from arm surgery; and arm problems reduced promising Haas to a two-game winner. Lary Sorensen (18-12) and Jerry Augustine (13-12) are two youngsters who round out a good, young staff. George Bamberger was hired as manager simply because he is a genius with pitchers, and he proved it. All the Brewers need now to challenge is to do better than the 17 saves they got out of their bullpen from their top two relievers, Bob McClure and Bill Castro. The addition of Reggie Cleveland could help.

FIELDING: The Brewers finished down the line in team defense, but there were extenuating circumstances. Cecil Cooper played only 84 games at first, Robin Yount missed 37 games at short and rookie Paul Molitor split his time between short and second. Sixto Lezcano missed 35 games in the outfield, but still managed to lead the league in assists with 18. And Gorman Thomas, noted more for his 32-homer bat, was a better than adequate center fielder.

OUTLOOK: More and more, baseball people are taking the Brewers seriously and there are many who think they are in the best position to challenge the Yankee dynasty. It is primarily a young team, which can only get better with experience. But sprinkled among the kids are a handful of solid veteran pros like Larry Hisle, Sal Bando, Ben Oglivie and Don Money, who can lead them to heights the folks of Sudsville never dreamed possible when the team was born out of expansion just 10 years ago.

MILWAUKEE BREWERS 1979 ROSTER

MANAGER George Bamberger
Coaches—Frank Howard, Harvey Kuenn, Cal McLish, Bob Rodgers

PITCHERS

No.	Name	1978 Club	W-L	IP	SO	ERA	B-T	Ht.	Wt.	Born
46	Augustine, Jerry	Milwaukee	13-12	188	59	4.55	L-L	6-0	185	7/24/52 Kewaunee, WI
—	Beare, Gary	Spokane	2-6	75	37	5.52	R-R	6-3	205	8/22/52 San Diego, CA
36	Bomback, Mark	Milwaukee	0-0	2	1	13-50	R-R	5-11	170	4/14/53 Portsmouth, VA
		Spokane	7-5	132	111	3.55				
48	Caldwell, Mike	Milwaukee	22-9	293	131	2.36	R-L	6-0	185	1/22/49 Tarboro, NC
35	Castro, Bill	Milwaukee	5-4	50	17	1.81	R-R	5-11	170	12/13/53 Dominican Republic
—	Cleveland, Reggie	Bos.-Tex.	5-8	76	46	3.08	R-R	6-1	200	5/23/48 Swift Current, Sask.
30	Haas, Moose	Milwaukee	2-3	31	32	6.10	R-R	6-0	170	4/22/56 Baltimore, MD
10	McClure, Bob	Milwaukee	2-6	65	47	3.74	B-L	5-11	170	4/29/53 Oakland, CA
40	Mueller, Willie	Milwaukee	1-0	13	6	6.23	R-R	6-4	220	8/30/56 West Bend, WI
		Holyoke	7-5	96	74	2.91				
27	Replogle, Andy	Milwaukee	9-5	149	41	3.99	R-R	6-5	205	10/7/53 South Bend, IN
23	Rodriguez, Ed	Milwaukee	5-5	105	51	3.94	R-R	6-0	180	3/6/52 Puerto Rico
—	Slaton, Jim	Detroit	17-11	234	92	4.12	R-R	6-0	185	6/19/50 Long Beach, CA
39	Sorenson, Lary	Milwaukee	18-12	281	78	3.20	R-R	6-2	205	10/4/55 Detroit, MI
43	Stein, Randy	Milwaukee	3-2	73	42	5.30	R-R	6-4	210	3/7/53 Pomona, CA
25	Travers, Bill	Milwaukee	12-11	176	66	4.45	L-L	6-6	200	10/27/52 Norwood, MA

CATCHERS

No.	Name	1978 Club	H	HR	RBI	Pct.	B-T	Ht.	Wt.	Born
13	Fosse, Ray	Milwaukee	on disabled list				R-R	6-2	210	4/4/47 Marion, IL
21	Martinez, Buck	Milwaukee	56	1	20	.219	R-R	5-11	190	11/7/48 Redding, CA
22	Moore, Charlie	Milwaukee	72	5	31	.269	R-R	5-11	180	6/21/53 Birmingham, AL
—	Yost, Ed	Spokane	70	7	42	.262	R-R	6-1	185	8/19/55 Eureka, CA

INFIELDERS

No.	Name	1978 Club	H	HR	RBI	Pct.	B-T	Ht.	Wt.	Born
6	Bando, Sal	Milwaukee	154	17	78	.285	R-R	6-0	195	2/13/44 Cleveland, OH
15	Cooper, Cecil	Milwaukee	127	13	54	.312	L-L	6-2	185	12/20/49 Brenham, TX
17	Gantner, Jim	Milwaukee	21	1	8	.216	L-R	5-11	175	1/5/53 Fond du Lac, WI
4	Molitor, Paul	Milwaukee	142	6	45	.273	R-R	6-0	175	8/22/56 St. Paul, MN
21	Money, Don	Milwaukee	152	14	54	.293	R-R	6-1	190	6/7/47 Washington, DC
1	Nordbrook, Tim	Tor.-Mil.	0	0	0	.000	R-R	6-1	170	7/17/49 Baltimore, MD
2	Sakata, Lenn	Milwaukee	15	0	3	.192	R-R	5-9	160	6/8/53 Honolulu, HI
		Spokane	42	0	20	.269				
—	Romero, Ed	Spokane	123	4	52	.280	R-R	5-11	160	12/9/57 Puerto Rico
19	Yount, Robin	Milwaukee	147	9	71	.293	R-R	6-0	165	9/16/55 Danville, IL

OUTFIELDERS

No.	Name	1978 Club	H	HR	RBI	Pct.	B-T	Ht.	Wt.	Born
26	Davis, Dick	Milwaukee	54	5	26	.248	R-R	6-3	190	9/25/53 Long Beach, CA
7	Hisle, Larry	Milwaukee	151	34	115	.290	R-R	6-2	195	5/5/47 Portsmouth, OH
16	Lezcano, Sixto	Milwaukee	129	15	61	.292	R-R	5-10	175	11/28/53 Puerto Rico
24	Oglivie, Ben	Milwaukee	142	18	72	.303	L-L	6-2	170	2/11/49 Panama
—	Smith, Bobby	Burlington	168	3	46	.332	L-L	5-10	175	1/23/56 Vallejo, CA
20	Thomas, Gorman	Milwaukee	111	32	86	.246	R-R	6-3	205	12/12/50 Charleston, SC
14	Wohlford, Jim	Milwaukee	35	1	19	.297	R-R	5-10	175	2/18/51 Visalia, CA
11	Yurak, Jeff	Milwaukee	0	0	0	.000	B-R	6-3	195	2/26/54 Pasadena, CA
		Holyoke	152	21	87	.321				

BREWER PROFILES

SAL BANDO 35 6-0 195   Bats R Throws R

Continues to be key cog in Brewer machine . . . Played important part in Team's remarkable rise in '78 . . . Cut down on strikeouts last year to increase effectiveness . . . "I thought about keeping the ball in play with two outs" . . . Spent nine seasons with Oakland before joining Brewers and is accustomed to pressure of pennant race . . . Born Feb. 13, 1944, in Cleveland . . . Attended Arizona State and was MVP in College World Series . . . A consistent clutch performer.

Year	Club	Pos	G	AB	R	H	2B	3B	HR	RBI	SB	Avg
1966	Kansas City	3B	11	24	1	7	1	1	0	1	0	.292
1967	Kansas City	3B	47	130	11	25	3	2	0	6	1	.192
1968	Oakland	3B-OF	162	605	67	152	25	5	9	67	13	.251
1969	Oakland	3B	162	609	106	171	25	3	31	113	1	.281
1970	Oakland	3B	155	502	93	132	20	2	20	75	6	.263
1971	Oakland	3B	153	538	75	146	23	1	24	94	3	.271
1972	Oakland	3B-2B	152	535	64	126	20	3	15	77	3	.236
1973	Oakland	3B	162	592	97	170	32	3	29	98	4	.287
1974	Oakland	3B	146	498	84	121	21	2	22	103	2	.243
1975	Oakland	3B	160	562	64	129	24	1	15	78	7	.230
1976	Oakland	3B-SS	158	550	75	132	18	2	27	84	20	.240
1977	Milwaukee	3B-2B-SS	159	580	65	145	27	3	17	82	4	.250
1978	Milwaukee	3B	152	540	85	154	20	6	17	78	3	.285
	Totals		1779	6265	887	1610	259	34	226	956	67	.257

DON MONEY 31 6-1 190   Bats R Throws R

Steady, solid and reliable . . . "He's one of the most steady ballplayers there is," says George Bamberger . . . Senior Brewer in terms of service, having spent six full years with club . . . Teased for his frugality by his teammates, who suggest his habits were inspired by his surname . . . Ironically, was originally signed by Syd Thrift, then with the Pirates . . . Born June 7, 1947, in Washington, D.C. . . . Owns two-acre farm in New Jersey . . . Has bounced from second to third, back to second and back to third . . . Calls self "expensive utility man" . . . Wrote book about former teammate Henry Aaron.

Year	Club	Pos	G	AB	R	H	2B	3B	HR	RBI	SB	Avg.
1968	Philadelphia......	SS	4	13	1	3	2	0	0	2	0	.231
1969	Philadelphia......	SS	127	450	41	103	22	2	6	42	1	.229
1970	Philadelphia......	3B-SS	120	447	66	132	25	4	14	66	4	.295
1971	Philadelphia......	3B-2B-OF	121	439	40	98	22	8	7	38	4	.223
1972	Philadelphia......	3B-SS	152	536	54	119	16	2	15	52	5	.222
1973	Milwaukee.......	3B-SS	145	556	75	158	28	2	11	61	22	.284
1974	Milwaukee.......	3B-2B	159	629	85	178	32	3	15	65	19	.283
1975	Milwaukee.......	3B-SS	109	405	58	112	16	1	15	43	7	.277
1976	Milwaukee.......	3B-SS	117	439	51	117	18	4	12	62	6	.267
1977	Milwaukee.......	2B-3B	152	570	86	159	28	3	25	83	8	.279
1978	Milwaukee.......	3B-1B-2B	137	518	88	152	30	2	14	54	3	.293
	Totals...........		1343	5002	645	1331	239	31	134	568	79	.266

CECIL COOPER 29 6-2 185   Bats L Throws L

Changed stance in 1978 after slow start, copying deep crouch used by Rod Carew . . . Frequently consults Carew, whom he calls "The Hitting Instructor" . . . Still strikes out too often to suit himself . . . Has trouble handling high fastball . . . Born Dec. 12, 1949, in Brehham, Tex. . . . Finally got opportunity to play every day with Brewers when Milwaukee traded George Scott . . . Has proved ability by putting together five solid seasons in a row . . . Drafted by Cardinals, but went to Red Sox because Cards had no room for him.

Year	Club	Pos	G	AB	R	H	2B	3B	HR	RBI	SB	Avg.
1971	Boston..........	1B	14	42	9	13	4	1	0	3	1	.310
1972	Boston..........	1B	12	17	0	4	1	0	0	2	0	.235
1973	Boston..........	1B	30	101	12	24	2	0	3	11	1	.238
1974	Boston..........	1B	121	414	55	114	24	1	8	43	2	.275
1975	Boston..........	1B	106	305	49	95	17	6	14	44	1	.311
1976	Boston..........	1B	123	451	66	127	22	6	15	78	7	.282
1977	Milwaukee.......	1B	160	643	86	193	31	7	20	78	13	.300
1978	Milwaukee.......	1B	107	407	60	127	23	2	13	54	3	.312
	Totals...........		673	2380	337	697	124	23	73	313	28	.293

ROBIN YOUNT 23 6-0 165   Bats R Throws R

Will have spent nearly six years in the big leagues by the time he turns 24 . . . Signed lucrative multi-year contract for undisclosed amount of cash after threatening to quit baseball and try his hand at pro golf tour . . . Enjoyed finest year of career in '78 . . . "I'm getting stronger as I get older. Not only physically, but mentally, too." . . . Born Sept. 16, 1955, in Danville, Ill. . . . "He has matured so much it's unbelievable" says coach Harvey Kuenn . . . One of outstanding shortstops in the game . . . Brewers' first round draft pick in June, 1973.

Year	Club	Pos	G	AB	R	H	2B	3B	HR	RBI	SB	Avg
1974	Milwaukee.......	SS	107	344	48	86	14	5	3	26	7	.25
1975	Milwaukee.......	SS	147	558	67	149	28	2	8	52	12	.26
1976	Milwaukee.......	SS-OF	161	638	59	161	19	3	2	54	16	.252
1977	Milwaukee.......	SS	154	605	66	174	34	4	4	49	16	.288
1978	Milwaukee.......	SS	127	502	66	147	23	9	9	71	16	.293
	Totals..........		696	2647	306	717	118	23	26	252	67	.271

LARRY HISLE 31 6-2 195   Bats R Throws R

Biggest of second batch of free agents, signing $3.1 million contract . . . Yet remains quiet, unassuming . . . "We view money as a means to bring our lives a measure of happiness. That's its only value." . . . Amateur photographer . . . Born May 5, 1947, in Portsmouth, Ohio . . . "I'm more interested in playing good on the field than seeing my name in headlines. I'd rather have RBIs than clippings." . . . And he's had a few of each . . . A former first round draft pick of the Phillies, he was given a big buildup as a rookie but was unable to cope with it emotionally . . . Later flunked trials with Dodgers and Cardinals before finding success with Twins.

Year	Club	Pos	G	AB	R	H	2B	3B	HR	RBI	SB	Avg.
1968	Philadelphia......	OF	7	11	1	4	1	0	0	1	0	.364
1969	Philadelphia......	OF	145	482	75	128	23	5	20	56	18	.266
1970	Philadelphia......	OF	126	405	52	83	72	4	10	44	5	.205
1971	Philadelphia......	OF	36	76	7	15	3	0	0	3	1	.197
1973	Minnesota	OF	143	545	88	148	25	6	15	64	11	.272
1974	Minnesota	OF	143	510	68	146	20	7	19	79	12	.286
1975	Minnesota	OF	80	255	37	80	9	2	11	51	17	.314
1976	Minnesota	OF	155	581	81	158	19	5	14	96	31	.272
1977	Minnesota	OF	141	546	95	165	36	3	28	119	21	.302
1978	Milwaukee.......	OF	142	520	96	151	24	0	34	115	10	.290
	Totals..........		1118	3931	600	1078	182	32	151	630	126	.274

GORMAN THOMAS 28 6-3 205   Bats R Throws R

Former flake, calmed down in 1978 and began clobbering home runs . . . Used to perch on top of his locker reading magazine or walk through the clubhouse mimicking Fonzie . . . Once tried to dye his hair from brown to blonde and it turned out orange . . . "I've calmed down quite a bit." . . . Born Dec. 12, 1950, in Charleston, S.C. . . .

Spent four years with Brewers before being relegated to Spokane in '77 . . . Finally put his game together in '78.

Year	Club	Pos	G	AB	R	H	2B	3B	HR	RBI	SB	Avg.
1973	Milwaukee	OF-3B	59	155	16	29	7	1	2	11	5	.187
1974	Milwaukee	OF	17	46	10	12	4	0	2	11	4	.261
1975	Milwaukee	OF	121	240	34	43	12	2	10	28	4	.179
1976	Milwaukee	OF-3B	99	227	27	45	9	2	8	36	2	.198
1978	Milwaukee	OF	137	452	70	111	24	1	32	86	3	.246
	Totals		433	1120	157	240	56	6	54	172	18	.214

BEN OGLIVIE 30 6-2 170   Bats L Throws L

The "Banana Man" . . . Enjoyed finest year of his career in 1978 when finally got opportunity to play full time after showing promise year after year in Boston and Detroit . . . "I got labeled," he says of his days in those two cities . . . Played much better than expected defensively . . . Born Feb. 11, 1949, in Colon, Panama . . . Was raised in New York City but struggled with English during the early days of his career . . . Intelligent, introspective man, loves to read poetry and study philosophy, although he admittedly doesn't always understand everything he reads . . . Used to wear the Brewers out when he played for Detroit, which was why Milwaukee wanted him.

Year	Club	Pos	G	AB	R	H	2B	3B	HR	RBI	SB	Avg.
1971	Boston	OF	14	38	2	10	3	0	0	4	0	.263
1972	Boston	OF	94	253	27	61	10	2	8	30	1	.241
1973	Boston	OF	58	147	16	32	9	1	2	9	1	.218
1974	Detroit	OF-1B	92	252	28	68	11	3	4	29	12	.270
1975	Detroit	OF-1B	100	332	45	95	14	1	9	36	11	.286
1976	Detroit	OF-1B	115	305	36	87	12	3	15	47	9	.285
1977	Detroit	OF	132	450	63	118	24	2	21	61	9	.262
1978	Milwaukee	OF	128	469	71	142	29	4	18	72	11	.303
	Totals		733	2246	288	613	112	16	77	288	54	.273

PAUL MOLITOR 22 6-0 175   Bats R Throws R

Was supposed to spend 1978 season at Spokane, learning to play the game . . . Instead, stunned Brewers and AL with his surprisingly strong performance . . . Started season at shortstop in absence of Robin Yount, later moved to second base where he became a star . . . "He really has a head on his shoulders," says George Bamberger . . . "He looks like he's played the game for 10 or 15 years." . . . Born Aug. 22, 1956, in St. Paul . . . The Brewers' No. 1 pick in June, 1977, draft . . . Spent only one year in minors, but was outstanding, winning every honor in sight . . . Was All-American at University of Minnesota, where arm injury forced him to abandon mound and become infielder.

Year	Club	Pos	G	AB	R	H	2B	3B	HR	RBI	SB	Avg.
1978	Milwaukee	2B	125	521	73	142	26	4	6	45	30	.273

LARY SORENSEN 23 6-2 205   Bats R Throws R

Could be outstanding pitcher for many years to come . . . One of Brewers many fine young pitchers who figure to keep club in thick of pennant race . . . Grew up in Detroit, worshipping Tigers . . . Still has chunk of Tiger Stadium sod torn up the night the team won 1968 pennant . . . Bypassed by his boyhood heroes but drafted on eighth round in 1976 by Brewers because Tigers didn't think he threw hard enough . . . "Milwaukee liked my attitude better than my stuff." . . . Born Oct. 4, 1955, in Detroit . . . Starred at University of Michigan . . . Joined Brewers midway through '77 season, but was plagued by tough luck.

Year	Club	G	IP	W	L	Pct.	SO	BB	H	ERA
1977	Milwaukee	23	142	7	10	.412	57	36	147	4.37
1978	Milwaukee	37	281	18	12	.600	78	50	277	3.20
	Totals	60	423	25	22	.532	135	86	424	3.60

MIKE CALDWELL 30 6-0 185   Bats R Throws L

The old man of the Brewer pitching staff . . . Ignored in winter when Brewers talked about '78 team . . . Yet led league in complete games with 23, finished second in wins and third in ERA . . . "A great competitor," says George Bamberger . . . Born Jan. 22, 1949, in Tarboro, N.C. . . . Finally has recovered from elbow surgery he underwent following 1974 season . . . Average stuff, but great control . . . Set Brewer record with six shutouts . . . Also broke club record for wins, complete games and ERA.

Year	Club	G	IP	W	L	Pct.	SO	BB	H	ERA
1971	San Diego	6	7	1	0	1.000	5	3	4	0.00
1972	San Diego	42	164	7	11	.389	102	49	183	4.01
1973	San Diego	55	149	5	14	.263	86	53	146	3.74
1974	San Francisco	31	189	14	5	.737	83	63	176	2.95
1975	San Francisco	38	163	7	13	.350	57	48	194	4.80
1976	San Francisco	50	107	1	7	.125	55	20	145	4.88
1977	Cincinnati	14	25	0	0	.000	11	8	25	3.96
1977	Milwaukee	21	94	5	8	.385	38	36	101	4.60
1978	Milwaukee	37	293	22	9	.710	131	54	258	2.37
	Totals	294	1190	62	67	.481	568	334	1232	3.62

TOP PROSPECTS

DICK DAVIS 25 6-3 190   **Bats R Throws R**
Appears ready to break into big league line-up . . . Continues
to show marked improvement at plate . . . Born Sept. 25, 1953,
in Long Beach, Cal. . . . Impressive minor league statistics . . .
Signed with Brewers as free agent in 1972 . . . Originally a first
baseman, can also play outfield or DH.

JIM GANTNER 26 5-11 175   **Bats L Throws R**
Talented infielder, has had three brief trials with Brewers . . .
Drafted on 12th round in 1974 . . . Born Jan. 5, 1953, in Fond
du Lac, Wisc. . . . Has hit consistently in minors . . . Must
prove he can do it in big time . . . Also has good speed on
bases.

MANAGER GEORGE BAMBERGER: Named by The Sporting
News as Manager of the Year . . . Responsi-
ble for remarkable rise of Brewers in '78, his
rookie season as a manager . . . Still plans to
retire at end of '79 season, though success
might tempt him to stick around a while . . .
Great handler of pitchers . . . Built Baltimore's fine pitching staffs . . . Born Aug. 1,
1925, on Staten Island, N.Y. . . . CB enthu-
siast . . . His handle is "Brew Master" . . . Easy-going, but can
explode at times . . . Impressed GM Harry Dalton with his
frankness and his ability to handle men . . . Brewers became
known as "Bambi's Bombers" last year.

GREATEST PITCHER

At age 19, he signed a contract with a team that was based in Seattle and known as the Pilots. By the time Jim Slaton surfaced in the big leagues two years later, the Pilots had moved to Milwaukee and changed their name to the Brewers.

It didn't take Slaton long to make a name for himself as he quickly won 10 games as an inexperienced rookie and served notice on the rest of the American League that they'd be seeing a lot more of him in the years to come.

And they did.

By the time the Brewers traded him to the Tigers following the 1977 season, the reliable right-hander ranked No. 1 in virtually every pitching department in the Brewer record book.

He appeared in more games (220), won more games (72), pitched more innings (1,449), struck out more enemy batters (701) and shut out more opponents (16) than anyone in Milwaukee's American League history. And now he is back with the Brewers to add to his records.

ALL-TIME BREWER LEADERS

BATTING: Cecil Cooper, .312, 1978
HRs: George Scott, 36, 1975
RBIs: Larry Hisle, 115, 1978
STEALS: Tommy Harper, 73, 1969
WINS: Mike Caldwell, 22, 1978
STRIKEOUTS: Marty Pattin, 161, 1971

BOSTON RED SOX

TEAM DIRECTORY: President: Mrs. Thomas A. Yawkey; VP-GM: Haywood Sullivan; VP: Edward "Buddy" LeRoux; Pub. Rel.: Bill Crowley; Trav. Sec.: John Rogers; Mgr.: Don Zimmer. Home: Fenway Park (33,543). Field distances: 315, l.f. line; 390, c.f.; 420, c.f. corner; 380, r.c.; 302, r.f. line. Spring training: Winter Haven, Fla.

SCOUTING REPORT

HITTING: Jim Rice is the one-man Boston wrecking crew who turned in one of the most awesome set of hitting statistics in

Jim Rice won MVP, but the Sox lost the pennant.

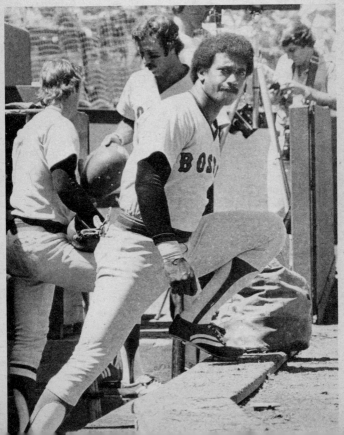

baseball history in only his fourth full year. At 26, he can only get better. His league-leading 46 homers, 139 RBIs, 15 triples, 213 hits and .600 slugging percentage puts him in a class with Jimmy Foxx, Hank Greenberg and Joe DiMaggio as a right-handed slugger and makes him a threat to Roger Maris' 61 home run record. Playing in Fenway Park doesn't hurt, either.

It should not be misconstrued that Rice gets no help from his Red Sox teammates. Fred Lynn, Carlton Fisk, Butch Hobson, George Scott and Carl Yastrzemski, still going strong after all these years (39 of them), continue to give the Sox the most devastating attack in the league. Especially at home.

PITCHING: How can a team, desperate for pitching, beaten in a playoff with the Yankees last year, let Luis Tiant walk away? And to the rival Yankees, no less. Subtracting Tiant's 13 victories and Bill Lee's 10, that's 23 victories the Sox must find this year. Can they expect more than 20 from Dennis Eckersley? Can Bob Stanley do better than 15-2? The hope is that Mike Torrez can improve on his disappointing 16-13 after going six weeks down the stretch without winning. And that young Allen Ripley (2-5) can take a regular turn. And that Jim Wright can improve on his 8-4. And that Bill Campbell can rebound from shoulder problems.

FIELDING: As always, there is strength up the middle—Fisk at catch, an excellent DP combo of Rick Burleson, short, and Jerry Remy, second, and Lynn in center—but the Sox are beginning to wear thin around the edges. George Scott is no longer the Gold Glove first baseman he used to be. Butch Hobson at third, was guilty of 43 errors, many because of an elbow injury. A beaning caused double vision for Dwight Evans, who made an uncharacteristic six errors in right. Yaz still plays the left field wall like he built it, but a bad back has curtailed his defensive skill somewhat. The Sox are also short on bench strength, which hurt last year when a rash of injuries depleted their formidable starting corps.

OUTLOOK: Their standstill attitude is difficult to comprehend, especially since all around them, the Red Sox' rivals were improving. Complacency can cost the Red Sox not only the pennant, but they will be hard pressed to fight off the improving Brewers and solid Orioles for second and third. Thin pitching, Yaz' age and lack of bench strength can prove costly this year, despite the potent bat of Rice, the most destructive hitter in either league.

BOSTON RED SOX 1979 ROSTER

MANAGER Don Zimmer
Coaches—Walt Hriniak, Al Jackson, John Pesky, Eddie Yost

PITCHERS

No.	Name	1978 Club	W-L	IP	SO	ERA	B-T	Ht.	Wt.	Born
16	Burgmeier, Tom	Boston	2-1	61	24	4.43	L-L	5-11	180	8/2/43 St. Paul, MN
22	Campbell, Bill	Boston	7-5	51	47	3.88	R-R	6-3	190	8/9/48 Highland Park, MI
41	Drago, Dick	Boston	4-4	77	42	3.04	R-R	6-2	200	6/24/45 Toledo, OH
43	Eckersley, Dennis	Boston	20-8	268	162	2.99	R-R	6-2	190	10/3/54 Oakland, CA
—	Finch, Joel	Pawtucket	11-8	167	101	3.17	R-R	6-2	175	8/20/56 South Bend, IN
31	Hassler, Andy	KC-Boston	3-5	88	49	3.89	L-L	6-5	215	10/18/51 Texas City, TX
28	LaRose, John	Pawtucket	10-5	73	44	1.60	L-L	6-1	185	— Pawtucket, RI
		Boston	0-0	2	0	22.50				
—	Rainey, Chuck	Pawtucket	13-7	170	104	2.91	R-R	5-11	195	7/14/54 San Diego, CA
—	Remmerswaal, Win	Pawtucket	8-6	155	108	4.48	R-R	6-2	160	3/3/54 Holland
—	Ripley, Allen	Boston	2-5	73	26	5.55	R-R	6-3	180	10/18/52 Norwood, MA
		Pawtucket	2-2	37	28	5.54				
—	Schneck, Steve	Bristol	15-7	205	180	2.15	R-R	6-0	180	— Benton Harbor, MI
47	Sprowl, Bobby	Bristol	9-3	103	102	2.71	L-L	6-2	195	— Tampa, FL
		Pawtucket	7-4	78	69	4.15				
		Boston	0-2	13	10	6.23				
46	Stanley, Bob	Boston	15-2	142	38	2.60	R-R	6-4	205	11/10/54 Portland, ME
—	Suter, Burk	Pawtucket	10-6	132	134	3.34	R-R	6-3	190	— Parkville, MD
21	Torrez, Mike	Boston	16-13	250	120	3.96	R-R	6-5	202	8/28/46 Topeka, KS
—	Tudor, John	Pawtucket	8-4	109	87	2.98	L-L	6-0	185	— Peabody, MA
45	Wright, Jim	Boston	8-4	116	56	3.57	R-R	6-1	165	12/21/50 Reed City, MI

CATCHERS

No.	Name	1978 Club	H	HR	RBI	Pct.	B-T	Ht.	Wt.	Born
26	Allenson, Gary	Pawtucket	133	20	76	.299	R-R	5-11	188	— Hawthorne, CA
27	Fisk, Carlton	Boston	162	20	88	.284	R-R	6-2	215	12/26/47 Bellows Falls, VT
10	Montgomery, Bob	Boston	7	0	5	.241	R-R	6-1	210	4/16/44 Nashville, TN
—	O'Berry, Mike	Bristol	79	6	41	.235	R-R	6-2	190	— Birmingham, AL

INFIELDERS

No.	Name	1978 Club	H	HR	RBI	Pct.	B-T	Ht.	Wt.	Born
3	Brohamer, Jack	Boston	57	1	25	.234	L-R	5-9	170	2/26/50 Maywood, CA
7	Burleson, Rick	Boston	155	5	49	.248	R-R	5-10	165	4/29/51 Lynwood, CA
17	Duffy, Frank	Boston	27	0	4	.260	R-R	6-1	180	10/14/46 Oakland, CA
4	Hobson, Butch	Boston	128	17	80	.250	R-R	6-1	190	8/17/51 Tuscaloosa, AL
—	Hoffman, Glenn	Pawtucket	116	2	48	.282	R-R	6-2	170	— Anaheim, CA
—	Papi, Stan	Montreal	35	0	11	.230	R-R	6-0	178	2/4/51 Fresno, CA
2	Remy, Jerry	Boston	162	2	44	.278	L-R	5-9	165	11/8/52 Fall River, MA
15	Scott, George	Boston	96	12	54	.233	R-R	6-2	210	3/23/44 Greenville, MS
—	Valdez, Julio	Bristol	104	7	55	.269	R-R	6-2	150	— Dominican Republic

OUTFIELDERS

No.	Name	1978 Club	H	HR	RBI	Pct.	B-T	Ht.	Wt.	Born
29	Bowen, Sam	Pawtucket	67	12	49	.252	R-R	5-9	167	9/18/52 Brunswick, GA
—	Easler, Mike	Columbus	148	18	84	.330	L-R	6-0	190	11/29/50 Cleveland, OH
24	Evans, Dwight	Boston	124	24	63	.247	R-R	6-3	205	11/3/51 Santa Monica, CA
38	Hancock, Garry	Pawtucket	94	8	44	.303	L-L	6-0	175	— Brandon, FL
		Boston	18	0	4	.225				
19	Lynn, Fred	Boston	161	22	82	.298	L-L	6-1	185	2/3/52 Chicago, IL
14	Rice, Jim	Boston	213	46	139	.315	R-R	6-2	200	3/8/53 Anderson, SC
8	Yastrzemski, Carl	Boston	145	17	81	.277	L-R	5-11	190	8/22/39 Southampton, NY

RED SOX PROFILES

CARL YASTRZEMSKI 39 5-11 190   Bats L Throws R

Captain Carl . . . An inspiration to all the Red Sox . . . Great in clutch . . . Was deeply saddened by death of mother prior to '78 season . . . "She was an incredible woman. She showed me what courage really is. Seeing the way she handled it shaped my life." . . . Hindered by bad back, forced to wear brace . . . Starting 19th season . . . Born Aug. 22, 1939, in Southampton, N.Y. . . . "I never get tired. Never. Maybe it's because I enjoy the game and never let myself get out of shape." . . . Very close to late Bosox owner Tom Yawkey . . . In all-time top 30 in games, at bats, doubles, homers, RBIs, walks . . . Master at playing Fenway Park's tricky left field wall.

Year	Club	Pos	G	AB	R	H	2B	3B	HR	RBI	SB	Avg.
1961	Boston	OF	148	583	71	155	31	6	11	80	6	.266
1962	Boston	OF	160	646	99	191	43	6	19	94	7	.296
1963	Boston	OF	151	570	91	183	40	3	14	68	8	.321
1964	Boston	OF-3B	151	567	77	164	29	9	15	67	6	.289
1965	Boston	OF	133	494	78	154	45	3	20	72	7	.312
1966	Boston	OF	160	594	81	165	39	2	16	80	8	.278
1967	Boston	OF	161	579	112	189	31	4	44	121	10	.326
1968	Boston	OF-1B	157	539	90	162	32	2	23	74	13	.301
1969	Boston	OF-1B	162	603	96	154	28	2	40	111	15	.255
1970	Boston	1B-OF	161	566	125	186	29	0	40	102	23	.329
1971	Boston	OF	148	508	75	129	21	2	15	70	8	.254
1972	Boston	OF-1B	125	455	70	120	18	2	12	68	5	.264
1973	Boston	1B-3B-OF	152	540	82	160	25	4	19	95	9	.296
1974	Boston	1B-OF	148	515	93	155	25	2	15	79	12	.301
1975	Boston	1B-OF	149	543	91	146	30	1	14	60	8	.269
1976	Boston	1B-OF	155	546	71	146	23	2	21	102	5	.267
1977	Boston	1B-OF	150	558	99	165	27	3	28	102	11	.296
1978	Boston	OF-1B	144	523	70	145	21	2	17	81	4	.277
	Totals		2715	9929	1571	2869	537	55	383	1526	165	.289

CARLTON FISK 31 6-2 215   Bats R Throws R

Compares job to that of football quarterback, although more difficult . . . Takes charge behind plate, encouraging pitchers, prodding them when they need it . . . "There just aren't enough words to total up what Fisk has done for us," says Don Zimmer . . . Sign over his locker reads: "Think" . . . Born Dec. 26, 1947, in Bellows Falls, Vt. . . . No longer blocks the plate the way he once did . . . When in doubt, he protects his body . . . "I'm the master of the ole tag." . . .

Nicknamed "Pudge" . . . Will always be remembered for dramatic game-winning HR in sixth game of '75 Series.

Year	Club	Pos	G	AB	R	H	2B	3B	HR	RBI	SB	Avg.
1969	Boston	C	2	5	0	0	0	0	0	0	0	.000
1971	Boston	C	14	48	7	15	2	1	2	6	0	.313
1972	Boston	C	131	457	74	134	28	9	22	61	5	.293
1973	Boston	C	135	508	65	125	21	0	26	71	7	.246
1974	Boston	C	52	187	36	56	12	1	11	26	5	.299
1975	Boston	C	79	263	47	87	14	4	10	52	4	.331
1976	Boston	C	134	487	76	124	17	5	17	58	12	.255
1977	Boston	C	152	536	106	169	26	3	26	102	7	.315
1978	Boston	C	157	571	94	162	39	5	20	88	7	.284
	Totals		856	3062	505	872	159	28	134	464	47	.285

JIM RICE 26 6-2 200   Bats R Throws R

Positively awesome at the plate . . . Led league in hits, triples, homers, RBIs, total bases, slugging percentage and at bats . . . Finished third in batting race behind Rod Carew . . . Finished first in MVP voting, though, ahead of Ron Guidry . . . "With the unlimited talent and strength he has, God only knows what he might accomplish in the future," says Don Zimmer. "There isn't any question but that he can be an all-time great." . . . Already compared to Jimmy Foxx and Hank Greenberg . . . Born March 8, 1953, in Anderson, S.C. . . . Strong, silent type . . . "I want to get better, I want to improve every year I play, and I think I can." . . . Once tried to check swing in Detroit and his strength snapped bat in half . . . Occasionally wears contact lenses at plate . . . Can play LF, RF or DH . . . Credits coach John Pesky and scout Sam Mele for success.

Year	Club	Pos	G	AB	R	H	2B	3B	HR	RBI	SB	Avg.
1974	Boston	OF	24	67	6	18	2	1	1	13	0	.269
1975	Boston	OF	144	564	92	174	29	4	22	102	10	.309
1976	Boston	OF	153	581	75	164	25	8	25	85	8	.282
1977	Boston	OF	160	644	104	206	29	15	39	114	5	.320
1978	Boston	OF	163	677	121	213	25	15	46	139	7	.315
	Totals		644	2533	398	775	110	43	133	453	30	.306

BOB STANLEY 24 6-4 205   Bats R Throws R

Emerged as unexpected ace of bullpen when Bill Campbell and Dick Drago were both hurt . . . Compiled second best winning percentage in league . . . Has nasty sinker, throws it at two or three different speeds . . . Thought he might be traded in spring training . . . Added slider to repertoire this season . . . Some think he has more raw talent than any pitcher on staff . . . "The talent was always there," says pitching coach Al Jackson. "Mostly it was a matter of watching it grow." . . . "Born Nov. 10, 1954, in Portland, Me. . . . "There's no telling how good he can be," says Don Zimmer . . . Made jump from Double-A to big leagues in '77 . . . Can start as well as relieve . . . Was No. 1 pick in January, 1974, free agent draft.

Year	Club	G	IP	W	L	Pct.	SO	BB	H	ERA
1977	Boston	41	151	8	7	.533	44	43	176	3.99
1978	Boston	52	142	15	2	.882	38	34	142	2.60
	Totals	93	293	23	9	.719	82	77	318	3.32

BUTCH HOBSON 27 6-1 190   Bats R Throws R

Underwent surgery following 1978 season to remove bone chips in elbow . . . Developed into Fenway Park favorite because of aggressive attitude . . . Dangerous in clutch . . . Replaced popular Rico Petrocelli at third . . . Quiet, drawling, extra polite . . . "He still says 'Yes, sir' and 'No, Sir,' " says veteran coach Johnny Pesky. "Not many of them do that these days." . . . Born Aug. 17, 1951, in Tuscaloosa, Ala. . . . Real name Clell Lavern Jr. . . . Quarterback of Alabama's 1972 Orange Bowl team against Nebraska . . . Bear Bryant remembers him as a "tough player and a quiet leader." . . . Swings heavy 34 ounce bat.

Year	Club	Pos	G	AB	R	H	2B	3B	HR	RBI	SB	Avg.
1975	Boston	3B	2	4	0	1	0	0	0	0	0	.250
1976	Boston	3B	76	269	34	63	7	5	8	34	0	.234
1977	Boston	3B	159	593	77	157	33	5	30	112	5	.265
1978	Boston	3B	147	512	65	128	26	2	17	80	1	.250
	Totals		384	1378	176	349	66	12	55	226	6	.253

FRED LYNN 27 6-1 185   Bats L Throws L

Went into late-season tailspin in '78 along with rest of Red Sox . . . "The hits just weren't falling in" . . . Hampered by injuries for last three years after storybook rookie season in '75 . . . Red Sox denied rumors that he might be traded . . . Still young enough to get his act together and become a superstar . . . One of the best center fielders in the game, famous for his diving, somersault catches . . . Born Feb. 2, 1952, in Chicago . . . Moved to California and starred at USC . . . Enjoyed best night of career in Detroit,

June 18, 1975, when he hit three homers, a triple, and a single, drove in 10 runs and tied record with 16 total bases.

Year	Club	Pos	G	AB	R	H	2B	3B	HR	RBI	SB	Avg.
1974	Boston	OF	15	43	5	18	2	2	2	10	0	.419
1975	Boston	OF	145	528	103	175	47	7	21	105	10	.331
1976	Boston	OF	132	507	76	159	32	8	10	65	14	.314
1977	Boston	OF	129	497	81	129	29	5	18	76	2	.260
1978	Boston	OF	150	541	75	161	33	3	22	82	3	.298
	Totals		571	2116	340	642	143	25	73	338	29	.303

GEORGE SCOTT 35 6-2 210   Bats R Throws R

Slumped at plate for second year in row in '78 . . . Plagued by injuries to back and finger . . . Confident he can come back and contribute . . . "I've been around the game too long to start worrying about things." . . . Went on special diet to control weight . . . Born March 23, 1944, in Greenville, Miss. . . . Nicknamed "Boomer" . . . Recently opened tennis boutique near Cape Cod home . . . Wife's name is Lucky . . . One of the most amusing, entertaining players in the big leagues when he's in the mood, which he usually is.

Year	Club	Pos	G	AB	R	H	2B	3B	HR	RBI	SB	Avg.
1966	Boston	1B-3B	162	601	73	147	18	7	27	90	4	.245
1967	Boston	1B-3B	159	565	74	171	21	7	19	82	10	.303
1968	Boston	1B-3B	124	350	23	60	14	0	3	25	3	.171
1969	Boston	3B-1B	152	549	63	139	14	5	16	52	4	.253
1970	Boston	3B-1B	127	480	50	142	24	5	16	63	4	.296
1971	Boston	1B	146	537	72	141	16	4	24	78	0	.263
1972	Milwaukee	1B-3B	152	578	71	154	24	4	20	88	16	.266
1973	Milwaukee	1B	158	604	98	185	30	4	24	107	9	.306
1974	Milwaukee	1B	158	604	74	170	36	2	17	82	9	.281
1975	Milwaukee	1B-3B	158	617	86	176	26	4	36	109	6	.285
1976	Milwaukee	1B	156	606	73	166	21	5	18	77	0	.274
1977	Boston	1B	157	584	103	157	26	5	33	95	1	.269
1978	Boston	1B	120	412	51	96	16	4	12	54	1	.233
	Totals		1929	7087	911	1904	276	56	265	1002	67	.269

DENNIS ECKERSLEY 24 6-2 190   Bats R Throws R

One of the keys to Boston's success in '78 . . . A flame thrower with unorthodox, slingshot delivery . . . But no longer relies exclusively on fastball . . . Has become a complete pitcher . . . Traded to Bosox from Cleveland during spring training . . . "I thought I was too valuable to be traded" . . . Promised Red Sox he'd win, and he did, 20 times . . . Born Oct. 3, 1954, in Oakland, Cal. . . . Has been called a showman, a hot-dog . . . Found consistency in '78 after struggling for three seasons in Cleveland.

Year	Club	G	IP	W	L	Pct.	SO	BB	H	ERA
1975	Cleveland...............	34	187	13	7	.650	152	90	147	2.60
1976	Cleveland...............	36	199	13	12	.520	200	78	155	3.44
1977	Cleveland...............	33	247	14	13	.519	191	54	214	3.53
1978	Boston..................	35	268	20	8	.714	162	71	258	2.99
	Totals..................	138	901	60	40	.600	705	293	774	3.16

MIKE TORREZ 32 6-5 202   Bats R Throws R

Was en route to outstanding season when suddenly became mired in late season slump . . . Went six weeks down the stretch without winning a game . . . "I'm no loser" . . . Joined Red Sox as free agent after pitching Yankees to '77 World Championship . . . "I feel comfortable pitching for this club and in this town" . . . Born Aug. 28, 1946, in Topeka, Kan. . . . "The thing I like about him is the way he battles," says Don Zimmer . . . Signed seven-year $2.5 million contract.

Year	Club	G	IP	W	L	Pct.	SO	BB	H	ERA
1967	St. Louis	3	6	0	1	.000	5	1	5	3.00
1968	St. Louis	5	19	2	1	.667	6	12	20	2.84
1969	St. Louis	24	108	10	4	.714	61	62	96	3.58
1970	St. Louis	30	179	8	10	.444	100	103	168	4.22
1971	St. L-Montreal	10	39	1	2	.333	10	31	45	5.54
1972	Montreal	34	243	16	12	.571	112	103	215	3.33
1973	Montreal	35	208	9	12	.429	90	115	207	4.46
1974	Montreal	32	186	15	8	.652	92	84	184	3.58
1975	Baltimore	36	271	20	9	.690	119	133	238	3.06
1976	Oakland................	39	266	16	12	.571	115	87	231	2.50
1977	Oak-N.Y. (AL)	35	243	17	13	.567	102	86	235	3.93
1978	Boston	36	250	16	13	.552	120	99	272	3.96
	Totals..................	319	2018	130	97	.573	932	916	1916	3.60

RICK BURLESON 27 5-10 165   Bats R Throws R

One of the Red Sox unsung heros . . . Teamed with second baseman Jerry Remy to form heart of dependable infield . . . "Hoot and Scoot" they called them . . . Steady fielder and a great competitor . . . Nicknamed "Rooster" . . . Born April 29, 1951, in Lynwood, Cal. . . . "He made himself a good hitter by hard work," says Don Zimmer . . . Boston's No. 1 pick in January, 1970, free agent draft.

Year	Club	Pos	G	AB	R	H	2B	3B	HR	RBI	SB	Avg.
1974	Boston	SS-2B-3B	114	384	36	109	22	0	4	44	3	.284
1975	Boston	SS	158	580	66	146	25	1	6	62	8	.252
1976	Boston	SS	152	540	75	157	27	1	7	42	14	.291
1977	Boston	SS	154	663	80	194	36	7	3	52	13	.293
1978	Boston	SS	145	626	75	155	32	5	5	49	8	.248
	Totals		723	2793	332	761	142	14	25	249	46	.272

TOP PROSPECTS

ALLEN RIPLEY 26 6-3 180   Bats R Throws R

Has the arm to be a winner in the big leagues . . . Appeared briefly with Red Sox in '78, winning two and losing five . . . Owned the best winning percentage in the International League in 1977 . . . Born Oct. 18, 1952, in Norwood, Mass. . . . Was a winner everywhere he pitched after his first year in the minors . . . Signed with Red Sox as undrafted free agent in 1973 when he was discovered pitching sandlot ball in Rhode Island.

SAM BOWEN 26 5-9 167   Bats R Throws R

Excellent outfielder, still must prove he can hit major league pitching . . . Improved as hitter in minors in '77, smacking 15 homers and driving in 49 runs at Pawtucket . . . Born Sept. 18, 1952, in Brunswick, Ga. . . . Was Boston's seventh pick in June, 1974, draft . . . Made All-America team while in college at Valdosta St.

MANAGER DON ZIMMER: Likeable, low-keyed guy who is popular with his players . . . "With him it's 'let's go out and play the game,'" says Mike Torrez . . . "Nobody tells me how to manage my team." . . . Born Jan. 17, 1931, in Cincinnati . . . Loves the race track . . . Once one of the most promising young players in the Brooklyn Dodgers farm system . . . Career curtailed by a couple of unfortunate beanings . . . Played 12 years for Dodgers, Cubs, Reds, Mets and Senators, doing whatever he was asked to do, including catching . . . Signed two-year contract with Bosox in late July . . . Hates artificial turf, calling it "the biggest joke in America."

GREATEST PITCHER

He pitched longer and won more games than anyone in big league history. And 193 of Cy Young's record 511 victories occurred while he was wearing the uniform of the Boston Red Sox. No Red Sox pitcher in history ever won more often.

He was undoubtedly the most durable pitcher of all time, throwing a baseball in the big leagues for 22 years in a total of 906 games. Yet he didn't begin his career until he was 23. He didn't retire until he was 44.

He played against Cap Anson, whose career began in 1871. And against Tris Speaker, who didn't retire until 1930. He spent 10 full years in each major league and saw the pitcher's mound change from a flat, square area 50 feet from the plate to a hill 60 feet 6 inches away.

They called him Cy because when he finished warming up, the wooden fence behind the catcher looked like a Cyclone had hit it.

He won 20 or more games 16 times, including 14 years in a row. He walked only 1,209 batters in 7,377 innings, averaging eight innings per start for 22 years. Yet he never made as much as $5,000 in any one season. One can only wonder what sort of pitcher Young would be if he was pitching today.

ALL-TIME RED SOX LEADERS

BATTING: Ted Williams, .406, 1941
HRs: Jimmy Foxx, 50, 1938
RBIs: Jimmy Foxx, 175, 1938
STEALS: Tommy Harper, 54, 1973
WINS: Joe Wood, 34, 1912
STRIKEOUTS: Joe Wood, 258, 1912

DETROIT TIGERS

TEAM DIRECTORY: Owner and Chairman: John Fetzer; Pres./GM: Jim Campbell; Consultant: Richard Ferrell; VP-Baseball: William Lajoie; VP-Operations: William Haase; Dir. Pub. Rel.: Hal Middlesworth; Trav. Sec.: Bill Brown; Mgr.: Les Moss. Home: Tiger Stadium (54,226). Field distances: 340, l.f. line; 365, l.c.; 440, c.f.; 370, r.c.; 325, r.f. line. Spring training: Lakeland, Fla.

SCOUTING REPORT

HITTING: Second in hitting in the American League last year, the Tigers figure to make a strong run at the leader—Milwaukee —because of the best young talent around. Only 35-year old Rusty Staub disturbs the youth movement, ut the veteran slugger, a professional hitter, has found new life as a DH. His 121

Restaurateur Rusty Staub knocked in career-high 121 runs.

RBIs, second to Jim Rice, was his highest total in a distinguished 16-year career, and his 24 homers are his greatest output since he slugged 30 for Montreal in 1970. Obviously, "Le Grand Orange" is not getting older, he's getting better.

Also getting better are the Tiger kids—Jason Thompson, Steve Kemp, Lance Parrish, Alan Trammell and Sweet Lou Whitaker. Thompson, in particular, is considered a certain star. Only 24, he has 51 homers and 201 RBIs in the last two seasons and can only improve.

Another young veteran is center fielder Ron LeFlore, a .297 hitter last year, his first season under .300 in the last three, falling just two hits short of the 200 mark. LeFlore continues to make the Tiger offense go with his speed, which accounted for a league-leading 68 stolen bases.

PITCHING: The Tigers won 86 games last season, but still finished 13½ games behind the Yankees, and it isn't difficult to figure out why. They got a total of 11 victories out of Mark (The Bird) Fidrych and Dave Rozema, expected to be their two top pitchers. Fidrych was a 19-game winner three seasons back; Rozema won 15 two seasons ago. Another bad break for the Tigers was the defection of Jim Slaton, who played out his option and returned to Milwaukee as a free agent.

It puts a lot of pressure on a staff made up of young arms. The exceptions are veterans Jack Billingham (a pleasant surprise with 15 victories) and John Hiller, one of the great relief pitchers of all-time. His nine victories and 15 saves made him a key man for the Tigers, as he is again this year, possibly his final season.

FIELDING: It is interesting to note that the Tigers led the AL with 177 double plays and did it with an all-rookie DP combination of Trammell and Whitaker that is certain to get better with experience. Flanking the kids are Aurelio Rodriguez, the league's leading third baseman with four errors in 311 chances and a .987 fielding percentage, and Jason Thompson at first.

The outfield defense is adequate. LeFlore may not be the most graceful center fielder, but his blazing speed outruns his mistakes.

OUTLOOK: But for arm injuries to Fidrych and Rozema, the Tigers could contend for their first championship in a decade. The rest of the team is solid, offensively and defensively, especially since a trade brought Jerry Morales to fill the only vacancy—a right-handed hitting right fielder.

DETROIT TIGERS 1979 ROSTER

MANAGER Les Moss
Coaches—Ed Brinkman, Gates Brown, John Grodzicki, Dick Tracewski

PITCHERS

No.	Name	1978 Club	W-L	IP	SO	ERA	B-T	Ht.	Wt.	Born
31	Baker, Steve	Evansville	8-1	101	87	3.22	R-R	6-0	185	8/30/56 Eugene, OR
		Detroit	2-4	63	39	4.57				
41	Billingham, Jack	Detroit	15-8	202	59	3.88	R-R	6-4	215	2/21/43 Orlando, FL
42	Burnside, Sheldon	Evansville	14-5	161	100	3.53	R-L	6-5	200	12/22/54 South Bend, IN
		Detroit	0-0	4	3	9.00				
20	Fidrych, Mark	Detroit	2-0	22	10	2.45	R-R	6-3	175	8/14/54 Worcester, MA
		Lakeland	1-1	13	6	3.46				
48	Glynn, Ed	Evansville	3-2	38	28	3.32	R-L	6-2	180	6/3/53 Flushing, NY
		Detroit	0-0	15	9	3.00				
49	Grafton, Garry	Evansville	4-6	80	56	3.95	R-R	6-2	195	9/15/55 Sewickley, PA
18	Hiller, John	Detroit	9-4	92	74	2.35	R-L	6-0	165	4/8/43 Scarborough, Ont.
—	Lopez, Aurelio	Springfield	6-6	76	81	3.55	R-R	6-0	200	9/21/48 Mexico
		St. Louis	4-2	65	46	4.29				
47	Morris, Jack	Detroit	3-5	106	48	4.33	R-R	6-3	195	5/16/55 St. Paul, MN
46	Petry, Dan	Montgomery	6-7	92	67	2.45	R-R	6-4	180	11/13/58 Palo Alto, CA
		Evansville	4-3	71	50	4.56				
19	Rozema, Dave	Detroit	9-12	209	57	3.14	R-R	6-4	190	8/5/56 Grand Rapids, MI
32	Taylor, Bruce	Detroit	0-0	1	0	0.00	R-R	6-0	175	4/16/53 Holden, MA
		Evansville	4-7	65	53	4.57				
38	Tobik, Dave	Evansville	4-4	77	67	3.51	R-R	6-1	190	3/2/53 Euclid, OH
		Detroit	0-0	12	11	3.75				
45	Treuel, Ralph	Montgomery	12-6	147	73	3.18	R-R	6-3	188	6/7/55 Elyria, OH
		Evansville	2-3	32	6	5.85				
40	Underwood, Pat	Evansville	5-5	104	73	4.17	L-L	6-0	175	2/9/57 Kokomo, IN
44	Weaver, Roger	Montgomery	1-0	12	4	1.50	R-R	6-3	190	10/6/54 Amsterdam, NY
39	Wilcox, Milt	Detroit	13-12	215	132	3.77	R-R	6-2	185	4/20/50 Honolulu, HI
37	Young, Kip	Evansville	11-3	140	88	3.02	R-R	5-11	175	10/20/54 Georgetown, OH
		Detroit	6-7	106	49	2.80				

CATCHERS

No.	Name	1978 Club	H	HR	RBI	Pct.	B-T	Ht.	Wt.	Born
11	Kimm, Bruce	Evansville	94	8	49	.242	R-R	5-11	170	6/29/51 Cedar Rapids, IA
12	May, Milt	Detroit	88	10	37	.250	L-R	6-0	190	8/1/50 Gary, IN
13	Parrish, Lance	Detroit	63	14	41	.219	R-R	6-3	195	6/15/56 McKeesport, PA
14	Wockenfuss, John	Detroit	53	7	22	.283	R-R	6-0	190	2/27/49 Welch, WV

INFIELDERS

No.	Name	1978 Club	H	HR	RBI	Pct.	B-T	Ht.	Wt.	Born
7	Dillard, Steve	Detroit	29	0	7	.223	R-R	6-1	180	2/8/51 Memphis, TN
2	Mankowski, Phil	Detroit	61	4	20	.275	L-R	6-0	180	1/9/53 Buffalo, NY
12	Manuel, Jerry	Evansville	113	7	50	.263	R-R	6-0	150	12/23/53 Hahira, GA
4	Rodriguez, Aurelio	Detroit	102	7	43	.265	R-R	5-11	180	12/28/47 Mexico
9	Scrivener, Chuck	Detroit	86	9	46	.262	R-R	5-9	170	10/3/47 Alexandria, VA
30	Thompson, Jason	Detroit	169	26	96	.287	L-L	6-4	200	7/6/54 Hollywood, CA
3	Trammell, Alan	Detroit	120	2	34	.268	R-R	6-0	160	2/21/58 Garden Grove, CA
5	Wagner, Mark	Detroit	26	0	6	.239	R-R	6-1	175	3/4/54 Conneaut, OH
1	Whitaker, Lou	Detroit	138	3	58	.285	L-R	5-11	160	5/12/57 New York, NY

OUTFIELDERS

No.	Name	1978 Club	H	HR	RBI	Pct.	B-T	Ht.	Wt.	Born
25	Corcoran, Tim	Detroit	86	1	27	.265	L-L	5-11	175	3/19/53 Glendale, CA
2	Gibson, Kirk	Lakeland	42	7	40	.240	L-L	6-3	215	5/28/57 Pontiac, MI
34	Gonzales, Dan	Evansville	11	6	66	.305	L-R	6-1	178	9/30/53 Whittier, CA
33	Kemp, Steve	Detroit	161	15	79	.277	L-L	6-0	185	8/7/54 San Angelo, TX
8	LeFlore, Ron	Detroit	198	12	62	.297	R-R	6-0	200	6/16/52 Detroit, MI
—	Morales, Jerry	St. Louis	109	4	46	.239	R-R	5-10	175	2/18/49 Puerto Rico
10	Staub, Rusty	Detroit	175	24	121	.273	L-R	6-2	205	4/1/44 New Orleans, LA
22	Stegman, Dave	Evansville	122	14	67	.264	R-R	5-11	190	1/30/54 Inglewood, CA
		Detroit	4	1	3	.286				

TIGER PROFILES

RUSTY STAUB 35 6-2 205   Bats L Throws R

Has adjusted to role as DH after distinguished outfield career . . . Ranked second in league in RBIs, topping century mark for second year in row . . . Highest paid Tiger in history, also oldest regular . . . "When I look around at my teammates, I feel downright ancient." . . . Contract recently extended through 1980 . . . Born April 1, 1944, in New Orleans . . . Teammates call him "Felix," because he's so fussy . . . "I know the kids on this team think I'm a fanatic—and they're right." . . . Still one of baseball's most eligible bachelors . . . Loves working on crossword puzzles . . . A gourmet cook, owns New York restaurant "Rusty's" . . . Serves as Tiger player rep.

Year	Club	Pos	G	AB	R	H	2B	3B	HR	RBI	SB	Avg.
1963	Houston	1B-OF	150	513	43	115	17	4	6	45	0	.224
1964	Houston	1B-OF	89	292	26	63	10	2	8	35	1	.216
1965	Houston	OF-1B	131	410	43	105	20	1	14	63	3	.256
1966	Houston	OF-1B	153	554	60	155	28	3	13	81	2	.280
1967	Houston	OF	149	546	71	182	44	1	10	74	0	.333
1968	Houston	1B-OF	161	591	54	172	37	1	6	72	2	.291
1969	Montreal	OF	158	549	89	166	26	5	29	79	3	.302
1970	Montreal	OF	160	569	98	156	23	7	30	94	12	.274
1971	Montreal	OF	162	599	94	186	34	6	19	97	9	.311
1972	New York (NL)	OF	66	239	32	70	11	0	9	38	0	.293
1973	New York (NL)	OF	152	585	77	163	36	1	15	76	1	.279
1974	New York (NL)	OF	151	561	65	145	22	2	19	78	2	.258
1975	New York (NL)	OF	155	574	93	162	30	4	19	105	2	.282
1976	Detroit	OF	161	589	73	176	28	3	15	96	3	.299
1977	Detroit	DH	158	623	84	173	34	3	22	101	1	.278
1978	Detroit	DH	162	642	75	175	30	1	24	121	3	.273
	Totals		2328	8436	1077	2364	430	44	258	1255	44	.280

RON LeFLORE 28 6-0 200   Bats R Throws R

Led AL in runs and stolen bases . . . Enjoyed league's longest hitting streak, a 27-gamer . . . Named to National Advisory Committee on Juvenile Justice and Delinquency Prevention . . . Tigers' best base stealer since Ty Cobb . . . One of top right-handed hitters in AL . . . "I always said I could hit." . . . Learned to play baseball while serving prison term for armed robbery . . . Discovered when then Tiger manager Billy Martin visited prison . . . Life story the subject of book "Breakout," and movie "One In a Million" . . . Born June 16, 1950, in Detroit . . . Plagued by slow starts last two years . . . Natural athlete, could probably have excelled at football or basketball.

Year	Club	Pos	G	AB	R	H	2B	3B	HR	RBI	SB	Avg.
1974	Detroit..........	OF	59	254	37	66	8	1	2	13	23	.260
1975	Detroit..........	OF	136	550	66	142	13	6	8	37	28	.258
1976	Detroit..........	OF	135	544	93	172	23	8	4	39	58	.316
1977	Detroit..........	OF	154	652	100	212	30	10	16	57	39	.325
1978	Detroit..........	OF	155	666	126	198	30	3	12	62	68	.297
	Totals..........		639	2666	422	790	104	28	42	208	216	.296

STEVE KEMP 24 6-0 185 — Bats L Throws L

Aggressive outfielder, aspires to be team leader . . . "I think I'm capable of being a team leader" . . . Intelligent and outspoken . . . Continues to improve, at plate and in field . . . Reminded former manager Ralph Houk of Mickey Mantle and Bobby Murcer . . . Picked for future stardom . . . Born Aug. 7, 1954, in San Angelo, Tex. . . . All-American at USC, where he was described as better than Fred Lynn . . . Signed with Tigers as No. 1 pick in nation in January, 1976, free agent draft . . . Best friend is teammate Jason Thompson . . . Knicknamed "Bubs" or "Gabby." . . . Could be Tigers' DH of future.

Year	Club	Pos	G	AB	R	H	2B	3B	HR	RBI	SB	Avg.
1977	Detroit..........	OF	151	552	75	142	29	4	18	88	3	.257
1978	Detroit..........	OF	159	582	75	161	18	4	15	79	2	.277
	Totals..........		310	1134	150	303	47	8	33	167	5	.267

JASON THOMPSON 24 6-4 200 — Bats L Throws L

Soft-spoken slugger, slumped at plate second half of season . . . Hindered by injuries . . . Named to AL all-star team past two years . . . One of the most feared young power hitters in league . . . "I don't think I'm close to my prime yet—I want to keep improving every year" . . . Born July 6, 1954, in Hollywood, Cal. . . . A pitcher in college, switched to first when hurt arm . . . Overlooked by Central Scouting Bureau . . . Tigers' No. 4 pick in June, 1975, free agent draft . . . Signed on advice of scout Dick Wiencek, who stumbled across him while scouting another athlete . . . Was playing first base for Tigers 10 months after he signed . . . Could be star for many years to come.

Year	Club	Pos	G	AB	R	H	2B	3B	HR	RBI	SB	Avg.
1976	Detroit	1B	123	412	45	90	12	1	17	54	2	.218
1977	Detroit	1B	158	585	87	158	24	5	31	105	0	.270
1978	Detroit	1B	153	589	79	169	25	3	26	96	0	.287
	Totals		434	1586	211	417	61	9	74	255	2	.253

MARK FIDRYCH 24 6-3 175   Bats R Throws R

Missed all but three games last year because of recurring tendinitis in arm . . . Still considered key to Tigers' future . . . Known as "The Bird" . . . Shot to national stardom as rookie in 1976 . . . Became toast of baseball, attracting crowds, talking to ball and winning wherever he went . . . Reigned as Rookie of Year . . . Hampered by injuries to knee and arm since . . . Born Aug. 14, 1954, in Worcester, Mass. . . . Worked during winter as salesman for firm owned by former Tiger Bill Freehan . . . Still one of the most popular players in the game . . . Loves rock music, pretty girls and working on car engines—not necessarily in that order.

Year	Club	G	IP	W	L	Pct.	SO	BB	H	ERA
1976	Detroit	31	250	19	9	.679	97	53	217	2.34
1977	Detroit	11	81	6	4	.600	42	12	82	2.89
1978	Detroit	3	22	2	0	1.000	10	5	17	2.45
	Totals	45	353	27	13	.675	149	70	316	2.47

JOHN HILLER 35 6-0 165   Bats R Throws L

One of the most courageous players in game . . . Once brash, cocky, overweight, battled back from heart attack in '71 to become one of most consistently successful relief pitchers in game . . . Honored last year for decade of service . . . "John Hiller," says Tiger GM Jim Campbell, "is a very special person." . . . Born April 8, 1943, in Scarborough, Ont. . . . Spent 21 days on disabled list with pulled muscle . . . Nicknamed "Ratso." . . . A clubhouse agitator . . . has 116 saves in 10 seasons . . . Plans to retire after '79 season . . . Says heart attack changed life and was best thing that ever happened to him.

Year	Club	G	IP	W	L	Pct.	SO	BB	H	ERA
1965	Detroit	5	6	0	0	.000	4	1	5	0.00
1966	Detroit	1	2	0	0	.000	1	2	2	9.00
1967	Detroit	23	65	4	3	.571	49	9	57	2.63
1968	Detroit	39	128	9	6	.600	78	51	92	2.39
1969	Detroit	40	99	4	4	.500	74	44	97	4.00
1970	Detroit	47	104	6	6	.500	89	46	82	3.03
1971	Detroit				(Did Not Play)					
1972	Detroit	24	44	1	2	.333	26	13	39	2.05
1973	Detroit	65	125	10	5	.667	124	39	89	1.44
1974	Detroit	59	150	17	14	.548	134	62	127	2.64
1975	Detroit	36	71	2	3	.400	87	36	52	2.15
1976	Detroit	56	121	12	8	.600	117	67	93	2.38
1977	Detroit	45	124	8	14	.364	115	61	120	3.56
1978	Detroit	51	92	9	4	.692	74	35	64	2.35
	Totals	491	1131	82	69	.543	972	466	919	2.63

LOU WHITAKER 21 5-11 160　　Bats L Throws R

"Sweet Lou" . . . Rookie of the Year, played second base like seasoned pro . . . Teammate Mickey Stanley thought he was a clubhouse attendant first time he saw him . . . Skinny, yet durable . . . Surprisingly consistent at plate in clutch . . . Born May 27, 1957, in New York City . . . Originally a third baseman, shifted to second in minors . . . Extremely popular with Tiger fans who chant "Lou! Lou! Lou!" whenever he gets a hit or makes outstanding play . . . Former manager Ralph Houk called him one of three best second baseman in AL . . . Chosen on fifth round of June, 1975, draft . . . Expected to be fixture in Tiger infield for many years to come.

Year	Club	Pos	G	AB	R	H	2B	3B	HR	RBI	SB	Avg.
1977	Detroit	2B	11	32	5	8	1	0	0	2	0	.250
1978	Detroit	2B	139	484	71	138	12	7	3	58	7	.285
	Totals		150	516	76	146	13	7	3	60	7	.283

AURELIO RODRIGUEZ 31 5-11 180　　Bats R Throws R

Outstanding defensive third baseman with good range and rifle for arm . . . Still uses same glove he had when he joined Tigers in 1971 . . . "I just can't use any other glove" . . . Carefree, always smiling, very popular with fans and teammates . . . Born Dec. 28, 1947, in Sonora, Mexico . . . Discovered by California Angels in Mexican League when 18 . . . Billed at time as "the most expensive ballplayer ever purchased from a Latin league" . . . Joined Tigers as partial payment for Denny McLain . . . Teammates call him "Chi Chi" . . . Only major leaguer with all five vowels in his first name.

Year	Club	Pos	G	AB	R	H	2B	3B	HR	RBI	SB	Avg.
1967	California........	3B	29	130	14	31	3	1	1	8	1	.238
1968	California........	3B-2B	76	223	14	54	10	1	1	16	0	.242
1969	California........	3B	159	561	47	130	17	2	7	49	5	.232
1970	Cal.-Wash........	3B-SS	159	610	70	152	33	7	19	83	15	.249
1971	Detroit..........	3B-SS	154	604	68	153	30	7	15	39	4	.253
1972	Detroit..........	3B-SS	153	601	65	142	23	5	13	56	2	.236
1973	Detroit..........	3B-SS	160	555	46	123	27	3	9	58	3	.222
1974	Detroit..........	3B	159	571	54	127	23	5	5	49	2	.222
1975	Detroit..........	3B	151	507	47	124	20	6	13	60	1	.245
1976	Detroit..........	3B	128	480	40	115	13	2	8	50	0	.240
1977	Detroit..........	3B-SS	96	306	30	67	14	1	10	32	1	.219
1978	Detroit..........	3B	134	385	40	102	25	2	7	43	0	.265
	Totals...........		1558	5533	535	1320	238	42	108	543	34	.239

ALAN TRAMMELL 21 6-0 160   Bats R Throws R

Emerged as leader Tigers have long lacked in infield, even though only a rookie . . . Remarkably poised young pro . . . Along with Whitaker, anchored heart of Tiger infield in first year in big leagues . . . "Getting drafted by the Tigers turned out to be the best thing that could have happened to me" . . . Born Feb. 21, 1958, in Garden Grove, Cal. . . . Began playing pro ball as soon as he graduated from high school . . . Broke Reggie Jackson's Southern League record for triples . . . Plays with chaw of tobacco in his cheek . . . Also basketball star while in high school . . . Tigers' No. 2 pick in June, 1976, free agent draft.

Year	Club	Pos	G	AB	R	H	2B	3B	HR	RBI	SB	Avg.
1977	Detroit..........	SS	19	43	6	8	0	0	0	0	0	.186
1978	Detroit..........	SS	139	448	49	120	14	6	2	34	3	.268
	Totals..........		158	491	55	128	14	6	2	34	3	.261

JACK BILLINGHAM 36 6-4 215   Bats R Throws R

Joined Tigers in spring training in exchange for two minor leaguers . . . Became surprise of starting staff, winning 15 . . . "I'm no Cy Young Award winner" . . . Dry humor makes him favorite with Tiger teammates . . . "He's a real model," says former manager Ralph Houk . . . Turned down trades that would have sent him to Cubs and Giants . . . Born Feb. 21, 1943, in Winter Park, Fla. . . . One of few pitchers to win 10 or more games in each of last nine years . . .

Distant relative of Christy Mathewson . . . Served up Hank Aaron's 714th HR . . . Outstanding in World Series with Reds.

Year	Club	G	IP	W	L	Pct.	SO	BB	H	ERA
1968	Los Angeles	50	71	3	0	1.000	46	30	54	2.15
1969	Houston	52	83	6	7	.462	71	29	.92	4.23
1970	Houston	46	188	13	9	.591	134	63	190	3.97
1971	Houston	33	228	10	16	.385	139	68	205	3.39
1972	Cincinnati	36	218	12	12	.500	137	64	197	3.18
1973	Cincinnati	40	293	19	10	.655	155	95	257	3.04
1974	Cincinnati	36	212	19	11	.633	103	64	233	3.95
1975	Cincinnati	33	208	15	10	.600	79	76	222	4.11
1976	Cincinnati	34	177	12	10	.545	76	62	190	4.32
1977	Cincinnati	36	162	10	10	.500	76	56	195	5.22
1978	Detroit	30	202	15	8	.652	59	65	218	3.88
	Totals	426	2042	134	103	.565	1075	672	2053	3.77

TOP PROSPECTS

DAVE STEGMAN 25 5-11 190   Bats R Throws R
Highly regarded young outfielder, joined Tigers for late-season trial . . . Batted .286 in eight games and impressed everyone with defensive ability . . . Can play right field or center . . . Signed with Tigers as their No. 1 draft pick in the secondary phase of June, 1976, free agent draft . . . Graduated from University of Arizona . . . Has spent three years in Tiger farm system.

STEVE BAKER 22 6-0 185   Bats R Throws R
Called up early in season when Tigers ran out of starting pitchers, then rejoined the club in September . . . Hard throwing right-hander reminds many of Denny McLain . . . Needs to work on his control . . . Impressed everyone with poise and explosive fastball . . . Signed by Tigers as undrafted free agent in May, 1976 . . . Parents are prominent newspaper publishers in Oregon . . . Attended University of Oregon and Grossmont (Cal.) JC.

MANAGER LES MOSS: Named to replace Ralph Houk who resigned at end of 1978 season . . . Highly successful minor league manager, winning four pennants in 11 years . . . Known as a hard worker and a strict disciplinarian . . . "I don't believe in sitting back and waiting for things to happen" . . . Spent 13 years in AL as a back-up catcher for St. Louis Browns, Boston Red Sox, Baltimore Orioles and Chi-

cago White Sox . . . Born May 14, 1925 in Tulsa, Okla. . . .
Coached White Sox and served as interim manager in Chicago
for five weeks in 1968 . . . Managed 17 of current Tigers while
they were in minor leagues.

GREATEST PITCHER

To hear him tell it, Mickey Lolich never received the credit
he deserved during his pitching days in Detroit. And he's right.

Perhaps it was his pot-belly that it made it so difficult for
people to fathom the fact he was the best pitcher the Tigers ever
possessed. Or maybe it was because he was so consistently
successful that most people took the tireless left-hander for
granted.

But his record speaks for itself.

Only George Mullin (211) and Hooks Dauss (220), a couple
of right-handers out of ancient history, won more games in a
Tiger uniform than "The Mick" (207).

Twice a 20-game winner, Lolich still holds team records for
starts and strikeouts in a season and career, and strikeouts in a
game. And his three victories in the 1968 World Series carried
the Tigers to a seven-game, come-from-behind victory over the
St. Louis Cardinals.

Before he was traded to the New York Mets following the
1975 season, he had replaced Hal Newhouser as the Tigers' all-
time top left-hander, and had established himself as one of the
premier pitchers in the game.

ALL-TIME TIGER LEADERS

BATTING: Ty Cobb, .420, 1911
HRs: Hank Greenberg, 58, 1938
RBIs: Hank Greenberg, 183, 1937
STEALS: Ty Cobb, 96, 1915
WINS: Denny McLain, 31, 1968
STRIKEOUTS: Mickey Lolich, 308, 1971

BALTIMORE ORIOLES

TEAM DIRECTORY: Chairman of the Board: Jerold C. Hoffberger; Chairman Exec. Comm. and Treas.: Zanvyl Krieger; VP: Frank Cashen; Exec. VP and Gen. Mgr.: Henry Peters; VP: Jack Dunn III; VP and Sec.: Joseph P. Hamper, Jr.; Pub. Rel.: Bob Brown; Trav. Sec.: Philip Itzoe; Mgr.: Earl Weaver. Home: Memorial Stadium (52,137). Field distances: 309, l.f. line; 385, l.c.; 405, c.f.; 385, r.c.; 309, r.f. line. Spring training: Miami, Fla.

SCOUTING REPORT

HITTING: Four men make up the bulk of the Orioles' attack, one on the rise, another on the decline and two holding steady.

Jim Palmer had his eighth 20-victory season in 1978.

Among them, Ken Singleton, Eddie Murray, Lee May and Doug DeCinces accounted for 100 homers and 336 RBIs. But is it enough? That's 70 percent of the team's home run production, 55 percent of its ribbies. Others must do their share, especially with May at age 36 and having his lowest RBI total since 1968. Murray (.285, 27 HRs, 95 RBIs) is one of the brightest young stars in the game and could take up the slack. But more help is needed, and badly.

PITCHING: Every year, it seems, the Orioles come up with a player to fill a need, plug a hole and keep them in contention. In recent years, it has been people like Don Stanhouse, Ross Grimsley, Rudy May, Ken Singleton, Lee May. This year, it could be Steve Stone (12-12 with the White Sox), who signed on as a free agent. If Stone is used as a starter, he will give manager Earl Weaver a five-man rotation that can match any in the game. It starts with Jim Palmer, as it has for the last decade. Only once (when he had arm trouble) in the last nine seasons has this premier right-hander failed to win 20 games.

After Palmer, comes a trio of youngsters who have already proved their ability to pitch and win. Among them, Mike Flanagan, Dennis Martinez and Scott McGregor won 50 games and figure to get better. The bullpen is in the capable hands of Stanhouse (24 saves, third best in the AL), with Tippy Martinez needed to get left-handed hitters out.

FIELDING: For the fifth year in a row, the Orioles led the league in fielding, an interesting note when you realize the turnover in personnel in that time. The one constant remains Mark Belanger, the peerless shortstop, better than ever at age 33. Over the past five years, he paired with first Bob Grich, now Rich Dauer, at second, and first with Brooks Robinson, now Doug DeCinces, at third. Dauer is a defensive whiz, having made only one error in 433 chances for a .998 percentage. He failed to qualify as fielding leader at his position, although he fielded 11 points higher than the leader. DeCinces has finally shaken the shadow of Robinson to rank as an outstanding third baseman in his own right, with just 10 errors in 401 tries. While the inner defense is solid, the outfield has weaknesses which must be corrected.

OUTLOOK: Never underestimate manager Earl Weaver's ability to get the most out of his players and to contend against more powerful opposition. His format is pitching and defense and he has both, in quantity, to stay in the race until the end.

BALTIMORE ORIOLES 1979 ROSTER

MANAGER Earl Weaver
Coaches—Jim Frey, Elrod Hendricks, Cal Ripkin, Frank
       Robinson

PITCHERS

No.	Name	1978 Club	W-L	IP	SO	ERA	B-T	Ht.	Wt.	Born
—	Eastian, Jose	Charlotte	8-4	126	90	2.71	R-R	6-0	158	12/2/56 Puerto Rico
		Rochester	0-1	21	11	3.86				
34	Briles, Nelson	Baltimore	4-4	54	30	4.67	R-R	5-11	205	8/5/43 Dorris, CA
46	Flanagan, Mike	Baltimore	19-15	281	167	4.04	L-L	6-0	185	12/16/51 Manchester, NH
37	Flinn, John	Rochester	1-0	38	36	5.17	R-R	6-1	180	9/2/54 Merced, CA
		Baltimore	1-1	16	8	7.88				
59	Ford, Dave	Rochester	11-6	156	74	3.80	R-R	6-4	210	12/29/56 Cleveland, OH
		Baltimore	1-0	15	5	0.00				
32	Kerrigan, Joe	Baltimore	3-1	72	41	4.75	R-R	6-5	210	1/30/54 Philadelphia, PA
30	Martinez, Dennis	Baltimore	16-11	276	142	3.55	R-R	6-1	170	5/14/55 Nicaragua
23	Martinez, Tippy	Baltimore	3-3	69	57	4.83	L-L	5-10	170	5/31/50 LaJunta, CO
39	McGregor, Scott	Baltimore	15-13	233	94	3.32	B-L	6-1	190	1/18/54 Inglewood, CA
22	Palmer, Jim	Baltimore	21-12	296	138	2.46	R-R	6-3	196	10/15/45 New York, NY
—	Rineer, Jeff	Rochester	9-5	125	64	4.75	L-L	6-4	210	7/3/55 Lancaster, PA
48	Stanhouse, Don	Baltimore	6-9	75	42	2.88	R-R	6-2	195	2/12/51 DuQuoin, IL
53	Stewart, Sammy	Rochester	13-10	173	111	3.79	R-R	6-3	207	10/28/54 Asheville, NC
		Baltimore	1-1	11	11	3.27				
49	Stoddard, Tim	Rochester	7-3	76	70	2.62	R-R	6-7	250	1/24/53 East Chicago, IN
		Baltimore	0-1	18	14	6.00				
—	Stone, Steve	Chicago (AL)	12-12	212	118	4.37	R-R	5-10	175	7/14/47 Cleveland, OH

CATCHERS

No.	Name	1978 Club	H	HR	RBI	Pct.	B-T	Ht.	Wt.	Born
24	Dempsey, Rick	Baltimore	114	6	32	.259	R-R	6-0	185	9/13/49 Fayetteville, TN
44	Hendricks, Elrod	Baltimore	6	1	1	.333	L-R	6-1	185	12/22/40 Virgin Islands
—	Kennedy, Kevin	Rochester	104	4	58	.254	R-R	6-2	195	9/26/54 Los Angeles, CA
8	Skaggs, Dave	Baltimore	13	0	2	.151	R-R	6-1	195	6/12/51 Santa Monica, CA

INFIELDERS

No.	Name	1978 Club	H	HR	RBI	Pct.	B-T	Ht.	Wt.	Born
7	Belanger, Mark	Baltimore	74	0	16	.213	R-R	6-2	170	6/8/44 Pittsfield, MA
—	Chism, Tom	Rochester	116	10	62	.317	L-L	6-1½	190	5/9/55 Chester, PA
10	Crowley, Terry	Baltimore	24	0	12	.253	L-L	6-0	175	2/16/47 Staten Island, NY
25	Dauer, Rich	Baltimore	121	6	46	.264	R-R	6-0	180	7/27/52 San Bernardino, CA
11	DeCinces, Doug	Baltimore	146	28	80	.286	R-R	6-2	190	8/29/50 Burbank, CA
3	Garcia, Kiko	Baltimore	49	0	13	.263	R-R	5-11	175	10/14/53 Martinez, CA
—	Krenchicki, Wayne	Rochester	154	12	71	.296	L-R	6-1	175	9/17/54 Trenton, NJ
14	May, Lee	Baltimore	137	25	80	.246	R-R	6-3	205	3/23/43 Birmingham, AL
33	Murray, Eddie	Baltimore	174	27	95	.285	B-R	6-2	180	2/24/56 Los Angeles, CA
2	Smith, Billy	Baltimore	65	5	30	.260	B-R	6-2½	185	7/14/53 Hodge, LA
—	Smith, Jim	Rochester	64	5	26	.221	R-R	6-1	180	9/8/54 Santa Monica, CA

OUTFIELDERS

No.	Name	1978 Club	H	HR	RBI	Pct.	B-T	Ht.	Wt.	Born
—	Corey, Mark	Rochester	81	5	40	.324	R-R	6-2	200	11/3/55 Tucumcari, NM
6	Harlow, Larry	Baltimore	112	8	26	.243	L-L	6-2	175	11/13/51 Colorado Springs, CO
18	Kelly, Pat	Baltimore	75	11	40	.274	L-L	6-1	190	7/30/44 Philadelphia, PA
9	Lopez, Carlos	Baltimore	46	4	20	.238	R-R	6-1	190	9/27/50 Mexico
—	Lowenstein, John	Texas	39	5	21	.222	L-R	5-11	165	1/27/47 Wolf Point, MD
27	Mora, Andres	Rochester	20	4	10	.227	R-R	6-0	200	5/25/55 Mexico
		Baltimore	49	8	14	.214				
35	Roenicke, Gary	Rochester	101	13	64	.307	R-R	6-3	200	12/5/54 Covina, CA
		Baltimore	15	3	15	.259				
29	Singleton, Ken	Baltimore	147	20	81	.293	B-R	6-4	213	6/10/47 New York, NY

ORIOLE PROFILES

JIM PALMER 33 6-3 196   Bats R Throws R

Master craftsman . . . Has won 20 or more games eight of last nine years . . . Career victories now stand at 215 . . . A student of pitching . . . Great help to young hurlers on staff . . . "He makes things so much easier for the rest of us," says Mike Flanagan . . . Born Oct. 15, 1945, in New York City but family moved when he was infant . . . Raised in California and Arizona . . . Led league in innings pitched . . . Occasionally at odds with organization and Earl Weaver . . . Criticized by some teammates during season . . . Came back twice in career from crippling injuries . . . Still plagued by nagging shoulder problems . . . Worked as TV commentator during AL playoffs.

Year	Club	G	IP	W	L	Pct.	SO	BB	H	ERA
1965	Baltimore	27	92	5	4	.556	75	56	75	3.72
1966	Baltimore	30	208	15	10	.600	147	91	176	3.46
1967	Baltimore	9	49	3	1	.750	23	20	34	2.94
1969	Baltimore	26	181	16	4	.800	123	64	131	2.34
1970	Baltimore	39	305	20	10	.667	199	100	263	2.71
1971	Baltimore	37	282	20	9	.690	184	106	231	2.68
1972	Baltimore	36	274	21	10	.677	184	70	219	2.07
1973	Baltimore	38	296	22	9	.710	158	113	225	2.40
1974	Baltimore	26	179	7	12	.368	84	69	176	3.27
1975	Baltimore	39	323	23	11	.676	193	80	253	2.09
1976	Baltimore	40	315	22	13	.629	159	84	255	2.51
1977	Baltimore	39	319	20	11	.645	193	99	263	2.91
1978	Baltimore	38	296	21	12	.636	138	97	246	2.46
	Totals	424	3119	215	116	.650	1860	1049	2547	2.63

DON STANHOUSE 28 6-2 195   Bats R Throws R

Ace of Oriole bullpen . . . Acquired from Montreal in exchange for Rudy May, although Earl Weaver objected to the deal . . . Turned out to be the best reliever Weaver has ever had . . . "He won't give in to the hitters, even when he gets behind on the count," says pitching coach Ray Miller . . . Outspoken and somewhat zany . . . Credits strong arm to his time spent playing third base, his original position . . . Born Feb. 12, 1951, in DuQuoin, Ill. . . . Was Oakland A's No.

draft pick in 1969 . . . Involved in deal that sent Denny McLain from Texas to Oakland . . . Good hitting pitcher, although never gets a chance to show it because of DH.

ear	Club	G	IP	W	L	Pct.	SO	BB	H	ERA
972	Texas	24	105	2	9	.182	78	73	83	3.77
973	Texas	21	70	1	7	.125	42	44	70	4.76
974	Texas	18	31	1	1	.500	26	17	38	4.94
975	Montreal	4	13	0	0	.000	5	11	19	8.31
976	Montreal	34	184	9	12	.429	79	92	182	3.77
977	Montreal	47	158	10	10	.500	89	84	147	3.42
978	Baltimore	56	75	6	9	.400	42	52	60	2.88
	Totals	204	636	29	48	.377	361	373	599	3.83

EDDIE MURRAY 23 6-2 180   Bats S Throws R

Proved performance as rookie was no fluke . . . Quiet, compared to Willie McCovey . . . Showed remarkable consistency from both sides of the plate . . . "As intelligent a hitter as I've ever seen," says Earl Weaver . . . Only Jim Gentile hit more home runs during first two years as an Oriole . . . Teammates call him "Young Eddie" . . . Born Feb. 24, 956, in Los Angeles . . . "The guy just likes to play," says Weaver . . . Has younger brother in Giants farm system . . . Got chance in '77 when Birds lost three free agents . . . Was named Rookie of Year . . . A natural right-hander, learned to switch hit in 1976 . . . Can DH or play first base.

ear	Club	Pos	G	AB	R	H	2B	3B	HR	RBI	SB	Avg.
977	Baltimore	OF-1B	160	611	81	173	29	2	27	88	0	.283
978	Baltimore	OF-1B	161	610	85	174	32	3	27	95	6	.285
	Totals		321	1221	166	347	61	5	54	183	6	.284

MIKE FLANAGAN 27 6-0 185   Bats L Throws L

Has the stuff to be an outstanding pitcher for many years to come . . . Earl Weaver says he has the tools to be "another Mickey Lolich" . . . Throws heavy fastball but can also get by with curve when has good stuff . . . Led league in starts . . . Slowed by tendinitis in left ankle . . . Born Dec. 16, 1951, in manchester, N.H. . . . His dad also played pro ball . . . Originally drafted by Houston, but decided to attend

college instead . . . Signed by Orioles after sophomore year a
Amherst . . . "The biggest difference between pitching her
and in the minors is that it's much tougher to go nine inning
up here."

Year	Club	G	IP	W	L	Pct.	SO	BB	H	E
1975	Baltimore	2	10	0	1	.000	7	6	9	2.
1976	Baltimore	20	85	3	5	.375	56	33	83	4.
1977	Baltimore	36	235	15	10	.600	149	70	235	3.
1978	Baltimore	40	281	19	15	.559	167	87	271	4.
	Totals	98	611	37	31	.544	379	196	598	3.

SCOTT McGREGOR 25 6-1 190   Bats S Throws

Frequently compared to former Oriole sta
Dave McNally . . . Recovered from sluggish
start to erase all doubts about ability to wi
in majors . . . Excellent curve . . . "Scotty i
just so knowledgeable for 25," says Ear
Weaver . . . Born Jan. 18, 1954, in Ingle
wood, Cal. . . . Picked up first big league wi
in first appearance, beating Wayne Garland
. . . Was Yankees No. 1 draft pick in June, 1972, free agen
draft . . . Acquired by Orioles in '76 as part of 10-player swap
. . . Was teammate of George Brett in high school.

Year	Club	G	IP	W	L	Pct.	SO	BB	H	ER
1976	Baltimore	3	15	0	1	.000	6	5	17	3.6
1977	Baltimore	29	114	3	5	.375	55	30	119	4.4
1978	Baltimore	35	233	15	13	.536	94	47	217	3.3
	Totals	67	362	18	19	.486	155	82	353	3.6

DENNIS MARTINEZ 23 6-1 170   Bats R Throws R

Fell short of expectations as he won six o
first nine then slipped into mysterious slump
. . . Excellent change-of-pace . . . "He's my
man," says pitching coach Ray Miller . .
Admires Jim Palmer and watches every move
Palmer makes and tries to duplicate it . .
Born May 14, 1955, in Granada, Nicaragua
. . . Has had difficulty adjusting to life in
U.S. and overcoming language barrier . . . "Could be another
Juan Marichal," says Earl Weaver . . . First Nicaraguan ever to

appear in major league game . . . Struck out first three batters
he faced in big league debut in '76.

Year	Club	G	IP	W	L	Pct.	SO	BB	H	ERA
1976	Baltimore	4	28	1	2	.333	18	8	23	2.57
1977	Baltimore	42	167	14	7	.667	107	64	157	4.10
1978	Baltimore	40	276	16	11	.593	142	93	257	3.55
	Totals	86	471	31	20	.608	267	165	437	3.69

DOUG DeCINCES 27 6-2 190   Bats R Throws R

Given the impossible task of replacing
Brooks Robinson . . . Ironically, hit three-
run HR on "Brooks Robinson Day" in Baltimore for biggest big league thrill . . . "They
all came out to see Brooks and on my first
time up I hit a three run homer" . . . Lanky
free-swinger, must cure bad habits of lunging
at balls and taking half-swings . . . Born
Aug. 29, 1950, in Burbank, Cal. . . . Undrafted after high
school, went to Pierce JC to further baseball career . . . Later
drafted by Padres but refused to sign because offer was too
small . . . Player of Month in July when he hit .336 with 10
HRs and 31 RBIs.

Year	Club	Pos	G	AB	R	H	2B	3B	HR	RBI	SB	Avg.
1973	Baltimore	3B-2B-SS	10	18	2	2	0	0	0	3	0	.111
1974	Baltimore	3B	1	1	0	0	0	0	0	0	0	.000
1975	Baltimore	3B-SS-2B-1B	61	167	20	42	6	3	4	23	0	.251
1976	Baltimore	3B-2B-SS-1B	129	440	36	103	17	2	11	42	8	.234
1977	Baltimore	3B-2B-1B	150	522	63	135	28	3	19	69	8	.259
1978	Baltimore	3B-2B	142	511	72	146	37	1	28	80	7	.286
	Totals		493	1659	193	428	88	9	62	217	23	.258

LEE MAY 36 6-3 205   Bats R Throws R

Former first baseman, now used as DH . . .
"I don't want anybody to get the impression
that just because I'm a DH I can't play anymore." . . . Streak hitter, can carry club
when hot . . . Has hit home run in every big
league park he's played in. And he's played
in 29 . . . Quiet man, paid to drive in runs,
and does it . . . Born March 23, 1943, in
Birmingham, Ala. . . . Brother of Carlos . . . Originally signed
with Reds, later traded to Houston and Orioles . . . Turned out

to be one of the best deals the Birds ever made, and they'v
made a few dandies.

Year	Club	Pos	G	AB	R	H	2B	3B	HR	RBI	SB	Avg
1965	Cincinnati	PH	5	4	1	0	0	0	0	0	0	.00
1966	Cincinnati	1B	25	75	14	25	5	1	2	10	0	.33
1967	Cincinnati	1B-OF	127	438	54	116	29	2	12	57	4	.26
1968	Cincinnati	1B-OF	146	559	78	162	32	1	22	80	4	.29
1969	Cincinnati	1B-OF	158	607	85	169	32	3	38	110	5	.27
1970	Cincinnati	1B	153	605	78	153	34	2	34	94	1	.25
1971	Cincinnati	1B	147	553	85	154	17	3	39	98	3	.27
1972	Houston	1B	148	592	87	168	31	2	29	98	3	.28
1973	Houston	1B	148	545	65	147	24	3	28	105	1	.27
1974	Houston	1B	152	556	59	149	26	0	24	85	1	.26
1975	Baltimore........	1B	146	580	67	152	28	3	20	99	1	.26
1976	Baltimore........	1B	148	530	61	137	17	4	25	109	4	.25
1977	Baltimore........	1B	150	585	75	148	15	2	27	99	2	.25
1978	Baltimore........	1B	148	556	56	137	16	1	25	80	5	.24
	Totals...........		1801	6785	865	1817	306	27	325	1124	34	.26

RICH DAUER 26 6-0 180   Bats R Throws R

Broke 30-year-old AL record for consecutive
errorless games by second baseman . .
Credits teammate Mark Belanger with teach-
ing him how to play hitters . . . Groomed tc
replace Bobby Grich but lost job temporarily
in '77 . . . Moved closer to plate last year,
and improved power . . . Has steadily improved . . . Born July 27, 1952, in San Berna-
dino, Cal. . . . A line drive hitter . . . Starred on two NCAA
championship teams at USC . . . Was college teammate of
Fred Lynn . . . Won International League batting title in '76
while at Rochester.

Year	Club	Pos	G	AB	R	H	2B	3B	HR	RBI	SB	Avg
1976	Baltimore........	2B	11	39	4	0	0	0	3	0	.103
1977	Baltimore........	2B-3B	96	304	38	74	15	1	5	25	1	.243
1978	Baltimore........	2B-3B	133	459	57	121	23	0	6	46	0	.264
	Totals...........		240	802	95	199	38	1	11	74	1	.248

KEN SINGLETON 31 6-4 213   Bats S Throws R

Overcame elbow surgery . . . Excellent
leadoff hitter because he makes good contact
and walks so often . . . "He's the kind of
hitter who can start a rally by getting on base
or end one by driving in the winning run,"
says Earl Weaver . . . Quiet, mild-mannered
. . . Learned to switch hit because he wanted
to imitate all of his boyhood idols on the
Giants . . . Born June 10, 1947, in New York City . . . "If you

talk about consistency, coming to the ballpark day in and day
out and getting the job done, then you have to rank Ken right
up there with the best of them," says Weaver.

Year	Club	Pos	G	AB	R	H	2B	3B	HR	RBI	SB	Avg.
1970	New York (NL) ...	OF	69	198	22	52	8	0	5	26	1	.263
1971	New York (NL) ...	OF	115	298	34	73	5	0	13	46	0	.245
1972	Montreal	OF	142	507	78	139	23	2	14	50	5	.274
1973	Montreal	OF	162	560	100	169	26	2	23	103	2	.302
1974	Montreal	OF	148	511	68	141	20	2	9	74	5	.276
1975	Baltimore........	OF	155	586	88	176	37	4	15	55	3	.300
1976	Baltimore........	OF	154	544	62	151	25	2	13	70	2	.278
1977	Baltimore........	OF	152	536	90	176	24	0	24	99	0	.328
1978	Baltimore........	OF	149	502	67	147	21	2	20	81	0	.293
	Totals..........		1246	4242	608	1224	189	14	136	604	18	.289

TOP PROSPECTS

SAMMY STEWART 24 6-3 207   Bats R Throws R

Set record by striking out seven straight batters in big league
debut Sept. 1 . . . Possesses all the pitches: Fastball, slow curve,
slider and change . . . Also can help himself with fielding . . .
Born Oct. 28, 1954, in Asheville, N.C. . . . Was drafted by
Royals while in junior college but didn't sign . . . Signed with
Orioles as undrafted free agent after attending tryout camp in
'75 . . . Had lowest ERA in nation (0.36) among junior college
pitchers in 1974.

GARY ROENICKE 24 6-3 200   Bats R Throws R

Keeps threatening to make it . . . Saw limited service in '78 and
impressed Orioles with bat . . . Problem may be finding a place
for him to play . . . Has hit well everywhere he's played in
minors . . . Born Dec. 5, 1954, in Covina, Cal. . . . Turned
down college football scholarships to play baseball . . . Came
to Orioles along with Don Stanhouse from Expos . . . Was
Montreal's top pick in June, 1973, free agent draft.

MANAGER EARL WEAVER: The "Apple Dumpling" . . . His
record speaks for itself . . . Third best winning percentage in major league history
among managers with five or more years of
service . . . Feisty, cocky and combative, de-
lights in baiting umpires . . . Always thinking
ahead, opponents say he never beats himself
. . . Born Aug. 14, 1930, in St. Louis . . . An
avid gardener, enjoys feeding his house

guests delicacies from his garden . . . Holds AL record for a total of 318 wins in three consecutive years . . . Never played major league ball . . . Has spent 22 years in Oriole organization, beginning in 1957 as a minor league playing-manager.

GREATEST PITCHER

Over the years, the Orioles have been famous for their many fine pitchers. And Jim Palmer has unquestionably been the best of an outstanding group.

Eight times in the last nine years he has won 20 or more games for the Birds, a feat surpassed only by Hall of Fame greats Cy Young, Christy Mathewson, Warren Spahn and Walter Johnson.

He is one of only three pitchers (Sandy Koufax and Tom Seaver are the others) who have won the coveted Cy Young Award three times.

His .650 lifetime winning percentage places him second only to Don Gullett among all active pitchers.

He holds every Oriole pitching record imaginable, including victories (215), innings pitched (3,119), strikeouts (1,860), and shutouts (51).

In addition, the intelligent, articulate right-hander is a serious student of the science of pitching.

No wonder he's regarded as one of the outstanding practitioners of his chosen profession of all time.

ALL-TIME ORIOLE LEADERS

BATTING: Ken Singleton, .328, 1977
HRs: Frank Robinson, 49, 1966
RBIs: Jim Gentile, 141, 1961
STEALS: Luis Aparicio, 57, 1964
WINS: Dave McNally, 24, 1970
     Mike Cuellar, 24, 1970
STRIKEOUTS: Dave McNally, 202, 1968

CLEVELAND INDIANS

TEAM DIRECTORY: Principal Owner: Steve O'Neill; Pres.: Gabe Paul; VP-GM: Phillip Seghi; VP-Treasurer: Dudley S. Blossom; Dir. of Admin.: Rich Rollins; Dir. of Scouting and Minor League Operations: Bob Quinn; Dir. Pub. Rel.: Harry Jones; Dir. Pub.: Joe Bick; Trav. Sec.: Mike Seghi; Mgr.: Jeff Torborg. Home: Cleveland Municipal Stadium (76,713). Field distances: 320, l.f. line; 385, r.c.; 320, r.f. line. Spring training: Tuscon, Ariz.

SCOUTING REPORT

HITTING: The Indians have committed themselves to a more potent offense in '79. It may not win more games, but it will be more fun for the fans. With the addition of Bobby Bonds (31 homers, 90 RBIs) and the development of Gary Alexander (27 homers, 84 RBIs), the Tribe can feature a trio of bombers who totaled 91 homers and 279 ribbies last year. The third musketeer, of course, is Andre Thornton who arrived in '78 with 33

Andre Thornton overcame wife's death for 33-HR season.

homers, tied for third in the AL, and 105 RBIs, fourth best in the league.

Also new to Cleveland is Toby Harrah, who had an off year in '78. The Indians are hoping he will play back to his 1977 form—27 homers, 87 ribbies.

And it doesn't stop there. Rick Manning is still around to cover center field and get on base. Duane Kuiper is a good contact hitter at second. Tom Veryzer had his best year at bat and at short. All in all, it promises more runs for the Indians, who scored 165 fewer than league-leading Milwaukee last year and were shut out 18 times.

PITCHING: Here is where the Indians have the shorts and must get lucky if they are to compete. They were fourth from the bottom last year, with little hope of improving. Much of that hope rests with Wayne Garland, the $2 million free agent who had arm problems the past two years and won only two games in '78. Also needed is for several young pitchers obtained from the Rangers to fulfill their potential.

Namely, they are hard-throwing Len Barker and Bobby Cuellar. Holdover starters include Rick Wise, Rick Waits, Mike Paxton, Don Hood and David Clyde. Together, they combined for a 47-62 record, and three of the five had ERAs over four, hardly the stuff of which winning teams are made. Gone, too, is the team's top reliever Jim Kern, but in his place is Victor Cruz, who did remarkable relief work with the lowly Blue Jays.

FIELDING: In their desire to strengthen their attack, the Indians weakened a defense that was fourth best in the American League last year. And when you weaken your defense, you hurt your pitching, of which the Tribe has little to begin with.

In trading Buddy Bell, the Indians let loose of a third baseman who received the imprimatur of the Yankees' Graig Nettles as one of the top fielding third basemen in the game. In his place is Toby Harrah, who is a better shortstop than he is a third baseman, but Tom Veryzer did a good job there. Elsewhere, the defense is solid with Duane Kuiper at second, Andre Thornton at first, and the prospect of good outfield play from Rick Manning, Bobby Bonds and Jim Norris.

OUTLOOK: Two years ago, the Indians went for pitching at the expense of offense. "You're going to play a lot of 2-1 games," someone chided GM Phil Seghi, who replied: "That's all right, if we have the 2." It wasn't all right. The Indians still lost, and were dull doing it. This year they won't be dull.

CLEVELAND INDIANS 1979 ROSTER

MANAGER Jeff Torborg
Coaches—Dave Duncan, Dave Garcia, Chuck Hartenstein,
    Joe Nossek

PITCHERS

No.	Name	1978 Club	W-L	IP	SO	ERA	B-T	Ht.	Wt.	Born
42	Andersen, Larry	Portland	10-7	99	65	3.45	R-R	6-3	180	5/6/53 Portland, OR
39	Barker, Len	Texas	1-5	52	33	4.85	R-R	6-4	235	7/7/55 Ft. Knox, KY
32	Clyde, David	Cleveland	8-11	153	83	4.29	L-L	6-1	185	4/22/55 Kansas City, KS
—	Cruz, Victor	Syracuse	3-2	42	57	4.54	R-R	5-9	175	12/24/55 Dominican Republic
		Toronto	7-3	47	51	1.72				
38	Cuellar, Bobby	Tucson	4-8	76	36	4.38	R-R	5-11	190	8/20/52 Alice, TX
17	Garland, Wayne	Cleveland	2-3	30	13	7.80	R-R	6-0	195	10/26/50 Nashville, TN
44	Hood, Don	Cleveland	5-6	155	73	4.47	L-L	6-2	180	10/16/49 Florence, SC
55	Melson, Gary	Chattanooga	7-3	74	49	3.89	R-R	6-1	185	2/27/53 New Albany, TN
		Portland	4-5	63	32	7.86				
43	Monge, Sid	Cleveland	4-3	85	54	2.75	B-L	6-2	195	4/11/51 Mexico
51	Narleski, Steve	Waterloo	9-2	55	46	3.11	R-R	6-3	195	9/12/55 Laurel Springs, NJ
48	Paxton, Mike	Cleveland	12-11	191	96	3.86	R-R	5-11	190	9/3/53 Memphis, TN
61	Puryear, Nate	Chattanooga	5-13	129	61	3.42	R-R	6-4	195	7/30/54 Biloxi, MS
		Portland	1-2	14	9	6.43				
41	Reuschel, Paul	Chicago (NL)	2-0	28	13	5.14	R-R	6-4	210	1/12/47 Quincy, IL
		Cleveland	2-4	90	24	3.10				
59	Spence, Sam	Waterloo	13-6	174	144	2.38	R-R	6-0	180	5/21/58 Brandon, FL
37	Spilliner, Dan	San Diego	1-0	26	16	4.50	R-R	6-1	190	11/27/51 Casper, WY
		Cleveland	3-1	56	48	3.70				
36	Waits, Rick	Cleveland	13-15	230	97	3.21	L-L	6-3	195	5/15/52 Atlanta, GA
56	Wihtol, Sandy	Portland	6-5	107	64	4.07	R-R	6-2	190	6/1/55 Palo Alto, CA
40	Wise, Rick	Cleveland	9-19	213	106	4.33	R-R	6-2	195	9/13/45 Jackson, MI

CATCHERS

No.	Name	1978 Club	H	HR	RBI	Pct.	B-T	Ht.	Wt.	Born
35	Alexander, Gary	Oak-Cleveland	112	27	84	.225	R-R	6-2	200	3/27/53 Los Angeles, CA
16	Diaz, Bo	Cleveland	30	2	11	.236	R-R	5-11	190	3/23/53 Venezuela
54	Glass, Tim	Waterloo	27	5	17	.171	R-R	6-2	215	4/23/58 Springfield, OH
9	Hassey, Ron	Cleveland	7	1	4	.226	L-R	6-2	195	2/27/53 Tucson, AZ
		Portland	76	12	52	.323				
13	Pruitt, Ron	Cleveland	44	6	17	.235	R-R	6-0	185	10/21/51 Flint, MI

INFIELDERS

No.	Name	1978 Club	H	HR	RBI	Pct.	B-T	Ht.	Wt.	Born
31	Cage, Wayne	Portland	102	18	69	.368	L-L	6-4	175	11/23/51 Monroe, LA
		Cleveland	24	4	13	.245				
11	Cox, Ted	Cleveland	53	1	19	.233	R-R	6-3	190	1/24/55 Oklahoma City, OK
50	DeLeon, Luis	Chattanooga	88	0	23	.227	R-R	6-1	165	1/13/56 Puerto Rico
—	Harrah, Toby	Texas	103	12	59	.229	R-R	6-0	180	10/26/48 Sissonville, WV
14	Kuiper, Duane	Cleveland	155	0	43	.283	L-R	6-0	175	6/19/50 Racine, WI
26	Oliver, Dave	Portland	127	2	54	.307	L-R	5-11	175	4/7/51 Stockton, CA
12	Rosello, Dave	Portland	123	9	71	.282	R-R	5-11	160	6/26/50 Puerto Rico
29	Thornton, Andre	Cleveland	133	33	105	.262	R-R	6-2	205	8/13/49 Tuskegee, AL
21	Veryzer, Tom	Cleveland	114	1	32	.271	R-R	6-1	185	2/11/53 Pt. Jefferson, NY

OUTFIELDERS

No.	Name	1978 Club	H	HR	RBI	Pct.	B-T	Ht.	Wt.	Born
22	Bonds, Bobby	Chi (AL)-Tex	151	31	90	.267	R-R	6-1	190	3/15/46 Riverside, CA
23	Briggs, Dan	Portland	168	20	109	.330	L-L	6-0	180	11/18/52 Scotia, CA
		Cleveland	8	1	1	.163				
00	Dade, Paul	Cleveland	78	3	20	.254	R-R	6-0	195	12/7/51 Seattle, WA
28	Manning, Rick	Cleveland	149	3	50	.263	L-R	6-1	180	9/2/54 Niagara Falls, NY
57	Norrid, Tim	Portland	112	10	66	.272	L-R	6-3	190	2/8/55 Ripley, NY
27	Norris, Jim	Cleveland	89	2	27	.283	L-L	5-10	190	12/20/48 Brooklyn, NY
30	Rivera, Dave	Tulsa	97	16	62	.231	R-R	5-11	175	8/9/57 King City, CA
20	Speed, Horace	Cleveland	24	0	4	.226	R-R	6-1	180	10/4/51 Los Angeles, CA

INDIAN PROFILES

BOBBY BONDS 33 6-1 190

Bats R Throws R

Probably the most frequently traded superstar in baseball history . . . Obtained from Texas in exchange for Jim Kern and Larvell Blanks following 1978 season . . . Born March 15, 1946 in Riverside, Cal. . . . Frequently compared to Reggie Jackson . . . "Reggie is just more flamboyant. He drives a Rolls Royce. I drive a '36 Dodge" . . . Ironically, his wife is Reggie's fifth cousin . . . Goal is to be the first player to hit 40 HRs and steal 40 bases in same season . . . "If it's done within the next three years, I'll be the one to do it." . . . Already member of exclusive 30-30 club . . . Combines speed and power like few players in history.

Year	Club	Pos	G	AB	R	H	2B	3B	HR	RBI	SB	Avg.
1968	San Francisco	OF	81	307	55	78	10	5	9	35	16	.254
1969	San Francisco	OF	158	622	120	161	25	6	32	90	45	.259
1970	San Francisco	OF	157	663	134	200	36	10	26	78	48	.302
1971	San Francisco	OF	155	619	110	178	32	4	33	102	26	.288
1972	San Francisco	OF	153	626	118	162	29	5	26	80	44	.259
1973	San Francisco	OF	160	643	131	182	34	4	39	96	43	.283
1974	San Francisco	OF	150	567	97	145	22	8	21	71	41	.256
1975	New York (AL)....	OF	145	529	93	143	26	3	32	85	30	.270
1976	California	OF	99	378	48	100	10	3	10	54	30	.265
1977	California	OF	158	592	103	156	23	9	37	115	41	.264
1978	Chi(AL)-Texas	OF	156	565	93	151	19	4	31	90	43	.267
	Totals		1572	6111	1102	1656	266	61	296	866	407	.271

RICK MANNING 24 6-1 180

Bats L Throws R

Recently signed five-year, $1.5 contract, making him highest paid Indian in history until Bobby Bonds came along . . . "This is more dollars than there are gallons of water in Niagara Falls" . . . Admits he got more money than he deserved . . . Hampered throughout career by injuries . . . Fractured vertebrae in lower back in '78 . . . Born Sept. 2, 1954, in Niagara Falls, N.Y. . . . Was No. 2 draft pick in nation in June, 1972 . . . Won Gold Glove in '76 at ripe old age of 21 . . . Excelled in football, basketball and baseball in high school.

Year	Club	Pos	G	AB	R	H	2B	3B	HR	RBI	SB	Avg.
1975	Cleveland	OF	120	480	69	137	16	5	3	35	19	.285
1976	Cleveland	OF	138	552	73	161	24	7	6	43	16	.292
1977	Cleveland	OF	68	252	33	57	7	3	5	18	9	.226
1978	Cleveland	OF	148	566	65	149	27	3	3	50	12	.263
	Totals		474	1850	240	504	74	18	17	146	56	.272

ANDRE THORNTON 29 6-2 205   Bats R Throws R

Physical and spiritual leader of Indians . . . Lost wife and daughter in tragic auto accident following 1977 season . . . Deeply religious, received Danny Thompson Memorial Award for "exemplary Christian spirit in baseball" in '78 . . . "The Lord will not use us in pro sports if we put anything before Him" . . . Nicknamed "Thunder," but teammates also kiddingly refer to "Andy's Doughnut and Bible Shop" because of his extra pounds. "Holy Doughnuts and Dunkin' Bibles" . . . Born Aug. 13, 1949, in Tuskeegee, Ala. . . . Originally with Phillies' organization, traded to Cubs and Expos before achieving stardom with Indians.

Year	Club	Pos	G	AB	R	H	2B	3B	HR	RBI	SB	Avg.
1973	Chicago (NL)	1B	17	35	3	7	3	0	0	2	0	.200
1974	Chicago (NL)	1B-3B	107	303	41	79	16	4	10	46	2	.261
1975	Chicago (NL)	1B-3B	120	372	70	109	21	4	18	60	3	.293
1976	Chi(NL) Montreal	1B-OF	96	268	28	52	11	2	11	38	4	.194
1977	Cleveland	1B	131	433	77	114	20	5	28	70	3	.263
1978	Cleveland	1B	145	508	97	133	22	4	33	105	4	.262
	Totals		616	1919	316	494	93	19	100	321	16	.257

TOBY HARRAH 30 6-0 180   Bats R Throws R

Returned to shortstop in mid-season, regaining position lost to Campy Campaneris . . . Slumped badly at plate in '78 . . . Repeatedly on Rangers' trading list, they finally dealt him to Indians during winter meetings to dismay of Texas fans . . . Born Oct. 26, 1948, in Sissonville, W. Va., one of nine children . . . Very durable, has spent eight full years in big leagues . . . Originally signed with Phils but became one of baseball's best bargains when Rangers drafted him from Phillies farm system in 1967 for $8,000.

Year	Club	Pos	G	AB	R	H	2B	3B	HR	RBI	SB	Avg.
1969	Washington	SS	8	1	4	0	0	0	0	0	0	.000
1971	Washington	SS-3B	127	383	45	88	11	3	2	22	10	.230
1972	Texas	SS	116	374	47	97	14	3	1	31	16	.259
1973	Texas	SS-3B	118	461	64	120	16	1	10	50	10	.260
1974	Texas	SS-3B	161	573	79	149	23	2	21	74	15	.260
1975	Texas	SS-3B-2B	151	522	81	153	24	1	20	93	23	.293
1976	Texas	SS-3B	155	584	64	152	21	1	15	67	8	.260
1977	Texas	3B-SS	159	539	90	142	25	5	27	87	27	.263
1978	Texas	3B-SS	139	450	56	103	17	3	12	59	31	.229
	Totals		1134	3887	530	1004	151	19	108	483	140	.258

DUANE KUIPER 28 6-0 175   Bats L Throws R

Co-captain of Tribe . . . Tied major league record with two bases loaded triples in game against Yankees . . . Has copied Rusty Staub's habit of choking up on the bat . . . A clubhouse leader who keeps the Indians loose . . . Described as "tremendous, amazing, fearless" . . . Born June 19, 1950, in Racine, Wis. . . . Drafted by Yankees, Pilots, White Sox, Reds and Red Sox before signing with Indians as their No. 1 pick in January, 1972 . . . Named Indians "Man of the Year" in '77 . . . Had what many considered the best defensive season of any player in Cleveland history that summer.

Year	Club	Pos	G	AB	R	H	2B	3B	HR	RBI	SB	Avg.
1974	Cleveland	2B	10	22	7	11	2	0	0	4	1	.500
1975	Cleveland	2B	90	346	42	101	11	1	0	25	19	.292
1976	Cleveland	2B-1B	135	506	47	133	13	6	0	37	10	.263
1977	Cleveland	2B	148	610	62	169	15	8	1	50	11	.277
1978	Cleveland	2B	149	547	52	155	18	6	0	43	4	.283
	Totals		532	2032	210	569	59	21	1	159	45	.280

TOM VERYZER 26 6-1 185   Bats R Throws R

Found fresh start with Tribe after falling from favor with Tigers . . . "I never knew he could play so well," said Jeff Torborg. "He's one guy on our club we can't afford to lose." . . . Shed pot belly that prompted much criticism in Detroit . . . "My weight isn't a problem except that it seems to be one to everyone else." . . . Born Feb. 11, 1953, in Port Jefferson, N.Y. . . . Choked up on bat last season to improve productivity . . . Was tabbed for future stardom from day Tigers made him their No. 1 pick in June, 1971, free agent draft . . . Tiger hitting instructor Wayne Blackburn predicted he'd become "best hitting shortstop since Honus Wagner" . . . Never lived up to expectations as a Tiger.

Year	Club	Pos	G	AB	R	H	2B	3B	HR	RBI	SB	Avg.
1973	Detroit	SS	18	20	1	6	0	1	0	2	0	.300
1974	Detroit	SS	22	55	4	13	2	0	2	9	1	.236
1975	Detroit	SS	128	404	37	102	13	1	5	48	2	.252
1976	Detroit	SS	97	354	31	83	8	2	1	25	1	.234
1977	Detroit	SS	125	350	31	69	12	1	2	28	0	.197
1978	Cleveland	SS	130	421	48	114	18	4	1	32	1	.271
	Totals		520	1604	152	387	53	9	11	144	5	.241

GARY ALEXANDER 26 6-2 200   Bats R Throws R

Obtained in trade from Oakland . . . Rose to prominence as Indians' No. 1 catcher . . . Long regarded as one of the best potential hitters in Giants' farm system . . . Nicknamed "Sleepy" . . . Named to major league rookie all-star team in '77 . . . Born March 27, 1953, in Los Angeles . . . Began pro career as an outfielder . . . Caught John Montefusco's no-hitter in 1977 . . . "I'm still learning to be a catcher" . . . Admittedly a free swinger, set Cleveland club record by striking out 166 times.

Year	Club	Pos	G	AB	R	H	2B	3B	HR	RBI	SB	Avg.
1975	San Francisco	C	3	3	1	0	0	0	0	0	0	.000
1976	San Francisco	C	23	73	12	13	1	1	2	7	1	.178
1977	San Francisco	C-OF	51	119	17	36	4	2	5	20	3	.303
1978	Oakland-Cleve.....	C-1B-OF	148	498	57	112	20	4	27	84	0	.225
	Totals...........		225	693	87	161	25	7	34	111	4	.232

JIM NORRIS 30 5-10 190   Bats L Throws L

Can play outfield or first base . . . Excellent speed . . . Finally made big leagues in '77 after six years in minors . . . Continues to improve at plate . . . Injury prone, has spent 66 weeks of his life in casts due to eight sports-related injuries including broken collarbone, shoulder, left arm, right arm, right hand and right thumb, not to mention torn cartilage and ligaments in his right knee . . . Born Dec. 20, 1948, in Brooklyn, N.Y. . . . Signed for mere $2,500 bonus . . . Excellent fielder . . . Starred at University of Maryland before career was slowed by injuries.

Year	Club	Pos	G	AB	R	H	2B	3B	HR	RBI	SB	Avg.
1977	Cleveland........	OF-1B	133	440	59	119	23	6	2	37	26	.270
1978	Cleveland........	OF-1B	113	315	41	89	14	5	2	27	12	.283
	Totals...........		246	755	100	208	37	11	4	64	38	.275

DAVID CLYDE 23 6-1 185   Bats L Throws L

The "Comeback Kid" . . . Returned to majors in '78 and enjoyed best season of career . . . Made major league debut as 18-year-old rookie in 1973 in front of capacity crowd in Texas, and beat Twins one month after he graduated from high school . . . Struggled for next year and a half, then was sent to minors to find himself . . . Underwent shoulder surgery in May, 1976 . . . Born April 22, 1955, in Kansas City, Kan. . . . "I've seen the highest peaks and I've hit rock bottom." . . . Traded to Cleveland in spring, '78 and regained effectiveness under Jeff Torborg, who got him to "slow down and go back to his original, natural delivery."

Year	Club	G	IP	W	L	Pct.	SO	BB	H	ERA
1973	Texas	18	93	4	8	.333	74	54	106	5.03
1974	Texas	28	117	3	9	.250	52	47	129	4.38
1975	Texas	1	7	0	1	.000	2	6	6	2.57
1978	Cleveland	28	153	8	11	.421	83	60	166	4.29
	Totals	75	370	15	29	.341	211	167	407	4.48

WAYNE GARLAND 28 6-0 195   Bats R Throws R

high-priced star attempting to bounce back from shoulder surgery . . . Signed 10-year $2.3 million contract with Indians after playing out option in Baltimore . . . "This shows what kind of unpredictable game that guy Abner Doubleday invented" . . . Was admittedly stunned by size of Indians' offer . . . Born Oct. 25, 1950, in Nashville . . . Signed as free agent with Orioles and hit jackpot by winning 20 games in '76 while playing without contract . . . Started slow in '77, under considerable pressure because of salary, but finished strong . . . Indians are counting on him to reestablish himself as one of the top pitchers in the league.

Year	Club	G	IP	W	L	Pct.	SO	BB	H	ERA
1973	Baltimore	4	16	0	1	.000	10	7	14	3.94
1974	Baltimore	20	91	5	5	.500	40	26	68	2.97
1975	Baltimore	29	87	2	5	.286	46	31	80	3.72
1976	Baltimore	38	232	20	7	.741	113	64	224	2.68
1977	Cleveland	38	283	13	19	.406	118	88	281	3.59
1978	Cleveland	6	30	2	3	.400	13	16	43	7.80
	Totals	135	739	42	40	.512	340	232	710	3.42

VICTOR CRUZ 21 5-9 175   Bats R Throws R

Just missed setting record for consecutive scoreless innings . . . No relation to Tommy, Jose, Hector, Henry or Julio Cruz . . . Obtained from Blue Jays last winter . . . Has a crackling fastball . . . Throws harder than anyone on staff . . . Has twisting, turning delivery similar to Luis Tiant's . . . Born Dec. 24, 1957, in Rancho Viejo LaVega, Dominican Republic . . . Has unusual tattoo on thigh . . . It reads, "If you don't like me, leave me alone" in Spanish . . .

Never spent a day in the big leagues until he was called by Blue Jays in late June.

Year	Club	G	IP	W	L	Pct.	SO	BB	H	ERA
1978	Toronto	32	47	7	3	.700	51	35	28	1.72

TOP PROSPECTS

WAYNE CAGE 27 6-4 175   **Bats L Throws L**

Showed signs that he may finally be developing into the major league hitter the Indians have long believed he could be . . . Batted .245 in 36 games with Tribe, smacking four homers and driving in 13 runs . . . Born Nov. 23, 1951, in Monroe, La. . . . Signed as Indians' No. 3 draft pick in June, 1971, after outstanding high school career . . . Entered pro ball as a pitcher, but moved to first base after he hurt his arm.

TED COX 24 6-3 190   **Bats R Throws R**

Principal problem may be finding a place for him to play . . . Obtained from Red Sox in spring of '78 . . . Promising right-handed hitter, was originally signed as shortstop, then moved to third base, then tried at first . . . Born Jan 24, 1955, in Oklahoma City . . . Was drafted by Red Sox ahead of Fred Lynn in 1973.

MANAGER JEFF TORBORG: One of youngest managers in the major leagues . . . Intelligent and an intense student of pitching mechanics . . . Skilled at finding out what's wrong with his pitchers, then correcting it . . . Sometimes criticized for being too nice, too logical . . . Some feel players take advantage of his good nature . . . Born Nov. 26, 1941, in Westfield, N.J. . . . Signed with Dodgers and caught no-hitters by Sandy Koufax, Bill Singer and Nolan Ryan, one less than major league record . . . Graduated from Rutgers, later earned masters degree in athletic administration at Montclair State in New Jersey . . . Has been mentioned as possible future general manager.

GREATEST PITCHER

To this day, every young pitcher with a blazing fastball is eventually compared to the man the baseball world once reverently referred to as "Rapid Robert," Bob Feller.

In his day, he was in a class by himself.

Some old-timers insist Walter Johnson could throw a ball harder. Today, some say Nolan Ryan may be quicker. But certainly no one was ever as spectacular as early in life as Feller, the world famous farm boy from Van Meter, Iowa.

By the time he was 11 years old, he could throw a ball harder than high school kids six and seven years older. By the time he was 14, he was drawing crowds of 1,000 or more every time he pitched.

At 16, he struck out 26 batters in a game—a game which was witnessed by 10,000 people. He threw five no-hitters in high school and averaged 19 strikeouts per game, pitching semi-pro ball.

In his major league debut with the Indians, he struck out eight batters in three innings of an exhibition game. In his first regular season start, he fanned 15.

By the time he was through, Feller pitched three no-hitters, and a dozen one-hitters. He led the American League in strikeouts seven times. He won 266 games and had six 20-game seasons. And he broke just about every pitching record in the Cleveland book by the time he completed 18 major league seasons in 1956.

ALL-TIME INDIAN LEADERS

BATTING: Joe Jackson, .408, 1911
HRs: Al Rosen, 43, 1953
RBIs: Hal Trosky, 162, 1936
STEALS: Ray Chapman, 52, 1917
WINS: Jim Bagby, 31, 1920
STRIKEOUTS: Bob Feller, 348, 1946

TORONTO BLUE JAYS

TEAM DIRECTORY: Chairman of the Board: R. Howard Webster; Pres.-Chief Oper. Officer: Peter Bavasi; VP-Baseball Operations: Pat Gillick; VP-Business Operations: Paul Beeston; Dir. Pub. Rel.: Howard Starkman; Dir. of Information: Joe Bodolai; Trav. Sec.: Mike Cannon; Mgr.: Roy Hartsfield. Home: Exhibition Stadium (43,737). Field distances: 330, l.f. line; 400, c.f.; 330, r.f. line. Spring training: Dunedin, Fla.

Roy Howell's .270 batting average was Blue Jays' best.

SCOUTING REPORT

HITTING: Not even the addition of a bonafide slugger like John Mayberry (22 homers, 70 RBIs to lead the club in both departments) could keep the Blue Jays from dropping off in every major offensive category—batting, runs, home runs, RBIs

—in their second season. And there is little hope for much improvement this year.

The Jays are committed to a youth movement and it will be still a few years before that commitment can begin to show dividends. There isn't a regular player, Mayberry included, who will be 30 before the end of the season. Many players are a good deal younger. Besides Mayberry, the attack will center around Bob Bailor, Roy Howell and Rick Bosetti. The pickings are slim, but in the future are names like Pat Kelly, Thad Wilborn, Pedro Hernandez, Willie Upshaw and Garth Iorg. When those become household names, if they become household names, the Blue Jays will have arrived.

PITCHING: Only the Mariners had a higher team ERA, fewer shutouts and fewer complete games. The Blue Jays recognize the problem and attempted to bolster their staff over the winter. First string catcher Alan Ashby was sacrificed to get Mark Lemongello, who won nine games for Houston last season. Of the holdovers, only two pitchers won in double figures for the Jays—Tom Underwood at 11, Jim Clancy at 10. Those two will head the staff, the remainder of the rotation to come from among Jerry Garvin, Jesse Jefferson, Dave Lemanczyk, Don Kirkwood and Lemongello. The bullpen, which accounted for only 23 saves, has been weakened by the trading of Victor Cruz, who had nine of those saves and also won seven. That leaves Tom Murphy (six wins, seven saves) as the No. 1 reliever.

FIELDING: The Jays fared better in this department than any other, finishing fifth in the league in team defense. That's a dramatic improvement over 1977, when they were 13th. Rick Bosetti helped by playing a sometimes spectacular, if reckless, center field, posting a .989 fielding percentage and cutting down 17 runners. Put that with Bob Bailor's 15 assists and 11 from Otto Velez, Al Woods and Willie Upshaw combined and you have 43 outfield assists. Another plus was the shortstop play of Luis Gomez, who fielded .977, made only 15 errors and took part in 97 double plays.

OUTLOOK: Not good. In their third year, the Blue Jays have no hope of rising above the cellar. To make things more embarrassing, their fellow expansionists, the Seattle Mariners, have a chance to move to fifth place in the weaker West Division. But it's Toronto's misfortune to play in a division in which four teams won 90 or more games and five teams finished above .500.

TORONTO BLUE JAYS 1979 ROSTER

MANAGER Roy Hartsfield
Coaches—Don Leppert, Jackie Moore, Harry Warner

PITCHERS

No.	Name	1978 Club	W-L	IP	SO	ERA	B-T	Ht.	Wt.	Born
44	Buskey, Tom	Syracuse	7-13	119	62	2.95	R-R	6-3	228	2/20/47 Harrisburg, PA
		Toronto	0-1	13	7	3.46				
27	Byrd, Jeff	Syracuse	0-3	31	18	8.22	R-R	6-3	185	11/11/56 La Mesa, CA
18	Clancy, Jim	Toronto	10-12	194	105	4.08	R-R	6-5	185	12/18/55 Chicago, IL
28	Darr, Mike	Syracuse	6-16	175	133	4.07	R-R	5-4	190	3/23/56 Pomona, CA
–	Edge, Butch	Syracuse	2-10	107	65	5.28	R-R	6-4	202	7/18/56 Houston, TX
–	Freisleben, Dave	San Diego	0-3	27	16	6.00	R-R	5-11	205	10/31/51 Corapolis, PA
		Cleveland	1-4	44	19	7.16				
36	Garvin, Jerry	Toronto	4-12	145	67	5.65	L-L	6-3	195	1/21/55 Oakland, CA
34	Jefferson, Jesse	Toronto	7-16	212	97	4.37	R-R	6-3	214	3/3/50 Midlothian, VA
32	Kirkwood, Don	Toronto	4-5	68	29	4.24	R-R	6-3	195	9/24/49 Pontiac, MI
23	Lemanczyk, Dave	Toronto	4-14	137	62	6.24	R-R	6-5	230	8/17/50 Syracuse, NY
–	Lemongello, Mark	Houston	9-14	210	77	3.94	R-R	6-1	180	7/21/55 Jersey City, NJ
38	Moore, Balor	Toronto	6-9	144	75	4.94	L-L	6-2	194	1/25/51 Smithville, TX
45	Murphy, Tom	Toronto	6-9	94	35	3.93	R-R	6-3	190	12/30/45 Cleveland, OH
22	Underwood, Tom	Toronto	6-14	198	140	4.09	L-L	5-11	170	12/22/53 Kokomo, IN
21	Wiley, Mark	Hawaii	11-11	159	80	4.36	R-R	6-2	205	2/28/48 National City, CA
		Toronto	0-0	3	2	6.00				
33	Willis, Mike	Toronto	3-7	101	52	4.54	L-L	6-2	200	12/26/50 Oklahoma City, OK

CATCHERS

No.	Name	1978 Club	H	HR	RBI	Pct.	B-T	Ht.	Wt.	Born
9	Cerone, Rick	Toronto	63	3	20	.223	R-R	5-11	184	5/9/54 Newark, NJ
6	Kelly, Pat	Syracuse	27	0	12	.161	R-R	6-3	210	8/27/55 Santa Maria, CA
3	Milner, Brian	Toronto	4	0	2	.444	R-R	6-2	200	11/17/59 Fort Worth, TX
		Medicine Hat	58	4	36	.307				
12	Whitt, Ernie	Syracuse	98	12	53	.246	L-R	6-2	201	6/13/52 Detroit, MI
		Toronto	0	0	0	.000				

INFIELDERS

No.	Name	1978 Club	H	HR	RBI	Pct.	B-T	Ht.	Wt.	Born
14	Alberts, Butch	Syracuse	91	9	71	.299	R-R	6-2	208	5/4/50 Williamsport, PA
		Toronto	5	0	0	.278				
25	Ault, Doug	Toronto	25	3	7	.240	R-L	6-3	200	3/9/50 Beaumont, TX
–	Griffin, Alfredo	Portland	138	5	48	.291	B-R	5-11	160	10/6/57 Dominican Republic
		Cleveland	2	0	0	.500				
11	Gomez, Luis	Toronto	92	0	32	.223	R-R	5-9	151	8/19/51 Mexico
1	Howell, Roy	Toronto	149	8	61	.270	L-R	6-1	190	12/18/53 Lompic, CA
29	Iorg, Garth	Toronto	8	0	3	.163	R-R	5-11	165	10/12/54 Arcata, CA
		Syracuse	70	6	25	.216				
17	Johnson, Tim	Mil.-Tor.	19	0	3	.232	L-R	6-1	185	7/22/49 Grand Forks, MD
10	Mayberry, John	Toronto	129	22	70	.250	L-L	6-3	220	2/18/50 Detroit, MI
39	McKay, Dave	Toronto	120	7	45	.238	B-R	6-2	195	3/14/50 Vancouver, BC

OUTFIELDERS

No.	Name	1978 Club	H	HR	RBI	Pct.	B-T	Ht.	Wt.	Born
1	Bailor, Bob	Toronto	164	1	52	.264	R-R	5-9	160	7/10/51 Connellsville, PA
22	Bosetti, Rick	Toronto	147	5	42	.259	R-R	5-11	185	8/5/53 Redding, CA
–	Mallory, Sheldon	Syracuse	86	10	40	.270	L-L	6-2	165	7/16/53 Argo, IL
–	Pisker, Don	Charleston	137	11	77	.287	L-L	6-2	190	12/29/53 Camden, NJ
26	Upshaw, Willie	Toronto	53	1	17	.237	L-L	6-0	185	4/27/57 Blanco, TX
19	Velez, Otto	Toronto	66	9	38	.266	R-R	6-0	195	11/29/50 Puerto Rico
20	Woods, Al	Syracuse	91	11	49	.313	L-L	6-3	199	8/8/53 Oakland, CA
		Toronto	53	3	25	.241				

BLUE JAY PROFILES

BOB BAILOR 27 5-9 160   Bats R Throws R

One of the outstanding young players in the league . . . Grew up idolizing Roberto Clemente . . . Can play shortstop or center field, as the situation demands . . . Was Blue Jays' MVP as a rookie in '77, the club's first year in existence . . . Born July 10, 1951, in Connellsville, Pa. . . . Overlooked in free agent draft, but signed in 1969 with Baltimore . . . Played shortstop, second base, third base, outfield and pitched in minors . . . Toronto's No. 1 pick in 1977 expansion draft, which turned out to be a wise choice.

Year	Club	Pos	G	AB	R	H	2B	3B	HR	RBI	SB	Avg.
1975	Baltimore	SS-2B	5	7	0	1	0	0	0	0	0	.143
1976	Baltimore	SS	9	6	2	2	0	1	0	0	0	.333
1977	Toronto	SS-OF	122	496	62	154	21	5	5	32	15	.310
1978	Toronto	OF-SS	154	621	74	164	29	7	1	52	5	.264
	Totals		290	1130	138	321	50	13	6	84	20	.284

ROY HOWELL 25 6-1 190   Bats L Throws R

Rangers once gave up on him as a third baseman, but he's now one of the more respected players in the league . . . Credits coach Bobby Doerr with improving his technique . . . Hampered by bone spur in his right ankle in '78 . . . Obtained in trade from Texas in 1977 . . . Was once shot in the right arm with a rifle in a hunting accident . . . Born Dec. 18, 1953, in Lompoc, Cal. . . . No. 1 draft pick in country in June, 1972 . . . Excellent offensive player . . . One of a handful of hitters in history to hit more than .300 with a first-year expansion club.

Year	Club	Pos	G	AB	R	H	2B	3B	HR	RBI	SB	Avg.
1974	Texas	3B	13	44	2	11	1	0	1	3	0	.250
1975	Texas	3B	125	383	43	96	15	2	10	51	2	.251
1976	Texas	3B	140	491	55	124	28	2	8	53	1	.253
1977	Texas-Toronto	3B-OF-1B	103	381	41	115	17	1	10	44	4	.302
1978	Toronto	3B-1B	140	551	67	149	28	3	8	61	0	.270
	Totals		521	1850	208	495	89	8	37	212	7	.268

JIM CLANCY 23 6-5 185   Bats R Throws R

One of the most promising young pitchers on Blue Jays' staff . . . Has impressed friend and foe alike with his stuff, poise, and ability to keep the ball down . . . When he's on, he's tough to hit . . . Originally in Texas farm system, although he never pitched for Rangers . . . Grabbed by Blue Jays on first round of expansion draft . . . Born Dec. 18, 1955, in Chicago . . . Caught pitching coach Bob Miller's eye with his performance in minor leagues.

Year	Club	G	IP	W	L	Pct.	SO	BB	H	ERA
1977	Toronto	13	77	4	9	.308	44	47	80	5.03
1978	Toronto	31	194	10	12	.455	106	91	199	4.08
	Totals	44	271	14	21	.400	150	138	279	4.35

OTTO VELEZ 28 6-0 195   Bats R Throws R

Never lived up to promise with Yankees, but never had a real chance . . . Has impressive power when he connects, but plays only part time for Blue Jays, usually against left-handed pitchers . . . Has made life miserable for Tigers' John Hiller on more than one occasion . . . Born Nov. 29, 1950, in Ponce, P.R. . . . Another Blue Jay who gives credit to hitting instructor Bobby Doerr . . . Appeared destined for certain stardom when he broke in with Yanks in 1973.

Year	Club	Pos	G	AB	R	H	2B	3B	HR	RBI	SB	Avg.
1973	New York (AL)	OF	23	77	9	15	4	0	2	7	0	.195
1974	New York (AL)	1B-OF-3B	27	67	9	14	1	1	2	10	0	.209
1975	New York (AL)	1B	6	8	0	2	0	0	0	1	0	.250
1976	New York (AL)	1B-OF-3B	49	94	11	25	6	0	2	10	0	.266
1977	Toronto	OF	120	360	50	92	19	3	16	62	4	.256
1978	Toronto	OF	91	248	29	66	14	2	9	38	1	.266
	Totals		316	854	108	214	44	6	31	128	5	.251

RICK BOSETTI 25 5-11 175   Bats R Throws R

Acquired from Cardinals in spring, blossomed into one of finest outfielders in AL . . . Showed up in Blue Jay training camp wearing T-shirt which read, "Toronto At Last" . . . Makes things happen when he's in the game . . . Originally an infielder in Phillies organization but moved to outfield because of Mike Schmidt . . . Born Aug. 5,

1953, in Redding, Cal. . . . "He covers center field like a mohair rug," says Roy Hartsfield . . . Has excellent speed on basepaths, leading several leagues while in minors.

Year	Club	Pos	G	AB	R	H	2B	3B	HR	RBI	SB	Avg.
1976	Philadelphia......	OF	13	18	6	5	1	0	0	0	3	.278
1977	St. Louis........	OF	41	69	12	16	0	0	0	3	4	.232
1978	Toronto.........	OF	136	568	61	147	25	5	5	42	6	.259
	Totals...........		190	655	79	168	26	5	5	45	13	.256

JOHN MAYBERRY 30 6-3 220   Bats L Throws L

The muscle man in the Blue Jays' batting order . . . Acquired from the Royals to put more punch in the lineup . . . Can hit a ball a mile when he makes contact . . . Knocked in seven runs in one game against Baltimore . . . Born Feb. 18, 1950, in Detroit . . . Attended same high school as Willie Horton and Alex Johnson . . . Fell from favor in Kansas City when his production tailed off and he missed final game of '77 playoff with a toothache . . . Once one of the most feared sluggers in the game.

Year	Club	Pos	G	AB	R	H	2B	3B	HR	RBI	SB	Avg.
1968	Houston..........	1B	4	9	0	0	0	0	0	0	0	.000
1969	Houston.........	PH	5	4	0	0	0	0	0	0	0	.000
1970	Houston..........	1B	50	148	23	32	3	2	5	14	1	.216
1971	Houston..........	1B	46	137	16	25	0	1	7	14	0	.182
1972	Kansas City......	1B	149	503	65	150	24	3	25	100	0	.298
1973	Kansas City......	1B	152	510	87	142	20	2	26	100	3	.278
1974	Kansas City......	1B	126	427	63	100	13	1	22	69	4	.234
1975	Kansas City......	1B	156	554	95	161	38	1	34	106	5	.291
1976	Kansas City......	1B	161	594	76	138	22	2	13	95	3	.232
1977	Kansas City......	1B	153	543	73	125	22	1	23	82	1	.230
1978	Toronto.........	1B	152	515	51	129	15	2	22	70	1	.250
	Totals...........		1154	3944	549	1002	157	15	177	650	18	.254

MARK LEMONGELLO 23 6-1 180   Bats R Throws R

Throws as many strikes as his cousin, pro bowler Mike Lemongello, and can be as vocal as singing cousin, Peter Lemongello . . . Got into shouting match with Astro manager Bill Virdon after being relieved in Chicago and nearly destroyed dugout . . . Born July 21, 1955, in Jersey City, N.J. . . . Lost first 11 decisions of 1977, bought a Mack Truck cap and beat Reds . . . Wore hat off field rest of season and finished 9-14, same as '78 . . . Was minor league roommate of Mark Fidrych, which probably explains his quick sense of humor. Came in winter trade to Toronto.

Year	Club	G	IP	W	L	Pct.	SO	BB	H	ERA
1976	Houston	4	29	3	1	.750	9	7	26	2.79
1977	Houston	34	215	9	14	.391	83	52	237	3.47
1978	Houston	33	210	9	14	.391	77	66	204	3.94
	Totals	71	454	21	29	.420	169	125	467	3.65

TOM UNDERWOOD 25 5-11 170   Bats R Throws L

A winning pitcher with Phillies, he struggled with Blue Jays last season . . . Admits coming to the AL from the NL was a difficult transition . . . "It's tough coming to a club when you don't know anyone on the roster, or the manager" . . . Born Dec. 22, 1953, in Kokomo, Ind. . . . Younger brother Pat is promising pitcher in Tiger farm system . . . Traded from Philly to St. Louis midway through '77 season . . . Used almost exclusively as starter by Blue Jays, but can also relieve . . . Was Phillies' second pick in June, 1972, draft.

Year	Club	G	IP	W	L	Pct.	SO	BB	H	ERA
1974	Philadelphia	7	13	1	0	1.000	8	5	15	4.85
1975	Philadelphia	35	219	14	13	.519	123	84	221	4.15
1976	Philadelphia	33	156	10	5	.667	94	63	154	3.52
1977	Phil.-St. L.	33	133	9	11	.450	86	75	148	5.01
1978	Toronto	31	198	6	14	.300	140	87	201	4.09
	Totals	139	719	40	43	.482	451	314	739	4.17

TOP PROSPECTS

BRIAN MILNER 19 5-11 175   Bats R Throws R

Signed with Blue Jays right out of high school last summer and broke in with a bang, batting .444 before he was sent to minors . . . Went three-for-five with an RBI and a triple in his second start . . . Optioned to Medicine Hat to refine his skills, but he'll be back . . . Maybe sooner than anyone expects.

BUTCH ALBERTS 28 6-2 205   Bats R Throws R

Finally made his major league debut in 1978 and indicated he may be ready for more . . . Batted .278 in brief trial with Blue Jays after spending nearly seven years in minors . . . Born May

4, 1950, in Williamsport, Pa. . . . Has outstanding minor league credentials . . . Has hit everywhere he's ever played . . . Formerly in the Pirate and Angel farm systems.

MANAGER ROY HARTSFIELD: Another in the long line of managers who grew up in the Dodger organization under Branch Rickey's influence . . . Has tremendous patience, which helps when you're building a team from the ground up the way the Blue Jays are . . . Seems to have the perfect disposition for the job . . . Born Oct. 25, 1925, in Chattahoochee, Ga. . . . Spent 17 seasons in pro ball as a player, but only three of those in the big leagues . . . Later managed for 15 years in the minors with outstanding success . . . Coached Dodgers for five years.

GREATEST PITCHER

With the Tigers, Dave Lemanczyk bounced from the bullpen to the starting rotation, back to the bullpen, never finding his niche. With the Orioles and White Sox, Jesse Jefferson was a pitcher who never lived up to his potential. With the Twins, Jerry Garvin was just another name on their minor league roster.

Then along came the Blue Jays and the opportunity for all three pitchers to prove themselves.

It would certainly be premature and admittedly a gross exaggeration to say that Lemanczyk, Jefferson and Garvin have become great pitchers for Toronto.

But they nevertheless were the best the Blue Jays had during their first two years in existence.

Lemanczyk led the expansion Jays in victories as they struggled to get the fledgling franchise off the ground. Garvin struck out more batters than anyone else on the staff. And Jefferson led the team in innings pitched, no small accomplishment considering the lack of support he frequently received.

ALL-TIME BLUE JAY LEADERS

BATTING: Bob Bailor, .310, 1977
HRs: John Mayberry, 22, 1978
RBIs: John Mayberry, 70, 1978
STEALS: Bob Bailor, 15, 1977
WINS: Dave Lemanczyk, 13, 1977
STRIKEOUTS: Tom Underwood, 140, 1978

John Mayberry slugged 22 homers, 70 RBIs for Blue Jay marks.

KANSAS CITY ROYALS

TEAM DIRECTORY: Pres.: Ewing Kaufman; Exec. VP-GM: Joe Burke; VP-Operations: Spencer Robinson; Pub. Rel.: Dean Vogelaar; Dir. Player Development: John Schuerholz; Trav. Sec.: Bill Beck; Mgr.: Whitey Herzog. Home: Royals Stadium (40,762). Field distances: 330, l.f. line; 385, l.c.; 410, c.f.; 385, r.c.; 330, r.f. line. Spring training: Fort Myers, Fla.

SCOUTING REPORT

HITTING: Where have you gone, Al Cowens? The most improved player in the league in 1977 when he raised his BA 47 points, increased his HRs by 20 and his RBIs by 53, Cowens went the other way in 1978. His BA dropped 38 points, his home runs were down 18, his RBIs down 49. It was a mystery.

The Royals were third in hitting, but without John Mayberry and with Cowens slipping, they were only one of four teams in the league who failed to hit 100 home runs. Only club leader Amos Otis (22), Darrell Porter (18) and Hal McRae (16) reached double figures in homers. It is for this reason that batting coach Charlie Lau was dismissed. He's a miracle worker at improving averages, but believes in hits at the expense of home runs.

Manager Whitey Herzog wants more long ball from such as George Brett (nine homers) and Clint Hurdle (seven).

PITCHING: Third best in the league last year and figures to be just as good again with the same cast. It cost $1.2 million to keep Larry Gura in KC after he posted a 16-4 mark with a 2.72 ERA, his best year ever. Dennis Leonard bounced back from an awful start to win 21, the club leader. And Paul Splittorff won his usual 19. Rookie Rich Gale was a find with 14 wins and the bullpen was solid, led by Al (The Mad Hungarian) Hrabosky's 20 saves and eight wins. Marty Pattin, Doug Bird and Steve Mingori round out a solid staff of young veterans.

FIELDING: Surprisingly, the Royals were second from last in the league in this category. This despite a Gold Glove at second in Frank White and excellent play from center fielder Otis, who made only two errors and led all AL outfielders with a .9949 percentage. Veteran shortstop Fred Patek had an off year with 32 errors, many on throws, and may have his job challenged by young U.L. Washington.

Royals re-signed free agent Larry Gura after 16-4 year.

OUTLOOK: The Royals were ready to be taken last year, with no home run production and many regulars having off years. But there was no team able to take them. They sputtered early, but won when they had to, the class of their division. The same seems true this time around. The Royals made no improvement, mainly because none was needed. They have enough talent to win again in a division that has few solid challengers.

The Royals should have little trouble winning in their division for the fourth straight year, because the competition is not strong. Once they get into the playoffs, that's where the competition gets tough, as it was the last three years.

KANSAS CITY ROYALS 1979 ROSTER

MANAGER Whitey Herzog
Coaches—Steve Boros, Galen Cisco, Chuck Hiller, John
Sullivan

PITCHERS

No.	Name	1978 Club	W-L	IP	SO	ERA	B-T	Ht.	Wt.	Born
29	Bird, Doug	Kansas City	6-6	99	48	5.27	R-R	6-4	180	3/5/50 Corona, CA
40	Busby, Steve	Kansas City	1-0	21	10	7.71	R-R	6-2	190	9/29/49 Burbank, CA
		Omaha	3-7	66	32	5.43				
41	Cvejdlik, Kent	Jacksonville	10-11	199	122	2.44	R-R	6-3	185	1/16/57 Omaha, NB
38	Gale, Rich	Omaha	1-1	21	24	4.29	R-R	6-7	225	1/19/54 Littleton, NH
		Kansas City	14-8	192	88	3.09				
48	Grzybek, Ben	Jacksonville	8-8	140	84	2.64	L-R	6-5	200	1/7/58 Miami Beach, FL
32	Gura, Larry	Kansas City	16-4	222	81	2.72	L-L	6-1	185	11/26/47 Joliet, IL
39	Hrabosky, Al	Kansas City	8-7	75	60	2.88	R-L	5-11	180	7/21/49 Oakland, CA
22	Leonard, Dennis	Kansas City	21-17	295	183	3.33	R-R	6-1	190	5/8/51 Brooklyn, NY
28	McGilberry, Randy	Omaha	1-4	38	25	2.84	R-R	6-1	195	10/29/53 Mobile, AL
		Kansas City	0-1	26	12	4.15				
23	Mingori, Steve	Kansas City	1-4	69	28	2.74	L-L	5-10	170	2/29/44 Kansas City, MO
42	Paschall, Bill	Omaha	14-9	186	80	3.64	R-R	6-0	175	4/22/54 Norfolk, VA
		Kansas City	0-1	8	5	3.38				
33	Pattin, Marty	Kansas City	3-3	79	30	3.30	R-R	5-10	180	4/6/43 Charleston, IL
34	Splittorff, Paul	Kansas City	19-13	262	76	3.40	L-L	6-3	210	10/8/46 Evansville, IN
35	Throop, George	Omaha	12-10	153	77	5.47	R-R	6-7	205	11/24/50 Pasadena, CA
		Kansas City	1-0	3	2	0.00				

CATCHERS

No.	Name	1978 Club	H	HR	RBI	Pct.	B-T	Ht.	Wt.	Born
37	Gaudet, Jim	Omaha	83	4	36	.222	R-R	6-0	185	6/3/55 New Orleans, LA
		Kansas City	0	0	0	.000				
15	Porter, Darrell	Kansas City	138	18	78	.265	L-R	6-0	193	1/17/52 Joplin, MO
12	Wathan, John	Kansas City	57	2	28	.300	R-R	6-2	205	10/4/49 Cedar Rapids, IA

INFIELDERS

No.	Name	1978 Club	H	HR	RBI	Pct.	B-T	Ht.	Wt.	Born
43	Barranca, German	Omaha	54	0	17	.236	L-R	6-0	160	10/19/56 Mexico
		Jacksonville	44	2	13	.242				
3	Braun, Steve	Sea-KC	53	3	29	.251	L-R	5-10	180	5/8/48 Trenton, NJ
5	Brett, George	Kansas City	150	9	62	.294	L-R	6-0	200	5/15/53 Glendale, WV
31	Cripe, Dave	Omaha	142	9	53	.300	R-R	6-0	180	4/7/51 Ramona, CA
		Kansas City	2	0	1	.154				
8	LaCock, Pete	Kansas City	95	5	48	.295	L-L	6-3	210	1/17/52 Burbank, CA
2	Patek, Fred	Kansas City	109	2	46	.248	R-R	5-4	145	10/9/44 Oklahoma City, OK
10	Quirk, Jamie	Spokane	100	12	63	.292	L-R	6-4	185	10/22/54 Whittier, CA
		Kansas City	6	0	2	.207				
1	Terrell, Jerry	Kansas City	27	0	8	.203	R-R	6-0	170	7/13/46 Waseca, MN
30	Washington, U.L.	Kansas City	34	0	9	.264	B-R	5-11	175	10/27/53 Otoka, OK
20	White, Frank	Kansas City	127	7	50	.275	R-R	5-11	170	9/4/50 Greenville, MS

OUTFIELDERS

No.	Name	1978 Club	H	HR	RBI	Pct.	B-T	Ht.	Wt.	Born
18	Cowens, Al	Kansas City	133	5	63	.274	R-R	6-2	200	10/25/51 Los Angeles, CA
9	Hurdle, Clint	Kansas City	110	7	56	.264	L-R	6-3	195	7/30/57 Big Rapids, MI
11	McRae, Hal	Kansas City	170	16	72	.273	R-R	5-11	180	7/10/46 Avon Park, FL
26	Otis, Amos	Kansas City	145	22	96	.298	R-R	5-11	166	4/26/47 Mobile, AL
25	Poquette, Tom	Kansas City	44	4	30	.216	L-R	5-11	175	10/30/51 Eau Claire, WI
17	Silverio, Luis	Omaha	106	19	57	.230	R-R	5-11	150	10/23/56 Dominican Republic
		Kansas City	6	0	3	.545				
6	Wilson, Willie	Kansas City	43	0	16	.217	B-R	6-3	190	7/9/55 Montgomery, AL
19	Zdeb, Joe	Kansas City	32	0	11	.252	R-R	5-11	185	6/27/53 Medota, IL
		Omaha	21	2	12	.304				

ROYAL PROFILES

AL COWENS 27 6-2 200   Bats R Throws R

No longer underrated . . . "He has shown us he can do everything," says Whitey Herzog. "Hit for average, hit with power, run and play outstanding defense." . . . Hobbled by knee injury in 1978 . . . Outstanding right fielder with excellent arm . . . Born Oct. 25, 1951, in Los Angeles . . . Has improved tremendously during past two years . . . "The ideal player," added Herzog . . . Was on verge of quitting baseball after he was passed over several times while in minors . . . Quiet, soft-spoken, almost shy . . . Has been one of Royals' most consistent performers since 1976, his first season as a regular.

Year	Club	Pos	G	AB	R	H	2B	3B	HR	RBI	SB	Avg.
1974	Kansas City	OF-3B	110	269	28	65	7	1	1	25	5	.242
1975	Kansas City	OF	120	328	44	91	13	8	4	42	12	.277
1976	Kansas City	OF	152	581	71	154	23	6	3	59	23	.265
1977	Kansas City	OF	162	606	98	189	32	14	23	112	16	.312
1978	Kansas City	OF	132	485	63	133	24	8	5	63	14	.274
	Totals		676	2269	304	632	99	37	36	301	70	.279

DENNIS LEONARD 27 6-1 190   Bats R Throws R

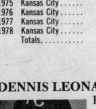

Ranks second behind Orioles' Jim Palmer in victories since 1975, his rookie year . . . Tied for league lead in starts in 1978 with 40 . . . Struggled early in season . . . Described experience as "frustrating" . . . "I was putting too much pressure on myself". . . Strong during Royals stretch drive to third straight Western Division title . . . Born May 18, 1951, in Brooklyn . . . Workhorse of staff . . . Advised to quit game while in college because of arm trouble . . . Gets better and better . . . Was Yankee fan as a kid . . . Has good fastball, slider and curve . . . Threw eight no-hitters in six years in sandlot, high school, college and minor league ball.

Year	Club	G	IP	W	L	Pct.	SO	BB	H	ERA
1974	Kansas City	5	22	0	4	.000	8	12	28	5.32
1975	Kansas City	32	212	15	7	.682	146	90	212	3.78
1976	Kansas City	35	259	17	10	.630	150	70	247	3.51
1977	Kansas City	38	293	20	12	.625	244	79	246	3.04
1978	Kansas City	40	295	21	17	.553	183	78	283	3.33
	Totals	150	1081	73	50	.593	731	329	1016	3.42

RICH GALE 25 6-7 225   Bats R Throws R

Was a leading candidate for Rookie of Year honors first half of season, but slumped during second half . . . Nevertheless, kept Royals in pennant race when most of their other pitchers weren't winning . . . "Thank God for Rich Gale," says Dennis Leonard . . . Called up April 29 to replace injured Steve Busby . . . Born Jan. 19, 1954, in Littleton, N.H. . . . Grew up idolizing Carl Yastrzemski . . . Yet held Yaz hitless in four trips the first time he faced him . . . "I said the heck with that idol stuff" . . . Explosive fastball and slider . . . Played basketball as well as baseball at University of New Hampshire.

Year	Club	G	IP	W	L	Pct.	SO	BB	H	ERA
1978	Kansas City	31	192	14	8	.636	88	100	171	3.09

AL HRABOSKY 29 5-11 180   Bats R Throws L

The "Mad Hungarian" . . . "I have a way to get myself mad. A sign that says Detroit or New York or Boston or any other city in the American League can do it." . . . No. 1 goal is to win the World Series . . . A power pitcher, relies on blazing fastball to make his madman act work . . . "I throw 'em fastballs, good fastballs." . . . Born July 21, 1949, in Oakland Cal. . . . Captured fancy of Royals' fans with ability to squelch rallies . . . Kept Royals in pennant race with his 20 saves . . . Fell from favor with Cardinals after reigning as their ace reliever . . . Claims his beard is essential to his act . . . "The best left-handed relief pitcher in the league," says Whitey Herzog.

Year	Club	G	IP	W	L	Pct.	SO	BB	H	ERA
1970	St. Louis	16	19	2	1	.667	12	7	22	4.74
1971	St. Louis	1	2	0	0	.000	2	0	2	0.00
1972	St. Louis	5	7	1	0	1.000	9	3	2	0.00
1973	St. Louis	44	56	2	4	.333	57	21	45	2.09
1974	St. Louis	65	88	8	1	.889	82	38	71	2.97
1975	St. Louis	65	97	13	3	.813	82	33	72	1.67
1976	St. Louis	68	95	8	6	.571	73	39	89	3.32
1977	St. Louis	65	86	6	5	.545	68	41	82	4.40
1978	Kansas City	58	75	8	7	.533	60	35	52	2.88
	Totals	387	525	48	27	.640	445	217	437	2.93

GEORGE BRETT 25 6-0 200   **Bats L Throws R**

Super guy, and outstanding player, too . . . Hampered by chipped bone in right thumb in 1978 . . . Became mired in worst slump of his life . . . Rose to the occasion, though, by belting three home runs in losing cause in third playoff game against the Yankees . . . Aggressive base runner . . . Born May 15, 1953, in Glendale, W. Va. . . . Has own post-game radio show, "Hot Corner" . . . "George Brett can hit snowballs on Christmas Day," says Whitey Herzog . . . Very close to older brother, big league pitcher Ken Brett . . . "He always gets the big hit when we need it," says Herzog. "He's one of the most consistent and aggressive hitters in baseball . . . Midway through a five-year, $1.5 million contract.

Year	Club	Pos	G	AB	R	H	2B	3B	HR	RBI	SB	Avg.
1973	Kansas City	3B	13	40	2	5	2	0	0	0	0	.125
1974	Kansas City	3B-SS	133	457	49	129	21	5	2	47	8	.282
1975	Kansas City	3B-SS	159	634	84	195	35	13	11	89	13	.308
1976	Kansas City	3B-SS	159	645	94	215	34	14	7	67	21	.333
1977	Kansas City	3B-SS	139	564	105	176	32	13	22	88	14	.312
1978	Kansas City	3B-SS	128	510	79	150	45	8	9	62	23	.294
	Totals		731	2850	413	870	169	53	51	353	79	.305

HAL McRAE 32 5-11 180   **Bats R Throws R**

An intense competitor . . . Played in more consecutive games than any active major leaguer . . . Suffered through one of the worst slumps of his career the first half of the season . . . Collected 1,000th hit and 500th RBI in 1978 . . . Claims trying to hit home runs messed up his swing . . . Born July 10, 1946, in Avon Park, Fla. . . . Signed with Reds, but became expendable because they had so many outstanding hitters . . . "Most of our players look to him for leadership and advice," says Whitey Herzog. "He gives you 110 percent every time he is on the field. He makes every play like it means the Series."

Year	Club	Pos	G	AB	R	H	2B	3B	HR	RBI	SB	Avg.
1968	Cincinnati	2B	17	51	1	10	1	0	0	2	1	.196
1970	Cincinnati	OF-3B-2B	70	165	18	41	6	1	8	23	0	.248
1971	Cincinnati	OF	99	337	39	89	24	2	9	34	3	.264
1972	Cincinnati	OF-3B	62	97	9	27	4	0	5	26	0	.278
1973	Kansas City	OF-3B	106	338	36	79	18	3	9	50	2	.234
1974	Kansas City	OF-3B	148	539	71	167	36	4	15	88	11	.310
1975	Kansas City	OF-3B	126	480	58	147	38	6	5	71	11	.306
1976	Kansas City	OF	149	527	75	175	34	5	8	73	22	.332
1977	Kansas City	OF	162	641	104	191	54	11	21	92	18	.298
1978	Kansas City	OF	156	623	90	170	39	5	16	72	17	.273
	Totals		1094	3798	501	1096	254	37	96	529	85	.289

PAUL SPLITTORFF 32 6-3 210 — Bats L Throws L

Believes he may have reached his peak . . . "The last three years, I believe I've pitched up to my potential" . . . Got off to the best start of his career in 1978 . . . "When Splitt is going good, he pitches baseball about as good as it can be pitched," says Whitey Herzog . . . Needs good control to be effective . . . Born Oct. 8, 1946, in Evansville, Ind. . . . First 20-game winner in Royals' history . . . Wears glasses on the mound . . . Sells real estate during the off-season . . . "He knows how to pitch to each batter," says Herzog. "He's a real student of the game and gets the maximum out of himself every time he goes to the mound."

Year	Club	G	IP	W	L	Pct.	SO	BB	H	ERA
1970	Kansas City	2	9	0	1	.000	10	5	16	7.00
1971	Kansas City	22	144	8	9	.471	80	35	129	2.69
1972	Kansas City	35	216	12	12	.500	140	67	189	3.12
1973	Kansas City	38	262	20	11	.645	110	78	279	3.98
1974	Kansas City	36	226	13	19	.406	90	75	252	4.10
1975	Kansas City	35	159	9	10	.474	76	56	156	3.17
1976	Kansas City	26	159	11	8	.578	59	59	169	3.96
1977	Kansas City	37	229	16	6	.727	99	83	243	3.69
1978	Kansas City	39	262	19	13	.594	76	62	244	3.40
	Totals	270	1666	108	89	.548	740	520	1677	3.58

DARRELL PORTER 27 6-0 193 — Bats L Throws R

Has found happiness and stardom in Kansas City after several unhappy years in Milwaukee . . . "Now everything is different and I feel happy. At the time of the trade I was what you call a bad guy. I was really messed up." . . . Was probably the most valuable Royal in 1978 . . . Credits weight program and winter training for improved performance . . . Born Jan. 17, 1952, in Joplin, Mo. . . . "Darrell is a gamer," says Whitey Herzog. "He comes to the park every day ready to play as hard as he can." . . . Collects unusual caps and displays his collection on top of his locker . . . Has strong arm and hits for power.

Year	Club	Pos	G	AB	R	H	2B	3B	HR	RBI	SB	Avg.
1971	Milwaukee	C	22	70	4	15	2	0	2	9	2	.214
1972	Milwaukee	C	18	56	2	7	1	0	1	2	0	.125
1973	Milwaukee	C	117	350	50	89	19	2	16	67	5	.254
1974	Milwaukee	C	131	432	59	104	15	4	12	56	8	.241
1975	Milwaukee	C	130	409	66	95	12	5	18	60	2	.232
1976	Milwaukee	C	119	389	43	81	14	1	5	32	2	.208
1977	Kansas City	C	130	425	61	117	21	3	16	60	1	.275
1978	Kansas City	C	150	520	77	138	27	6	18	78	0	.265
	Totals		817	2651	362	646	111	21	88	364	20	.244

AMOS OTIS 31 5-11 166   Bats R Throws R

Likes to be called "A.O." . . . Called 1978 his "most satisfying year." . . . Holds almost every Kansas City offensive record . . . Rumored on trading block last spring to make room for rookie Willie Wilson . . . "They might give Willie my job, but he's not going to take it from me" . . . Born April 26, 1947, in Mobile, Ala., the same city that produced Willie Mays, Willie McCovey, Hank Aaron, Cleon Jones and Tommy Agee . . . "A.O. is a pro," says Whitey Herzog . . . Outstanding center fielder, has excellent arm and seldom makes a mistake in outfield . . . Combines speed and power.

Year	Club	Pos	G	AB	R	H	2B	3B	HR	RBI	SB	Avg.
1967	New York (NL) ...	OF-3B	19	59	6	13	2	0	0	1	0	.220
1969	New York (NL) ...	OF-3B	48	93	6	14	3	1	0	4	1	.151
1970	Kansas City......	OF	159	620	91	176	36	9	11	58	33	.284
1971	Kansas City......	OF	147	555	80	167	26	4	15	79	52	.301
1972	Kansas City......	OF	143	540	75	158	28	2	11	54	28	.293
1973	Kansas City......	OF	148	583	89	175	21	4	26	93	13	.300
1974	Kansas City......	OF	146	552	87	157	31	9	12	73	18	.284
1975	Kansas City......	OF	132	470	87	116	26	6	9	46	39	.247
1976	Kansas City......	OF	153	592	93	165	40	2	18	86	26	.279
1977	Kansas City......	OF	142	478	85	120	20	8	17	78	23	.251
1978	Kansas City......	OF	141	486	74	145	30	7	22	96	32	.298
	Totals..........		1378	5028	773	1406	263	52	141	668	265	.280

FRANK WHITE 28 5-11 170   Bats R Throws R

Smooth as silk in the field . . . The best second baseman in the league . . . "I feel I'm valuable and that's what's important." . . . Has been Royals regular for past three years . . . "Frank is one of the best I've ever seen," says Whitey Herzog. "You just can't appreciate how good he is defensively unless you see him play every day. His range is unbelievable." . . . Also starting to be aggressive at the plate . . . Born Sept. 4, 1950, in Greenville, Miss. . . . Grew up and went to school a block from Royals' old Municipal Stadium . . . Graduated from Royals' ill-fated baseball academy.

Year	Club	Pos	G	AB	R	H	2B	3B	HR	RBI	SB	Avg.
1973	Kansas City	SS-2B	51	139	20	31	6	1	0	5	3	.223
1974	Kansas City	2B-SS-3B	99	204	19	45	6	3	1	18	3	.221
1975	Kansas City	2B-3B-SS-C	111	304	43	76	10	2	7	36	11	.250
1976	Kansas City	2B-SS	152	446	39	102	17	6	2	46	20	.229
1977	Kansas City	2B-SS	152	474	59	116	21	5	5	50	23	.245
1978	Kansas City	2B-SS	143	461	66	127	24	6	7	50	13	.275
	Totals..........		708	2028	246	497	84	23	22	205	73	.245

TOP PROSPECTS

LUIS SILVERIO 22 5-11 150   **Bats R Throws R**
Hit with unexpected authority during brief trial with Royals in
1978, batting .545 for eight games . . . Speedy outfielder is best
known for his defense and his aggressive style on the base paths
. . . Born Oct. 23, 1956, in Villa Gonzalez, Dominican Republic
. . . Signed with Royals as free agent in 1974.

GEORGE THROOP 28 6-7 205   **Bats R Throws R**
In a position to make a place for himself in Royals' bullpen
. . . "He comes in there and throws strikes and gets the ground
balls," says Whitey Herzog. "That's what you want a reliever to
do." . . . Born Nov. 24, 1950, in Sierra Madre, Cal. . . . Has
had three brief trials with Royals . . . Won the only game he
appeared in in 1978.

MANAGER WHITEY HERZOG: Has taken Royals to playoff
three years in a row, only to lose to Yankees
each time . . . After last loss, he wondered
aloud if maybe the Royals might be better off
with a new manager . . . Sincere, outspoken
and well-liked . . . Born Nov. 9, 1931, in
New Athens, Ill. . . . Real name Dorrel Norman Elvert Herzog . . . Affectionately referred to around the league as "The White
Rat." . . . Previously managed Texas and California . . . Spent
eight years in major leagues as a player with Washington, Kansas City, Baltimore and Detroit.

GREATEST PITCHER

He is certainly not an overpowering pitcher. He doesn't pos-
sess a blazing fastball or a baffling, sharp-breaking curve. The
truth is, if you bumped into him out of uniform away from the
ballpark, you probably wouldn't even know he was a ballplayer.
But don't let those glasses and his pleasant demeanor fool
you.
When Paul Splittorff is in the groove, there are few better
pitchers in the American League.
And he has the credentials to prove it.

Without attracting a great deal of fanfare or acclaim, the tall left-hander has quietly accumulated more victories (108), more strikeouts (730), and more shutouts (17) than any pitcher in Kansas City history.

In time, other pitchers will undoubtedly come along, catch and pass Splittorff, erasing his name from the Royals' record book.

But Royals fans will never forget how much he has meant to their club for the past several years.

ALL-TIME ROYAL LEADERS

BATTING: George Brett, .333, 1976
HRs: John Mayberry, 34, 1975
RBIs: Al Cowens, 112, 1977
STEALS: Fred Patek, 53, 1977
WINS: Steve Busby, 22, 1974
STRIKEOUTS: Dennis Leonard, 244, 1977

Royals' Freddie Patek stole club-record 53 bases in 1977.

TEXAS RANGERS

TEAM DIRECTORY: Chairman of the Board: Brad Corbett; Exec. VP: Eddie Robinson; GM: Dan O'Brien; Farm Dir.: Hal Keller; Trav. Sec. and News Media Director: Burton Hawkins; Promotions Dir.: Dan McDonald; Mgr.: Pat Corrales. Home: Arlington Stadium (41,000). Field distances: 330, l.f. line; 400, c.f.; 330, r.f. line. Spring training: Pompano Beach, Fla.

SCOUTING REPORT

HITTING: The big gamble was a bomb. Brad Corbett tried to buy a pennant, just as George Steinbrenner did, but still wound up third best in the AL West. He spent $2.7 million on Richie Zisk, traded for high-salaried Al Oliver and Bobby Bonds, without the desired results.

Dissatisfied, Corbett began moving bodies. Gone are Mike

Club-record 52 steals show Bump Wills heeds father Maury.

Hargrove, Juan Beniquez, Toby Harrah, Bonds and manager Billy Hunter; coming are Buddy Bell, Oscar Gamble, Sparky Lyle and manager Pat Corrales.

Zisk and Oliver are the constants and they will form the center of the Rangers' attack, as they did last year when they combined for 36 homers and 174 RBIs, Oliver also finishing second in batting, nine points behind Rod Carew. The Rangers are hoping a return to the AL will perk up Gamble's bat. He went from 31 homers, 83 RBIs in the AL in '77 to seven homers, 47 RBIs in the NL last year. Improvement is also expected from Bump Wills (.250) at second and at short, where Campy Campaneris slumped off to .186 and will be replaced by rookie Nelson Norman, .284 at Tucson.

PITCHING: This was the most pleasant surprise for the Rangers and yet, despite finishing second in the league in team ERA, there is room for improvement. Jon Matlack continues to be an enigma, his 2.30 ERA being second best to Ron Guidry, but his record was a disappointing 15-13.

The Rangers figure Doyle Alexander is better than his 9-10 record indicates and that Dock Ellis is better than his 9-7. The other Doc, Medich, gave the Rangers only nine wins on a $1 million contract.

Fergy Jenkins popped up as the surprise of the year, an 18-game winner and the ace of the staff at age 34. It was his highest victory total since 1974.

The biggest problem was out of the bullpen, where they had a team total of 25 saves. So they went out and got Jim Kern from the Indians and Sparky Lyle from the Yankees. On a good year, Sparky gets that many himself and, with a chance to be the No. 1 man once again, he can have that big year with the Rangers and put them over the top.

FIELDING: The Rangers were third from last in fielding and much of that can be placed on Campy Campaneris, the aging shortstop. The left side of the infield will be all-new, with Buddy Bell at third and Nelson Norman at short. Bell is a proven quantity, and quality, one of the top third sackers in the game. Norman must prove himself. Jim Sundberg remains the top defensive catcher in the league, but the Rangers must replace Juan Beniquez, a defensive whiz in center.

OUTLOOK: The top two priorities for the Rangers were to improve their bullpen and their defense. They have done both, but they might have done it at the expense of their offense.

TEXAS RANGERS 1979 ROSTER

MANAGER Pat Corrales
Coaches—Jackie Brown, Fred Koenig, Frank Lucchesi, Connie Ryan

PITCHERS

No.	Name	1978 Club	W-L	IP	SO	ERA	B-T	Ht.	Wt.	Born
33	Alexander, Doyle	Texas	9-10	191	81	3.86	R-R	6-3	205	9/4/50 Cordova, AL
24	Allard, Brian	Tulsa	7-10	155	102	4.24	R-R	6-3	175	1/3/58 Spring Valley, IL
28	Comer, Steve	Texas	11-5	117	65	2.31	R-R	6-3	195	1/13/54 Minneapolis, MN
44	Darwin, Danny	Texas	1-0	9	8	4.50	R-R	6-3	190	10/25/55 Bonham, TX
		Tucson	8-9	125	126	6.26				
17	Ellis, Dock	Texas	9-7	141	45	4.21	B-R	6-3	203	3/11/45 Los Angeles, CA
—	Farmer, Ed	Milwaukee	1-0	11	6	0.82	R-R	6-0	205	10/18/49 Evergreen Park, IL
		Spokane	9-7	90	50	6.00				
30	Finch, Steve	Tulsa	1-2	29	24	4.97	R-R	6-3	160	3/9/55 Escondido, CA
31	Jenkins, Fergie	Texas	18-8	249	157	3.04	R-R	6-5	210	12/13/43 Chatham, Ont.
41	Kern, Jim	Cleveland	10-10	99	95	3.09	R-R	6-5	205	3/15/49 Gladwin, MI
38	Lyle, Sparky	New York (AL)	9-3	112	33	3.46	L-L	6-1	208	7/22/44 Reynoldsville, PA
32	Matlack, Jon	Texas	15-13	270	157	2.30	L-L	6-3	205	1/19/50 West Chester, PA
36	McCall, Larry	Tacoma	10-4	138	81	2.93	L-R	6-2	182	9/8/52 Asheville, NC
		New York (AL)	1-1	16	7	5.63				
42	Medich, Doc	Texas	9-8	171	71	3.68	R-R	6-5	227	12/9/48 Aliquippa, PA
29	Moret, Roger	Texas	0-1	15	5	4.80	B-R	6-4	175	9/16/49 Puerto Rico
27	Rajsich, Dave	Tacoma	8-4	81	59	3.56	L-L	6-5	180	9/28/51 Youngstown, OH
		New York (AL)	0-0	13	9	4.15				
40	Umbarger, Jim	Texas	5-8	98	60	4.51	L-L	6-6	200	2/17/53 Burbank, CA

CATCHERS

No.	Name	1978 Club	H	HR	RBI	Pct.	B-T	Ht.	Wt.	Born
9	Ellis, John	Texas	23	3	17	.245	R-R	6-2	210	8/21/48 New London, CT
2	Heath, Mike	West Haven	64	8	27	.295	R-R	5-11	175	2/5/55 Tampa, FL
		New York (AL)	21	0	8	.228				
14	Roberts, Dave	Hawaii	32	5	31	.267	R-R	6-4	200	2/17/51 Lebanon, OR
		San Diego	21	1	7	.216				
10	Sundberg, Jim	Texas	144	6	58	.278	R-R	6-0	190	5/18/51 Galesburg, IL

INFIELDERS

No.	Name	1978 Club	H	HR	RBI	Pct.	B-T	Ht.	Wt.	Born
—	Bell, Buddy	Cleveland	157	6	62	.282	R-R	6-2	185	8/27/51 Pittsburgh, PA
6	Blanks, Larvell	Cleveland	49	2	20	.254	R-R	5-8	165	1/28/50 Del Rio, TX
25	Bucci, Mike	Tucson	124	4	65	.331	R-R	5-11	180	7/5/53 Reading, PA
1	Campaneris, Bert	Texas	50	1	17	.186	R-R	5-10	160	3/9/42 Cuba
21	Duran, Dan	Tulsa	66	7	40	.330	L-L	5-11	190	3/16/54 Palo Alto, CA
		Tucson	84	10	55	.327				
23	Gray, Gary	Tucson	126	13	98	.316	R-R	6-0	203	9/21/52 New Orleans, LA
		Texas	12	2	6	.240				
—	Holle, Gary	Spokane	66	8	40	.300	R-L	6-6	208	8/11/54 Albany, NY
		Holyoke	66	10	44	.258				
35	Jorgensen, Mike	Texas	19	1	9	.196	L-L	6-0	192	8/16/48 Passaic, NJ
4	Norman, Nelson	Tucson	133	2	76	.284	R-R	6-2	160	5/23/58 Dominican Republic
		Texas	9	0	1	.265				
18	Putnam, Pat	Tucson	138	21	96	.309	L-R	6-1	214	12/3/53 Bethel, VT
		Texas	7	1	2	.152				
20	Ramos, Domingo	West Haven	31	1	11	.254	R-R	5-10	154	3/29/58 Puerto Rico
		Tacoma	74	0	30	.236				
		New York (AL)	0	0	0	.000				
15	Washington, LaRue	Tucson	166	4	74	.324	R-R	6-0	170	9/7/53 Long Beach, CA
		Texas	0	0	0	.000				
1	Wills, Bump	Texas	135	9	57	.250	B-R	5-9	170	7/27/52 Washington, DC

OUTFIELDERS

No.	Name	1978 Club	H	HR	RBI	Pct.	B-T	Ht.	Wt.	Born
12	Gamble, Oscar	San Diego	103	7	47	.275	L-R	5-11	170	12/20/49 Ramer, AL
6	Grubb, John	Cleve-Texas	113	15	67	.276	L-R	6-3	188	8/4/48 Richmond, VA
0	Oliver, Al	Texas	170	14	89	.324	L-L	6-1	190	10/14/46 Portsmith, OH
7	Sample, Bill	Tucson	170	18	99	.352	R-R	5-9	175	4/2/55 Roanoke, VA
		Texas	7	0	3	.467				
22	Zisk, Richie	Texas	134	22	85	.262	R-R	6-1	208	2/6/49 Brooklyn, NY

RANGER PROFILES

RICHIE ZISK 30 6-1 208   Bats R Throws R

Enjoyed productive year after signing with Rangers for $2,955,000 for 10 years . . . "I dread to think where we'd be without him," says teammate Al Oliver . . . One of premier right-handed power hitters in AL . . . Fled Chicago when White Sox owner Bill Veeck refused to meet his salary demands . . . Born Feb. 6, 1949, in Brooklyn, N.Y. . . . Moved to Parsipanny, N.J., where he starred in basketball, baseball, and soccer . . . Signed with Pirates, then traded to White Sox, when he refused to sign Pittsburgh contract . . . Attended Seton Hall University.

Year	Club	Pos	G	AB	R	H	2B	3B	HR	RBI	SB	Avg.
1971	Pittsburgh	OF	7	15	2	3	1	0	1	2	0	.200
1972	Pittsburgh	OF	17	37	4	7	3	0	0	4	0	.189
1973	Pittsburgh	OF	103	333	44	108	23	7	10	54	0	.324
1974	Pittsburgh	OF	149	536	75	168	30	3	17	100	1	.313
1975	Pittsburgh	OF	147	504	69	146	27	3	20	75	0	.290
1976	Pittsburgh	OF	155	581	91	168	35	2	21	89	1	.289
1977	Chicago (AL)	OF	141	531	78	154	17	6	30	101	0	.290
1978	Texas	OF	140	511	68	134	19	1	22	85	3	.262
	Totals		859	3048	431	888	155	22	121	510	5	.291

JIM SUNDBERG 27 6-0 190   Bats R Throws R

The best defensive catcher in the AL . . . "He's the best catcher in baseball," said KC manager Whitey Herzog . . . "Give me him and I've got the start of a helluva team." . . . Blossomed into a steady hitter last two seasons . . . "Confidence means more than anything else," he says . . . Born May 18, 1951, in Galesburg, Ill. . . . Played in 140 or more games four years in a row . . . Excellent arm, adept at picking runners off first base as well as nailing those who try to steal . . . Nicknamed "Sonny Boone," by his teammates because he's so clean-cut . . . Former Gold Glove winner.

Year	Club	Pos	G	AB	R	H	2B	3B	HR	RBI	SB	Avg.
1974	Texas	C	132	368	45	91	13	3	3	36	2	.247
1975	Texas	C	155	472	45	94	9	0	6	36	3	.199
1976	Texas	C	140	448	33	102	24	2	3	34	0	.228
1977	Texas	C	149	453	61	132	20	3	6	65	2	.291
1978	Texas	C	149	518	54	144	23	6	6	58	2	.278
	Totals		725	2259	238	563	89	14	24	129	9	.249

OSCAR GAMBLE 29 5-11 170   Bats L Throws R

Keeps his suitcase packed, having played for Chicago (NL), Philadelphia, Cleveland, New York (AL), Chicago (AL) and finally signing as a free agent with San Diego before 1978 and now he is back in the American League, coming in off-season trade for Mike Hargrove . . . In-and-out player all season due to injuries and platooning . . . Hit only seven homers, first time under double figures since 1973 . . . Hit a career-high 31 for White Sox in 1977 . . . Born Dec. 20, 1949, in Ramer, Ala. . . . Slapped the last hit in old Connie Mack Stadium in Philadelphia . . . Wife, Juanita, is a singer and sang the National Anthem at Yankee Stadium several times, including once before a playoff game in 1976.

Year	Club	Pos	G	AB	R	H	2B	3B	HR	RBI	SB	Avg.
1969	Chicago (NL)	OF	24	71	6	16	1	1	1	5	0	.225
1970	Philadelphia	OF	88	275	31	72	12	4	1	19	5	.262
1971	Philadelphia	OF	92	280	24	62	11	1	6	23	5	.221
1972	Philadelphia	OF-1B	74	135	17	32	5	2	1	13	0	.237
1973	Cleveland	OF	113	390	56	104	11	3	20	44	3	.267
1974	Cleveland	OF	135	454	74	132	16	4	19	59	5	.291
1975	Cleveland	OF	121	348	60	91	16	3	15	45	11	.261
1976	New York (AL)	OF	110	340	43	79	13	1	17	57	5	.232
1977	Chicago (AL)	OF	137	408	75	121	22	2	31	83	1	.297
1978	San Diego	OF	126	375	46	103	15	3	7	47	1	.275
	Totals		1020	3076	432	812	122	24	118	395	36	.264

BUDDY BELL 27 6-2 185   Bats R Throws R

Became youngest Indian ever to reach 1,000 hits in '78 . . . "I've had so many bad years, my first hit seems like a long time ago" . . . Was traded to Rangers over the winter . . . "He's like a good growth stock," says Indian coach Joe Nossek. "Every year you see steady improvement" . . . Born Aug. 27, 1951, in Pittsburgh where his dad, Gus, was starring for the Pirates . . . Almost overlooked in free agent draft, not chosen until 16th round . . . Originally an infielder, he was moved to center field because Indians had Graig Nettles . . . Transferred back to third when Nettles was traded.

Year	Club	Pos	G	AB	R	H	2B	3B	HR	RBI	SB	Avg.
1972	Cleveland	OF-3B	132	466	49	119	21	1	9	36	5	.255
1973	Cleveland	3B-OF	156	631	86	169	23	7	14	59	7	.268
1974	Cleveland	3B	116	423	51	111	15	1	7	46	1	.262
1975	Cleveland	3B	153	553	66	150	20	4	10	59	6	.271
1976	Cleveland	3B-1B	159	604	75	170	26	2	7	60	3	.281
1977	Cleveland	3B-OF	129	479	64	140	23	4	11	64	1	.292
1978	Cleveland	3B	142	556	71	157	27	8	6	62	1	.282
	Totals		987	3712	462	1016	155	27	64	386	24	.274

DOC MEDICH 30 6-5 227 Bats R Throws R

Had disappointing year for Rangers after signing four-year, $1 million contract as free agent . . . Attends University of Pittsburgh medical school in the off-season and plans to practice medicine when baseball career ends . . . Was credited with saving life of fan in the stands in Baltimore July 17, when he left the field to revive heart attack victim . . . Born Dec. 9, 1948, in Aliquippa, Pa. . . . Began career with Yankees, later pitched for Pittsburgh, Oakland, Seattle and Mets before signing with Rangers . . . Real name is George Francis Medich . . . Has begun internship in orthopedics and will receive $50,000 a year for four years as Rangers' medical consultant when he retires.

Year	Club	G	IP	W	L	Pct.	SO	BB	H	ERA
1972	New York (AL)	1	0	0	0	.000	0	2	2	
1973	New York (AL)	34	235	14	9	.609	145	74	217	2.95
1974	New York (AL)	38	280	19	15	.559	154	91	275	3.60
1975	New York (AL)	38	272	16	16	.500	132	72	271	3.51
1976	Pittsburgh	29	179	8	11	.421	86	48	193	3.52
1977	Oakland-Seattle	29	170	12	6	.667	77	53	181	4.55
1977	New York (NL)	1	7	0	1	.000	3	1	6	3.86
1978	Texas	28	171	9	8	.529	71	52	166	3.68
	Totals	198	1314	78	66	.542	668	393	1311	3.60

JIM KERN 30 6-5 205 Bats R Throws R

Flame-throwing right-hander, acquired from Cleveland in exchange for Bobby Bonds . . . Before he left, he signed three-year contract with Indians worth $330,000 . . . "You can be loyal to a team all you want and that loyalty is liable to put you on the street corner selling papers when you're 35." . . . Spent eight seasons in minor leagues before finally reaching Cleveland in 1975 . . . Born March 15, 1949, in Gladwin, Mich. . . . Saved 46 games last three years . . . Once fanned 20 in American Legion state tournament . . . Studies chemical engineering at Michigan State during off-season.

Year	Club	G	IP	W	L	Pct.	SO	BB	H	ERA
1974	Cleveland	4	15	0	1	.000	11	14	16	4.80
1975	Cleveland	13	72	1	2	.333	55	45	60	3.75
1976	Cleveland	50	118	10	7	.588	111	50	91	2.36
1977	Cleveland	60	92	8	10	.444	91	47	85	3.42
1978	Cleveland	58	99	10	10	.500	95	58	77	3.09
	Totals	185	396	29	30	.492	363	214	329	3.14

BUMP WILLS 26 5-9 170   Bats S Throws R

Son of former infield star Maury, and a chip off the old block . . . Says "hard work and dedication" not natural ability got him to the big leagues . . . Good speed and a steady fielder . . . "I'm not as smooth as Frank White, that's for sure, but I get the job done." . . . Slumped along with rest of Ranger infield in '78 . . . Goal is to hit .300 . . . Born July 27, 1952, in Washington, D.C., which is where Rangers come from, too . . . Won second base job from Lenny Randle in spring of '77 . . . Frequently phones dad for advice . . . Will never match Maury's 104 stolen bases, but is all-around ballplayer.

Year	Club	Pos	G	AB	R	H	2B	3B	HR	RBI	SB	Avg.
1977	Texas	2B	152	541	87	155	28	6	9	62	28	.287
1978	Texas	2B	157	539	78	135	17	4	9	57	52	.250
	Totals		309	1080	165	290	45	10	18	119	80	.269

AL OLIVER 32 6-1 190   Bats L Throws L

No. O in your programs . . . "The O stands for Oliver" . . . An instant hit with Texas fans who fell in love with easy-going outfielder . . . Made late season charge at perennial batting king Rod Carew before settling for second . . . A legitimate .300 hitter and an all-star outfielder . . . "The fans made me feel like Texas has been my home forever." . . . Came to Rangers in trade from Pittsburgh last winter . . . Born Oct. 14, 1946, in Portsmouth, Ohio . . . Can play left field, center field or first base . . . Can carry club with his bat when he's hot . . . Active in various community projects during the off-season.

Year	Club	Pos	G	AB	R	H	2B	3B	HR	RBI	SB	Avg.
1968	Pittsburgh	OF	4	8	1	1	0	0	0	0	0	.125
1969	Pittsburgh	1B-OF	129	463	55	132	19	2	17	70	8	.285
1970	Pittsburgh	OF-1B	151	551	63	149	33	5	12	83	1	.270
1971	Pittsburgh	OF-1B	143	529	69	149	31	7	14	64	4	.282
1972	Pittsburgh	OF-1B	140	565	88	176	27	4	12	89	2	.312
1973	Pittsburgh	OF-1B	158	654	90	191	38	7	20	99	6	.292
1974	Pittsburgh	OF-1B	147	617	96	198	38	12	11	85	10	.321
1975	Pittsburgh	OF-1B	155	628	90	176	39	8	18	84	4	.280
1976	Pittsburgh	OF-1B	121	443	62	143	22	5	12	61	6	.323
1977	Pittsburgh	OF	154	568	75	175	29	6	19	82	13	.308
1978	Texas	OF	133	525	65	170	35	5	14	89	8	.324
	Totals		1435	5551	754	1660	311	61	149	806	62	.299

FERGIE JENKINS 35 6-5 210   Bats R Throws R

Returned to Texas after two years with Boston and regained magic touch . . . Was supposedly washed-up when left Boston, having been banished to Don Zimmer's doghouse . . . Feels performance in '78 proved former manager wrong . . . Third in lifetime victories among all active major leaguers, trailing Gaylord Perry and Jim Kaat . . . Born Dec. 13, 1943, in Chatham, Ont. . . . Preferred basketball and hockey as youngster, didn't play baseball in high school . . . Father urged him to take up the game . . . Has lost some of zip in fastball but relies on control . . . Ninth on the all-time strikeout list . . . Operates his farm during off-season.

Year	Club	G	IP	W	L	Pct.	SO	BB	H	ERA
1965	Philadelphia	7	12	2	1	.667	10	2	7	2.25
1966	Phil.-Chi. (NL)	61	184	6	8	.429	150	52	150	3.33
1967	Chicago (NL)	38	289	20	13	.606	236	83	230	2.80
1968	Chicago (NL)	40	308	20	15	.571	260	65	255	2.63
1969	Chicago (NL)	43	311	21	15	.583	273	71	284	3.21
1970	Chicago (NL)	40	313	22	16	.579	274	60	265	3.39
1971	Chicago (NL)	39	325	24	13	.649	263	37	304	2.77
1972	Chicago (NL)	36	289	20	12	.625	184	62	253	3.21
1973	Chicago (NL)	38	271	14	16	.467	170	57	267	3.89
1974	Texas	41	328	25	12	.676	225	45	286	2.83
1975	Texas	37	270	17	18	.486	157	56	261	3.93
1976	Boston	30	209	12	11	.522	142	43	201	3.27
1977	Boston	28	193	10	10	.500	105	36	190	3.68
1978	Texas	34	249	18	8	.692	157	41	228	3.04
	Totals	512	3551	231	168	.579	2606	710	3181	3.19

JON MATLACK 29 6-3 205   Bats L Throws L

Boasted the second lowest earned run average in the AL, second only to Yankee sensation Ron Guidry . . . Expected to be traded before Mets sent him to Rangers, but didn't know where . . . "They could have told me I was going to Texas, Honolulu or Moscow and I wouldn't have known the difference" . . . Ranger owner Brad Corbett promised him a minimum of five runs per game . . . "I sure wish I had gotten that in writing." . . . Born Jan. 19, 1950, in West Chester, Pa. . . . Was N.L. Rookie of Year in 1972 . . . twice led NL in shutouts . . . Lack of support and shoulder problems have prevented him from realizing goal of 20 victories . . . So protective of pitching arm he won't even draw blinds with left hand during season.

Year	Club	G	IP	W	L	Pct.	SO	BB	H	ERA
1971	New York (NL)	7	37	0	3	.000	24	15	31	4.14
1972	New York (NL)	34	244	15	10	.600	169	71	215	2.32
1973	New York (NL)	34	242	14	16	.467	205	99	210	3.20
1974	New York (NL)	34	265	13	15	.464	195	76	221	2.41
1975	New York (NL)	33	229	16	12	.571	154	58	224	3.42
1976	New York (NL)	35	262	17	10	.630	153	57	236	2.95
1977	New York (NL)	26	169	7	15	.318	123	43	175	4.21
1978	Texas	35	270	15	13	.536	157	51	252	2.30
	Totals	238	1718	97	94	.508	1180	470	1564	2.92

SPARKY LYLE 34 6-1 208   Bats L Throws L

Went from "Cy Young to Sayonara" in the words of Graig Nettles . . . Spent latter part of season plus World Series watching from bullpen . . . Expected to be traded during off-season, and was . . . Needs to work a lot to be effective . . . Resented arrival of Rich Gossage because that meant less work for him . . . Born July 22, 1944, in Dubois, Pa. . . . Free-spirited and outspoken . . . A notorious practical joker . . . Became first relief pitcher in AL history to win Cy Young Award in '77.

Year	Club	G	IP	W	L	Pct.	SO	BB	H	ERA
1967	Boston	27	43	1	2	.333	42	14	33	2.30
1968	Boston	49	66	6	1	.857	52	14	67	2.73
1969	Boston	71	103	8	3	.727	93	48	91	2.53
1970	Boston	63	67	1	7	.125	51	37	62	3.90
1971	Boston	50	52	6	4	.600	37	23	41	2.77
1972	New York (AL)	59	108	9	5	.643	75	29	84	1.92
1973	New York (AL)	51	82	5	9	.357	63	18	66	2.51
1974	New York (AL)	66	114	9	3	.750	89	43	93	1.66
1975	New York (AL)	49	89	5	7	.417	65	36	94	3.13
1976	New York (AL)	64	104	7	8	.467	61	42	82	2.25
1977	New York (AL)	72	137	13	5	.722	68	33	131	2.17
1978	New York (AL)	59	112	9	3	.750	33	33	116	3.46
	Totals	680	1077	79	57	.581	729	367	960	2.55

TOP PROSPECTS

STEVE COMER 25 6-3 195   Bats S Throws R

Signed with Rangers as undrafted free agent in 1976 . . . Shut Minnesota out 2-0 for first win in late August . . . Ignored by Twins even though he compiled a 30-9 record while pitching for the University of Minnesota . . . "I throw the same now as I did in college." . . . Born Jan. 13, 1954, in Minneapolis . . . "The kid's a helluva pitcher," says Oriole manager Earl Weaver . . . Was working on a construction job when Rangers signed him.

DAVE RAJSICH 27 6-5 180   Bats L Throws L

Summoned from Syracuse to start two games when Yankees ran out of pitchers at midseason . . . Can relieve as well as start . . . Has good fastball, plus curve and forkball . . . Born Sept. 28, 1951, in Youngstown, Ohio . . . Was basketball and baseball star in high school and college . . . Signed with Yanks as free agent in 1974, traded to Texas with Sparky Lyle.

MANAGER PAT CORRALES: Named to succeed Billy Hunter when Hunter was fired on final day of 1978 season . . . Had been a Ranger coach since 1976 . . . Texas owner Brad Corbett calls him "a very tough individual" . . . Hired to crack down on players, also to improve communication between the clubhouse and the front office . . . "I have two rules: Be on time and hustle." . . . Born March 20, 1941, in Los Angeles . . . A former catcher, he spent eight years in the big leagues, playing for the Phillies, Cardinals, Reds and Padres . . . Compiled .216 batting average as a reserve . . . Managed one year (1975) in minors.

GREATEST PITCHER

The Boston Red Sox decided he was finished after the 1977 season, so they shipped him back to Texas, convinced he couldn't pitch anymore.

But Fergie Jenkins showed 'em. And the Rangers were understandably delighted to have him back.

After all, even though he has only pitched for Texas for three of his 13 years in the big leagues, Jenkins has established himself as the most successful pitcher in Ranger history.

He arrived in Texas in 1974, supposedly in the twilight of what had been a brilliant career in the National League, and immediately won 25 games to help lift the Rangers out of the doldrums and up into second place.

He pitched for the Rangers again in '75, then was traded to Boston where he spent two disappointing seasons before returning to Texas in 1978. Back in a Ranger uniform, Jenkins regained his old touch, winning 18 times.

He has won 20 or more games in seven different seasons, six of those in a row while he pitched for the Cubs. And he ranks eighth on baseball's all-time strikeout list.

Al Oliver set Rangers' batting mark first year on team.

ALL-TIME RANGER LEADERS

BATTING: Al Oliver, .324, 1978
HRs: Jeff Burroughs, 30, 1973
RBIs: Jeff Burroughs, 118, 1974
STEALS: Bump Wills, 52, 1978
WINS: Ferguson Jenkins, 25, 1974
STRIKEOUTS: Gaylord Perry, 233, 1975

CALIFORNIA ANGELS

TEAM DIRECTORY: Chairman of the Board-Pres.: Gene Autry; VP-Asst. Chairman of the Board: Red Patterson; VP-GM: Buzzie Bavasi; Dir. of Pub. Rel./Trav. Sec.: Tom Seeberg; Mgr.: Jim Fregosi. Home: Anaheim Stadium (43,250). Field distances: 333, l.f. line; 386, l.c.; 404, c.f.; 386, r.c.; 333, r.f. line. Spring training: Holtville and Palm Springs, Cal.

SCOUTING REPORT

HITTING: Pity the poor Angels. All of Gene Autry's money cannot put Humpty-Dumpty back together again. Everything that can go wrong has gone wrong. Injuries, slumps and the tragedy of Lyman Bostock.

Batters see double against 18-game winner Frank Tanana.

Signed for almost $3 million as a free agent, Bostock got off to a terrible start. He was hitting below .200 in May and offered to give back his month's pay if he did not begin to hit. By the beginning of September, he had hiked his average up to .296, when he was gunned down in a senseless, sickening shooting incident while visiting friends in Gary, Ind.

Now the Angels, ninth in the league in hitting last year, must put the pieces together once more. Toward that end, they traded for Minnesota's Dan Ford (.274, 11 homers, 82 RBIs) to play right field. But to challenge the Royals, they must get continued production from Don Baylor (34 homers, 99 RBIs), big years from veterans Joe Rudi and Bob Grich, and increased production from youngsters Ken Landreaux and third baseman Carney Lansford.

PITCHING: "Everybody's worried about Frank Tanana except me," says manager Jim Fregosi. "There's nothing wrong with his arm. He won 18 games last year. I wish I had five more just like him."

Actually, Fregosi is very high on his pitching. "I've got six starters," he boasts, naming Tanana, Nolan Ryan, Don Aase, Dave Frost, Chris Knapp and Paul Hartzell. In addition, the bullpen is in capable hands, led by Dave LaRoche (10 wins, 25 saves) with Ken Brett, Dyar Miller and Jim Barr, acquired from the Giants, backing him up.

FIELDING: Trading of Tony Solaita and Ron Jackson will necessitate moving Joe Rudi from left field, where he had the third highest fielding percentage in the league, to first base. But the outfield will be manned by Gold Glove Rick Miller in center, speedy Ken Landreaux in left and veteran Dan Ford in right. Not bad.

Rudi has proven he is a capable first baseman and Bob Grich, after a back operation, is almost back to his Baltimore form at second. Short and third will be handled by a pair of youngsters, Rance Mulliniks and Carney Lansford, who have wonderful promise and can only get better.

OUTLOOK: Jim Fregosi did a marvelous job as a rookie manager after taking over from Dave Garcia. He's a positive thinker who has excellent rapport with his men and can only get better with a year under his belt. Fregosi thinks the Angels can make a strong run at the Royals this year, with a little bit of luck. The fates have dealt the Angels a series of bad blows over the last two seasons, maybe they have run out of bad breaks.

CALIFORNIA ANGELS 1979 ROSTER

MANAGER Jim Fregosi
Coaches—Deron Johnson, Bobby Knoop, Jimmie Reese, Larry Sherry

PITCHERS

No.	Name	1978 Club	W-L	IP	SO	ERA	B-T	Ht.	Wt.	Born
44	Aase, Don	California	11-8	179	93	4.02	R-R	6-4	185	9/8/54 Orange, CA
33	Barlow, Mike	S. Lake City	6-5	77	38	3.16	R-R	6-6	215	4/30/48 Stamford, NY
		California	0-0	2	1	4.50				
—	Barr, Jim	San Francisco	8-11	163	44	3.53	R-R	6-3	215	2/10/48 Lynwood, CA
43	Botting, Ralph	El Paso	7-5	93	74	7.06	L-L	6-0	195	5/12/55 Houlton, ME
34	Brett, Ken	California	3-5	100	43	4.95	L-L	5-11	195	9/18/48 Brooklyn, NY
—	Clear, Mark	Salinas	3-5	53	55	5.43	R-R	6-4	200	5/27/56 Los Angeles, CA
		El Paso	4-2	52	80	2.42				
—	Dorsey, Jim	El Paso	5-2	59	56	5.76	R-R	6-2	190	8/2/55 Chicago, IL
		S. Lake City	11-7	132	83	3.34				
—	Eddy, Steve	El Paso	6-10	137	85	4.74	R-R	6-2	185	8/21/57 Sterling, IL
37	Frost, Dave	S. Lake City	6-4	91	53	3.96	R-R	6-6	235	11/17/52 Long Beach, CA
		California	5-4	80	30	2.59				
45	Hartzell, Paul	California	6-10	157	55	3.44	R-R	6-5	200	11/2/53 Bloomsburg, PA
42	Knapp, Chris	California	14-8	188	126	4.21	R-R	6-5	195	9/16/53 Cherry Point, NC
17	LaRoche, Dave	California	10-9	96	70	2.81	L-L	6-2	195	5/14/48 Colorado Springs, CO
41	Miller, Dyar	California	6-2	85	34	2.65	R-R	6-0	215	5/29/46 Batesville, IN
30	Ryan, Nolan	California	10-13	235	260	3.71	R-R	6-2	180	1/31/47 Refugio, TX
40	Tanana, Frank	California	18-12	239	137	3.65	L-L	6-3	180	7/3/53 Detroit, MI

CATCHERS

No.	Name	1978 Club	H	HR	RBI	Pct.	B-T	Ht.	Wt.	Born
23	Cliburn, Stan	S. Lake City	31	3	16	.209	R-R	6-0	190	12/19/56 Jackson, MS
		El Paso	18	4	16	.194				
8	Donohue, Tom	S. Lake City	91	10	57	.291	R-R	6-0	195	11/15/52 Westbury, NY
5	Downing, Brian	California	105	7	46	.255	R-R	5-10	185	10/9/50 Los Angeles, CA
15	Hampton, Ike	California	3	1	4	.214	R-R	6-1	185	8/22/51 Camden, SC
		S. Lake City	26	3	18	.248				
9	Humphrey, Terry	California	25	1	9	.219	R-R	6-3	190	8/4/49 Chickasha, OK

INFIELDERS

No.	Name	1978 Club	H	HR	RBI	Pct.	B-T	Ht.	Wt.	Born
22	Aikens, Willie	S. Lake City	153	29	110	.326	L-R	6-2	220	10/14/54 Seneca, SC
14	Anderson, Jim	S. Lake City	64	5	32	.258	R-R	6-0	170	2/23/57 Los Angeles, CA
		California	21	0	7	.194				
7	Chalk, Dave	California	119	1	34	.253	R-R	5-10	175	8/30/50 Del Rio, TX
6	Fairly, Ron	California	51	10	40	.217	L-L	5-10	180	7/12/38 Macon, GA
4	Grich, Bobby	California	122	6	42	.251	R-R	6-2	180	1/15/49 Muskegon, MI
12	Lansford, Carney	California	133	8	52	.294	R-R	6-2	195	2/7/57 San Jose, CA
18	Mulliniks, Rance	California	22	1	6	.185	L-R	6-0	170	1/15/56 Tulare, CA
		S. Lake City	39	3	21	.307				
—	Ramirez, Orlando	El Paso	109	5	50	.282	R-R	5-10	170	9/28/51 Colombia
		S. Lake City	5	0	4	.217				
—	Rayford, Floyd	El Paso	151	17	87	.313	R-R	5-10	195	7/27/57 Memphis, TN
—	Slater, Bob	El Paso	149	9	43	.290	R-R	5-10	170	10/26/55 Amsterdam, NY
—	Thon, Dickie	S. Lake City	113	1	47	.257	R-R	5-11	150	6/20/58 South Bend, IN

OUTFIELDERS

No.	Name	1978 Club	H	HR	RBI	Pct.	B-T	Ht.	Wt.	Born
25	Baylor, Don	California	151	34	99	.255	R-R	6-1	190	6/28/49 Austin, TX
32	Clark, Bob	El Paso	155	31	111	.316	R-R	6-0	190	6/13/55 Sacramento, CA
—	Ford, Dan	Minnesota	162	11	82	.274	R-R	6-1	185	5/19/52 Los Angeles, CA
19	Landreaux, Ken	California	58	5	23	.223	L-R	5-11	170	12/22/54 Los Angeles, CA
1	Miller, Rick	California	125	1	37	.263	L-L	6-0	185	4/19/48 Grand Rapids, MI
8	Rettenmund, Merv	California	29	1	14	.269	R-R	5-11	190	6/6/43 Flint, MI
26	Rudi, Joe	California	127	17	79	.256	R-R	6-2	200	9/7/46 Modesto, CA

ANGEL PROFILES

FRANK TANANA 25 6-3 180   Bats L Throws L

"When they talk about the best pitcher in baseball, I want Frank Tanana's name to come to mind first" . . . Pitched all of 1978 with a sore arm . . . Lost some speed off his fastball as a result . . . Still one of best in the business . . . "He's the best three-pitch pitcher in baseball," says Sal Bando . . . "He's the best pitcher in baseball," agrees Milwaukee manager George Bamberger . . . Born July 3, 1953, in Detroit . . . Donated $10 for every strikeout in 1978 to a children's hospital . . . Refreshingly open and honest . . . Has shed carefree playboy image since getting married.

Year	Club	G	IP	W	L	Pct.	SO	BB	H	ERA
1973	California	4	26	2	2	.500	22	8	20	3.12
1974	California	39	269	14	19	.424	180	77	262	3.11
1975	California	34	257	16	9	.640	269	73	211	2.63
1976	California	34	288	19	10	.655	261	73	212	2.44
1977	California	31	241	15	9	.625	205	61	201	2.54
1978	California	33	239	18	12	.600	137	60	239	3.65
	Totals	275	1320	84	61	.579	1074	352	1145	2.86

NOLAN RYAN 32 6-2 180   Bats R Throws R

Struggled to maintain consistency in 1978 . . . Nevertheless, led league in strikeouts with 260 . . . "He could throw a ball through a car wash without getting it wet," says umpire Durwood Merrill . . . Ryan says his incredible speed "is basically a gift" . . . When he's throwing well, fans can actually hear him grunt as he releases the ball . . . Born Jan. 31, 1947, in Refugio, Tex. . . . An intense competitor, with an immense amount of pride . . . Continues to move upward on all-time strikeout list . . . Owns four-no-hitters and best strikeout per innings pitched ratio in baseball history . . . When he has his control he's virtually unbeatable.

Year	Club	G	IP	W	L	Pct.	SO	BB	H	ERA
1966	New York (NL)	2	3	0	1	.000	6	3	5	15.00
1968	New York (NL)	21	134	6	9	.400	133	75	93	3.09
1969	New York (NL)	25	89	6	3	.667	92	53	60	3.54
1970	New York (NL)	27	132	7	11	.389	125	97	86	3.41
1971	New York (NL)	30	152	10	14	.417	137	116	125	3.97
1972	California	39	284	19	16	.543	329	157	166	2.28
1973	California	41	326	21	16	.568	383	162	238	2.87
1974	California	42	333	22	16	.578	367	202	221	2.89
1975	California	28	198	14	12	.538	186	132	152	3.45
1976	California	39	284	17	18	.486	327	183	193	3.36
1977	California	37	299	19	16	.543	341	204	198	2.77
1978	California	31	235	10	13	.435	260	148	183	3.71
	Totals	362	2469	151	145	.510	2686	1532	1720	3.12

JOE RUDI 32 6-2 200   **Bats R Throws R**

Quiet, genuine nice guy who prefers to let his bat do his talking for him . . . Warm and affable, yet a man of few words . . . His hobby is operating his ham radio . . . Recently purchased 200 acre ranch in Oregon with some of the $2 million he received when he signed with Angels as a free agent . . . Born Sept. 7, 1946, in Modesto, Cal. . . . One of best defensive left fielders in the league . . . "Joe Rudi is the most fundamentally sound ballplayer of our generation," says admirer Billy Martin . . . "I got my values from my parents. I've always been quiet. I don't step on anyone's toes. I try to treat people the way they want to be treated.

Year	Club	Pos	G	AB	R	H	2B	3B	HR	RBI	SB	Avg.
1967	Kansas City......	OF	19	43	2	8	2	0	0	1	0	.186
1968	Oakland.........	OF	68	181	10	32	5	1	1	12	1	.177
1969	Oakland.........	OF-1B	35	122	10	23	3	1	2	6	1	.189
1970	Oakland.........	OF-1B	106	350	40	108	23	2	11	42	3	.309
1971	Oakland.........	OF-1B	127	513	62	137	23	4	10	52	3	.267
1972	Oakland.........	OF-3B	147	593	94	181	32	9	19	75	3	.305
1973	Oakland.........	1B-OF	120	437	53	118	25	1	12	66	0	.270
1974	Oakland.........	1B-OF	158	593	73	174	39	4	22	99	2	.293
1975	Oakland.........	1B-OF	126	468	66	130	26	6	21	75	2	.278
1976	Oakland.........	1B-OF	130	500	54	135	32	3	13	94	6	.270
1977	California.......	OF	64	242	48	64	13	2	13	53	1	.264
1978	California.......	OF	133	497	58	127	27	1	17	79	2	.256
	Totals..........		1233	4539	572	1237	250	34	141	654	24	.273

DAVE CHALK 28 5-10 175   **Bats R Throws R**

Started fast in 1978 for a change, instead of waiting until August to come alive . . . Played three positions, third base, shortstop and second, and played all three well . . . Copied Tiger Rusty Staub's practice of choking up on bat . . . Underwent knee surgery during off-season . . . Born Aug. 30, 1950, in Del Rio Tex. . . . Has always been excellent fielder, improving with bat . . . "This game isn't as easy as I thought it was" . . . No. 1 pick in nation in June, 1972, draft . . . Some experts think he could be the next Brooks Robinson.

Year	Club	Pos	G	AB	R	H	2B	3B	HR	RBI	SB	Avg.
1973	California........	SS	24	69	14	16	2	0	0	6	0	.232
1974	California........	SS-3B	133	465	44	117	9	3	5	31	10	.252
1975	California........	3B	149	513	59	140	24	2	3	56	6	.273
1976	California........	SS-3B	142	438	39	95	14	1	0	33	0	.217
1977	California........	SS-3B-2B	149	519	58	144	27	2	3	45	12	.277
1978	California........	SS-3B	135	470	42	119	12	0	1	34	5	.253
	Totals..........		732	2474	256	631	88	8	12	205	33	.255

DAVE LaROCHE 30 6-2 195 Bats L Throws L

Loves to be a relief pitcher . . . "I'd rather have a save than a victory" . . . Last year he had 25 of them . . . Shuns attempts to nickname him "The Vulture" . . . "Can't I just be plain 'Roachie?' " . . . Transformed image of Angel bullpen from arson squad to rescue squad . . . Born May 14, 1948, in Colorado Springs . . . Born David Garcia but changed his name in grade school because classmates kidded him about being related to David Garcia, the fat Mexican Army sergeant in the TV series "Zorro" that was popular at the time.

Year	Club	G	IP	W	L	Pct.	SO	BB	H	ERA
1970	California	38	50	4	1	.800	44	21	41	3.42
1971	California	56	72	5	1	.833	63	27	55	2.50
1972	Minnesota	62	95	5	7	.417	79	39	72	2.84
1973	Chicago (NL)	45	54	4	1	.800	34	29	55	5.83
1974	Chicago (NL)	49	92	5	6	.455	49	47	103	4.79
1975	Cleveland	61	82	5	3	.625	94	57	61	2.20
1976	Cleveland	61	96	1	4	.200	104	49	57	2.25
1977	Clev.-Cal.	59	100	8	7	.533	79	44	79	3.51
1978	California	59	96	10	9	.526	70	48	73	2.81
	Totals	490	737	47	39	.547	616	361	596	3.25

DON BAYLOR 29 6-1 190 Bats R Throws R

Relaxed in 1978 after suffering pressure that accompanied signing $2.5 million contract with Angels as free agent in '77 . . . And his production soared accordingly . . . "In 1977 I put too much pressure on myself. It was pretty sad." . . . Credits coaches John McNamara and Bob Skinner with his turnaround . . . "They told me to quit worrying and do the best I could." . . . Born June 28, 1949, in Austin, Tex. . . . Would still prefer to return to the outfield but is adjusting to role of DH . . . Minor league star before reaching bigs with Orioles in 1972.

Year	Club	Pos	G	AB	R	H	2B	3B	HR	RBI	SB	Avg.
1970	Baltimore	OF	8	17	4	4	0	0	0	4	1	.235
1971	Baltimore	OF	1	2	0	0	0	0	0	1	0	.000
1972	Baltimore	OF-1B	102	319	33	81	13	3	11	38	24	.254
1973	Baltimore	OF-1B	118	405	64	116	20	4	11	51	32	.286
1974	Baltimore	OF-1B	137	489	66	133	22	1	10	59	29	.272
1975	Baltimore	OF-1B	145	524	79	148	21	6	25	76	32	.282
1976	Oakland	OF-1B	157	595	85	147	25	1	15	68	52	.247
1977	California	OF-1B	154	561	87	141	27	0	25	75	26	.251
1978	California	OF	158	591	103	151	26	0	34	99	22	.255
	Totals		1000	3504	521	921	154	15	131	471	218	.263

RICK MILLER 30 6-0 185   **Bats L Throws L**

Defensive specialist . . . Decided to sign with Angels as free agent when they traded Bobby Bonds, opening up right field . . . "I guess a good right fielder can save a club 80 runs over a season . . . Finally got chance to play regularly after sitting on bench in Boston for six years . . . Born April 19, 1949, in Grand Rapids, Mich., birthplace of another outstanding defensive outfielder, Tigers' Mickey Stanley . . . Married to former teammate Carlton Fisk's sister . . . Would prefer to play center field and may get chance in 1979.

Year	Club	Pos	G	AB	R	H	2B	3B	HR	RBI	SB	Avg.
1971	Boston	OF	15	33	9	11	5	0	1	7	0	.333
1972	Boston	OF	89	98	13	21	4	1	3	15	0	.214
1973	Boston	OF	143	441	65	115	17	7	6	43	12	.261
1974	Boston	OF	114	280	41	73	8	1	5	22	13	.261
1975	Boston	OF	77	108	21	21	2	1	0	15	3	.194
1976	Boston	OF	105	269	40	76	15	3	0	27	11	.283
1977	Boston	OF	86	189	34	48	9	3	0	24	11	.254
1978	California	OF	132	475	66	125	25	4	1	37	3	.263
	Totals		761	1893	289	490	85	20	16	190	53	.259

BOBBY GRICH 30 6-2 180   **Bats R Throws R**

Thought he had completely recovered from back surgery, but discovered he hadn't . . . "I didn't believe it when the doctors said I'd have problems." . . . Confidence returned late in year and looking forward to outstanding season in 1979 . . . Born Jan. 15, 1949, in Muskegon, Mich. . . . Another of the Angels' millionaire free agents who has not yet lived up to expectations . . . Signed by Orioles as shortstop, but was converted to second base where he won Gold Glove . . . Angels returned him to shortstop, which is position he prefers . . . Once regarded as one of the best players in AL.

Year	Club	Pos	G	AB	R	H	2B	3B	HR	RBI	SB	Avg.
1970	Baltimore	SS-2B-3B	30	95	11	20	1	3	0	8	1	.211
1971	Baltimore	SS-2B	7	30	3	9	0	0	1	6	1	.300
1972	Baltimore	SS-2B-1B-3B	133	460	66	128	21	3	12	50	13	.278
1973	Baltimore	2B	162	581	82	146	29	7	12	50	17	.251
1974	Baltimore	2B	160	582	92	152	29	6	19	82	17	.261
1975	Baltimore	2B	150	524	81	136	26	4	13	57	14	.262
1976	Baltimore	2B-3B	144	518	93	138	31	4	13	54	14	.266
1977	California	SS	52	181	24	44	6	0	7	23	6	.243
1978	California	2B	144	487	68	122	16	2	6	42	4	.251
	Totals		982	3458	525	895	159	29	83	371	87	.259

CARNEY LANSFORD 22 6-2 195   Bats R Throws R

One of the best rookies ever to wear Angels' uniform . . . Impressed new manager Jim Fregosi with his consistency . . . Fastest man on club . . . Favorite of scout Bill Rigney . . . "That kid is a major leaguer," said Rig, first time he saw him . . . "A complete player," says ex-manager Dave Garcia . . . Combines speed and size . . . Also a good listener and learner . . . Born Feb. 7, 1957, in San Jose, Cal. . . . "He has a good attitude," says Bobby Grich. "He's serious, he observes, he asks questions." . . . Admits he was a "million to one shot" when he made the team last spring.

Year	Club	Pos	G	AB	R	H	2B	3B	HR	RBI	SB	Avg.
1978	California........	3B-2B	121	453	62	133	23	2	8	52	20	.294

CHRIS KNAPP 25 6-5 195   Bats R Throws R

Bespectacled stringbean . . . Quit for two weeks in mid-season because of contract dispute . . . "I don't think I have to explain it, really. I just did what I had to do at the time." . . . Felt he was worth more than $40,000 Angels were paying him and wanted to renegotiate his contract . . . Later apologized to teammates . . . Born Sept. 16, 1953, in Cherry Point, N.C. . . . Traded to Angels by White Sox as partial payment for Bobby Bonds . . . Starred at Central Michigan University before signing with Sox.

Year	Club	G	IP	W	L	Pct.	SO	BB	H	ERA
1975	Chicago (AL).............	2	2	0	0	.000	3	4	2	4.50
1976	Chicago (AL).............	11	52	3	1	.750	41	32	54	4.85
1977	Chicago (AL).............	27	146	12	7	.632	103	61	166	4.81
1978	California.................	30	188	14	8	.636	126	67	178	4.21
	Totals..................	70	388	29	16	.644	273	164	400	4.52

DAN FORD 26 6-1 185   Bats R Throws R

Moved to center field last season to replace Lyman Bostock and astounded Twins with his defense . . . Made so many long, running catches, writers named him "Whooshmobile." . . . Enjoyed best year of career in 1978 . . . Almost traded to Mets following '77 season . . . "Disco Dan" . . . Born May 19, 1952, in Los Angeles . . . Collected seven RBIs in

12-inning game against A's . . . Originally drafted by A's and traded to Twins . . . "A truly gifted athlete," says Gene Mauch . . . Consistent hitter who regularly comes through in the clutch.

Year	Club	Pos	G	AB	R	H	2B	3B	HR	RBI	SB	Avg.
1975	Minnesota	OF	130	440	72	123	21	1	15	59	6	.280
1976	Minnesota	OF	145	514	87	137	24	7	20	86	17	.267
1977	Minnesota	OF	144	453	66	121	25	7	11	60	6	.267
1978	Minnesota	OF	151	592	78	162	36	10	11	82	7	.274
	Totals		570	1999	303	543	106	25	57	287	36	.272

TOP PROSPECT

JOHN CANEIRA 26 6-4 200　　　　　**Bats R Throws R**
Husky right-hander could make a place for himself on Angel pitching staff this season . . . Started a couple of games in 1978 but didn't get the decisions . . . Also up briefly with Angels in '77 . . . Born Oct. 7, 1952, in Naugatuck, Conn. . . . Angels' No. 1 pick in secondary phase of June, 1974, draft . . . Impressive college and minor league credentials.

MANAGER JIM FREGOSI: Easy going, fun-loving guy in first full season as manager of Angels . . . Popular with players because he has no rules . . . "If you don't have any rules, they can't break them" . . . Has been looking forward to managing and has been preparing himself for it since 1964 when he was 22 years old . . . "The only goal I ever set for myself was to be a manager in the big leagues" . . . Born April 4, 1942, in San Francisco . . . Youngest manager in majors . . . "He's one of my very, very best and closest friends," says owner Gene Autry, who personally picked Jim to replace Dave Garcia . . . Wears same No. 11 he wore as a player . . . Three times winner of owner's trophy as Most Valuable Angel as a player . . . Made the all-star team six times . . . One of few managers who would like to be able to use a designated runner.

GREATEST PITCHER

In the dugouts around the American League, they still tell the story about the first time umpire Durwood Merrill worked behind home plate when Nolan Ryan was on the mound.

Elrod Hendricks was the batter and after Ryan's first fastball whistled by him, Ellie turned to Merrill and asked, "Where was it?"

"I don't know," the umpire replied.

"Well, what was it?" inquired Hendricks.

"I don't know," Merrill responded again.

"Well, what are you going to call it?" Hendricks wanted to know.

"A ball," the umpire said.

"Why?" asked Hendricks.

"I don't know," answered Merrill with a smile.

Such is the caliber of Nolan Ryan's fastball—the pitch that has made him baseball's seventh leading strikeout artist of all-time. If he merely maintains his present pace for another four or five years, he'll surpass the immortal Walter Johnson as the all-time strikeout king.

Meanwhile, Ryan, who came to the Angels from the Mets following the 1971 season in one of the greatest steals ever, continues to enhance his status as the most successful pitcher who has ever worn a California uniform.

ALL-TIME ANGEL LEADERS

BATTING: Alex Johnson, .329, 1970
HRs: Leon Wagner, 37, 1962
    Bobby Bonds, 37, 1977
RBIs: Bobby Bonds, 115, 1977
STEALS: Mickey Rivers, 70, 1975
WINS: Clyde Wright, 22, 1970
    Nolan Ryan, 22, 1974
STRIKEOUTS: Nolan Ryan, 383, 1973

MINNESOTA TWINS

TEAM DIRECTORY: Chairman of the Board and Pres.: Calvin R. Griffith; VP/Asst. Treas.: Mrs. Thelma Griffith Haynes; VP-Sec. Treas.: Clark Griffith; VP: Bruce Haynes; VP: William Robertson; VP: James Robertson; VP: George Brophy; Dir. Pub. Rel.: Tom Mee; VP and Trav. Sec.: Howard T. Fox Jr.; Mgr.: Gene Mauch. Home: Metropolitan Stadium, Bloomington, Minn. (45,919). Field distances: 343, l.f. line; 402, c.f.; 330, r.f. line. Spring training: Orlando, Fla.

SCOUTING REPORT

HITTING: Whither Rod Carew? Is he in or is he out of the Twins' lineup? Everyone waits for the Minnesota hitting machine to make up his mind, while Twins' manager Gene Mauch contemplates a season without Carew.

"It won't be the first time I've managed with tears in my eyes," he says.

For Rod Carew, .333 was an off year.

Unable to sign Carew, the Twins decided to trade him. But any deal needed Rod's approval and he remained in limbo. And so did Mauch, who had to make out two lineups, one with Carew, one without the seven-time batting champion. He began preparing for life without Carew by shipping Dan Ford to the Angels for Ron Jackson and Danny Goodwin.

"We've lost so many players over the past few years (Bostock, Hisle, Campbell)," says Mauch, "we've got to get numbers back."

Jackson (.297 with the Angels) and Goodwin (.360 at El Paso) can hit. They are weak defensively, but Mauch is excellent at deploying his players. He platooned a .270 out of Bob Randall and a .266 out of Rob Wilfong at second base; got .282 from Mike Cubbage by using him judiciously at third; and came up with enough offense by shuffling outfielders Rich Chiles, Glenn Adams, Willie Norwood and Hosken Powell. The one constant, without Carew, is shortstop Roy Smalley (.273, 19 homers, 77 RBIs). Mauch will build his team around Smalley and catcher Butch Wynegar, who's a better hitter than his .229.

PITCHING: Mets' general manager Joe McDonald knew he made a bad deal when he sent veteran Jerry Koosman to the Twins for two young pitchers. But Koosman, 3-15, had the Mets over the barrel. He might have quit unless he was traded to Minnesota, his home.

"I know he can still pitch, despite his record," said McDonald. Baltimore scout Jim Russo called Kooz, "the best three-game winner in baseball."

Jerry will move into the starting rotation with Dave Goltz, who fell off from a 20-game winner in '77 to 15 in '78, Roger Erickson (14-13) and Geoff Zahn (14-14) to give the Twins a good starting staff. And Mike Marshall will be back in relief.

FIELDING: The Twins were somewhere in the middle of the pack, not good, not bad. The infield is solid with Smalley at short, Randall or Wilfong at second, Cubbage at third and with or without Carew at first. Wynegar continues to improve at catcher. The crying need is for a steady center fielder, who may come if Carew goes.

OUTLOOK: On paper, the Twins cannot compete with the Royals and Angels and even the Rangers. But don't underestimate Gene Mauch's miracle-working powers. He manages to compete while losing star players who, if they had remained, could have brought the Twins a championship.

MINNESOTA TWINS 1979 ROSTER

MANAGER Gene Mauch
Coaches—Karl Kuehl, Tony Oliva, Camilo Pascual, Jerry Zimmerman

PITCHERS

No.	Name	1978 Club	W-L	IP	SO	ERA	B-T	Ht.	Wt.	Born
19	Erickson, Roger	Minnesota	14-13	266	121	3.96	R-R	6-3	180	8/30/56 Springfield, IL
48	Felton, Terry	Toledo	9-9	162	80	3.49	R-R	6-1	180	10/29/57 Baker, LA
30	Goltz, Dave	Minnesota	15-10	220	116	2.50	R-R	6-4	210	6/23/49 Pelican Rapids, MN
36	Holly, Jeff	Orlando	6-0	—	41	0.77	L-L	6-5	215	3/1/53 Torrance, CA
		Minnesota	1-1	35	12	3.60				
31	Jackson, Darrell	Orlando	4-3	75	68	1.80	L-L	5-10	150	4/3/56 Los Angeles, CA
		Minnesota	4-6	92	54	4.50				
21	Johnson, Tom	Minnesota	1-4	33	21	5.45	R-R	6-1	185	4/2/51 St. Paul, MN
28	Marshall, Mike	Minnesota	10-12	99	56	2.54	R-R	5-10	180	1/15/43 Adrian, MI
—	Koosman, Jerry	New York (NL)	3-15	235	160	3.75	R-L	6-2	208	12/23/43 Appleton, MN
39	Perzanowski, Stan	Toledo	5-2	84	50	2.46	R-R	6-3	190	8/25/50 Syracuse, IN
		Minnesota	2-7	57	31	5.21				
17	Redfern, Pete	Minnesota	0-2	10	4	6.30	R-R	6-2	190	8/25/54 Glendale, CA
		Toledo	9-8	128	81	3.74				
20	Serum, Gary	Minnesota	9-9	184	80	4.11	R-R	6-1	175	10/24/56 Alexandria, MN
51	Sheehan, Terry	Orlando	16-8	—	134	3.10	L-R	6-3	195	3/2/54 Boise, ID
40	Sutton, Johnny	Toledo	4-6	46	22	3.91	R-R	5-11	185	11/13/52 Dallas, TX
		Minnesota	0-0	44	18	3.48				
23	Thormodsgard, Paul	Minnesota	1-6	66	23	5.05	R-R	6-2	190	11/10/53 San Francisco, CA
		Toledo	4-0	36	26	1.98				
38	Zahn, Geoff	Minnesota	14-14	252	106	3.04	L-L	6-1	175	12/19/46 Baltimore, MD

CATCHERS

No.	Name	1978 Club	H	HR	RBI	Pct.	B-T	Ht.	Wt.	Born
14	Borgmann, Glenn	Minnesota	26	3	15	.211	R-R	6-2	210	5/25/50 Paterson, NJ
—	Goodwin, Dan	El Paso	130	25	89	.360	L-R	6-1	195	9/2/53 Peoria, IL
		California	16	2	10	.276				
34	Morales, Jose	Minnesota	76	2	38	.314	R-R	6-0	195	12/30/44 Virgin Islands
16	Wynegar, Butch	Minnesota	104	4	45	.229	B-R	6-0	195	3/14/56 York, PA

INFIELDERS

No.	Name	1978 Club	H	HR	RBI	Pct.	B-T	Ht.	Wt.	Born
29	Carew, Rod	Minnesota	188	5	70	.333	L-R	6-0	182	10/1/45 Panama
2	Castino, John	Orlando	128	10	58	.268	R-R	5-11	175	10/23/54 Kenilworth, IL
26	Cubbage, Mike	Minnesota	111	7	57	.282	L-R	6-0	180	7/21/50 Charlottesville, VA
37	Graham, Dan	Toledo	125	22	81	.275	L-R	6-1	212	7/19/54 Phoenix, AZ
22	Kusick, Craig	Minnesota	33	4	20	.173	R-R	6-3	225	9/30/48 Milwaukee, WI
—	Jackson, Ron	California	115	6	57	.297	R-R	6-0	205	5/9/53 Birmingham, AL
11	Perlozzo, Sam	Toledo	116	4	34	.244	R-R	5-9	174	3/4/51 Cumberland, MD
32	Randall, Bobby	Minnesota	89	0	21	.270	R-R	6-3	180	6/10/48 Norton, KS
5	Smalley, Roy	Minnesota	160	19	77	.273	B-R	6-1	185	10/25/52 Los Angeles, CA
18	Soderholm, Dale	Toledo	71	10	37	.208	R-R	6-2	188	7/13/52 Miami, FL
7	Wilfong, Rob	Minnesota	53	1	11	.266	L-R	6-1	177	9/1/53 Pasadena, CA
1	Wolfe, Larry	Minnesota	55	3	25	.234	R-R	5-11	180	3/2/53 Rancho Cordova, CA

OUTFIELDERS

No.	Name	1978 Club	H	HR	RBI	Pct.	B-T	Ht.	Wt.	Born
8	Adams, Glenn	Minnesota	80	7	35	.258	L-R	6-0	185	10/4/47 Northbridge, MA
12	Chiles, Rich	Minnesota	53	1	22	.268	L-L	6-0	175	11/22/49 Sacramento, CA
34	Douglas, Steve	Visalia	192	19	106	.343	R-R	5-11	175	1/17/57 Alexandria, VA
33	Edwards, Dave	Toledo	120	16	70	.262	R-R	6-0	172	2/24/54 Los Angeles, CA
		Minnesota	11	1	3	.250				
24	Norwood, Willie	Minnesota	109	8	46	.255	R-R	6-0	185	11/7/50 Long Beach, CA
10	Powell, Hosken	Minnesota	94	3	31	.247	L-L	6-1	180	5/14/55 Pensacola, FL
9	Rivera, Bombo	Minnesota	68	3	23	.271	R-R	5-10	186	8/2/52 Puerto Rico
46	Sofield, Rick	Toledo	10	0	4	.164	L-R	6-1	193	12/16/56 Morris Plains, NJ
		Orlando	47	5	23	.275				
50	Ward, Gary	Toledo	150	14	79	.294	R-R	6-2	195	12/6/53 Compton, CA

TWIN PROFILES

ROD CAREW 33 6-0 182   Bats L Throws R

The best hitter in baseball, bar none . . . Won seventh batting title in 1978 although his average "slipped" to .333 . . . Eligible to become free agent at end of season, and probably will . . . Prides himself on defense, too, since moved from second base to first . . . Born Oct. 1, 1945, on a train in Gatun, Panama . . . Named after doctor who delivered him . . . Raised in New York City . . . Soft-spoken and articulate . . . A cinch to enter Hall of Fame when he finally stops winning batting championships and retires.

Year	Club	Pos	G	AB	R	H	2B	3B	HR	RBI	SB	Avg.
1967	Minnesota	2B	137	514	66	150	22	7	8	51	5	.292
1968	Minnesota	2B-SS	127	461	46	126	27	2	1	42	12	.273
1969	Minnesota	2B	123	458	79	152	30	4	8	56	19	.332
1970	Minnesota	2B-1B	51	191	27	70	12	3	4	28	4	.366
1971	Minnesota	2B-3B	147	577	88	177	16	10	2	48	6	.307
1972	Minnesota	2B	142	535	61	170	21	6	0	51	12	.318
1973	Minnesota	2B	149	580	98	203	30	11	6	62	41	.350
1974	Minnesota	2B	153	599	86	218	30	5	3	55	38	.364
1975	Minnesota	2B-1B	143	535	89	192	24	4	14	80	35	.359
1976	Minnesota	1B-2B	156	605	97	200	29	12	9	90	49	.331
1977	Minnesota	1B-2B	155	616	128	239	38	16	14	100	23	.388
1978	Minnesota	1B	152	564	85	188	26	10	5	70	27	.333
	Totals		1635	6235	950	2085	305	90	74	733	271	.334

BUTCH WYNEGAR 23 6-0 195   Bats S Throws R

Three full years in the big leagues behind him, and still only 23 . . . Because of his age, his position, and the fact that he's a switch-hitter, he's one of the most valuable properties in baseball . . . There's virtually no limit to what he might accomplish . . . Slumped at plate in '78 but Twins are counting on him to come back strong . . . Born March 14, 1956, in York, Pa. . . . "He's a beautiful kid," says Gene Mauch . . . "Baseball is my entire life. I do nothing but sleep, eat, watch TV and go to the park." . . . Has strong, accurate arm that is respected by enemy runners . . . Started switch-hitting at age nine because his favorite player, Mickey Mantle, "hit that way" . . . The Twins are certainly glad he did.

Year	Club	Pos	G	AB	R	H	2B	3B	HR	RBI	SB	Avg.
1976	Minnesota	C	149	534	58	139	21	2	10	69	0	.260
1977	Minnesota	C-3B	144	532	76	139	22	3	10	79	2	.261
1978	Minnesota	C-3B	135	454	36	104	22	1	4	45	1	.229
	Totals		428	1520	170	382	65	6	24	193	3	.251

DAVE GOLTZ 29 6-4 210   Bats R Throws R

Plagued by one injury after another all year . . . Cracked ribs in April, burned right index finger in barbeque accident in June, stumbled on mound and suffered lower back injury later in season . . . Still managed to win 15 games . . . The veteran leader of the Twins' pitching staff . . . Born June 23, 1949, in Pelican Rapids, Minn. . . . Was spotted by Twins' scout throwing a baseball in his back yard, and signed . . . Could be one of big winners in league if he ever stays healthy and consistent all season . . . Famous for his fast finishes in August and September.

Year	Club	G	IP	W	L	Pct.	SO	BB	H	ERA
1972	Minnesota	15	91	3	3	.500	38	26	75	2.67
1973	Minnesota	32	106	6	4	.600	65	32	138	5.26
1974	Minnesota	28	174	10	10	.500	89	45	192	3.26
1975	Minnesota	32	243	14	14	.500	128	72	235	3.67
1976	Minnesota	36	249	14	14	.500	133	91	239	3.36
1977	Minnesota	39	303	20	11	.645	186	91	284	3.36
1978	Minnesota	29	220	15	10	.600	116	67	209	2.50
	Totals	211	1386	82	66	.554	755	424	1372	3.36

ROY SMALLEY 26 6-1 185   Bats S Throws R

Voted the Most Valuable Twin in 1978 . . . Hit career high 19 HRs . . . Has received more verbal abuse than perhaps any player in Twins' history because of the fact that manager Gene Mauch is his uncle . . . Yet never complained . . . "He's a man and he acts like one," says Mauch . . . The most improved player on the team last year . . . Born Oct. 25, 1952, in Los Angeles . . . Only major league shortstop to regularly bat clean-up in '78 . . . Lifted weights during offseason to build up strength and stamina . . . Developed overnight into a good hitter . . . Father, Roy Sr., played short for Cubs, Braves and Phillies . . . No. 1 draft pick in nation in January, 1973, after standout career at USC.

Year	Club	Pos	G	AB	R	H	2B	3B	HR	RBI	SB	Avg.
1975	Texas	SS-2B-C	78	250	22	57	8	0	3	33	4	.228
1976	Texas-Minnesota	SS-2B	144	513	61	133	18	3	3	44	2	.259
1977	Minnesota	SS	150	584	93	135	21	5	6	56	5	.231
1978	Minnesota	SS	158	586	80	160	31	3	19	77	2	.273
	Totals		530	1933	256	485	78	11	31	210	13	.251

MIKE CUBBAGE 28 6-0 180   Bats L Throws R

Bespectacled infielder, resembles John Denver . . . Became only fifth Twin ever to hit for cycle in 1978 . . . Came to Twins from Texas, along with Smalley in Bert Blyleven trade . . . Found himself a position at third base . . . Noted more for his bat than his glove . . . Born July 21, 1950, in Charlottesville, Va. . . . Star quarterback at University of Virginia . . . "There were times I feared for my life because I didn't have big strong linemen in front of me. They were the ones chasing me. You had to have a quick release to survive." . . . Uses quick release in baseball to compensate for rather weak arm.

Year	Club	Pos	G	AB	R	H	2B	3B	HR	RBI	SB	Avg.
1974	Texas	2B-3B	9	15	0	0	0	0	0	0	0	.000
1975	Texas	2B-3B	58	143	12	32	6	0	4	21	0	.224
1976	Tex.-Min.	3B-2B	118	374	42	96	19	5	3	49	1	.257
1977	Minnesota	3B	129	417	60	110	16	5	9	55	1	.264
1978	Minnesota	3B	125	394	40	111	12	7	7	57	3	.282
	Totals		439	1343	154	349	53	17	23	182	5	.260

HOSKEN POWELL 23 6-1 180   Bats L Throws L

Appears destined for stardom . . . "He's going to be more than just an average major league ballplayer," says Gene Mauch. "There's no reason why he can't be an exceptional player." . . . Made place for himself in lineup with strong performance as a rookie in 1978 . . . Born May 14, 1955, in Salem, Ala. . . . Never batted less than .326 during three seasons in minors . . . Twins' No. 1 pick in secondary phase of June, 1975, free agent draft . . . Was branded a blue chipper from day he signed with Twins.

Year	Club	Pos	G	AB	R	H	2B	3B	HR	RBI	SB	Avg.
1978	Minnesota	OF	121	381	55	94	20	2	3	31	11	.247

ROGER ERICKSON 22 6-3 180   Bats R Throws R

Made team as a non-roster rookie last spring . . . Together with Wynegar, formed youngest battery in major leagues . . . Billed as "The new Bird," in reference to Tigers' Mark Fidrych, because of his zany antics . . . Talks to his arm instead of to ball . . . Worked as groundskeeper during summers while in college . . . Born Aug. 30, 1956, in Springfield,

Ill. . . . "I've never seen a kid that young with so little experience come into camp and throw like he did," says Gene Mauch . . . Nicknamed "Pudge" . . . "When I was three years old, I had a teddy bear that had a pug nose and my brother started calling me Pudge." . . . Best first year pitcher in Twins' history.

Year	Club	G	IP	W	L	Pct.	SO	BB	H	ERA
1978	Minnesota	37	266	14	13	.519	121	79	268	3.96

GEOFF ZAHN 32 6-1 175   Bats L Throws L

Victim of more than his fair share of tough luck in 1978 . . . Pitched better than record indicates . . . Released by Cubs in 1976 because of sore arm, won job with Twins as free agent in spring of '77 . . . Born Dec. 19, 1946, in Baltimore . . . Holds degree in education from University of Michigan . . . Originally drafted by Dodgers in 1968 . . . Deeply religious . . . Full name is Geoffrey Clayton . . . Enjoyed best year in big leagues with Twins in 1977.

Year	Club	G	IP	W	L	Pct.	SO	BB	H	ERA
1973	Los Angeles	6	13	1	0	1.000	9	2	5	1.38
1974	Los Angeles	21	80	3	5	.375	33	16	78	2.03
1975	L.A.-Chi. (NL)	18	66	2	8	.200	22	31	69	4.64
1976	Chicago (NL)	3	8	0	1	.000	4	2	16	11.25
1977	Minnesota	34	198	12	14	.462	88	66	234	4.68
1978	Minnesota	35	252	14	14	.500	106	81	260	3.04
	Totals	117	617	32	42	.432	262	198	662	3.68

JERRY KOOSMAN 35 6-2 208   Bats R Throws L

After winning 21 in 1976, has an 11-35 record past two seasons, including unbelievable 3-15 in 1978 . . . Mets didn't give him many runs to work with, but club was consistent in that regard with all its pitchers . . . Still second to Tom Seaver in virtually all club pitching records . . . Born Dec. 23, 1943, in Appleton, Minn. . . . Took two months to match career high of 13 strikeouts in 1977 when he started July 13 game against Cubs, but game was suspended by New York City power outage, then resumed Sept. 16 and Kooz fanned two in final two innings . . . Mets heard about him through letters from Shea Stadium father-son usher team recounting his exploits with Fort Bliss service team . . . Has won 104 games since fearing his career was over twice in 1969, first after scalding his pitching hand in New Year holiday kitchen accident, then when arm went dead pitching April 29 to Montreal's John Bateman . . . Was second in Cy Young balloting to Randy Jones in 1976 . . . Now home with the Twins.

Year	Club	G	IP	W	L	Pct.	SO	BB	H	ERA
1967	New York (NL)	9	22	0	2	.000	11	19	22	6.14
1968	New York (NL)	35	264	19	12	.613	178	69	221	2.08
1969	New York (NL)	32	241	17	9	.654	180	68	187	2.28
1970	New York (NL)	30	212	12	7	.632	118	71	189	3.14
1971	New York (NL)	26	166	6	11	.353	96	51	160	3.04
1972	New York (NL)	34	163	11	12	.478	147	52	155	4.14
1973	New York (NL)	35	263	14	15	.483	156	76	234	2.84
1974	New York (NL)	35	265	15	11	.577	188	85	258	3.36
1975	New York (NL)	36	240	14	13	.519	173	98	234	3.41
1976	New York (NL)	34	247	21	10	.677	200	66	205	2.70
1977	New York (NL)	32	227	8	20	.286	192	81	195	3.49
1978	New York (NL)	38	235	3	15	.167	160	84	221	3.75
	Totals	376	2540	140	137	.505	1799	820	2281	3.10

TOP PROSPECTS

DARRELL JACKSON 22 5-10 150   **Bats S Throws L**
Skinny, hard-throwing left-hander, made major league debut in 1978 after less than one full season in minors . . . Erratic, but has plenty of promise . . . Called a hot dog and showboat by some because of unbridled enthusiasm . . . "I just try to be myself" . . . Born April 3, 1956, in Los Angeles . . . Drafted by Twins out of high school, but chose to attend Arizona State instead . . . Threw no-hitter in first pro start at Orlando.

JOHNNY SUTTON 26 5-11 185   **Bats R Throws R**
Knocking on door again . . . Appeared in 17 games for Twins in '78 . . . Born Nov. 13, 1952, in Dallas . . . Plucked out of Cardinals farm system in 1977 draft . . . Originally in Rangers farm system . . . A starter his first season in pro ball, has been used strictly as a reliever since then.

DANNY GOODWIN 25 6-1 195   **Bats L Throws R**
Promising young left-handed slugger . . . May be Twins' DH or first baseman in near future . . . Was leading Texas League in hitting when called up in 1978 . . . "I didn't feel any pressure." . . . Born Sept. 2, 1953, in Peoria, Ill. . . . Was twice the No. 1 draft pick in the nation . . . Drafted out of high school by White Sox, but went to USC instead . . . A catcher by trade . . . Determined to become a doctor . . . Accepted $125,000 bonus to sign with Angels in 1975.

MANAGER GENE MAUCH: A perfectionist who has never realized his dream of winning a pennant and World Series . . . Frustrated by loss of free agents Bill Campbell, Larry Hisle and Lyman Bostock, he wanted to flee to California . . . Instead signed in 1978 to manage Twins for three more years . . . Born Nov. 18, 1925, in Salina, Kan. . . . Long considered one of the smartest, most innovative managers in game . . Has surprising sense of humor for one who is so intense . . "I don't want a contending team. I want to win." . . . Spent eight rather undistinguished seasons in big leagues as a player . . . Beginning 20th consecutive season as a major league manager.

GREATEST PITCHER

Bert Blyleven . . . Camilo Pasqual . . . Jim Perry—yes, the Minnesota Twins have had more than a few outstanding pitchers on their side. But none was ever nearly as successful as Jim Kaat.

During the dozen years he wore a Twins uniform, the lanky left-hander won more games (189), pitched more innings (2,958), and struck out more opponents (1,824) than any pitcher in Twins history.

More than that, though, he ranks in baseball's all-time top 25 in games, wins, starts, strikeouts and innings pitched.

He broke in with the Twins in 1959 when they were still known as Senators and called Washington, D.C. home. He accompanied them to Minnesota in 1961 and he helped pitch them into the World Series in 1965 and to the Western half of the American League pennant in 1970.

Of course, if one takes the Twins back to their days as the Washington Senators, then Walter "Big Train" Johnson, who is second on the all-time victory list with 414, first in career shutouts with 113, and first in career strikeouts with 3,508, gets the nod.

ALL-TIME TWIN LEADERS

BATTING: Rod Carew, .388, 1977
HRs: Harmon Killebrew, 49, 1964, 1969
RBIs: Harmon Killebrew, 140, 1969
STEALS: Rod Carew, 49, 1976
WINS: Jim Kaat, 25, 1966
STRIKEOUTS: Bert Blyleven, 258, 1973

SEATTLE MARINERS

TEAM DIRECTORY: General Partners: Stanley Golub, Danny Kaye, Walter Schoenfeld, Lester Smith, James Stillwell, James Walsh; Exec. Dir.: Kip Horsburgh; GM: Lou Gorman; Dir. Bus.: Jeff Odenwald; Dir. Marketing: Jack Carvalho; Dir. Pub. Rel.: Randy Adamack; Mgr.: Darrell Johnson. Home: Kingdome (59,059). Field distances: 316, l.f. line; 405, c.f.; 316, r.f. line. Spring training: Tempe, Ariz.

SCOUTING REPORT

HITTING: Only Oakland batted lower, only Minnesota hit fewer homers, still the Mariners saw fit to deal shortstop Craig Reynolds, their second leading hitter. That's because there are

Ruppert Jones remains Seattle favorite despite poor year.

so many holes, the Mariners decided they can fill them one at a time. Pitching and defense come first.

The Mariners think they have a nucleus of hitters not to miss Reynolds, counting on catcher Bob Stinson, outfielders Ruppert Jones, Leon Roberts and Bruce Bochte and first baseman Danny Meyer to handle the attack. Among them, those five struck 60 homers with Meyer and Jones down from 22 and 24 respectively, to eight apiece. In Jones' case, injury caused him to miss 33 games.

PITCHING: "We feel we must improve our pitching, even at the expense of some offense," said Lou Gorman, the Mariners' director of operations. "We think we have done that."

Gorman had just announced the second of two trades during baseball's winter meetings. In one, he got pitchers Odell Jones and Rafael Vasquez from the Pirates. In another, he got Floyd Bannister from the Astros, the nation's No. 1 draft choice a few years ago. The Mariners continue to hope for the arrival of youngsters like Mike Parrott, Paul Mitchell, Byron MacLaughlin, Dick Pole, Glenn Abbott and Gary Wheelock.

In dealing with the Pirates, the Mariners got rid of veteran reliever Enrique Romo, who was not only their leading winner (11), he was their ace out of the bullpen with 10 of the team's 20 saves. Romo will be missed, but the Mariners think they have his successor in left-hander Shane Rawley.

FIELDING: The trade with the Pirates brought shortstop Mario Mendoza. "He won't hit much," says Lou Gorman, "but he's an excellent defensive player."

Gorman figures Mendoza will give the Mariners better shortstop play than Reynolds and the hitting will take care of itself. Mendoza will team with second baseman Julio Cruz, whose .987 fielding percentage led all AL second basemen. Bill Stein is adequate at third and Stinson, converted to catcher by Dodger manager Tom LaSorda, has developed into a fine receiver with regular work. An outfield of Jones, Bochte and Roberts is a good one and accounted for 27 assists.

OUTLOOK: The Mariners, who finished ahead of Oakland in their first season, took a backward step last year when several players had a reduction in their offensive production, notably Lee Stanton, Ruppert Jones and Danny Meyer. They are young enough to bounce back and under the patient guidance of Darrell Johnson, the Mariners could surprise a few teams this year and move up a couple of notches in the standings.

SEATTLE MARINERS 1979 ROSTER

MANAGER Darrell Johnson
Coaches—Don Bryant, Vada Pinson, Wes Stock

PITCHERS

No.	Name	1978 Club	W-L	IP	SO	ERA	B-T	Ht.	Wt.	Born
17	Abbott, Glenn	Seattle	7-15	155	67	5.28	R-R	6-6	200	2/16/51 Little Rock, AR
—	Bannister, Floyd	Houston	3-9	110	94	4.83	L-L	6-1	188	6/10/55 Pierre, SD
42	Brown, Tom	San Jose	7-8	90	65	3.70	R-R	6-1	170	8/10/49 Lafayette, LA
		Seattle	0-0	13	8	4.15				
39	Burke, Steve	Seattle	0-1	49	16	3.49	R-R	6-2	200	3/5/55 Stockton, CA
		San Jose	1-1	67	22	6.18				
40	Honeycutt, Rick	Seattle	5-11	134	50	4.90	L-L	6-1	190	6/29/54 Chattanooga, TN
29	House, Tom	Seattle	5-4	116	29	4.73	L-L	5-10	175	4/29/47 Seattle, WA
—	Jones, Odell	Columbus	12-9	181	69	4.57	R-R	6-3	180	1/13/53 Tulare, CA
		Pittsburgh	2-0	9	10	2.00				
—	Lindblad, Paul	Tex-NY (AL)	1-1	58	34	3.88	L-L	6-2	195	8/9/41 Chanute, KS
24	MacCormack, Frank	San Jose	4-12	134	76	6.31	R-R	6-4	210	9/21/54 Jersey City, NJ
30	McLaughlin, Byron	San Jose	5-2	54	52	3.50	R-R	6-1	175	9/29/55 Van Nuys, CA
		Seattle	4-8	107	87	4.37				
34	Mitchell, Paul	Seattle	8-14	168	75	4.23	R-R	6-1	195	8/19/50 Worcester, MA
25	Montague, John	Seattle	1-3	44	14	6.14	R-R	6-2	205	9/12/57 Newport News, VA
20	Parrott, Mike	Seattle	1-5	82	41	5.16	R-R	6-4	205	12/6/54 Oxnard, CA
13	Pole, Dick	Seattle	4-11	99	41	6.45	R-R	6-3	194	10/13/50 Trout Creek, MI
		San Jose	0-4	32	19	4.22				
41	Rawley, Shane	Seattle	4-9	111	66	4.14	L-L	6-0	155	7/27/55 Racine, WI
27	Todd, Jim	Seattle	3-4	107	37	3.87	L-R	6-2	195	9/21/47 Lancaster, PA
—	Vasquez, Rafael	Shreveport	14-9	184	—	3.22	R-R	6-0	162	— Dominican Republic
16	Wheelock, Gary	San Jose	1-12	116	32	6.98	R-R	6-3	210	11/29/51 Bakersfield, CA

CATCHERS

No.	Name	1978 Club	H	HR	RBI	Pct.	B-T	Ht.	Wt.	Born
18	Pasley, Kevin	San Jose	94	3	43	.261	R-R	6-0	185	7/22/53 Bronx, NY
		Seattle	13	1	5	.241				
15	Stinson, Bob	Seattle	94	11	55	.258	B-R	5-11	185	10/11/45 Elkin, NC

INFIELDERS

No.	Name	1978 Club	H	HR	RBI	Pct.	B-T	Ht.	Wt.	Born
11	Beamon, Charlie	San Jose	170	5	62	.328	L-L	6-0	170	12/4/53 Oakland, CA
		Seattle	2	0	0	.182				
26	Bernhardt, Juan	San Jose	26	2	16	.284	R-R	6-0	175	8/31/53 Dominican Republic
		Seattle	38	2	12	.230				
2	Cruz, Julio	Seattle	129	1	25	.235	B-R	5-9	160	12/2/54 Brooklyn, NY
—	Mendoza, Mario	Pittsburgh	12	1	3	.218	R-R	5-11	185	12/26/50 Mexico
7	Meyer, Dan	Seattle	101	8	56	.227	L-R	5-11	180	8/3/52 Hamilton, OH
10	Milbourne, Larry	Seattle	53	2	20	.226	B-R	6-0	155	2/14/51 Port Norris, NJ
6	Robertson, Bob	Seattle	40	8	28	.230	R-R	6-1	210	10/2/46 Frostburg, MD
1	Stein, Bill	Seattle	105	4	37	.261	R-R	5-10	170	1/21/47 Battle Creek, MI

OUTFIELDERS

No.	Name	1978 Club	H	HR	RBI	Pct.	B-T	Ht.	Wt.	Born
23	Bochte, Bruce	Seattle	128	11	51	.264	L-L	6-3	200	11/12/50 Pasadena, CA
5	DelGado, Luis	San Jose	136	2	49	.252	R-L	5-11	170	2/2/54 Puerto Rico
44	Hale, John	Seattle	36	4	22	.171	L-R	6-2	195	8/5/53 Fresno, CA
9	Jones, Ruppert	Seattle	101	8	46	.235	L-L	5-10	170	3/12/55 Dallas, TX
—	Potter, Mike	Springfield	111	22	90	.266	R-R	6-1	195	5/16/51 Montebello, CA
8	Roberts, Leon	Seattle	142	22	91	.301	R-R	6-3	200	4/10/46 Vicksburg, MI
36	Stanton, Lee	Seattle	55	3	24	.182	R-R	6-1	200	4/10/46 Latta, SC
—	Thompson, Bobby	Texas	27	2	12	.225	B-R	5-10	175	11/3/53 Meck City, NC

MARINER PROFILES

JULIO CRUZ 24 5-9 160   Bats S Throws R

Speedy second baseman, set club record by swiping three bases in game in 1978 . . . A flawless fielder . . . A natural right-handed batter, began switch-hitting to take advantage of his speed . . . Stole 15 bases in a row without being caught early in the season . . . Born Dec. 2, 1954, in Brooklyn . . . Now makes his home in California where he grew up . . . Was never drafted . . . Signed with Angels and later claimed by Mariners from expansion pool . . . Loves to devour cheesecake and work on cars . . . An excellent hitter throughout his minor league career.

Year	Club	Pos	G	AB	R	H	2B	3B	HR	RBI	SB	Avg.
1977	Seattle..........	2B	60	199	25	51	3	1	1	7	15	.256
1978	Seattle..........	2B	147	550	77	129	14	1	1	25	59	.235
	Totals...........		207	749	102	180	17	2	2	32	74	.240

DANNY MEYER 26 5-11 180   Bats L Throws R

Pleasant, personable young man . . . Found security with Mariners, signing five-year, $500,000 contract . . . Bought a home in Seattle and works for club during off-season . . . Once the heir apparent to Willie Horton's left field job in Detroit . . . Also flunked trial at first base with Tigers . . . Born Aug. 3, 1952, in Hamiliton, Ohio . . . His friends call him "Whitey" because of light blond hair . . . Slumped at plate in 1978 after strong showing the year before . . . Outstanding potential as a hitter, led all professional players with .396 average at Bristol in 1972.

Year	Club	Pos	G	AB	R	H	2B	3B	HR	RBI	SB	Avg.
1974	Detroit..........	OF	13	50	5	10	1	1	3	7	1	.200
1975	Detroit..........	OF-1B	122	470	56	111	17	3	8	47	8	.236
1976	Detroit..........	OF-1B	105	294	37	74	8	4	2	16	10	.252
1977	Seattle..........	1B	159	582	75	159	24	4	22	90	11	.273
1978	Seattle..........	1B	123	444	38	101	18	1	8	56	7	.227
	Totals...........		522	1840	211	455	68	13	43	216	37	.247

RUPPERT JONES 24 5-10 170   Bats L Throws L

Idol of the Mariner fans . . . One of best defensive outfielders in the league . . . No. 1 pick in the expansion draft, and obviously well worth it . . . Part-time sportscaster, tapes interviews for Seattle radio station . . . Born March 12, 1955, in Dallas . . . Signed a five-year $500,000 contract after rookie season . . . Plucked off the roster of Royals . . . "With Kansas City I probably would have been sent back to the minors" . . . Instead became a star . . . Center field fans at Kingdome are known as "Rupe's Troops".

Year	Club	Pos	G	AB	R	H	2B	3B	HR	RBI	SB	Avg.
1976	Kansas City	OF	28	51	9	11	1	1	1	7	0	.216
1977	Seattle	OF	160	597	85	157	26	8	24	76	13	.263
1978	Seattle	OF	129	472	48	111	24	3	6	46	22	.235
	Totals		317	1120	142	279	51	12	31	129	35	.249

BRUCE BOCHTE 28 6-3 200   Bats L Throws L

Signed with Mariners as a free agent for $504,000, spread over four years . . . Former Angel star, was traded to Indians before claiming his freedom . . . Holds a degree in finance from Santa Clara where he also excelled in basketball and baseball . . . Born Nov. 11, 1950, in Pasadena, Cal. . . . Angel's No. 2 pick in June, 1972, amateur draft . . . Considering his unusually high batting average, he should drive in more runs than he does.

Year	Club	Pos	G	AB	R	H	2B	3B	HR	RBI	SB	Avg.
1974	California	OF-1B	57	196	24	53	4	1	5	26	6	.270
1975	California	1B	107	375	41	107	19	3	3	48	3	.285
1976	California	OF-1B	146	466	53	120	17	1	2	49	4	.258
1977	Cal.-Cle.	OF-1B	137	492	64	148	23	1	7	51	6	.301
1978	Seattle	OF	140	486	58	128	25	3	11	51	3	.263
	Totals		587	2015	240	556	88	9	28	225	22	.276

LEON ROBERTS 28 6-3 200   Bats R Throws R

Never lived up to expectations with Tigers and got caught in shuffle at Houston, but emerged as star with Mariners . . . Does not appreciate his nickname "Goober" . . . Admits he's "an exercise fanatic" especially during the winter . . . "I want to be remembered as some one who gave 100 percent, used his ability and came to play." . . . Born Jan. 22,

1951, in Vicksburg, Mich. . . . Always regarded as a solid hitter, has improved defensively . . . Repeatedly asked Astros to trade him, and they finally did . . . A steal for Seattle . . . All-American football player in high school, went to University of Michigan on a football scholarship . . . But never set foot on the gridiron at Michigan . . . Played baseball instead and was All-Big Ten twice.

Year	Club	Pos	G	AB	R	H	2B	3B	HR	RBI	SB	Avg.
1974	Detroit	OF	17	63	5	17	3	2	0	7	0	.270
1975	Detroit	OF	129	447	51	115	17	5	10	38	3	.257
1976	Houston	OF	87	235	31	68	11	2	7	33	1	.289
1977	Houston	OF	19	27	1	2	0	0	0	2	0	.074
1978	Seattle	OF	134	472	78	142	21	7	22	92	6	.301
	Totals		386	1244	166	344	52	16	39	172	10	.277

BILL STEIN 32 5-10 170   Bats R Throws R

Steady player, contributes to Mariners in many ways . . . Played five different positions for White Sox, but settled down at third base in Seattle . . . Born Jan. 21, 1947, in Battle Creek, Mich. . . . Raised in Cocoa, Fla. . . . Star infielder in college at Brevard (Fla.) JC and Southern Illinois . . . Earned All-America honors at SIU . . . Originally signed with Cardinals . . . First major league hit was HR . . . Traded to Angels and later to Chisox . . . Had best year of career in 1977.

Year	Club	Pos	G	AB	R	H	2B	3B	HR	RBI	SB	Avg.
1972	St. Louis	3B-OF	14	35	2	11	0	1	2	3	1	.314
1973	St. Louis	1B-3B-OF	32	55	4	12	2	0	0	2	0	.218
1974	Chicago (AL)	3B	13	43	5	12	1	0	0	5	0	.279
1975	Chicago (AL)	2B-3B-OF	76	226	23	61	7	1	3	21	2	.270
1976	Chicago (AL)	INF-OF	117	392	32	105	15	2	4	36	4	.268
1977	Seattle	3B-SS	151	556	53	144	26	5	13	67	3	.259
1978	Seattle	3B	114	403	41	105	24	4	4	37	1	.261
	Totals		517	1710	160	450	75	13	26	171	11	.263

BOB STINSON 33 5-11 185   Bats S Throws R

Third string catcher with Royals, but No. 1 in Seattle . . . "God bless expansion" . . . Nicknamed "Scrap Iron" because of his durability . . . Born Oct. 11, 1945, in Elkin, N.C. . . . "I'm like good wine, I improve with age" . . . Hit first grand slam of career in 1978 . . . "I hit one in college once but I lost it because I forgot to step on first base" . . .

Began pro career in Dodger organization as an outfielder . . . converted to catcher by Tom Lasorda, his minor league manager, in 1967 . . . Later caught for Cardinals, Houston and Montreal.

Year	Club	Pos	G	AB	R	H	2B	3B	HR	RBI	SB	Avg.
1969	Los Angeles	C	4	8	1	3	0	0	0	2	0	.375
1970	Los Angeles	C-OF	4	3	1	0	0	0	0	0	0	.000
1971	St. Louis	C-OF	17	19	3	4	1	0	0	1	0	.211
1972	Houston	C-OF	27	35	3	6	1	0	0	2	0	.171
1973	Montreal	3B-C	48	111	12	29	6	1	3	12	0	.261
1974	Montreal	C	38	87	4	15	2	0	1	6	1	.172
1975	Kansas City	C-OF-2B-1B	63	147	18	39	9	1	1	9	1	.265
1976	Kansas City	C	79	209	26	55	7	1	2	25	3	.263
1977	Seattle	C	105	297	27	80	11	1	8	32	0	.269
1978	Seattle	C	124	364	46	94	14	3	11	55	2	.258
	Totals		509	1280	141	325	51	7	26	144	7	.254

SHANE RAWLEY 24 6-0 155   Bats L Throws L

Slender, hard-throwing left-handed reliever . . . One of few bright spots on Mariner pitching staff . . . Hindered by sore shoulder in 1978 . . . Club officials cringed when he took flying lessons during off-season . . . Born July 27, 1954, in Racine, Wis. . . . Spent four years in Expos' organization before joining Mariners . . . Primarily a starting pitcher until he joined Mariners . . . Could become one of the top relief experts in the league.

Year	Club	G	IP	W	L	Pct.	SO	BB	H	ERA
1978	Seattle	52	111	4	9	.308	66	51	114	4.14

TOP PROSPECTS

CHARLIE BEAMON 25 6-0 170   Bats L Throws L

This could be his year . . . Appeared in 10 games with Mariners in 1978 . . . Signed with Royals after attending junior college . . . Drafted out of Royals' farm system in 1976 . . . Born Dec. 4, 1953, in Oakland, Cal. . . . Father, Charlie Sr., pitched for Orioles in '50s . . . Was a baseball sensation in high school . . . Has good speed but must improve hitting.

STEVE BURKE 24 6-2 200   Bats R Throws R

Compiled impressive 3.49 ERA in 18-game trial with Mariners

in 1978 . . . Claimed in expansion draft from Red Sox . . .
Born March 5, 1955, in Stockton, Cal. . . . Spent three seasons
at Class A level in Red Sox organization . . . Could be used in
short or long relief.

MANAGER DARRELL JOHNSON Entrusted with difficult task

of building Mariners into bona fide pennant
contenders . . . Ideally suited for the task
. . . Patient and hard-working . . . Another
former backup catcher who has made good as
a manager . . . Guided Red Sox to AL pennant in 1975, only to lose to Reds in seven-
game Series . . . Born Aug. 25, 1927, in Fort
Ord, Neb. . . . Played for seven teams in six
years in big leagues, but appeared in only 134 games . . . Was
once involved in 17-player trade between Orioles and Yankees
. . . Also coached Cardinals, Orioles, Yankees and Red Sox, in
addition to learning trade as minor league manager.

Dan Meyer hopes to rebound to 1977 form for Mariners.

GREATEST PITCHER

Granted, to call anyone the greatest pitcher in Mariner history is a dubious distinction at best. It is like bragging about owning the fastest Edsel on your street.

However, the Mariners shudder to think about what their first two years in the American League would have been like if they hadn't had Enrique Romo.

Ironically, if it hadn't been for the birth of the Mariners, Romo would most probably still be laboring in Mexico, unknown outside of his native land.

For 11 years, Romo pitched in obscurity south of the border. Then the Mariners, who were desperately in need of pitching help, invited the mustachioed right-hander to spring training in 1977.

Nineteen victories and 26 saves later, he is regarded as one of the outstanding relief pitchers in baseball.

ALL-TIME MARINER LEADERS

BATTING: Leon Roberts, .301, 1978
HRs: Lee Stanton, 27, 1977
RBIs: Leon Roberts, 92, 1978
STEALS: Julio Cruz, 59, 1978
WINS: Glenn Abbott, 12, 1977
STRIKEOUTS: Enrique Romo, 105, 1977

CHICAGO WHITE SOX

TEAM DIRECTORY: President: Bill Veeck; VP: Roland Hemond; Business Mgr: Rudy Schaffer; Dir. of Player Development: Paul Richards; Pub. Rel.: Don Unferth; Trav. Sec.: Glen Rosenbaum; Mgr.: Don Kessinger. Home: Comiskey Park (44,-492). Field distances: 352, l.f. line; 375, l.c.; 445, c.f.; 375, r.c.; 352, r.f. line. Spring training: Sarasota, Fla.

SCOUTING REPORT

HITTING: Have all Bill Veeck's dreams gone up in smoke? Has his rent-a-player plan backfired? Has he lost his touch?

The White Sox even failed to make a deal during the winter meetings, but somehow you keep expecting the redoubtable

Don Kessinger is the majors' only player-manager.

Veeck to come up with something. He had better do it fast. The Sox are on a downward trend, going from 90 victories in 1977 to 71 last year.

Veeck's trump card was to name shortstop Don Kessinger as player-manager and to remind one and all that at one time he had a player-manager named Lou Boudreau, also a shortstop, who led the Cleveland Indians to the 1948 pennant. Unfortunately, Kessinger doesn't have Feller, Lemon and Doby on his side.

What he has is a bunch of people who have talent, but are coming off poor years. Only Chet Lemon (.300) and Wayne Nordhagen (.301) lived up to potential. There is room for improvement from Lamar Johnson (.273 and only eight homers), Alan Bannister (.224), Ron Blomberg (.231), Jorge Orta (.274), Eric Soderholm (.258, but 20 HRs), Ralph Garr (.275) and Claudell Washington (.264).

PITCHING: A major overhauling is needed here after defections by Steve Stone (12-12) and Wilbur Wood (10-10). With them, the Sox were third from the bottom of the AL in pitching. The only remaining double figure winner is Ken Kravec (11-16) and he will head a staff that includes Francisco Barrios (9-15), Ron Schueler (3-5) and a handful of prospects.

The bullpen, at least, is in capable hands with Lerrin LaGrow, six wins, 16 saves, as ace, and in reserve, lefties Rich Hinton and Pablo Torrealba, and righties Mike Proly and Jack Kucek.

FIELDING: The best thing about the White Sox, especially in center, where Chet Lemon roams the wide open spaces with the best of them. The infield is steady, if unspectacular, particularly if manager Kessinger can continue to play as well as he has, or if Harry Chappas, only 5-foot-3, can replace the boss. Johnson at first and Soderholm at third are acceptable and Orta is sure-handed at second. But the Sox', and Orta's, biggest weakness is in turning the double play. They made only 130 last year, less than any other American League club.

OUTLOOK: There isn't much hope for the poor, long-suffering folks of Chicago unless Veeck can come up with a couple of trades that can reverse the downward trend. Rent-a-player didn't work and the White Sox' lease is up. Pity Veeck, who tries and brings excitement to his fans. But there is no substitute for winning. Also pity Kessinger, a nice man who deserves better. But there is no substitute for talent.

CHICAGO WHITE SOX 1979 ROSTER

MANAGER Don Kessinger
Coaches—Joe Sparks, Bobby Winkles, Fred Martin

PITCHERS

No.	Name	1978 Club	W-L	IP	SO	ERA	B-T	Ht.	Wt.	Born
46	Barrios, Francisco	Chicago (AL)	9-15	196	79	4.04	R-R	6-3	195	6/10/53 Mexico
—	Baumgarten, Ross	Appleton	9-1	74	73	1.82	L-L	6-1	180	5/27/55 Highland Park, IL
		Knoxville	2-1	25	14	3.24				
		Iowa	5-4	66	54	3.29				
		Chicago (AL)	2-2	23	15	5.87				
—	Burns, Britt	Appleton	3-2	30	28	2.40	R-L	6-5	215	6/8/59 Houston, TX
		Knoxville	1-1	21	17	4.29				
		Chicago (AL)	0-2	8	3	12.38				
47	Hinton, Rich	Iowa	4-0	33	26	2.70	L-L	6-2	185	5/22/47 Tucson, AZ
		Chicago (AL)	2-6	81	48	4.00				
—	Howard, Fred	Knoxville	12-6	139	109	2.78	R-R	6-3	190	9/2/56 Portland, MN
—	Hoyt, Lamarr	Appleton	18-4	189	115	2.90	R-R	6-3	195	1/1/55 Columbia, SC
27	Kravec, Ken	Iowa	1-1	12	14	3.75	L-L	6-2	185	7/29/51 Cleveland, OH
		Chicago (AL)	11-16	203	154	4.08				
55	Kucek, Jack	Iowa	9-8	150	115	2.47	R-R	6-2	190	6/8/53 Warren, OH
		Chicago (AL)	2-3	52	30	3.29				
36	LaGrow, Lerrin	Chicago (AL)	6-5	88	42	4.40	R-R	6-5	230	7/8/48 Phoenix, AZ
24	Proly, Mike	Iowa	6-2	66	41	2.59	R-R	6-0	185	12/15/50 Jamaica, NY
		Chicago (AL)	5-2	66	19	2.73				
37	Schueler, Ron	Chicago (AL)	3-5	82	40	4.28	R-R	6-4	204	4/18/48 Hays, KS
35	Torrealba, Pablo	Chicago (AL)	2-4	57	23	4.73	L-L	5-10	178	4/28/48 Venezuela
—	Trout, Steve	Knoxville	8-3	71	48	1.65	L-L	5-4	195	7/30/57 Detroit, MI
		Iowa	3.4	56	38	5.38				
		Chicago (AL)	3-0	22	11	4.09				
—	Wortham, Rick	Iowa	5-8	138	73	3.99	R-L	6-0	185	10/22/53 Odessa, TX
		Chicago (AL)	3-2	59	25	3.05				

CATCHERS

No.	Name	1978 Club	H	HR	RBI	Pct.	B-T	Ht.	Wt.	Born
—	Colbern, Mike	Iowa	71	12	44	.283	R-R	6-3	205	4/19/55 Santa Monica, CA
		Chicago (AL)	38	2	20	.270				
—	Foley, Marvis	Knoxville	93	1	44	.275	L-R	6-0	185	8/29/53 Stanford, KY
		Chicago (AL)	12	0	6	.353				
15	Nahorodny, Bill	Chicago (AL)	82	8	35	.236	R-R	6-2	190	8/31/53 Hamtramck, MI

INFIELDERS

No.	Name	1978 Club	H	HR	RBI	Pct.	B-T	Ht.	Wt.	Born
7	Bannister, Alan	Chicago (AL)	24	0	8	.224	R-R	5-11	175	9/3/51 Buena Park, CA
8	Bell, Kevin	Iowa	65	12	40	.213	R-R	6-0	185	7/13/55 Los Angeles, CA
		Chicago (AL)	13	2	5	.191				
10	Blomberg, Ron	Chicago (AL)	36	5	22	.231	R-L	6-1	205	8/23/48 Atlanta, GA
1	Chappas, Harry	Appleton	149	1	62	.302	B-R	5-3	150	10/26/57 Mt. Rainier, MD
		Chicago (AL)	20	0	6	.267				
—	Gates, Joe	Knoxville	159	4	53	.333	L-R	5-7	175	10/3/54 Gary, IN
		Chicago (AL)	6	0	1	.250				
—	Hill, A.J.	Iowa	8	0	3	.119	R-R	6-1	165	11/12/58 Los Angeles, CA
		Knoxville	99	2	30	.251				
23	Johnson, Lamar	Chicago (AL)	136	8	72	.273	R-R	6-2	225	9/2/50 Bessemer, AL
11	Kessinger, Don	Chicago (AL)	110	1	31	.255	B-R	6-1	170	7/17/42 Forrest City, AR
4	Orta, Jorge	Chicago (AL)	115	13	53	.274	L-R	5-10	170	11/26/50 Mexico
—	Perez, Joel	Durango	178	15	93	.358	R-R	5-9	150	4/1/55 Sonora, TX
26	Pryor, Greg	Chicago (AL)	58	2	15	.261	R-R	6-0	175	10/2/49 Marietta, OH
12	Soderholm, Eric	Chicago (AL)	118	20	67	.258	R-R	5-11	190	9/24/48 Cortland, NY
—	Squires, Mike	Iowa	140	5	48	.312	L-L	5-11	185	3/5/52 Kalmazoo, MI
		Chicago (AL)	42	0	19	.280				
—	White, Dave	Appleton	9	1	5	.120	R-R	6-0	180	10/1/60 Habira, GA

OUTFIELDERS

No.	Name	1978 Club	H	HR	RBI	Pct.	B-T	Ht.	Wt.	Born
22	Bosley, Thad	Iowa	52	3	15	.291	L-L	6-3	175	9/17/56 Oceanside, CA
		Chicago (AL)	59	2	13	.269				
48	Garr, Ralph	Chicago (AL)	122	3	29	.275	L-R	5-11	197	12/12/45 Monroe, LA
44	Lemon, Chet	Chicago (AL)	107	13	55	.300	R-R	6-0	190	2/12/55 Jackson, MI
5	Molinaro, Bob	Chicago (AL)	75	6	27	.262	L-R	6-0	180	5/21/50 Newark, NJ
20	Nordhagen, Wayne	Chicago (AL)	62	5	35	.301	R-R	6-2	195	7/4/48 Thief River Falls, MN
—	Scott, John	Springfield	141	12	57	.279	R-R	6-2	165	1/24/52 Jackson, MI
21	Torres, Rusty	Tucson	37	7	39	.346	B-R	5-11	180	9/30/48 Puerto Rico
		Iowa	90	16	55	.280				
		Chicago (AL)	14	3	6	.318				
18	Washington, Claudell	Texas-Chi. (AL)	90	6	33	.253	L-L	6-0	190	8/31/54 Los Angeles, CA

WHITE SOX PROFILES

JORGE ORTA 28 5-10 170   Bats L Throws R

Splendid hitter . . . Showed marked improvement in field, thanks to coaching of new player-manager Don Kessinger . . . Has very quick bat . . . Signed with Sox because of GM Roland Hemond's friendship with Mexican League officials . . . Born Nov. 26, 1950, in Mazatlan, Mexico . . . Father was known as "Babe Ruth of Cuba" . . . Played basketball so well in high school he was recruited by UCLA . . . Broke in with Sox as raw rookie in 1972 but returned to minors to improve technique.

Year	Club	Pos	G	AB	R	H	2B	3B	HR	RBI	SB	Avg.
1972	Chicago (AL)	SS-2B-3B	51	124	20	25	3	1	3	11	1	.202
1973	Chicago (AL)	2B-SS	128	425	46	113	9	10	6	40	8	.266
1974	Chicago (AL)	2B-SS	139	525	73	166	31	2	10	67	9	.316
1975	Chicago (AL)	2B	140	542	64	165	26	10	11	83	16	.304
1976	Chicago (AL)	OF-2B	158	636	74	174	29	8	14	72	24	.274
1977	Chicago (AL)	2B	144	564	71	159	27	8	11	84	4	.282
1978	Chicago (AL)	OF-2B	117	420	45	115	19	2	13	53	1	.274
	Totals		877	3236	393	917	144	41	68	410	63	.283

ERIC SODERHOLM 30 5-11 190   Bats R Throws R

Has written a book about his remarkable comeback . . . Missed all of '76 because of two operations to repair damaged cartilage in left knee . . . Rehabilitated himself with weight program . . . Bill Veeck, who has himself battled a handicap, was inspired to give Eric a chance . . . Rewarded Sox owner's confidence with another impressive performance in '78 . . . Born Sept. 24, 1948, in Cortland, N.Y. . . . AL Comeback Player of the Year in '77 . . . Originally an infielder with Twins, played out his option and signed with Sox as free agent . . . Younger brother, Dale, is shortstop in Twins' farm system.

Year	Club	Pos	G	AB	R	H	2B	3B	HR	RBI	SB	Avg.
1971	Minnesota	3B	21	64	9	10	4	0	1	4	0	.156
1972	Minnesota	3B	93	287	28	54	10	0	13	39	3	.188
1973	Minnesota	3B-SS	35	111	22	33	7	2	1	9	1	.297
1974	Minnesota	3B-SS	141	464	63	128	18	3	10	51	7	.276
1975	Minnesota	3B	117	419	62	120	17	2	11	58	3	.286
1976					(Did Not Play)							
1977	Chicago (AL)	3B	130	460	77	129	20	3	25	67	7	.280
1978	Chicago (AL)	3B	143	457	57	118	16	1	20	67	2	.258
	Totals		680	2262	318	592	92	11	81	295	18	.262

CHET LEMON 24 6-0 190   Bats R Throws R

One of AL's fastest rising young stars . . . Plagued by nagging groin injury in 1978, finally placed on disabled list . . . "I was taped up like a mummy." . . . Consistent hitter and one of top defensive centerfielders in the league . . . Plays extremely shallow . . . Many clubs have asked White Sox if Lemon might be available in trade . . . Born Feb. 12, 1955, in Jackson, Miss. . . . Credits ex-manager Lary Doby with helping improve his hitting . . . Hit career high .300 last year . . . Broke two fielding records in '77, for most chances and putouts . . . Both had been set by Dom DiMaggio in 1948 . . . Was Oakland's No. 1 draft pick in June, 1972 . . . Traded to Sox for pitcher Stan Bahnsen in one of Charley Finley's worst deals ever.

Year	Club	Pos	G	AB	R	H	2B	3B	HR	RBI	SB	Avg.
1975	Chicago (AL)	3B-OF	9	35	2	9	2	0	0	1	1	.257
1976	Chicago (AL)	OF	132	451	46	111	15	5	4	38	13	.246
1977	Chicago (AL)	OF	150	553	99	151	38	4	19	67	8	.273
1978	Chicago (AL)	OF	105	357	51	107	24	6	13	55	5	.300
	Totals		396	1396	198	378	79	15	36	161	27	.271

LERRIN LaGROW 30 6-5 230   Bats R Throws R

Nicknamed "Lurch" . . . Blossomed into ace of Chisox bullpen after struggling as a starter with the Tigers . . . Finally fell from favor with Tiger management, which kept expecting greatness from him . . . Has saved 41 games for Sox in past two years . . . Born July 8, 1948, in Phoenix, Ariz. . . . Led Arizona State to NCAA title in 1969 . . . Gained national attention when he hit Campy Campaneris, on orders from then Tiger manager Billy Martin, in 1972 playoff . . . Campy retaliated by hurling his bat at LaGrow . . . Another Bill Veeck reclamation project . . . Was seriously thinking of quitting when traded to White Sox . . . "I wasn't getting anywhere" . . . Has had to learn to control temper, which used to get him into trouble on mound when things went bad.

Year	Club	G	IP	W	L	Pct.	SO	BB	H	ERA
1970	Detroit	10	12	0	1	.000	7	6	16	7.50
1972	Detroit	16	27	0	1	.000	9	6	22	1.33
1973	Detroit	21	54	1	5	.167	33	23	54	4.33
1974	Detroit	37	216	8	19	.296	85	80	245	4.67
1975	Detroit	32	164	7	14	.333	75	66	183	4.39
1976	St. Louis	8	24	0	1	.000	10	7	21	1.50
1977	Chicago (AL)	66	99	7	3	.700	63	35	81	2.45
1978	Chicago (AL)	52	88	6	5	.545	42	38	85	4.40
	Totals	242	684	29	49	.372	324	261	707	4.03

LAMAR JOHNSON 28 6-2 225   Bats R Throws R

Slowed by leg injuries in 1978 . . . "I'm an aggressive hitter" . . . Extremely strong . . . Bill Veeck calls him "the second best hitter in the league next to Rod Carew" . . . Earned job as Sox first baseman with impressive display of power in minor leagues . . . Born Sept. 2, 1950, in Bessemer, Ala. . . . Sang National Anthem prior to game in '77, then hit two homers to lead Sox to victory over A's . . . Also starred in football while in high school . . . Turned down several football scholarships to concentrate on baseball career.

Year	Club	Pos	G	AB	R	H	2B	3B	HR	RBI	SB	Avg.
1974	Chicago (AL)	1B	10	29	1	10	0	0	0	2	0	.345
1975	Chicago (AL)	1B	8	30	2	6	3	0	1	1	0	.200
1976	Chicago (AL)	1B-OF	82	222	29	71	11	1	4	33	2	.320
1977	Chicago (AL)	1B	118	374	52	113	12	5	18	65	1	.302
1978	Chicago (AL)	1B-OF	148	498	52	136	23	2	8	72	6	.273
	Totals		366	1153	136	336	49	8	31	173	9	.291

RALPH GARR 33 5-11 197   Bats L Throws R

Compact, muscular slugger . . . Built more like football running back than baseball star . . . Notorious bad ball hitter, yet still hits close to .300 every year . . . Supposedly not too dependable in clutch though . . . "I swing at anything. People say I'm a lousy looking hitter. That doesn't bother me. I'd rather have a pretty average." . . . A liability on defense, sometimes . . . Born Dec. 12, 1945, in Monroe, La. . . . The "Road Runner" . . . Says teammate Chet Lemon: "Ralph is more than a great player; he's a great human being." . . . Hero is Pete Rose . . . Graduated from Grambling College . . . Enjoyed phenomenal college and minor league career . . . Originally surfaced with Braves in 1968.

Year	Club	Pos	G	AB	R	H	2B	3B	HR	RBI	SB	Avg.
1968	Atlanta	PH	11	7	3	2	0	0	0	0	1	.286
1969	Atlanta	OF	22	27	6	6	1	0	0	2	1	.222
1970	Atlanta	OF	37	96	18	27	3	0	0	8	5	.281
1971	Atlanta	OF	154	639	101	219	24	6	9	44	30	.343
1972	Atlanta	OF	134	554	87	180	22	0	12	53	25	.325
1973	Atlanta	OF	148	668	94	200	32	6	11	55	35	.299
1974	Atlanta	OF	143	606	87	214	24	17	11	54	26	.353
1975	Atlanta	OF	151	625	74	174	26	11	6	31	14	.278
1976	Chicago (AL)	OF	136	527	63	158	22	6	4	36	14	.300
1977	Chicago (AL)	OF	134	543	78	163	29	7	10	54	12	.300
1978	Chicago (AL)	OF	118	443	67	122	18	9	3	29	7	.275
	Totals		1188	4735	678	1465	201	62	66	366	170	.309

KEN KRAVEC 27 6-2 185   Bats L Throws L

Strikeout artist . . . Probably has not yet reached peak . . . Earned himself promotion to Sox and a spot in starting rotation midway through 1977 season . . . Has been there ever since . . . Born July 29, 1951, in Cleveland, Ohio. . . . Impressive minor league career . . . Once fanned 11 A's in 2-0 shutout . . . Struck on 10 Angels on another occasion.

Year	Club	G	IP	W	L	Pct.	SO	BB	H	ERA
1975	Chicago (AL)	2	4	0	1	.000	1	8	1	6.75
1976	Chicago (AL)	9	50	1	5	.167	38	32	49	4.86
1977	Chicago (AL)	26	167	11	8	.579	125	57	161	4.10
1978	Chicago (AL)	30	203	11	16	.407	154	95	188	4.08
	Totals	67	424	23	30	.434	318	192	399	4.20

RON SCHUELER 30 6-4 204   Bats R Throws R

Veteran right-hander, can start or relieve . . . Originally drafted by Pirates in 1966 but didn't sign . . . Later signed with Braves, who traded him to Phillies . . . Played out his option with Twins and came to Chisox in 1977 free agent auction . . . Born April 18, 1948, in Hays, Kan. . . . Attended Ft. Hays St. College . . . Won career-high 11 games in 1974, making 27 starts for Phillies.

Year	Club	G	IP	W	L	Pct.	SO	BB	H	ERA
1972	Atlanta	37	145	5	8	.385	96	60	122	3.66
1973	Atlanta	39	186	8	7	.533	124	66	179	3.87
1974	Philadelphia	44	203	11	16	.407	109	98	202	3.72
1975	Philadelphia	46	93	4	4	.500	69	40	88	5.23
1976	Philadelphia	35	50	1	0	1.000	43	16	44	2.88
1977	Minnesota	52	135	8	7	.533	77	61	131	4.40
1978	Chicago (AL)	30	82	3	5	.375	40	39	76	4.28
	Totals	283	894	40	47	.460	558	380	842	4.01

BOB MOLINARO 28 6-0 180   Bats L Throws R

Another former Tiger who has found a home in Chicago . . . Confident, outgoing outfielder . . . Insists he was unjustly buried for 10 years in Tiger farm system . . . "I want to set an example for minor league players, to prove to them there's always hope. One team believed in me; that's all you need." . . . Became free agent at end of 1977 because of contract technicality and signed with Sox . . . Born May 21,

1950, in Newark N.J. . . . Has worked as black-jack dealer in Las Vegas during off-season . . . Good speed and good power . . . Can play right field, left field or DH.

Year	Club	Pos	G	AB	R	H	2B	3B	HR	RBI	SB	Avg.
1975	Detroit	OF	6	19	2	5	0	1	0	1	2	.263
1977	Det.-Chic. (AL)	OF	5	6	0	2	1	0	0	0	1	.333
1978	Chicago (AL)	OF	105	286	39	75	5	5	6	27	22	.262
	Totals		116	311	41	82	6	6	6	28	25	.264

TOP PROSPECTS

MIKE PROLY 28 6-0 185   **Bats R Throws R**
Most impressive during limited stay with White Sox in 1978, winning five games, while losing only two . . . Another bargain Bill Veeck uncovered at the 1977 free agent auction . . . Born Dec. 15, 1950, in Jamaica, N.Y. . . . Originally drafted by Cardinals in June, 1972 . . . Minor league success, as a starter and as a reliever, earned him trial with Cards in '76 . . . Claimed by Twins in minor league draft, but played out his option rather than sign with Minnesota.

MIKE COLBERN 23 6-3 205   **Bats R Throws R**
Could be Chisox' catcher of the future . . . Hit .270 during trial with Sox in 1978 . . . Drove in three runs with three hits in game against Detroit . . . Born April 19, 1955, in Santa Monica, Cal. . . . Has showed marked improvement at plate in each of last three years . . . Starred at Arizona State before signing with Sox . . . Played for U.S. all-star team in Japan in 1976.

MANAGER DON KESSINGER: The AL's only player-manager . . . Named to replace Lary Doby during off-season . . . White Sox team leader as a player in 1978 . . . "He's our MVP," said Steve Stone . . . Teammates said he did more for club on day-to-day basis than anyone else on team . . . Born July 17, 1942, in Forrest City, Ark. . . . "I don't think I'll play a lot." . . . "He is the man ideally suited to manage our club," says Bill Veeck . . . His popularity with

White Sox fans was also a factor in his selection . . . Never
thought about managing until late last year . . . Was star infielder with Cubs and Cardinals for 12 years before joining
Chisox midway through 1977 season . . . Owns two racquetball
emporiums.

Year	Club	Pos	G	AB	R	H	2B	3B	HR	RBI	SB	Avg.
1964	Chicago (NL)	SS	4	12	1	2	0	0	0	0	0	.167
1965	Chicago (NL)	SS	106	309	19	62	4	3	0	14	1	.201
1966	Chicago (NL)	SS	150	533	50	146	8	2	1	43	13	.274
1967	Chicago (NL)	SS	145	580	61	134	10	7	0	42	6	.231
1968	Chicago (NL)	SS	160	655	63	157	14	7	1	32	9	.240
1969	Chicago (NL)	SS	158	664	109	181	38	6	4	53	11	.273
1970	Chicago (NL)	SS	154	631	100	168	21	14	1	39	12	.266
1971	Chicago (NL)	SS	155	617	77	159	18	6	2	38	15	.258
1972	Chicago (NL)	SS	149	577	77	158	20	6	1	39	8	.274
1973	Chicago (NL)	SS	160	577	52	151	22	3	0	43	6	.262
1974	Chicago (NL)	SS	153	599	83	155	20	7	1	42	7	.259
1975	Chicago (NL)	SS-3B	154	601	77	146	26	10	0	46	4	.243
1976	St. Louis	SS-2B-3B	145	502	55	120	22	6	1	40	3	.239
1977	St. Louis	SS-2B-3B	59	134	14	32	4	0	0	7	0	.239
1977	Chicago (AL)	SS-2B-3B	39	119	12	28	3	2	0	11	2	.235
1978	Chicago (AL)	SS-2B-3B	131	431	35	110	18	1	1	31	2	.255
	Totals		2022	7541	885	1909	248	80	13	520	99	.253

GREATEST PITCHER

For 21 years, Ted Lyons pitched as though the White Sox
were in pursuit of the pennant. But popular right-hander was
only pretending.

During his first 11 years work, the Chisox never once
emerged from the American League's second division. Yet
Lyons kept pitching—and winning.

Finally, in 1936, he got a little help as teammate Luke Appling won the batting title. And Lyons made the most of the
opportunity, winning enough games to lift Chicago into the first
division for the first time since he joined the club.

Most of the time, though, Lyons made his living pitching to
people like Babe Ruth, Lou Gehrig, Jimmy Foxx, Hank Greenberg and Joe DiMaggio. And most of the time, he was sur-
rounded by mediocre teams that were out of the pennant race
from opening day.

Even so, Lyons won more games (260) and pitched more
innings (4,162) than anyone in White Sox history. The world
will never know how great his statistics might have been, had he
been privileged to pitch for a championship team.

Luis Aparicio sparked new stealing era with 56 in 1959.

ALL-TIME WHITE SOX LEADERS

BATTING: Luke Appling, .388, 1936
HRs: Dick Allen, 37, 1972
RBIs: Zeke Bonura, 138, 1936
STEALS: Wally Moses, 56, 1943
             Luis Aparicio, 56, 1959
WINS: Ed Walsh, 40, 1908
STRIKEOUTS: Ed Walsh, 269, 1908

OAKLAND A'S

TEAM DIRECTORY: Pres.: Charles O. Finley; Sec. Treas.: Charles O. Finley Jr.; Dir. Minor League Oper.: Norm Koselke; Controller: Charles Cottonaro; Dir. Pub. Rel.: Carl Finley; Trav. Sec.: Robert Hoffman. Home: Oakland Coliseum (50,000). Field distances: 330, l.f.; 375, l.c; 400, c.f.; 375, r.c.; 330, r.f. Spring training: Mesa, Ariz.

SCOUTING REPORT

HITTING: Everything is in limbo out in Oakland. The proposed sale of the club never materialized and, while waiting, Charlie Finley let his manager (Jack McKeon) go and did

Mitchell Page's .285 was bright spot for weak-hitting A's.

nothing to improve his sad-sack club. He failed to draft at the re-entry or the major league draft, and never even showed up at the winter meetings.

Charlie has proved to be an excellent horse (or mule?) trader. The last two years he showed signs of patching up his once-mighty A's, acquiring Jim Essian, Mitchell Page, Taylor Duncan, Dave Revering, Miguel Dilone and Joe Wallis in trades, and signing Mario Guerrero as a free agent. Revering and Page combined for 33 homers and 116 RBIs last year and Guerrero hit a respectable .275. But Finley can't stop there. A few more deals like the ones he made can put the A's back on the right track, instead of off the track, where they are now.

PITCHING: Two fine young pitchers, Matt Keough (8-15 with a 3.24 ERA) and John Johnson, 11-10, give the A's a start. Behind them, there is little, especially since Elias Sosa (8-2 with 14 saves) opted for free agency. That leaves Bob Lacey (8-9, five saves and a 3.01 ERA) as the probable ace of the bullpen. Others on the staff are Rick Langford, Dave Heaverlo and Mike Norris and a handful of young hopefuls, among them Mike Morgan, the high school senior who was the nation's No. 1 draft pick last summer.

FIELDING: Dead last in fielding last year, the A's committed 177 errors, the only club in the league to make more than one boot a game. It's counterproductive for a team like the A's to allow the opposition an average of one more out per game.

To complicate matters, the A's found that their best fielders cannot hit and their best hitters had weaknesses afield. There was, however, a measure of respectability at three key positions. Jim Essian gave the A's the best catching they have had in years and Mario Guerrero and Mike Edwards, at short and second, were at times a nifty pair. Edwards, in particular, showed wonderful promise for a second-year man.

OUTLOOK: As Pittsburgh West, the A's seemed headed for something good following a few good trades with the Pirates, engineered by Charlie O. But Finley has lost his desire, or his interest, and things are at a standstill. The A's didn't even have a manager at the winter meetings.

"I'm not going to name a manager," said Finley, "until I know how the sale of the club is going to be resolved."

It's that kind of stand-still attitude, understandable, yet destructive, that will result in the A's being mired in the cellar in the AL West.

OAKLAND A'S 1979 ROSTER

PITCHERS

No.	Name	1978 Club	W-L	IP	SO	ERA	B-T	Ht.	Wt.	Born
37	Conroy, Tim	Oakland	0-0	5	0	7.20	L-L	6-0	178	4/3/60 Monroeville, PA
		Vancouver	0-1	9	3	16.00				
60	Heaverlo, Dave	Oakland	3-6	130	71	3.25	R-R	6-1	195	8/25/50 Ellensburg, WA
38	Johnson, John	Oakland	11-10	186	91	3.39	L-L	6-2	185	8/21/56 Houston, TX
27	Keough, Matt	Oakland	8-15	197	108	3.24	R-R	6-2	175	7/3/55 Pomona, CA
50	Kingman, Brian	Modesto	0-1	20	19	2.70	R-R	6-1	190	7/27/54 Los Angeles, CA
3	Lacey, Bob	Oakland	8-9	120	60	3.00	R-L	6-5	190	8/25/53 Fredericksburg, VA
22	Langford, Rick	Oakland	7-13	176	92	3.43	R-R	6-0	180	3/20/52 Farmville, VA
54	McCatty, Steve	Vancouver	7-4	55	51	3.11	R-R	6-3	195	3/20/54 Detroit, MI
		Oakland	0-0	20	10	4.50				
32	Minetto, Craig	Vancouver	10-4	134	78	4.30	L-L	6-0	185	4/25/54 Stockton, CA
		Oakland	0-0	12	3	3.75				
29	Mitchell, Craig	Vancouver	12-9	155	67	3.60	R-R	6-3	190	4/14/54 Santa Rosa, CA
15	Morgan, Mike	Oakland	0-3	12	0	7.50	R-R	6-1	180	10/8/59 Tulare, CA
		Vancouver	5-6	92	31	5.58				
17	Norris, Mike	Vancouver	3-3	42	32	5.79	R-R	6-2	172	3/19/55 San Francisco, CA
		Jersey City	2-6	66	51	3.41				
		Oakland	0-5	49	36	5.51				
—	Sosa, Elias	Oakland	8-2	109	61	2.64	R-R	6-2	190	6/10/50 Dominican Republic
30	Wirth, Alan	Vancouver	4-2	73	43	4.19	R-R	6-5	190	12/8/56 Mesa, AZ
		Oakland	5-6	81	31	3.44				

CATCHERS

No.	Name	1978 Club	H	HR	RBI	Pct.	B-T	Ht.	Wt.	Born
18	Essian, Jim	Oakland	62	3	26	.223	R-R	6-1	187	1/2/51 Detroit, MI
26	Meyer, Scott	Jersey City	39	5	22	.247	R-R	6-1	195	8/19/57 Midlothian, IL
		Oakland	1	0	0	.111				
5	Newman, Jeff	Oakland	64	9	32	.239	R-R	6-2	218	9/11/48 Ft. Worth, TX
48	Robinson, Bruce	Vancouver	109	10	73	.299	L-R	6-2	195	4/16/54 La Jolla, CA
		Oakland	21	0	8	.250				

INFIELDERS

No.	Name	1978 Club	H	HR	RBI	Pct.	B-T	Ht.	Wt.	Born
16	Duncan, Taylor	Vancouver	48	3	29	.302	R-R	5-11	180	5/12/53 Memphis, TN
		Oakland	82	2	37	.257				
7	Edwards, Mike	Oakland	113	1	23	.274	R-R	5-10	152	8/27/52 Ft. Lewis, WA
10	Gross, Wayne	Vancouver	23	3	10	.411	L-R	6-2	205	1/14/52 Riverside, CA
		Oakland	57	7	23	.199				
3	Guerrero, Mario	Oakland	139	3	38	.275	R-R	5-10	155	9/28/49 Dominican Republic
47	Klutts, Mickey	New York (AL)	2	0	0	1.000	R-R	5-11	189	9/30/54 Montebello, CA
		Vancouver	12	4	14	.293				
8	Picciolo, Rob	Vancouver	23	2	17	.256	R-R	6-2	185	2/4/53 Santa Monica, CA
		Oakland	21	2	7	.226				
24	Revering, Dave	Oakland	141	16	46	.271	L-R	6-4	205	2/12/53 Roseville, CA
4	Tabb, Jerry	Oakland	1	0	1	.111	L-R	6-2	195	3/17/52 Altus, OK
		Vancouver	122	18	75	.357				

OUTFIELDERS

No.	Name	1978 Club	H	HR	RBI	Pct.	B-T	Ht.	Wt.	Born
13	Alston, Dell	Tac-Vancou.	97	7	42	.353	R-R	6-0	174	9/22/52 White Plains, NY
		NY (AL)-Oak.	36	1	10	.205				
11	Armas, Tony	Oakland	51	2	13	.213	R-R	6-1	182	7/12/53 Venezuela
14	Burke, Glenn	Los Angeles	4	0	2	.211	R-R	6-0	205	11/16/52 Oakland, CA
		Oakland	47	1	14	.235				
25	Cosey, Ray	Jersey City	124	11	87	.268	L-L	5-11	185	2/15/56 San Rafael, CA
19	Dilone, Miguel	Oakland	59	1	14	.228	B-R	6-0	161	11/1/54 Dominican Republic
35	Henderson, Rickey	Jersey City	136	0	33	.310	R-L	5-10	180	12/25/58 Chicago, IL
36	Murphy, Dwayne	Vancouver	39	7	17	.264	L-R	6-1	180	3/18/55 Merced, CA
		Oakland	10	0	5	.192				
20	Murray, Larry	Vancouver	123	9	63	.284	B-R	5-11	180	3/1/53 Chicago, IL
		Oakland	1	0	0	.083				
6	Page, Mitchell	Oakland	147	17	70	.285	L-R	6-2	205	10/15/51 Compton, CA
9	Wallis, Joe	Chicago (NL)	17	1	6	.309	B-R	5-10	195	1/9/52 E. St. Louis, IL
		Oakland	66	6	26	.237				

A's PROFILES

MIKE EDWARDS 26 5-10 152   Bats R Throws R

Was destined to spend 1978 season in Pirates' farm system until traded to Oakland in spring . . . Took advantage of opportunity to become one of A's brightest young stars . . . Tied team record with 17-game hitting streak . . . Credits religion for his success . . . "I am a man of faith." . . . Born Aug. 27, 1952, in Fort Lewis, Wash. . . . Only player in AL to score five runs in a game in '78 . . . Led Pac-8 in hitting while at UCLA . . . Has played both second base and shortstop . . . Has excellent speed and surprising power.

Year	Club	Pos	G	AB	R	H	2B	3B	HR	RBI	SB	Avg.
1977	Pittsburgh	2B	7	6	1	0	0	0	0	0	0	.000
1978	Oakland	2B-3B-SS	142	413	48	113	16	2	1	23	27	.274
	Totals		149	419	49	113	16	2	1	23	27	.270

MITCHELL PAGE 27 6-2 205   Bats L Throws L

Proved performance as a rookie was no fluke . . . "Everything I am, I made all by myself." . . . Convinced Charlie Finley to spend $1,800 for a video tape machine and spent hours studying movies of himself . . . Still believes he should have been Rookie of Year in 1977 . . . Would like to sign a five-year contract for $1.5 million . . . Born Oct. 15, 1951, in Compton, Cal. . . . Was honorable mention All-America in college at Cal Poly . . . Originally signed with Pirates in '73 . . . Has played first base and outfield . . . Had outstanding minor league statistics.

Year	Club	Pos	G	AB	R	H	2B	3B	HR	RBI	SB	Avg.
1977	Oakland	OF	145	501	85	154	28	8	21	75	42	.307
1978	Oakland	OF	147	516	62	147	25	7	17	70	23	.285
	Totals		292	1017	147	301	53	15	38	145	65	.296

DAVE REVERING 26 6-4 205   Bats L Throws R

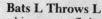

Another player who finally got his chance after he was traded to the A's . . . Too outspoken in minor leagues for straight-laced Reds . . . Traded to Oakland by Cincinnati twice, but Bowie Kuhn vetoed the first deal that would have sent Vida Blue to the Reds . . . Later, Cincinnati settled for Doug Bair and cash . . . Born Feb. 12, 1953, in Roseville, Cal. . . . Averaged 26 homers a year for three years in Triple-A yet didn't spend one day in majors . . . Gives Willie Horton credit for helping him with his hitting . . . Plays first base, but could DH.

Year	Club	Pos	G	AB	R	H	2B	3B	HR	RBI	SB	Avg.
1978	Oakland.........	1B	152	521	48	141	21	3	16	46	0	.271

JOE WALLIS 27 5-10 195   Bats S Throws R

Known as "Tarzan" because of his reputation for being a "wild man" . . . Traded from Cubs to Indians to A's in 1978 . . . Excellent defensive center fielder . . . Once dove from a hotel room window into a swimming pool . . . "Just make sure you clear the cement" . . . Born Jan. 9, 1952, in East St. Louis, Ill. . . . Originally drafted by Houston but didn't sign . . . All-America in college at Southern Illinois . . . Has good speed.

Year	Club	Pos	G	AB	R	H	2B	3B	HR	RBI	SB	Avg.
1975	Chicago (NL).....	OF	16	56	9	16	2	2	1	4	2	.286
1976	Chicago (NL).....	OF	121	338	51	86	11	5	5	21	3	.254
1977	Chicago (NL).....	OF	56	80	14	20	3	0	2	8	0	.250
1978	Chicago (NL).....	OF	28	55	7	17	2	1	1	6	0	.309
1978	Oakland.........	OF	85	279	28	66	16	1	6	26	1	.237
	Totals...........		306	808	109	205	34	9	15	65	6	.254

MIGUEL DILONE 24 6-0 161   Bats S Throws R

This speedster finished fourth in league in stolen bases with 50 . . . Another player who was rescued from Pirates' farm system by Charley Finley . . . Has the speed to be one of the most exciting runners in baseball . . . Averaged 64 stolen bases a season for six years in Pirate organization . . . Born Nov. 1, 1954, in Santiago, Dominican Republic . . . Signed with Pirates as free agent in 1971 . . . Outstanding minor league hitter, too.

Year	Club	Pos	G	AB	R	H	2B	3B	HR	RBI	SB	Avg.
1974	Pittsburgh	OF	12	2	3	0	0	0	0	0	2	.000
1975	Pittsburgh	OF	18	6	8	0	0	0	0	0	2	.000
1976	Pittsburgh	OF	16	17	7	4	0	0	0	0	5	.235
1977	Pittsburgh	OF	29	44	5	6	0	0	0	0	12	.136
1978	Oakland.........	OF	135	259	34	59	8	0	1	14	50	.228
	Totals...........		210	328	57	69	8	0	1	14	71	.210

JOHN JOHNSON 22 6-2 185   Bats L Throws L

Another of the fine young players Charley Finley "stole" from Giants to rebuild his ballclub . . . Half Indian, and proud of it . . . "They're the ones who made America." . . . Wears hair like Harpo Marx . . . Posted 27-4 record in two years in minors but all Giants promised him was a promotion to AA . . . A's made him a star . . . Born Aug. 21, 1956, in Austin, Tex. . . . First went out for sports in high school because "all my friends were in it" . . . "I didn't even know who was playing back then" . . . Signed with Giants in 1974 and assumed they wanted him to be an outfielder . . . No wonder . . . His high school pitching record read: Five wins, six losses.

Year	Club	G	IP	W	L	Pct.	SO	BB	H	ERA
1978	Oakland	33	186	11	10	.524	91	82	164	3.39

BOB LACEY 25 6-5 200   Bats R Throws L

Led league in appearances (74) and in chatter . . . Backs up words with performance on the mound . . . Yet called 1978 season "disgusting" . . . Known as "Spacey Lacey" . . . A real flake . . . "Lacey is flakier than hell," says Whitey Herzog. "But he's also a helluva relief pitcher" . . . Kansas City's Darrell Porter called him "an immature punk" . . . Born Aug. 25, 1953, in Fredricksburg, Va. . . . Taunted Reggie Jackson when he faced that famous slugger in his major league debut . . . Then proceeded to strike Jackson out twice . . . A's sixth pick in January, 1972, free agent draft.

Year	Club	G	IP	W	L	Pct.	SO	BB	H	ERA
1977	Oakland	64	122	6	8	.429	69	43	100	3.02
1978	Oakland	74	120	8	9	.471	60	35	126	3.00
	Totals	138	242	14	17	.452	129	78	226	3.01

MARIO GUERRERO 29 5-10 155   Bats R Throws R

Got the chance to play every day with A's and made the most of the opportunity, enjoying the best year of his big league career . . . Played out his option with Angels ("They treated me like a dog") and signed with Giants . . . Traded to A's in spring as partial payment for Vida Blue . . . Born Sept. 28, 1949, in Santo Domingo . . . Known for his

ability with a bat as well as his defensive skills . . . Once highly
regarded by Red Sox, later played for Cardinals and Angels
. . . Originally signed with Yankees.

Year	Club	Pos	G	AB	R	H	2B	3B	HR	RBI	SB	Avg.
1973	Boston..........	SS-2B	66	219	19	51	5	2	0	11	2	.233
1974	Boston..........	SS	93	284	18	70	6	2	0	23	3	.246
1975	St. Louis	SS	64	184	17	44	9	0	0	11	0	.239
1976	California........	SS-2B	83	268	24	76	12	0	1	18	0	.284
1977	California........	SS-2B	86	244	17	69	8	2	1	28	0	.283
1978	Oakland.........	SS-2B	143	505	28	139	18	4	3	38	0	.275
	Totals...........		535	1704	123	449	58	10	5	129	5	.263

ELIAS SOSA 28 6-2 190   Bats R Throws R

Traded to A's last spring by Pirates, who had
acquired him from Dodgers on waivers during the winter . . . "Being in Oakland was
the best thing that ever happened to me."
. . . Appeared in 68 games, saving 14 . . .
"Work, I've got to have work, that's all I
need" . . . Born June 10, 1950, in La Vega,
Dominican Republic . . . Was Dodgers' top
reliever in 1977 . . . Originally signed with Giants in 1968 . . .
Enjoyed finest season as rookie in '73 when he saved 18 games
and won 10 others . . . Later traded to Cardinals and Braves.

Year	Club	G	IP	W	L	Pct.	SO	BB	H	ERA
1972	San Francisco	8	16	0	1	.000	10	12	10	2.25
1973	San Francisco	71	107	10	4	.714	70	41	95	3.28
1974	San Francisco	68	101	9	7	.563	48	45	94	3.48
1975	St. L.-Atl.................	57	90	2	5	.286	46	43	92	4.30
1976	Atl.-L.A.................	45	69	6	8	.429	52	25	71	4.43
1977	Los Angeles..............	44	64	2	2	.500	47	12	42	1.97
1978	Oakland.................	68	109	8	2	.800	61	44	106	2.64
	Totals..................	361	556	37	29	.561	334	222	510	3.32

TOP PROSPECTS

MIKE MORGAN 18 6-1 180   Bats R Throws R

Made major league debut with A's, seven days after he graduated from high school . . . Lost 3-0 to Orioles, but went all the
way . . . Started two more games but lost them both before he
was sent to the minors to sharpen his skills . . . Was A's No. 1
draft pick . . . Signed for bonus in excess of $50,000 . . . Hard-
throwing right-hander . . . Fastball clocked at 90 mph . . . "I
wouldn't mind going for the Cy Young one of these years" . . .
His friends call him "Big Mo."

BRUCE ROBINSON 24 6-2 195   **Bats L Throws R**

Promising young catcher . . . Batted .250 during brief trial with
A's in 1978 . . . Was A's. No. 1 draft pick in June, 1975 . . .
Has steadily improved in minors . . . Holds degree in econom-
ics from Stanford . . . Born April 16, 1954, in LaJolla, Cal. . . .
Played on national championship semi-pro teams in Alaska for
three years.

GREATEST PITCHER

To single out one man as the greatest pitcher in Oakland
history, would mean choosing between Catfish Hunter and Vida
Blue. And that would be an impossible task.

On the one hand, Hunter won seven more games than Blue
(131 to 124) and compiled a slightly lower earned run average
(3.05 to 3.18) while wearing an Oakland uniform.

But Blue struck out more batters (1,315 to 1,139), pitched
more innings and started more games.

Actually, the two complemented one another quite nicely
during the four years they were on the same side.

Hunter, of course, went on to greater riches and still more
glory with the Yankees while Blue eventually moved across the
bay to San Francisco and out from under the oppressive thumb
of Charlie Finley.

But both men built their reputations in Oakland, making the
A's the dominant team in the American League in the early
'70s. And they set the standard by which future Oakland pitchers will be judged.

Of course, if you go back to the original Philadelphia A's of
Connie Mack, Robert Moses "Lefty" Grove rates as the greatest
pitcher. Before being traded to the Boston Red Sox where he
completed his 300-victory, Hall of Fame career, Grove won 195
games for the A's. He had back-to-back seasons of 28-5 and
31-4 in 1930 and 1931.

ALL-TIME A's LEADERS

BATTING: Napoleon Lajoie, .422, 1901
HRs: Jimmy Foxx, 58, 1932
RBIs: Jimmy Foxx, 169, 1932
STEALS: Eddie Collins, 81, 1910
WINS: John Coombs, 31, 1910
　　　　Lefty Grove, 31, 1931
STRIKEOUTS: Rube Waddell, 349, 1904

Lefty Grove was AL's first MVP in 1931 with 31-4 record.

By HAL McCOY
Dayton News

	East	West
PREDICTED ORDER OF FINISH	Philadelphia Phillies	Los Angeles Dodgers
	Pittsburgh Pirates	San Francisco Giants
	Montreal Expos	Cincinnati Reds
	St. Louis Cardinals	San Diego Padres
	Chicago Cubs	Houston Astros
	New York Mets	Atlanta Braves

Playoff Winner: Philadelphia

RUN FOR THE ROSE

103rd Running, National League Race. Distance, 162 games, plus playoff. Purse: $12,000 per winning player, division; $15,000 added, pennant; $6,000 added, World Championship. A field of 12 entered in two divisions.

Track Record 116 wins—Chicago 1906

EAST DIVISION		Owner			Morning Line Manager
1	**PHILLIES** crimson & white	R.R.M. Carpenter		1978 W 90 L 72	**2-1** Danny Ozark
	Class of field.				
2	**PIRATES** old gold, white & black	John Galbreath		1978 W 88 L 73	**9-5** Chuck Tanner
	Losing distance fast.				
3	**EXPOS** scarlet, white & royal blue	Charles Bronfman		1978 W 76 L 86	**5-1** Dick Williams
	Ready for strong finish.				
4	**CARDINALS** red & white	August A. Busch		1978 W 69 L 93	**10-1** Ken Boyer
	Better than previous showings.				
5	**CUBS** royal blue & white	Phillip K. Wrigley		1978 W 79 L 83	**20-1** Herman Franks
	No finishing stamina.				
6	**METS** orange, white & blue	Mrs. Vincent de Roulet		1978 W 66 L 96	**100-1** Joe Torre
	Longest of long shots.				

PHILLIES should lead from the gate to wire. **PIRATES** will start slowly and close at the finish. **EXPOS** should hang near the middle of the pack throughout the race. **CARDS** will run neck-and-neck with **EXPOS**, but fade in stretch. **CUBS** will break fast but drop to rear by mid-race. **METS** will stumble in starting gate and at the attendance gate.

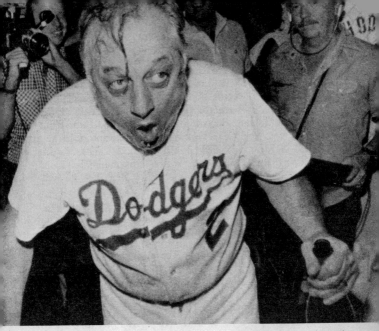

Tom Lasorda hopes to take Dodgers to another pennant party.

WEST DIVISION		Owner			Morning Line Manager
1	**DODGERS** royal blue & white	Walter O'Malley		1978 W 95 L 67	**3-1** Tom Lasorda
	Winning is habit forming.				
2	**GIANTS** white, orange & black	Robert Lurie		1978 W 89 L 73	**4-1** Joe Altobelli
	Won't fade this time out.				
3	**REDS** red & white	Louis Nippert		1978 W 92 L 69	**6-1** John McNamara
	No longer classy.				
4	**PADRES** brown, gold & white	Ray A. Kroc		1978 W 84 L 78	**10-1** Roger Craig
	Moving up fast.				
5	**ASTROS** orange & white	T.H. Neyland		1978 W 74 L 88	**25-1** Bill Virdon
	Never lives up to promises.				
6	**BRAVES** royal blue & white	Ted Turner		1978 W 69 L 93	**100-1** Bobby Cox
	Young and not ready to win.				

DODGERS will break from gate quickly and build insurmountable lead. **GIANTS** follow **DODG-ERS** from start to finish, making move in the stretch but falling short. **REDS** limp home to third after a slow start. **PADRES** make early move but the field is too fast. **ASTROS** languish at rear of the pack, never challenging. **BRAVES** sink quickly to last and stay there.

PHILADELPHIA PHILLIES

TEAM DIRECTORY: Chairman of the Board: R.R.M. Carpenter, Jr.; Pres.: R.R.M. Carpenter III; Exec. VP: William Y. Giles; VP and Director of Player Personnel: Paul Owens; VP and Director of Finances: George F.H. Harrison; Director of Minor Leagues and Scouting: Dallas Green; Pub. Rel.: Larry Shenk; Trav. Sec.: Ed Ferenz; Mgr.: Danny Ozark. Home: Veterans Stadium (56,581) Field distances: 330 l.f. line; 408, c.f.; 330, r.f. line. Spring training: Clearwater, Fla.

SCOUTING REPORT

HITTING: The strong get much, much stronger. The addition of Pete Rose's base-hit bat and his penchant for getting on base from the leadoff spot will benefit the offense. Rose will have no difficulty achieving his yearly goal of scoring 100 runs with Mike Schmidt and Greg Luzinski batting behind him. Phillies trailed only the Reds in homers (136 to 133) and doubles (270 to 248) but should pass Cincinnati in doubles since Rose is always near the top of the league.

Phillies will have no trouble scoring runs by any method, the long ball from Schmidt and Luzinski, or the short ball from Rose, Larry Bowa (.294), Bake McBride and Garry Maddox. The Phils are so rich in hitting that a good hitting catcher like Tim McCarver sits on the bench waiting for Steve Carlton to pitch because "Lefty" prefers pitching to McCarver. And,

Larry Bowa plays like friend and new teammate Pete Rose.

there's nothing wrong with regular catcher Bob Boone's bat.

When Boone catches, McCarver's productive bat is ready on the bench, along with Richie Hebner, Jose Cardenal and Davey Johnson. Phillies can play Rose in the outfield, at first base, at second base . . . anywhere . . . and not weaken themselves. In fact, it strengthens the bench.

PITCHING: Steve Carlton is still the word when you mention pitching, though his record was only 16-13. His earned run average, though, was 2.84, eighth best in the league. When manager Danny Ozark is faced with a big game, Carlton is the man he wants holding the baseball. Phillies have always been known as an "outscore 'em, 10-8," team, but that's changing. Dick Ruthven won 15 games, Larry Christenson won 13 games, Randy Lerch won 11. Aging Jim Kaat and aging Jim Lonborg are fading, but Philadelphia's youngsters are capable of picking up the slack. Tug McGraw is still the chairman of the bullpen.

FIELDING: The Phillies led the National League in fielding (.983) and their defense is overshadowed by their large bats. Speed in the outfield and sticky gloves in the infield help keep the opposition's run total down in The Vet, where balls fly into the stratosphere. Anything in the park is caught by Maddox and McBride, with Maddox's speed in center helping to overcome the slow bulk of Luzinski in left.

Schmidt stops everything at third and has the arm, but is sometimes wild. Bowa is baseball's most underrated shortstop and isn't far off when he says, "I'm the best shortstop in baseball." Put Carlton or Kaat on the mound and you have fifth infielders. Boone is decent behind the plate, too, leading the league (.991) and being charged with only five passed balls and six errors. Other Phillie defensive league leaders were Bowa at short (.986) with only 10 errors and McBride in the outfield (.996) with one error. Any more questions about the Phillie defense?

OUTLOOK: The Phillies didn't need to add anything, but when they added Rose, they added enthusiasm, team leadership, a relentless bat and perhaps a world's championship. The Phillies have lost three straight National League playoffs, one to Cincinnati and two to Los Angeles, but there is no reason to repeat that act in 1979. Rose should be living proof to the claim made by W.C. Fields, "On the whole, I'd rather be in Philadelphia." That's where the National League pennant, and perhaps the World Series trophy, may reside after '79.

PHILADELPHIA PHILLIES 1979 ROSTER

MANAGER Danny Ozark
Coaches—Billy DeMars, Herm Starrette, Tony Taylor, Bob
Tiefenauer, Bobby Wine

PITCHERS

No.	Name	1978 Club	W-L	IP	SO	ERA	B-T	Ht.	Wt.	Born
46	Boltano, Dan	Okla. City	7-10	132	71	4.02	R-R	6-0	190	3/22/53 Sacramento, CA
		Philadelphia	0-0	1	0	0.00				
—	Botelho, Derek	Reading	15-7	178	130	3.34	R-R	6-3	160	8/2/56 Long Beach, CA
40	Brusstar, Warren	Philadelphia	6-3	89	60	2.33	R-R	6-3	200	2/2/52 Oakland, CA
32	Carlton, Steve	Philadelphia	16-13	247	161	2.84	L-L	6-5	210	12/22/44 Miami, FL
38	Christenson, Larry	Philadelphia	13-14	228	131	3.24	R-R	6-2	210	11/10/53 Everett, WA
49	Eastwick, Rawly	New York (AL)	2-1	25	13	3.24	R-R	6-3	172	10/24/50 Camden, NJ
		Philadelphia	2-1	40	14	4.05				
39	Kaat, Jim	Philadelphia	8-5	140	48	4.11	L-L	6-5	224	11/7/38 Zeeland, MI
48	Larson, Dan	Charleston	14-6	202	115	3.75	R-R	6-0	180	7/4/54 Los Angeles, CA
		Philadelphia	0-0	1	2	9.00				
47	Lerch, Randy	Philadelphia	11-8	184	96	3.96	L-L	6-3	—	10/9/54 Sacramento, CA
41	Lonborg, Jim	Philadelphia	8-10	114	48	5.21	R-R	6-5	206	4/16/43 Santa Maria, CA
—	Mack, Henry	Peninsula	15-4	158	158	2.79	R-R	6-2	185	11/10/58 Winchester, KY
—	Martinez, Jose	Peninsula	13-2	148	131	2.07	R-R	6-3	176	5/24/57 Puerto Rico
45	McGraw, Tug	Philadelphia	8-7	90	63	3.20	R-L	6-0	185	8/30/44 Martinez, CA
42	Reed, Ron	Philadelphia	3-4	109	85	2.23	R-R	6-6	225	11/1/42 LaPorte, IN
44	Ruthven, Dick	Atl-Phil.	15-11	232	120	3.38	R-R	6-2	195	3/27/51 Sacramento, CA
33	Saucier, Kevin	Okla. City	7-12	173	58	4.63	R-L	6-1	190	8/9/56 Pensacola, FL
		Philadelphia	0-1	2	2	18.00				
37	Wright, Jim	Okla. City	1-1	20	10	4.95	R-R	6-6	220	3/3/55 St. Joseph, MO

CATCHERS

No.	Name	1978 Club	H	HR	RBI	Pct.	B-T	Ht.	Wt.	Born
8	Boone, Bob	Philadelphia	123	12	62	.283	R-R	6-2	208	11/19/47 San Diego, CA
9	Foote, Barry	Philadelphia	9	1	4	.158	R-R	6-3	200	2/16/52 Smithfield, NC
11	McCarver, Tim	Philadelphia	36	1	14	.247	L-R	6-0	200	10/16/41 Memphis, TN
—	McCormack, Don	Reading	78	3	35	.320	R-R	6-3	195	9/18/55 Omak, WA
		Okla. City	46	7	31	.313				
34	Moreland, Keith	Okla. City	145	16	98	.289	R-R	6-0	186	5/2/54 Dallas, TX
		Philadelphia	0	0	0	.000				
—	Virgil, Ozzie	Peninsula	124	29	98	.303	R-R	6-1	195	12/7/56 Puerto Rico

INFIELDERS

No.	Name	1978 Club	H	HR	RBI	Pct.	B-T	Ht.	Wt.	Born
10	Bowa, Larry	Philadelphia	192	3	43	.294	B-R	5-10	155	12/6/45 Sacramento, CA
1	Cardenal, Jose	Philadelphia	50	4	33	.249	R-R	5-10	156	10/7/43 Cuba
16	Cruz, Todd	Okla. City	120	11	69	.261	R-R	6-0	170	11/23/55 Highland Park, MI
		Philadelphia	2	0	2	.500				
18	Hebner, Richie	Philadelphia	123	17	71	.283	R-R	6-1	193	11/26/47 Boston, MA
24	Mackanin, Pete	Denver	142	17	112	.276	R-R	6-2	190	8/1/51 Chicago, IL
		Philadelphia	2	0	1	.250				
28	Moreno, Jose	Reading	95	6	48	.262	B-R	6-0	175	11/2/57 Dominican Rep.
		Okla. City	16	3	9	.239				
15	Morrison, Jim	Okla. City	52	10	28	.275	R-R	5-11	178	9/23/52 Pensacola, FL
		Philadelphia	17	3	10	.157				
—	Poff, John	Okla. City	131	20	79	.300	L-L	6-2	190	10/23/52 Chillicothe, OH
14	Rose, Pete	Cincinnati	198	7	52	.302	B-R	5-11	200	4/14/41 Cincinnati, OH
20	Schmidt, Mike	Philadelphia	129	21	78	.251	R-R	6-2	198	9/27/49 Dayton, OH
6	Sizemore, Ted	Philadelphia	77	0	25	.219	R-R	5-10	157	4/15/45 Gadsen, AL

OUTFIELDERS

No.	Name	1978 Club	H	HR	RBI	Pct.	B-T	Ht.	Wt.	Born
29	Iseles, Orlando	Reading	98	7	47	.263	R-R	5-9	174	12/22/59 Puerto Rico
19	Luzinski, Greg	Philadelphia	143	35	101	.265	R-R	6-1	225	11/22/50 Chicago, IL
31	Maddox, Garry	Philadelphia	172	11	68	.288	R-R	6-3	175	9/1/49 Cincinnati, OH
25	Martin, Jerry	Philadelphia	72	9	36	.271	R-R	6-1	195	5/11/49 Columbia, SC
21	McBride, Bake	Philadelphia	127	10	49	.269	L-R	6-2	190	2/3/49 Fulton, MO
27	Smith, Lonnie	Okla. City	151	7	43	.315	R-R	5-9	170	12/22/55 Chicago, IL
		Philadelphia	0	0	0	.000				

HILLIE PROFILES

MIKE SCHMIDT 29 6-2 198   Bats R Throws R

Only guy in history to force removal of a stadium speaker when one of his towering blasts struck a speaker suspended from Astrodome roof . . . Believed to be baseball's first single-season half-millionaire with $556,000 salary . . . Earns it with supreme power, base-running instincts, rocket arm and dexterity at third base . . . Born Sept. 27, 1949, n Dayton, Ohio . . . Works harder for higher batting average than distance on homers . . . Usually bats third, but was leadoff hitter during NL playoffs with LA . . . Better-than-average basketball and tennis player and runs charity bowling tournament with teammate Garry Maddox in off-season . . . Off-year for him was 21 homers and 77 RBIs.

Year	Club	Pos	G	AB	R	H	2B	3B	HR	RBI	SB	Avg.
1972	Philadelphia......	3B-2B	13	34	2	7	0	0	1	3	0	.206
1973	Philadelphia......	3B-2B-1B-SS	132	367	43	72	11	0	18	52	8	.196
1974	Philadelphia......	3B	162	568	108	160	28	7	36	116	23	.282
1975	Philadelphia......	3B-SS	158	562	93	140	34	3	38	95	29	.249
1976	Philadelphia......	3B	160	584	112	153	31	4	38	107	14	.262
1977	Philadelphia......	3B	154	544	114	149	27	11	38	101	15	.274
1978	Philadelphia......	3B	145	513	93	129	27	2	21	78	19	.251
	Totals..........		924	3172	565	810	158	27	190	552	108	.255

LARRY BOWA 33 5-10 155   Bats S Throws R

Too little to play baseball and be a team leader, but doesn't believe it and proves it . . . Push hitter who finds holes even when outfield bunches in on him . . . Batted over .300 most of the season before dropping to .294 at the end . . . Argues with Cincinnati shortstop Dave Concepcion over who is better . . . Got off all-time quip when he asked Concepcion if his name was Elmer because every time he looked in a Cincinnati box score it said, "E-Concepcion" . . . Born Dec. 6, 1945, in Sacramento . . . Overlooked in 1965 draft and signed as free agent . . . Quick on bases, stole home twice in 1970, his rookie season . . . An off-season talk radio host.

Year	Club	Pos	G	AB	R	H	2B	3B	HR	RBI	SB	Avg.
1970	Philadelphia......	2B	145	547	50	137	17	6	0	34	24	.250
1971	Philadelphia......	SS	159	650	74	162	18	5	0	25	28	.249
1972	Philadelphia......	SS	152	579	67	145	11	13	1	31	17	.250
1973	Philadelphia......	SS	122	446	42	94	11	3	0	23	10	.211
1974	Philadelphia......	SS	162	669	97	184	19	10	1	36	39	.275
1975	Philadelphia......	SS	136	583	79	178	18	9	2	38	24	.305
1976	Philadelphia......	SS	156	624	71	155	15	9	0	49	30	.248
1977	Philadelphia......	SS	154	624	93	175	19	3	4	41	32	.280
1978	Philadelphia......	SS	156	654	78	192	31	5	3	43	27	.294
	Totals..........		1342	5376	651	1422	159	53	11	320	231	.265

GREG LUZINSKI 28 6-1 225   Bats R Throws R

Looks as if he doesn't belong on a baseball field, but everybody is afraid to tell him . . . Proves he belongs when he swings hefty bat, but also hits for average . . . Looks like a football player and could have been before Phils stole him away from Kansas State scholarship in 1968 draft . . . Hurt knees hurt his defense in left field, but he makes up for it at plate with 129 homers and 446 RBIs past four seasons . . . Born Nov. 22, 1950, in Chicago . . . Bought over $20,000 in tickets last two seasons for underprivileged children to see Phillies and sit in portion of left field stands called "The Bull Ring" . . . Part owner of tennis club in Cherry Hill, N.J.

Year	Club	Pos	G	AB	R	H	2B	3B	HR	RBI	SB	Avg.
1970	Philadelphia......	1B	8	12	0	2	0	0	0	0	0	.167
1971	Philadelphia......	1B	28	100	13	30	8	0	3	15	2	.300
1972	Philadelphia......	OF-1B	150	563	66	158	33	5	18	68	0	.281
1973	Philadelphia......	OF	161	610	76	174	26	4	29	97	3	.285
1974	Philadelphia......	OF	85	302	29	82	14	1	7	48	3	.272
1975	Philadelphia......	OF	161	596	85	179	35	3	34	120	3	.300
1976	Philadelphia......	OF	149	533	74	162	28	1	21	95	1	.304
1977	Philadelphia......	OF	149	544	99	171	35	3	39	130	3	.309
1978	Philadelphia......	OF	155	540	85	143	32	2	35	101	8	.265
	Totals..........		1046	3800	527	1101	211	19	186	674	23	.290

STEVE CARLTON 34 6-5 210   Bats L Throws L

Only pitcher in baseball with personal caddy, preferring backup catcher Tim McCarver to catch his games . . . Missed third straight 20-victory season by four games, but still considered Philadelphia's "Mr. Reliable" . . . Shares major league record for strikeouts in a game, 19, with Tom Seaver . . . Born Dec. 22, 1944, in Miami . . . Since joining the

hillies from St. Louis in 1972, he has won 131 games . . . Has
itched three one-hitters . . . Helps himself win games with a
otent bat . . . Won Cy Young Award twice with Phillies (1972
hen he won 27, 1977 when he won 23).

ear	Club	G	IP	W	L	Pct.	SO	BB	H	ERA
965	St. Louis	15	25	0	0	.000	21	8	27	2.52
966	St. Louis	9	52	3	3	.500	25	18	56	3.12
967	St. Louis	30	193	14	9	.609	168	62	173	2.98
968	St. Louis	34	232	13	11	.542	162	61	214	2.99
969	St. Louis	31	236	17	11	.607	210	93	185	2.17
970	St. Louis	34	254	10	19	.345	193	109	239	3.72
971	St. Louis	37	273	20	9	.690	172	98	275	3.56
972	Philadelphia	41	346	27	10	.730	310	87	257	1.98
973	Philadelphia	40	293	13	20	.394	223	113	293	3.90
974	Philadelphia	39	291	16	13	.552	240	136	249	3.22
975	Philadelphia	37	225	15	14	.517	192	104	217	3.56
976	Philadelphia	35	253	20	7	.741	195	72	224	3.13
977	Philadelphia	36	283	23	10	.697	198	89	229	2.64
978	Philadelphia	34	247	16	13	.552	161	63	228	2.84
	Totals	452	3233	207	149	.582	2470	1113	2866	3.04

GARRY MADDOX 29 6-3 175   Bats R Throws R

Patrols center field like a minesweeper; if it's
there, he'll find it and catch it . . . But
dropped fly ball and misplayed another that
allowed Dodgers to win last game of playoffs
. . . Never met an outfielder he couldn't run
on . . . So unhappy in San Francisco he was
hitting .159 when Phils gave up Willie Montanez to get him in 1975 and his average
climbed to .272 . . . Owns .291 career average and hit near that
again in 1978 . . . A Vietnam veteran honored in Washington
n 1977 by No Greater Love Committee as one of four Vietnam
veterans who have distinguished themselves in public life . . .
Born Sept. 1, 1949, in Cincinnati . . . Has won four consecutive
Gold Gloves and twice finished third in the NL in hitting (.319
n 1973 and .330 in 1976).

ear	Club	Pos	G	AB	R	H	2B	3B	HR	RBI	SB	Avg.
972	San Francisco	OF	125	458	62	122	26	7	12	58	13	.266
973	San Francisco	OF	144	587	81	187	30	10	11	76	24	.319
974	San Francisco	OF	135	538	74	153	31	3	8	50	21	.284
975	S.F.-Phil.	OF	116	426	54	116	26	8	5	50	25	.272
976	Philadelphia	OF	146	531	75	175	37	6	6	68	29	.330
977	Philadelphia	OF	139	571	85	167	27	10	14	74	22	.292
978	Philadelphia	OF	155	598	62	172	34	3	11	68	33	.288
	Totals		960	3709	493	1092	211	47	67	444	167	.294

BAKE McBRIDE 30 6-2 190   Bats L Throws R

Always bothered by injuries and 1978 was no exception . . . When healthy, runs swiftly, chases fly balls niftily and hits for average . . . Contact hitter, tough to strike out . . . Born Feb. 3, 1949, in Fulton, Mo. . . . Clocked in 9.8 for the 100 at Westminster (Mo.) College . . . Real name is Arnold Ray McBride, nicknamed "Bake" by his father . . . Ability to get on base several ways, including the bunt, makes him ideal leadoff hitter . . . Was NL Rookie of Year with St. Louis in 1974 with .300 average and 30 steals . . . Came to Philadelphia in mid-1977 in trade with Cardinals for Tommy Underwood, Rick Bosetti and Dane Iorg.

Year	Club	Pos	G	AB	R	H	2B	3B	HR	RBI	SB	Avg
1973	St. Louis	OF	40	63	8	19	3	0	0	5	0	.30
1974	St. Louis	OF	150	559	81	173	19	5	6	56	30	.30
1975	St. Louis	OF	116	413	70	124	10	9	5	36	26	.30
1976	St. Louis	OF	72	272	40	91	13	4	3	24	10	.33
1977	St. L-Phil.	OF	128	402	76	127	25	6	15	61	36	.31
1978	Philadelphia	OF	122	472	68	127	20	4	10	49	28	.26
	Totals		628	2181	343	661	90	28	39	231	130	.30

DICK RUTHVEN 28 6-2 195   Bats R Throws R

Call him "Round Robin Dick" . . . Signed by the Phillies, but traded away, only to return for 1978 and win career-high 15 . . . Was a No. 1 draft choice twice, first by Minnesota, then the next year by Philadelphia . . . Went right from Fresno State College to big leagues . . . Traded twice within three days at 1975 winter meetings, Phillies sending him to White Sox, who dispatched him to Atlanta . . . Born March 27, 1951, in Sacramento . . . In two years with Braves he took part in seven shutouts . . . Pitched four of them himself and was Atlanta's only all-star in 1976 . . . Married to twin sister of big leaguer Tommy Hutton.

Year	Club	G	IP	W	L	Pct.	SO	BB	H	ERA
1973	Philadelphia	25	128	6	9	.400	98	75	125	4.22
1974	Philadelphia	35	213	9	13	.409	153	116	182	4.01
1975	Philadelphia	11	41	2	2	.500	26	22	37	4.17
1976	Atlanta	36	240	14	17	.452	142	90	255	4.20
1977	Atlanta	25	151	7	13	.350	84	62	158	4.23
1978	Atl.-Phil.	33	232	15	11	.577	120	56	214	3.38
	Totals	165	1005	53	65	.449	623	421	971	3.98

'UG McGRAW 34 6-0 185   Bats R Throws L

Self-proclaimed "Screwball," acts like one and throws one . . . Talks in a language of his own but sportswriters love it . . . Trademark is slapping glove on his thigh as he leaves the mound after baffling another hitter with a screwball . . . Popular in New York where he played on 1969 and 1973 World Series teams with Mets . . . Born Aug. 30, 944, in Martinez, Cal. . . . Writes weekly syndicated newspaer column during season and not afraid to criticize teammates . . Real name is Frank Edwin, but picked up nickname beause he was always tugging on things as a child . . . Brother, lank, was catcher-outfielder in four different NL organizations.

ear	Club	G	IP	W	L	Pct.	SO	BB	H	ERA
965	New York (N.L.)	37	98	2	7	.222	57	48	88	3.31
966	New York (N.L.)	15	62	2	9	.182	34	25	72	5.37
967	New York (N.L.)	4	17	0	3	.000	18	13	13	7.94
969	New York (N.L.)	42	100	9	3	.750	92	47	89	2.25
970	New York (N.L.)	57	91	4	6	.400	81	49	77	3.26
971	New York (N.L.)	51	111	11	4	.733	109	41	73	1.70
972	New York (N.L.)	54	106	8	6	.571	92	40	71	1.70
973	New York (N.L.)	60	119	5	6	.455	81	55	106	3.86
974	New York (N.L.)	41	89	6	11	.353	54	32	96	4.15
975	Philadelphia	56	103	9	6	.600	55	36	84	2.97
976	Philadelphia	58	97	7	6	.538	76	42	81	2.51
977	Philadelphia	45	79	7	3	.700	58	24	62	2.62
978	Philadelphia	55	90	8	7	.533	63	23	82	3.20
	Totals	575	1162	78	77	.503	870	475	994	3.06

ETE ROSE 37 5-11 200   Bats S Throws R

Baseball's most newsworthy character during the season . . . Reached 3,000 career hits with single off Montreal's Steve Rogers on May 5 . . . Turned the nation into Pete Rose fans by embarking on incredible 44-game hitting streak, setting a modern National League record and tying Wee Willie Keeler's all-time NL record set in 1897 . . . Then, he played out option with Reds and hit the road as a traveling salesman –selling himself . . . Hit jackpot with Phillies, getting $3.2 million for four years . . . After all, he offered 13 seasons over 300 and a devil-may-care playing style that earned him the nickname of "Charlie Hustle" . . . Missed setting all-time record of 10 seasons of 200 or more hits when he finished with 198, the Reds losing one game to rain . . . Born April 14, 1941, in Cincinnati . . . Now the man who plays the child's game like a kid leaves home for the first time.

Year	Club	Pos	G	AB	R	H	2B	3B	HR	RBI	SB	Avg
1963	Cincinnati	2B-OF	157	623	101	170	25	9	6	41	13	.27
1964	Cincinnati	2B	136	516	64	139	13	2	4	34	4	.26
1965	Cincinnati	2B	162	670	117	209	35	11	11	81	8	.31
1966	Cincinnati	2B-3B	156	654	97	205	38	5	16	70	4	.31
1967	Cincinnati	OF-2B	148	585	86	176	32	8	12	76	11	.30
1968	Cincinnati	OF-2B-1B	149	626	94	210	42	6	10	49	3	.33
1969	Cincinnati	OF-2B	156	627	120	218	33	11	16	82	7	.34
1970	Cincinnati	OF	159	649	120	205	37	9	15	52	12	.31
1971	Cincinnati	OF	160	632	86	192	27	4	13	44	13	.30
1972	Cincinnati	OF	154	645	107	198	31	11	6	57	10	.30
1973	Cincinnati	OF	160	680	115	230	36	8	5	64	10	.33
1974	Cincinnati	OF	163	652	110	185	45	7	3	51	2	.28
1975	Cincinnati	3B-OF	162	662	112	210	47	4	7	74	0	.31
1976	Cincinnati	3B-OF	162	665	130	215	42	6	10	63	9	.32
1977	Cincinnati	3B	655	95	204	38	7	9	64	16	.31	
1978	Cincinnati	3B	159	655	103	198	51	3	7	52	13	.30
	Totals		2505	10196	1657	3164	572	111	150	954	135	.31

LARRY CHRISTENSON 25 6-2 210   Bats R Throws R

Though he is now 25, still carries same baby-face appearance he had the day he was 19 and beat the Mets in his first major league start in 1973 . . . Phils' No. 1 draft selection in 1972 because of a live fast ball but can help with the bat, too . . . Owns grand slam homer . . . Born Nov. 10, 1953, in Everett, Wash. . . . Has won 56 games in last four seasons, losing only 34 . . . Was unhittable at the end of 1977, winning 15 of last 16 decisions, including the division-clincher . . . Owns two two-hitters . . . Golf and basketball fanatic.

Year	Club	G	IP	W	L	Pct.	SO	BB	H	ERA
1973	Philadelphia	10	34	1	4	.200	11	20	53	6.62
1974	Philadelphia	10	23	1	1	.500	18	15	20	4.30
1975	Philadelphia	29	172	11	6	.647	88	45	149	3.66
1976	Philadelphia	32	169	13	8	.619	54	42	199	3.67
1977	Philadelphia	34	219	19	6	.760	118	69	229	4.07
1978	Philadelphia	33	228	13	14	.482	131	47	209	3.24
	Totals	148	845	58	39	.598	420	238	859	3.79

BOB BOONE 31 6-2 208   Bats R Throws R

Even though Steve Carlton prefers pitching to backup catcher Tim McCarver, he is an all-star catcher . . . Enjoyed second straight season hitting above .280 and over 10 homers . . . Astute, no-nonsense guy who serves as NL player representative . . . Father Ray played shortstop 12 years in majors and wore uniform No. 8 like his son . . . Father was originally a catcher converted to an infielder, Bob was an infielder converted to a catcher . . . Born Nov. 19, 1947, in San Diego . . . Led NL in catching assists in 1973 rookie season with 89 . . . Loves racquetball and supervised construction of own courts in South Jersey.

Year	Club	Pos	G	AB	R	H	2B	3B	HR	RBI	SB	Avg.
1972	Philadelphia......	C	16	51	4	14	1	0	1	4	1	.275
1973	Philadelphia......	C	145	521	42	136	20	2	10	61	3	.261
1974	Philadelphia......	C	146	488	41	118	24	3	3	52	3	.242
1975	Philadelphia......	C-3B	97	289	28	71	14	2	2	20	1	.246
1976	Philadelphia......	C	121	361	40	98	18	2	4	54	2	.271
1977	Philadelphia......	C	132	440	55	125	26	4	11	66	5	.284
1978	Philadelphia......	C	132	435	48	123	18	4	12	62	2	.283
	Totals..........		789	2585	258	685	121	17	43	319	17	.265

TOP PROSPECT

OSSIE VIRGIL JR. 22 6-1 195   **Bats R Throws R**
Famous name—son of Montreal coach of the same name who played on five different teams from 1956 through 1966 as an infielder . . . Ossie Jr. is a catcher and sixth round draft pick in the June, 1976, free agent draft . . . Born Dec. 7, 1956, in Mayaguez, Puerto Rico, raised in Glendale, Ariz. . . . Batted .303 with 29 homers, 98 runs batted in in 126 games at Class A Peninsula in 1978 . . . Strong arm and strong bat, plus possesses rare commodity for a catcher—he can run.

MANAGER DANNY OZARK: Should play tough-guy part in movies, but his tough, no-nonsense stance is no act . . . Has won three straight NL East titles, but fickle Philly fans are restless, saying he should do better after his teams lost three straight playoffs to Cincinnati and Los Angeles . . . Spent 31 years in Dodger organization, 17 of them unsuccessfully trying to make the majors as a player . . . Finally went to Philadelphia in 1973 to replace Frank Lucchesi and is the National League's senior manager in terms of longevity . . . Born Nov. 26, 1923, in Buffalo . . . Was signed by the Dodgers in Dec. 1941, by Heinie Groh as a second baseman, but switched to first base and played in 10 different minor league towns . . . Known for his running battles with Philadelphia writers and his ability to mix metaphors and use malaprops.

GREATEST PITCHER

Pitching lore is rich with the Philadelphia Phillies.

Robin Roberts, Steve Carlton, Grover Cleveland Alexander.

Roberts owns the most career victories for the Phillies, 234. He pitched in Philadelphia 14 years—winning 20, 21, 28, 23, 23 and 23 in one six-year stretch.

Still active, Carlton owns 130 Philadelphia victories in seven years, with 27, 20 and 23-victory seasons to his credit.

All very nice.

But the legend is Grover Cleveland Alexander, who won 190 games in seven incredible seasons (1911-1917), an average of 27 victories a season. Then, he went on to win 128 more games with the Cubs and 55 for the Cardinals.

Ol' Grover was 31-10, 33-12 and 30-13 in 1915-16-17, completing an unbelievable 38 games in 1916, a year during which he pitched 399 innings, a club record.

Although Roberts pitched almost 1,200 more innings for the Phils than Alexander, Grover pitched 61 shutouts to 35 for Roberts.

Truly, Grover Cleveland Alexander is the Phillies' all-time master.

ALL-TIME PHILLIE LEADERS

BATTING: Frank O'Doul, .398, 1929
HRs: Chuck Klein, 43, 1929
RBIs: Chuck Klein, 170, 1930
STEALS: Sherry Magee, 55, 1906
WINS: Grover Alexander, 33, 1916
STRIKEOUTS: Steve Carlton, 310, 1972

PITTSBURGH PIRATES

TEAM DIRECTORY: Chairman: John Galbreath; Pres.: Daniel Galbreath; VP-Player Personnel: Harding Peterson; VP-Business Administration: Joseph O'Toole; Minor Leagues/Scouting: Murray Cook; Trav. Sec.: Charlie Muse; Pub. Rel.: Bill Guilfoile; Mgr.: Chuck Tanner. Home: Three Rivers stadium (50,364). Field distances: 335, l.f. line; 400, c.f.; 335, r.f. line. Spring training: Bradenton, Fla.

Broken cheekbone couldn't keep Dave Parker from MVP.

SCOUTING REPORT

HITTING: The Pirates take a walk grudgingly. They're up there to hit, and hit hard, which they do often. The Pirates not only hit for distance, they hit for average. And, what they don't get with their bats, they get with their larcenous feet. Rennie Stennett, Frank Taveras and Omar Moreno ping the opposition to death with singles and stolen bases, then Dave Parker, Willie Stargell and Bill Robinson plaster foes with the long ball.

Of course, Parker does it both, winning his second straight batting title with a .334 average, 18 points ahead of closest pursuer, LA's Steve Garvey. And, Parker mixed in 30 home runs and 117 RBIs. As if those weren't enough for an MVP title, he swiped 20 bases to totally epitomize the Pirate offense.

Parker can't make up his mind if he wants to hit for average or be a slugger, so he is doing both rather well. Robinson, one of baseball's unappreciated talents, bounces around between outfield, third base and first base, always producing with the bat, most often when it's needed. Pirates seldom are hurting for runs.

PITCHING: As usual, the Bucs were as inept afield as they are adept at bat. Defense is a bother, a nuisance they perform to get to bat again. The Pirates were last in National League fielding (.973) with 167 errors. They don't give Gold Gloves in Pittsburgh, they give Iron Gloves . . . and the Pirates use them. Frank Taveras at short and Rennie Stennett at second are a good doubleplay combination, but the Pirates are historically weak at the corners.

Parker needn't apologize to any outfielder for impersonating a defender. His speed enables him to chase down balls in the gap, his height enables him to go high up the right field wall, and his arm produces bullet throws. But, he did make a league-high 13 errors, most with errant throws attempting to gun down daring base runners. He also had 12 assists and participated in three double plays—one behind league-leader Reggie Smith's four. Defense is Pittsburgh's Achilles heel and hasn't improved, making it doubtful the hitting can overtake the defensive mistakes . . . and that's why the Pirates won't catch the Phillies.

FIELDING: On paper, Pittsburgh's pitching seems good. But paper can't throw strikes. Bert Blyleven, John Candelaria, Jerry Reuss and Jim Rooker all were off past performances. History says all should do better in '79.

The bullpen was overused last season and Kent Tekulve, "His Royal Skinniness," responded adeptly, as did Grant Jackson. Bruce Kison was another subpar actor, though. The main bright spot was rookie Don Robinson's 14-6 record.

OUTLOOK: The Pirates are more than overstuffed with proper hitting and blessed with outstanding speed and base-stealing ability, which manager Chuck Tanner uses to the utmost. The bullpen is in the good right hand of Tekulve, but he could use help. The starters should revert to better form, but what the pitchers don't give up, the defense probably will. The Pirates haven't done enough improving to catch Philadelphia.

PITTSBURGH PIRATES 1979 ROSTER

MANAGER Chuck Tanner
Coaches—Joe Lonnett, Al Monchak, Don Osborn, Bob Skinner

PITCHERS

No.	Name	1978 Club	W-L	IP	SO	ERA	B-T	Ht.	Wt.	Born
26	Bibby, Jim	Pittsburgh	8-7	107	72	3.53	R-R	6-5	250	10/10/44 Franklinton, NC
22	Blyleven, Bert	Pittsburgh	14-10	244	182	3.02	R-R	6-3	207	4/6/51 Holland
—	Breining, Fred	Columbus	2-2	55	34	6.38	R-R	6-3	180	11/15/55 San Francisco, CA
		Shreveport	3-6	56	–	3.67				
45	Candelaria, John	Pittsburgh	12-11	189	94	3.24	L-L	6-7	215	11/6/53 New York, NY
—	Holland, Al	Columbus	8-5	91	65	5.36	R-L	5011	213	8/16/52 Roanoke, VA
23	Jackson, Grant	Pittsburgh	7-5	77	45	3.27	L-L	6-0	204	9/28/42 Fostoria, OH
—	Jones, Rick	San Jose	7-8	135	85	3.87	L-L	6-5	195	4/16/56 Jacksonville, FL
		Seattle	0-2	12	11	6.00				
25	Kison, Bruce	Pittsburgh	6-6	96	62	3.19	R-R	6-4	173	2/18/50 Pasco, WA
—	Pentz, Gene	Houston	0-0	15	8	6.00	R-R	6-0	215	6/21/53 Johnstown, PA
—	Perez, Pascual	Salem	11-7	152	–	2.61	R-R	6-2	162	– Dominican Republic
		Columbus	0-0	5	–	0.00				
41	Reuss, Jerry	Pittsburgh	3-2	83	42	4.88	L-L	6-5	217	6/19/49 St. Louis, MO
43	Robinson, Don	Pittsburgh	14-6	228	135	3.47	R-R	6-4	225	6/8/57 Ashland, KY
—	Romo, Enrique	Seattle	11-7	107	62	3.70	R-R	5-11	185	7/15/57 Mexico
19	Rooker, Jim	Pittsburgh	9-11	163	76	4.25	R-L	6-0	193	9/23/42 Lakeview, OR
—	Scurry, Rod	Columbus	3-3	63	57	5.71	L-L	6-2	180	3/17/56 Sacramento, CA
		Shreveport	1-4	29	–	4.71				
27	Tekulve, Kent	Pittsburgh	8-7	135	77	2.33	R-R	6-4	167	3/5/47 Cincinnati, OH
31	Whitson, Ed	Columbus	2-2	51	55	3.71	R-R	6-3	190	5/19/55 Johnson City, TX
		Pittsburgh	5-6	74	64	3.28				

CATCHERS

No.	Name	1978 Club	H	HR	RBI	Pct.	B-T	Ht.	Wt.	Born
—	Nicosia, Steve	Columbus	118	12	74	.322	R-R	5-10	185	8/6/55 Paterson, NJ
		Pittsburgh	0	0	0	.000				
14	Ott, Ed	Pittsburgh	102	9	38	.269	L-R	5-10	190	7/11/51 Muncy, PA
—	Pena, Tony	Shreveport	–	8	42	.230	R-R	6-0	175	– Dominican Republic
—	Saferight, Harry	Columbus	84	9	50	.247	L-R	6-0	190	– Richmond, VA
35	Sanguillen, Manny	Pittsburgh	58	3	16	.264	R-R	6-0	193	3/21/44 Panama

INFIELDERS

No.	Name	1978 Club	H	HR	RBI	Pct.	B-T	Ht.	Wt.	Born
—	Berra, Dale	Columbus	–	18	63	.280	R-R	6-0	190	12/13/56 Ridgewood, NJ
		Pittsburgh	28	6	14	.207				
—	Boyland, Dorian	Columbus	118	12	61	.291	L-L	6-4	204	– Chicago, IL
		Pittsburgh	2	0	1	.250				
3	Garner, Phil	Pittsburgh	138	10	66	.261	R-R	5-10	177	4/30/50 Jefferson, City, TN
—	Hargis, Gary	Columbus	105	10	45	.283	R-R	5-11	160	11/2/56 Minneapolis, MN
8	Stargell, Willie	Pittsburgh	115	28	97	.295	L-L	6-2	228	3/6/41 Earlsboro, OK
6	Stennett, Rennie	Pittsburgh	81	3	35	.243	R-R	5-11	175	4/5/51 Panama
10	Taveras, Frank	Pittsburgh	182	0	38	.278	R-R	6-0	170	12/24/50 Dominican Republic

OUTFIELDERS

No.	Name	1978 Club	H	HR	RBI	Pct.	B-T	Ht.	Wt.	Born
—	Cotes, Eugenia	Shreveport	–	13	67	.280	R-R	5-11	162	– Dominican Republic
		Columbus	–	0	4	.278				
—	Littleton, Larry	Shreveport	–	19	76	.264	R-R	6-1	186	– Atlanta, GA
—	Lois, Alberto	Columbus	46	6	20	.254	R-R	5-9	160	5/6/56 Dominican Republic
		Salem	–	1	11	.284				
		Pittsburgh	1	0	0	.250				
16	Milner, John	Pittsburgh	80	6	38	.271	L-L	6-0	183	12/28/49 Fort Wayne, IN
18	Moreno, Omar	Pittsburgh	121	2	33	.235	L-L	6-3	175	10/24/52 Panama
39	Parker, Dave	Pittsburgh	194	30	117	.334	R-L	6-5	220	6/9/51 Cincinnati, OH
28	Robinson, Bill	Pittsburgh	123	14	80	.246	R-R	6-3	200	6/26/43 Elizabeth, PA

PIRATE PROFILES

WILLIE STARGELL 38 6-2 228　　　　　**Bats L Throws L**

Plays less, hits as well as ever and as far as ever . . . Mr. Pittsburgh, even though he modestly claims Dave Parker is now in command of the Pirate ship . . . Entering 17th season with Pirates after signing with club as a free agent on Aug. 7, 1958 . . . Extremely active in national fight against sickle cell anemia . . . Born Wilver Dornell Stargell on March 6, 1941, in Earlsboro, Okla. . . . Has won practically every award presented to baseball players for character—Roberto Clemente Award, Brian Piccolo-YMCA Award, Lou Gehrig Award, Arthur J. Rooney Award, Ernie Mehl Award . . . Totally awesome man on and off the field . . . All-time Pirate home run leader and 17th player in baseball history with 400 or more . . . Holds NL record of four extra-base hits in four different games.

Year	Club	Pos	G	AB	R	H	2B	3B	HR	RBI	SB	Avg.
1962	Pittsburgh	OF	10	31	1	9	3	1	0	4	0	.290
1963	Pittsburgh	OF-1B	108	304	34	74	11	6	11	47	0	.243
1964	Pittsburgh	OF-1B	117	421	53	115	19	7	21	78	1	.273
1965	Pittsburgh	OF-1B	144	533	68	145	25	8	27	107	1	.272
1966	Pittsburgh	OF-1B	140	485	84	153	30	0	33	102	2	.315
1967	Pittsburgh	OF-1B	134	462	54	125	18	6	20	73	1	.271
1968	Pittsburgh	OF-1B	128	435	57	103	15	1	24	67	5	.237
1969	Pittsburgh	OF-1B	145	522	89	160	31	6	29	92	1	.307
1970	Pittsburgh	OF-1B	136	474	70	125	18	3	31	85	0	.264
1971	Pittsburgh	OF	141	511	104	151	26	0	48	125	0	.295
1972	Pittsburgh	1B-OF	138	495	75	145	28	2	33	112	1	.293
1973	Pittsburgh	OF	148	522	106	156	43	3	44	119	0	.299
1974	Pittsburgh	OF	140	508	90	153	37	4	25	96	0	.301
1975	Pittsburgh	1B	124	461	71	136	32	2	22	90	0	.295
1976	Pittsburgh	1B	117	428	54	110	20	3	20	65	2	.257
1977	Pittsburgh	1B	63	186	29	51	12	0	13	35	0	.274
1978	Pittsburgh	1B	122	390	60	115	18	2	28	97	3	.295
	Totals		2055	7168	1099	2026	386	54	429	1394	17	.283

DAVE PARKER 27 6-5 220　　　　　**Bats L Throws R**

The supreme compliment: A young Willie Stargell . . . Even though he altered his swing to get more loft and hit more homers, still won second straight NL batting title, tacked nine more homers to his 1977 total and drove in 29 more runs than in '77 . . . And was NL MVP . . . Called "The Cobra," and opposing pitchers know why . . . Converted from pitcher, but still uses arm to obliterate the few base-runners who test it . . . Born June 9, 1951, in Cincinnati . . . A nine-letter winner at Cincinnati Courter Tech in baseball, football and basketball and could have starred in any sport in college, but signed after Pirates drafted him 14th in June, 1970, free agent draft . . . Line drive doubles and tape measure homers his specialty.

Year	Club	Pos	G	AB	R	H	2B	3B	HR	RBI - SB	Avg.
1973	Pittsburgh	OF	54	139	17	40	9	1	4	14	1	.288
1974	Pittsburgh	OF-1B	73	220	27	62	10	3	4	29	3	.282
1975	Pittsburgh	OF	148	558	75	172	35	10	25	101	8	.308
1976	Pittsburgh	OF	138	537	82	168	28	10	13	90	19	.313
1977	Pittsburgh	OF-2B	159	637	107	215	44	8	21	88	17	.338
1978	Pittsburgh	OF	148	581	102	194	32	12	30	117	20	.334
	Totals..........		720	2672	410	851	158	44	97	439	68	.318

KENT TEKULVE 32 6-4 167　　　　Bats R Throws R

So skinny, when he stands on the mound he looks like a center field foul pole . . . Physique doesn't stop manager Chuck Tanner from using him over and over, good for 31 saves, second behind Rollie Fingers in NL . . . "He gets mad at me if I skip him a day," says Tanner . . . Whippy sidearm fastball brutal on right-handed hitters . . . Born Mar. 5, 1947, in Cincinnati . . . Set club record in 1977 by appearing in 72 games . . . "Teke" has won 23 games, all in relief, in past three seasons . . . Was cut from high school team at Hamilton (O.) Catholic High School, but made the team at Marietta (O.) College and led it in strikeouts four straight years.

Year	Club	G	IP	W	L	Pct.	SO	BB	H	ERA
1974	Pittsburgh	8	9	1	1	.500	6	5	12	6.00
1975	Pittsburgh	34	56	1	2	.333	28	23	43	2.25
1976	Pittsburgh	64	103	5	3	.625	68	25	91	2.45
1977	Pittsburgh	72	103	10	1	.909	59	33	89	3.06
1978	Pittsburgh	91	135	8	7	.533	77	55	115	2.33
	Totals..................	269	406	25	14	.641	238	141	350	2.62

FRANK TAVERAS 28 6-0 170　　　　Bats R Throws R

Stole 17 bases in 1975, then was tutored over winter by Maury Wills and swiped 58, 70 and 46 next three seasons on thieving Pirate team . . . Stealing total was down but batting average was career high by 20 points . . . Born Frank Fabian Taveras on Dec. 24, 1950, in Villa Vasquez, Dominican Republic . . . Once stole 27 straight bases until he was obliterated on a pitchout . . . Was 70 of 88 in stolen bases in 1977, but slipped to 46 of 72 in 1978 . . . Defense at shortstop needs work, but he is trying to improve . . . His only major league home run was an inside-the-park grand slam and teammate Willie Stargell faked passing out in the dugout at his display of power.

Year	Club	Pos	G	AB	R	H	2B	3B	HR	RBI	SB	Avg.
1971	Pittsburgh	PR	1	0	0	0	0	0	0	0	0	.000
1972	Pittsburgh	SS	4	3	0	0	0	0	0	0	0	.000
1974	Pittsburgh	SS	126	333	33	82	4	2	0	26	13	.246
1975	Pittsburgh	SS	134	378	44	80	9	4	0	23	17	.212
1976	Pittsburgh	SS	144	519	76	134	8	6	0	24	58	.258
1977	Pittsburgh	SS	147	544	72	137	20	10	1	29	70	.252
1978	Pittsburgh	SS	157	654	81	182	31	9	0	38	46	.278
	Totals		713	2431	306	615	72	31	1	140	204	.253

OMAR MORENO 26 6-3 175   Bats L Throws L

No tentmaker, this guy, just a runmaker . . . Frank Taveras held the Pirate stolen base record one year, then watched Omar Renan Moreno run to 71 thefts in 92 attempts in 1978 . . . Stole 53 in 1977 after swiping 15 in only 48 games in '76, giving him 140 in less than three seasons . . . Instantaneous acceleration and long, slender legs enable him to seemingly outrun baseballs on the basepaths and in center field . . . Born Oct. 24, 1952, in Puerto Armuelles, Panama . . . Adept bunter, but hasn't hit for average or could easily steal 100 . . . Theft total rose in 1978 because bases on balls doubled from 38 to 79 . . . Like Taveras, Moreno was tutored by Maury Wills in winter ball.

Year	Club	Pos	G	AB	R	H	2B	3B	HR	RBI	SB	Avg.
1975	Pittsburgh	OF	6	6	1	1	0	0	0	0	1	.167
1976	Pittsburgh	OF	48	122	24	33	4	1	2	12	15	.270
1977	Pittsburgh	OF	150	492	69	118	19	9	7	34	53	.240
1978	Pittsburgh	OF	155	515	95	121	15	7	2	33	71	.235
	Totals		359	1135	189	273	38	17	11	79	140	.241

DON ROBINSON 21 6-4 225   Bats R Throws R

Rookie makes good . . . After winning 22 games in little more than two minor league seasons, he stuck with the Pirates in 1978, despite no major league experience, and tied Bert Blyleven for most victories on the season . . . Sizzling fastball enabled him to get non-roster invite to spring training in 1977 after he was Pirate's second pick in June, 1975,

ee agent draft . . . Born June 8, 1957, in Ashland, Ky. . . .
alks-strikeouts ratio, 57 to 134, unusually good for rookie . . .
itched only one game in Triple-A for Columbus and threw a
ve-inning shutout for a victory.

ar	Club	G	IP	W	L	Pct.	SO	BB	H	ERA
78	Pittsburgh	35	228	14	6	.700	135	57	203	3.47

LL ROBINSON 35 6-3 200   Bats R Throws R

Never counted upon, always produces . . .
Plays wherever needed—third base, first base,
any outfield position and never embarrasses
himself . . . Always billed as "The Next
Somebody," the next Hank Aaron when he
played for Atlanta and the next Mickey
Mantle when he played for Yankees, but only
wanted to be himself . . . Born June 26, 1943
a Elizabeth, Pa. . . . Big day was June 5, 1976, against San
Diego—three homers, four-for-eight and 13 total bases . . . De-
pite seldom playing regularly anywhere, owns 121 career
omers and 489 RBIs . . . Very personable and a new-born
Christian.

ear	Club	Pos	G	AB	R	H	2B	3B	HR	RBI	SB	Avg.
966	Atlanta	OF	6	11	1	3	0	1	0	3	0	.273
967	New York (AL)	OF	116	342	31	67	6	1	7	29	2	.196
968	New York (AL)	OF	107	342	34	82	16	7	6	40	7	.240
969	New York (AL)	OF-1B	87	222	23	38	11	2	3	21	3	.171
972	Philadelphia	OF	82	188	19	45	9	1	8	21	2	.239
973	Philadelphia	3B-OF	124	452	62	130	32	1	25	65	5	.288
974	Philadelphia	OF	100	280	32	66	14	1	5	29	5	.236
975	Pittsburgh	OF	92	200	26	56	12	2	6	33	3	.280
976	Pittsburgh	OF-3B-1B	122	393	55	119	22	3	21	64	2	.303
977	Pittsburgh	1B-OF-3B	137	507	74	154	32	1	26	104	12	.304
978	Pittsburgh	1B-OF-3B	136	499	70	123	36	2	14	80	14	.246
	Totals		1109	3436	427	883	190	22	121	489	55	.257

ERT BLYLEVEN 28 6-3   Bats R Throws R

Always in double figures in victories, but
never seems to reach the potential of his
pitches . . . Tied Don Robinson in club victories, 14, about his average for nine years in
the majors . . . Perplexing case because hitters swear his stuff is almost unhittable, but
he is barely over .500 for his career at 136-123
. . . Born Rik Aalbert Blyleven in Zeist, Hol-
and, April 6, 1951, but grew up in California . . . Pitched
o-hitter Sept. 22, 1977, facing one hitter over the minimum
. . . Has won 12 1-0 games, a feat matched by only eight
itchers in baseball history, none active . . . After Minnesota

traded him to Texas on June 1, 1976, his first two games wer
1-0 victories over Oakland in 10 innings, a one-hitter, and ove
Chicago in 10 innings.

Year	Club	G	IP	W	L	Pct.	SO	BB	H	E
1970	Minnesota	27	164	10	9	.526	135	47	143	3.
1971	Minnesota	38	278	16	15	.516	224	59	267	2.
1972	Minnesota	39	287	17	17	.500	228	69	247	2.
1973	Minnesota	40	325	20	17	.541	258	67	296	2.
1974	Minnesota	37	281	17	17	.500	249	77	244	2.
1975	Minnesota	35	276	15	10	.600	233	84	219	3.
1976	Minnesota-Tex.	36	298	13	16	.448	219	81	283	2.
1977	Texas	30	235	14	12	.538	182	69	181	2.
1978	Pittsburgh	34	244	14	10	.583	182	66	217	3.
	Totals	316	2388	136	123	.525	1910	619	2097	2.

JOHN CANDELARIA 25 6-7 215   Bats L Throws

The "Candy Man" was bothered by injurie
throughout 1978, sinking to 12-11 after 2
and 16-victory seasons the previous two year
. . . Owns 56 major league victories and onl
29 defeats despite young age . . . Mad
splash rookie season when he struck out 1
Reds in 1975 playoffs . . . Threw a no-hitte
against Dodgers on Aug. 8, 1976, first Pirat
to do it in Pittsburgh since 1907 . . . Born Nov. 6, 1953, in New
York City . . . Became embroiled in media squabble in mid
season and refused to talk to the press . . . Didn't play high
school baseball because school dropped program but is second
on New York Catholic high school all-time rebounding list t
Lew Alcindor, now Kareem Abdul-Jabbar . . . Was invited t
play for Puerto Rican Olympic basketball team (his parents ar
from Puerto Rico) but signed with Pirates after June, 1972, fre
agent draft as club's second selection.

Year	Club	G	IP	W	L	Pct.	SO	BB	H	ER
1975	Pittsburgh	18	121	8	6	.571	95	36	95	2.7
1976	Pittsburgh	32	220	16	7	.696	138	60	173	3.1
1977	Pittsburgh	33	231	20	5	.800	133	50	197	2.3
1978	Pittsburgh	30	189	12	11	.522	94	49	191	3.2
	Totals	113	761	56	29	.659	460	195	656	2.8

ENRIQUE ROMO 31 5-11 185   Bats R Throws R

"Call me 'Henry' " . . . Emerged as one o
the best right-handed relievers in AL . .
Led Seattle in victories . . . Spent 11 years i
oblivion of Mexican League before Mariner
bought him for $75,000 and brought him t
big leagues . . . Born July 15, 1947, in Santa
Rosalia, Mexico . . . Came to Bucs in winte
trade . . . A starting pitcher in Mexico, con

rted to relief because Mariners needed help there . . . Made
am in spring training 1977 even though he wasn't on the
ajor league roster.

r	Club	G	IP	W	L	Pct.	SO	BB	H	ERA
7	Seattle	58	114	8	10	.444	105	39	93	2.84
8	Seattle	56	107	11	7	.611	62	39	88	3.70
	Totals	114	221	19	17	.528	167	78	181	3.26

ENNIE STENNETT 28 5-11 175   Bats R Throws R

Victim of injuries . . . After finishing second
to Dave Parker in NL batting title chase in
1977, fell 40 points below career average in
1978 . . . One of many Pirates with base
thievery always on his mind, also fields well
. . . Fell eight chances short of all-time
record in 1974 when he completed 410 plays
without an error, a record for second base-
en held by Chicago's Ken Hubbs . . . Born April 5, 1951, in
olon, Panama . . . Set modern record in 1975 when he went
even-for-seven, first man to do it since 1892 . . . Had two hits
an inning twice in that game, tying major league record, and
ored five runs . . . Put together an 18-game hitting streak his
okie season (1971) when he was 20.

ar	Club	Pos	G	AB	R	H	2B	3B	HR	RBI	SB	Avg.
71	Pittsburgh	2B	50	153	24	54	5	4	1	15	1	.353
72	Pittsburgh	2B-OF-SS	109	370	43	106	14	5	3	30	4	.286
73	Pittsburgh	2B-OF-SS	128	466	45	113	18	3	10	55	2	.242
74	Pittsburgh	2B-OF	157	673	84	196	29	3	7	56	8	.291
75	Pittsburgh	2B	148	616	89	176	25	7	7	62	5	.286
76	Pittsburgh	2B-SS	157	654	59	168	31	9	2	60	18	.257
77	Pittsburgh	2B	116	453	53	152	20	4	5	51	28	.336
78	Pittsburgh	2B	106	333	30	81	9	2	3	35	2	.243
	Totals		971	3718	427	1046	151	37	38	364	68	.281

OP PROSPECT

DORIAN BOYLAND 24 6-4 204   Bats L Throws L

Willie Stargell's replacement? . . . He's big enough and strong
nough, but must cut down strikeouts, a Stargell specialty . . .
Hit .291 for Columbus in Triple A in 1978, with 12 homers and
1 RBIs in 113 games . . . Born Jan. 6, 1955, in Chicago and
vas Pittsburgh's second pick in June, 1976, free agent draft . . .
Hit .330 at Shreveport in 1977 with 11 homers and 60 RBIs, but
truck out 107 times in 119 games while walking only 26 times.

MANAGER CHUCK TANNER: Became Pittsburgh managvia trade . . . Pirates wanted him from Oak land, so Charlie Finley demanded, an received, catcher Manny Sanguillen plu $100,000 to give Tanner his release to sig with Pittsburgh . . . Managed seven seaso in American League at Chicago and Oaklan . . . Began undistinguished major leagu career of 396 games by homering on the fir big league pitch he saw . . . Born July 4, 1929, in New Castl Pa., 60 miles from Pittsburgh's Three Rivers Stadium and ha the optimism and enthusiasm a guy born on the Fourth of Jul should have . . . His 1978 team got off to a miserable start an languished low for three-fourths of the season, but he promise his team would be in the race before it ended and he was rigl . . . Phillies put the Pirates away in the final series of th season.

GREATEST PITCHER

Wilbur Cooper or Bob Friend? You pick it.

Cooper pitched 13 years for the Pirates, from 1912 to 192 and the 175-pound lefty was 202-159. Friend pitched 15 yea for the Pirates from 1951 to 1965 and the 190-pound righ hander was 191-218.

Both names are prominent in the Buc record books.

Cooper is the all-time leader in games started for a lefty, 46 while Friend is the all-time leader period, 477. Cooper owns th Pirates' complete-game record with 263, but relief pitchin wasn't the art it is now, or in Friend's day when he had Elro Face to clean up for him.

Friend is Pittsburgh's strikeout leader with 1,682, but ha only one 20-victory season, a 22-14 mark in 1958, though h won 13 or more games in nine of 10 seasons from '55 throug '64. Cooper won 20 or more four times and twice won 19.

Okay, let's make Coop the all-time lefty and Friend the all time righty.

ALL-TIME PIRATE LEADERS

BATTING: Arky Vaughan, .385, 1935
HRs: Ralph Kiner, 54, 1949
RBIs: Paul Waner, 131, 1927
STEALS: Omar Moreno, 71, 1978
WINS: Jack Chesbro, 28, 1902
STRIKEOUTS: Bob Veale, 276, 1965

ONTREAL EXPOS

AM DIRECTORY: Chairman of the Board: Charles Bronf-
n; Pres.-GM: John McHale; Asst. to Pres.: Danny Menen-
:; VP-Player Development and Scouting: Jim Fanning;
-Marketing: Roger Landry; VP-Sec.-Treas.: Harry Renaud;
s. Pub. Rel.: Richard Griffin, M. Giroux; Trav. Sec.: Gene
by; Mgr.: Dick Williams. Home: Olympic Stadium (60,476).
ld distances: 325. l.f.; 404, c.f.; 325, r.f. Spring training:
ytona Beach, Fla.

COUTING REPORT

TTING: The Expos have put together a batting order to
tch the awesomeness of the massive concrete edifice in which
y play their games. With Warren Cromartie, Ellis Valentine
d Andre Dawson, there is no room in the outfield for inter-
ers.

Valentine hits for both average and power, Dawson matches
lentine's home run bat—25 each last season—but Andre
esn't hit as steadily for average. Cromartie just missed .300.
d, the most important item . . . one can count on seeing

Ross Grimsley became Expos' first 20-game winner ever.

Cromartie, Dawson and Valentine in the lineup daily. Crom
tie played 159 games, Dawson 157 and Valentine 151.

There's no letup elsewhere, either—not with Dave Ca
steady Tony Perez and Gary Carter in the lineup. Cash is o
of baseball's best leadoff men, a guy with an electric eye. Pe
is one of baseball's consistent clutch RBI men. Carter suffer
an off-season, hitting only .255, but still hit 20 homers a
drove in 72 runs. Just when pitchers think most of the mayhe
is over, Chris Speier and Larry Parrish have nasty habits
breaking up a game here and there.

PITCHING: Does Bill Lee have any French phrases bounci
around his "Spaceman" mind? Lee should make a strong pitc
ing staff extra-strong, especially from the left side where t
Expos already had Ross Grimsley and Rudy May.

And, that's without even mentioning right-hander Steve Ro
ers, only one of baseball's best pitchers. With Lee and Grimsl
on the same staff—two resident flakes—pitching coach Ji
Brewer is in for a fun season.

There are some other names mixed in to make the Expo
staff prodigious . . . names like Bill Atkinson, Stan Bahnse
Hal Dues, Woodie Fryman, Mike Garman, Dan Schatzeder a
Wayne Twitchell. Manager Dick Williams has a proble
though—finding enough innings to keep a staff like that conter

FIELDING: Getting the other team out is no Montreal pro
lem. The Expos tied New York with the National Leagu
second best fielding record, .979. But, the Expos don't just n
make errors, they also make things happen, especially the ou
fielders.

Cromartie and Valentine each contributed 24 assists, tying f
the National League lead. Fourth was another Expo, Dawsc
with 17. The word is: Don't even think about trying to take a
extra base on Montreal.

Cash is the league's best second baseman and Speier is r
slouch at shortstop, close to Larry Bowa and Dave Concepcio
The Expos aren't sensational at the corners with Parrish ar
Perez, but more than adequate. Carter makes up for lack of ra
ability behind the plate with guts and determination.

OUTLOOK: The Expos improve every year and their youn
lineup may be mature enough to make a serious run at the to
especially with a much-improved pitching staff. On pape
Montreal has everything but the proven know-how to win.
the Expos can stay close until September, watch out.

MONTREAL EXPOS 1979 ROSTER

MANAGER Dick Williams

Coaches—Felipe Alou, Jim Brewer, Pat Mullin, Norm Sherry, Vern Rapp, Ossie Virgil

PITCHERS

No.	Name	1978 Club	W-L	IP	SO	ERA	B-T	Ht.	Wt.	Born
42	Atkinson, Bill	Montreal	2-2	45	32	4.40	R-R	5-8	165	10/4/54 Chatham, Ont.
		Denver	1-3	34	18	7.49				
22	Bahnsen, Stan	Montreal	1-5	75	44	3.84	R-R	6-3	198	12/15/44 Council Bluffs, IA
28	Dues, Hal	Montreal	5-6	99	36	2.36	R-R	6-3	190	9/22/54 Dickinson, TX
35	Fryman, Woodie	Chi. (NL)-Mont.	7-11	150	81	4.20	R-L	6-2	215	4/12/40 Ewing, KY
29	Garman, Mike	L.A. (NL)-Mont.	4-7	78	28	4.38	R-R	6-3	208	9/16/49 Cladwell, ID
48	Grimsley, Ross	Montreal	20-11	263	84	3.05	L-L	6-3	200	1/7/50 Topeka, KS
—	Horn, Larry	Memphis	5-4	87	66	3.83	R-R	6-2	200	11/24/56 Dallas, TX
20	James, Bob	W. Palm Beach	10-7	127	139	3.11	R-R	6-4	215	8/15/58 Glendale, CA
		Memphis	2-1	19	25	0.47				
		Montreal	0-1	4	3	9.00				
—	Keener, Joe	Denver	11-7	159	67	4.30	R-R	6-2	189	4/21/53 San Pedro, CA
—	Lee, Bill	Boston	10-10	177	44	3.46	L-L	6-3	205	12/28/46 Burbank, CA
43	May, Rudy	Montreal	8-10	144	87	3.88	L-L	6-2	195	7/18/44 Coffeyville, KS
47	Miller, Randy	Denver	7-5	100	95	4.14	R-R	6-1	180	3/18/53 Oxnard, CA
		Montreal	0-1	7	6	10.29				
46	Palmer, David	W. Palm Beach	4-2	51	58	1.94	R-R	6-1	195	10/19/57 Glens Falls, NY
		Memphis	8-10	129	78	3.05				
		Montreal	0-1	10	7	2.70				
45	Rogers, Steve	Montreal	13-10	219	126	2.47	R-R	6-1	177	10/26/49 Jefferson City, MO
21	Sanderson, Scott	Memphis	5-3	58	45	4.03	R-R	6-5	195	7/22/56 Northbrook, IL
		Denver	4-2	49	36	6.02				
		Montreal	4-2	61	50	2.51				
36	Schatzeder, Dan	Denver	3-0	28	19	2.89	L-L	6-0	195	12/1/54 Elmhurst, IL
		Montreal	7-7	144	69	3.07				
33	Twitchell, Wayne	Montreal	4-12	112	69	5.38	R-R	6-6	225	3/10/48 Portland, OR

CATCHERS

No.	Name	1978 Club	H	HR	RBI	Pct.	B-T	Ht.	Wt.	Born
8	Carter, Gary	Montreal	136	20	72	.255	R-R	6-2	210	4/8/54 Culver City, CA
—	Dyer, Duffy	Pittsburgh	37	0	13	.211	R-R	6-0	198	8/15/45 Dayton, OH
39	Fry, Jerry	Denver	79	6	40	.294	R-R	6-0	185	2/29/56 Springfield, IL
		Montreal	0	0	0	.000				
44	Ramos, Roberto	Denver	7	0	2	.179	R-R	5-11	190	11/5/55 Cuba
		Memphis	87	9	49	.264				
		Montreal	0	0	0	.000				
9	Reece, Bob	Montreal	2	0	3	.182	R-R	6-1	190	1/5/51 Sacramento, CA
		Denver	45	1	21	.296				

INFIELDERS

No.	Name	1978 Club	H	HR	RBI	Pct.	B-T	Ht.	Wt.	Born
—	Bernazard, Tony	Denver	137	9	65	.286	B-R	5-9	160	8/24/56 Puerto Rico
30	Cash, Dave	Montreal	166	3	43	.252	R-R	5-11	170	6/11/48 Utica, NY
—	Cox, Jim	Denver	101	10	64	.299	R-R	5-11	180	5/28/50 Bloomington, IL
38	Frias, Pepe	Montreal	4	0	5	.267	B-R	5-11	165	7/14/48 Dominican Republic
37	Hutton, Tom	Toronto	44	2	9	.254	L-L	5-11	170	4/20/46 Los Angeles, CA
		Montreal	12	0	5	.203				
—	Mason, Jim	Texas	20	0	3	.190	L-R	6-2	190	8/14/50 Mobile, AL
15	Parrish, Larry	Montreal	144	15	70	.277	R-R	6-3	200	11/10/53 Winter Haven, FL
24	Perez, Tony	Montreal	158	14	78	.290	R-R	6-2	215	5/14/42 Cuba
—	Solaita, Tony	California	21	1	14	.223	L-L	6-0	215	1/15/47 American Samoa
4	Speier, Chris	Montreal	126	5	51	.251	R-R	6-1	182	6/28/50 Alameda, CA

OUTFIELDERS

No.	Name	1978 Club	H	HR	RBI	Pct.	B-T	Ht.	Wt.	Born
49	Cromartie, Warren	Montreal	180	10	56	.297	L-L	6-0	190	9/29/53 Miami, FL
10	Dawson, Andre	Montreal	154	25	72	.253	R-R	6-3	180	7/10/54 Miami, FL
—	Gates, Eddie	Memphis	113	25	57	.323	R-R	6-0	186	11/20/54 Mobile, AL
—	Hart, Jim	Denver	142	19	98	.320	B-R	6-3	185	12/20/51 Kalamazoo, MI
—	Scott, Rodney	Wichita	67	4	17	.262	B-R	6-0	160	10/16/53 Indianapolis, IN
		Chicago (NL)	64	0	15	.282				
17	Valentine, Ellis	Montreal	165	25	76	.289	R-R	6-4	205	7/30/54 Helena, AR
—	White, Jerry	Mont.-Chi. (NL)	39	1	10	.267	B-R	5-11	165	8/23/52 Shirley, MA

EXPO PROFILES

STEVE ROGERS 29 6-1 177   Bats R Throws

Gave up Pete Rose's 3,000th career hit an
was one of Rose's victims during 44-gam
hitting streak, but those are about the on
negative things about this hard-throwin
hard-luck pitcher . . . Expos scored only
runs during his 17 losses in 1976 . . . Le
club in most pitching departments in 19
and was overshadowed by Grimsley in 19
despite his best season, including the seventh best ERA in th
NL . . . Born Oct. 27, 1949, in Jefferson City, Mo. . . . Varie
interests include collecting coins and Indian arrowheads an
working crossword puzzles . . . Could have been a Yankee, b
passed them up to complete education at Tulsa University
obtain B.S. degree in petroleum engineering.

Year	Club	G	IP	W	L	Pct.	SO	BB	H	
1973	Montreal	17	134	10	5	.667	64	49	93	1
1974	Montreal	38	254	15	22	.405	154	80	225	4
1975	Montreal	35	252	11	12	.478	137	88	248	3
1976	Montreal	33	230	7	17	.292	150	69	212	3
1977	Montreal	40	302	17	16	.515	206	81	272	3
1978	Montreal	30	219	13	10	.565	126	64	186	2
	Totals	193	1391	73	82	.471	837	431	1266	3

WARREN CROMARTIE 25 6-0 190   Bats L Throws

Loves to play the drums, shoot pool or liste
to rock music, any of the three of which N
pitchers would pay him to do instead c
swing his lethal bat at them . . . Was leadin
hitter on a club full of hitters . . . His 17
hits were only five short of Rusty Staub's clu
record . . . Born Sept. 29, 1953, in Miam
. . . Played only one year in minors afte
Expos drafted him in first round of secondary phase of June
1973, free agent draft . . . An All-American at Miami-Dad
North Community College . . . Had a five-for-five game i
1976, tying club record held by Staub, Willie Davis and Larr
Parrish.

Year	Club	Pos	G	AB	R	H	2B	3B	HR	RBI	SB	A
1974	Montreal	OF	8	17	2	3	0	0	0	0	1	.1
1976	Montreal	OF	33	81	8	17	1	0	0	2	1	.2
1977	Montreal	OF	155	620	64	175	41	7	5	50	10	.28
1978	Montreal	OF	159	607	77	180	32	6	10	56	8	.29
	Totals		355	1325	151	375	74	13	15	108	20	.28

ELLIS VALENTINE 24 6-4 205   Bats R Throws R

Fast becoming Montreal's first superstar . . . Hits for power, hits for average and owns legendary arm capable of throwing line drives from right field corner to third base . . . Can also run, once stealing 14 straight bases, including three in one game . . . Challenges Cromartie for title of club pool champion, but is the indisputed chess champion . . . Played only 88 games in the outfield in 1976, finishing fourth in assists for NL outfielders with 12, then got only 12 for 127 games in 1977 because runners refused to challenge him . . . Born July 30, 1954, in Helena, Ark. . . . Showed running ability by twice hitting inside-the-park-homers in Olympic Stadium in 1977.

Year	Club	Pos	G	AB	R	H	2B	3B	HR	RBI	SB	Avg.
1975	Montreal	OF	12	33	2	12	4	0	1	3	0	.364
1976	Montreal	OF	94	305	36	85	15	2	7	39	14	.279
1977	Montreal	OF	127	508	63	149	28	2	25	76	13	.293
1978	Montreal	OF	151	570	75	165	35	2	25	76	13	.289
	Totals		384	1416	176	411	82	6	58	194	40	.290

ROSS GRIMSLEY 29 6-3 200   Bats L Throws L

Doesn't throw hard enough to ruffle the Charmin, but keeps the ball in the park . . . Attained first 20-victory season and passed 100-victory level . . . Unlimited ability, but has played for three clubs because he is his own man, a free spirit . . . Refused to knuckle under to rigid rules set by the Cincinnati club and was traded to Baltimore, then played out his contract with Orioles and Expos signed him as free agent on Dec. 5, 1977 . . . Born Jan. 7, 1950, in Topeka, Kan. . . . Father, Ross Grimsley Sr., pitched for White Sox in 1951 . . . Tied a record when he won two games in relief for the Reds in 1972 World Series, a record for a six-game Series . . . Long, frizzy hair and big mustache his pride and joy.

Year	Club	G	IP	W	L	Pct.	SO	BB	H	ERA
1971	Cincinnati	26	161	10	7	.588	67	43	151	3.58
1972	Cincinnati	30	198	14	8	.636	79	50	194	3.05
1973	Cincinnati	38	242	13	10	.565	90	68	245	3.24
1974	Baltimore	40	296	18	13	.581	158	76	267	3.07
1975	Baltimore	35	197	10	13	.435	89	47	210	4.07
1976	Baltimore	28	137	8	7	.533	41	35	143	3.94
1977	Baltimore	34	218	14	10	.583	53	74	230	3.96
1978	Montreal	36	263	20	11	.645	84	67	237	3.05
	Totals	267	1712	107	79	.575	661	460	1677	3.43

ANDRE DAWSON 24 6-3 180   Bats R Throws R

Third member of Expos' very young and very talented outfield (Dawson is 24, Ellis Valentine 24 and Warren Cromartie 25) . . . Off year in average, but tied Valentine for club home run leadership and finished six behind Tony Perez in RBIs . . . Chosen in 11th round of 1975 draft, but showed potential by hitting seven homers in his first six Class AAA games at Denver in 1976 . . . NL Rookie of Year in 1977 . . . Born July 10, 1954, in Miami and played high school ball with Cromartie . . . Opened major league career with a single off Steve Carlton

Year	Club	Pos	G	AB	R	H	2B	3B	HR	RBI	SB	Avg.
1976	Montreal	OF	24	85	9	20	4	1	0	7	1	.235
1977	Montreal	OF	139	525	64	148	26	9	19	65	21	.282
1978	Montreal	OF	157	609	84	154	24	8	25	72	28	.253
	Totals		296	1134	148	302	50	17	44	137	49	.266

TONY PEREZ 36 6-2 215   Bats R Throws R

The "Happy Cuban," always smiles through all adversity . . . Reds gave up on him two years ago, but he keeps pouring out the RBIs, leading the Expos in 1978 and hitting for second highest average on club . . . Owns 1,197 career RBIs, most of any active player, and missed his 12th straight year of 90 or more by 12, but that's because Valentine, Dawson and Cromartie didn't leave many men on base . . . Born May 14, 1942, in Camaguey, Cuba . . . Cincinnati's Joe Morgan says Reds haven't won NL West last two years because of Perez's absence . . . Hit three homers against Boston in 1975 World Series . . . Clubhouse comedian who keeps younger players loose.

Year	Club	Pos	G	AB	R	H	2B	3B	HR	RBI	SB	Avg.
1964	Cincinnati	1B	12	25	1	2	1	0	0	1	0	.080
1965	Cincinnati	1B	104	281	40	73	14	4	12	47	0	.260
1966	Cincinnati	1B	99	257	25	68	10	4	4	39	1	.265
1967	Cincinnati	3B-1B-2B	156	600	78	174	28	7	26	102	0	.290
1968	Cincinnati	3B	160	625	93	176	25	7	18	92	3	.282
1969	Cincinnati	3B	160	629	103	185	31	2	37	122	4	.294
1970	Cincinnati	3B-1B	158	587	107	186	28	6	40	129	8	.317
1971	Cincinnati	3B-1B	158	609	72	164	22	3	25	91	4	.269
1972	Cincinnati	1B	136	515	64	146	33	7	21	90	4	.283
1973	Cincinnati	1B	151	564	73	177	33	3	27	101	3	.314
1974	Cincinnati	1B	158	596	81	158	28	2	28	101	1	.265
1975	Cincinnati	1B	137	511	74	144	28	3	20	109	1	.282
1976	Cincinnati	1B	139	527	77	137	32	6	19	91	10	.260
1977	Montreal	1B	154	559	71	158	32	6	19	91	4	.283
1978	Montreal	1B	148	544	63	158	38	3	14	78	2	.290
	Totals		2030	7429	1022	2106	383	63	310	1284	45	.283

GARY CARTER 25 6-2 210   **Bats R Throws R**

Only 25, but already playing his fifth major league season . . . Was NL Rookie of Year in 1975 . . . Pete Rose is his idol and he displays Pete's mannerisms, including a sprint to first base on a walk . . . Likes being the captain, was captain of Fullerton (Cal.) Sunny Hills High School baseball, basketball and football teams . . . Born April 8, 1954, in Culver City, Cal. . . . Strong arm behind the plate, strong bat at the plate with 75 career homers . . . Was selected top catcher in all Class AAA baseball in 1974 while playing at Memphis . . . First Expo to hit three homers in one game.

Year	Club	Pos	G	AB	R	H	2B	3B	HR	RBI	SB	Avg.
1974	Montreal	C-OF	9	27	5	11	0	1	1	6	2	.407
1975	Montreal	OF-C-3B	144	503	58	136	20	1	17	68	5	.270
1976	Montreal	C-OF	91	311	31	68	8	1	6	38	0	.219
1977	Montreal	C-OF	154	522	86	148	29	2	31	84	5	.284
1978	Montreal	C-OF	157	533	76	136	27	1	20	72	10	.255
	Totals		555	1896	256	499	84	6	75	268	22	.263

DAVE CASH 30 5-11 170   **Bats R Throws R**

A winner and a leader, something Expos needed and paid handsomely to get, $1 million in free agent draft when he played out his option with Philadelphia in 1976 . . . An ideal leadoff hitter who seldom strikes out, always searching for ways to get on base, then steal a base . . . Came to plate 658 times, hit his normal three homers, but who needs 'em with Dawson, Valentine, Cromartie and Perez in the lineup to drive him home . . . Born June 11, 1948, in Utica, N.Y. . . . Coined Philadelphia's 1974 slogan, "Yes we can." . . . Believer in transcendental meditation and overt leadership.

Year	Club	Pos	G	AB	R	H	2B	3B	HR	RBI	SB	Avg.
1970	Pittsburgh	2B	64	210	30	66	7	6	1	28	5	.314
1971	Pittsburgh	2B-3B-SS	123	478	79	138	17	4	2	34	13	.289
1972	Pittsburgh	2B	99	425	58	120	22	4	3	30	9	.282
1973	Pittsburgh	2B-3B	116	436	59	118	21	2	2	31	2	.271
1974	Philadelphia	2B	162	687	89	206	26	11	2	58	20	.300
1975	Philadelphia	2B	162	699	111	213	40	3	4	57	13	.305
1976	Philadelphia	2B	160	666	92	189	14	12	1	56	10	.284
1977	Montreal	2B	153	650	91	188	42	7	0	43	21	.289
1978	Montreal	2B	159	658	66	166	26	3	3	43	12	.252
	Totals		1216	4970	683	1421	218	53	18	384	107	.286

LARRY PARRISH 25 6-3 200   Bats R Throws R

One of the underrated . . . Another of Expos' young veterans, only 25 but playing in his fourth full season . . . Hit for power and average almost 30 points above career mark . . . Was five-for-five in 1977 game against St. Louis, scoring five and driving in five, hitting homers in his last three at bats, then hit safely in his next two at bats the following day . . . Born Nov. 10, 1953, in Winter Haven, Fla. . . . Was originally an outfielder, but Expos converted him to third base and he won the job for good in 1975 with fancy glovework, strong arm and wide range . . . After being bypassed in 1971 draft he enrolled at Seminole Junior College in Sanford, Fla., hit .455 as an outfielder, then signed with Expos.

Year	Club	Pos	G	AB	R	H	2B	3B	HR	RBI	SB	Avg.
1974	Montreal	3B	25	69	9	14	5	0	0	4	0	.203
1975	Montreal	3B-2B-SS	145	532	50	146	32	5	10	65	4	.274
1976	Montreal	3B	154	543	65	126	28	5	11	61	2	.232
1977	Montreal	3B	123	402	50	99	19	2	11	46	2	.246
1978	Montreal	3B	144	520	68	144	39	4	15	70	2	.277
	Totals		591	2066	242	529	123	16	47	246	10	.256

CHRIS SPEIER 28 6-1 182   Bats R Throws R

A veteran of eight years, but only 28, and a three-time all-star at shortstop . . . Played only one year in the minors, then became San Francisco's regular shortstop, making the all-star team in 1972-73-74 . . . Struggled when Giants began platooning him at short in 1977, but found new life when Expos traded Tim Foli to get him in April, 1977 . . . Born June 28, 1950, in Alameda, Cal. . . . Played college baseball at University of California at Santa Barbara, hitting .314 in 42 games . . . Active in Fellowship of Christian Athletes and peddles insurance in off-season.

Year	Club	Pos	G	AB	R	H	2B	3B	HR	RBI	SB	Avg.
1971	San Francisco	SS	157	601	74	141	17	6	8	46	4	.235
1972	San Francisco	SS	150	562	74	151	25	2	15	71	9	.269
1973	San Francisco	SS-2B	153	542	58	135	17	4	11	71	4	.249
1974	San Francisco	SS-2B	141	501	55	125	19	5	9	53	3	.250
1975	San Francisco	SS-3B	141	487	60	132	30	5	10	69	4	.271
1976	San Francisco	INF	145	495	51	112	18	4	3	40	2	.226
1977	S.F.-Mtl.	SS	145	548	59	128	31	6	5	38	1	.234
1978	Montreal	SS	150	501	47	126	18	3	5	51	1	.251
	Totals		1182	4237	478	1050	175	35	66	439	28	.248

TOP PROSPECT

BILL GULLICKSON 20 6-3 198   **Bats R Throws R**
The "No-Hit Kid" . . . Signed as No. 1 draft pick, June, 1977,
right out of Joliet (Ill.) High School after throwing six no-hitters
. . . Was 12-0 with 0.43 earned run average his senior year . . .
Born Feb. 20, 1959, in Marshall, Minn. . . . Was 1-4 with 3.04
earned run average at Memphis (AA), then went to Florida
Instruction League and gave up three earned runs in his first
inning, then pitched 22 straight scoreless innings . . . Expos
consider him their No. 1 pitching prospect and a fast developer.

MANAGER DICK WILLIAMS: A thinking man's manager,
adept at tactics and gamesmanship . . . Took
1967 Boston team to the World Series and
was named AL Manager of the Year . . .
Led Oakland to World Series victories in
1972 and 1973, first non-Yankee manager to
win back-to-back since Connie Mack . . .
Yankees signed him after that, but Charlie
Finley fought it in court and won, forcing
Williams to honor contract with A's . . . Managed unsuccessfully for California 1974, 1975 and parts of 1976, then hired by
the Expos for the 1977 season to build a contender with youth
. . . Born May 7, 1929, in St. Louis . . . Began successful run in
the minors by managing Toronto to two straight Governors
Cups in the International League in 1965 and 1966 before
becoming Boston manager . . . Played 14 years in the majors as
an outfielder and infielder with Brooklyn, Baltimore, Cleveland, Kansas City and Boston, after first signing with the Dodgers . . . Batted .260 for 1,023 games . . . A tough guy on and
off the field.

GREATEST PITCHER

One might be inclined to believe Steve Rogers is more infa-
mous than famous.

One would be wrong.

Just because Rogers lost 22 games in 1974, just because Rogers gave up Pete Rose's 3,000th hit, just because Rogers gave up
a single to extend Rose's hitting streak to 36 last season, don't
make the mistake of believing he can't pitch.

As a six-year member of the Montreal pitching staff, Rogers is 73-82, and since he is only 29 and the young Expos are getting better quickly, Rogers stands to win a lot more games.

Even though he lost 22 games in 1974, he won 15. And, 1978 was his best season, 13-10, with a 2.47 earned run average that was second best in the National league.

Rogers holds the Montreal club record for complete games (66), shutouts (16) and strikeouts (837) and is living up to his first-year impression when he compiled a 1.54 ERA and a 10-5 record, never pitching less than five-and-one half innings.

ALL-TIME EXPO LEADERS

BATTING: Rusty Staub, .311, 1971
HRs: Gary Carter, 31, 1977
RBIs: Ken Singleton, 103, 1973
STEALS: Larry Lintz, 50, 1974
WINS: Ross Grimsley, 20, 1978
STRIKEOUTS: Bill Stoneman, 251, 1971

Gary Carter led NL catchers with 781 putouts in 1978.

ST. LOUIS CARDINALS

TEAM DIRECTORY: Chairman of the Board and Pres.: August A. Busch Jr.; Sen. VP and Chief Operating Officer: John Claiborne; Senior VP: Stan Musial; Dir. Player Personnel: Jim Bayens; Dir. Pub. Rel.: Jim Toomey; Trav. Sec.: Lee Thomas; Mgr.: Ken Boyer. Home: Busch Memorial Stadium (50,100). Field distances: 330. l.f. line; 404, c.f.; 330, r.f. line. Spring training: St. Petersburg, Fla.

Ted Simmons dipped to .287, but had career-high 22 HRs.

SCOUTING REPORT

HITTING: The Cardinals put out an all-points bulletin this winter to find their missing bats. Somewhere, the Cardinals lost 20 points off their team batting average with a team that should have gained 20. The Cardinals had nobody in the top 15 in National League hitting, a shock. At the very least, catcher Ted Simmons is usually battling for the batting title and some experts predicted yearly .300 averages for Garry Templeton.

Simmons hit .287 and Templeton staged an incredible late-season comeback to reach .280 after floundering near .120 for a couple of months. Having George Hendrick for a full season should help the dismal Cardinal offensive production and Ken Reitz can be pesky at times.

Jerry Mumphrey, Jerry Morales and Tony Scott were far below what people expect of them and Lou Brock sunk with them, making one wonder how much longer the graceful and smooth Lou can hang on. The Cardinal batting order never was heavyweight in calibre in recent years, but in 1978 it was lightweight. It is capable of much better.

PITCHING: After Bob (No-Hit) Forsch and Pete Vuckovich, you've about said it all, and that includes in-and-out John Denny. Those three were the only Cardinals to reach double figures in victories—Denny leading with 14 while Vuckovich won 12 and Forsch 11. Unfortunately, Forsch also lost 17.

Mark Littell and Buddy Schultz were the steadies out of the bullpen, but not steady enough, so the Cardinals have added right-hander Jim Willoughby to give them help. The Cardinals like Silvio Martinez, who showed promise after a midseason callup from Springfield by winning nine games. The pitching staff is populated by some good arms, but there is no depth.

FIELDING: Ken Reitz, Mike Tyson and Keith Hernandez are all near the top at their positions. Reitz led the league in fielding at third (.973) and makes all the plays and all the throws. Tyson is smooth at second and covers plenty of territory. Hernandez is fancy out of the Willie Montanez mold at first base and lost the fielding title to Cincinnati's Dan Driessen by .002 points. But, the Cardinals are weak defensively in the infield where it counts most—shortstop. Templeton, perhaps letting his dismal offensive beginning last year affect his fielding, made an ungodly 40 errors, most in the National League.

On the plus side, Templeton participated in 108 doubleplays, tops for any shortstop.

Simmons never has been known as a glove behind the plate. His batting glove is more well-known than his catcher's mitt. The Cardinal outfield won't dazzle, even though it has speed afoot.

OUTLOOK: The Cardinals were the surprise of the National League East last season, surprisingly bad. They changed managers early, but it didn't help much. It's nothing that won't be cured by improved pitching, improved hitting and improved defense in the outfield. If that doesn't happen, the Cardinals will drown in their owner's beer, and finish the same as last season—a few steps above the hopeless Mets.

ST. LOUIS CARDINALS 1979 ROSTER

MANAGER Ken Boyer
Coaches—Red Schoendienst, Dal Maxvill, Jack Krol, Dave Ricketts, Clause Osteen

PITCHERS

No.	Name	1978 Club	W-L	IP	SO	ERA	B-T	Ht.	Wt.	Born
49	Bruno, Tom	Springfield	5-10	127	105	4.41	R-R	6-5	210	1/26/53 Chicago, IL
		St. Louis	4-3	50	33	1.98				
36	Denny, John	St. Louis	14-11	234	103	2.96	R-R	6-3	185	11/18/52 Prescott, AZ
26	Dressler, Bob	Phoenix	9-8	140	80	3.54	R-R	6-3	195	2/2/54 Portland, OR
		Springfield	1-4	41	20	5.88				
		St. Louis	0-1	13	4	2.08				
33	Edelen, Joe	Arkansas	5-2	54	40	3.64	R-R	6-0	165	9/16/55 Durant, OK
		Springfield	2-5	62	37	4.91				
31	Forsch, Bob	St. Louis	11-17	234	114	3.69	R-R	6-4	200	1/13/50 Sacramento, CA
43	Frazier, George	Springfield	6-5	69	52	3.39	R-R	6-5	205	10/13/54 Oklahoma City, OK
		St. Louis	0-3	22	8	4.09				
—	Fulgham, John	Arkansas	9-7	154	119	4.02	R-R	6-2	205	6/9/56 St. Louis, MO
32	Littell, Mark	St. Louis	4-8	106	130	2.80	L-R	6-3	210	1/17/53 Cape Girardeau, MO
35	Martinez, Silvio	Springfield	5-2	54	42	2.15	R-R	5-11	160	8/31/55 Dominican Republic
		St. Louis	9-8	138	45	3.65				
—	Murphy, Jack	Evansville	5-1	70	49	3.20	L-L	6-3	185	8/7/57 Brooklyn, NY
34	O'Brien, Dan	Arkansas	12-3	118	91	2.75	R-R	6-4	215	4/22/54 St. Petersburg, FL
		Springfield	4-1	55	40	3.42				
		St. Louis	0-2	22	12	4.50				
—	Seaman, Kim	Jackson	10-4	99	117	2.09	L-L	6-3	205	5/6/57 Pascagoula, MS
22	Schultz, Buddy	St. Louis	2-4	83	70	3.80	R-L	6-0	175	9/19/50 Cleveland, OH
—	Sykes, Bob	Evansville	4-0	32	12	1.41	B-L	6-2	200	12/11/54 Neptune, NJ
		Detroit	6-6	94	58	3.93				
38	Urrea, John	St. Louis	4-9	99	61	5.36	R-R	6-3	205	2/9/55 Los Angeles, CA
		Springfield	2-1	45	39	5.76				
46	Vuckovich, Pete	St. Louis	12-12	198	149	2.55	R-R	6-4	220	10/27/52 Johnstown, PA
—	Willoughby, Jim	Chicago (AL)	1-6	92	36	3.87	R-R	6-2	205	1/31/49 Salinas, CA

CATCHERS

No.	Name	1978 Club	H	HR	RBI	Pct.	B-T	Ht.	Wt.	Born
16	Kennedy, Terry	Arkansas	71	10	55	.293	L-R	6-4	220	6/4/56 Mesa, AZ
		Springfield	76	10	46	.330				
		St. Louis	5	0	2	.172				
22	Simmons, Ted	St. Louis	148	22	80	.287	B-R	6-0	200	8/9/49 Highland Park, MI
2	Swisher, Steve	St. Louis	32	1	10	.278	R-R	6-2	205	8/9/51 Parkersburg, WV

INFIELDERS

No.	Name	1978 Club	H	HR	RBI	Pct.	B-T	Ht.	Wt.	Born
47	Castillo, Manny	Springfield	96	2	39	.251	B-R	5-9	160	4/1/57 Dominican Republic
15	Farkas, Ron	Springfield	97	6	49	.274	R-R	6-0	180	7/30/53 Cleveland, OH
—	Durham, Leon	Arkansas	116	12	70	.316	L-L	6-1	185	7/31/57 Cincinnati, OH
7	Freed, Roger	St. Louis	22	2	20	.239	R-R	6-2	205	6/2/46 Los Angeles, CA
37	Hernandez, Keith	St. Louis	138	11	64	.255	L-L	6-0	185	10/20/53 San Francisco, CA
28	Herr, Tom	Arkansas	100	3	46	.296	B-R	6-0	175	4/4/56 Lancaster, PA
		Springfield	24	0	8	.279				
24	Oberkfell, Ken	Springfield	69	6	28	.285	L-R	6-1	185	5/4/56 Highland, IL
		St. Louis	6	0	0	.120				
5	Phillips, Mike	St. Louis	44	1	28	.268	L-R	6-1	185	8/19/50 Beaumont, TX
33	Ramsey, Mike	Springfield	92	2	30	.241	B-R	6-1	170	3/29/54 Roanoke, VA
		St. Louis	1	0	0	.200				
44	Reitz, Ken	St. Louis	133	10	75	.246	R-R	6-0	185	6/24/51 San Francisco, CA
1	Templeton, Garry	St. Louis	181	2	47	.280	B-R	5-11	170	3/24/56 Lockey, TX
10	Tyson, Mike	St. Louis	88	3	26	.233	R-R	5-9	170	1/13/50 Rocky Mount, NC

OUTFIELDERS

No.	Name	1978 Club	H	HR	RBI	Pct.	B-T	Ht.	Wt.	Born
20	Brock, Lou	St. Louis	66	0	12	.221	L-L	5-11	170	6/18/39 El Dorado, AR
—	Grieve, Tom	New York (NL)	21	2	8	.208	R-R	6-2	190	3/4/48 Pittsfield, MA
27	Hendrick, George	S.D.-St. Louis	137	20	75	.278	R-R	6-3	195	10/18/49 Los Angeles, CA
19	Iorg, Dane	St. Louis	23	0	4	.271	L-R	6-0	180	5/11/50 Eureka, CA
		Springfield	128	24	87	.371				
21	Lentine, Jim	Arkansas	34	1	13	.291	R-R	6-0	175	7/16/54 Los Angeles, CA
		Springfield	139	11	63	.342				
		St. Louis	2	0	1	.182				
29	Mumphrey, Jerry	St. Louis	96	2	37	.262	B-R	6-2	185	9/9/52 Tyler, TX
—	Pennial, Dave	Arkansas	102	6	59	.301	R-R	5-10	175	9/26/54 Coronado, CA
30	Scott, Tony	St. Louis	50	1	14	.228	B-R	6-0	175	9/18/51 Cincinnati, OH

CARDINAL PROFILES

GEORGE HENDRICK 29 6-3 195   Bats R Throws R

George's way, or no way at all . . . After loafing along in San Diego for 36 games in 1978, the Padres traded him to St. Louis for Eric Rasmussen and the deal was beneficial for both sides . . . Silent George, who refuses to talk to sportswriters, hit .288 for the Cardinals in 102 games, blasting 17 or his 20 homers in St. Louis . . . Teammates on the Cardinals liked him and the Cardinal pitchers loved to see him at the plate with his booming bat . . . Born Oct. 18, 1949, in Los Angeles . . . Moody, brooding demeanor has led him to four major league cities already, too many for a man of his talents . . . Was sensation with Padres in 1977 after Pads gave up Johnny Grubb, Fred Kendall and Hector Torres to get him from Cleveland . . . Hit three homers for Tribe against Detroit in 1973 game . . . Was AL all-star in 1974 and 1975.

Year	Club	Pos	G	AB	R	H	2B	3B	HR	RBI	SB	Avg.
1971	Oakland	OF	42	114	8	27	4	1	0	8	0	.237
1972	Oakland	OF	58	121	10	22	1	1	4	15	3	.182
1973	Cleveland	OF	113	440	64	118	18	0	21	61	7	.268
1974	Cleveland	OF	139	495	65	138	23	1	19	67	6	.279
1975	Cleveland	OF	145	561	82	145	21	2	24	86	6	.258
1976	Cleveland	OF	149	551	72	146	20	3	25	81	4	.265
1977	San Diego	OF	152	541	75	168	25	2	23	81	11	.311
1978	San Diego	OF	138	493	64	137	31	1	20	75	2	.278
	Totals		846	3316	440	901	143	11	136	474	39	.272

TED SIMMONS 29 6-0 200   Bats S Throws R

Best hitting catcher in baseball and one of baseball's best switch-hitters . . . Nothing wrong as defensive catcher, either . . . Survived early-season shouting match with manager Vern Rapp . . . Rapp was fired, Simmons played on . . . Consistent hitter from both sides, hitting .284 right-handed and .288 left-handed . . . Led feeble Cardinals in homers, RBIs and doubles . . . Was walked intentionally 17 times and struck out only 39 times in 516 at-bats . . . Born Aug. 9, 1949, in Highland Park, Mich. . . . Once owned long, stringy hair but trimmed it ultra-short after it caught fire as he burned leaves . . . Known as "Simba" and is a camera buff, taking pictures on the road that appeared in Cardinal yearbook . . .

Received football scholarship offers from Ohio State, Michigan, Michigan State, Purdue and Colorado, but signed with Cardinals as No. 1 draft choice in June, 1967.

Year	Club	Pos	G	AB	R	H	2B	3B	HR	RBI	SB	Avg.
1968	St. Louis	C	2	3	0	1	0	0	0	0	0	.333
1969	St. Louis	C	5	14	0	3	0	1	0	3	0	.214
1970	St. Louis	C	82	284	29	69	8	2	3	24	2	.243
1971	St. Louis	C	133	510	64	155	32	4	7	77	1	.304
1972	St. Louis	C-1B	152	594	70	180	36	6	16	96	1	.303
1973	St. Louis	C-1B-OF	161	619	62	192	36	2	13	91	2	.310
1974	St. Louis	C-1B	152	599	66	163	33	6	20	103	0	.272
1975	St. Louis	C-1B-OF	157	581	80	193	32	3	18	100	1	.332
1976	St. Louis	C-1B-OF-3B	150	546	60	159	35	3	5	75	0	.291
1977	St. Louis	C-OF	150	516	82	164	25	3	21	95	2	.318
1978	St. Louis	C-OF	152	516	71	148	40	5	22	80	1	.287
	Totals		1296	4782	584	1427	277	35	125	744	10	.298

BOB FORSCH 29 6-4 200   Bats R Throws R

They said he couldn't hit as a third baseman, so they made him a pitcher . . . He can pitch —and hit . . . Pitched a seven-inning no-hitter at Tulsa over Memphis in Triple-A, then did better in 1978 by throwing a nine-inning no-hitter for the Cardinals . . . Not only did he win 20 games in 1977, but he batted .308 to lead all NL pitchers in hitting . . . Was a victim of team's collapse in 1978, winning only 11 despite pitching well . . . Born Jan. 13, 1950, in Sacramento . . . Brother of Houston pitcher Ken Forsch . . . Low, low draft pick, 38th by Cardinals in June, 1968, free agent draft . . . Eloquent off-season speaker and speaks eloquently on the mound with loud-sounding fast ball.

Year	Club	G	IP	W	L	Pct.	SO	BB	H	ERA
1974	St. Louis	19	100	7	4	.636	39	34	84	2.97
1975	St. Louis	34	230	15	10	.600	108	70	213	2.86
1976	St. Louis	33	194	8	10	.444	76	71	209	3.94
1977	St. Louis	35	217	20	7	.741	95	69	210	3.48
1978	St. Louis	34	234	11	17	.393	114	97	205	3.69
	Totals	155	975	61	48	.560	432	341	921	3.42

GARRY TEMPLETON 23 5-11 170   Bats S Throws R

Can outrun a tornado, and once looked like one circling the bases on an inside-the-park home run that was a ground ball between short and second . . . Made tremendous mid-season comeback after batting near .180 for two months . . . Excellent defensive short-stop able to cut off any ground ball between second and third and lethal arm to finish off the play . . . Hit .401 for 42 games at Double-A Little Rock in Texas League in 1975 with 16 stolen bases . . . Born March 24, 1956, in Lockey, Tex. . . . Led the club with 34 stolen bases in 1978, but defense suffered with 40 errors . . . Father, Spiavia, played for Kansas City Monarchs of Negro League . . . Nick-named "Jump Steady."

Year	Club	Pos	G	AB	R	H	2B	3B	HR	RBI	SB	Avg.
1976	St. Louis	SS	53	213	32	62	8	2	1	17	11	.291
1977	St. Louis	SS	153	621	94	200	19	18	8	79	28	.322
1978	St. Louis	SS	155	647	82	181	31	13	2	47	34	.280
	Totals		361	1481	208	443	58	33	11	143	73	.299

LOU BROCK 39 5-11 170   Bats L Throws L

Slowing down, but hanging on . . . Exactly 100 hits away from 3,000 and owns 917 stolen bases, tops on baseball's all-time list . . . A part-time player, but still dangerous both at the plate and on the basepaths . . . Broke Maury Wills' single-season theft record with 118 in 1974, but hasn't topped 56 since, stealing only 17 in 1978 . . . Shows flashes of power with 156 career homers. . . Born June 18, 1939, in El Dorado, Ark. . . . Owns Lu-Wan Enterprises to market world-wide the "BroccaBrella" umbrella hat he designed . . . Played only 128 games in the minors before Cubs called him up, then traded him in 1964 to St. Louis for Ernie Broglio, Bobby Shantz and Doug Clemens, a deal the Cardinals still call their "all-time steal."

Year	Club	Pos	G	AB	R	H	2B	3B	HR	RBI	SB	Avg.
1961	Chicago (NL)	OF	4	11	1	1	0	0	0	0	0	.091
1962	Chicago (NL)	OF	123	434	73	114	24	7	9	35	16	.263
1963	Chicago (NL)	OF	148	547	79	141	19	11	9	37	24	.258
1964	Chi. (NL)-St.L.	OF	155	634	111	200	20	11	14	58	43	.315
1965	St. Louis	OF	155	631	107	182	35	8	16	69	63	.288
1966	St. Louis	OF	156	643	94	183	24	12	15	46	74	.285
1967	St. Louis	OF	159	689	113	206	32	12	21	76	52	.299
1968	St. Louis	OF	159	660	92	184	46	14	6	51	62	.279
1969	St. Louis	OF	157	655	97	195	33	10	12	47	53	.298
1970	St. Louis	OF	155	664	114	202	29	5	13	57	51	.304
1971	St. Louis	OF	157	640	126	200	37	7	7	61	64	.313
1972	St. Louis	OF	153	621	81	193	26	8	3	42	63	.311
1973	St. Louis	OF	160	650	110	193	29	8	7	63	70	.297
1974	St. Louis	OF	153	635	105	194	25	7	3	48	118	.306
1975	St. Louis	OF	136	528	78	163	27	6	3	47	56	.309
1976	St. Louis	OF	133	498	73	150	24	5	4	67	56	.301
1977	St. Louis	OF	141	489	69	133	22	6	2	46	35	.272
1978	St. Louis	OF	92	298	31	66	9	0	0	12	17	.221
	Totals		2496	9927	1554	2900	471	137	144	862	917	292

KEITH HERNANDEZ 25 6-0 185   Bats L Throws L

The picture player—a stylish hitter and flashy first baseman . . . Suffered an off-season at the plate, hitting far below his .289 career average . . . A first baseman because Willie McCovey was his boyhood idol and he used to sneak into Candlestick Park to watch "Stretch" play first base . . . Born Oct. 20, 1953, in San Francisco . . . Rare find because he was drafted 40th by the Cardinals in June, 1971, free agent draft . . . Was first athlete in San Francisco Capuchino High School history to make all-league in three major sports as quarterback in football, guard in basketball and with a .500 batting average in baseball . . . Likes to paint as he listens to music.

Year	Club	Pos	G	AB	R	H	2B	3B	HR	RBI	SB	Avg.
1974	St. Louis	1B	14	34	3	10	1	2	0	2	0	.294
1975	St. Louis	1B	64	188	20	47	8	2	3	20	0	.250
1976	St. Louis	1B	129	374	54	108	21	5	7	46	4	.289
1977	St. Louis	1B	161	560	90	163	41	4	15	91	7	.291
1978	St. Louis	1B	159	542	90	138	32	4	11	64	13	.255
	Totals..........		527	1698	257	466	103	17	36	223	24	.274

KEN REITZ 27 6-0 185   Bats R Throws R

Anything that goes by him at third base goes high over his head because he stops everything . . . Cardinals traded him to San Francisco for 1976 season, realized the error, and got him back for 1977 by trading Lynn McGlothen . . . Short stature misleading because he has hit 27 homers past two seasons and driven in 154 runs . . . Born June 24, 1951, in San Francisco . . . Nicknamed "The Zamboni Machine" because of his ability to suck up grounders off the AstroTurf . . . Was Cardinals' captain in 1978 . . . Set defensive record for third baseman in 1977 with only nine errors in 450 chances . . . Once drove in eight runs in one game, the only NL player ever to do it in St. Louis.

Year	Club	Pos	G	AB	R	H	2B	3B	HR	RBI	SB	Avg.
1972	St. Louis	3B	21	78	5	28	4	0	0	10	0	.359
1973	St. Louis	SS-3B	147	426	40	100	20	2	6	42	0	.235
1974	St. Louis	3B-SS-2B	154	579	48	157	28	2	7	54	0	.271
1975	St. Louis	3B	161	592	43	159	25	1	5	63	1	.269
1976	San Francisco	3B-SS	155	577	40	154	21	1	5	66	5	.267
1977	St. Louis	3B	157	587	58	153	36	1	17	79	2	.261
1978	St. Louis	3B	150	540	41	133	26	2	10	75	1	.246
	Totals..........		945	3379	275	884	160	9	50	389	9	.262

JOHN DENNY 26 6-3 185   Bats R Throws R

Second-leading winner on the pitching staff best percentage . . . Led club in innings pitched, complete games (11 in 33 starts) . . . Another of many low draft picks by the Cardinals to make it, 29th in June, 1970, free agent draft . . . First NL complete game was five-hit 4-0 shutout over Mets in 1975 and singled to start rally that saw Ted Simmons hit grand slam for all the runs . . . Born Nov. 8, 1952, in Prescott, Ariz. . . . Has had only one losing season in eight-year professional career . . . Pitched the only no-hitter in 1973 Texas League for Arkansas . . . Won NL ERA title in 1976 (2.52) when he was 23, tying two others as youngest right-hander ever to do it.

Year	Club	G	IP	W	L	Pct.	SO	BB	H	ERA
1974	St. Louis	2	2	0	0	.000	1	0	3	0.00
1975	St. Louis	25	136	10	7	.588	72	51	149	3.97
1976	St. Louis	30	207	11	9	.550	74	74	189	2.52
1977	St. Louis	26	150	8	8	.500	60	62	165	4.50
1978	St. Louis	33	234	14	11	.560	103	74	200	2.96
	Totals	116	729	43	35	.551	310	261	706	3.29

JERRY MUMPHREY 26 6-2 185   Bats S Throws R

One of four switch-hitters on Cardinal roster, but hit much better left-handed (.270) than he did right-handed (.244) . . . Also one of several "Fast Eddies" on the team, a close man afoot with Garry Templeton . . . His improvement enabled Cardinals to dispose of Bake McBride, but McBride has done better thus far at Philadelphia than Mumphrey has done at St. Louis . . . Caught stealing 10 of his 24 attempts, a disappointment . . . Born Sept. 9, 1952, in Tyler, Tex. . . . Only two years in minors after stealing 40 bases for Double-A Arkansas team . . . A 12-letter man at Chapel Hill High School in Tyler, Tex., for baseball, basketball, football and track . . . Led American Association at Tulsa with 44 steals in 1975.

Year	Club	Pos	G	AB	R	H	2B	3B	HR	RBI	SB	Avg.
1974	St. Louis	OF	5	2	2	0	0	0	0	0	0	.000
1975	St. Louis	OF	11	16	2	6	2	0	0	1	0	.375
1976	St. Louis	OF	112	384	51	99	15	5	1	26	22	.258
1977	St. Louis	OF	145	463	73	133	20	10	2	38	22	.287
1978	St. Louis	OF	125	367	41	96	13	4	2	37	14	.262
	Totals		398	1232	169	334	50	19	5	102	58	.270

PETE VUCKOVICH 26 6-4 220   **Bats R Throws R**

Resembles tight end, with demeanor to match . . . Great acquisition for Cardinals from Toronto in December, 1977, for Tom Underwood and Victor Cruz . . . Didn't give up many runs, but didn't get many, either, as .500 record shows despite fourth best ERA of all NL starters . . . Versatile, split season between bullpen and starting, 23 starts and 22 relief appearances . . . Born Oct. 27, 1952, in Johnstown, Pa. . . . Pitched first shutout in Toronto history, 2-0, over Orioles and Jim Palmer . . . Was football and baseball star at Clarion State (Pa.) Teachers College . . . No-nonsense guy who says his hobby is "trying to enjoy life and all it has to offer."

Year	Club	G	IP	W	L	Pct.	SO	BB	H	ERA
1975	Chicago (AL)	4	10	0	1	.000	5	7	17	13.50
1976	Chicago (AL)	33	110	7	4	.636	62	60	122	4.66
1977	Toronto	53	148	7	7	.500	123	59	143	3.47
1978	St. Louis	45	198	12	12	.500	149	59	187	2.55
	Totals	135	466	26	24	.520	339	185	469	3.57

TOP PROSPECT

DAVE PENNIAL 24 5-10 175   **Bats R Throws R**

Passed over in 1976 draft after injuries kept him out of action his senior year in high school . . . Cardinals decided to take a chance and now consider him an excellent prospect after signing him as a free agent . . . Born Sept. 26, 1954, in Los Angeles . . . After signing, promptly hit .406 at Sarasota in Florida Rookie League, then .380 at Johnson City in Appalachian League . . . Followed those with .321 at St. Petersburg in 1977 and .312 last season at Arkansas . . . Strong-armed outfielder.

MANAGER KEN BOYER: Replaced Vern Rapp last April 29 after Rapp lost a disagreement with catcher Ted Simmons . . . Retired as active player in 1969, spending most of his 15-year career as a St. Louis third baseman . . . Began managing in the Cardinal organization in 1970 and won a pennant at Tulsa in 1974 . . . Born May 20, 1931, in Liberty, Mo. . . . Father, Dave, and five brothers (Clete, Cloyd, Len, Ron and

Wayne) all played baseball professionally . . . Won five Gold
Gloves for defense and was NL MVP for 1964 with a .294
average, 119 RBIs and 24 homers . . . Capped off that season
with a grand slam home run in '64 World Series . . . Was a
member of the National League all-star team 11 times (twice in
1959, 1960 and 1962 when two games were played each year)
. . . Originally signed by the Cardinals as a pitcher and was 5-1
his first year with Lebanon in the North Atlantic League, but
was switched to the infield in 1951.

Bob Gibson's 1.12 ERA in 1968 stands as majors' record.

GREATEST PITCHER

Clearly, the most colorful pitcher in Cardinal history was Dizzy Dean. And, Ol' Diz probably was the second best pitcher in the club's long, storied existence.

But, the best all-time pitcher was "Bullet" Bob Gibson. Dean was a comedian on the mound, making hitters laugh as he whisked them aside. There was nothing funny about Gibson. He was deadly serious.

In 15 big league seasons, all with the Cardinals, Gibson won 261 games, threw 56 shutouts and won 20 games five times over a span of six seasons. In addition, he put together a 1.12 earned run average in 1968 when he was 22-9 and struck out 274 in 1970 when he was 23-7.

During the unbelievable 1968 season, Gibson's sizzling fast ball, sometimes neatly tucked under a crowding hitter's chin, helped him throw 13 shutouts and win 15 straight games. And, in 1971, Gibson threw an 11-0 no-hitter at the Pittsburgh Pirates.

As good as Gibson was during the season, he was unmatchable in the World Series. When the Cardinals beat the Yankees, four games to three in 1964, Gibson was 2-1 with 31 strikeouts in 27 innings, winning the seventh game with his third complete game, 7-5, and striking out nine.

Gibson was even better in 1968 when Detroit beat the Cardinals in seven games. Once more he was 2-1, but his time he struck out 35 in 27 innings (three complete games), losing the final game, 4-1, though his 35 strikeouts gave him a World Series record. He also set a World Series record by fanning 17 Tigers in one game, breaking by two the mark Sandy Koufax set in 1963.

ALL-TIME CARDINAL LEADERS

BATTING: Rogers Hornsby, .424, 1924
HRs: Johnny Mize, 43, 1940
RBIs: Joe Medwick, 154, 1937
STEALS: Lou Brock, 118, 1974
WINS: Dizzy Dean, 30, 1934
STRIKEOUTS: Bob Gibson, 274, 1970

CHICAGO CUBS

TEAM DIRECTORY: Chairman of Exec. Committee: William Wrigley; Pres.: William J. Hagenah Jr.; Exec., VP: Bob Kennedy; VP: Charles Grimm; Dir. of Player Development: C.V. Davis; Dir. of Scouting: Vedie Himsl; Dir. Pub. Rel.: Buck Pedan; Dir. Park Operations: E.R. Saltwell; Mgr.: Herman Franks. Home: Wrigley Field (37,471). Field distances: 355, l.f. line; 400, c.f.; 353, r.f. line. Spring training: Mesa, Ariz.

SCOUTING REPORT

HITTING: It was as big of a surprise as Guess Who's Coming To Dinner? Guess who led the National League in hitting in 1978? Not the Reds. Not the Phillies. Not the Pirates. It was the Chicago Cubs with .264, leading the second place Dodgers by 26 hits. There were no Cubs in the top 15, but Bill Buckner hit .323, second to league-leading Dave Parker. But Buckner fell a few at-bats short of qualifying for the listings.

Dave Kingman terrorized residents along Waveland Avenue behind the left field wall with some gargantuan home runs early in the season, then tailed off as injuries struck, finishing with 28

Cubs' savior, Bruce Sutter, has 68 saves in three seasons.

homers and 79 RBIs. Ol' reliable, Bobby Murcer, climbs out of his clubhouse rocking chair to hit steadily, while Gene Clines and Greg Gross punch a few key hits here and there.

Ivan DeJesus and Manny Trillo, "The Latin Infield Connection," hit better than most people ask of them and Larry Biittner has his moments. The only surefire outs in the lineup came when one of the light-hitting catchers walked to the plate. If the Cubs can match their bat potency this season, they could hang near the top again, and maybe this time not disappoint their ever-loyal fans with a fadeout. It's not likely, though.

PITCHING: Rick Reuschel and Ray Burris are capable of great games and lousy games in the same week. If Reuschel could face the Cincinnati Reds every time out, he'd win 30 games. But he has to face the other 10 clubs and doesn't do as well, though he can be counted on every year to win at least twice as many as he loses. Reuschel is the one man every team seems to have on its staff—the guy the team doesn't score runs for when he pitches.

A full season from Ken Holtzman, rescued last season from the Yankees, may be beneficial for the Cubs and Holtzman. Mike Krukow started fast last season and finished 9-3. Dennis Lamp also started quickly, but faded to 7-15. But, Krukow and Lamp give the Cubs youthful pitching with bright possibilities, along with 25-year-old Donnie Moore.

Still there to bail out the starters is tireless Bruce Sutter. Although 8-10 with a 3.18 ERA last season, he is still recognized as the National League's premier relief pitcher. Sutter, though, is the only reliable commodity out of the bullpen and Herman Franks saves him for game-saving situations.

FIELDING: As long as Kingman is in the lineup, the team will be weakened on defense. When they ask Kingman what position he plays, he should answer, "Batter." Trillo and DeJesus aren't the best doubleplay combination, but they're not the worst, either—which is why the Cubs were near the middle in team defense, making 144 errors and turning 154 doubleplays, both near the middle of the pack.

OUTLOOK: Recent Cub history indicates a fast start, a stay on top, then a quick exit, stage right, to once again disappoint their fans. The pitching is adequate, the hitting isn't as good as the numbers indicate and the fielding is below average—all of which says the Cubs will argue with St. Louis for fourth and fifth.

CHICAGO CUBS 1979 ROSTER

MANAGER Herman Franks
Coaches—Joe Amalfitano, Harry Lowrey, Mike Roarke, Cookie Rojas

PITCHERS

No.	Name	1978 Club	W-L	IP	SO	ERA	B-T	Ht.	Wt.	Born
34	Burris, Ray	Chicago (NL)	7-13	199	94	4.75	R-R	6-5	195	8/22/50 Idabel, OK
36	Caudill, Bill	Wichita	8-9	158	124	5.53	R-R	6-1	175	7/13/56 Santa Monica, CA
46	Geisel, Dave	Wichita	6-9	107	62	4.95	L-L	6-3	210	1/18/55 Windber, PA
		Chicago (NL)	1-0	23	15	4.30				
38	Hernandez, Willie	Chicago (NL)	8-2	60	38	3.75	L-L	6-2	180	11/14/55 Puerto Rico
30	Holtzman, Ken	New York (AL)	1-0	18	3	4.00	R-L	6-2	190	11/3/45 St. Louis, MO
		Chicago (NL)	0-3	53	36	6.11				
39	Krukow, Mike	Wichita	2-3	53	29	3.91	R-R	6-4	195	1/21/52 Long Beach, CA
		Chicago (NL)	9-3	138	81	3.91				
47	Lamp, Dennis	Chicago (NL)	7-15	224	73	3.29	R-R	6-3	190	9/23/52 Los Angeles, CA
40	McGlothen, Lynn	S.F.-Chi.	5-3	93	69	3.29	L-R	6-2	195	3/27/50 Monroe, LA
49	Moore, Donnie	Chicago (NL)	9-7	103	50	4.11	L-R	6-0	170	2/13/54 Lubbock, TX
46	Reuschel, Rick	Chicago (NL)	14-15	243	115	3.41	R-R	6-3	230	5/16/49 Quincy, IL
33	Riley, George	Midland	5-3	69	50	4.41	L-L	6-2	200	10/6/56 Philadelphia, PA
		Wichita	3-5	36	17	7.25				
43	Segelke, Herman	Midland	8-8	143	58	4.61	R-R	6-4	215	4/24/58 San Mateo, CA
37	Seoane, Manny	Wichita	12-9	174	131	4.51	R-R	6-0	190	6/26/55 Tampa, FL
		Chicago (NL)	1-0	8	5	5.63				
42	Sutter, Bruce	Chicago (NL)	8-10	99	106	3.18	R-R	6-2	190	1/8/53 Lancaster, PA
44	Wilkerson, Byron	Wichita	0-3	47	37	3.61	R-R	6-3	165	2/4/55 Evansville, IN

CATCHERS

No.	Name	1978 Club	H	HR	RBI	Pct.	B-T	Ht.	Wt.	Born
9	Blackwell, Tim	Wichita	54	8	33	.293	B-R	5-11	185	8/19/52 San Diego, CA
		Chicago (NL)	23	0	7	.223				
6	Cox, Larry	Chicago (NL)	34	2	18	.281	R-R	5-11	190	9/11/47 Bluffton, OH
23	Gordon, Mike	Wichita	39	8	32	.179	B-R	6-3	215	9/11/53 Leominster, MA
		Chicago (NL)	1	0	0	.200				
52	Keatley, Greg	Midland	78	8	38	.226	R-R	6-2		9/12/53 Princeton, NJ
8	Rader, Dave	Chicago (NL)	62	3	36	.203	L-R	6-0	175	12/26/48 Claremore, OK

INFIELDERS

No.	Name	1978 Club	H	HR	RBI	Pct.	B-T	Ht.	Wt.	Born
26	Biittner, Larry	Chicago (NL)	88	4	50	.257	L-L	6-2	200	7/27/47 Pocahontas, IA
22	Buckner, Bill	Chicago (NL)	144	5	74	.323	L-L	6-1	185	12/14/49 Vallejo, CA
51	Davis, Steve	Wichita	132	13	70	.270	R-R	6-1	200	12/30/53 Oakland, CA
11	DeJesus, Ivan	Chicago (NL)	172	3	35	.278	R-R	5-11	175	1/9/53 Puerto Rico
20	Kelleher, Mick	Chicago (NL)	24	0	6	.253	R-R	5-9	175	7/25/47 Seattle, WA
16	Ontiveros, Steve	Chicago (NL)	67	1	22	.243	B-R	6-1	185	10/26/51 Bakersfield, CA
17	Putman, Ed	Wichita	102	24	81	.268	R-R	6-1	190	9/25/53 Los Angeles, CA
		Chicago (NL)	5	0	3	.200				
56	Seibert, Kurt	Midland	145	5	41	.291	B-R	6-0	190	10/16/55 Cheverly, MD
29	Sember, Mike	Wichita	98	13	57	.239	R-R	6-0	185	2/24/53 Hammond, IN
		Chicago (NL)	1	0	0	.333				
19	Trillo, Manny	Chicago (NL)	144	4	55	.261	R-R	6-1	160	12/25/50 Venezuela

OUTFIELDERS

No.	Name	1978 Club	H	HR	RBI	Pct.	B-T	Ht.	Wt.	Born
18	Clines, Gene	Chicago (NL)	59	0	17	.258	R-R	5-9	170	10/6/46 San Pablo, CA
21	Gross, Greg	Chicago (NL)	92	1	39	.265	L-L	5-11	170	8/1/52 York, PA
30	Kingman, Dave	Chicago (NL)	105	28	79	.266	R-R	6-6	210	12/21/48 Pendleton, OR
–	Mejias, Sam	Montreal	13	0	6	.232	R-R	6-0	168	5/9/52 Dominican Republic
7	Murcer, Bobby	Chicago (NL)	140	9	64	.281	L-R	5-11	180	5/20/46 Oklahoma City, OK
45	Pagel, Karl	Wichita	124	23	86	.268	L-L	6-2	188	3/29/55 Madison, WI
		Chicago (NL)	0	0	0	.000				
25	Thompson, Scot	Wichita	169	10	64	.326	L-L	6-3	175	12/7/55 Grove City, PA
		Chicago (NL)	15	0	2	.417				
27	Vail, Mike	Portland	22	4	19	.393	R-R	6-0	185	11/10/51 San Francisco, CA
		Cleveland	8	0	2	.235				
		Chicago (NL)	60	4	33	.333				

CUB PROFILES

BRUCE SUTTER 26 6-2 190   Bats R Throws R

An "off year"—only 27 saves and an 8-10 record, the fourth-rated relief pitcher in the NL . . . Considered an off year because he was 7-3 with 31 saves in 1977 after coming up as a midseason rookie in 1976 to win six (tops out of the bullpen) and save 10 . . . Gets hitters out with a forkball he calls a "split-fingered fastball . . ." Had lowest ERA in the majors in 1977 (1.35), but it climbed to 3.19 in 1978 . . . Born Jan. 8, 1953, in Lancaster, Pa. . . . Seldom walks a hitter in crucial times, usually strikes him out . . . Signed by the Cubs off a semi-pro team in Pennsylvania's Lebanon Valley called Hippey's Raiders . . . Trained from beginning as a relief pitcher, in Arizona Instructional League in 1974 he was 3-0 with seven saves and an 0.90 ERA.

Year	Club	G	IP	W	L	Pct.	SO	BB	H	ERA
1976	Chicago (NL)	52	83	6	3	.667	73	26	63	2.71
1977	Chicago (NL)	62	107	7	3	.700	129	23	69	1.35
1978	Chicago (NL)	64	99	8	10	.444	106	34	82	3.18
	Totals	178	289	21	16	.568	308	83	214	2.37

KEN HOLTZMAN 33 6-2 190   Bats R Throws L

The Yankees finally granted him a pardon . . . After New York manager Billy Martin let him sit and rust for two seasons, Yankees finally traded him for a minor league player named Ron Davis on June 10, 1978 . . . Holtzman loved it, having started his career with the Cubs in 1965 before they dealt him to Oakland for the 1972 season . . . A's traded him to Baltimore in 1976, where he started 13 games before being shipped to New York—and obscurity . . . Players involved in Holtzman deals have included Rick Monday, Reggie Jackson, Mike Torrez, Rudy May . . . Born Nov. 2, 1945, in St. Louis . . . In 1967, he was 9-0 for the Cubs, pitching only on weekend passes from the Army . . . Owns two no-hitters, one for Cubs against Atlanta and another for Cubs against Cincinnati . . . Never won fewer than 18 games in four years with A's

. . . Refuses to talk about bad times with Martin and Yanks, saying, "I'll talk about it when my career is over."

Year	Club	G	IP	W	L	Pct.	SO	BB	H	ERA
1965	Chicago (NL)	3	4	0	0	.000	3	3	2	2.25
1966	Chicago (NL)	34	221	11	16	.407	171	68	194	3.79
1967	Chicago (NL)	12	93	9	0	1.000	62	44	76	2.52
1968	Chicago (NL)	34	215	11	14	.440	151	76	201	3.35
1969	Chicago (NL)	39	261	17	13	.567	176	93	248	3.59
1970	Chicago (NL)	39	288	17	11	.607	202	94	271	3.38
1971	Chicago (NL)	30	195	9	15	.375	143	64	213	4.48
1972	Oakland	39	265	19	11	.633	134	52	232	2.51
1973	Oakland	40	297	21	13	.618	157	66	275	2.97
1974	Oakland	39	255	19	17	.528	117	51	273	3.07
1975	Oakland	39	266	18	14	.563	122	108	217	3.15
1976	Balt.-N.Y. (AL)	34	247	14	11	.560	66	70	265	3.64
1977	New York (AL)	18	72	2	3	.400	14	24	105	5.75
1978	New York (AL)	5	18	1	0	1.000	3	9	21	4.00
1978	Chicago (NL)	23	53	0	3	.000	36	35	61	6.11
	Totals	428	2750	168	141	.544	1557	857	2654	3.47

BILL BUCKNER 29 6-1 185   Bats L Throws L

Forgotten in Los Angeles, loved in Wrigley . . . Possesses one of baseball's prettiest swings and used it to lead Cubs in hitting at .323, but fell short of at-bats to qualify for possible batting title, though he was second behind Dave Parker in average . . . Came to Cubs in 1977 in deal that sent Rick Monday and Mike Garman to LA . . . Natural first baseman, but no room for him at LA with Steve Garvey there and two outfield spots taken by Dusty Baker and Reggie Smith . . . Born Dec. 14, 1949 in Vallejo, Calif. . . . Not only difficult to get out, but almost impossible to strike out because he'll swing at anything close . . . Wide receiver at Napa (Cal.) High School, so good he was elected to state's prep Hall of Fame . . . Passed up 60 collegiate football offers to sign with Dodgers.

Year	Club	Pos	G	AB	R	H	2B	3B	HR	RBI	SB	Avg.
1969	Los Angeles	PH	1	1	0	0	0	0	0	0	0	.000
1970	Los Angeles	OF-1B	28	68	6	13	3	1	0	4	0	.191
1971	Los Angeles	OF-1B	108	358	37	99	15	1	5	41	4	.277
1972	Los Angeles	OF-1B	105	383	47	122	14	3	5	37	10	.319
1973	Los Angeles	1B-OF	140	575	68	158	20	0	8	46	12	.275
1974	Los Angeles	OF-1B	145	580	83	182	30	3	7	58	31	.314
1975	Los Angeles	OF	92	288	30	70	11	2	6	31	8	.243
1976	Los Angeles	1B-OF	154	642	76	193	28	4	7	60	28	.301
1977	Chicago (NL)	1B	122	426	40	121	27	0	11	60	7	.284
1978	Chicago (NL)	1B	117	446	47	144	26	1	5	74	7	.323
	Totals		1012	3767	434	1102	174	15	54	411	107	.293

BOBBY MURCER 32 6-1 180   **Bats L Throws R**

Has a Will Rogers-type humor, issued from the comfort of his homemade rocking chair he carts around the league . . . Had a power outage in 1978, losing home run stroke and missing double figures for first time in 12-year career . . . Began with Yankees as shortstop, but switched to outfield and was Mickey Mantle's successor in center field . . . Yankees traded him to San Francisco for Bobby Bonds in 1975, then landed in Chicago for '77 season in deal involving Bill Madlock . . . Born May 20, 1946, in Oklahoma City . . . Once hit four consecutive homers in doubleheader for Toledo in minors, then matched it in majors by hitting four straight for New York in doubleheader with Cleveland . . . Hit three homers in one game against Kansas City in 1973 and hit for the cycle against Texas in 1972 . . . Receives more fan mail than any other Cub.

Year	Club	Pos	G	AB	R	H	2B	3B	HR	RBI	SB	Avg.
1965	New York (AL)....	SS	11	37	2	9	0	1	1	4	0	.243
1966	New York (AL)....	SS	21	69	3	12	1	1	0	5	2	.174
1967	New York (AL)....		In Military Service									
1968	New York (AL)....		In Military Service									
1969	New York (AL)....	OF-3B	152	564	82	146	24	4	26	82	7	.259
1970	New York (AL)....	OF	159	581	95	146	23	3	23	78	15	.251
1971	New York (AL)....	OF	146	529	94	175	25	6	25	94	14	.331
1972	New York (AL)....	OF	153	585	102	171	30	7	33	96	11	.292
1973	New York (AL)....	OF	160	616	83	187	29	2	22	95	6	.304
1974	New York (AL)....	OF	156	606	69	166	25	4	10	88	14	.274
1975	San Francisco	OF	147	526	80	157	29	4	11	91	9	.298
1976	San Francisco	OF	147	533	73	138	20	2	23	90	12	.259
1977	Chicago (NL).....	OF	154	554	90	147	18	3	27	89	16	.265
1978	Chicago (NL).....	OF	146	499	66	140	22	6	9	64	14	.281
	Totals...........		1552	5699	839	1594	246	43	210	876	118	.280

DAVE KINGMAN 30 6-6 210   **Bats R Throws R**

The John Hancock Tower of Wrigley . . . Signed as free agent for $1.4 million and quickly became Wrigley Field favorite by knocking down buildings behind left field ivy with patented lunar shots . . . Started quickly, hitting 20 homers early in the season, then tailed off . . . Still a definite liability in the outfield, but not much ground to cover in Wrigley . . . Born Dec. 21, 1948, in Pendleton, Ore. . . . Played with four teams in 1977—New York Mets, San Diego Padres, California Angels, New York Yankees—and was unhappy at each stop . . . Claims happiness in Chicago . . . Nicknamed

"King Kong," usually it's a home run or a strike out when he swings . . . Hit 600-foot homer in Wrigley that landed on a porch and once hit three homers against LA.

Year	Club	Pos	G	AB	R	H	2B	3B	HR	RBI	SB	Avg.
1971	San Francisco	1B-OF	41	115	17	32	10	2	6	24	5	.278
1972	San Francisco	3B-1B-OF	135	472	65	106	17	4	29	83	16	.225
1973	San Francisco	3B-1B-P	112	305	54	62	10	1	24	55	8	.203
1974	San Francisco	1B-3B-OF	121	350	41	78	18	2	18	55	8	.223
1975	New York (NL) . . .	OF-1B-3B	134	502	65	116	22	1	36	88	7	.231
1976	New York (NL) . . .	OF-1B	123	474	70	113	14	1	37	86	7	.238
1977	NY (NL)-SD	OF-1B	114	379	38	84	16	0	20	67	5	.222
1977	Calif-NY (AL)	1B-DH-OF	18	60	9	13	4	0	6	11	0	.217
1978	Chicago (NL)	1B-OF	119	395	65	105	17	4	28	79	3	.266
	Totals		917	3052	424	709	128	15	204	548	59	.232

MANNY TRILLO 28 6-1 160   Bats R Throws R

A one-season hitting flash (.280 in 1977), but continues to impress as an aggressive second baseman, particularly for a man who started career as a catcher . . . Came to Cubs from Oakland in deal that sent Billy Williams (Mr. Cub II behind Ernie Banks) to A's . . . Born on Christmas Day, 1950, in Caritito, Venezuela, his given name is Jesus . . . Phillies signed him as catcher, but A's drafted him out of the organization and made him a second baseman . . . Led NL second basemen in assists in 1975 with 509, then did better in '76 with 527 and made only 17 errors . . . Once went 42 games without an error . . . Played on NL all-star team in 1977 . . . Was a high school volleyball star.

Year	Club	Pos	G	AB	R	H	2B	3B	HR	RBI	SB	Avg.
1973	Oakland	2B	17	12	0	3	2	0	0	3	0	.250
1974	Oakland	2B	21	33	3	5	0	0	0	2	0	.152
1975	Chicago (NL)	2B-SS	154	545	55	135	12	2	7	70	1	.248
1976	Chicago (NL)	2B-SS	158	582	42	139	24	3	4	59	17	.239
1977	Chicago (NL)	2B	152	504	51	141	18	5	7	57	3	.280
1978	Chicago (NL)	2B	152	552	53	144	17	5	4	55	0	.261
	Totals		654	2228	204	567	73	15	22	246	21	.255

RICK REUSCHEL 29 6-3 230   Bats R Throws R

An off-year, but still managed 14 victories to lead club, his seventh straight in double figures for the Cubs . . . Despite boyish looks, he is mean and ugly on the mound and hates hitters taking liberties . . . Big, portly body to back it up—looks fat, but isn't . . . Keeps ball inside cozy Wrigley with sinker that coaxes grounders . . . Born May 16, 1949, in Quincy,

...ll. . . . Brother, Paul, used to pitch for Cubs and they combined for a shutout over the Dodgers in 1976, Rick getting the victory and Paul the save . . . Was 10-0 with a 1.29 ERA his senior season at Western Illinois University . . . Started fast in majors, striking out Bobby Bonds as the first man he faced and hitting a double his first time up . . . Specializes in beating Cincinnati.

Year	Club	G	IP	W	L	Pct.	SO	BB	H	ERA
1972	Chicago (NL)	21	129	10	8	.556	87	29	127	2.93
1973	Chicago (NL)	36	237	14	15	.483	168	62	244	3.00
1974	Chicago (NL)	41	241	13	12	.520	160	83	262	4.29
1975	Chicago (NL)	38	234	11	17	.393	155	67	244	3.73
1976	Chicago (NL)	38	260	14	12	.538	146	64	260	3.46
1977	Chicago (NL)	39	252	20	10	.667	166	74	233	2.79
1978	Chicago (NL)	35	243	14	15	.483	115	54	235	3.41
	Totals	348	1596	96	89	.519	997	433	1605	3.40

MIKE KRUKOW 27 6-4 195   Bats R Throws R

Began 1978 perfectly, 5-0, and finished niftily, 9-3, although his ERA was nothing to excite the Bleacher Bums . . . Wrote a song for teammate Bruce Sutter's wedding . . . Pitched at Cal Poly and was a composite 25-7 with a 1.93 ERA and 274 strikeouts in 274 innings . . . Once threw a sandlot no-hitter —and walked 17 batters . . . Born Jan. 21, 1952, in Long Beach, Cal. . . . Received Texas League's Gene Lawing Memorial Award for contributions to baseball on and off the field . . . Threw a four-hit shutout at Montreal his rookie season . . . Owns exceptional fast ball.

Year	Club	G	IP	W	L	Pct.	SO	BB	H	ERA
1976	Chicago (NL)	2	4	0	0	.000	1	2	6	9.00
1977	Chicago (NL)	34	172	8	14	.364	106	61	195	4.40
1978	Chicago (NL)	27	138	9	3	.750	81	53	125	3.91
	Totals	63	314	17	17	.500	188	116	326	4.24

IVAN DeJESUS 26 5-11 175   Bats R Throws R

A throw-in from LA in the Bill Buckner-Rick Monday deal, the Cubs threw him in at shortstop and he batted 619 times, compiling a .278 average . . . Played almost every day the past two seasons and played well . . . Signed out of Puerto Rican high school by Dodgers . . . Teams with second baseman Manny Trillo to form what Cub fans call "The Latin Connection" . . . Stole three bases in one game in

1977 and although he is no power hitter, opened the '77 season with a homer . . . Born Jan. 9, 1953, in Santurce, Puerto Rico . . . Played Class A ball for four years at Daytona Beach and Bakersfield learning the game . . . When finally elevated to Triple-A Albuquerque he hit .298 and made the Pacific Coast League all-star team.

Year	Club	Pos	G	AB	R	H	2B	3B	HR	RBI	SB	Avg.
1974	Los Angeles	SS	3	3	1	1	0	0	0	0	0	.333
1975	Los Angeles	SS	63	87	10	16	2	1	0	2	1	.184
1976	Los Angeles	SS-3B	22	41	4	7	2	1	0	2	0	.171
1977	Chicago (NL)	SS	155	624	91	166	31	7	3	40	24	.266
1978	Chicago (NL)	SS	160	619	104	172	24	7	3	35	41	.278
	Totals		403	1374	210	362	59	16	6	79	66	.263

RAY BURRIS 28 6-5 195   Bats R Throws R

Hard-thrower with penchant for plunking hitters who crowd home plate . . . Failed to reach 14 victories for first time since joining Cubs full-time for 1975 season . . . Reached the majors in his second pro season and promptly won his first start on April 18, 1973, pitching five shutout innings against the Mets . . . Made the club for good as a starter in 1975 . . . After starting 3-11 in 1976, he was named NL Pitcher of the Month in August with a 6-1 record and 1.89 ERA that saved his season . . . Born Aug. 22, 1950, in Idabel, Okla. . . . A good enough hitter to see some pinch-hitting duties . . . Pitched one of baseball's longest games when New York suffered its July, 1977, blackout and he finished the 5-2 victory in September.

Year	Club	G	IP	W	L	Pct.	SO	BB	H	ERA
1973	Chicago (NL)	31	65	1	1	.500	57	27	65	2.91
1974	Chicago (NL)	40	75	3	5	.375	40	26	91	6.60
1975	Chicago (NL)	36	238	15	10	.600	108	73	259	4.12
1976	Chicago (NL)	37	249	15	13	.536	112	70	251	3.11
1977	Chicago (NL)	39	221	14	16	.467	105	67	270	4.72
1978	Chicago (NL)	40	199	7	13	.350	94	79	210	4.75
	Totals	223	1047	55	58	.487	516	342	1146	4.23

TOP PROSPECT

SCOT THOMPSON 23 6-3 175   Bats L Throws L
Plays first base, outfield or tight end . . . High school didn't have baseball, so he once caught three touchdown passes in a football game . . . Played last two seasons at Wichita, hitting

305 in '77 and .326 in '78 . . . Born Dec. 7, 1955, in Grove City, Pa. . . . After setting Wichita club record with 169 hits last season, Cubs called him up Sept. 1 and he batted .417 (19 for 36) . . . Good defensive player, splitting time between first base and outfield in 1976 at Midland (Tex.), and made only 12 errors in 116 games.

MANAGER HERMAN FRANKS: Cigar-chomping champion of the National League . . . Moody and irascible, especially in defeat . . . Doesn't need baseball because of independent wealth in real estate business, but loves the game . . . Managed the San Francisco Giants to four second place finishes with a 367-280 record from 1965 through 1968 . . . An astute investor, Franks helps players as much off the field as on and Willie Mays gives him credit for helping more than anybody else . . . Born Jan. 4, 1915, at Price, Utah . . . Was general manager of the Salt Lake City team and gave Bob Kennedy his first managerial job . . . Kennedy then offered the Chicago job to Franks when Kennedy became club vice president . . . Spent six years in the majors . . . Started as a 17-year-old catcher with the Hollywood Stars of the Pacific Coast League . . . Played in the majors with the St. Louis Cardinals, Brooklyn Dodgers, Philadelphia Athletics and New York Giants.

GREATEST PITCHER

No, it wasn't Grover Cleveland Alexander, even though he won 128 games in a little more than eight seasons for the 1918-1925 Chicago Cubs.

Ferguson Arthur (Fergie) Jenkins did even better . . . doing it in Wrigley Field, where most pitchers regard a walk to the mound about the same as the walk to the gallows.

In seven-plus seasons (1966-73) with mostly mediocre Cub teams, Jenkins won 147 games.

Even so, Jenkins suffered from home runs flying out of the Wrigley brickyard, leading the league in gophers five times, tying a major league record. And, in 1968, he tied another major league record by losing five 1-0 games—yet he was 20-15, one of six 20-victory seasons, all in a row from 1967 to 1972.

Ferguson Jenkins had six straight 20-win seasons for Cubs.

And, when the Cubs shipped him to Texas in the American League in 1974, Jenkins showed he still had it with a 25-12 record, leading the league with 29 complete games.

That was nothing new . . . complete games were his specialty, completing what he started 31 times in 1971.

But then, does anybody remember John Clarkson? He won 52 games for the pennant-winning Cubs in 1885.

ALL-TIME CUB LEADERS

BATTING: Rogers Hornsby, .380, 1929
HRs: Hack Wilson, 56, 1930
RBIs: Hack Wilson, 190, 1930
STEALS: Frank Chance, 67, 1903
WINS: Mordecai Brown, 29, 1908
STRIKEOUTS: Ferguson Jenkins, 274, 1970

EW YORK METS

TEAM DIRECTORY: Chairman of the Board-Pres.: Mrs. Vincent de Roulet; GM: Joe McDonald; Dir. of Minor League Oper.: Pete Gebrian; Dir. of Player Devel.: Dick Gernert; Dir. Pub. Rel.: Arthur Richman; Trav. Sec.: Lou Niss; Mgr.: Joe Torre. Home: Shea Stadium (55,300). Field distances: 341, l.f. line; 410, c.f.; 341, r.f. line. Spring training: St. Petersburg, Fla.

SCOUTING REPORT

HITTING: The Mets own two of baseball's best hitters—Willie Mays and Joe Torre, their special coach and manager. Those two probably still can hit better than most men on the roster, but they won't be doing it, which is the reason the club once again will be near the bottom of the National League in hitting (.245), near the bottom in runs scored (607) and near the bottom in home runs (86).

Young Steve Henderson is a potential hitting star, but other than Willie Montanez, he doesn't have much protection in the lineup. Lee Mazzilli, Elliott Maddox and Lenny Randle are capable hitters, but not the type to carry a club on their shoulders from last place into a contending position. There are too

Lee Mazzilli was most consistent Met batter with .273 BA.

many automatic outs in the lineup to put many big innings together.

PITCHING: For years, when you said pitching you meant the New York Mets. You meant Tom Seaver and you meant Jon Matlack and you meant Jerry Koosman. All three are dearly-departed now and it's all up to Craig Swan and Pat Zachry and Nino Espinosa.

Like the hitting, the pitching was near the bottom of the National League with a 3.87 earned run average. The Mets got only 21 complete games, second worst to Cincinnati and everybody knows ex-Cincinnati manager Sparky Anderson went to his bullpen at first sign of distress.

Swan and Zachry, with a little help from their hitting friends, could be big winners for any team. Swan led the league with a 2.43 ERA and was 9-6 for his 29 starts, pitching five complete games. Zachry was rolling merrily along—until stubbing his toe. He was 10-6 in late July when his old bugaboo, his temper, got to him. After giving up a seventh-inning single to Pete Rose, extending Rose's hitting streak to 37 games, Zachry was lifted from the game. On his way to the shower, he angrily kicked the dugout step, fracturing a toe and didn't pitch again in 1978. The Mets need him to keep all 10 toes healthy.

FIELDING: Light-hitting Doug Flynn is vastly underrated at second base, making only eight errors in 128 games, three less than Montreal's Dave Cash, the acknowledged best at the position. Montanez can do anything you ask of him with a glove —and some things you don't ask. Tim Foli is dependable at shortstop and John Stearns isn't afraid of anything or anybody behind the plate.

The Met outfield won't dazzle anybody, though Lee Mazzilli makes it exciting by playing the shallowest center field in baseball and has learned the basket catch method from Mays. Maddox will play as well as his creaky knees will permit and Henderson is learning left field quickly, though his judgment on fly balls is still shaky.

OUTLOOK: If the Mets could use Torre and Mays in the lineup, the Cardinals and Cubs might be in trouble. But, that isn't possible, so the only people in trouble are Met fans, who must wait for the young players to develop and hope for good things from within the minor league system. The pitching is thin, the hitting is thinner and the defense is thinning out. By April 10, Met fans can start saying, "Wait'll next year."

NEW YORK METS 1979 ROSTER

MANAGER Joe Torre
Coaches—Chuck Cottier, Willie Mays, Joe Pignatano, Dick Sisler, Rube Walker

PITCHERS

No. Name	1978 Club	W-L	IP	SO	ERA	B-T	Ht.	Wt.	Born
46 Allen, Neil	Jackson	5-9	120	111	2.09	R-R	6-2	185	1/24/58 Kansas City, KS
	Tidewater	2-7	57	30	4.42				
34 Apodaca, Bob	New York (NL)	on disabled list				R-R	5-11	175	1/31/50 Los Angeles, CA
48 Berenguer, Juan	Tidewater	10-7	147	130	3.68	R-R	5-11	186	11/30/54 Panama
	New York (NL)	0-2	13	8	8.31				
28 Bernard, Dwight	Tidewater	5-3	44	21	1.64	R-R	6-2	170	5/31/52 Vernon, IL
	New York (NL)	1-4	48	26	4.31				
26 Bruhert, Mike	Tidewater	3-1	24	4	4.18	R-R	6-6	220	6/24/51 Jamaica, NY
	New York (NL)	4-11	134	56	4.77				
39 Espinosa, Nino	New York (NL)	11-15	204	76	4.72	R-R	6-0	184	8/15/53 Dominican Republic
— Falcone, Pete	St. Louis	2-7	75	28	5.76	L-L	6-2	185	10/1/53 Brooklyn, NY
— Field, Greg	Toledo	6-6	113	68	4.94	R-R	6-4	190	1/6/57 West Palm Beach, FL
	Orlando	2-2	—	20	3.66				
32 Hausman, Tom	Tidewater	5-2	74	42	1.22	R-R	6-5	200	3/31/53 Mobridge, SD
	New York (NL)	3-3	52	16	4.67				
31 Jackson, Roy Lee	Tidewater	11-10	176	132	3.74	R-R	6-2	195	5/1/54 Opelika, AL
	New York (NL)	0-0	13	6	9.00				
49 Kobel, Kevin	Tidewater	2-1	26	17	2.39	R-L	6-1	183	10/2/53 Buffalo, NY
	New York (NL)	5-6	108	51	2.92				
38 Lockwood, Skip	New York (NL)	7-13	91	73	3.56	R-R	6-0	200	8/17/46 Boston, MA
22 Murray, Dale	Cin-NY (NL)	9-6	119	62	3.78	R-R	6-4	205	2/2/50 Cuero, TX
44 Myrick, Bob	New York (NL)	0-3	25	13	3.24	R-L	6-1	200	10/1/52 Hattiesburg, MS
	Tidewater	4-8	94	64	3.83				
20 Pacella, John	Tidewater	4-11	102	77	4.96	R-R	6-2	184	9/15/56 Brooklyn, NY
	Jackson	4-3	43	44	2.64				
30 Scott, Mike	Tidewater	10-10	192	93	4.03	R-R	6-3	215	4/26/55 Santa Monica, CA
27 Swan, Craig	New York (NL)	9-6	207	125	2.43	R-R	6-3	225	11/30/50 Van Nuys, CA
40 Zachry, Pat	New York (NL)	10-6	138	78	3.33	R-R	6-5	175	4/24/52 Richmond, TX

CATCHERS

No. Name	1978 Club	H	HR	RBI	Pct.	B-T	Ht.	Wt.	Born
15 Benton, Butch	Jackson	99	6	44	.275	R-R	6-1	193	8/24/57 Tampa, FL
	New York (NL)	2	0	2	.500				
42 Hodges, Ron	New York (NL)	26	0	7	.255	L-R	6-1	185	6/22/49 Franklin Co., VA
35 Rosado, Luis	Tidewater	98	6	42	.270	R-R	6-0	180	12/6/55 Puerto Rico
12 Stearns, John	New York (NL)	126	15	73	.264	R-R	6-0	185	8/21/51 Denver, CO
29 Trevino, Alex	Tidewater	77	5	37	.294	R-R	5-10	165	8/26/57 Mexico
	New York (NL)	3	0	0	.250				

INFIELDERS

No. Name	1978 Club	H	HR	RBI	Pct.	B-T	Ht.	Wt.	Born
10 Chapman, Kelvin	Jackson	130	8	42	.266	R-R	5-11	172	6/2/56 Willits, CA
23 Flynn, Doug	New York (NL)	126	0	36	.237	R-R	5-11	165	4/18/51 Lexington, KY
19 Foli, Tim	New York (NL)	106	1	27	.257	R-R	6-0	176	12/8/50 Culver City, CA
7 Kranepool, Ed	New York (NL)	17	3	19	.210	L-L	6-3	215	11/8/44 Bronx, NY
25 Montanez, Willie	New York (NL)	156	17	96	.256	L-L	6-1	193	4/1/48 Puerto Rico
3 Ramirez, Mario	Tidewater	81	5	41	.208	R-R	5-9	153	9/12/57 Puerto Rico
11 Randle, Len	New York (NL)	102	2	35	.233	B-R	5-10	169	2/12/49 Long Beach CA
1 Valentine, Bobby	New York (NL)	43	1	18	.269	R-R	5-10	185	5/13/50 Stamford, CT
18 Youngblood, Joel	New York (NL)	67	7	30	.252	R-R	5-11	175	8/28/51 Houston, TX

OUTFIELDERS

No. Name	1978 Club	H	HR	RBI	Pct.	B-T	Ht.	Wt.	Born
4 Boisclair, Bruce	New York (NL)	48	4	15	.224	L-L	6-2	200	12/9/52 Putnam, CT
17 Flores, Gil	S. Lake City	79	2	33	.279	R-R	6-0	180	10/27/52 Puerto Rico
	Tidewater	27	0	6	.270				
	New York (NL)	8	0	1	.276				
5 Henderson, Steve	New York (NL)	156	10	65	.266	R-R	6-1	197	11/18/52 Houston, TX
21 Maddox, Elliott	New York (NL)	100	2	39	.257	R-R	5-11	181	12/21/48 E. Orange, NJ
16 Mazzilli, Lee	New York (NL)	148	16	61	.273	B-R	6-1	180	3/25/55 New York, NY
6 Norman, Dan	Tidewater	133	18	66	.281	R-R	6-2	195	1/11/55 Los Angeles, CA
	New York (NL)	17	4	10	.266				

MET PROFILES

WILLIE MONTANEZ 31 6-1 193   Bats L Throws I

Does tricks with bat as he approaches plate
but wasn't much of a treat for Mets once a
pitcher threw the ball . . . Struggled through
worst batting season since first three years in
majors with Philadelphia, hitting 26 points
below career average . . . A magician with
the glove, probably best defensive first baseman in baseball . . . Prefers to be called
Guillermo . . . Born April 1, 1948, in Catano, Puerto Rico, but
he's been no April Fool's joke to most pitchers through his
career . . . Increased power output with 37 homers past two
seasons and his 17 led light-hitting Mets in 1978 . . . Mets gave
up Jon Matlack and John Milner on Dec. 8, 1977, to get him
. . . Lasted one winter with Cardinals (1969-70) but Cards gave
him to Philadelphia after Curt Flood refused to report to
Phillies.

Year	Club	Pos	G	AB	R	H	2B	3B	HR	RBI	SB	Avg
1966	California	1B	8	2	2	0	0	0	0	0	1	.000
1970	Philadelphia	OF-1B	18	25	3	6	0	0	0	3	0	.240
1971	Philadelphia	OF-1B	158	599	78	153	27	6	30	99	4	.255
1972	Philadelphia	OF-1B	147	531	60	131	39	3	13	64	1	.247
1973	Philadelphia	1B-OF	146	552	69	145	16	5	11	65	2	.263
1974	Philadelphia	1B-OF	143	527	55	160	33	1	7	79	3	.304
1975	Phil.-San Fran.	1B	156	602	61	182	34	2	10	101	6	.302
1976	San Fran.-Atl.	1B	163	650	74	206	29	2	11	84	2	.317
1977	Atlanta	1B	136	544	70	156	31	1	20	68	1	.287
1978	New York (NL)	1B	159	609	66	156	32	0	17	96	9	.256
	Totals		1234	4641	538	1295	241	20	119	659	29	.279

LENNY RANDLE 30 5-10 169   Bats S Throws R

Gained undeserved reputation as bad guy
after 1977 spring altercation with Texas manager Frank Lucchesi . . . Actually polite,
soft-spoken guy willing to play anywhere, any
time, as he has done—playing third, second,
short and was even an outfielder on 1969
NCAA champion Arizona State . . . Installed
as third baseman when Joe Torre took over
as Met manager . . . Born Feb. 12, 1949, in Long Beach, Cal.
. . . Average took a 71-point nose dive in 1978 . . . Was sensa-

tion in 1977, leading the Mets in batting average, hits, runs, triples, stolen bases and game-winning RBIs . . . Was No. 1 draft choice of old Washington Senators in secondary phase of 1970 free agent draft and never played below Triple-A ball . . . Graduate of Compton Centennial High School, which also produced Roy White, Reggie Smith, Don Wilson and Wayne Simpson.

Year	Club	Pos	G	AB	R	H	2B	3B	HR	RBI	SB	Avg.
1971	Washington	2B	75	215	27	47	11	0	2	13	1	.219
1972	Texas	2B-SS-OF	74	249	23	48	13	0	2	21	4	.193
1973	Texas	2B-OF	10	29	3	6	1	1	1	1	0	.207
1974	Texas 3B-2B-OF-SS		151	520	65	157	17	4	1	49	26	.302
1975	Texas 2B-OF-3B-SS-C		156	601	85	166	24	7	4	57	16	.276
1976	Texas	2B-OF-3B	142	539	53	121	11	6	1	51	30	.224
1977	New York (NL) ...	3B-OF-2B	136	513	78	156	22	7	5	27	33	.304
1978	New York (NL) ...	3B-OF-2B	132	437	53	102	16	8	2	35	14	.233
	Totals..........		876	3103	387	803	115	33	18	254	124	.259

PAT ZACHRY 26 6-5 175   Bats R Throws R

Was disappointed with Reds when they gave up on him to obtain Tom Seaver from Mets, saying, "I really thought I could be the No. 1 pitcher on Cincinnati's staff." . . . Temper is own worst enemy and proved it July 24, 1978, in seventh inning of game with Reds . . . Gave up single to Pete Rose, extending his streak to 37 games, then gave up two more hits and a walk . . . When taken out of the game, he kicked the dugout step, fracturing his foot and didn't appear in another game . . . Born April 24, 1952, in Richmond, Tex. . . . Once set a minor league record by giving up third straight game-winning homer in three nights. He heaved his glove over the grandstands he was so mad . . . When not upset, owns dry sense of humor delivered with Texas drawl . . . Has great stuff . . . After beating Yankees in 1976 World Series he gained national attention by saying "I'm gonna dump my World Series money on my bed and wallow in it."

Year	Club	G	IP	W	L	Pct.	SO	BB	H	ERA
1976	Cincinnati	38	204	14	7	.667	143	83	170	2.74
1977	Cincinnati-N.Y. (NL)	31	195	10	13	.435	99	77	207	4.25
1978	New York (NL)	21	138	10	6	.625	78	60	120	3.33
	Totals.................	90	537	34	26	.567	320	220	497	3.44

STEVE HENDERSON 26 6-1 197   Bats R Throws R

Once considered top prospect in Cincinnati organization, but Reds couldn't find room for him in their outfield and included him in deal for Tom Seaver . . . Reds had no choice because Mets wouldn't make deal unless he was included . . . Carries normally potent bat, but became infected with the non-hitting ailment that struck entire club lineup . . . Born Nov. 18, 1952, in Houston . . . Reds drafted him No. 5 in June, 1974, free agent draft out of Prairie View A&M University . . . Led 1976 Eastern League at Three Rivers (Canada) in total bases, triples and hits . . . Despite playing only 99 games after trade to Mets in 1977, he led the club in RBIs and tied in homers . . . Lost Rookie of Year honors by one vote.

Year	Club	Pos	G	AB	R	H	2B	3B	HR	RBI	SB	Avg.
1977	New York (NL) ...	OF	99	350	67	104	16	6	12	65	6	.297
1978	New York (NL) ...	OF	157	587	83	156	30	9	10	65	13	.266
	Totals...........		256	937	150	260	46	15	22	130	19	.277

DOUG FLYNN 28 5-11 165   Bats R Throws R

Used both at shortstop and second base, but may be best all-around defensive second baseman in NL . . . Never much threat with the bat with .235 career average and only two homers in almost 1,200 major league at-bats . . . Was reserve infielder in Cincinnati until Reds shipped him to New York with Steve Henderson, Pat Zachry and Dan Norman for Tom Seaver on June 15, 1977 . . . Was playing sandlot softball when Reds signed him in 1971 . . . Born April 18, 1951, in Lexington, Ky. . . . Father, Bobby, was basketball star at University of Dayton and Doug played basketball at University of Kentucky before disagreeing with Uncle Adolph Rupp and transferring to Somerset (Ky.) Community College . . . Was all-star in Eastern League in 1973 and American Association in 1974.

Year	Club	Pos	G	AB	R	H	2B	3B	HR	RBI	SB	Avg.
1975	Cincinnati	3B-2B-SS	89	127	17	34	7	0	1	20	3	.268
1976	Cincinnati	2B-3B-SS	93	219	20	62	5	2	1	20	2	.283
1977	Cin.-N.Y. (NL)	SS-2B-3B	126	314	14	62	7	2	0	19	1	.197
1978	New York (NL) ...	SS-2B-3B	156	532	37	126	12	8	0	36	3	.237
	Totals...........		464	1192	88	284	31	12	2	95	9	.238

ELLIOTT MADDOX 30 5-11 181   Bats R Throws R

Club invested $1 million in him in 1977 free agent draft when he played out option in Baltimore after Yankees dealt him there in Paul Blair deal . . . Still hampered by knee problems that began when he slipped on Shea Stadium grass in 1975 while Yanks played there during Yankee Stadium refurbishing . . . Born Dec. 21, 1948, in East Orange, N.J. . . . Batted 389 times in 1978 after making only 153 plate appearances in 1976 and 1977 . . . Good defensive player . . . Has no power . . . Former Big Ten batting champion at University of Michigan, where he took pre-law courses . . . Signed for $40,000 with Detroit Tigers in 1968 and tied for league lead in double plays by third baseman in Carolina League with 18 in 1969 . . . Was in deal that sent him to Washington for Denny McLain in 1970.

Year	Club	Pos	G	AB	R	H	2B	3B	HR	RBI	SB	Avg.
1970	Detroit	3B-OF-SS-2B	109	258	30	64	13	4	3	24	2	.248
1971	Washington	OF-3B	128	258	38	56	8	2	1	18	10	.217
1972	Texas	OF	98	294	40	74	7	2	0	10	20	.252
1973	Texas	OF-3B	100	172	24	41	1	0	1	17	5	.238
1974	New York (AL)	OF-2B-3B	137	466	75	141	26	2	3	45	6	.303
1975	New York (AL)	OF-2B	55	218	36	67	10	3	1	23	9	.307
1976	New York (AL)	OF	18	46	4	10	2	0	0	3	0	.217
1977	Baltimore	OF	49	107	14	28	7	0	2	9	2	.262
1978	New York (NL)	OF-3B	119	389	43	100	18	2	2	39	2	.257
	Totals		813	2208	304	581	92	15	13	188	56	.263

LEE MAZZILLI 24 6-1 180   Bats S Throws R

Contest between him and Houston's Terry Puhl as to who plays shallowest center field . . . Confident in his ability to go back and make the catch, usually a basket catch taught him by coach Willie Mays . . . Swift afoot, both afield and on the basepaths . . . Jumped from Double-A ball to Mets in 1976, but played first full season in 1977, appearing in 159 games and stealing 22 bases . . . Born March 25, 1955, in New York City . . . Ripped three-run pinch-hit homer in his second big league at-bat . . . Just 12 days later, he ruined Pittsburgh's 1976 pennant hopes by blasting a game-winning two-run homer with two outs in the ninth . . . A high school All-American at Brooklyn's Abraham Lincoln High school, where he "switch-threw" as well as switch-hit . . . On June 8, 1975, at San Jose, set what may be all-time professional base-

ball record by stealing seven bases in seven-inning game . . .
Mets first draft pick in June, 1973, free agent draft.

Year	Club	Pos	G	AB	R	H	2B	3B	HR	RBI	SB	Avg.
1976	New York (NL) ...	OF	24	77	9	15	2	0	2	7	5	.195
1977	New York (NL) ...	OF	159	537	66	134	24	3	6	46	22	.250
1978	New York (NL) ...	OF	148	542	78	148	28	5	16	61	20	.273
	Totals..........		331	1156	153	297	54	8	24	114	47	.257

JOHN STEARNS 27 6-0 185   Bats R Throws R

Played reckless, mad dog type defense in
football at University of Colorado and liter-
ally earned nickname "Mad Dog" . . . Plays
baseball like football, mean and tough . . .
Acquired from Philadelphia in deal that sent
Tug McGraw to Phillies, then asked to be
sent to minors so he could play every day and
hit .310 at Tidewater . . . Came back and
took over catching from Jerry Grote, with Grote instructing him
. . . Born Aug. 21, 1951, in Denver . . . Was nation's second
draft pick by Phillies behind Rangers' David Clyde in 1973 free
agent draft . . . Oakland picked him ninth in '69 draft but he
opted for Colorado football scholarship and played in four
straight post-season bowl games as defensive back . . . Won Big
Eight batting title in 1972 and NCAA home run title with 15 in
1973.

Year	Club	Pos	G	AB	R	H	2B	3B	HR	RBI	SB	Avg.
1974	Philadelphia......	C	1	2	0	1	0	0	0	0	0	.500
1975	New York (NL) ...	C	59	169	25	32	5	1	3	10	4	.189
1976	New York (NL) ...	C-3B	32	103	13	27	6	0	2	10	1	.262
1977	New York (NL) ...	C-1B	139	431	52	108	25	1	12	55	9	.251
1978	New York (NL) ...	C-1B	143	477	65	126	24	1	15	73	25	.264
	Totals..........		373	1182	155	294	61	3	32	148	39	.249

CRAIG SWAN 28 6-3 225   Bats R Throws R

Great individual numbers lost in the swirl of
poor team numbers . . . ERA was the lowest
in NL and walks-to-strikeouts ratio was su-
perb . . . First time in six major league seasons his won-lost record was above .500 and
it was accomplished with probably the worst
team he's had behind him . . . Born Nov. 30,
1950, in Van Nuys, Cal. . . . Highly devel-
oped slider taught to him by Tom Seaver . . . An Arizona State

product . . . Has survived numerous physical problems, including peritonitis following an appendectomy in 1973 and a stress fracture injury of the pitching elbow in 1974 . . . Won 47 games, struck out 459 and pitched 457 innings at Arizona State, all school records, and lost only one game in 17 senior-year decisions . . . Hobbies include collecting food in his stomach.

Year	Club	G	IP	W	L	Pct.	SO	BB	H	ERA
1973	New York (NL)	3	8	0	1	.000	4	2	16	9.00
1974	New York (NL)	7	30	1	3	.250	10	21	28	4.50
1975	New York (NL)	6	31	1	3	.250	19	13	38	6.39
1976	New York (NL)	23	132	6	9	.400	89	44	129	3.55
1977	New York (NL)	26	147	9	10	.474	71	56	153	4.22
1978	New York (NL)	29	207	9	6	.600	125	58	164	2.43
	Totals................	94	555	26	32	.448	318	194	528	3.60

TOP PROSPECT

NEIL ALLEN 21 6-2 195   **Bats R Throws R**
Only an 11th round draft pick in June, 1976, but quickly attracted Mets' attention by throwing three three-hitters in his first three starts as a pro at Marion (Rookie) and Wausau (A) . . . His blind father taught him to pitch . . . Born Jan. 24, 1958, in Kansas City, Kan. . . . Began '78 at Jackson (AA) and led the league in ERA and had 111 strikeouts in 120 innings . . . Was 10-2 with a 2.79 ERA at Lynchburg (A) in 1977 with 126 strikeouts in 142 innings . . . Very hard thrower . . . Turned down scholarships from every Big 8 football coach to sign with Mets.

MANAGER JOE TORRE: Young and in touch enough to still be one of the boys, but big and tough enough to handle all situations . . . A knowledgeable baseball man with a quick, cutting sense of humor delivered from behind dark, flashing eyes . . . Retired to the dugout after serving last part of 1977 as first player-manager in NL since Solly Hemus in 1960 . . . Born July 18, 1940, in Brooklyn . . . NL MVP for Cardinals in 1971 with .363 batting average that included 24 homers and 137 RBIs . . . Never managed a day in the minors after having played in nine All-Star Games . . . During 1971 MVP season, led NL in four hitting departments—average, hits, RBIs and total bases—first to lead the league in four categories since Stan Musial in 1948 . . . Began as catcher in 1960, but moved to third base in 1970 . . . Joined the Mets after 1974 season, in time for a trip to Japan and was named MVP on the excursion.

GREATEST PITCHER

Some might say the greatest pitcher in Met history had to be Roger Craig, who somehow managed to win 15 games in 1962 and 1963 for a team whose folk hero was Marv Throneberry.

Of course, Craig lost 46 games in those two laughable seasons.

But, the epic hero of all Met pitchers is George Thomas Seaver, the pitching scientist still active with the Cincinnati Reds.

Tom Seaver owns every positive pitching record imaginable for the Mets . . . most victories (189), most shutouts (42), most

Tom Seaver holds virtually all of Mets' pitching records.

strikeouts (2,406), most complete games (166), lowest earned run average (2.49).

It wasn't until Seaver put on the crimson of the Cincinnati Reds that he pitched his first no-hitter, but he pitched five one-hitters as a Met, including two no-hit games that went into the ninth inning before being ruined.

The former University of Southern California star is a three-time Cy Young Award winner (1969, 1973 and 1975). And he led the Mets to a world's championship in 1969 and to the National League pennant in 1973.

Seaver won 20 games four times with the Mets, including 25-7 in 1969, and 20-10 in 1971 when he put together a 1.76 earned run average.

"I've always found pitching a creative art and that's why I find it so stimulating. In fact, I'm still learning," he says.

ALL-TIME MET LEADERS

BATTING: Cleon Jones, .340, 1969
HRs: Dave Kingman, 37, 1976
RBIs: Rusty Staub, 105, 1975
STEALS: Len Randle, 33, 1977
WINS: Tom Seaver, 25, 1969
STRIKEOUTS: Tom Seaver, 289, 1971

LOS ANGELES DODGERS

TEAM DIRECTORY: Chairman: Walter O'Malley; Pres.: Peter O'Malley; Vice-Pres., Player Personnel: Al Campanis; Vice-Pres., Public Relations: Fred Claire; Vice-Pres., Minor Leagues: Bill Schweppe; Publicity: Steve Brener; Trav. Sec.: Lee Scott; Mgr.: Tom Lasorda. Home: Dodger Stadium (56,000). Field distances: 330 l.f. line; 400, c.f.; 330, r.f. line. Spring training: Vero Beach, Fla.

SCOUTING REPORT

HITTING: The Dodgers don't get much hitting out of their catchers, but seven out of eight isn't bad. Just ask manager Tom Lasorda and not only will he convince you the seven others are Ted Williams and Babe Ruth combined, he'll convince you catchers Steve Yeager and Joe Ferguson are potential .300 hitters.

They aren't, of course, but the other seven guys ARE hitters —from Steve Garvey, a yearly .300 hitter, right on through the hit-infested lineup. Beginning at the top, not only does Davey Lopes hit and steal bases, he developed a penchant for the long ball, which the Yankees discovered in the World Series. Bill Russell isn't the most feared man in knickers, but ask the Phillies if he ever gets any clutch hits.

Reggie Smith and Garvey are twin terrors in the middle of the lineup, both hitting for average and power. If a pitcher is fortunate enough to escape those two dangers, up waddles the

Dodgers shot to NL pennant when Reggie Smith's bat got hot.

"Penguin," Ron Cey, a compact man with a long-ball stroke. If a pitcher thinks it gets easier after that . . . well, there's Dusty Baker and Rick Monday and . . . well, it just never ends. Simply stated, the Dodgers are loaded from both sides of the plate—Lopes, Russell, Garvey, Cey, Baker on the right side; Monday from the left side; and Smith switch-hitting from both sides.

PITCHING: Tommy John is gone, a staggering loss for most teams. For the Dodgers, it is but a minor irritation because of Don Sutton, Burt Hooton, Doug Rau and Rick Rhoden. Rau, 15-9 last year, always seems to be overlooked come playoffs and World Series, but suddenly he becomes the big left-hander in the Dodgers' rotation.

In addition, the Dodgers own a couple of youngsters who figure immensely, especially Bob Welch, a World Series participant despite being a college pitcher two years ago. And, Robert Castillo is said to be able to throw a ball through the Iron Curtain without guards detecting it. The bullpen? Well-stuffed, of course, with Charlie Hough and Terry Forster and Lance Rautzhan. That's why the Dodgers could afford to let John pass through the free agent draft without so much as a whimper.

FIELDING: In the outfield, Baker chases fly balls with radar in left, Monday crashes into walls to stop potential doubles in center, and Smith throws out baserunners from the right field corner. OK, so how about the infield? "Yeah, how about it?" says Lasorda. "It's the best." Who's to argue.

The stiff-legged, stiff-armed Cey is an all-star third baseman, as much for his glove as his bat. Russell isn't the best shortstop, even if Lasorda believes it, but he can play on any team. Lopes isn't as good as Montreal's Dave Cash at second, but neither is anybody else. Just say if Cash is No. 1, Lopes is No. 1A. Garvey doesn't have a lot of range at first base, but he handles his mitt as if it were a surgeon's operating glove. Yeager can throw from behind the plate and Joe Ferguson can too. All this is to say the Dodger defense is always in eighteen good hands.

OUTLOOK: The National League West should be LA, then the other five, and not too many teams could say that after losing a pitcher like John. But, when the lineup is populated by so many all-stars and so much talent-in-the-rough, the Dodgers can't help but win. They'll jump to the front early, as they always do because they leave for spring training ready for the season, and they'll stay there.

LOS ANGELES DODGERS 1979 ROSTER

MANAGER Tom Lasorda
Coaches—Red Adams, Monty Basgall, Mark
Cresse, Preston Gomez, Jim Lefebvre

PITCHERS

No.	Name	1978 Club	W-L	IP	SO	ERA	B-T	Ht.	Wt.	Born
41	Castillo, Robert	Albuquerque	5-3	82	65	5.38	R-R	5-10	170	4/18/55 Los Angeles, CA
		Los Angeles	0-4	34	30	3.97				
51	Forster, Terry	Los Angeles	5-4	65	46	1.94	L-L	6-3	210	1/14/52 Sioux Falls, SD
29	Hannahs, Gerald	Los Angeles	0-0	2	5	9.00	L-L	6-3	200	3/6/52 Binghamton, NY
		San Antonio	9-5	109	95	2.57				
		Memphis	1-3	35	31	4.63				
46	Hooton, Burt	Los Angeles	19-10	236	104	2.71	R-R	6-1	200	2/7/50 Greenville, TX
49	Hough, Charlie	Los Angeles	5-5	93	66	3.29	R-R	6-2	190	1/5/48 Honolulu, HI
56	Landreth, Larry	Albuquerque	6-3	86	45	6.28	R-R	6-1	175	3/11/55 Stratford, ONT.
		Denver	1-3	29	20	5.52				
25	Power, Ted	San Antonio	6-5	101	97	4.01	R-R	6-4	220	1/31/55 Tulsa, OK
31	Rau, Doug	Los Angeles	15-9	199	95	3.26	L-L	6-2	175	12/15/48 Columbus, TX
38	Rautzhan, Lance	Los Angeles	2-1	61	25	2.95	R-L	6-1	200	8/20/52 Pottsville, PA
		Albuquerque	3-2	25	15	3.96				
36	Rhoden, Rick	Los Angeles	10-8	165	79	3.65	R-R	6-3	195	5/16/53 Boynton Beach, FL
48	Stewart, Dave	Los Angeles	0-0	2	1	0.00	R-R	6-2	200	2/19/57 Oakland, CA
		San Antonio	14-12	193	130	3.69				
43	Sutcliffe, Rick	Los Angeles	0-0	2	0	0.00	L-R	6-6	200	6/21/56 Independence, MO
		Albuquerque	13-6	184	99	4.45				
20	Sutton, Don	Los Angeles	15-11	238	154	3.55	R-R	6-2	185	4/2/45 Clio, AL
47	Tennant, Mike	San Antonio	4-2	72	71	2.88	R-R	6-3	190	10/14/55 Humansville, MO
35	Welch, Bob	Los Angeles	7-4	111	66	2.03	R-R	6-3	190	11/3/56 Detroit, MI
		Albuquerque	5-1	69	53	3.78				

CATCHERS

No.	Name	1978 Club	H	HR	RBI	Pct.	B-T	Ht.	Wt.	Born
13	Ferguson, Joe	Houston-LA	78	14	50	.224	R-R	6-2	215	9/19/46 San Francisco, CA
40	Gulden, Brad	Los Angeles	0	0	0	.000	L-R	5-11	170	6/10/56 New Ulm, MN
		Albuquerque	128	8	72	.294				
5	Oates, Johnny	Los Angeles	23	0	6	.307	L-R	6-0	185	1/21/46 Sylvia, NC
22	Scioscia, Mike	San Antonio	61	2	34	.299	L-R	6-2	200	11/27/58 Upper Darby, PA
7	Yeager, Steve	Los Angeles	44	4	23	.193	R-R	6-0	190	11/24/48 Huntington, WV

INFIELDERS

No.	Name	1978 Club	H	HR	RBI	Pct.	B-T	Ht.	Wt.	Born
10	Cey, Ron	Los Angeles	150	23	84	.270	R-R	5-10	185	2/15/48 Tacoma, WA
6	Garvey, Steve	Los Angeles	202	21	113	.316	R-R	5-10	190	12/22/48 Tampa, FL
57	Guerrero, Pedro	Los Angeles	5	0	1	.625	R-R	5-11	176	6/29/56 Dominican Republic
		Albuquerque	166	14	116	.337				
15	Lopes, Davey	Los Angeles	163	17	58	.278	R-R	5-10	170	5/3/46 E. Providence, RI
23	Martinez, Teddy	Los Angeles	14	1	5	.255	R-R	6-0	160	12/10/47 Dominican Republic
18	Russell, Bill	Los Angeles	179	3	46	.286	R-R	6-0	180	10/21/48 Pittsburg, KA
4	Snider, Kelly	San Antonio	142	13	91	.293	L-L	6-0	187	4/12/55 Springfield, MO
34	Thomas, Derrel	San Diego	80	3	26	.227	B-R	6-0	160	1/14/51 Los Angeles, CA

OUTFIELDERS

No.	Name	1978 Club	H	HR	RBI	Pct.	B-T	Ht.	Wt.	Born
12	Baker, Dusty	Los Angeles	137	11	66	.262	R-R	6-2	195	6/15/49 Riverside, CA
55	Bradley, Mark	San Antonio	56	3	30	.042	R-R	6-1	180	12/3/56 Elizabethtown, KY
		Lodi	27	2	11	.248				
33	Davalillo, Vic	Los Angeles	24	1	11	.312	L-L	5-8	155	7/31/39 Venezuela
3	Law, Rudy	Los Angeles	3	0	1	.250	L-L	6-1	165	10/7/56 Waco, TX
		Albuquerque	179	4	72	.312				
16	Monday, Rick	Los Angeles	87	19	57	.254	L-L	6-3	200	11/20/45 Batesville, AR
11	Mota, Manny	Los Angeles	10	0	6	.303	R-R	5-11	168	2/18/38 Dominican Republic
17	Simpson, Joe	Los Angeles	2	0	1	.400	L-L	6-3	175	12/31/51 Purcell, OK
		Albuquerque	163	5	73	.309				
8	Smith, Reggie	Los Angeles	132	23	93	.295	B-R	6-0	195	4/2/45 Shreveport, LA
52	White, Myron	Los Angeles	7	0	1	.500	L-L	5-10	180	8/1/57 Long Beach, CA
		San Antonio	108	15	66	.244				

DODGER PROFILES

REGGIE SMITH 34 6-0 195   Bats S Throws R

Shaved mustache off for World Series, but Yankees recognized him anyway and pitched him carefully . . . Dodgers staggered when he missed 30 games with assorted injuries, but he led the club in homers with 29 and was second in RBIs . . . Born April 2, 1945, in Shreveport, La. . . . His definition of pressure? "When you have two kids, a car, a house and you're trying to make it on unemployment. . . ." Will never be unemployed because he dabbles in so many things—real estate, training quarter horses, playing seven musical instruments, scuba diving, flying airplanes, cooking, playing tennis, working in a morgue, and playing right field masterfully.

Year	Club	Pos	G	AB	R	H	2B	3B	HR	RBI	SB	Avg.
1966	Boston	OF	6	26	1	4	1	0	0	0	0	.154
1967	Boston	OF-2B	158	565	78	139	24	6	15	61	16	.246
1968	Boston	OF	155	558	78	148	37	5	15	69	22	.265
1969	Boston	OF	143	543	87	168	29	7	25	93	7	.309
1970	Boston	OF	147	580	109	176	32	7	22	74	10	.303
1971	Boston	OF	159	618	85	175	33	2	30	95	11	.283
1972	Boston	OF	131	467	75	126	25	4	21	74	15	.270
1973	Boston	OF-1B	115	423	79	128	23	2	21	69	3	.303
1974	St. Louis	OF-1B	143	517	79	160	26	9	23	100	4	.309
1975	St. Louis	OF-1B-3B	135	477	67	144	26	3	19	76	9	.302
1976	St. L.-L.A.	OF-1B-3B	112	395	55	100	15	5	18	49	3	.253
1977	Los Angeles	OF	148	488	104	150	27	4	32	87	7	.307
1978	Los Angeles	OF	128	447	82	132	27	2	29	93	12	.295
	Totals		1680	6104	979	1750	325	56	270	941	119	.287

STEVE GARVEY 30 5-10 190   Bats R Throws R

Mr. Personality and Mr. Consistency . . . Started the season with 21-game hitting streak . . . Made big news with clubhouse scrap with teammate Don Sutton, over which Sutton later apologized . . . Finished the season by hitting .430 in September, but ran out of hits at World Series time . . . Born Dec. 22, 1948, in Tampa, Fla. . . . Father still drives team bus in spring training, as did way back for the "boys of summer" . . . Was Most Valuable Player in All-Star Game . . . Durable, playing in every Dodger game for third straight season . . . Had more than 200 hits for fourth time in five years . . . Junior high school in Lindsay, Cal., is named Steve Garvey Junior High School and its nickname is Dodgers.

Colors? Dodger blue and white, of course . . . Great friend of New York's Reggie Jackson.

Year	Club	Pos	G	AB	R	H	2B	3B	HR	RBI	SB	Avg.
1969	Los Angeles......	3B	3	3	0	1	0	0	0	0	0	.333
1970	Los Angeles......	3B-2B	34	93	8	25	5	0	1	6	1	.269
1971	Los Angeles......	3B	81	225	27	51	12	1	7	26	1	.227
1972	Los Angeles......	3B-1B	96	294	36	79	14	2	9	30	4	.269
1973	Los Angeles......	1B-OF	114	349	37	106	17	3	8	50	0	.304
1974	Los Angeles......	1B	156	642	95	200	32	3	21	111	5	.312
1975	Los Angeles......	1B	160	659	85	210	38	6	18	95	11	.319
1976	Los Angeles......	1B	162	631	85	200	37	4	13	80	19	.317
1977	Los Angeles......	1B	162	646	91	192	25	3	33	115	9	.297
1978	Los Angeles......	1B	162	639	89	202	36	9	21	113	10	.316
	Totals............		1130	4181	553	1266	216	31	131	626	60	.303

DAVEY LOPES 32 5-10 170   Bats R Throws R

Displayed inspirational and outstanding play in World Series, hitting with power and playing with verve in memory of good friend Jim Gilliam, Dodger coach who died two days before the World Series began . . . Is Dodger captain . . . Born May 3, 1946, in East Providence, R.I. . . . Was consistent with hitting streaks of 12, 10 and nine games . . . Twice has stolen four bases in a game . . . "You don't want Lopes on base if you're a pitcher," says manager Tommy Lasorda. "He makes things happen like Lou Brock . . ." Was originally an outfielder, but moved to second base prior to 1971 season by his Spokane minor league manager, Lasorda. Has 11 brothers and sisters, which might explain quick hands.

Year	Club	Pos	G	AB	R	H	2B	3B	HR	RBI	SB	Avg.
1972	Los Angeles......	2B	11	42	6	9	4	0	0	1	4	.214
1973	Los Angeles......	2B-OF-SS-3B	142	535	77	147	13	5	6	37	36	.275
1974	Los Angeles......	2B	145	530	95	141	26	3	10	35	59	.266
1975	Los Angeles......	2B-OF-SS	155	618	108	162	24	6	8	41	77	.262
1976	Los Angeles......	2B-OF	117	427	72	103	17	7	4	20	63	.241
1977	Los Angeles......	2B	134	502	85	142	19	5	11	53	47	.283
1978	Los Angeles......	2B	151	587	93	163	25	4	17	58	45	.278
	Totals............		855	3241	536	867	128	30	56	245	331	.268

RON CEY 31 5-10 185   Bats R Throws R

Despite short, stubby stature and a waddle that earned him the nickname "Penguin" from his teammates, he hit 23 homers, the fourth straight season of hitting 20 or more . . . Has averaged more than 90 RBIs over last five seasons . . . Born Feb. 15, 1948, in Tacoma, Wash. . . . Stiff-legged and stiff-armed afield, but acknowledged as good defensive third baseman . . . "I'm never satisfied with my accomplishments because you can always do better," he says. "Team accomplishments are more important anyway . . ." An all-star five straight years . . . Once drove in eight runs in one game . . . Since 1958, 53 men have played third base for the Dodgers, but Cey has been there regularly since 1973.

Year	Club	Pos	G	AB	R	H	2B	3B	HR	RBI	SB	Avg.
1971	Los Angeles......	PH	2	2	0	0	0	0	0	0	0	.000
1972	Los Angeles......	3B	11	37	3	10	1	0	1	3	0	.270
1973	Los Angeles......	3B	152	507	60	124	18	4	15	80	1	.245
1974	Los Angeles......	3B	159	577	88	151	20	2	18	97	1	.262
1975	Los Angeles......	3B	158	566	72	160	29	2	25	101	5	.283
1976	Los Angeles......	3B	145	502	69	139	18	3	23	80	0	.277
1977	Los Angeles......	3B	153	564	77	136	22	3	30	110	3	.241
1978	Los Angeles......	3B	159	555	84	150	32	0	23	84	2	.270
	Totals..........		939	3310	453	870	140	14	135	555	12	.263

DUSTY BAKER 29 6-2 195   Bats R Throws R

Power production slipped from 30 homers in 1977 to 11 homers in 1978, but contributed heavily in clutch . . . Batted .378 during 13-game hitting streak from Aug. 21 to Sept. 7 while Dodgers were holding off the Reds . . . A young underachiever, he almost gave up baseball at age 10 because he wasn't making Little League all-star teams. His dad talked him out of quitting to take a paper route . . . Born June 15, 1949, in Riverside, Cal. . . . Once broke into tears on April 1 when manager Tom Lasorda called him into his office and told him he was traded to Cleveland, enough to make anybody cry. Lasorda told him it was an April Fool's joke . . . Baker's strong outfield play and clutch hitting is never a joke.

Year	Club	Pos	G	AB	R	H	2B	3B	HR	RBI	SB	Avg.
1968	Atlanta..........	OF	6	5	0	2	0	0	0	0	0	.400
1969	Atlanta..........	OF	3	7	0	0	0	0	0	0	0	.000
1970	Atlanta..........	OF	13	24	3	7	0	0	0	4	0	.292
1971	Atlanta..........	OF	29	62	2	14	2	0	0	4	0	.226
1972	Atlanta..........	OF	127	446	62	143	27	2	17	76	4	.321
1973	Atlanta..........	OF	159	604	101	174	29	4	21	99	24	.288
1974	Atlanta..........	OF	149	574	80	147	35	0	20	69	18	.256
1975	Atlanta..........	OF	142	494	63	129	18	2	19	72	12	.261
1976	Los Angeles......	OF	112	384	36	93	13	0	4	39	2	.242
1977	Los Angeles......	OF	153	533	86	155	26	1	30	86	2	.291
1978	Los Angeles......	OF	149	522	62	137	24	1	11	66	12	.262
	Totals..........		1042	3655	495	1001	174	10	122	515	74	.274

RICK MONDAY 33 6-3 200   Bats L Throws L

After a fantastic April during in which he hit .353 and slapped eight homers, good for NL Player of the Month, he sustained injuries that bothered him season-long . . . A national hero a few years back while playing for the Cubs when he physically stopped two people from burning an American flag in center field of Dodger Stadium . . . Not the reason LA traded for him after the 1976 season . . . Born Nov. 20, 1945, in Batesville, Ark. . . . Was 1965 College Player of the Year at Arizona State and was the first college player drafted that year, by the A's . . . Former Marine and is vice president of a real estate firm, a natural position for a center fielder.

Year	Club	Pos	G	AB	R	H	2B	3B	HR	RBI	SB	Avg.
1966	Kansas City	OF	17	41	4	4	1	1	0	2	1	.098
1967	Kansas City	OF	124	406	52	102	14	6	14	58	3	.251
1968	Oakland	OF	148	482	56	132	24	7	8	49	14	.274
1969	Oakland	OF	122	399	57	108	17	4	12	54	12	.271
1970	Oakland	OF	112	376	63	109	19	7	10	37	11	.290
1971	Oakland	OF	116	355	53	87	9	3	18	56	6	.245
1972	Chicago (NL)	OF	138	434	68	108	22	5	11	42	12	.249
1973	Chicago (NL)	OF	149	554	93	148	24	5	26	56	5	.267
1974	Chicago (NL)	OF	142	538	84	158	19	7	20	58	7	.294
1975	Chicago (NL)	OF	136	491	89	131	29	4	17	60	8	.267
1976	Chicago (NL)	OF-1B	137	534	107	145	20	5	32	77	5	.272
1977	Los Angeles	OF	118	392	47	90	13	1	15	48	1	.230
1978	Los Angeles	OF	119	342	54	87	14	1	19	57	2	.254
	Totals		1578	5344	827	1409	225	56	202	654	93	.264

BILL RUSSELL 30 6-0 180   Bats R Throws R

Manager Tom Lasorda calls him the best shortstop in the National League, but Dave Concepcion (Cincinnati) and Larry Bowa (Philadelphia) dispute the claim . . . For sure, Russell was outstanding as a hitter in the playoffs and World Series, banging the winning hit in deciding game of playoffs with Phillies . . . But he was anything but slick in the field during the Series . . . Born Oct. 21, 1948, in Pittsburg, Kan. . . . Was second on the club in hits with 179 and his .286 average was 25 points higher than his previous high . . . Performed the incredible in his first major league game for the Dodgers when he hit for the cycle—single, double, triple, homer . . . "I've never thought of myself in the same class with PeeWee Reese and Maury Wills, but if some people put me there, that's great with me," he says.

Year	Club	Pos	G	AB	R	H	2B	3B	HR	RBI	SB	Avg.
1969	Los Angeles	OF	98	212	35	48	6	2	5	15	4	.226
1970	Los Angeles	OF-SS	81	278	30	72	11	9	0	28	9	.259
1971	Los Angeles	2B-OF-SS	91	211	29	48	7	4	2	15	6	.227
1972	Los Angeles	SS-OF	129	434	47	118	19	5	4	34	14	.272
1973	Los Angeles	SS	162	615	55	163	26	3	4	56	15	.265
1974	Los Angeles	SS-OF	160	553	61	149	18	6	5	65	14	.269
1975	Los Angeles	SS	84	252	24	52	9	2	0	14	5	.206
1976	Los Angeles	SS	149	554	53	152	17	3	5	65	15	.274
1977	Los Angeles	SS	153	634	84	176	28	6	4	51	16	.278
1978	Los Angeles	SS	155	625	72	179	32	4	3	46	10	.286
	Totals		1262	4368	460	1157	173	44	32	389	108	.265

BURT HOOTON 29 6-1 200　　　Bats R Throws R

Dodgers call him Happy because he never smiles and never seems to be happy . . . Hitters facing his knuckle curve aren't happy, either . . . Led the NL in ERA and his 19 victories was a career high . . . Giants hate him because he was 4-and-0 against them . . . Two is his magic number because he has pitched four two-hitters in the majors . . . Born on Feb. 7, 1950, in Greenville, Tex., and stayed in the state to pitch for the University of Texas, where he was a three-time All-American with a 35-3 record and 1.14 ERA . . . Signed by the Cubs and appeared in the minors only briefly in 1971 . . . Won 12 straight games for LA in 1975, erasing Sandy Koufax's club record of 11.

Year	Club	G	IP	W	L	Pct.	SO	BB	H	ERA
1971	Chicago (NL)	3	21	2	0	1.000	22	10	8	2.14
1972	Chicago (NL)	33	218	11	14	.440	132	81	201	2.81
1973	Chicago (NL)	42	240	14	17	.452	134	73	248	3.68
1974	Chicago (NL)	48	176	7	11	.389	94	51	214	4.81
1975	Chi (NL)-L.A.	34	235	18	9	.667	153	68	190	3.06
1976	Los Angeles	33	227	11	15	.423	116	60	203	3.25
1977	Los Angeles	32	223	12	7	.632	153	60	184	2.62
1978	Los Angeles	32	236	19	10	.655	104	61	196	2.71
	Totals	257	1576	94	83	.531	908	464	1444	3.22

DON SUTTON 34 6-2 185　　　Bats R Throws R

Ol' reliable of the Dodger pitching staff, tied Don Drysdale for all-time shutouts in LA history with 49 . . . Reached 200th career victory with six-hitter over Pirates July 18 and became LA's all-time strikeout leader on June 29 . . . Now has 2,378 . . . Leads all-time LA pitching list in eight categories, but made bigger news during the season with celebrated clubhouse wrestling match with Steve Garvey . . . Born

May 2, 1945, in Clio, Ala. . . . Grew up wanting to pitch for the Yankees and admitted rooting for Notre Dame even though he grew up a confirmed Southern Baptist . . . Clubhouse humorist who hones his wit as an LA disc jockey during the off-season.

Year	Club	G	IP	W	L	Pct.	SO	BB	H	ERA
1966	Los Angeles	37	226	12	12	.500	209	52	192	2.99
1967	Los Angeles	37	233	11	15	.423	169	57	223	3.94
1968	Los Angeles	35	208	11	15	.423	162	59	179	2.60
1969	Los Angeles	41	293	17	18	.486	217	91	269	3.47
1970	Los Angeles	38	260	15	13	.536	201	78	251	4.08
1971	Los Angeles	38	265	17	12	.586	194	55	231	2.55
1972	Los Angeles	33	273	19	9	.679	207	63	186	2.08
1973	Los Angeles	33	256	18	10	.643	200	56	196	2.43
1974	Los Angeles	40	276	19	9	.679	179	80	241	3.23
1975	Los Angeles	35	254	16	13	.552	175	62	202	2.87
1976	Los Angeles	35	268	21	10	.677	161	82	231	3.06
1977	Los Angeles	33	240	14	8	.636	150	69	207	3.19
1978	Los Angeles	34	238	15	11	.577	154	54	228	3.55
	Totals	469	3290	205	155	.569	2378	858	2836	3.08

TOP PROSPECT

MIKE SCIOSCIA 19 6-2 195   Bats L Throws R

Just a baby, but moving up quickly as fast-maturing catcher . . . Signed as No. 1 1976 draft pick and played in a rookie league at 17, then played at Class A Clinton (Ia.) at 18 and Class AA San Antonio at 19 . . . Dodgers say he'll probably play this season at Class AAA Albuquerque . . . Born July 10, 1959, in Philadelphia . . . Began 1978 season catching for San Antonio and was hitting .360 for six weeks, then underwent knee surgery . . . Came back late in the season as a designated hitter and batted over .300 . . . Dodgers say he'll hit with power in the big leagues and can do everything required but run fast.

MANAGER TOM LASORDA: As one writer put it, "With Tom Lasorda, you get egg rolls." . . . Keeps endless supply of egg rolls under clubhouse desk and passes them out to an equally endless stream of celebrities and hangers-on . . . In 29 years as a member of the Dodger organization he has yet to utter first negative word about anything or anybody connected with it . . . A Dale Carnegie graduate—remembers everybody's name, from Frank Sinatra and Don Rickles down to lowliest member of a grounds crew . . . Born Sept. 22, 1927,

in Norristown, Pa. . . . Hugs and kisses; positive words to his
players are his trademark, besides bleeding Dodger Blue . . .
Was Manager of the Year in 1977 after becoming only the 19th
manager in history to win a pennant in his first year . . .
Succeeded Walter Alston . . . Spent 11 years as a pitcher in the
organization, playing in the majors briefly.

GREATEST PITCHER

It says here . . . Don Drysdale.

It could also say Don Sutton, or Sandy Koufax, or even
Dazzy Vance.

For the last four years of his 12-year career, Koufax was
clearly the best—25-5, 19-5, 26-8, 27-9 for a 97-27 record from
1963 through 1966. But his earlier career precludes any designa-
tion as the all-time greatest.

Sutton is still going, 205-155 for his 13-year career, and only
four career victories ahead is big, bad Drysdale. For seven
straight years, from 1922 through 1928, Vance led the National
League in strikeouts, and he won 190 games in 11 years.

But, for overall consistency, for better or for worse, the selection as all-time greatest belongs to Donald Scott (Big D) Drysdale, who was 6-feet-5 inches, 190 pounds of meanness on the
mound.

For 14 years, all with the Brooklyn-Los Angeles Dodgers,
Drysdale was 209-166, with two 20-victory seasons, including a
25-9 mark in 1962.

Drysdale owns Dodger club records for victories (209), shutouts (tied with Sutton at 49), strikeouts (2,486), innings pitched
(3,432) and is second behind Koufax's run average (2.95 to
2.76).

The pick is Drysdale, with Koufax, Sutton and Vance listed
as 1A, 1B and 1C.

ALL-TIME DODGER LEADERS

BATTING: Babe Herman, .393, 1930
HRs: Duke Snider, 43, 1956
RBIs: Tommy Davis, 153, 1962
STEALS: Maury Wills, 104, 1962
WINS: Joe McGinnity, 29, 1900
STRIKEOUTS: Sandy Koufax, 382, 1965

SAN FRANCISCO GIANTS

TEAM DIRECTORY: Co-Chairmen: Bob Lurie and Bud Herseth; GM: Spec Richardson; Asst. GM: Charles Feeney Jr.; Dir. of Scouting and Minor League Oper.: Jack Schwarz; Consultant; Jerry Donovan; Trav. Sec.: Frank Bergonzi; Dir. Pub. Rel.: Stu Smith; Mgr.: Joe Altobelli. Home: Candlestick Park (58,000). Field distances: 335, l.f. line; 410, c.f.; 225 r.f. line. Spring training: Phoenix, Ariz.

Jack Clark's slugging makes Giants a pennant contender.

SCOUTING REPORT

HITTING: Jack Clark is a hitter and Bill Madlock is a hitter and Terry Whitfield is a hitter. Willie McCovey is a part-time hitter, a doggone good part-time hitter. But, there were several holes in the lineup, holes which became caverns as the Giants dropped from first to third as the days dwindled in the National League West last season.

When Madlock plays, he can hit blind-folded, and he surprised by shedding his singles-hitter tag with 15 homers. Clark is a legitimate big league hitter, both for average (.306) and for power, (25 HRs). Whitfield proved he can hit (.289) if given a chance every day.

Mike Ivie was invaluable as a pinch-hitter and a sharecropper at first base with McCovey, hitting .308 in 117 games. He is too valuable not to play every day, but first base and catcher are his only positions . . . and he prefers not to catch. Darrell Evans was productive at third base. Roger Metzger hit well after joining the Giants from Houston in midseason, but can't be counted on to hit with regularity. Now, if only Rod Carew . . .

PITCHING: The Giants live, or die, with an excellent young pitching staff revolving around veteran left-hander Vida Blue. The addition of pitching coach Larry Shepard, an excellent handler of young arms, will help the Giants.

Starting with Blue, the Giants are well-populated with pitchers. Bob Knepper gives the Giants two excellent left-handed starters. And, with Ed Halicki and John Montefusco, the Giants should be strong from the right side—but both Halicki and Montefusco must rebound from so-so seasons. With Gary Lavelle and Randy Moffitt in the bullpen, the Giants have the ability to stop any enemy uprising. Lavelle was involved in 23 decisions (13-10), showing how much manager Joe Altobelli thrusts him into crucial game-on-the-line situations. Terry Cornutt and Greg Minton are a couple of younger arms that could figure.

FIELDING: The Giants filled a cavity when they obtained Metzger to play shortstop. Whether he plays second base or third base, Madlock is no Gold Glover. He'd rather bat than field, but he manages to get in the way of as many grounders as possible. Neither McCovey nor Ivie has much range at first, making the Giant infield somewhat suspect. The Giants made 179 errors in 1977 and Altobelli vowed to slice that figure drastically and the Giants reduced it to 146, but still were only ninth in National League fielding. Clark has vastly improved in the outfield, but still has all his pictures taken with a bat in his hand. Defense isn't something they talk about positively in Candlestick.

OUTLOOK: As long as the pitching staff holds up, the Giants will be in excellent condition. Pitching is so important in baseball and the Giants have it. The rest of the team gained immense confidence with their fine showing last season and the Giants are ready—for second place.

SAN FRANCISCO GIANTS 1979 ROSTER

MANAGER Joe Altobelli
Coaches—Jim Davenport, Tom Haller, Dave Bristol, Larry
        Shepard

PITCHERS

No.	Name	1978 Club	W-L	IP	SO	ERA	B-T	Ht.	Wt.	Born
14	Blue, Vida	San Francisco	18-10	259	173	2.75	B-L	6-0	192	7/28/49 Mansfield, LA
42	Cornutt, Terry	Phoenix	8-5	86	37	3.87	R-R	6-2	195	10/2/52 Roseburg, OR
		San Francisco	0-0	3	0	0.00				
40	Curtis, John	San Francisco	4-3	63	38	3.71	L-L	6-1½	190	3/9/48 Newton, MA
—	Glinatsis, Michael	Waterbury	9-13	162	88	4.39	R-R	6-3	210	4/22/55 Youngstown, OH
28	Halicki, Ed	San Francisco	9-10	199	105	2.85	R-R	6-7	220	10/4/50 Newark, NJ
39	Knepper, Bob	San Francisco	17-11	260	147	2.63	L-L	6-2	180	5/25/54 Akron, OH
46	Lavelle, Gary	San Francisco	13-10	98	63	3.31	B-L	6-1	190	1/3/49 Scranton, PA
38	Minton, Greg	Phoenix	7-4	92	32	4.50	B-R	6-2	190	7/29/51 Lubbock, TX
		San Francisco	0-1	16	6	7.88				
17	Moffitt, Randy	San Francisco	8-4	82	52	3.29	R-R	6-3	190	10/13/48 Long Beach, CA
26	Montefusco, John	San Francisco	11-9	239	177	3.80	R-R	6-1	180	5/25/50 Keansburg, NJ
25	Nastu, Phil	Phoenix	9-8	160	114	4.67	L-L	6-2	180	3/8/55 Bridgeport, CT
		San Francisco	0-1	8	5	5.63				
37	Plank, Ed	Phoenix	8-8	90	35	2.10	R-R	6-1	195	4/9/52 Chicago, IL
		San Francisco	0-0	7	1	3.86				

CATCHERS

No.	Name	1978 Club	H	HR	RBI	Pct.	B-T	Ht.	Wt.	Born
2	Hill, Marc	San Francisco	87	3	36	.243	R-R	6-3	210	2/18/52 Louisiana, MO
47	Littlejohn, Dennis	Phoenix	57	4	31	.256	R-R	6-2	200	10/4/54 Santa Monica, CA
		San Francisco	0	0	0	.000				
3	Sadek, Mike	San Francisco	26	2	9	.239	R-R	5-10	170	5/30/46 Minneapolis, MN
30	Tamargo, John	St. Lou.-San Fran.	22	1	8	.224	B-R	5-10	180	11/7/51 Tampa, FL

INFIELDERS

No.	Name	1978 Club	H	HR	RBI	Pct.	B-T	Ht.	Wt.	Born
21	Andrews, Rob	San Francisco	39	1	11	.220	R-R	5-11	180	12/11/52 Santa Monica, CA
4	Evans, Darrell	San Francisco	133	20	78	.243	L-R	6-2	200	5/26/47 Pasadena, CA
32	Heintzelman, Tom	Phoenix	65	5	41	.272	R-R	6-0	189	11/3/46 St. Charles, MO
		San Francisco	8	2	6	.229				
15	Ivie, Mike	San Francisco	98	11	55	.308	R-R	6-4	210	8/8/52 Decatur, IL
34	James, Skip	Phoenix	41	1	24	.259	L-L	6-0	190	10/21/49 Elmhurst, IL
		San Francisco	2	0	3	.095				
—	Kuecker, Mark	Waterbury	87	3	33	.215	R-R	5-10	150	11/26/57 Brenham, TX
10	LeMaster, Johnnie	San Francisco	64	1	14	.235	R-R	6-2	160	6/19/54 Portsmouth, OH
18	Madlock, Bill	San Francisco	138	15	44	.309	R-R	5-11	180	1/12/51 Memphis, TN
44	McCovey, Willie	San Francisco	80	12	64	.228	L-L	6-4	210	1/10/38 Mobile, AL
42	Metzger, Roger	Hou.-San Fran.	88	0	23	.246	B-R	6-0	165	10/10/47 Fredricksburg, TX
29	Murray, Rich	Phoenix	124	5	58	.281	R-R	6-4	195	7/6/57 Los Angeles, CA
—	Rex, Michael	Waterbury	143	5	52	.304	R-R	5-10	170	8/8/54 Lebanon, OR
—	Strain, Joe	Phoenix	171	3	52	.305	R-R	5-10	165	4/30/54 Denver, CO

INFIELDERS

No.	Name	1978 Club	H	HR	RBI	Pct.	B-T	Ht.	Wt.	Born
22	Clark, Jack	San Francisco	181	25	98	.306	R-R	6-1	170	11/10/55 Brighton, PA
9	Cruz, Heity	Chi. (NL)-S.F.	62	8	33	.227	R-R	5-11	180	4/2/53 Arroyo, PR
36	Dwyer, Jim	St. L.-S.F.	53	6	26	.223	L-L	5-10	175	1/3/50 Evergreen Park, IL
35	Gardner, Art	Phoenix	132	8	88	.267	L-L	5-11	180	9/21/52 Madden, MS
		San Francisco	0	00	00	.000				
31	Herndon, Larry	San Francisco	122	1	32	.259	R-R	6-3	190	11/3/53 Sunflower, MS
—	Johnston, Gregory	Phoenix	142	6	69	.274	L-L	6-0	175	2/12/55 Los Angeles, CA
45	Whitfield, Terry	San Francisco	141	10	32	.289	L-R	6-1	197	1/12/53 Blythe, CA

GIANT PROFILES

JACK CLARK 23 6-1 170   Bats R Throws R

Probably would have been NL MVP if Giants hadn't folded in September . . . Was outstanding offensively and improved enough defensively so that no pitcher asked, or demanded, that he be taken out of right field in mid-game, as Ed Halicki did in once in 1977 . . . Had the misfortune of putting together a 26-game hitting streak that was almost ignored because it came during Pete Rose's 44-game streak . . . Born Nov. 10, 1955, in New Brighton, Pa. . . . Took right field job from Bobby Murcer . . . Signed as a pitcher but quickly converted to third baseman, then outfielder, when his bat was more useful than a pitching toe.

Year	Club	Pos	G	AB	R	H	2B	3B	HR	RBI	SB	Avg.
1975	San Francisco	OF-3B	8	17	3	4	0	0	0	2	1	.235
1976	San Francisco	OF	26	102	14	23	6	2	2	10	6	.225
1977	San Francisco	OF	136	413	64	104	17	4	13	51	12	.252
1978	San Francisco	OF	156	592	90	181	46	8	25	98	15	.306
	Totals..........		326	1124	171	312	69	14	40	161	34	.278

ED HALICKI 28 6-7 220   Bats R Throws R

Record was only 9-10, but pitched 199 innings with a 2.85 earned run average . . . Suffered from malnutrition of runs . . . Bore down hardest against Reds after he shut them out early in the season and Cincinnati manager Sparky Anderson promised the world, "We'll beat his brains out next time . . ." They didn't . . . Born Oct. 4, 1950, in Newark, N.J. . . . Giants call him Ho Ho in deference to his height and resemblance to The Jolly Green Giant . . . Throws a fastball that he seemingly delivers from 10 feet in front of home plate with long, whippy arm.

Year	Club	G	IP	W	L	Pct.	SO	BB	H	ERA
1974	San Francisco	16	74	1	8	.111	40	31	84	4.26
1975	San Francisco	24	160	9	13	.409	153	59	143	3.49
1976	San Francisco	32	186	12	14	.462	130	61	171	3.63
1977	San Francisco	37	258	16	12	.571	168	70	241	3.31
1978	San Francisco	29	199	9	10	.474	105	45	166	2.85
	Totals..................	138	877	47	57	.452	596	266	805	3.39

VIDA BLUE 29 6-0 192   Bats S Throws R

Found listed in most publications in 1978 as a member of the Cincinnati Reds, including the Official 1978 Cincinnati Reds Media Fact Book . . . Never wore uniform No. 40 assigned to him (he wanted No. 14, but Pete Rose owned it) because commissioner Bowie Kuhn ruled against a trade that sent Blue from Oakland to Cincinnati for first baseman Dave Revering and $1.75 million . . . Charlie Finley then traded him to San Francisco for Gary Thomasson, Gary Alexander, Dave Heaverlo, Alan Wirth, John Johnson, Phil Huffman and a player to be named later . . . Kuhn approved . . . Blue disappeared for a week, shortly after March 15, 1978, trade but was found at home solving some personal problems . . . Born July 28, 1949, in Mansfield, La. . . . Won both Cy Young and MVP in 1971 with 24-8 record at Oakland and owns eight career games of giving up two or less hits, including one no-hitter . . . Credited with pushing Giants into a contender both with his arm and his advice to young pitchers . . . Wears first name on back of jersey in honor of his father, Vida Sr. . . . Once refused Finley's request to change his first name to "True."

Year	Club	G	IP	W	L	Pct.	SO	BB	H	ERA
1969	Oakland	12	42	1	1	.500	24	18	49	6.21
1970	Oakland	6	39	2	0	1.000	35	12	20	2.08
1971	Oakland	39	312	24	8	.750	301	88	209	1.82
1972	Oakland	25	151	6	10	.375	111	48	117	2.80
1973	Oakland	37	264	20	9	.690	158	105	214	3.27
1974	Oakland	40	282	17	15	.531	174	98	246	3.26
1975	Oakland	39	278	22	11	.667	189	99	243	3.01
1976	Oakland	37	298	18	13	.581	166	63	268	2.35
1977	Oakland	38	280	14	19	.424	157	86	284	3.83
1978	San Francisco	35	258	18	10	.643	171	70	233	2.79
	Totals	308	2204	142	96	.597	1486	687	1883	2.92

BOB KNEPPER 24 6-2 180   Bats L Throws L

One of three players Giants put on untouchable list in off-season dealings, and for good reason . . . Was half of one-two left handed pitching punch with Vida Blue, winning 17 games to Vida's 18 and topping Blue's ERA —2.63 to 2.83 . . . Refined pitching techniques by watching and listening to Vida . . . Born May 25, 1954, in Akron, Ohio . . . Giants signed him out of Calistoga (Cal.) High School as a second round draft pick after he struck out 19 in a seven-inning game and 22 in a nine-inning game . . . Once threw only 81 pitches in complete-game victory over Pittsburgh . . . Came up with reputation of wildness, but walked only 85 in 260 innings, using mostly hard-breaking curve balls.

Year	Club	G	IP	W	L	Pct.	SO	BB	H	ERA
1976	San Francisco	4	25	1	2	.333	11	7	26	3.24
1977	San Francisco	27	166	11	9	.550	100	72	151	3.36
1978	San Francisco	36	260	17	11	.607	147	85	218	2.63
	Totals	67	451	29	22	.569	258	164	395	2.93

WILLIE McCOVEY 41 6-4 210   Bats L Throws L

"You're only old as you feel, and I don't feel old," said the grand old man of Candlestick Park . . . Timeliness was godliness for "Stretch" . . . Had only 80 hits, but drove in 64 runs . . . Was worth his weight in advice to youth-dotted Giant lineup . . . While Giants led NL West through most of the season, correctly predicted what would happen by saying, "If it's close late in the year, the Dodgers or Reds will beat us because they've been there, they have the experience. We'll learn from it, though." . . . Born Jan. 10, 1938, in Mobile, Ala. . . . Two seasons away from goal of playing in four different decades, which only six other men have done . . . Designed his own custom home on San Francisco Peninsula.

Year	Club	Pos	G	AB	R	H	2B	3B	HR	RBI	SB	Avg.
1959	San Francisco	1B	52	192	32	68	9	5	13	38	2	.354
1960	San Francisco	1B	101	260	37	62	15	3	13	51	1	.238
1961	San Francisco	1B	106	328	59	89	12	3	18	50	1	.271
1962	San Francisco	OF-1B	91	229	41	67	6	1	20	54	3	.293
1963	San Francisco	OF-1B	152	564	103	158	19	5	44	102	1	.280
1964	San Francisco	OF-1B	130	364	55	80	14	1	18	54	2	.220
1965	San Francisco	1B	160	540	93	149	17	4	39	92	0	.276
1966	San Francisco	1B	150	502	85	148	26	6	36	96	2	.295
1967	San Francisco	1B	135	456	73	126	17	4	31	91	3	.276
1968	San Francisco	1B	148	523	81	153	16	4	36	105	4	.293
1969	San Francisco	1B	149	491	101	157	26	2	45	126	0	.320
1970	San Francisco	1B	152	495	98	143	39	2	39	126	0	.289
1971	San Francisco	1B	105	329	45	91	13	0	18	70	0	.277
1972	San Francisco	1B	81	263	30	56	8	0	14	35	0	.213
1973	San Francisco	1B	130	383	52	102	14	3	29	75	1	.266
1974	San Diego	1B	128	344	53	87	19	1	22	63	1	.253
1975	San Diego	1B	122	413	43	104	17	0	23	68	1	.252
1976	San Diego	1B	71	202	20	41	9	0	7	36	0	.203
1976	Oakland	DH	11	24	0	5	0	0	0	0	0	.208
1977	San Francisco	1B	141	478	54	134	21	0	28	86	3	.280
1978	San Francisco	1B	108	351	32	80	19	2	12	64	1	.228
	Totals		2423	7731	1187	2100	336	46	505	1482	26	.272

BILL MADLOCK 28 5-11 180   Bats R Throws R

Injuries limited his plate appearances, but he hit .309, a normal occurrence for the man with a seeing-eye bat . . . It was his fifth straight season above .300 . . . Never expected to make it after being drafted No. 268 by the Washington Senators . . . Born Jan. 12, 1951, in Memphis . . . Once went six-for-six in Albuquerque . . . An off-season sportscaster in Sacramento . . . Won 1976 batting title on last day, beating Cincinnati's Ken Griffey with a four-for-four day . . . Moved from third base to second base in 1978 to make room for Darrell Evans at third.

Year	Club	Pos	G	AB	R	H	2B	3B	HR	RBI	SB	Avg.
1973	Texas	3B	21	77	16	27	5	3	1	5	3	.351
1974	Chicago (NL)	3B	128	453	65	142	21	5	9	54	11	.313
1975	Chicago (NL)	3B	130	514	77	182	29	7	7	64	9	.354
1976	Chicago (NL)	3B	142	514	68	174	36	4	15	84	15	.339
1977	San Francisco	2B-3B	140	533	70	161	28	1	12	46	13	.302
1978	San Francisco	2B-3B	122	447	76	138	26	3	15	44	16	.309
	Totals		683	2538	372	824	145	20	59	297	67	.325

JOHN MONTEFUSCO 28 6-1 180   Bats R Throws R

Injuries slowed "The Count" so much he even went out of the predicting business . . . Does controversial things like predict shutouts publicly . . . Sometimes it worked, sometimes not . . . Once said he would strike out Johnny Bench four times, but Bench's first appearance turned into a three-run homer . . . Undaunted, "The Count" said, "I'll get him next time." . . . Actively campaigned for NL Rookie of the Year after 15-9 season in 1975, saying, "I deserve it." . . . He won it . . . Born May 25, 1950, in Keansburg, N.J., and was signed out of a New Jersey industrial league . . . Pitched a no-hitter against Atlanta in 1976 after discovering the sinker ball, which he said he used to keep former teammate Willie Montanez hitless on a bet, not knowing he'd keep all the Braves hitless.

Year	Club	G	IP	W	L	Pct.	SO	BB	H	ERA
1974	San Francisco	7	39	3	2	.600	34	19	41	4.85
1975	San Francisco	35	244	15	9	.625	215	86	210	2.88
1976	San Francisco	37	253	16	14	.533	172	74	224	2.85
1977	San Francisco	26	157	7	12	.368	110	46	170	3.50
1978	San Francisco	36	239	11	9	.550	177	68	233	3.80
	Totals	141	932	52	46	.531	708	283	878	3.29

GARY LAVELLE 30 6-1 190 Bats S Throws L

One of baseball's premier relief pitchers, called the best left-handed relief pitcher by ex-Cincy manager Sparky Anderson . . . Was 13-10, all in relief, as manager Joe Altobelli generally had him finishing games . . . An ex-Marine, he is deeply religious . . . Born Jan. 3, 1949, in Scranton, Pa. . . . Bounced around the minors for eight years, mostly as a starter, before findng his niche as relief specialist . . . Had 14 saves to go with 13 victories, placing his talented left hand in 27 San Francisco wins.

Year	Club	G	IP	W	L	Pct.	SO	BB	H	ERA
1974	San Francisco	10	17	0	3	.000	12	10	14	2.12
1975	San Francisco	65	82	6	3	.667	51	48	80	2.96
1976	San Francisco	65	110	10	6	.625	71	52	102	2.70
1977	San Francisco	73	118	7	7	.500	93	37	106	2.06
1978	San Francisco	67	98	13	10	.565	63	44	96	3.31
	Totals	280	425	36	29	.554	290	191	396	2.69

RANDY MOFFITT 30 6-3 190 Bats R Throws R

The right-handed half of San Francisco's A and 1-A bullpen punch with lefty Gary Lavelle . . . Also one-half of the A and 1-A family sports punch as he is a brother of tennis legend Billie Jean (Moffitt) King . . . Sinker ball makes him adept at getting inning-ending double plays . . . Born Oct. 13, 1948, in Long Beach, Cal. . . . Since 1972, has averaged 55 appearances and 11 saves, an exception to Casey Stengel's rule that relief pitchers are only effective every other season . . . Like Lavelle, began minor league career as starter, but switched to bullpen and has made only one major league start.

Year	Club	G	IP	W	L	Pct.	SO	BB	H	ERA
1972	San Francisco	40	71	1	5	.167	37	30	72	3.68
1973	San Francisco	60	100	4	4	.500	65	31	86	2.43
1974	San Francisco	61	102	5	7	.417	49	29	99	4.50
1975	San Francisco	55	74	4	5	.444	39	32	73	3.89
1976	San Francisco	58	103	6	6	.500	50	35	92	2.27
1977	San Francisco	64	88	4	9	.308	68	39	91	3.58
1978	San Francisco	70	82	8	4	.667	52	33	79	3.29
	Totals	408	620	32	40	.444	360	229	592	3.34

DARRELL EVANS 31 6-2 200   Bats L Throws R

Furnished power to team's attack . . . Never much on average, but good in clutch . . . Underrated on defense, setting a major league record in 1974 for third baseman by taking part in 45 double plays . . . Hit 41 homers in Atlanta in 1973 . . . Born May 26, 1947, in Pasadena, Cal. . . . Became an immediate San Francisco hero in his first appearance at Candlestick with six RBIs on a triple and two homers . . . Finely tuned eye, leading NL in walks in 1973 and 1974, and set an NL record in 1976 by drawing walks in 15 straight games . . . Dabbles in real estate.

Year	Club	Pos	G	AB	R	H	2B	3B	HR	RBI	SB	Avg.
1971	Atlanta	3B-OF	89	260	42	63	11	1	12	38	2	.242
1972	Atlanta	3B	125	418	67	106	12	0	19	71	4	.254
1973	Atlanta	3B-1B	161	595	114	167	25	8	41	104	6	.281
1974	Atlanta	3B	160	571	99	137	21	3	25	79	4	.240
1975	Atlanta	3B-1B	156	567	82	138	22	2	22	73	12	.243
1976	Atl.-S.F.	1B-3B	136	396	53	81	9	1	11	46	9	.205
1977	San Francisco	OF-1B-3B	144	461	64	117	18	3	17	72	9	.254
1978	San Francisco	OF-1B-3B	159	547	82	133	24	2	20	78	4	.243
	Totals		1154	3885	610	962	143	21	167	571	50	.248

TOP PROSPECT

JOE STRAIN 24 5-10 165   Bats R Throws R

Ready to step into second base if it's available after hitting .305 with 35 stolen bases last year at Phoenix . . . Owns good eye, striking out only 30 times in 561 at bats . . . Born April 30, 1954, in Denver . . . Helped University of Northern Colorado to four straight Great Plains Athletic Conference championships with a .338 career average over 144 games . . . Was MVP for Great Falls when it won the Pioneer League pennant in 1976, leading the league in stolen bases (32) and fielding for second basemen (.953) . . . Led the California League in hits at Fresno in 1977 (188).

MANAGER JOE ALTOBELLI: Took a team most people said would finish fourth and kept it in first place in the NL West for most the 1978 season before slowly sinking to third behind LA and Cincinnati . . . Effort earned him Manager of the Year Award in his second season . . . Weeded out recalcitrants from first season and blended the remnants into closely-knit, talented team . . . Another of the ever-increasing no-nonsense, do-it-my-way, discipline-pushing managers, and gets away with it . . . Born May 26, 1932, in Detroit . . . Spent five years at Rochester in Baltimore organization, managing it to four pennants and one fourth before realizing Earl Weaver was in Baltimore to stay and taking San Francisco's offer . . . Also another of the many successful managers who were not successful as major league players . . . Played professionally 17 years, mostly as a Triple-A star, but only briefly in the majors with Cleveland and Minnesota, hitting .210 for 166 games.

GREATEST PITCHER

From Factoryville, Pa., came the 6-foot-1½ inch 195-pound "Big Six"—Christy Mathewson. In 1900, when he was 20, Mathewson was 0-and-3 for the New York Giants.

He won 20 in 1901, slipped to 14-17 in 1902, then never won fewer than 22 for the next 12 years, all with the Giants, en route to a career 373-188 record.

Four times Christy won more than 30, his best a 37-11 with a 1.43 ERA in 1908 and a 31-8 with a 1.27 ERA in 1905.

Mathewson started 551 games and completed 434 for the Giants, throwing 83 shutouts and striking out 2,502.

Mathewson's first World Series appearance was 1905, a five-game Series the Giants won four games to one. A rain delay permitted Christy to pitch three games—all shutouts—two four-hitters and a six-hitter.

ALL-TIME GIANT LEADERS

BATTING: Bill Terry, .401, 1930
HRs: Willie Mays, 52, 1965
RBIs: Mel Ott, 151, 1929
STEALS: George Burns, 62, 1914
WINS: Christy Mathewson, 37, 1908
STRIKEOUTS: Christy Mathewson, 267, 1903

CINCINNATI REDS

TEAM DIRECTORY: Chairman of the Board: Louis Nippert; Pres.: Dick Wagner; Scouting Director: Joe Bowen; Publicity: Jim Ferguson; Trav. Sec.: Doug Bureman; Mgr.: John McNamara. Home: Riverfront Stadium (51,963). Field distances: 330, l.f. line; 404, c.f.; 330, r.f. line. Spring training: Tampa, Fla.

SCOUTING REPORT

HITTING: When The Big Red Machine is healthy, it can hit with anybody. The trouble is, The Machine has been rusted with injuries the past two seasons and age is setting in. And, with Pete Rose defecting to the Phillies, the Reds lost a .300 batting average and 100 runs scored every year.

Johnny Bench and Joe Morgan spent more time in the training room than in the batter's box and creeping age is catching up with both. A healthy Bench devastated the Japanese in October, but nagging injuries inherent with catchers keep cropping up to slow down Bench's effectiveness. Morgan is coming off two straight horrid seasons and told Cincinnati management he would refuse any trade so he could show Reds' fans he still has it. If his legs are gone, Morgan is gone, too.

Ken Griffey, George Foster and Dave Concepcion are Cincinnati's main offensive weapons now. Griffey offers immense speed with occassional power outbursts. Foster is the power outlet, but hits for average, too. Concepcion has blossomed into a .300 hitter and probably will take over Rose's leadoff spot. In clutch situations, Concepcion is one of the best. Dan Driessen is a picture hitter, but also spent most of 1978 wrapped in tape. Cesar Geronimo is no offensive threat and if Ray Knight takes Rose's place at third the Reds will lose considerable offense.

PITCHING: Well, there's Tom Seaver and . . . uh, well, uh . . . there's Tom Seaver. And, the Reds didn't give him enough runs to win the 16 games he managed to win. The second best pitcher is Bill Bonham, and he underwent elbow surgery in the off-season and his return to form is suspect. The Reds keep waiting for Paul Moskau and Tom Hume to develop, but both erase flashes of brilliance with periods of mediocrity. Doug Bair was one of baseball's best out of the bullpen, but he suffered from overuse and needs help.

The Reds never can seem to decide if Fred Norman is a starter or a relief pitcher and he does well either way, but would like to know which job the Reds want him to do. Pedro Borbon

George Foster again led NL in homers (40) and RBIs (120).

is no longer dependable out of the bullpen. The Reds won't win too many games with dazzling pitching—other than the days they can get Seaver some runs.

FIELDING: Like the hitting, fielding was once Cincinnati's strong suit. Now, there are too many cavities. Bench is still the best behind the plate and Concepcion may be the best at shortstop. Driessen is vastly underrated at first and led the National League in fielding. That's not because he imitates a statue at first; he is one of the best going to his right. When he gets to the ball, Morgan is dependable at second, but his range is limited and his arm skimpy. Third base is a big hole.

In the outfield, the Reds are limited. Geronimo, once one of the best, suddenly has trouble judging fly balls and throws erratically. Foster is adequate in left and Griffey can chase them down in right.

OUTLOOK: The Big Red Machine is in need of a major overhaul, but did nothing positive at the winter meetings. The Reds lost Rose and for some reason fired manager Sparky Anderson. It's a weaker team than the one that finished behind the Dodgers the last two seasons.

CINCINNATI REDS 1979 ROSTER

MANAGER John McNamara
Coaches—Russ Nixon, Ron Plaza, Bill Fischer

PITCHERS

No.	Name	1978 Club	W-L	IP	SO	ERA	B-T	Ht.	Wt.	Born
40	Bair, Doug	Cincinnati	7-6	100	91	1.98	R-R	5-10	185	8/22/49 Melrose, OH
38	Berenyi, Bruce	Nashville	10.5	–	–	2.47	R-R	6-3	205	8/21/54 Bryan, OH
42	Bonham, Bill	Cincinnati	11-5	140	83	3.54	R-R	6-3	195	10/1/48 Glendale, CA
34	Borbon, Pedro	Cincinnati	8-2	99	35	5.00	R-R	6-2	200	12/2/46 Dominican Republic
44	Capilla, Doug	Indianapolis	10-6	132	87	5.47	L-L	5-8	175	1/7/52 Honolulu, HI
		Cincinnati	0-1	11	9	9.82				
48	Combe, Geoff	Nashville	11-6	95	61	1.99	R-R	6-2	185	2/1/56 Melrose, MA
49	Dawley, Bill	Nashville	7-12	–	–	3.98	R-R	6-4	205	2/6/58 Norwich, CT
50	Dumoulin, Dan	Indianapolis	12-6	123	79	4.17	R-R	6-0	185	8/20/53 Kokomo, IN
		Cincinnati	1-0	5	2	1.80				
43	Howell, Jay	Nashville	8-14	–	–	3.17	R-R	6-3	200	11/26/55 Miami, FL
47	Hume, Tom	Cincinnati	8-11	174	90	4.14	R-R	6-1	180	3/29/53 Cincinnati, OH
51	LaCoss, Mike	Indianapolis	11-5	130	67	3.47	R-R	6-4	190	5/30/56 Glendale, CA
		Cincinnati	4-8	96	31	4.50				
54	Moore, David	Indianapolis	12-6	140	75	4.83	R-R	6-2	185	9/19/54 Lexington, KY
31	Moskau, Paul	Indianapolis	1-1	26	27	3.08	R-R	6-2	210	12/20/53 St. Joseph, MO
		Cincinnati	6-4	145	88	3.97				
32	Norman, Fred	Cincinnati	11-9	177	111	3.71	B-L	5-8	170	8/20/42 San Antonio, TX
53	Pastore, Frank	Nashville	6-8	–	–	3.43	R-R	6-2	205	8/21/57 Alhambra, CA
45	Sarmiento, Manny	Cincinnati	9-7	127	72	4.39	R-R	5-11	170	2/2/56 Venezuela
41	Seaver, Tom	Cincinnati	16-14	260	226	2.87	R-R	6-1	208	11/17/44 Fresno, CA
36	Soto, Mario	Indianapolis	9-12	160	121	5.02	R-R	6-0	180	7/12/56 Dominican Republic
		Cincinnati	1-0	18	13	2.50				
37	Tomlin, Dave	Cincinnati	9-1	62	32	5.81	L-L	6-3	185	6/22/49 Maysville, KY

CATCHERS

No.	Name	1978 Club	H	HR	RBI	Pct.	B-T	Ht.	Wt.	Born
5	Bench, John	Cincinnati	102	23	73	.260	R-R	6-1	215	12/7/47 Oklahoma City, OK
9	Correll, Vic	Indianapolis	27	6	19	.260	R-R	5-9	175	2/5/46 Florence, SC
		Cincinnati	25	1	6	.238				
7	Werner, Don	Cincinnati	17	0	11	.150	R-R	6-1	185	3/8/53 Appleton, WI
		Indianapolis	30	3	22	.240				

INFIELDERS

No.	Name	1978 Club	H	HR	RBI	Pct.	B-T	Ht.	Wt.	Born
23	Auerbach, Rick	Cincinnati	18	2	5	.327	R-R	6-0	175	2/15/50 Glendale, CA
13	Concepcion, Dave	Cincinnati	170	6	67	.301	R-R	6-2	175	6/17/48 Venezuela
58	DeFreites, Arturo	Indianapolis	153	32	101	.327	R-R	6-2	195	4/26/53 Dominican Republic
		Cincinnati	4	1	2	.200				
22	Driessen, Dan	Cincinnati	131	16	70	.250	L-R	5-11	187	7/29/51 Hilton Head, SC
26	Kennedy, Junior	Cincinnati	40	0	11	.255	R-R	6-0	185	8/9/50 Fort Gibson, OK
25	Knight, Ray	Cincinnati	13	1	4	.200	R-R	6-2	185	12/28/52 Albany, GA
8	Morgan, Joe	Cincinnati	104	13	75	.236	L-R	5-7	165	9/19/43 Bonham, TX
16	Oester, Ron	Indianapolis	133	7	49	.259	R-R	6-1	175	5/5/56 Cincinnati, OH
		Cincinnati	3	0	1	.375				
57	Santo Domingo, Rafael	Nashville	–	2	6	.200	B-R	6-0	160	11/24/55 Puerto Rico
		Indianapolis	36	2	15	.265				
12	Spilman, Harry	Indianapolis	144	13	79	.295	L-R	6-0	180	7/18/54 Albany, GA
		Cincinnati	1	0	0	.250				

OUTFIELDERS

No.	Name	1978 Club	H	HR	RBI	Pct.	B-T	Ht.	Wt.	Born
29	Collins, Dave	Cincinnati	22	0	7	.216	B-L	5-10	175	10/20/52 Rapid City, SD
15	Foster, George	Cincinnati	170	40	120	.281	R-R	6-1	185	12/1/48 Tuscaloosa, AL
22	Geronimo, Cesar	Cincinnati	67	5	27	.226	L-L	6-2	175	3/11/48 Dominican Republic
30	Griffey, Ken	Cincinnati	177	10	63	.288	L-L	5-11	200	4/10/50 Donora, PA
19	Henderson, Ken	NY (NL)-Cin	29	4	23	.175	B-R	6-3	190	6/15/46 Manning, IA
56	Householder, Paul	Tampa	–	9	42	.248	R-R	6-2	180	9/4/58 North Haven, CT
55	Milner, Eddie	Tampa	–	8	44	.284	L-L	6-0	170	5/21/55 Griffin, GA
28	Summers, Champ	Indianapolis	170	34	124	.368	L-R	6-2	205	6/15/48 Bremerton, WA
		Cincinnati	9	1	3	.257				

RED PROFILES

TOM SEAVER 34 6-1 208   Bats R Throws R

Was a victim of gross non-support by The Big Red Machine . . . Eight times while he was in the game, the Reds furnished him with no runs; seven times with only one run; seven times with only two runs . . . Finally achieved one of the few things he hadn't done when he pitched a no-hitter against St. Louis on June 16 to go along with five one-hitters . . . George Thomas Seaver was born Nov. 17, 1944, in Fresno, Cal. . . . Has more than 200 career victories . . . "And, I'm definitely thinking about 300," he says . . . Was once the bedrock of the New York Mets, but team failed to build around him and he was dealt to Reds in controversial trade in 1977 . . . Was color man on World Series telecasts . . . Studied Journalism at USC and plans TV career after baseball . . . Pitched Reds' opener on fall tour of Japan, showing the world that yes, Japanese slugger Saduharu Oh can hit home runs off the best American pitchers.

Year	Club	G	IP	W	L	Pct.	SO	BB	H	ERA
1967	New York (NL)	35	251	16	13	.552	170	78	224	2.76
1968	New York (NL)	36	278	16	12	.571	205	48	224	2.20
1969	New York (NL)	36	273	25	7	.781	208	82	202	2.21
1970	New York (NL)	37	291	18	12	.600	283	83	230	2.81
1971	New York (NL)	36	286	20	10	.667	289	61	210	1.76
1972	New York (NL)	35	262	21	12	.636	249	77	215	2.92
1973	New York (NL)	36	290	19	10	.655	251	64	219	2.07
1974	New York (NL)	32	236	11	11	.500	201	75	199	3.20
1975	New York (NL)	36	280	22	9	.710	243	88	217	2.38
1976	New York (NL)	35	271	14	11	.560	235	77	211	2.59
1977	New York (NL)-Cincinnati	33	261	21	6	.778	196	66	199	2.59
1978	Cincinnati	36	260	16	14	.533	226	89	218	2.87
	Totals	423	3239	219	127	.633	2756	888	2568	2.51

JOHNNY BENCH 31 6-1 215   Bats R Throws R

Despite chronic sore back, a fractured ankle and other injuries, Bench caught in more than 100 games for the 11th straight season, a National League record . . . Hit 300th career homer, second only to Yogi Berra's 358 on the all-time catcher's list . . . Selected for all-star team for the 11th straight year, but declined because of injuries in magnanimous move . . . Born Dec. 7, 1947 in Oklahoma City . . . Made nationwide news in August by publicly stating that manager

Sparky Anderson was too nice to the Reds, saying the team needed some stern discipline . . . Loves country music, golf and grand slam homers, of which he has eight . . . Near scratch golfer.

Year	Club	Pos	G	AB	R	H	2B	3B	HR	RBI	SB	Avg.
1967	Cincinnati	C	26	86	7	14	3	1	1	6	0	.163
1968	Cincinnati	C	154	564	67	155	40	2	15	82	1	.275
1969	Cincinnati	C	148	532	83	156	23	1	26	90	6	.293
1970	Cincinnati	C-OF-1B-3B	158	605	97	177	35	4	45	148	5	.293
1971	Cincinnati	C-1B-OF-3B	149	562	80	134	19	2	27	61	2	.238
1972	Cincinnati	C-OF-1B-3B	147	538	87	145	22	2	40	125	6	.270
1973	Cincinnati	C-OF-1B-3B	152	557	83	141	17	3	25	104	4	.253
1974	Cincinnati	C-3B-1B	160	621	108	174	38	2	33	129	5	.280
1975	Cincinnati	C-OF-1B	142	530	83	150	39	1	28	110	11	.283
1976	Cincinnati	C-OF-1B	135	465	62	109	24	1	16	74	13	.234
1977	Cincinnati	C-OF-1B-3B	142	494	67	136	34	2	31	109	2	.275
1978	Cincinnati	C-OF-1B	120	393	52	102	17	1	23	73	4	.260
	Totals		1633	5947	876	1593	311	22	310	1111	59	.268

JOE MORGAN 35 5-7 165   Bats L Throws R

Injuries, mostly to groin and stomach, severely curtailed his offensive output . . . Couldn't run to steal bases and couldn't swing hard to hit homers, which more than anything else prevented the Reds from overtaking the Dodgers . . . Contributed defensively at second base by establishing major league record for second baseman with 91 consecutive errorless games . . . Born in Bonham, Tex., Sept. 19, 1943 . . . Called by LA second baseman Davey Lopes, "Most powerful hitter, pound for pound, in baseball." . . . Student of the game with managerial aspirations . . . Keeps book on every pitcher in the National League . . . Has base-stealing down to a precise science.

Year	Club	Pos	G	AB	R	H	2B	3B	HR	RBI	SB	Avg.
1963	Houston	2B	8	25	5	6	0	1	0	3	1	.240
1964	Houston	2B	10	37	4	7	0	0	0	0	0	.189
1965	Houston	2B	157	601	100	163	22	12	14	40	20	.271
1966	Houston	2B	122	425	60	121	14	8	5	42	11	.285
1967	Houston	2B-OF	133	494	73	136	27	11	6	42	29	.275
1968	Houston	2B-OF	10	20	6	5	0	1	0	0	3	.250
1969	Houston	2B-OF	147	535	94	126	18	5	15	43	49	.236
1970	Houston	2B	144	548	102	147	28	9	8	52	42	.268
1971	Houston	2B	160	583	87	149	27	11	13	56	40	.256
1972	Cincinnati	2B	149	552	122	161	23	4	16	73	58	.292
1973	Cincinnati	2B	157	576	116	167	35	2	26	82	67	.290
1974	Cincinnati	2B	149	512	107	150	31	3	22	67	58	.293
1975	Cincinnati	2B	146	498	107	163	27	6	17	94	67	.327
1976	Cincinnati	2B	141	472	113	151	30	5	27	111	60	.320
1977	Cincinnati	2B	153	521	113	150	21	6	22	78	49	.288
1978	Cincinnati	2B	132	441	68	104	27	0	13	75	19	.236
	Totals		1918	6840	1277	1906	330	84	204	858	573	.280

KEN GRIFFEY 28 5-11 200   Bats L Throws L

Speediest Red and master of the infield hit . . . Developed into power hitter but average suffered for it . . . Once asked where he got his speed, he said, "If you had grown up in my neighborhood, you'd be fast, too . . ." Born April 19, 1950, in Donora, Pa., home of Stan Musial, but says he didn't know who Musial was when he was a kid . . . A lowly 29th round pick in 1969 free agent draft . . . Pleasant, easy-going guy with permanent smile . . . Speed makes him exceptional outfielder with ability to go after deep balls . . . Hit with power to all fields . . . Line drive hitter . . . Hit below .300 for first time in four seasons.

Year	Club	Pos	G	AB	R	H	2B	3B	HR	RBI	SB	Avg.
1974	Cincinnati	OF	88	227	24	57	9	5	2	19	9	.251
1975	Cincinnati	OF	132	463	95	141	15	9	4	46	16	.305
1976	Cincinnati	OF	148	562	111	189	28	9	6	74	34	.336
1977	Cincinnati	OF	154	585	117	186	35	8	12	57	17	.318
1978	Cincinnati	OF	158	614	90	177	33	8	10	63	23	.288
	Totals...........		705	2537	456	783	125	40	37	273	103	.309

BILL BONHAM 30 6-3 195   Bats R Throws R

Was 8-1 early in the season, but injured his elbow during complete game victory in Los Angeles . . . Was in and out of the rotation from then on, finally undergoing surgery last week of the season from Dr. Frank Jobe, the same surgeon who restored Tommy John and Randy Jones . . . Born Oct. 1, 1948, in Glendale, Cal. . . . Owns psychology degree from UCLA and spends road hours deeply engrossed in his books . . . Also runs up to 10 miles a day . . . Owns one of the top changeups in baseball and specializes in coaxing ground balls out of hitters . . . Faced long winter of rehabilitation.

Year	Club	G	IP	W	L	Pct.	SO	BB	H	ERA
1971	Chicago (NL).............	33	60	2	1	.667	41	36	38	4.65
1972	Chicago (NL).............	19	58	1	1	.500	49	25	56	3.10
1973	Chicago (NL).............	44	152	7	5	.583	121	64	126	3.02
1974	Chicago (NL).............	44	243	11	22	.333	191	109	246	3.85
1975	Chicago (NL).............	38	229	13	15	.464	165	109	254	4.72
1976	Chicago (NL).............	32	196	9	13	.409	110	96	215	4.27
1977	Chicago (NL).............	34	215	10	13	.435	134	82	207	4.35
1978	Cincinnati	23	140	11	5	.688	83	50	151	3.54
	Totals.................	267	1293	64	75	.460	894	571	1318	4.02

GEORGE FOSTER 30 6-1 185   Bats R Throws R

Led the league in RBIs for third straight year and homers for second straight, reaching 40 on last day of season with two, including two-run belt in 14th inning to beat Atlanta . . . Physical fitness devotee with huge upper body to go with 30-inch waist . . . Only nine balls have been hit into Riverfront Stadium's upper deck in left field and Foster has four of them . . . Born Dec. 1, 1948, in Ralph, Ala. . . . Deeply religious, reads Bible every night . . . Does not smoke, drink or swear, but is hung up on ice cream and milkshakes . . . Has hit two or more homers in one game 15 times . . . Started career with Giants as another of those many "next Willie Mays," but sat the bench until traded to the Reds, where hypnosis alleviated his introverted personality.

Year	Club	Pos	G	AB	R	H	2B	3B	HR	RBI	SB	Avg
1969	San Francisco	OF	9	5	1	2	0	0	0	1	0	.40
1970	San Francisco	OF	9	19	2	6	1	1	1	4	0	.31
1971	S.F.-Cin..........	OF	140	473	50	114	23	4	13	58	7	.24
1972	Cincinnati	OF	59	145	15	29	4	1	2	12	2	.20
1973	Cincinnati	OF	17	39	6	11	3	0	4	9	0	.28
1974	Cincinnati	OF	106	276	31	73	18	0	7	41	3	.26
1975	Cincinnati	OF-1B	134	463	71	139	24	4	23	78	2	.30
1976	Cincinnati	OF	144	562	86	172	21	9	29	121	17	.30
1977	Cincinnati	OF	158	615	124	197	31	2	52	149	6	.32
1978	Cincinnati	OF	158	604	97	170	26	7	40	120	4	.28
	Totals..........		934	3201	483	913	151	28	171	593	41	.285

DOUG BAIR 30 5-10 185   Bats R Throws R

The bullpen savior with 28 saves and a 1.98 earned run average, first Cincinnati pitcher below 2.00 since 1972 (Gary Nolan) . . . "I shudder to think where we would have been without Bair," said manager Sparky Anderson . . . Born Aug. 22, 1949, in Defiance, Ohio . . . Pitched a no-hitter for Bowling Green State University against Miami (O.) University and Buddy Schultz of the Cardinals . . . Obtained in spring of 1978 from Oakland for Dave Revering after Commissioner Bowie Kuhn negated Cincinnati's deal of Revering and $1.75 million for Vida Blue . . . Wore No. 40, uniform number first assigned to Blue.

Year	Club	G	IP	W	L	Pct.	SO	BB	H	ERA
1976	Pittsburgh	4	6	0	0	.000	4	5	4	6.00
1977	Oakland................	45	83	4	6	.400	68	57	78	3.47
1978	Cincinnati	70	100	7	6	.538	91	38	87	1.98
	Totals..................	119	189	11	12	.478	163	100	169	2.76

DAVE CONCEPCION 30 6-2 175   Bats R Throws R

Called by ex-manager Sparky Anderson, "Our Most Valuable Player in 1978." Became the first Cincinnati shortstop since 1913 to hit .300 . . . Recognized as baseball's finest defensive shortstop, but suffered off-year defensively . . . Born June 17, 1948, in Aragua, Venezuela . . . An all-around player who can steal bases as well as hit for power . . . Best athlete on the team; he can dunk a basketball . . . Normally a lower half of the order hitter, batted second and third at times due to injuries to the team and hit better . . . LA scouting report calls him most dangerous Cincinnati hitter in the clutch.

Year	Club	Pos	G	AB	R	H	2B	3B	HR	RBI	SB	Avg.
1970	Cincinnati	SS-2B	101	265	38	69	6	3	1	19	10	.260
1971	Cincinnati	SS-2B-3B-OF	130	327	24	67	4	4	1	20	9	.205
1972	Cincinnati	SS	119	378	40	79	13	2	2	29	13	.209
1973	Cincinnati	SS-OF	89	328	39	94	18	3	8	46	22	.287
1974	Cincinnati	SS-OF	160	594	70	167	25	1	14	82	41	.281
1975	Cincinnati	SS-3B	140	507	62	139	23	1	5	49	33	.274
1976	Cincinnati	SS	152	576	74	162	28	7	9	69	21	.281
1977	Cincinnati	SS	156	572	59	155	26	3	8	64	29	.271
1978	Cincinnati	SS	153	565	75	170	33	4	6	67	23	.301
	Totals		1200	4112	481	1102	176	28	54	445	201	.268

DAN DRIESSEN 27 5-11 187   Bats L Throws R

Cincinnati's strong, silent man . . . Never speaks unless spoken to and spends spare time sleeping . . . Under severe pressure as Tony Perez's replacement at first base, but has responded . . . Was hitting .325 first two months until plunked by San Diego's Bob Shirley . . . Despite very painful elbow, played anyway and average steadily dwindled . . . Born July 29, 1951, in Hilton Head, S.C. . . . Carries bad defensive rap due to horrendous season at third base his rookie year . . . He had never played third before . . . Had outstanding defensive year at first base . . . Particularly adept at going to his right . . . Hits for power and owns picturesque swing.

Year	Club	Pos	G	AB	R	H	2B	3B	HR	RBI	SB	Avg.
1973	Cincinnati	3B-1B	102	366	49	110	15	2	4	47	8	.301
1974	Cincinnati	3B-1B-OF	150	470	63	132	23	6	7	56	10	.281
1975	Cincinnati	1B-OF	88	210	38	59	8	1	7	38	10	.281
1976	Cincinnati	1B-OF	98	219	32	54	11	1	7	44	14	.247
1977	Cincinnati	1B	151	536	75	161	31	4	17	91	31	.300
1978	Cincinnati	1B	153	524	68	131	23	3	16	70	28	.250
	Totals		742	2325	325	647	111	17	58	346	101	.278

TOP PROSPECT

HARRY SPILMAN 24 6-1 180   Bats L Throws R
Focused attention on himself in 1977 by hitting over .400 into
the middle of July at Class AA Three Rivers in Eastern League
before settling to .373 with 16 homers and 78 RBIs . . . Promoted to Triple-A Indianapolis for 1978 and switched from first
base to third base as the eventual replacement for Pete Rose
and batted .295 with 13 homers . . . Born July 18, 1954, in
Albany, Ga., and grew up with Cincinnati utility infielder Ray
Knight, with whom he spent many hours taking batting practice
from a pitching machine placed in front of their home-made
batting cage.

MANAGER JOHN McNAMARA: Will The Big Red Machine

become McNamara's Band? . . . The Reds
better play to beat the band, because their
new manager is under a heap of pressure,
having replaced the popular Sparky Anderson after a shocking late-November decision
by Cincinnati president-general manager
Dick Wagner to fire Anderson, a man who
averaged 97 victories in his nine seasons and
finished lower than second only once . . . Opinion polls con-
ducted in Cincinnati area were four to one against the firing of
Anderson, but nobody was upset about the hiring of the new
soft-spoken, easy-going manager . . . Born June 4, 1932, in
Sacramento . . . Worked his way through Sacramento State
College by becoming a minor league manager at age 25 at
Lewiston, Idaho . . . Played 17 years in the minors as a catcher
and managed nine years in the minors, sometimes as player-
manager . . . Oakland's Charlie Finley hired him to manage
the 1970 team and it finished second in the AL West with an
89-73 record, best finish and record for any A's team in 38 years
. . . His reward? Finley fired him . . . Managed San Diego
from 1974 to early 1977, advancing the team from a first-year
60-102 record to 73-89 in 1976 . . . When 1977 team started
20-28, owner Ray Kroc ordered him fired against the wishes of
GM Buzzie Bavasi, who said, "Mac comes from the same mold
as Walter Alston . . ."

GREATEST PITCHER

Johnny Vander Meer is the only man in major league history to pitch back-to-back no-hitters, a staggering accomplishment he glued together for the 1938 Cincinnati Reds.

But, that doesn't make him the greatest Cincinnati pitcher.

On the same day Vander Meer pitched his second no-hitter, June 15, Bucky Walters became a Cincinnati Red, traded from the Philadelphia Phillies.

The next year, Walters was the team's best pitcher, winning a still-standing club record 27 games and leading the league with a 2.29 earned run average.

Walters went on to pitch 10 years for the Reds and won 160 games. Along the way, he threw a club record 32 shutouts, 195 complete games (second on Cincinnati's all-time list) and had a career 2.93 ERA for the Reds.

Walters always permitted a lot of hits, but silenced bats with men on base. For five straight seasons, he gave up at least 240 hits, but won 97 games in that span and pitched more than 300 innings in three of those seasons.

After retiring with 198 career victories, Walters managed the 1949 Reds . . . quite a career for a guy who began his major league career as an infielder.

ALL-TIME RED LEADERS

BATTING: Cy Seymour, .377, 1905
HRs: George Foster, 52, 1977
RBIs: George Foster, 149, 1977
STEALS: Bob Bescher, 80, 1911
WINS: Adolpho Luque, 27, 1923
          Bucky Walters, 27, 1939
STRIKEOUTS: Jim Maloney, 265, 1963

SAN DIEGO PADRES

TEAM DIRECTORY: Board Chairman-President: Ray Kroc; VP-GM: Bob Fontaine; Minor League Admin: Jim Weigel; Trav. Sec.: John Mattei; Dir. Pub. Rel.: Bob Chandler; Mgr.: Roger Craig. Home: San Diego Stadium (51,362). Field distances: 330, l.f. line; 420, c.f.; 330, r.f. line. Spring training: Yuma, Ariz.

SCOUTING REPORT

HITTING: After Dave Winfield and Gene Richards, there isn't much in the hitting department—nothing that makes one think of a Big Mac Attack. If Winfield or Richards aren't batting, fans spend more time watching the KGB chicken than Padre hitters. Can Ronald McDonald swing a bat?

Winfield is everything in San Diego, bigger than any aircraft carrier at the naval base. He hits for average and he hits for power. He fields his position and he takes care of San Diego's youth. Winfield and Richards both hit .308, then it drops down to Jerry Turner's .280. Gene Tenace suffered through another atrocious season in the batter's box and took some well-aimed barbs from The Big Mac himself, Ray Kroc.

San Diego's other hitting threats, George Hendrick and Oscar Gamble, fell in disfavor with Mr. Kroc and were sent away like a hamburger wrapper. Rookie Ozzie Smith punches a few singles here and there, and that's what the entire infield does.

Battery mates: Gene Tenace, Cy Young king Gaylord Perry.

Mike Hargrove, acquired from Texas, can be expected to hit near .300. Padres hit only 75 homers all season, 24 by Winfield, who is a big man, but not big enough to carry an entire franchise on his bat.

PITCHING: What the Padres lack in hitting they make up with pitching, starting with amazing 40-year-old Cy Young winner Gaylord Perry, a 21-game winner. Randy Jones struggled to reach .500, but is still capable of winning 20 if his light-hitting teammates provide some offense. Bob Owchinko and Bob Shirley, two young left-handers, were coveted by other teams, but the Padres chose to keep them, a wise decision.

And, Rollie Fingers still rules the bullpen. He might get some help from 38-year-old Mickey Lolich, if he stays healthy.

Eric Rasmussen joins Perry as a right-handed starter and Rasmussen pitched well after joining the Padres in a trade that sent George Hendrick to St. Louis. The Padres were next-to-last in 1977 team earned run average, but completely reversed that in 1978 with a 3.28 that placed them second to the Dodgers. Padre pitchers gave up only 74 homers, lowest in the league —and one less than their hitters gave them to work with.

Fingers, of course, likes work. But, with San Diego's improved pitching, he may get less of it, which is good for the Padres.

FIELDING: In one season, the Padres reduced their errors by 29, but their 160 errors still were the second most in the league. Only Pittsburgh made more. And, once again, the Padres were next to last (.975) in National League fielding. Winfield, the right fielder, is the only guy in the outfield capable of daily spectacular plays. Turner and Richards are below average on defense. The Padres improved their infield with Smith, a spectacular shortstop who may quickly move into the class of Dave Concepcion and Larry Bowa. The rest of the infielders, Hargrove, Bill Almon, Tucker Ashford, Mike Champion, Fernando Gonzalez, Broderick Perkins—whomever the Padres use at third, second and first—are average.

Tenace is nothing great behind the plate, or at first base, and Rick Sweet is still learning as a catcher. Defense is not the Padres' best offense.

OUTLOOK: A lot of youngsters will have to play above their heads for the Padres to move up . . . and just how long can Perry keep it up? San Diego's success depends upon its pitching and another great season from Winfield, with help from Hargrove, Richards and Turner.

SAN DIEGO PADRES 1979 ROSTER

MANAGER Roger Craig
Coaches—Chuck Estrada, Billy Herman, Doug Rader,
Whitey Wietelmann, Don Williams

PITCHERS

No.	Name	1978 Club	W-L	IP	SO	ERA	B-T	Ht.	Wt.	Born
39	Bernal, Vic	San Diego	5-7	85	47	4.66	R-R	6-0	175	10/6/53 Los Angeles, CA
16	D'Acquisto, John	San Diego	4-3	93	104	2.13	R-R	6-2	195	12/24/51 San Diego, CA
38	Eichelberger, Juan	San Diego	0-0	3	2	12.00	R-R	6-2	195	10/21/53 St. Louis, MO
		Hawaii	8-13	156	106	4.50				
58	Fierbaugh, Randy	San Diego	5-6	114	45	5.37	L-R	6-3	205	10/16/52 Mansfield, OH
34	Fingers, Rollie	San Diego	6-13	107	72	2.52	R-R	6-3	195	8/25/46 Steubenville, OH
35	Jones, Randy	San Diego	13-14	253	71	2.88	R-L	6-0	180	1/12/50 Brea, CA
48	Kinney, Dennis	Cleveland	0-2	39	19	4.38	L-L	6-1	170	2/26/52 Toledo, OH
		Hawaii	3-3	42	23	3.86				
		San Diego	0-1	7	2	6.43				
42	Lee, Mark	Hawaii	0-0	5	1	0.00	R-R	6-4	225	6/14/53 Inglewood, CA
		San Diego	5-1	85	31	3.28				
29	Lolich, Mickey	San Diego	2-1	35	13	1.54	R-L	6-0	225	9/12/40 Portland, OR
59	Mura, Steve	Hawaii	10-16	177	158	4.17	R-R	6-2	188	2/12/55
		San Diego	0-2	8	5	11.25				
44	Owchinko, Bob	San Diego	10-13	202	194	3.56	L-L	6-2	185	1/1/55 Detroit, MI
36	Perry, Gaylord	San Diego	21-6	261	154	2.72	R-R	6-4	215	9/15/38 Williamston, NC
41	Rasmussen, Eric	St.L-SD	14-15	207	91	4.09	R-R	6-3	205	3/22/52 Racine, WI
32	Shirley, Bob	San Diego	8-11	166	102	3.69	R-L	5-11	185	6/25/54 Oklahoma City, OK
49	Tellman, Tom	Amarillo	5-6	76	48	2.61	R-R	6-3	185	3/29/54
24	Wehrmeister, Dave	Hawaii	2-11	129	59	5.65	R-R	6-4	195	11/9/52 Berwyn, IL
		San Diego	1-0	7	2	6.43				

CATCHERS

No.	Name	1978 Club	H	HR	RBI	Pct.	B-T	Ht.	Wt.	Born
27	Castillo, Tony	Hawaii	—	0	25	.211	R-R	6-2	185	6/14/57 Dominican Republic
		San Diego	1	0	1	.125				
3	Fahey, Bill	Tucson	53	2	19	.250	L-R	6-0	200	6/14/50 Detroit, MI
2	Sweet, Rick	San Diego	50	1	11	.221	B-R	6-0	190	9/7/52 Longview, WA
18	Tenace, Gene	San Diego	90	16	61	.224	R-R	6-0	190	10/10/46 Russellton, PA

INFIELDERS

No.	Name	1978 Club	H	HR	RBI	Pct.	B-T	Ht.	Wt.	Born
6	Almon, Bill	San Diego	102	0	21	.252	R-R	6-3	170	11/21/52 Providence, RI
12	Ashford, Tucker	Hawaii	14	0	6	.311	R-R	6-1	180	12/4/54 Memphis, TN
		San Diego	38	3	26	.245				
11	Baker, Chuck	San Diego	12	0	3	.207	R-R	5-11	175	12/6/52 Seattle, WA
7	Bevacqua, Kurt	Texas	55	6	30	.221	R-R	6-1	185	1/23/47 Miami Beach, FL
10	Champion, Mike	Hawaii	102	2	34	.325	R-R	6-0	180	2/10/55 Montgomery, AL
		San Diego	12	0	4	.226				
8	Evans, Barry	Amarillo	157	10	67	.305	R-R	6-1	180	11/30/56
		San Diego	24	0	4	.267				
13	Gonzalez, Fernando	Pitts-SD	84	2	29	.250	R-R	5-10	178	6/19/50 Puerto Rico
21	Hargrove, Mike	Texas	124	7	40	.251	L-L	6-0	195	10/26/49 Perryton, TX
15	Perkins, Broderick	Hawaii	83	3	42	.291	L-L	5-10	180	11/23/54
		San Diego	52	2	33	.240				
1	Smith, Ozzie	San Diego	152	1	46	.258	B-R	5-10	150	12/26/54 Mobile, AL

OUTFIELDERS

No.	Name	1978 Club	H	HR	RBI	Pct.	B-T	Ht.	Wt.	Born
14	Beswick, Jim	Amarillo	112	17	69	.305	B-R	6-1	175	2/12/58
		San Diego	1	0	0	.050				
43	Derryberry, Tim	Amarillo	—	6	61	.245	L-R	6-1	185	4/21/58 Pomona, CA
46	Dyes, Andrew	Hawaii	107	13	51	.323	R-R	6-2	205	12/2/53 Richmond, CA
37	Greer, Brian	Amarillo	—	6	19	.175	R-R	6-3	210	5/13/59 Lynwood, CA
26	Reynolds, Don	San Diego	22	0	10	.253	R-R	5-8	180	4/16/53 Arkadelphia, AR
19	Richards, Gene	San Diego	171	4	45	.308	L-L	6-0	175	9/29/53 Monticello, SC
20	Turner, Jerry	San Diego	63	8	37	.280	L-L	5-9	177	1/17/54 Texarkana, AR
25	Wilhelm, Jim	Hawaii	131	10	73	.284	R-R	6-3	190	9/20/52 Greenbrae, CA
		San Diego	7	0	4	.368				
31	Winfield, Dave	San Diego	181	24	97	.308	R-R	6-6	220	10/3/51 St. Paul, MN

PADRE PROFILES

GAYLORD PERRY 40 6-4 215   Bats R Throws R

 If life doesn't exactly begin at 40, at least it continued merrily on its way for this 22-game, Cy Young Award winner . . . The author of "Me and the Spitter" has 267 lifetime victories, most of any active pitcher . . . Finished the season with a flurry, striking out 11 Dodgers to hike career total to 3,001, trailing only Walter Johnson (3,508) and Bob Gibson (3,117) on the all-time list . . . Born Sept. 15, 1938, in Williamston, N.C. . . . Concluded 1978 with seven straight victories and 10 of last 11 . . . Defeated every NL team at least once, including Houston four times . . . Was a steal, obtained from Texas Rangers for Dave Tomlin and cash before the season.

Year	Club	G	IP	W	L	Pct.	SO	BB	H	ERA
1962	San Francisco	13	43	3	1	.750	20	14	54	5.23
1963	San Francisco	31	76	1	6	.143	52	29	84	4.03
1964	San Francisco	44	206	12	11	.522	155	43	179	2.75
1965	San Francisco	47	196	8	12	.400	170	70	194	4.18
1966	San Francisco	36	256	21	8	.724	201	40	242	2.99
1967	San Francisco	39	293	15	17	.469	230	84	231	2.61
1968	San Francisco	39	291	16	15	.516	173	59	240	2.44
1969	San Francisco	40	325	19	14	.576	233	91	290	2.49
1970	San Francisco	44	329	23	13	.639	214	84	292	3.20
1971	San Francisco	37	280	16	12	.571	158	67	255	2.76
1972	Cleveland	41	343	24	16	.600	234	82	253	1.92
1973	Cleveland	41	344	19	19	.500	238	115	315	3.38
1974	Cleveland	37	322	21	13	.618	216	99	230	2.52
1975	Cleve.-Texas	37	306	18	17	.514	233	70	277	3.24
1976	Texas	32	250	15	14	.517	143	52	232	3.24
1977	Texas	34	238	15	12	.556	177	56	239	3.37
1978	San Diego	37	261	21	6	.778	154	66	241	2.72
	Totals	626	4359	267	206	.564	3001	1121	3848	2.92

OZZIE SMITH 24 5-10 150   Bats R Throws R

 Wasn't listed in San Diego press guide before season, with good reason . . . Had only one year in pro ball after attending Cal Poly, a season at Walla Walla where he hit .303 with 30 stolen bases and led Northwest League shortstops with 40 double plays . . . By the end of 1978, Padres pushed him for NL Rookie of the Year, also with good reason . . . Played 155 games and hit .258 with 40 stolen bases . . . Born Dec. 26, 1954, in Mobile, Ala. . . . Manager Roger Craig said, "He's not only Rookie of the Year in my book, but our

MVP . . ." Said LA's Davey Lopes, "He does things on defense it takes years to learn in this business . . ."

Year	Club	Pos	G	AB	R	H	2B	3B	HR	RBI	SB	Avg.
1978	San Diego	SS	159	590	69	152	17	6	1	46	40	.258

ROLLIE FINGERS 32 6-3 195   Bats R Throws R

Once again baseball's best relief pitcher, winning NL Relief Man of the Year award for second straight season . . . Tied Clay Carroll's National League record with 37 saves . . . In two years, Fingers amassed a record 72 saves and has at least 20 saves in six of last seven years . . . Born Aug. 25, 1946, in Steubenville, Ohio . . . Picked up by Padres in free agent re-entry draft after playing out his option with A's after 1976 . . . Holds World Series record for career relief appearances (16) and set American League Championship Series record for appearances (11) and games finished (eight) . . . Wasn't always a relief pitcher, starting 19 times for Oakland in 1970.

Year	Club	G	IP	W	L	Pct.	SO	BB	H	ERA
1968	Oakland	1	1	0	0	.000	0	1	4	36.00
1969	Oakland	60	119	6	7	.462	61	41	116	3.71
1970	Oakland	45	148	7	9	.438	79	48	137	3.65
1971	Oakland	48	129	4	6	.400	98	30	94	3.00
1972	Oakland	65	111	11	9	.550	113	33	85	2.51
1973	Oakland	62	127	7	8	.467	110	39	107	1.92
1974	Oakland	76	119	9	5	.643	95	29	104	2.65
1975	Oakland	75	127	10	6	.625	115	33	95	2.98
1976	Oakland	70	135	13	11	.542	113	40	118	2.53
1977	San Diego	78	132	8	9	.471	113	36	123	3.00
1978	San Diego	67	107	6	13	.316	72	29	84	2.52
	Totals..................	647	1255	81	83	.494	969	358	1057	2.88

DAVE WINFIELD 27 6-6 220   Bats R Throws R

The epitome of an athlete, drafted professionally in three sports—Padres in baseball, Minnesota in football and Utah (ABA) in basketball . . . Never played a day in the minors after making All-American at University of Minnesota and MVP in 1973 College World Series . . . Hit safely in first six games in big leagues . . . Born Oct. 3, 1951 in St. Paul, Minn. . . . Strong arm and good speed, hits for power despite difficulty of hitting homers in San Diego Stadium

. . . Throws pre-game parties in bleachers for San Diego's underprivileged youth.

Year	Club	Pos	G	AB	R	H	2B	3B	HR	RBI	SB	Avg.
1973	San Diego	OF-1B	56	141	9	39	4	1	3	12	0	.277
1974	San Diego	OF	145	498	57	132	18	4	20	75	9	.265
1975	San Diego	OF	143	509	74	136	20	2	15	76	23	.267
1976	San Diego	OF	137	492	81	139	26	4	13	69	26	.283
1977	San Diego	OF	157	615	104	169	29	7	25	92	16	.275
1978	San Diego	OF	158	587	88	181	30	5	24	97	21	.308
	Totals...........		796	2842	413	796	127	23	100	421	95	.280

GENE TENACE 32 6-0 190　　　　Bats R Throws R

Endured second straight disappointing season and was subject of owner Ray Kroc's dissertation on free agents not producing . . . Split time between catching and first base, but better at first . . . Hits for power, but never much for average and his .222 in 1978 was second lowest of major league career (.211 for Oakland in 1974) . . . Born Fury Gene Tenace on Oct. 10, 1946, in Russellton, Pa. . . . Known as outstanding post-season player with four homers in 1972 World Series against Cincinnati and homers in his first two Series at-bats, a record.

Year	Club	Pos	G	AB	R	H	2B	3B	HR	RBI	SB	Avg.
1969	Oakland	C	16	38	1	6	0	0	1	2	0	.158
1970	Oakland	C	38	105	19	32	6	0	7	20	0	.305
1971	Oakland	C-OF	65	179	26	49	7	0	7	25	2	.274
1972	Oakland	C-OF-INF	82	227	22	51	5	3	5	32	0	.225
1973	Oakland	1B-C-2B	160	510	83	132	18	2	24	84	2	.259
1974	Oakland	1B-C	158	484	71	102	17	1	26	73	2	.211
1975	Oakland	1B-C	158	498	83	127	17	0	29	87	7	.255
1976	Oakland	1B-C	128	417	64	104	19	1	22	66	5	.249
1977	San Diego	C-1B	147	437	66	102	24	4	15	61	5	.233
1978	San Diego	C-1B	142	401	60	90	18	4	16	61	6	.224
	Totals...........		1094	3296	495	795	131	15	152	511	29	.241

RANDY JONES 29 6-0 180　　　　Bats R Throws L

Suffered second straight below .500 season, but barely. Was victim of low run-production by teammates and ERA was a respectable 2.88 . . . Hardly ever strikes anybody out (71 in 253 innings) but hardly ever walks anybody, either (64), relying on sinker to get ground balls . . . Born Jan. 12, 1950, in Fullerton, Cal. . . . So successful against Pete Rose that switch-hitter Rose once batted left handed against him, and was still unsuccessful . . . Holds nine club pitching records and won the Cy Young Award in 1976 with 22-14 record . . . Very quick worker, averaging just over two hours per game when he pitches complete game, of which he had club record 25 in 1976.

Year	Club	G	IP	W	L	Pct.	SO	BB	H	ERA
1973	San Diego	20	140	7	6	.538	77	37	129	3.15
1974	San Diego	40	208	8	22	.267	124	78	217	4.46
1975	San Diego	37	285	20	12	.625	103	56	242	2.24
1976	San Diego	40	315	22	14	.611	93	50	274	2.74
1977	San Diego	27	147	6	12	.333	44	36	173	4.59
1978	San Diego	37	253	13	14	.481	71	64	253	2.88
	Totals	201	1348	76	80	.487	512	321	1288	3.17

ERIC RASMUSSEN 27 6-3 205   Bats R Throws R

Born Harry Rasmussen, but changed first name legally to Eric and came up with career-high 14 victories after mid-season trade from St. Louis, to whom the Padres sent silent George Hendrick . . . Says last two syllables of his last name rhyme with fussin' and changed his first name to keep with his Nordic ancestry . . . Born March 22, 1952, in Racine, Wisc. . . . Pitched a seven-hit shutout in his first major league appearance—against the Padres . . . Was 11-17 with Cardinals in 1977 and all 11 victories were complete games on a staff that had only 26 complete games . . . Likes the nickname The Great Dane.

Year	Club	G	IP	W	L	Pct.	SO	BB	H	ERA
1975	St. Louis	14	81	5	5	.500	59	20	86	3.78
1976	St. Louis	43	150	6	12	.333	76	54	139	3.54
1977	St. Louis	34	233	11	17	.393	120	63	223	3.48
1978	St. L.-S.D.	37	207	14	15	.483	91	63	215	4.09
	Totals	128	671	36	49	.424	346	200	663	3.72

GENE RICHARDS 25 6-0 175   Bats L Throws L

Very good hit, very bad field . . . Reached his .300 goal in second big league season after just missing in 1977 . . . Outstanding base stealer, swiping 85 in his first professional season at Reno in 1975, as well as hitting .381 . . . Quit South Carolina State to sign with Padres after school dropped baseball to provide funds for women's athletics . . . Set a record with 56 stolen bases for a rookie in 1977 . . . Born Sept.

29, 1953, in Monticello, S.C. . . . Tied a major league record by going six-for-seven in an extra-inning game against Montreal . . . Plays mostly in left field, but being trained at first base.

Year	Club	Pos	G	AB	R	H	2B	3B	HR	RBI	SB	Avg.
1977	San Diego	OF-1B	146	525	79	152	16	11	5	32	56	.290
1978	San Diego	OF-1B	154	555	90	171	26	12	4	45	37	.308
	Totals		300	1080	169	323	42	23	9	77	93	.299

MIKE HARGROVE 29 6-0 195   Bats L Throws R

Texas' favorite son was upset at trade that brought him to Padres for Oscar Gamble . . . Led AL in walks with 107 . . . Also a natural hitter . . . "I can do everything a leadoff man is supposed to do except run with speed." . . . Promoted to lead-off spot in '77 by former Texas manager Billy Hunter on advice of Oriole manager Earl Weaver . . . Has batted every position in order from first to ninth . . . "That's got to tie a record, at least." . . . Born Oct. 26, 1949, in Perryton, Tex. . . . Slumped at plate in '78 . . . Was AL Rookie of Year in 1974 . . . Never played high school baseball, but father insisted he play in college . : . Was 577th pick in the nation in 1972 free agent draft, going on 25th round.

Year	Club	Pos	G	AB	R	H	2B	3B	HR	RBI	SB	Avg.
1974	Texas	1B-OF	131	415	57	134	18	6	4	66	0	.323
1975	Texas	1B-OF	145	519	82	157	22	2	11	62	4	.303
1976	Texas	1B	151	541	80	155	30	1	7	58	2	.287
1977	Texas	1B	153	525	98	160	28	4	18	69	2	.305
1978	Texas	1B	146	494	63	124	24	1	7	40	2	.251
	Totals		726	2494	380	730	122	14	47	295	10	.293

BOB SHIRLEY 24 5-11 185   Bats R Throws L

Very tough on left handed hitters . . . Cincinnati's Ken Griffey said, "If I ever get a hit off him, I'm gonna stop the game and ask for the ball." . . . It hasn't happened yet . . . In his major league debut in 1977 against the Reds, he struckout 11 . . . He beat the Reds four times in '77 . . . Used both as a starter and relief pitcher . . . Spent only one year in the minors and split that time between Amarillo and Hawaii in 1976, pitching for two teams that won league championships . . . Born June 25, 1954, in Cushing, Okla. . . . Pitched at University of Oklahoma and drafted by the Giants in 1975, but didn't sign . . . Padres signed him in secondary phase of January, 1976, free agent draft.

Year	Club	G	IP	W	L	Pct.	SO	BB	H	ERA
1977	San Diego	39	214	12	18	.400	146	100	215	3.70
1978	San Diego	50	166	8	11	.421	102	61	164	3.69
	Totals	89	380	20	29	.408	248	161	379	3.69

TOP PROSPECT

JIM BESWICK 21 6-1 175   Bats S Throws R

Chance to be super major league hitter despite rough first game after call up last Aug. 12 from Double-A Amarillo, when Padres were short on outfielders . . . Faced LA lefty Doug Rau in debut, striking out twice and grounding into two double plays . . . Born Feb. 12, 1958, in Ardmore, Pa. . . . Was hitting .305 with 17 homers and 69 RBIs when called up from Amarillo after 103 games . . . Because of strong San Diego outfield, probably will play 1979 in Triple-A Hawaii, but was on Padres' spring roster and is considered their No. 1 prospect.

MANAGER ROGER CRAIG: Succeeded Alvin Dark in early  1978 when Dark and Padre owner Ray Kroc had a blowout . . . Craig was pitching coach, but was named interim manager, then manager-for-real after doing excellent job with young team . . . Was an exceptional pitcher in the Dodger organization, but earned everlasting fame with the woebegotten expansionist Mets in 1962 by losing 24 games . . . But, he was 11-5 with a 2.06 earned run average with Los Angeles in 1959 . . . Born Feb. 17, 1931, in Durham, N.C. . . . Retains Southern drawl and homespun sense of humor . . . After career ended, spent 1967 as Dodger scout, then began managerial career at Albuquerque in 1968, leading the Dukes to second place in the Texas League and pitching four innings . . . Was San Diego pitching coach for Preston Gomez from 1969 through 1973, but left when Don Zimmer took over, going to Houston as Gomez's pitching coach . . . Returned to San Diego for the 1976 season.

GREATEST PITCHER

There have been 70 pitchers who have worn a San Diego uniform since the franchise was born in Mission Valley in 1969, and only one has won more than 52 games.

Pitching since 1973 for a less-than-productive team, Randall Leo (Randy) Jones owns 76 victories against 80 defeats—many, many of those defeats by one or two runs.

Jones has been so good, his teammates seem to relax and let Randy work hard for his victories.

Jones doesn't throw hard enough to make water ripple, but his sinker drives hitters up clubhouse walls. Jones coaxes ground ball after ground ball from batters.

The little left-hander owns the highest honor ever bestowed upon a Padre, the Cy Young Award, which he won in 1976 with a 22-14 record. But, his 1975 record was probably better—20-12 with a 2.24 ERA. His 1976 ERA was 2.74, but he lost the '75 Cy Young vote to Tom Seaver.

Not only do hitters find it difficult to extract base hits off Jones, they can't get bases on balls, either. In 1976, he tied a Christy Mathewson record by going 68 straight innings without giving up a walk.

Jones also qualifies for a courage award after developing a sore arm that forced Los Angeles surgeon Dr. Frank Jobe to reconstruct his elbow. Randy bounced back to win 13 games in 1978.

ALL-TIME PADRE LEADERS

BATTING: Clarence Gaston, .318, 1970
HRs: Nate Colbert, 38, 1970
RBIs: Nate Colbert, 111, 1972
STEALS: Gene Richards, 56, 1977
WINS: Randy Jones, 22, 1976
STRIKEOUTS: Clay Kirby, 231, 1971

HOUSTON ASTROS

TEAM DIRECTORY: Pres.-GM: Tal Smith; Admin. Asst.: Donald Davidson; Asst. to GM: John Mullen; Dir. of Scouting: Lynwood Stallings; Dir. Pub. Rel.: Art Perkins; Trav. Sec.: Gerry Hunsicker; Mgr.: Bill Virdon. Home: Astrodome (45,-000). Field distances: 340, l.f. line; 406, c.f.; 340, r.f. line; 390 power alleys. Spring training: Cocoa, Fla.

J.R. Richard fanned 303, NL record for right-handers.

SCOUTING REPORT

HITTING: The Astros talked big in spring training of 1978, talking National League West championship. But, they were counting on a healthy Cesar Cedeno and Bob Watson. Neither was healthy. Cedeno spent most of the season with a plaster of Paris cast on his knee. Watson played, but he needed a specially-designed NASA glove on an injured hand and suffered for it. Watson managed 139 games and hit an amazing .289, including 14 homers and 79 RBIs. With a healed hand, he can do better.

Cedeno played only 50 games and the Astros aren't about to be successful without his all-around abilities in the lineup. Jose Cruz has established himself as a bright major league hitter and Terry Puhl flirted with .300 all season, finishing at .289 with a spray-hitting style. With a healthy Cedeno, the Astros have an excellent hitting outfield.

Enos Cabell is another potential .300 hitter and Art Howe came close to that mark, giving the Astros a couple of fine hitting infielders to go with first baseman Watson. There are no hitters at shortstop or behind the plate.

PITCHING: The Astros gave up on a couple of promising youngsters, Mark Lemongello and Floyd Bannister. Lemongello and his manager, Virdon, didn't enjoy each other's company and guess who got shipped out?

But, J.R. Richard is not only baseball's tallest pitcher, he is close to the best. Beating Cincinnati and Los Angeles is his specialty, but he has lapses against lesser teams. No matter who he pitches against, though, he strikes out a bunch—303 last season. Ken Forsch is still around and capable of a big season with his excellent pitching repertoire. And, Joe Niekro befuddles opposition hitters with his hard knuckler. The Astros consider young Tom Dixon a future star.

In the bullpen, Joe Sambito is the star, but is coming off a so-so season. The Astros haven't given up on Joaquin Andujar, either.

FIELDING: Up the middle, where good teams are strong, the Astros are weak. Only center fielder Cedeno can hold up his end, and he more than holds it up. The catchers are Reggie Baldwin, Bruce Bochy, Alan Ashby and Luis Pujols—take your pick. None remind you of Johnny Bench. The Astros are still searching for a big league shortstop and Howe is no Gold Glove second baseman. Cabell is adequate at third, but wild of arm, and Watson covers little ground around first base. Richard takes care of the defensive deficiencies by striking out a lot of people, but all pitchers can't do that.

OUTLOOK: It all hinges on a good pitching staff and an injury-free season for Cedeno and Watson, two legitimate stars. The Astros still need a catcher and a big league shortstop to move into the upper echelon of the National League West.

HOUSTON ASTROS 1979 ROSTER

MANAGER Bill Virdon

Coaches—Deacon Jones, Bob Lillis, Tony Pacheco, Mel Wright

PITCHERS

No.	Name	1978 Club	W-L	IP	SO	ERA	B-T	Ht.	Wt.	Born
47	Andujar, Joaquin	Houston	5-7	111	55	3.32	B-R	5-11	180	12/21/52 Dominican Republic
37	Dixon, Tom	Houston	7-11	140	66	3.99	R-R	6-0	183	4/23/55 Orlando, FL
43	Forsch, Ken	Houston	10-6	133	71	2.71	R-R	6-4	205	9/8/46 Sacramento, CA
39	McLaughlin, Bo	Charleston	8-5	138	63	3.73	R-R	6-5	205	10/23/53 Oakland, CA
		Houston	0-1	23	10	5.09				
54	Mendoza, Mike	Columbus	9-8	133	101	2.75	R-R	6-5	215	11/26/55 Inglewood, CA
		Charleston	2-5	42	23	9.29				
36	Niekro, Joe	Houston	14-14	203	97	3.86	R-R	6-1	190	11/7/44 Martins Ferry, OH
—	Niemann, Randy	Columbus	9-5	123	53	2.05	L-L	6-4	200	11/15/55 Furtuna, CA
—	Pladson, Gordon	Columbus	10-9	165	109	3.71	R-R	6-4	210	7/31/56 Newestminster, BC
—	Riccelli, Frank	Springfield	3-3	50	51	3.06	L-L	6-3	200	2/24/53 Syracuse, NY
		Charleston	9-7	123	93	2.79				
		Houston	0-0	3	1	0.00				
50	Richard, J.R.	Houston	18-11	275	303	3.11	R-R	6-8	220	3/7/50 Vienna, LA
—	Ruhle, Vern	Columbus	4-1	39	25	1.85	R-R	6-1	187	1/25/51 Coleman, MI
		Charleston	4-4	94	48	2.78				
		Houston	3-3	68	27	2.12				
35	Sambito, Joe	Houston	4-9	88	96	3.07	L-L	6-1	190	6/28/52 Brooklyn, NY
—	Warthen, Dan	Oklahoma City	13-8	196	144	4.09	B-L	6-0	200	12/1/52 Omaha, NB
		Houston	0-1	11	2	4.09				
—	Wilson, Gary	Charleston	14-7	184	87	3.87	R-R	6-2	180	11/21/54 Camden, AR

CATCHERS

No.	Name	1978 Club	H	HR	RBI	Pct.	B-T	Ht.	Wt.	Born
8	Ashby, Alan	Toronto	69	9	29	.261	B-R	6-1	190	7/8/51 Long Beach, CA
—	Baldwin, Reggie	Columbus	43	1	23	.323	R-R	6-1	195	8/19/54 River Rouge, MI
		Houston	17	-1	11	.254				
—	Bochy, Bruce	Columbus	69	6	32	.271	R-R	6-4	210	4/16/55 France
		Houston	41	3	15	.266				
—	Pujols, Luis	Charleston	43	3	24	.219	R-R	6-1	195	11/18/55 Dominican Republic
		Houston	20	1	11	.131				

INFIELDERS

No.	Name	1978 Club	H	HR	RBI	Pct.	B-T	Ht.	Wt.	Born
—	Bergman, Dave	Houston	43	0	12	.231	L-L	6-2	185	6/6/53 Evanston, IL
23	Cabell, Enos	Houston	195	7	71	.295	R-R	6-4	185	10/8/49 Ft. Riley, KA
15	Drumright, Keith	Charleston	159	1	49	.311	L-R	5-10	160	10/21/54 Springfield, MO
		Houston	9	0	2	.164				
10	Fischlin, Mike	Charleston	59	0	19	.211	B-R	6-1	165	9/13/55 Sacramento, CA
		Houston	10	0	0	.116				
9	Gonzalez, Julio	Charleston	11	0	2	.367	R-R	5-11	165	12/25/53 Puerto Rico
		Houston	52	1	16	.233				
11	Hernandez, Pedro	Daytona	58	0	13	.267	R-R	6-1	160	4/4/59 Dominican Republic
		Sarasota	29	0	9	.287				
18	Howe, Art	Houston	123	7	55	.293	R-R	6-2	190	12/15/46 Pittsburgh, PA
17	Landestoy, Rafael	Albuquerque	76	1	35	.274	B-R	5-9	163	5/28/53 Dominican Republic
		Houston	58	0	9	.266				
19	Obradovich, Jim	Charleston	129	21	85	.306	L-L	6-2	200	9/13/49 Ft. Campbell, KY
		Houston	3	0	2	.176				
—	Reynolds, Craig	Seattle	160	5	44	.292	L-R	6-1	175	12/27/52 Houston, TX
24	Sexton, Jimmy	Houston	29	2	6	.206	R-R	5-11	175	12/15/51 Mobile, AL
27	Watson, Bob	Houston	133	14	79	.289	R-R	6-2	205	4/10/46 Los Angeles, CA

OUTFIELDERS

No.	Name	1978 Club	H	HR	RBI	Pct.	B-T	Ht.	Wt.	Born
12	Alou, Jesus	Houston	45	2	19	.324	R-R	6-2	195	3/24/43 Dominican Republic
20	Cannon, Joe	Charleston	152	8	75	.293	L-R	6-2	185	7/13/53 Camp LeJeune, NC
		Houston	4	0	1	.222				
28	Cedeno, Cesar	Houston	54	7	23	.281	R-R	6-2	190	2/25/51 Dominican Republic
25	Cruz, Jose	Houston	178	10	83	.315	L-L	6-0	175	8/8/47 Puerto Rico
26	Howard, Wilbur	Houston	34	1	13	.230	B-R	6-2	175	1/8/49 Lowell, NC
—	Leonard, Jeff	Albuquerque	183	11	93	.365	R-R	6-2	200	9/22/55 Philadelphia, PA
		Houston	10	0	4	.385				
21	Puhl, Terry	Houston	169	3	35	.289	L-R	6-1	190	7/8/56 Melville, Sask.
29	Walling, Denny	Houston	62	3	36	.251	L-R	6-1	185	4/17/54 Neptune, NJ
—	Wiedenbauer, Tom	Columbus	25	0	6	.269	R-R	6-1	175	11/5/58 Menomonie, WI
—	Woods, Gary	Syracuse	136	13	45	.270	R-R	6-2	190	7/20/53 Santa Barbara, CA
		Toronto	3	0	0	.158				

ASTRO PROFILES

J.R. RICHARD 29 6-8 220 **Bats R Throws R**

Tallest player in the National League, with shortest fastball . . . Arrives like an express train, enabling him to strike out league and career high 303 hitters . . . Gave indication of what was to come by striking out 15 Giants in first major league start . . . His ERA in high school at Lincoln High, Ruston, La., was 0.00 in 1969 and in one game he hit four straight homers and drove in 10 runs as Lincoln beat Jonesboro Jackson, 48-0 . . . Doesn't hit that well any more, but pitches almost that well . . . Born March 7, 1950, in Vienna, La. . . . A positive thinker and a Bible reader when not helping to tend to five children.

Year	Club	G	IP	W	L	Pct.	SO	BB	H	ERA
1971	Houston	4	21	2	1	.667	29	16	17	3.43
1972	Houston	4	6	1	0	1.000	8	8	10	13.50
1973	Houston	16	72	6	2	.750	75	38	54	4.00
1974	Houston	15	65	2	3	.400	42	36	58	4.15
1975	Houston	33	203	12	10	.545	176	138	178	4.34
1976	Houston	39	291	20	15	.571	214	151	221	2.75
1977	Houston	36	267	18	12	.600	214	104	212	2.97
1978	Houston	36	275	18	11	.621	303	141	192	3.11
	Totals	183	1200	79	54	.594	1061	632	942	3.38

ART HOWE 32 6-2 190 **Bats R Throws R**

Member of the "Bald is Beautiful" sect . . . Has lost hair, but gained range as second baseman who can contribute with a bat . . . Started his major league career correctly by singling in his first at bat off Atlanta's Carl Morton in 1974 . . . Not known for power, but once had 11 extra base hits in 12 at bats in minors at Memphis . . . Born Dec. 15, 1946, in Pittsburgh . . . Played football at the University of Wyoming, but gave it up to play baseball and handball . . . Led International League third basemen in double plays with 24 in 1972, but was transferred to second base after Astros traded Tommy Helms to Pittsburgh for player to be named later. That was how Howe became an Astro.

Year	Club	Pos	G	AB	R	H	2B	3B	HR	RBI	SB	Avg.
1974	Pittsburgh	3B-SS	29	74	10	18	4	1	1	5	0	.243
1975	Pittsburgh	3B-SS	63	146	13	25	9	0	1	10	1	.171
1976	Houston	3B-2B	21	29	0	4	1	0	0	0	0	.138
1977	Houston	2B-3B-SS	125	413	44	109	23	7	8	58	0	.264
1978	Houston	2B-3B-SS	119	420	46	123	33	3	7	55	2	.293
	Totals		357	1082	113	279	70	11	17	128	3	.258

BOB WATSON 33 6-2 205   Bats R Throws R

One of baseball's genuine nice guys, and has been for his 13-year Houston career . . . Hand injury slowed him all year, forcing him to wear special NASA-designed glove . . . Always good in the clutch and hits with power to all fields . . . Still considers scoring millionth run in baseball history his outstanding achievement after hitting a homer and sprinting the bases to accomplish it . . . Born Apr. 10, 1946 in Los Angeles . . . His 1,419 career hits is tops all-time for Astros . . . Averaged 90 RBI for past seven seasons.

Year	Club	Pos	G	AB	R	H	2B	3B	HR	RBI	SB	Avg.
1966	Houston	PH	1	1	0	0	0	0	0	0	0	.000
1967	Houston	1B	6	14	1	3	0	0	1	2	0	.214
1968	Houston	OF	45	140	13	32	7	0	2	8	1	.229
1969	Houston	OF-1B-C	20	40	3	11	3	0	0	3	0	.275
1970	Houston	1B-C-OF	97	327	48	89	19	2	11	61	1	.272
1971	Houston	OF-1B	129	468	49	135	17	3	9	67	0	.288
1972	Houston	OF-1B	147	548	74	171	27	4	16	86	1	.312
1973	Houston	OF-1B-C	158	573	97	179	24	3	16	94	1	.312
1974	Houston	OF-1B	150	524	69	156	19	4	11	67	3	.298
1975	Houston	1B-OF	132	485	67	157	27	1	18	85	3	.324
1976	Houston	1B	157	585	76	183	31	3	16	102	3	.313
1977	Houston	1B	151	554	77	160	38	6	22	110	5	.289
1978	Houston	1B	139	461	51	133	25	4	14	79	3	.289
	Totals		1332	4720	625	1409	237	30	136	764	21	.299

ENOS CABELL 29 6-4 185   Bats R Throws R

Born with built-in smile . . . So skinny, looks naked without a flag on him . . . Adequate third baseman, but very deadly hitter who hit .295, career high . . . Long legs move fast, making him base-stealing threat . . . Born Oct. 8, 1949, in Fort Riley, Kan. . . . Won two batting titles in the minor leagues and took third base away from Doug Rader when Astros traded Lee May for him . . . Clubhouse comedian . . . Hit 23 homers last two seasons despite slender build and dead air of Astrodome.

Year	Club	Pos	G	AB	R	H	2B	3B	HR	RBI	SB	Avg.
1972	Baltimore	1B	3	5	0	0	0	0	0	1	0	.000
1973	Baltimore	1B-3B	32	47	12	10	2	0	1	3	1	.213
1974	Baltimore	1B-OF-3B-2B	80	174	24	42	4	2	3	17	5	.241
1975	Houston	OF-1B-3B	117	348	43	92	17	6	2	43	12	.264
1976	Houston	3B-1B	144	586	85	160	13	7	2	43	35	.273
1977	Houston	3B	150	625	101	176	36	7	16	68	42	.282
1978	Houston	3B	162	660	92	195	31	8	7	71	33	.295
	Totals		688	2445	357	675	103	30	31	246	128	.276

CESAR CEDENO 28 6-2 190   Bats R Throws R

Pre-season prediction of .300 batting average, 30 homers and 60 stolen bases died on the surgeon's table where he underwent knee surgery early in the season . . . Has it all: Power, speed and a gun for an arm . . . "I was afraid I'd see him pinch-hit with his cast on," said ex-Cincinnati manager Sparky Anderson, a Cedeno booster . . . Born Feb. 25, 1951, in Santo Domingo . . . Despite injury-filled career, is in the top three in every offensive category in Astro history and won Gold Gloves from 1972 through 1976, then made only one error in 1977 and didn't win a Gold Glove.

Year	Club	Pos	G	AB	R	H	2B	3B	HR	RBI	SB	Avg.
1970	Houston	OF	90	355	46	110	21	4	7	42	17	.310
1971	Houston	OF-1B	161	611	85	161	40	6	10	81	20	.264
1972	Houston	OF	139	559	103	179	39	8	22	82	55	.320
1973	Houston	OF	139	525	86	168	35	2	25	70	56	.320
1974	Houston	OF	160	610	95	164	29	5	26	102	57	.269
1975	Houston	OF	131	500	93	144	31	3	13	63	50	.288
1976	Houston	OF	150	575	89	171	26	5	18	83	58	.297
1977	Houston	OF	141	530	92	148	36	8	14	71	61	.279
1978	Houston	OF	50	192	31	54	8	2	7	23	23	.281
	Totals		1161	4457	720	1299	265	43	142	617	397	.291

JOSE CRUZ 31 6-0 175   Bats L Throws L

Oldest and best-hitting of three baseball-playing brothers . . . Career high .315 in 1978 was third straight year over .299 . . . Fits Houston mold of outfielders with base-stealing speed and strong arm . . . Born Aug. 8, 1947, in Arroyo, P.R. . . . Was Houston's MVP in 1977 . . . Played four years in St. Louis, but never blossomed and was purchased by Astros for 1975 season . . . Houston coach Deacon Jones quickly turned him into aggressive combination power and spray hitter, depending upon the situation.

Year	Club	Pos	G	AB	R	H	2B	3B	HR	RBI	SB	Avg.
1970	St. Louis	OF	6	17	2	6	1	0	0	1	0	.353
1971	St. Louis	OF	83	292	46	80	13	2	9	27	6	.274
1972	St. Louis	OF	117	332	33	78	14	4	2	23	9	.235
1973	St. Louis	OF	132	406	51	92	22	5	10	57	10	.227
1974	St. Louis	OF-1B	107	161	24	42	4	3	5	20	4	.261
1975	Houston	OF	120	315	44	81	15	2	9	49	6	.257
1976	Houston	OF	133	439	49	133	21	5	4	61	28	.303
1977	Houston	OF	157	579	87	173	31	10	17	87	44	.299
1978	Houston	OF	153	565	79	178	34	9	10	83	37	.315
	Totals		1008	3106	415	863	155	40	66	408	144	.278

ALAN ASHBY 27 6-1 190   Bats S Throws R

Switch-hitting catcher with excellent arm . . .
Enjoyed best season at plate, by far, in '78
. . . First player Blue Jays traded for follow-
ing 1977 expansion draft . . . Born July 8,
1951, in Long Beach, Cal. . . . Many people
thought he'd be bigger star than he is . . .
Cleveland's third draft pick in 1969 . . . A
Dodger fan as a youngster, he witnessed two
of Sandy Koufax's four no-hitters . . . Played amateur ball with
Garry Maddox of Phillies.

Year	Club	Pos	G	AB	R	H	2B	3B	HR	RBI	SB	Avg.
1973	Cleveland	C	11	29	4	5	1	0	1	3	0	.172
1974	Cleveland	C	10	7	1	1	0	0	0	0	0	.143
1975	Cleveland	C-1B-3B	90	254	32	57	10	1	5	32	3	.224
1976	Cleveland	3B-1B-C	89	247	26	59	5	1	4	32	0	.239
1977	Toronto	C	124	396	25	83	16	3	2	29	0	.210
1978	Toronto	C	81	264	27	69	15	0	9	29	1	.261
	Totals		405	1197	115	274	47	5	21	125	4	.229

TERRY PUHL 22 6-1 190   Bats L Throws R

Flirted with .300 most of season . . . Contact
hitter, very difficult to strike out . . . Fast, a
base-stealer and covers considerable ground
in center field . . . Canadian-born . . . Born
July 8, 1956 in Melville, Sask. . . . Was
caught stealing in his first major league at-
tempt, then swiped 10 straight . . . Swiftness
enables him to play extremely shallow center
field . . . Rookie season, 1977, hit in 17 straight games and five
times during the streak got two or more hits.

Year	Club	Pos	G	AB	R	H	2B	3B	HR	RBI	SB	Avg.
1977	Houston	OF	60	229	40	69	13	5	0	10	10	.301
1978	Houston	OF	149	585	87	169	25	6	3	35	32	.289
	Totals		209	814	127	238	38	11	3	45	42	.292

JOE NIEKRO 34 6-1 190   Bats R Throws R

Like brother, Phil, drives hitters to distraction
with fluttery knuckleball, but throws it harder
than his older brother . . . Is one up on more
famous brother, defeating him in their one
confrontation on May 29, 1967, 4-3, on a
four-hitter and hit a home run . . . Born
Nov. 7, 1944, in Martins Ferry, Ohio . . .
Pitched a perfect game in Triple A for To-

ledo against Tidewater in 1972 . . . Effective as both starter and relief pitcher . . . Was one out away from pitching a no-hitter for Detroit in 1970 when New York's Horace Clarke singled.

Year	Club	G	IP	W	L	Pct.	SO	BB	H	ERA
1967	Chicago (N.L.)	35	170	10	7	.588	77	32	171	3.34
1968	Chicago (N.L.)	34	177	14	10	.583	65	59	204	4.32
1969	Chi. (N.L.)S.D.	41	221	8	18	.308	62	51	237	3.71
1970	Detroit	38	213	12	13	.480	101	72	221	4.06
1971	Detroit	31	122	6	7	.462	43	49	136	4.50
1972	Detroit	18	47	3	2	.600	24	8	62	3.83
1973	Atlanta	20	24	2	4	.333	12	11	23	4.13
1974	Atlanta	27	43	3	2	.600	31	18	36	3.56
1975	Houston	40	88	6	4	.600	54	39	79	3.07
1976	Houston	36	118	4	8	.333	77	56	107	3.36
1977	Houston	44	181	13	8	.619	101	64	155	3.03
1978	Houston	35	203	14	14	.500	97	73	190	3.86
	Totals	400	1607	95	97	.495	744	532	1621	3.73

JOE SAMBITO 26 6-1 190   Bats L Throws L

One of NL's better left-handers out of the bullpen . . . Pitched 142 innings in 1977, making 54 appearances, but was used for only 88 innings in 1978 after bitter contract squabble which was resolved late in the season . . . Born June 28, 1952, in Brooklyn, N.Y. . . . Was a 17th round draft selection in 1973 . . . Made rapid advancement after leading the Southern League at Columbus in wild pitches with 14 in 1975 . . . Was baseball All-American at Adelphi University in 1973.

Year	Club	G	IP	W	L	Pct.	SO	BB	H	ERA
1976	Houston	20	53	3	2	.600	26	14	45	3.57
1977	Houston	54	89	5	5	.500	67	24	77	2.33
1978	Houston	62	88	4	9	.308	96	32	85	3.07
	Totals	136	230	12	16	.429	189	70	207	2.90

CRAIG REYNOLDS 26 6-1 175   Bats R Throws R

Surprised everyone with his fine performance at the plate in 1978 . . . Once highly regarded by the Pirates, who had no place for him to play . . . The first player the Mariners traded for after completing the expansion draft . . . Good-looking, friendly, All-American boy . . . Deeply religious, doesn't smoke, drink or swear . . . Born Dec. 27, 1952, in Houston . . . Drafted and signed as an outfielder, but later converted to shortstop . . . Pirates No. 1 draft pick in June, 1971 . . . A star after only two full years in the big leagues.

Year	Club	Pos	G	AB	R	H	2B	3B	HR	RBI	SB	Avg.
1975	Pittsburgh.......	SS	31	76	8	17	3	0	0	4	0	.224
1976	Pittsburgh.......	SS-2B	7	4	1	1	0	0	1	1	0	.250
1977	Seattle.........	SS	135	420	41	104	12	3	4	28	6	.248
1978	Seattle.........	SS	148	548	57	160	16	7	5	44	9	.292
	Totals..........		321	1048	107	282	31	10	10	77	15	.269

TOP PROSPECT

JEFF LEONARD 24 6-2 200   **Bats R Throws R**
Just what the Astros need—another fleet outfielder . . . Obtained last season as "the player to be named later" when Astros sent catcher Joe Ferguson to Los Angeles . . . Born Sept. 22, 1955, in Philadelphia and played basketball at Overbrook High School where Wilt Chamberlain once roamed . . . Was Albuquerque (Pacific Coast-AAA) batting champion with .365, 11 homers, 93 RBIs and 36 stolen bases . . . Astros consider him an outstanding offensive threat with bat and legs, but needs work on defense.

MANAGER BILL VIRDON: After much talk about a possible challenge for the NL West championship, Astros lost Cesar Cedeno early, Bob Watson played despite season-long hand miseries, and Houston sank to fifth place . . . But, it wasn't Virdon's fault . . . He worked miracles with strangers in the lineup . . . No matter how good or how bad his teams play, you can't tell it from his demeanor . . . Remains gentlemanly and soft-spoken under all circumstances . . . Born June 9, 1931, in Hazel Park, Mich. . . . Was NL Rookie of the Year with Cardinals in 1955, but made reputation at Pittsburgh as smooth-fielding center fielder with a .267 lifetime average for 12 seasons . . . Loved by writers as nice guy, but doesn't say much controversially to grab headlines . . . Started major league managerial run with Pittsburgh in 1972, but was fired in 1973 with club in second place . . . Yankees picked him up in 1974 and he was Manager of the Year with second place finish

. . . Ran afoul of owner George Steinbrenner and was fired midway through 1975 . . . Picked up by Houston on Aug. 19, 1975, and took Astros to two straight third places in 1976 and 1977.

GREATEST PITCHER

Before he hangs up his rather large spikes, 6-foot-7-inch J.R. Richard may become Houston's greatest all-time pitcher.

He is close now with a 79-54 record and 1,061 strikeouts, but the all-time honor still belongs to Larry Dierker, winner of 137 games in 12 seasons with the Astros.

No matter where you look in the pitching records section of the Astrolog you find Dierker's name.

He tops the Astros in innings pitched (2,295), complete games (106), strikeouts (1,487) and shutouts (25). Of course, he also leads the Astros in defeats (117), but he was around for the lean expansion years in the early and mid-sixties.

Dierker owns the last no-hitter pitched by an Astro, defeating Montreal in the Astrodome, 6-0, on July 9, 1976, his last season with Houston before he was traded to St. Louis.

A broken leg and sore shoulder slowed Dierker to a 2-6 crawl in 1977 for the Cardinals, but the Cardinals were merely happy to get him away from Houston, where he was 4-0 against St. Louis in 1976.

Dierker pitched only 39 innings in the minors before coming to Houston in 1964 on his 18th birthday. The hard-throwing right-hander's best season was 20-13 in 1969.

ALL-TIME ASTRO LEADERS

BATTING: Rusty Staub, .333, 1967
HRs: Jimmy Wynn, 37, 1967
RBIs: Bob Watson, 110, 1977
STEALS: Cesar Cedeno, 61, 1977
WINS: Larry Dierker, 20, 1969
       J.R. Richard, 20, 1976
STRIKEOUTS: J.R. Richard, 303, 1978

ATLANTA BRAVES

TEAM DIRECTORY: Chairman of the Board: Bill Bartholomay; Pres.: Ted Turner; Dir. Player Personnel: Bill Lucas; Dir Player Development: Hank Aaron; Trav. Sec.: Pete Van Wieren; Pub. Rel.: Bob Hope; Mgr.: Bobby Cox. Home: Atlanta Stadium (52,870). Field distances: 330, l.f. line; 400, c.f.; 330, r.f. line. Spring training: West Palm Beach, Fla.

SCOUTING REPORT

HITTING: At the end of the season, you couldn't even tell the Braves' lineup with a program as flamboyant owner Ted Turner fiddled with a youth movement. There are still a couple of recognizable names in the lineup—Jeff Burroughs and Gary Matthews—both capable of big batting averages and lots of homers.

The headlines, though, belonged to Bob Horner, a curly-headed blond drafted out of Arizona State University in June. Horner talked director of player personnel Bill Lucas into keeping him on the major league roster instead of shipping him to the minors.

Lucas agreed and Horner put together an incredible half-season—23 homers and 63 RBIs in only 89 games, good for Rookie of the Year. The Braves will be strengthened by the

Bob Horner, playing half season, was NL Rookie of Year.

return of outfielder Brian Asselstine, an early-season casualty when his leg lost an argument with the outfield fence. If the names Eddie Miller, Larry Whisenton and Barry Bonnell are unfamiliar, well, those are some of the fresh faces manager Bobby Cox used in the outfield late in the season.

In the infield, there are unfamiliars like Glenn Hubbard, Chico Ruiz and Bob Beall gathered around veteran shortstop Darrel Chaney. The catchers are strangers, too—Joe Nolan and Bruce Benedict. Just how many squeeze into the lineup remains to be seen. One thing for sure, big guy Dale Murphy will wriggle into the lineup either at first base or behind the plate. The hitting, though, still must come from Burroughs, Matthews, Horner and Asselstine.

PITCHING: Phil Niekro just keeps fluttering along, frustrating hitters with that butterfly ball, the knuckler. One of the finest pitching rookies was Larry McWilliams, already famous for helping stop Pete Rose's 44-game hitting streak, along with bullpen ace Gene Garber. Niekro was 19-18 and McWilliams was 9-3. After those two, the starting corps was wafer thin, which is why the Atlanta pitching staff was last in the National League with a 4.08 earned run average, giving up a league-leading 132 homers.

After Niekro and McWilliams as starters, and Garber out of the bullpen, it's anybody's guess who Cox will come up with. Mickey Mahler? Duane Theiss? Rick Camp? Craig Skok? Adrian Devine? Stay tuned, but keep your radio turned low or the sound of bat on ball may be deafening.

FIELDING: Who can say, with so many young players? But, if the Atlanta kids are typical, expect a bundle of errors. The Braves made 153 errors last season, third most. But there should be different people in there this season. Expect more errors until experience sets in. Burroughs has never been accused of playing glowing defense. Neither has Matthews. The infield is shaky and so is the catching. If Turner's yacht was as leaky as the Atlanta defense, it would swiftly sink.

OUTLOOK: In a word, dismal. Turner's youth movement will keep the Braves buried in the depths from start to finish. Even Niekro might have trouble staying above .500. And there's no way the Braves can reach .500. Maybe not .300. The Braves have a chance to lead the league in two categories . . . defeats and errors.

ATLANTA BRAVES 1979 ROSTER

MANAGER Bobby Cox
Coaches—Tommie Aaron, Cloyd Boyer, Mark Cresse, Bobby Dews, Alex Grammas

PITCHERS

No.	Name	1978 Club	W-L	IP	SO	ERA	B-T	Ht.	Wt.	Born
—	Boggs, Tommy	Richmond	5-1	54	29	2.83	R-R	6-2	200	10/25/55 Poughkeepsie, NY
		Atlanta	2-8	59	21	6.71				
—	Bradford, Larry	Richmond	7-9	107	56	4.88	R-L	6-1	200	12/21/51 Chicago, IL
33	Camp, Rick	Atlanta	2-4	74	23	3.77	R-R	198	6/10/53 Trion, GA
32	Campbell, Dave	Atlanta	4-4	69	45	4.83	R-R	6-3	210	9/3/51 Princeton, IN
—	Chiti, Dom	Savannah	9-10	131	47	3.44	L-L	6-2	180	12/10/58 Independence, MO
—	Davey, Mike	Richmond	3-3	79	37	2.96	R-L	6-2	190	6/2/52 Spokane, WA
		Atlanta	0-0	3	0	0.00				
28	Devine, Adrian	Atlanta	5-4	65	26	5.95	R-R	6-4	205	12/2/51 Galveston, TX
45	Easterly, Jamie	Atlanta	3-6	78	42	5.65	L-L	5-9	179	2/17/53 Houston, TX
26	Garber, Gene	Phil-Atl	6-5	117	85	2.15	R-R	5-10	175	11/13/47 Lancaster, PA
49	Hanna, Preston	Atlanta	7-13	140	90	5.14	R-R	6-1	185	9/10/54 Pensacola, FL
—	LaCorte, Frank	Richmond	6-7	130	100	4.22	R-R	6-1	180	10/13/51 San Jose, CA
		Atlanta	0-1	15	7	3.60				
24	Mahler, Mickey	Atlanta	4-11	135	92	4.67	B-L	6-3	190	7/30/52 Montgomery, AL
—	McLaughlin, Joey	Richmond	9-13	179	84	3.97	R-R	6-2	192	7/11/56 Tulsa, OK
—	McWilliams, Larry	Richmond	6-5	108	78	2.83	L-L	6-5	175	2/10/54 Wichita, KN
		Atlanta	9-3	99	42	2.82				
35	Niekro, Phil	Atlanta	19-18	334	248	2.88	R-R	6-1	180	4/1/39 Blaine, OH
37	Solomon, Buddy	Atlanta	4-6	106	64	4.08	R-R	6-3	190	2/9/51 Perry, GA
—	Theiss, Duane	Richmond	6-2	68	51	3.57	R-R	6-3	185	11/20/53 Zanesville, OH
		Atlanta	0-0	6	3	1.50				

CATCHERS

No.	Name	1978 Club	H	HR	RBI	Pct.	B-T	Ht.	Wt.	Born
—	Benedict, Bruce	Richmond	97	2	34	.280	R-R	6-1	175	8/18/55 Birmingham, AL
		Atlanta	13	0	1	.250				
3	Murphy, Dale	Atlanta	120	23	79	.226	R-R	6-4	185	3/12/56 Portland, OR
11	Nolan, Joe	Atlanta	49	4	22	.230	L-R	5-11	175	5/12/51 St. Louis, MO
4	Pocoroba, Biff	Atlanta	70	6	34	.242	B-R	5-10	170	7/25/53 Los Angeles, CA

INFIELDERS

No.	Name	1978 Club	H	HR	RBI	Pct.	B-T	Ht.	Wt.	Born
25	Beall, Bob	Atlanta	41	1	16	.243	B-L	5-10	175	4/24/48 Portland, OR
15	Chaney, Darrell	Atlanta	55	3	20	.224	B-R	6-1	190	3/9/48 Hammond, IN
19	Gilbreath, Rod	Atlanta	80	3	31	.245	R-R	6-2	190	9/24/52 Laurel, MS
5	Horner, Bob	Atlanta	86	23	63	.266	R-R	6-1	195	8/1/57 Junction City, KS
—	Hubbard, Glenn	Richmond	101	14	36	.336	R-R	5-8	150	9/25/57 Hann AFB, Germany
		Atlanta	42	2	13	.258				
—	Macha, Mike	Richmond	127	17	69	.259	R-R	5-11	180	2/17/54 Victoria, TX
—	Maddox, Jerry	Richmond	96	10	44	.238	R-R	6-2	200	7/28/53 Whittier, CA
		Atlanta	3	0	1	.214				
9	Rockett, Pat	Richmond	5	0	7	.179	R-R	5-10	165	1/9/55 San Antonio, TX
		Atlanta	20	0	4	.141				
1	Royster, Jerry	Atlanta	137	2	35	.259	R-R	6-0	165	10/18/52 Sacramento, CA
—	Ruiz, Chico	Richmond	62	2	28	.219	R-R	5-11	170	11/2/51 Puerto Rico
		Atlanta	13	0	2	.283				
—	Small, Hank	Richmond	148	25	101	.289	R-R	6-3	205	7/31/53 Atlanta, GA
		Atlanta	0	0	0	.000				

OUTFIELDERS

No.	Name	1978 Club	H	HR	RBI	Pct.	B-T	Ht.	Wt.	Born
30	Asselstine, Brian	Atlanta	28	2	13	.272	L-R	6-1	175	9/23/53 Santa Barbara, CA
2	Bonnell, Barry	Atlanta	73	1	16	.240	R-R	6-3	190	10/27/53 Milford, OH
7	Burroughs, Jeff	Atlanta	147	23	77	.301	R-R	6-2	193	3/7/51 Long Beach, CA
—	Cooper, Gary	Savannah	83	4	30	.220	B-R	6-0	175	12/22/56 Savannah, GA
36	Matthews, Gary	Atlanta	135	18	62	.285	R-R	6-3	180	7/5/50 San Fernando, CA
—	Miller, Ed	Richmond	124	2	39	.249	B-R	5-9	170	6/29/57 San Pablo, CA
		Atlanta	3	0	2	.143				
22	Office, Rowland	Atlanta	101	9	40	.250	L-L	6-0	170	10/25/52 Sacramento, CA
—	Whisenton, Larry	Richmond	114	10	55	.241	L-L	6-1	190	7/3/56 St. Louis, MO
		Atlanta	3	0	2	.188				

BRAVE PROFILES

BOB HORNER 21 6-1 195   Bats R Throws R

Rookie of Year . . . Hit 48 home runs in 1978, 25 at Arizona State University and 23 from June 16 through the end of the season with Atlanta . . . No. 1 draft pick in June, then talked Braves into keeping him on major league roster . . . Hit home run in third major league at bat off Bert Blyleven while father listened via long distance telephone to radio broadcast . . . Drove in five runs in one game . . . Hit homers in last three games against Cincinnati, then underwent corrective surgery on left shoulder . . . Born Aug. 1, 1957, in Junction City, Kan. . . . Broke all of Reggie Jackson's records at Arizona State and set NCAA record with 58 career homers at ASU and batted .386 . . . Rate of homers and RBIs per at-bat better than any former National League Rookie of the Year.

Year	Club	Pos	G	AB	R	H	2B	3B	HR	RBI	SB	Avg.
1978	Atlanta..........	3B	89	323	50	86	17	1	23	63	0	.266

JEFF BURROUGHS 28 6-2 193   Bats R Throws R

Carries highly-productive bat and hit for average and power in 1978 for first time since 1974 with Texas Rangers . . . One of the old Washington Senators, signing for $88,000 in 1969 out of Long Beach City College . . . Came to Atlanta for five players and $250,-000 and Braves consider him a bargain . . . Born March 7, 1951, in Long Beach, Cal. . . . Once hit three grand slam homers in a 10-day span for Rangers in 1973 and missed records held by Babe Ruth and Mel Ott by one game when he drove in runs in 10 straight games in 1974 . . . Established himself quickly by hitting homer off Houston's J.R. Richard in first NL at bat, then hit one off Houston's Mark Lemongello in first at bat in Atlanta.

Year	Club	Pos	G	AB	R	H	2B	3B	HR	RBI	SB	Avg.
1970	Washington	OF	6	12	1	2	0	0	0	1	0	.167
1971	Washington	OF	59	181	20	42	9	0	5	25	1	.232
1972	Texas	OF-1B	22	65	4	12	1	0	1	3	0	.185
1973	Texas	OF-1B	151	526	71	147	17	1	30	85	0	.279
1974	Texas	OF	152	554	84	167	33	2	25	118	2	.301
1975	Texas	OF	152	585	81	132	20	0	29	94	4	.226
1976	Texas	OF	158	604	71	143	22	2	18	86	0	.237
1977	Atlanta..........	OF	154	579	91	157	19	1	41	114	4	.271
1978	Atlanta..........	OF	153	488	72	147	30	6	23	77	1	.301
	Totals..........		1007	3594	495	949	151	12	152	603	12	.264

PHIL NIEKRO 40 6-1 180   Bats R Throws R

The older he gets, the better he gets, as 19 victories and 247 strikeouts, second highest of his career, attests to that . . . No. 2 all-time Braves' winner with 197 victories . . . Only remaining original Atlanta Brave and has spent entire 15-year major league career in Braves' organization . . . Born April 1, 1939, in Blaine, Ohio . . . Fluttery knuckler difficult to catch, more difficult to hit . . . Established unusual record in 1969 when he gave up no sacrifice flies the entire season . . . Also has led league twice with wild pitches and once with hit batsmen . . . Hosts pre-game live TV show and interviewed Pete Rose before giving up single to stretch Rose's hitting streak to 44 . . . Brother is Houston's Joe Niekro.

Year	Club	G	IP	W	L	Pct.	SO	BB	H	ERA
1964	Milwaukee	10	15	0	0	.000	8	7	15	4.80
1965	Milwaukee	41	75	2	3	.400	40	26	73	2.88
1966	Atlanta	28	50	4	3	.571	17	23	48	4.14
1967	Atlanta	46	207	11	9	.550	129	55	164	1.87
1968	Atlanta	37	257	14	12	.538	140	45	228	2.50
1969	Atlanta	40	284	23	13	.639	193	57	235	2.57
1970	Atlanta	34	230	12	18	.400	168	68	222	4.27
1971	Atlanta	42	269	15	14	.517	173	70	248	2.98
1972	Atlanta	38	282	16	12	.571	164	53	254	3.06
1973	Atlanta	42	245	13	10	.565	131	89	214	3.31
1974	Atlanta	41	302	20	13	.606	195	88	249	2.38
1975	Atlanta	39	276	15	15	.500	144	72	285	3.20
1976	Atlanta	38	271	17	11	.607	173	101	249	3.29
1977	Atlanta	44	330	16	20	.444	262	164	315	4.04
1978	Atlanta	44	334	19	18	.514	248	102	295	2.88
	Totals	564	3427	197	171	.535	2194	1020	3094	3.07

LARRY McWILLIAMS 25 6-5 175   Bats L Throws L

A midseason call-up from Savannah and instant success, winning first six games . . . Made national headlines by combining with Gene Garber to stop Pete Rose's 44-game hitting streak . . . Sat next to Rose for 20 minutes during post-game interview and Rose didn't recognize him . . . Most National League hitters recognize him now . . . Born Feb. 10, 1954, at Wichita, Kan. . . . Selected in first round of January, 1974, draft and signed out of Paris (Tex.) Junior College . . . Moving fast ball, struck out 352 men in 437 minor league innings . . . Likes riding motorcycles and strumming guitars, but not at same time.

Year	Club	G	IP	W	L	Pct.	SO	BB	H	ERA
1978	Atlanta	15	99	9	3	.750	42	35	84	2.82

GENE GARBER 31 5-10 175   Bats R Throws R

Became Atlanta's big man out of the bullpen after obtained from Phillies . . . Third best ERA in NL . . . Struck out Pete Rose in the ninth to end his 44-game hitting streak . . . Threw a changeup, making Rose bitter enough to say, "I hope I face him again and drill one through the box, hard." . . . Born Nov. 13, 1947, in Lancaster, Pa. . . . Sidewinding, side-arm style, turns back on the hitter during windup . . . Was Philadelphia's Relief Man of the Year in both 1976 and 1977 . . . Owns political science and history degree from Elizabethtown College . . . Big on the banquet circuit, with Rose incident a big topic last winter.

Year	Club	G	IP	W	L	Pct.	SO	BB	H	ERA
1969	Pittsburgh	2	5	0	0	.000	3	1	6	5.40
1970	Pittsburgh	14	22	0	3	.000	7	10	22	5.32
1972	Pittsburgh	4	6	0	0	.000	3	3	7	7.50
1973	Kansas City	48	153	9	9	.500	60	49	164	4.24
1974	Kansas City	17	28	1	2	.333	14	13	35	4.82
1974	Philadelphia	34	48	4	0	1.000	27	31	39	2.06
1975	Philadelphia	71	110	10	12	.455	69	27	104	3.60
1976	Philadelphia	59	93	9	3	.750	92	30	78	2.81
1977	Philadelphia	64	103	8	6	.571	78	23	82	2.36
1978	Phil-Atlanta	65	117	6	5	.545	84	24	84	2.15
	Totals	378	685	47	40	.540	437	211	621	3.25

DALE MURPHY 23 6-4 185   Bats R Throws R

Didn't hit for average, but was power threat in rookie season . . . Counted on as backup catcher, but played regularly at first base and also caught . . . Outstanding athlete once recruited for football by Ohio State's Woody Hayes, though he didn't play high school football . . . Born March 12, 1956, in Portland, Ore. . . . First round selection in 1974 free agent draft after leading his high school basketball team to Oregon state tournament and making All-Metro Portland . . . Called up for the end of 1977 season and hit first and second major league homers in same game off Randy Jones and Rollie Fingers, respectively.

Year	Club	Pos	G	AB	R	H	2B	3B	HR	RBI	SB	Avg.
1976	Atlanta	C	19	65	3	17	6	0	0	9	0	.262
1977	Atlanta	C	18	76	5	24	8	1	2	14	0	.316
1978	Atlanta	C-1B	151	530	66	120	14	3	23	79	11	.226
	Totals		188	671	74	161	28	4	25	102	11	.240

ROD GILBREATH 26 6-2 190   Bats R Throws R

Moved from third base to second to make room for Bob Horner and played well . . . Once a power hitter, changed style to line drive hitter after leading the NL in sacrifice flies in 1976 with 20 . . . Born Sept. 24, 1952, in Laurel, Miss. . . . Turned down scholarship offers to quarterback at Ole Miss to sign with Braves after third round draft in 1970 . . . Runs a baseball clinic during the winter in hometown Laurel that attracts more than 1,000 youngsters . . . An antique collector, but there are few antiques on Atlanta roster.

Year	Club	Pos	G	AB	R	H	2B	3B	HR	RBI	SB	Avg.
1972	Atlanta	2B-3B	18	38	2	9	1	0	0	1	1	.237
1973	Atlanta	3B	29	74	10	21	2	1	0	2	2	.284
1974	Atlanta	2B	3	6	2	2	0	0	0	0	1	.333
1975	Atlanta	2B-3B-SS	90	202	24	49	3	1	2	16	5	.243
1976	Atlanta	2B-3B-SS	116	383	57	96	11	8	1	32	7	.251
1977	Atlanta	2B-3B	128	407	47	99	15	2	8	43	3	.243
1978	Atlanta	2B-3B	116	326	22	80	13	3	3	31	7	.245
	Totals		500	1436	164	356	45	15	14	125	25	.248

JERRY ROYSTER 26 6-0 165   Bats R Throws R

Jeron Kenis Royster is the only man left from a 1975 deal that brought him, Jimmy Wynn, Lee Lacy and Tom Paciorek to Atlanta for Dusty Baker and Ed Goodson . . . A swift base-stealer, was Pacific Coast League Player of the Year in 1975 at Albuquerque, where he led the league in hitting (.333), runs (91) and stolen bases (33) . . . Born Oct. 18, 1952, in Sacramento, Cal. . . . A numbers man, changing uniform digits from 4 to 13 to 1 in three years with Braves . . . Likes things picture-perfect because he works as a cameraman in the off-season . . . A three-sport high school star with basketball offers from UCLA and LSU . . . Was signed by the Dodgers out of a summer league.

Year	Club	Pos	G	AB	R	H	2B	3B	HR	RBI	SB	Avg.
1973	Los Angeles	3B-2B	10	19	1	4	0	0	0	2	1	.211
1974	Los Angeles	2B-3B-OF	6	0	2	0	0	0	0	0	0	.000
1975	Los Angeles	OF-2B-3B-SS	13	36	2	9	2	1	0	1	1	.250
1976	Atlanta	3B-SS	149	533	65	132	13	1	5	45	24	.248
1977	Atlanta	3B-SS-2B-OF	140	445	64	96	10	2	6	28	28	.216
1978	Atlanta	3B-SS-2B-OF	140	529	67	137	17	8	2	35	27	.259
	Totals		458	1562	201	378	42	12	13	111	81	.242

GARY MATTHEWS 28 6-3 180 　　　Bats R Throws R

May be most consistent offensive player in baseball . . . Statistics the past two seasons amazingly close and match his career totals in all offensive categories . . . NL Rookie of the Year with Giants in 1973, but came to the Braves in 1977 amid much fuss . . . Played out contract with Giants and was claimed by 12 teams in re-entry draft, but Atlanta owner Ted Turner was so anxious to get him, he was suspended and fined for tampering . . . Born July 5, 1950, in San Fernando, Cal. . . . An aggressive player with no fear of outfield fences and can reach any base rapidly with throws from deepest part of outfield.

Year	Club	Pos	G	AB	R	H	2B	3B	HR	RBI	SB	Avg.
1972	San Francisco	OF	20	62	11	18	1	1	4	14	0	.290
1973	San Francisco	OF	148	540	74	162	22	10	12	58	17	.300
1974	San Francisco	OF	154	561	87	161	27	6	16	82	11	.287
1975	San Francisco	OF	116	425	67	119	22	3	12	58	13	.280
1976	San Francisco	OF	156	587	79	164	28	4	20	84	12	.279
1977	Atlanta..........	OF	148	555	89	157	25	5	17	64	22	.283
1978	Atlanta..........	OF	129	474	75	134	20	5	18	62	8	.283
	Totals...........		871	3204	482	915	145	34	99	422	83	.286

ROWLAND OFFICE 26 6-0 170 　　　Bats L Throws L

Offensive statistics down for second year but still considered an outstanding defensive outfielder . . . Credited with making Atlanta Stadium's best all-time catch by climbing over the center field fence to take a homer away from Mike Ivie . . . Good off the bench, setting club record with five straight pinch-hits in 1975 . . . Born Oct. 25, 1952, in Sacramento, Cal. . . . Former manager Dave Bristol once called him in from center field to play right behind second base as a fifth infielder and he threw a runner out at the plate . . . Put together a 29-game hitting streak in 1976.

Year	Club	Pos	G	AB	R	H	2B	3B	HR	RBI	SB	Avg.
1972	Atlanta..........	OF	2	5	1	2	0	0	0	0	0	.400
1974	Atlanta..........	OF	131	248	20	61	16	1	3	31	5	.246
1975	Atlanta..........	OF	126	355	30	103	14	1	3	30	2	.290
1976	Atlanta..........	OF	99	359	51	101	17	1	4	34	2	.281
1977	Atlanta..........	OF	124	428	42	103	13	1	5	39	2	.241
1978	Atlanta..........	OF	146	404	40	101	13	1	9	40	8	.250
	Totals...........		628	1799	184	471	73	5	24	174	19	.262

TOP PROSPECT

ED MILLER 21 5-9 170   **Bats R Throws R**
Speedy outfielder who could provide the speed on the base
paths that is missing on young Atlanta team . . . In three minor
league seasons, swiped 175 bases to lead leagues at Sarasota
(Class A), Asheville (Class AA) and Tulsa (Class AAA), also
hitting .294 while swiping 80 bases at Tulsa in 1977 . . . Born
June 29, 1957, in San Pablo, Cal., came to Braves as part of
three-way deal with Rangers and Mets involving Willie Montanez . . . Received 70 football scholarship offers as a running
back.

MANAGER BOBBY COX: Fits right in with youngest team in
 the National League because he is the young-
est manager in the NL . . . Completed a full
season under owner Ted Turner after Turner
took him away from the Yankees on Nov. 22
'1977, where he was a coach . . . Managed six
years in the Yankee organization and never
finished lower than fourth, winning pennants
with West Haven of the Eastern League in
1972 and with Syracuse of the International League in 1976 . .
Born May 21, 1941, in Tulsa, Okla. . . . Signed to play in
Dodger organization as an infielder and once hit .337 with 19
homers and 85 RBIs at Great Falls . . . Was traded into Braves
organization and Atlanta dealt him to Yankees, where he became the regular third baseman in 1969 until he lost the job to
his roommate, Bobby Murcer . . . Has five children aged 14,
13, 12, 11 and 10 and is no relation to ex-Dodger third baseman
Billy Cox.

GREATEST PITCHER

The pitching section of the Braves' Press Guide should be
labeled The Warren Spahn Page.
There are 10 categories listed under career pitching records
and Spahnie's name is next to nine of them . . . and he wasn't
eligible for the 10th category: "Most victories, right-hander."
Spahn, of course, was left-handed, so Phil Niekro's 197 victories put him in the record book.
The rest belongs to Spahn . . . most seasons (20), most games

Warren Spahn's 363 victories rank sixth on all-time list.

(714), most games started (635), most complete games (374), most shutouts (63), most victories (356), most victories, left-hander (356), most innings (5,048) and most strikeouts (2,493).

There will be no pop quiz here as to who is the Braves' greatest pitcher. It's no contest.

In his 22 years with the Boston-Milwaukee Braves (1942-1964), the tall, skinny lefty had only two losing seasons (14-19 in 1952 and 6-13 in 1964 when he was 43 years old). And, he won 20 or more 13 times. His best was 23-7 with a 2.10 ERA in 1953, the Braves' first year in Milwaukee, and Spahnie couldn't buy a beer anywhere in town. They were all on the house.

ALL-TIME BRAVE LEADERS

BATTING: Rogers Hornsby, .387, 1928
HRs: Eddie Mathews, 47, 1953
　　　Hank Aaron, 47, 1971
RBIs: Eddie Mathews, 135, 1953
STEALS: Ralph Meyers, 57, 1913
WINS: Vic Willis, 27, 1902
　　　Charles Pittinger, 27, 1902
　　　Dick Rudolph, 27, 1914
STRIKEOUTS: Phil Niekro, 262, 1977

1979 OFFICIAL AMERICAN LEAGUE SCHEDULE

BOLD = SUNDAYS   [ ] = HOLIDAYS   * = NIGHT GAMES   TN = TWI-NIGHT DOUBLEHEADERS   (2) or (2) = DOUBLEHEADERS

	AT SEATTLE	AT OAKLAND	AT CALIFORNIA	AT TEXAS	AT KANSAS CITY	AT MINNESOTA	AT CHICAGO
SEATTLE		April 16*, 17*, **18** July 27*, 28, **29**	July 30*, 31*, Aug. 1* Aug. 10*, 11*, **12**	May 25 TN, 26*, 27* Sept. 10*, 11*, 12*	May 21*, 22*, 24* Sept. 14*, 15*, **16**	April 20*, 21, **22** July 2*, 3*,[4*],**5**	June 18*, 19*, 20*, 21* Sept. 28*, **29**, **30**
OAKLAND	April 9*, 10*, 11*, 12* Aug. 3*, 4*, **5**		April 20*, 21*, **22** July 2*, 3*,[4*],**5**	June 29*, 30* July 1* Sept. 25*, 26*, 27*	June 26*, 27*, 28* Sept. 28*, 29*, **30**	May [28], 29*, 30*, 31 Aug. 10*, 11, **12**	May 22*, 23*, 24* Sept. 14*, 15, **16**
CALIFORNIA	April 4*, 6*, 7*, **8** May 29*, 30*, 31*	April 13*, 14, **15** Aug. 6*, 7*, **8**		June 26*, 27*, 28* Sept. 28*, 29*, **30**	June 29*, 30* July 1 Sept. 17*, 18*, 19*, 20*	April 17, 18, 19 Aug. 3*, 4, **5(2)**	May 25*, 26, **27(2)** Sept. 11*, 12*
TEXAS	May 18*, 19*, **20** Sept.[3],4*,5*	June 22*, 23, **24(2)** Sept. 17*, 18*, 19	June 18*, 19*, 20*, 21* Sept. 21*, 22, 23		April 30* May 1*, 2* July 12*, 13*, 14*, **15**	May 14*, 15*, 16* Sept. 7*, 8*, **9**	April 27*, 28*, **29** July 9*, 10*, 11*
KANSAS CITY	May 14*, 15 TN, 16* Sept. 7*, 8*, **9**	June 18*, 19*, 20*, **21** Sept. 21*, 22, 23	June 22*, 23*, 24 Sept. 24*, 25*, 26*	May 7*, 8*, 9* July 21*, 22*, 23*		May 25*, 26, **27** Sept. [3], 4*, 5*	May 10*, 11*, 12*, **13** July 24*, 25*, 26*
MINNESOTA	April 13*, 14*, **15** Aug. 6*, 7*, **8**	April 6*, 7, **8** July 30*, 31* Aug. 1	April 10*, 11*, 12* July 27*, 28*, **29**	May 21*, 22*, 23* Sept. 13*, 14*, 15*, **16**	May 17*, 18*, 19*, **20** Sept. 10*, 11*, 12*		June 22*, 23, **24(2)** Sept. 17*, 18*, 19
CHICAGO	June 26*, 27*, 28 Sept. 21*, 22*, 23	May 15*, 16*, 17 Sept. 7*, 8, **9(2)**	May 18*, 19*, **20** Sept.[3],4*,5*,**6**	May 3*, 4*, 5*, **6** July 19 TN, 20*	April 23*, 24*, 25* July 6*, 7*, **8**	June 29*, **30** July 1* Sept. 25*, 26*, 27	

MILWAUKEE	June 22*, 23*, 24 Sept. 17*, 18*, 19*	May 18*, 19, 20(2) Sept. [3], 5*	May 15*, 16*, 17* Sept. 7*, 8*, 9	June 12*, 13*, 14* Aug. 24*, 25*, 26*	June 1*, 2, 3 Aug. 27*, 28*, 29*	June 26*, 27*, 28 Sept. 28*, 29, 30	June 4*, 5* Aug. 30*, 31* Sept. 1*, 2
DETROIT	June 4*, 5* 6* Aug. 17*, 18*, 19	June 1*, 2, 3 Aug. 20*, 21* 22	June 8*, 9*, 10 Aug. 13*, 14*, 15*	April 13*, 14*, 15 July 30*, 31* Aug. 1*	April 9*, 10*, 11* Aug. 10*, 11*, 12	May 3*, 4*, 5, 6 July 19*, 20*	May 1*, 2* July 12*, 13*, 14*, 15
CLEVELAND	June 8*,9* 10 Aug. 13*, 14*, 15	June 4*, 5* 6* Aug. 17*, 18, 19	June 1*, 2, 3 Aug. 20*, 21*, 22	April 10*, 11*, 12* Aug. 10*, 11*, 12*	April 26*, 27*, 28*, 29 July 19*, 20*	May 11*, 12, 13 July 24*, 25*, 26	May [28], 29*, 30* July 27*, 28*, 29
TORONTO	June 1*, 2* 3 Aug. 20*, 21*, 22*	June 8*, 9, 10 Aug. 13*, 14*, 15	June 4*, 5*, 6* Aug. 17*, 18*, 19	April 23*, 24*, 25* July 6*, 7*, 8*	April 5*, 7*, 8 July 30*, 31* Aug. 1*	May 7*, 8*, 9* July 21, 22, 23*	April 10, 11 Aug. 10*, 11, 12(2)
BALTIMORE	April 30* May 1*, 2* July 13*, 14*, 15	April 27*, 28, 29 July 9*, 10*, 11	April 24*, 25*, 26* July 6*, 7*, 8	June 1*, 2*, 3* July 2*, 3*, [4*]	May [28*], 29*, 30* July 27*, 28*, 29	June 15, 16, 17 Aug. 27*, 28*, 29	June 11*, 12*, 13* Aug. 24*, 25*, 26
NEW YORK	April 27*, 28*, 29* July 10*, 11*, 12*	April 24*, 25*, 26* July 6*, 7, 8	April 30* May 1*, 2* July 13*, 14*, 15	June 15*, 16*, 17* Aug. 27*, 28*, 29	June 8*, 9, 10 Aug. 20*, 21*, 22*	June 12*, 13*, 14* Aug. 24*, 25*, 26	April 13, 14, 15 July 30*, 31* Aug. 1*
BOSTON	April 24*, 25*, 26* July 6*, 7*, 8	April 30* May 1*, 2* July 13*, 14, 15	April 27*, 28*, 29 July 9, 10*, 11*	May [28*], 29*, 30* July 27*, 28*, 29*	June 11*, 12*, 13* Aug. 24*, 25, 26	June 1*, 2, 3 Aug. 20*, 21*, 22*	June 15*, 16*, 17 Aug. 27*, 28*, 29*

ALL STAR GAME AT SEATTLE, JULY 17
HALL OF FAME GAME, COOPERSTOWN, N.Y., AUGUST 6 — TEXAS vs. SAN DIEGO

1979 OFFICIAL AMERICAN LEAGUE SCHEDULE

BOLD = SUNDAYS   [ ] = HOLIDAYS   * = NIGHT GAMES   TN = TWI-NIGHT DOUBLEHEADERS   (2) or (2) = DOUBLEHEADERS

	AT MILWAUKEE	AT DETROIT	AT CLEVELAND	AT TORONTO	AT BALTIMORE	AT NEW YORK	AT BOSTON
SEATTLE	June 29*, 30* July 1 Sept. 25*, 26*, 27*	June 13*, 14* Aug. 24*, 25, 26(2)	June 15*, 16*, 17 Aug. 27*, 28*, 29	June 11*, 12* Aug. 30, 31 Sept. 1, 2	May 11*, 12*, 13 July 24*, 25*, 26*	May 7*, 8*, 9*, 10 July 22, 23*	May 4*, 5, 6 July 19*, 20*, 21
OAKLAND	May 25*, 26*, 27 Sept. 11*, 12*, 13*	June 11*, 12* Aug. 30*, 31* Sept. 1, 2	June 13*, 14* Aug. 23*, 24*, 25*, 26	June 15*, 16*, 17 Aug. 27, 28, 29	May 7*, 8*, 9*, 10* July 22, 23*	May 4*, 5, 6 July 19*, 20*, 21	May 11*, 12, 13 July 24*, 25*, 26
CALIFORNIA	May 22*, 23*, 24 Sept. 14*, 15*, 16	June 15*, 16, 17 Aug. 27*, 28*, 29*	June 11*, 12* Aug. 30*, 31* Sept. 1, 2	June 13(TN), 14* Aug. 24, 25, 26	May 4*, 5, 6 July 19*, 20*, 21	May 11*, 12, 13 July 24*, 25*, 26	May 7*, 8*, 9*, 10* July 22, 23*
TEXAS	June 6*, 7 Aug. 16*, 17*, 18*, 19	April 5, 7, 8 Aug. 7*, 8*, 9*	April 17, 18 Aug. 3*, 4, 5(2)	May 11*, 12, 13(2) July 25*, 26*	June 8*, 9*, 10 Aug. 20*, 21*, 23*	April 20*, 21, 22 Aug. 13*, 14*, 15*	June 4*, 5* Aug. 30*, 31* Sept. 1, 2
KANSAS CITY	June 15*, 16, 17 Aug. 13*, 14*, 15*	April 16, 17 Aug. 3 TN, 4, 5	May 4*, 5, 6 July 9*, 10*, 11*	April 13, 14, 15 Aug. 6*, 7*, 9*	June 6*, 7* Aug. 16*, 17*, 18*, 19	June 4*, 5* Aug. 30*, 31* Sept. 1, 2	June 20, 21, 22 July 3*, [4*], 5
MINNESOTA	June 19*, 20*, 21 Sept. 21*, 22, 23	April 27*, 28, 29 July 9*, 10*, 11*	April 24, 25 July 6*, 7, 8(2)	April 30* May 1*, 2* July 13*, 14, 15	June 4*, 5* Aug. 30*, 31* Sept. 1, 2	June 6*, 7 Aug. 16*, 17*, 18*, 19	June 8*, 9, 10 Aug. 13*, 14*, 15*
CHICAGO	June 8*, 9*, 10 Aug. 20*, 21*, 22*	May 7*, 8*, 9* July 21*, 22, 23*	April 20*, 21, 22 July 3*, [4], 5*	April 16, 17, 18 Aug. 3*, 4*, 5	April 6, 7, 8 Aug. 13*, 14*, 15*	June 1*, 2*, 3 Aug. 7*, 8*, 9*	June 6*, 7* Aug. 16*, 17*, 18, 19

	C1	C2	C3	C4	C5	C6	C7
MILWAUKEE	April 24, 25, 26 / July 6*, 7, 8(2)	May 11*, 12, 13 / July 24*, 25*, 26*	April 30* / May 1*, 2* / July 21, 22(2), 23*	April 27*, 28, 29(2) / July 9*, 11*, 12*	April 20*, 21, 22(2) / Aug. 7*, 8*, 9*	April 5, 7, 8 / July 3*, [4*], 5	April 17, 18, 19 / Aug. 10*, 11, 12
DETROIT	May 8*, 9*, 10 / July 13*, 14*, 15	June 29*, 30 / July 1, 2* / Sept. 11*, 12*, 13*	May 18*, 19, 20 / Sept. [3], 4*, 5*	May 28*, 29*, 30*, 31 / July 27*, 28*, 29	June 22*, 23 TN, 24 / Sept. 25*, 26*	May 14*, 15*, 16* / Sept. 14*, 15, 16	June 18*, 19*, 20*, 21* / Sept. 21*, 22, 23
CLEVELAND	May 3*, 4*, 5, 6 / July 19*, 20*	April 20, 21, 22 / July 3*, [4*], 5*	June 25*, 26*, 27*, 28* / Sept. 21*, 22*, 23	May 21, 22*, 23* / Sept. 14*, 15, 16	June 22*, 23*, 24 / Sept. 25*, 26*, 27*		April 5 / April 14, 15, 16 / Aug. 7*, 8*, 9*
TORONTO	April 13, 14, 15 / July 30*, 31* / Aug. 1*	May 25*, 26, 27(2) / Sept. 17*, 18*, 19*	May 14*, 15*, 16*, 17 / Sept. 7*, 8, 9	June 29 TN, 30 / July 1 / Sept. [3](2), 5*	June 19*, 20 TN, 21 / Sept. 28*, 29, 30	June 19*, 20 TN, 21 / Sept. 28*, 29, 30	June 22, 23, 24 / Sept. 25*, 26*, 27*
BALTIMORE	May [28], 29*, 30*, 31* / July 27*, 28*, 29	May 21*, 22*, 23* / Sept. 6*, 7*, 8, 9	June 18*, 19*, 20* / Sept. 28*, 29, 30	May 18*, 19, 20 / Sept. 11*, 12*, 13*	April 17, 18*, 19 / Aug. 3*, 4*, 5	April 17, 18*, 19 / Aug. 3*, 4*, 5	May 14*, 15*, 16*, 17* / Sept. 7*, 8, 9
NEW YORK	May 21*, 22*, 23* / Sept. 6*, 7*, 8, 9	May 25*, 26*, 27*, 28* / Sept. 17*, 18*, 19*	June 25*, 26*, 28* / Sept. 21*, 22, 23	April 10*, 11*, 12* / Aug. 10*, 11*, 12	May 22*, 23*, 24* / Sept. 14*, 15*, 16	May 22*, 23*, 24* / Sept. 14*, 15*, 16	May 18*, 19, 20 / Sept. 11*, 12*, 13*
BOSTON	April 10, 12 / Aug. 2*, 3*, 4, 5(2)	June 26*, 27*, 28* / Sept. 28*, 29, 30	April 7, 8 / July 30*, 31 TN / Aug. 1*	May 25*, 26, 27 / Sept. 17*, 18*, 19*, 20*	May 22*, 23*, 24* / Sept. 14*, 15*, 16	June 29*, 30 / July 1, 2* / Sept. [3], 4*, 5*	

ALL STAR GAME AT SEATTLE, JULY 17
HALL OF FAME GAME, COOPERSTOWN, N.Y., AUGUST 6 — TEXAS vs. SAN DIEGO

OFFICIAL NATIONAL LEAGUE SCHEDULE — 1979

E A S T

	At CHICAGO	At MONTREAL	At NEW YORK
CHICAGO		April 14, 15, 16 Aug. 1*, 2 Sept. 11(TN), 12*, 13*	May 22*, 23*, 24* July 27*, 28, 29(2) Sept. 17*, 18*
MONTREAL	April 20, 21, 22 July 2, 3, 4, 5 Sept. 5, 6		April 9, 10, 11 Aug. 10*, 11, 12(2) Sept. 19*, 20*
NEW YORK	April 5, 7, 8 June 29, 30 July 1 Sept. 24, 25, 26	April 17. 18 Aug. 3*, 4*, 5(2) Sept. 3(2), 4	
PHILADELPHIA	May 15, 16, 17 June 25, 26, 27 Sept. 7, 8, 9	May 29*, 30*, 31 June 22*, 23*, 24 Sept. 28*, 29, 30	April 12, 14, 15(2) Aug. 1, 2* Sept. 11*, 12*, 13*
PITTSBURGH	May 18, 19, 20 Aug. 7, 8, 9 Sept. 21, 22, 23	May 21, 22, 23* July 27(TN), 28*, 29 Sept. 17*, 18*	May 25*, 26, 27, 28 June 25*, 26* Sept. 7*, 8, 9
ST. LOUIS	April 17, 18, 19 Aug. 3, 4, 5(2) Sept. 3, 4	May 25*, 26, 27(2) July 30*, 31* Sept. 14*, 15*, 16	May 18*, 19*, 20 Aug. 7*, 8, 9* Sept. 21*, 22, 23
ATLANTA	May 4, 5, 6 July 19, 20, 21	June 11*, 13*, 14* Aug. 17*, 18*, 19	June 15*, 16*, 17 Aug. 27*, 28*, 29
CINCINNATI	May 8, 9, 10 July 22(2), 23	June 18*, 19*, 20* Aug. 31* Sept. 1*, 2	June 11*, 12*, 13* Aug. 24*, 25, 26
HOUSTON	April 24, 25, 26 July 6, 7, 8	June 15*, 16*, 17 Aug. 27*, 28*, 29*	June 8*, 9, 10 Aug. 20*, 21*, 22
LOS ANGELES	June 8, 9, 10 Aug. 20, 21, 22	April 30 May 1 July 6*, 7*, 8, 9*	April 27*, 28, 29 July 10*, 11, 12*
SAN DIEGO	June 5, 6, 7 Aug. 17, 18, 19	April 24, 25 July 13(TN), 14*, 15	April 30* May 1* July 6*, 7, 8(2)
SAN FRANCISCO	June 1, 2, 3 Aug. 14, 15, 16	April 27, 28, 29 July 10*, 11*, 12*	April 24*, 25*, 26* July 13*, 14, 15
	13 Sundays 0 Night Games 2 Holidays (July 4 – Labor Day)	13 Sundays 44 Night Games 1 Holiday (Labor Day)	13 Sundays 42 Night Games 1 Holiday (Memorial Day)

* NIGHT GAME   Underlined dates denote Sunday game
               NIGHT GAME: Any game starting after 5:00PM

OFFICIAL NATIONAL LEAGUE SCHEDULE — 1979

EAST

	At PHILADELPHIA	At PITTSBURGH	At ST. LOUIS
CHICAGO	May 25*, 26*, 27, 28* July 30*, 31* Sept. 14*, 15*, 16	May 29*, 30*, 31* June 22*, 23*, 24 Sept. 28*, 29, 30	April 10*, 11 Aug. 10(TN), 11*, 12, 13* Sept. 19*, 20*
MONTREAL	May 18*, 19*, 20 Aug. 7*, 8*, 9 Sept. 21*, 22*, 23	April 6, 7, 8 June 29*, 30 July 1(2) Sept. 25*, 26*	May 15*, 16*, 17 June 25*, 26*, 27* Sept. 7*, 8*, 9
NEW YORK	April 20*, 21*, 22 July 2*, 3*, 4*, 5* Sept. 5*, 6*	May 15*, 16*, 17* June 27*, 28* July 30*, 31* Sept. 15, 16	May 29*, 30*, 31 June 22*, 23*, 24 Sept. 28*, 29, 30
PHILADELPHIA		April 16*, 17*, 18* Aug. 3*, 4, 5(2) Sept. 3(2)	April 6*, 7, 8 June 29*, 30 July 1(2) Sept. 17*, 18*
PITTSBURGH	April 9*, 11* Aug. 10(TN), 11, 12*, 13* Sept. 19*, 20*		May 4*, 5*, 6 July 2*, 3*, 4, 5* Sept. 5*, 6*
ST. LOUIS	May 21*, 22*, 23* July 27*, 28*, 29 Sept. 24*, 25*, 26*	April 12*, 13*, 14, 15 Aug. 1*, 2* Sept. 11*, 12*, 13*	
ATLANTA	June 8*, 9*, 10 Aug. 20*, 21*, 22*	May 1*, 2*, 3 July 22(2), 23*	May 11*, 12*, 13 July 24*, 25*, 26*
CINCINNATI	June 15*, 16*, 17 Aug. 27*, 28*, 29*	May 11*, 12, 13 July 24*, 25*, 26*	April 20*, 21*, 22 July 19*, 20*, 21
HOUSTON	June 11*, 12*, 13* Aug. 24*, 25*, 26*	April 27*, 28, 29 July 19*, 20*, 21	April 30* May 1*, 2*, 3 July 22, 23*
LOS ANGELES	April 23*, 24*, 25* July 13*, 14, 15	June 4*, 5*, 6* Aug. 17*, 18*, 19	June 1*, 2*, 3 Aug. 14*, 15*, 16
SAN DIEGO	April 27*, 28*, 29 July 10*, 11*, 12*	June 1*, 2*, 3 Aug. 14*, 15*, 16*	June 8*, 9*, 10 Aug. 20*, 21*, 22*
SAN FRANCISCO	April 30* May 1* July 6*, 7*, 8, 9*	June 8*, 9*, 10 Aug. 20*, 21*, 22	June 5*, 6*, 7* Aug. 17*, 18*, 19
	13 Sundays 66 Night Games 2 Holidays (July 4 - Memorial Day)	13 Sundays 51 Night Games 1 Holiday (Labor Day)	13 Sundays 57 Night Games 1 Holiday (July 4)

July 17 - ALL-STAR GAME AT SEATTLE STADIUM

OFFICIAL NATIONAL LEAGUE SCHEDULE — 1979

WEST

	At ATLANTA	At CINCINNATI	At HOUSTON
CHICAGO	April 27*, 28*, 29 July 9*, 10*, 11*	May 1*, 2* July 12*, 13*, 14*, 15	May 11*, 12(TN), 13 July 24*, 25*
MONTREAL	June 4*, 5*, 6* Aug. 24*, 25*, 26*	June 8*, 9*, 10 Aug. 20*, 21*, 22*	June 1*, 2*, 3* Aug. 13*, 14*, 15*
NEW YORK	June 1*, 2*, 3* Aug. 14*, 15*, 16*	June 4*, 5*, 6* Aug. 17*, 18*, 19	June 18*, 19*, 20* Aug. 31* Sept. 1*, 2
PHILADELPHIA	June 18*, 19*, 20* Aug. 31* Sept. 1*, 2	June 1*, 2*, 3(2) Aug. 14*, 15*	June 4*, 5*, 6* Aug. 17*, 18*, 19
PITTSBURGH	May 7*, 8*, 9* July 13*, 14*, 15*	April 24*, 25 July 6*, 7*, 8(2)	April 20*, 21*, 22 July 10*, 11*, 12*
ST. LOUIS	April 23*, 24*, 25* July 6*, 7*, 8*	April 27*, 28, 29 July 9*, 10*, 11*	May 8*, 9*, 10* July 13*, 14*, 15
ATLANTA		April 17*, 19* Aug. 6*, 7*, 8*, 9 Sept. 28*, 29, 30	April 6*, 7*, 8 Aug. 3*, 4(TN), 5* Sept. 19*, 20*
CINCINNATI	April 9*, 10*, 11* July 27*, 28(TN), 29* Sept. 3*,4*		May 29*, 30*, 31* June 25(TN), 26* Sept. 21*, 22*, 23
HOUSTON	May 21*, 22*, 23* Aug. 10*, 11*, 12* Sept. 24*, 25*, 26*	May 4*, 5*, 6(2) July 3*, 4, 5* Sept. 11*, 12*	
LOS ANGELES	May 15*, 16*, 17* June 21*, 22*, 23, 24* Sept. 5*, 6*	May 18*, 19*, 20 July 30*, 31* Aug. 1* Sept. 7*, 8, 9	April 9*, 10*, 11* July 26*, 27*, 28*, 29* Sept. 3*, 4*
SAN DIEGO	April 20*, 21*, 22 July 31* Aug. 1*, 2* Sept. 7*, 8*, 9	May 14*, 15*, 16 Aug. 3*, 4*, 5 Sept. 25*, 26*, 27*	May 18*, 19*, 20(2) June 22*, 23*, 24 Sept. 5*, 6*
SAN FRANCISCO	May 18*, 19(TN), 20 July 3*, 4*, 5* Sept. 22*, 23	April 4, 6*, 7, 8 June 22*, 23, 24 Sept. 5*, 6*	May 15*, 16*, 17* July 30*, 31* Aug. 1* Sept. 7*, 8*, 9
	13 Sundays 73 Night Games 2 Holidays (July 4 – Labor Day)	13 Sundays 53 Night Games 1 Holiday (July 4)	13 Sundays 67 Night Games 1 Holiday (Labor Day)

* NIGHT GAME   Underlined dates denote Sunday game
NIGHT GAME: Any game starting after 5:00PM

OFFICIAL NATIONAL LEAGUE SCHEDULE — 1979

W E S T

	At LOS ANGELES	At SAN DIEGO	At SAN FRANCISCO
CHICAGO	June 18*, 19* August 30*, 31* Sept. 1*, 2	June 15*, 16*, 17 Aug. 27*, 28*, 29*	June 12*, 13*, 14* Aug. 24*, 25, 26
MONTREAL	May 11*, 12*, 13 July 19*, 20*, 21*	May 3*, 4*, 5*, 6 July 24*, 25*	May 8*, 9, 10 July 22(2), 23*
NEW YORK	May 7*, 8*, 9*, 10* July 22, 23*	May 11*, 12*, 13 July 19*, 20*, 21*	May 3, 4*, 5, 6 July 24*, 25
PHILADELPHIA	May 3*, 4*, 5*, 6 July 24*, 25	May 7*, 8*, 9*, 10 July 22, 23*	May 11*, 12, 13 July 19*, 20*, 21
PITTSBURGH	June 15*, 16*, 17 Aug. 27*, 28*, 29*	June 12*, 13*, 14* Aug. 24*, 25*, 26	June 19*, 20 Aug. 31* Sept. 1(2), 2
ST. LOUIS	June 11*, 12*, 13* Aug. 24, 25*, 26	June 18*, 19*, 20* Aug. 31* Sept. 1*, 2	June 15*, 16, 17 Aug. 28*, 29, 30
ATLANTA	April 12*, 13*, 14*, 15 June 29*, 30* July 1 Sept. 17*, 18*	May 29(TN), 30*, 31 June 27*, 28 Sept. 14*, 15*, 16	May 25*, 26, 27, 28 June 25*, 26* Sept. 11*, 12, 13
CINCINNATI	May 25*, 26, 27, 28 June 27*, 28* Sept. 14*, 15, 16	April, 13*, 14*, 15(2) Aug. 10*, 12(2) Sept. 19*, 20*	May 22*, 23*, 24* June 29*, 30 July 1(2) Sept. 17*, 18*
HOUSTON	April 16*, 17*, 18* Aug. 7*, 8*, 9 Sept. 28*, 29, 30	May 25*, 26*, 27, 28* June 29*, 30* July 1 Sept. 17*, 18*	April 13*, 14, 15(2) June 27*, 28 Sept. 14*, 15, 16
LOS ANGELES		May 21*, 22*, 23* July 2*, 3*, 4* Sept. 21*, 22*, 23	April 20*, 21*, 22 Aug. 10*, 11, 12 Sept. 25*, 26*, 27*
SAN DIEGO	April 5, 6*, 7*, 8 June 25*, 26* Sept. 11*, 12*, 13*		April 10, 11*, 12 Aug. 7*, 8, 9 Sept. 28*, 29, 30
SAN FRANCISCO	May 29*, 30*, 31 Aug. 3*, 4*, 5, 6* Sept. 19*, 20*	April 17*, 18*, 19 July 26*, 27*, 28*, 29 Sept. 3*, 4	
	13 Sundays 61 Night Games 1 Holiday (Memorial Day)	13 Sundays 60 Night Games 3 Holidays (Memorial Day – July 4 – Labor Day)	13 Sundays 36 Night Games 1 Holiday (Memorial Day)

July 17 – ALL-STAR GAME AT SEATTLE STADIUM

MAJOR LEAGUE YEAR-BY-YEAR LEADERS

NATIONAL LEAGUE MVP

Year	Player, Club
1931	Frank Frisch, St. Louis Cardinals
1932	Chuck Klein, Philadelphia Phillies
1933	Carl Hubbell, New York Giants
1934	Dizzy Dean, St. Louis Cardinals
1935	Gabby Hartnett, Chicago Cubs
1936	Carl Hubbell, New York Giants
1937	Joe Medwick, St. Louis Cardinals
1938	Ernie Lombardi, Cincinnati Reds
1939	Buck Walters, Cincinnati Reds
1940	Frank McCormick, Cincinnati Reds
1941	Dolph Camilli, Brooklyn Dodgers
1942	Mort Cooper, St. Louis Cardinals
1943	Stan Musial, St. Louis Cardinals
1944	Marty Marion, St. Louis Cardinals
1945	Phil Cavaretta, Chicago Cubs
1946	Stan Musial, St. Louis Cardinals
1947	Bob Elliott, Boston Braves
1948	Stan Musial, St. Louis Cardinals
1949	Jackie Robinson, Brooklyn Dodgers
1950	Jim Konstanty, Philadelphia Phillies
1951	Roy Campanella, Brooklyn Dodgers
1952	Hank Sauer, Chicago Cubs
1953	Roy Campanella, Brooklyn Dodgers
1954	Willie Mays, New York Giants
1955	Roy Campanella, Brooklyn Dodgers
1956	Don Newcombe, Brooklyn Dodgers
1957	Hank Aaron, Milwaukee Braves
1958	Ernie Banks, Chicago Cubs
1959	Ernie Banks, Chicago Cubs
1960	Dick Groat, Pittsburgh Pirates

Year	Player, Club
1961	Frank Robinson, Cincinnati Reds
1962	Maury Wills, Los Angeles Dodgers
1963	Sandy Koufax, Los Angeles Dodgers
1964	Ken Boyer, St. Louis Cardinals
1965	Willie Mays, San Francisco Giants
1966	Roberto Clemente, Pittsburgh Pirates
1967	Orlando Cepeda, St. Louis Cardinals
1968	Bob Gibson, St. Louis Cardinals
1969	Willie McCovey, San Francisco Giants
1970	Johnny Bench, Cincinnati Reds
1971	Joe Torre, St. Louis Cardinals
1972	Johnny Bench, Cincinnati Reds
1973	Pete Rose, Cincinnati Reds
1974	Steve Garvey, Los Angeles Dodgers
1975	Joe Morgan, Cincinnati Reds
1976	Joe Morgan, Cincinnati Reds
1977	George Foster, Cincinnati Reds
1978	Dave Parker, Pittsburgh Pirates

AMERICAN LEAGUE MVP

Year	Player, Club
1931	Lefty Grove, Philadelphia Athletics
1932	Jimmy Foxx, Philadelphia Athletics
1933	Jimmy Foxx, Philadelphia Athletics
1934	Mickey Cochrane, Detroit Tigers
1935	Hank Greenberg, Detroit Tigers
1936	Lou Gehrig, New York Yankees
1937	Charley Gehringer, Detroit Tigers
1938	Jimmy Foxx, Boston Red Sox
1939	Joe DiMaggio, New York Yankees
1940	Hank Greenberg, Detroit Tigers
1941	Joe DiMaggio, New York Yankees
1942	Joe Gordon, New York Yankees
1943	Spud Chandler, New York Yankees
1944	Hal Newhouser, Detroit Tigers
1945	Hal Newhouser, Detroit Tigers
1946	Ted Williams, Boston Red Sox
1947	Joe DiMaggio, New York Yankees
1948	Lou Boudreau, Cleveland Indians
1949	Ted Williams, Boston Red Sox
1950	Phil Rizzuto, New York Yankees
1951	Yogi Berra, New York Yankees
1952	Bobby Shantz, Philadelphia Athletics

Year	Player, Club
1953	Al Rosen, Cleveland Indians
1954	Yogi Berra, New York Yankees
1955	Yogi Berra, New York Yankees
1956	Mickey Mantle, New York Yankees
1957	Mickey Mantle, New York Yankees
1958	Jackie Jensen, Boston Red Sox
1959	Nellie Fox, Chicago White Sox
1960	Roger Maris, New York Yankees
1961	Roger Maris, New York Yankees
1962	Mickey Mantle, New York Yankees
1963	Elston Howard, New York Yankees
1964	Brooks Robinson, Baltimore Orioles
1965	Zolio Versalles, Minnesota Twins
1966	Frank Robinson, Baltimore Orioles
1967	Carl Yastrzemski, Boston Red Sox
1968	Dennis McLain, Detroit Tigers
1969	Harmon Killebrew, Minnesota Twins
1970	Boog Powell, Baltimore Orioles
1971	Vida Blue, Oakland A's
1972	Dick Allen, Chicago White Sox
1973	Reggie Jackson, Oakland A's
1974	Jeff Burroughs, Texas Rangers
1975	Fred Lynn, Boston Red Sox
1976	Thurman Munson, New York Yankees
1977	Rod Carew, Minnesota Twins
1978	Jim Rice, Boston Red Sox

NATIONAL LEAGUE
Batting Champions

Year	Player, Club	Avg.
1876	Roscoe Barnes, Chicago	.403
1877	James White, Boston	.385
1878	Abner Dalrymple, Milwaukee	.356
1879	Cap Anson, Chicago	.407
1880	George Gore, Chicago	.365
1881	Cap Anson, Chicago	.399
1882	Dan Brouthers, Buffalo	.367
1883	Dan Brouthers, Buffalo	.371
1884	Jim O'Rourke, Buffalo	.350
1885	Roger Connor, New York	.371
1886	Mike Kelly, Chicago	.388
1887	Cap Anson, Chicago	.421

Year	Player, Club	Avg.
1888	Cap Anson, Chicago	.343
1889	Dan Brouthers, Boston	.373
1890	Jack Glassock, New York	.336
1891	Billy Hamilton, Philadelphia	.338
1892	Cupid Childs, Cleveland	.335
	Dan Brouthers, Brooklyn	.335
1893	Hugh Duffy, Boston	.378
1894	Hugh Duffy, Boston	.438
1895	Jesse Burkett, Cleveland	.423
1896	Jesse Burkett, Cleveland	.410
1897	Willie Keeler, Baltimore	.432
1898	Willie Keeler, Baltimore	.379
1899	Ed Delahanty, Philadelphia	.408
1900	Honus Wagner, Pittsburgh	.380
1901	Jesse Burkett, St. Louis Cardinals	.382
1902	C.H. Beaumont, Pittsburgh Pirates	.357
1903	Honus Wagner, Pittsburgh Pirates	.355
1904	Honus Wagner, Pittsburgh Pirates	.349
1905	J. Seymour Bentley, Cincinnati Reds	.377
1906	Honus Wagner, Pittsburgh Pirates	.339
1907	Honus Wagner, Pittsburgh Pirates	.350
1908	Honus Wagner, Pittsburgh Pirates	.354
1909	Honus Wagner, Pittsburgh Pirates	.339
1910	Sherwood Magee, Philadelphia Phillies	.331
1911	Honus Wagner, Pittsburgh Pirates	.334
1912	Heinie Zimmerman, Chicago Cubs	.372
1913	Jake Daubert, Brooklyn Dodgers	.350
1914	Jake Daubert, Brooklyn Dodgers	.329
1915	Larry Doyle, New York Giants	.320
1916	Hal Chase, Cincinnati Reds	.339
1917	Edd Roush, Cincinnati Reds	.341
1918	Zack Wheat, Brooklyn Dodgers	.335
1919	Edd Roush, Cincinnati Reds	.321
1920	Rogers Hornsby, St. Louis Cardinals	.370
1921	Rogers Hornsby, St. Louis Cardinals	.397
1922	Rogers Hornsby, St. Louis Cardinals	.401
1923	Rogers Hornsby, St. Louis Cardinals	.384
1924	Rogers Hornsby, St. Louis Cardinals	.424
1925	Rogers Hornsby, St. Louis Cardinals	.403
1926	Bubbles Hargrave, Cincinnati Reds	.353
1927	Paul Waner, Pittsburgh Pirates	.380
1928	Rogers Hornsby, Boston Braves	.387
1929	Lefty O'Doul, Philadelphia Phillies	.398
1930	Bill Terry, New York Giants	.401

Year	Player, Club	Avg.
1931	Chick Hafey, St. Louis Cardinals	.349
1932	Lefty O'Doul, Brooklyn Dodgers	.368
1933	Chuck Klein, Philadelphia Phillies	.368
1934	Paul Waner, Pittsburgh Pirates	.362
1935	Arky Vaughn, Pittsburgh Pirates	.385
1936	Paul Waner, Pittsburgh Pirates	.373
1937	Joe Medwick, St. Louis Cardinals	.374
1938	Ernie Lombardi, Cincinnati Reds	.342
1939	Johnny Mize, St. Louis Cardinals	.349
1940	Debs Garms, Pittsburgh Pirates	.355
1941	Pete Reiser, Brooklyn Dodgers	.343
1942	Ernie Lombardi, Boston Braves	.330
1943	Stan Musial, St. Louis Cardinals	.330
1944	Dixie Walker, Brooklyn Dodgers	.357
1945	Phil Cavarretta, Chicago Cubs	.355
1946	Stan Musial, St. Louis Cardinals	.365
1947	Harry Walker, St. L. Cardinals-Phila. Phillies	.363
1948	Stan Musial, St. Louis Cardinals	.376
1949	Jackie Robinson, Brooklyn Dodgers	.342
1950	Stan Musial, St. Louis Cardinals	.346
1951	Stan Musial, St. Louis Cardinals	.355
1952	Stan Musial, St. Louis Cardinals	.336
1953	Carl Furillo, Brooklyn Dodgers	.344
1954	Willie Mays, New York Giants	.345
1955	Richie Ashburn, Philadelphia Phillies	.338
1956	Hank Aaron, Milwaukee Braves	.328
1957	Stan Musial, St. Louis Cardinals	.351
1958	Richie Ashburn, Philadelphia Phillies	.350
1959	Hank Aaron, Milwaukee Braves	.328
1960	Dick Groat, Pittsburgh Pirates	.325
1961	Roberto Clemente, Pittsburgh Pirates	.351
1962	Tommy Davis, Los Angeles Dodgers	.346
1963	Tommy Davis, Los Angeles Dodgers	.326
1964	Roberto Clemente, Pittsburgh Pirates	.339
1965	Roberto Clemente, Pittsburgh Pirates	.329
1966	Matty Alou, Pittsburgh Pirates	.342
1967	Roberto Clemente, Pittsburgh Pirates	.357
1968	Pete Rose, Cincinnati Reds	.335
1969	Pete Rose, Cincinnati Reds	.348
1970	Rico Carty, Atlanta Braves	.366
1971	Joe Torre, St. Louis Cardinals	.363
1972	Billy Williams, Chicago Cubs	.333
1973	Pete Rose, Cincinnati Reds	.338
1974	Ralph Garr, Atlanta Braves	.353

Year	Player, Club	Avg.
1975	Bill Madlock, Chicago Cubs	.354
1976	Bill Madlock, Chicago Cubs	.339
1977	Dave Parker, Pittsburgh Pirates	.338
1978	Dave Parker, Pittsburgh Pirates	.334

AMERICAN LEAGUE
Batting Champions

Year	Player, Club	Avg.
1901	Napoleon Lajoie, Philadelphia Athletics	.422
1902	Ed Delahanty, Washington Senators	.376
1903	Napoleon Lajoie, Cleveland Indians	.355
1904	Napoleon Lajoie, Cleveland Indians	.381
1905	Elmer Flick, Cleveland Indians	.306
1906	George Stone, St. Louis Browns	.358
1907	Ty Cobb, Detroit Tigers	.350
1908	Ty Cobb, Detroit Tigers	.324
1909	Ty Cobb, Detroit Tigers	.377
1910	Ty Cobb, Detroit Tigers	.385
1911	Ty Cobb, Detroit Tigers	.420
1912	Ty Cobb, Detroit Tigers	.410
1913	Ty Cobb, Detroit Tigers	.390
1914	Ty Cobb, Detroit Tigers	.368
1915	Ty Cobb, Detroit Tigers	.370
1916	Tris Speaker, Cleveland Indians	.386
1917	Ty Cobb, Detroit Tigers	.383
1918	Ty Cobb, Detroit Tigers	.382
1919	Ty Cobb, Detroit Tigers	.384
1920	George Sisler, St. Louis Browns	.407
1921	Harry Heilmann, Detroit Tigers	.393
1922	George Sisler, St. Louis Browns	.420
1923	Harry Heilmann, Detroit Tigers	.398
1924	Babe Ruth, New York Yankees	.378
1925	Harry Heilmann, Detroit Tigers	.393
1926	Heinie Manush, Detroit Tigers	.377
1927	Harry Heilmann, Detroit Tigers	.398
1928	Goose Goslin, Washington Senators	.379
1929	Lew Fonseca, Cleveland Indians	.369
1930	Al Simmons, Philadelphia Athletics	.381
1931	Al Simmons, Philadelphia Athletics	.390
1932	David Alexander, Detroit Tigers-Boston Red Sox	.367
1933	Jimmy Foxx, Philadelphia Athletics	.356

Year	Player, Club	Avg.
1934	Lou Gehrig, New York Yankees	.365
1935	Buddy Myer, Washington Senators	.349
1936	Luke Appling, Chicago White Sox.	.388
1937	Charlie Gehringer, Detroit Tigers	.371
1938	Jimmy Foxx, Boston Red Sox.	.349
1939	Joe DiMaggio, New York Yankees	.381
1940	Joe DiMaggio, New York Yankees	.352
1941	Ted Williams, Boston Red Sox.	.406
1942	Ted Williams, Boston Red Sox.	.356
1943	Luke Appling, Chicago White Sox.	.328
1944	Lou Boudreau, Cleveland Indians	.327
1945	Snuffy Stirnweiss, New York Yankees	.309
1946	Mickey Vernon, Washington Senators	.353
1947	Ted Williams, Boston Red Sox.	.343
1948	Ted Williams, Boston Red Sox.	.369
1949	George Kell, Detroit Tigers	.343
1950	Billy Goodman, Boston Red Sox.	.354
1951	Ferris Fain, Philadelphia Athletics	.344
1952	Ferris Fain, Philadelphia Athletics	.327
1953	Mickey Vernon, Washington Senators	.337
1954	Bobby Avila, Cleveland Indians.	.341
1955	Al Kaline, Detroit Tigers.	.340
1956	Mickey Mantle, New York Yankees	.353
1957	Ted Williams, Boston Red Sox.	.388
1958	Ted Williams, Boston Red Sox.	.328
1959	Harvey Kuenn, Detroit Tigers	.353
1960	Pete Runnels, Boston Red Sox.	.320
1961	Norm Cash, Detroit Tigers	.361
1962	Pete Runnels, Boston Red Sox.	.326
1963	Carl Yastrzemski, Boston Red Sox.	.321
1964	Tony Oliva, Minnesota Twins.	.323
1965	Tony Oliva, Minnesota Twins.	.321
1966	Frank Robinson, Baltimore Orioles.	.316
1967	Carl Yastrzemski, Boston Red Sox.	.326
1968	Carl Yastrzemski, Boston Red Sox.	.301
1969	Rod Carew, Minnesota Twins	.332
1970	Alex Johnson, California Angels	.329
1971	Tony Oliva, Minnesota Twins.	.337
1972	Rod Carew, Minnesota Twins	.318
1973	Rod Carew, Minnesota Twins	.350
1974	Rod Carew, Minnesota Twins	.364
1975	Rod Carew, Minnesota Twins	.359
1976	George Brett, Kansas City Royals	.333
1977	Rod Carew, Minnesota Twins	.388
1978	Rod Carew, Minnesota Twins	.333

NATIONAL LEAGUE
Home Run Leaders

Year	Player, Club	HRs
1900	Herman Long, Boston	12
1901	Sam Crawford, Cincinnati Reds	16
1902	Tom Leach, Pittsburgh Pirates	6
1903	Jim Sheckard, Brooklyn Dodgers	9
1904	Harry Lumley, Brooklyn Dodgers	9
1905	Fred Odwell, Cincinnati Reds	9
1906	Tim Jordan, Brooklyn Dodgers	12
1907	Dave Brian, Boston	10
1908	Tim Jordan, Brooklyn Dodgers	12
1909	Jim Murray, New York Giants	7
1910	Fred Beck, Boston	10
	Frank Schulte, Chicago Cubs	10
1911	Frank Schulte, Chicago Cubs	21
1912	Heinie Zimmerman, Chicago Cubs	14
1913	Gavvy Cravath, Philadelphia Phillies	19
1914	Gavvy Cravath, Philadelphia Phillies	19
1915	Gavvy Cravath, Philadelphia Phillies	24
1916	Dave Robertson, New York Giants	12
	Cy Williams, Chicago Cubs	12
1917	Gavvy Cravath, Philadelphia Phillies	12
	Dave Robertson, New York Giants	12
1918	Gavvy Cravath, Philadelphia Phillies	8
1919	Gavvy Cravath, Philadelphia Phillies	12
1920	Cy Williams, Philadelphia Phillies	15
1921	George Kelly, New York Giants	23
1922	Rogers Hornsby, St. Louis Cardinals	39
1923	Cy Williams, Philadelphia Phillies	41
1924	Jack Fournier, Brooklyn Dodgers	27
1925	Rogers Hornsby, St. Louis Cardinals	39
1926	Hack Wilson, Chicago Cubs	21
1927	Cy Williams, Philadelphia Phillies	30
	Hack Wilson, Chicago Cubs	30
1928	Jim Bottomley, St. Louis Cardinals	31
	Hack Wilson, Chicago Cubs	31
1929	Chuck Klein, Philadelphia Phillies	43
1930	Hack Wilson, Chicago Cubs	56
1931	Chuck Klein, Philadelphia Phillies	31
1932	Chuck Klein, Philadelphia Phillies	38
	Mel Ott, New York Giants	38
1933	Chuck Klein, Philadelphia Phillies	43

Year	Player, Club	HRs
1934	Rip Collins, St. Louis Cardinals	35
	Mel Ott, New York Giants	35
1935	Wally Berger, Boston Braves	34
1936	Mel Ott, New York Giants	33
1937	Joe Medwick, St. Louis Cardinals	31
	Mel Ott, New York Giants	31
1938	Mel Ott, New York Giants	36
1939	Johnny Mize, St. Louis Cardinals	28
1940	Johnny Mize, St. Louis Cardinals	43
1941	Dolph Camilli, Brooklyn Dodgers	34
1942	Mel Ott, New York Giants	30
1943	Bill Nicholson, Chicago Cubs	29
1944	Bill Nicholson, Chicago Cubs	33
1945	Tommy Holmes, Boston Braves	28
1946	Ralph Kiner, Pittsburgh Pirates	23
1947	Ralph Kiner, Pittsburgh Pirates	51
	Johnny Mize, New York Giants	51
1948	Ralph Kiner, Pittsburgh Pirates	40
	Johnny Mize, New York Giants	40
1949	Ralph Kiner, Pittsburgh Pirates	54
1950	Ralph Kiner, Pittsburgh Pirates	47
1951	Ralph Kiner, Pittsburgh Pirates	42
1952	Ralph Kiner, Pittsburgh Pirates	37
	Hank Sauer, Chicago Cubs	37
1953	Eddie Mathews, Milwaukee Braves	47
1954	Ted Kluszewski, Cincinnati Reds	49
1955	Willie Mays, New York Giants	51
1956	Duke Snider, Brooklyn Dodgers	43
1957	Hank Aaron, Milwaukee Braves	44
1958	Ernie Banks, Chicago Cubs	47
1959	Eddie Mathews, Milwaukee Braves	46
1960	Ernie Banks, Chicago Cubs	41
1961	Orlando Cepeda, San Francisco Giants	46
1962	Willie Mays, San Francisco Giants	49
1963	Hank Aaron, Milwaukee Braves	44
	Willie McCovey, San Francisco Giants	44
1964	Willie Mays, San Francisco Giants	47
1965	Willie Mays, San Francisco Giants	52
1966	Hank Aaron, Atlanta Braves	44
1967	Hank Aaron, Atlanta Braves	39
1968	Willie McCovey, San Francisco Giants	36
1969	Willie McCovey, San Francisco Giants	45
1970	Johnny Bench, Cincinnati Reds	45
1972	Willie Stargell, Pittsburgh Pirates	48

Year	Player, Club	HRs
1972	Johnny Bench, Cincinnati Reds	40
1973	Willie Stargell, Pittsburgh Pirates	44
1974	Mike Schmidt, Philadelphia Phillies	36
1975	Mike Schmidt, Philadelphia Phillies	38
1976	Mike Schmidt, Philadelphia Phillies	38
1977	George Foster, Cincinnati Reds	52
1978	George Foster, Cincinnati Reds	40

AMERICAN LEAGUE
Home Run Leaders

Year	Player, Club	HRs
1901	Napoleon Lajoie, Philadelphia Athletics	13
1902	Ralph Seybold, Philadelphia Athletics	16
1903	John Freeman, Boston Red Sox	13
1904	Harry Davis, Philadelphia Athletics	10
1905	Harry Davis, Philadelphia Athletics	8
1906	Harry Davis, Philadelphia Athletics	12
1907	Harry Davis, Philadelphia Athletics	8
1908	Sam Crawford, Detroit Tigers	7
1909	Ty Cobb, Detroit Tigers	9
1910	Garland Stahl, Boston Red Sox	10
1911	Home Run Baker, Philadelphia Athletics	9
1912	Home Run Baker, Philadelphia Athletics	10
1913	Home Run Baker, Philadelphia Athletics	12
1914	Home Run Baker, Philadelphia Athletics	8
	Sam Crawford, Detroit Tigers	8
1915	Bob Roth, Cleveland Indians	7
1916	Wally Pipp, New York Yankees	12
1917	Wally Pipp, New York Yankees	9
1918	Babe Ruth, Boston Red Sox	11
	Clarence Walker, Philadelphia Athletics	11
1919	Babe Ruth, Boston Red Sox	29
1920	Babe Ruth, New York Yankees	54
1921	Babe Ruth, New York Yankees	59
1922	Ken Williams, St. Louis Browns	39
1923	Babe Ruth, New York Yankees	43
1924	Babe Ruth, New York Yankees	46
1925	Bob Meusel, New York Yankees	33
1926	Babe Ruth, New York Yankees	47
1927	Babe Ruth, New York Yankees	60
1928	Babe Ruth, New York Yankees	54
1929	Babe Ruth, New York Yankees	46

Year	Player, Club	HRs
1930	Babe Ruth, New York Yankees	49
1931	Babe Ruth, New York Yankees	46
	Lou Gehrig, New York Yankees	46
1932	Jimmy Foxx, Philadelphia Athletics	58
1933	Jimmy Foxx, Philadelphia Athletics	48
1934	Lou Gehrig, New York Yankees	49
1935	Hank Greenberg, Detroit Tigers	36
	Jimmy Foxx, Philadelphia Athletics	36
1936	Lou Gehrig, New York Yankees	49
1937	Joe DiMaggio, New York Yankees	49
1938	Hank Greenberg, Detroit Tigers	46
1939	Jimmy Foxx, Boston Red Sox	35
1940	Hank Greenberg, Detroit Tigers	41
1941	Ted Williams, Boston Red Sox	37
1942	Ted Williams, Boston Red Sox	36
1943	Rudy York, Detroit Tigers	34
1944	Nick Etten, New York Yankees	22
1945	Vern Stephens, St. Louis Browns	24
1946	Hank Greenberg, Detroit Tigers	44
1947	Ted Williams, Boston Red Sox	32
1948	Joe DiMaggio, New York Yankees	39
1949	Ted Williams, Boston Red Sox	43
1950	Al Rosen, Cleveland Indians	37
1951	Gus Zernial, Philadelphia Athletics	33
1952	Larry Doby, Cleveland Indians	32
1953	Al Rosen, Cleveland Indians	43
1954	Larry Doby, Cleveland Indians	32
1955	Mickey Mantle, New York Yankees	37
1956	Mickey Mantle, New York Yankees	56
1957	Roy Sievers, Washington Senators	42
1958	Mickey Mantle, New York Yankees	42
1959	Rocky Colavito, Cleveland Indians	42
	Harmon Kilabrew, Washington Senators	42
1960	Mickey Mantle, New York Yankees	40
1961	Roger Maris, New York Yankees	61
1962	Harmon Killebrew, Minnesota Twins	48
1963	Harmon Killebrew, Minnesota Twins	45
1964	Harmon Killebrew, Minnesota Twins	49
1965	Tony Conigliaro, Boston Red Sox	32
1966	Frank Robinson, Baltimore Orioles	49
1967	Carl Yastrzemski, Boston Red Sox	44
	Harmon Killebrew, Minnesota Twins	44
1968	Frank Howard, Washington Senators	44
1969	Harmon Killebrew, Minnesota Twins	49

Year	Player, Club	HRs
1970	Frank Howard, Washington Senators	44
1971	Bill Melton, Chicago White Sox	33
1972	Dick Allen, Chicago White Sox	37
1973	Reggie Jackson, Oakland A's	32
1974	Dick Allen, Chicago White Sox	32
1975	George Scott, Milwaukee Brewers	36
	Reggie Jackson, Oakland A's	36
1976	Graig Nettles, New York Yankees	32
1977	Jim Rice, Boston Red Sox	39
1978	Jim Rice, Boston Red Sox	46

Tony Conigliaro led American League with 32 HRs in 1965.

CY YOUNG AWARD WINNERS

Year	Player, Club
1956	Don Newcombe, Brooklyn Dodgers
1957	Warren Spahn, Milwaukee Braves
1958	Bob Turley, New York Yankees
1959	Early Wynn, Chicago White Sox
1960	Vernon Law, Pittsburgh Pirates
1961	Whitey Ford, New York Yankees
1962	Don Drysdale, Los Angeles Dodgers
1963	Sandy Koufax, Los Angeles Dodgers
1964	Dean Chance, Los Angeles Angels
1965	Sandy Koufax, Los Angeles Dodgers
1966	Sandy Koufax, Los Angeles Dodgers

AMERICAN LEAGUE

Year	Player, Club
1967	Jim Lonborg, Boston Red Sox
1968	Dennis McLain, Detroit Tigers
1969	Mike Cuellar, Baltimore Orioles
	Dennis McLain, Detroit Tigers
1970	Jim Perry, Minnesota Twins
1971	Vida Blue, Oakland A's
1972	Gaylord Perry, Cleveland Indians
1973	Jim Palmer, Baltimore Orioles
1974	Jim Hunter, Oakland A's
1975	Jim Palmer, Baltimore Orioles
1976	Jim Palmer, Baltimore Orioles
1977	Sparky Lyle, New York Yankees
1978	Ron Guidry, New York Yankees

NATIONAL LEAGUE

Year	Player, Club
1967	Mike McCormick, San Francisco Giants
1968	Bob Gibson, St. Louis Cardinals
1969	Tom Seaver, New York Mets
1970	Bob Gibson, St. Louis Cardinals
1971	Ferguson Jenkins, Chicago Cubs
1972	Steve Carlton, Philadelphia Phillies
1973	Tom Seaver, New York Mets
1974	Mike Marshall, Los Angeles Dodgers
1975	Tom Seaver, New York Mets
1976	Randy Jones, San Diego Padres
1977	Steve Carlton, Philadelphia Phillies
1978	Gaylord Perry, San Diego Padres

NATIONAL LEAGUE
Rookie of Year

Year	Player, Club
1947	Jackie Robinson, Brooklyn Dodgers
1948	Al Dark, Boston Braves
1949	Don Newcombe, Brooklyn Dodgers
1950	Sam Jethroe, Boston Braves
1951	Willie Mays, New York Giants
1952	Joe Black, Brooklyn Dodgers
1953	Junior Gilliam, Brooklyn Dodgers
1954	Wally Moon, St. Louis Cardinals
1955	Bill Virdon, St. Louis Cardinals
1956	Frank Robinson, Cincinnati Reds
1957	Jack Sanford, Philadelphia Phillies
1958	Orlando Cepeda, San Francisco Giants
1959	Willie McCovey, San Francisco Giants
1960	Frank Howard, Los Angeles Dodgers
1961	Billy Williams, Chicago Cubs
1962	Kenny Hubbs, Chicago Cubs
1963	Pete Rose, Cincinnati Reds
1964	Richie Allen, Philadelphia Phillies
1965	Jim Lefebvre, Los Angeles Dodgers
1966	Tommy Helms, Cincinnati Reds
1967	Tom Seaver, New York Mets
1968	Johnny Bench, Cincinnati Reds
1969	Ted Sizemore, Los Angeles Dodgers
1970	Carl Morton, Montreal Expos
1971	Earl Williams, Atlanta Braves
1972	Jon Matlack, New York Mets
1973	Gary Matthews, San Francisco Giants
1974	Bake McBride, St. Louis Cardinals
1975	John Montefusco, San Francisco Giants
1976	Pat Zachry, Cincinnati Reds
	Butch Metzger, San Diego Padres
1977	Andre Dawson, Montreal Expos
1978	Bob Horner, Atlanta Braves

AMERICAN LEAGUE
Rookie of Year

Year	Player, Club
1949	Roy Sievers, St. Louis Browns
1950	Walt Dropo, Boston Red Sox
1951	Gil McDougald, New York Yankees
1952	Harry Byrd, Philadelphia Athletics
1953	Harvey Kuenn, Detroit Tigers
1954	Bob Grim, New York Yankees
1955	Herb Score, Cleveland Indians
1956	Luis Aparicio, Chicago White Sox
1957	Tony Kubek, New York Yankees
1958	Albie Pearson, Washington Senators
1959	Bob Allison, Washington Senators
1960	Ron Hansen, Baltimore Orioles
1961	Don Schwall, Boston Red Sox
1962	Tom Tresh, New York Yankees
1963	Gary Peters, Chicago White Sox
1964	Tony Oliva, Minnesota Twins
1965	Curt Blefary, Baltimore Orioles
1966	Tommie Agee, Chicago White Sox
1967	Rod Carew, Minnesota Twins
1968	Stan Bahnsen, New York Yankees
1969	Lou Piniella, Kansas City Royals
1970	Thurman Munson, New York Yankees
1971	Chris Chambliss, Cleveland Indians
1972	Carlton Fisk, Boston Red Sox
1973	Al Bumbry, Baltimore Orioles
1974	Mike Hargrove, Texas Rangers
1975	Fred Lynn, Boston Red Sox
1976	Mark Fidrych, Detroit Tigers
1977	Eddie Murray, Baltimore Orioles
1978	Lou Whitaker, Detroit Tigers

WORLD SERIES RESULTS

Year	A. L. Champion	N. L. Champion	World Series Winner
1903	Boston Red Sox	Pittsburgh Pirates	Boston, 5-3
1905	Philadelphia Athletics	New York Giants	New York, 4-1
1906	Chicago White Sox	Chicago Cubs	Chicago (AL), 4-2
1907	Detroit Tigers	Chicago Cubs	Chicago, 4-0-1
1908	Detroit Tigers	Chicago Cubs	Chicago, 4-1
1909	Detroit Tigers	Pittsburgh Pirates	Pittsburgh, 4-3
1910	Philadelphia Athletics	Chicago Cubs	Philadelphia, 4-1
1911	Philadelphia Athletics	New York Giants	Philadelphia, 4-2
1912	Boston Red Sox	New York Giants	Boston, 4-3-1
1913	Philadelphia Athletics	New York Giants	Philadelphia, 4-1
1914	Philadelphia Athletics	Boston Braves	Boston, 4-0
1915	Boston Red Sox	Philadelphia Phillies	Boston, 4-1
1916	Boston Red Sox	Brooklyn Dodgers	Boston, 4-1
1917	Chicago White Sox	New York Giants	Chicago, 4-2
1918	Boston Red Sox	Chicago Cubs	Boston, 4-2
1919	Chicago White Sox	Cincinnati Reds	Cincinnati, 5-2
1920	Cleveland Indians	Brooklyn Dodgers	Cleveland, 5-2
1921	New York Yankees	New York Giants	New York (NL), 5-3
1922	New York Yankees	New York Giants	New York (NL), 4-0-1
1923	New York Yankees	New York Giants	New York (AL), 4-2
1924	Washington Senators	New York Giants	Washington, 4-2
1925	Washington Senators	Pittsburgh Pirates	Pittsburgh, 4-3
1926	New York Yankees	St. Louis Cardinals	St. Louis, 4-3
1927	New York Yankees	Pittsburgh Pirates	New York, 4-0
1928	New York Yankees	St. Louis Cardinals	New York, 4-0
1929	Philadelphia Athletics	Chicago Cubs	Philadelphia, 4-2
1930	Philadelphia Athletics	St. Louis Cardinals	Philadelphia, 4-2
1931	Philadelphia Athletics	St. Louis Cardinals	St. Louis, 4-3
1932	New York Yankees	Chicago Cubs	New York, 4-0
1933	Washington Senators	New York Giants	New York, 4-1
1934	Detroit Tigers	St. Louis Cardinals	St. Louis, 4-3
1935	Detroit Tigers	Chicago Cubs	Detroit, 4-2
1936	New York Yankees	New York Giants	New York (AL), 4-2
1937	New York Yankees	New York Giants	New York (AL), 4-1
1938	New York Yankees	Chicago Cubs	New York, 4-0
1939	New York Yankees	Cincinnati Reds	New York, 4-0
1940	Detroit Tigers	Cincinnati Reds	Cincinnati, 4-3
1941	New York Yankees	Brooklyn Dodgers	New York, 4-1
1942	New York Yankees	St. Louis Cardinals	St. Louis, 4-1
1943	New York Yankees	St. Louis Cardinals	New York, 4-1
1944	St. Louis Browns	St. Louis Cardinals	St. Louis (NL), 4-2
1945	Detroit Tigers	Chicago Cubs	Detroit, 4-3
1946	Boston Red Sox	St. Louis Cardinals	St. Louis, 4-3
1947	New York Yankees	Brooklyn Dodgers	New York, 4-3
1948	Cleveland Indians	Boston Braves	Cleveland, 4-2
1949	New York Yankees	Brooklyn Dodgers	New York, 4-1
1950	New York Yankees	Philadelphia Phillies	New York, 4-0
1951	New York Yankees	New York Giants	New York (AL), 4-2
1952	New York Yankees	Brooklyn Dodgers	New York, 4-3

Nelson Briles and Roberto Clemente led Bucs to '71 title.

Year	A. L. Champion	N. L. Champion	World Series Winner
1953	New York Yankees	Brooklyn Dodgers	New York, 4-2
1954	Cleveland Indians	New York Giants	New York, 4-0
1955	New York Yankees	Brooklyn Dodgers	Brooklyn, 4-3
1956	New York Yankees	Brooklyn Dodgers	New York, 4-3
1957	New York Yankees	Milwaukee Braves	Milwaukee, 4-3
1958	New York Yankees	Milwaukee Braves	New York, 4-3
1959	Chicago White Sox	Los Angeles Dodgers	Los Angeles, 4-2
1960	New York Yankees	Pittsburgh Pirates	Pittsburgh, 4-3
1961	New York Yankees	Cincinnati Reds	New York, 4-1
1962	New York Yankees	San Francisco Giants	New York, 4-3
1963	New York Yankees	Los Angeles Dodgers	Los Angeles, 4-0
1964	New York Yankees	St. Louis Cardinals	St. Louis, 4-3
1965	Minnesota Twins	Los Angeles Dodgers	Los Angeles, 4-3
1966	Baltimore Orioles	Los Angeles Dodgers	Baltimore, 4-0
1967	Boston Red Sox	St. Louis Cardinals	St. Louis, 4-3
1968	Detroit Tigers	St. Louis Cardinals	Detroit, 4-3
1969	Baltimore Orioles	New York Mets	New York, 4-1
1970	Baltimore Orioles	Cincinnati Reds	Baltimore, 4-1
1971	Baltimore Orioles	Pittsburgh Pirates	Pittsburgh, 4-3
1972	Oakland A's	Cincinnati Reds	Oakland, 4-3
1973	Oakland A's	New York Mets	Oakland, 4-3
1974	Oakland A's	Los Angeles Dodgers	Oakland, 4-1
1975	Boston Red Sox	Cincinnati Reds	Cincinnati, 4-3
1976	New York Yankees	Cincinnati Reds	Cincinnati, 4-0
1977	New York Yankees	Los Angeles Dodgers	New York, 4-2
1978	New York Yankees	Los Angeles Dodgers	New York, 4-2

TV/RADIO ROUNDUP

NETWORK COVERAGE

ABC-TV: ABC will televise the World Series. In addition, the network will televise Monday night games.

NBC-TV: The American and National League playoff games and the All-Star Game will be televised by NBC. The network will also cover the Saturday Game of the Week.

NATIONAL LEAGUE

ATLANTA BRAVES: WSB (750) and WTCG (Channel 17) are the flagship stations for networks covering the South. Ernie Johnson, Pete Van Wieren and Skip Caray provide the coverage on both TV and radio.

CINCINNATI REDS: Joe Nuxhall and Marty Brennaman call the action over WLW (700). Bill Brown handles the TV coverage on WLWT (Channel 5).

CHICAGO CUBS: Jack Brickhouse, Vince Lloyd and Lou Boudreau are at the mikes for WGN (720) and WGN (Channel 9) and a 13-station network.

HOUSTON ASTROS: KRIV (Channel 26) heads the TV network and KPRC (950) the radio network. Gene Elston and DeWayne Staats do the play-by-play for both radio and television.

LOS ANGELES DODGERS: Vin Scully, Ross Porter and Jerry Doggett broadcast over KABC (790) and KTTV (Channel 11). Spanish coverage is done by Jaime Jarrin and Rudy Hoyos on XEGM (950).

MONTREAL EXPOS: Dave Van Horne and Duke Snider provide English coverage on CFCF (600) and the CBC-TV network. Jacques Doucet and Claude Raymond do French broadcasts on CKAC (730) and 16 other provincial stations, and Guy Ferron and Jean-Pierre Roy provide the French play-by-play on CBC-TV (French) network.

NEW YORK METS: Ralph Kiner and Bob Murphy handle TV originating at WOR-TV (Channel 9) and radio over WMCA (570).

PHILADELPHIA PHILLIES: WPHL (Channel 17) originates telecasts while KYW (1060) heads up the radio network. Andy Musser, Richie Ashburn, Chris Wheeler and Harry Kalas do the announcing.

PITTSBURGH PIRATES: Milo Hamilton and Larry Frattare are the broadcasters over KDKA (1020) and KDKA-TV (Channel 2).

SAN DIEGO PADRES: Jerry Coleman and Dave Campbell handle the play-by-play on radio KOGO (600).

SAN FRANCISCO GIANTS: The Giants can be heard on radio station KBM (680) and seen on television station Channel 2 (KTVU).

ST. LOUIS CARDINALS: Bob Starr, Mike Shannon and Jack Buck are on KMOX radio (1120); Starr, Shannon, Jay Randolph and Buck handle TV on KSD (Channel 5).

AMERICAN LEAGUE

BALTIMORE ORIOLES: Chuck Thompson and Bill O'Donnell call the action over radio station WBAL (1090) and WJZ-TV (Channel 13).

BOSTON RED SOX: Ken Coleman and Rico Petrocelli broadcast over radio station WITS (1510). Ned Martin and Ken Harrelson handle television chores over Channel 38 (WSBK-TV).

CALIFORNIA ANGELS: Flagship station KMPC (710) carries the Angels on radio, while KTLA (Channel 5) televises the Angels. Dick Enberg, Don Drysdale and Al Wisk are the announcers.

CHICAGO WHITE SOX: Harry Caray, Jimmy Piersall, and Lorn Brown provide the coverage over WMAQ (670) and WSNS-TV (Channel 44).

CLEVELAND INDIANS: Joe Tait and Herb Score describe the action on three-state radio network with WWWE (1100) as flagship. Eddie Doucette and Jim Mueller handle TV coverage on WJKW (channel 8).

DETROIT TIGERS: Ernie Harwell and Paul Carey are the Tiger broadcasters on a 50-station radio network originating on WJR (760). WDIV-TV (Channel 4) and a seven-station network have George Kell and Al Kaline behind the mikes.

KANSAS CITY ROYALS: Five-state TV network originates with KBMA (Channel 41). Radio network headed by KMBZ (980) in K.C. and WIBW (580) in Topeka with Fred White and Denny Matthews.

MILWAUKEE BREWERS: WTMJ (620) and WTMJ-TV (Channel 4) head radio and TV networks covering five states. Merle Harmon, Mike Hegan and Bob Uecker describe the action.

MINNESOTA TWINS: Joe Boyle and Harmon Killebrew telecast for WTCN-TV (Channel 11). Joe McConnell and Herb Carneal call the plays on a 32-station radio network headed by WCCO (830).

NEW YORK YANKEES: Frank Messer, Bill White and Phil Rizzuto share duties on a television network headed by WPIX-TV (Channel 11). Fran Healy joins the same crew on a radio network headed by WINS (1010).

OAKLAND A's: Radio and television arrangements were not completed at press time.

SEATTLE MARINERS: The Mariners can be heard over radio station KVI (570) and seen on Channel 5, KING-TV. Dave Niehaus and Ken Wilson describe the action.

TEXAS RANGERS: Jon Miller, Bill Merrill and Frank Glieber broadcast over WBAP (820) and KXAS-TV (Channel 5).

TORONTO BLUE JAYS: Tom Cheek and Early Wynn broadcast for a network headed by radio station CKFH. Don Chevrier, Tom McKee and Tony Kubek handle coverage for CBC-TV.

OFFICIAL 1978 AMERICAN LEAGUE AVERAGES

compiled by

SPORTS INFORMATION CENTER

STANDING OF CLUBS AT CLOSE OF SEASON

AMERICAN LEAGUE WEST

	Won	Lost	Pct.	Games Behind
Kansas City	92	70	.568	
California	87	75	.537	5.0
Texas	87	75	.537	5.0
Minnesota	73	89	.451	19.0
Chicago	71	90	.441	20.5
Oakland	69	93	.426	23.0
Seattle	56	104	.350	35.0

AMERICAN LEAGUE EAST

	Won	Lost	Pct.	Games Behind
New York	100	63	.613	
Boston	99	64	.607	1.0
Milwaukee	93	69	.574	6.5
Baltimore	90	71	.559	9.0
Detroit	86	76	.531	13.5
Cleveland	69	90	.434	29.0
Toronto	59	102	.366	40.0

CHAMPIONSHIP SERIES: New York defeated Kansas City 3 games to 1

TOP FIFTEEN QUALIFIERS FOR BATTING CHAMPIONSHIP
(Rankings Based on 502 Plate Appearances)

*Bats Lefthanded †Switch Hitter

Batter	PCT	G	AB	R	H	TB	2B	3B	HR	RBI	SH	SF	SB	CS	SLG PCT	TBB	IBB	HP	SO	GIDP
Carew, Rod, Minn.*	.333	152	564	85	188	249	26	10	5	70	2	6	27	9	.441	78	19	1	62	18
Oliver, Al, Tex.*	.324	133	525	65	170	257	35	5	14	89	2	6	5	7	.490	31	6	2	40	7
Rice, Jim, Bos.	.315	163	677	121	213	406	25	15	46	139	1	5	7	5	.600	58	8	5	126	15
Piniella, Lou, N.Y.	.314	130	472	67	148	210	34	5	6	69	4	3	3	1	.445	30	8	2	36	12
Oglivie, Ben, Milw.	.303	128	469	71	142	233	29	4	18	72	3	3	11	2	.497	52	10	0	69	10
Roberts, Leon, Sea.	.301	134	472	78	142	243	21	7	22	92	1	6	7	4	.515	41	7	4	54	7
Otis, Amos, K.C.	.298	141	486	74	145	255	30	7	22	96	1	6	32	8	.525	66	7	8	54	10
Lynn, Fred, Bos.*	.298	150	541	75	161	266	33	3	22	82	4	6	3	1	.492	75	11	4	50	9
LeFlore, Ron, Det.	.297	155	666	126	198	270	30	3	12	62	1	5	68	16	.405	65	7	4	104	11
Munson, Thurman, N.Y.	.297	154	617	73	183	230	27	1	6	71	4	10	2	3	.373	35	6	3	71	20
Bostock, Lyman, Calif.*	.296	147	568	74	168	215	24	4	5	62	14	6	15	2	.379	59	8	2	36	26
Brett, George, K.C.*	.294	128	510	79	150	238	45	8	9	62	3	5	23	7	.467	39	6	1	35	6
Money, Don, Milw.	.293	137	518	88	152	228	30	2	14	54	2	4	3	0	.440	48	2	7	70	10
Singleton, Ken, Balt.†	.293	149	502	67	147	232	21	2	20	81	2	4	2	0	.462	97	5	2	94	14
Yount, Robin, Milw.	.293	127	502	66	147	215	23	9	9	71	13	5	16	5	.428	24	1	1	43	5

INDIVIDUAL BATTING
(All Players – Listed Alphabetically)

*Bats Lefthanded †Switch Hitter

Batter	PCT	G	AB	R	H	TB	2B	3B	HR	RBI	SH	SF	SB	CS	SLG PCT	TBB	IBB	HP	SO	GIDP
Adams, Glenn, Minn.*	.258	116	310	27	80	121	18	1	7	35	2	0	0	0	.390	17	0	0	32	10
Adams, Mike, Oak.	.200	15	15	5	3	4	1	0	0	0	0	0	0	1	.267	7	0	0	2	0
Alberts, Butch, Tor.	.278	6	18	1	5	6	1	0	0	0	0	0	0	0	.333	0	0	0	2	0
Alexander, Gary, 58-Oak., 90-Clev.	.225	148	498	57	112	221	20	4	27	84	1	5	0	5	.444	57	5	2	166	11
Alomar, Sandy, Tex.†	.207	24	29	3	6	7	1	0	0	0	0	0	0	0	.241	1	0	0	10	1
Alston, Dell,* 3-N.Y., 58-Oak.	.205	61	176	17	36	41	2	0	1	10	4	0	11	10	.233	10	0	0	23	1
Anderson, Mike, Balt.	.094	53	32	2	3	5	0	0	0	3	1	0	0	0	.156	9	0	0	10	0
Anderson, Jim, Calif.	.194	48	108	6	21	28	7	0	0	7	7	1	2	1	.259	11	0	0	16	5
Armas, Tony, Oak.	.213	91	239	17	51	65	6	1	9	13	2	1	1	1	.272	14	2	1	62	5
Ashby, Alan, Tor.†	.261	81	264	27	69	111	15	0	9	29	4	1	0	0	.420	28	4	1	32	10
Aut, Doug, Tor.	.240	54	104	10	25	37	1	1	3	7	2	0	0	0	.356	17	1	1	14	6
Baez, Jose, Sea.	.160	23	50	8	8	10	1	0	0	2	2	0	2	1	.200	5	0	1	7	0
Bailey, Bob, Bos.	.191	43	94	12	18	33	3	0	4	9	0	2	0	0	.351	19	1	0	19	2
Bailor, Bob, Tor.	.264	154	621	74	164	210	29	7	1	52	9	3	5	6	.338	38	1	5	21	8

*Bats Lefthanded   †Switch Hitter

Batter	PCT	G	AB	R	H	TB	2B	3B	HR	RBI	SH	SF	SB	CS	SLG PCT	TBB	IBB	HP	SO	GI DP
Bando, Sal, Milw.	.285	152	540	85	154	237	20	6	17	78	4	7	3	3	.439	72	4	6	52	11
Bannister, Alan, Chgo.	.224	49	107	16	24	31	3	2	0	8	0	0	3	2	.290	11	1	2	12	2
Bass, Randy, K.C.*	.000	2	2	0	0	0	0	0	0	0	0	0	0	0	.000	0	0	0	0	0
Baylor, Don, Calif.	.255	158	591	103	151	279	26	4	34	99	0	12	22	9	.472	56	9	18	71	15
Beamon, Charlie, Sea.*	.182	10	11	2	2	2	0	0	0	0	0	0	0	0	.182	1	0	0	1	0
Belanger, Mark, Balt.	.213	134	348	39	74	87	13	0	0	16	7	7	6	6	.250	40	1	0	55	4
Bell, Kevin, Chgo.	.191	54	68	9	13	19	0	0	2	5	2	0	1	0	.279	5	0	1	19	3
Bell, Buddy, Clev.	.282	142	556	71	157	218	27	8	11	62	0	4	2	1	.392	39	1	1	43	24
Beniquez, Juan, Tex.	.260	127	473	61	123	179	17	3	11	50	10	4	10	12	.378	20	1	3	59	10
Bernhardt, Juan, Sea.	.230	54	165	13	38	53	9	0	2	12	4	3	1	1	.321	9	1	1	10	3
Bevacqua, Kurt, Tex.	.222	90	248	21	55	85	12	0	6	30	2	1	2	1	.343	18	0	0	31	8
Blair, Paul, N.Y.	.176	74	125	10	22	33	5	0	2	13	2	0	1	1	.264	9	0	0	17	4
Blanks, Larvell, Clev.	.254	70	193	19	49	65	10	0	2	20	5	1	0	0	.337	10	2	0	16	7
Blomberg, Ron, Chgo.*	.231	61	156	16	36	58	7	0	5	22	1	2	0	1	.372	11	1	2	17	1
Bochte, Bruce, Sea.*	.263	140	486	58	128	192	25	3	11	51	7	3	0	0	.395	60	3	1	47	12
Bonds, Bobby, 26-Chgo. 151-Tex.	.267	156	565	93	151	271	19	4	31	90	3	8	43	22	.480	79	7	2	121	14
Borgmann, Glenn, Minn.	.211	49	128	16	26	41	4	1	3	15	3	0	0	0	.333	18	0	1	17	0
Boseti, Rick, Tor.	.259	136	568	61	147	197	25	5	5	42	5	2	12	11	.347	30	1	0	65	5
Bosley, Thad, Chgo.*	.269	66	219	25	59	72	5	1	2	13	2	2	11	2	.329	13	1	0	32	4
Bostock, Lyman, Calif.*	.296	147	568	74	168	215	24	4	14	71	4	4	15	12	.379	59	8	2	36	26
Bowen, Sam, Bos.	.143	6	7	3	1	4	0	0	1	1	0	0	0	0	.571	2	0	0	2	0
Braun, Steve, 32-Sea. 64-Tex.*	.251	96	211	27	53	78	14	1	3	29	1	2	4	2	.370	37	2	0	21	5
Breazeale, Jim, Chgo.*	.208	25	72	8	15	27	3	0	3	13	0	0	0	0	.375	8	0	0	10	2
Brett, George, K.C.*	.294	128	510	79	150	238	45	8	9	62	3	5	23	7	.467	39	6	2	35	6
Briggs, Dan, Clev.*	.163	15	49	4	8	13	0	0	1	1	0	0	0	0	.265	4	0	1	9	2
Brohamer, Jack, Bos.*	.234	81	244	34	57	76	14	1	1	25	4	0	0	0	.311	25	2	0	13	6
Budaska, Mark, Oak.†	.250	4	4	0	1	2	1	0	0	1	0	0	0	0	.500	1	0	0	2	0
Bumbry, Al, Balt.*	.237	33	114	21	27	42	5	2	2	14	6	0	2	2	.368	17	0	0	15	4
Burke, Glenn, Oak.	.235	78	200	19	47	58	6	1	2	14	6	1	15	8	.290	10	1	0	27	0
Burleson, Rick, Bos.	.248	145	626	75	155	212	32	5	5	49	10	8	8	8	.339	40	2	4	71	16
Cage, Wayne, Clev.*	.245	36	98	11	24	44	6	1	3	13	1	0	0	0	.449	9	0	2	28	2
Campaneris, Bert, Tex.	.186	98	269	30	50	64	5	3	1	17	25	3	27	4	.238	20	0	2	37	6
Carbo, Bernie, 17-Bos., 60-Clev.*	.282	77	220	28	62	88	11	0	5	22	1	1	7	1	.400	28	1	0	39	9
Carew, Rod, Minn.*	.333	152	564	85	188	249	26	10	5	70	2	6	27	7	.441	78	19	1	62	8
Carty, Rico, 104-Tor., 41-Oak.	.281	145	528	51	149	265	21	0	31	99	0	5	0	2	.502	23	7	0	32	15
Cerone, Rick Tor.	.223	88	282	25	63	84	8	2	3	20	7	2	0	1	.298	38	0	0	34	7
Chalk, Dave, Calif.	.253	135	470	42	119	134	12	1	0	34	1	0	8	8	.285	17	0	0	57	6
Chambliss, Chris, N.Y.*	.274	162	625	81	171	239	26	3	12	90	1	5	1	1	.382	41	3	5	60	6

Chappas, Harry, Chgo.†	.267	20	75	11	20	21	1	0	0	6	3	3	1	2	.280	6	0	1	11	0
Chiles, Rich, Minn.*	.268	87	198	22	53	68	12	0	1	22	0	5	1	2	.343	20	2	2	25	9
Colbern, Mike, Chgo.	.270	48	141	11	38	51	5	1	2	20	0	2	0	1	.362	1	0	2	36	1
Cooper, Cecil, Milw.*	.312	107	407	60	127	193	23	2	13	54	5	4	3	4	.474	32	3	0	72	5
Corcoran, Tim, Det.*	.265	116	324	37	86	104	13	1	1	27	6	4	3	2	.321	24	2	5	27	10
Cowens, Al, K.C.	.274	132	485	63	133	188	24	8	5	63	1	11	14	6	.388	31	3	6	54	7
Cox, Ted, Clev.	.233	82	227	14	53	63	7	0	1	19	8	1	0	1	.278	16	1	1	30	4
Cripe, Dave, K.C.	.154	7	13	1	2	2	0	0	0	1	0	0	0	0	.154	0	0	0	2	0
Crowley, Terry, Balt.*	.253	62	95	9	24	26	2	0	0	12	0	1	0	0	.274	8	0	1	12	4
Cruz, Henry, Chgo.*	.221	53	77	13	17	27	2	1	2	10	0	3	0	1	.351	8	0	1	11	2
Cruz, Julio, Sea.†	.235	147	550	77	129	148	14	1	1	25	10	4	59	10	.269	69	0	1	66	8
Cubbage, Mike, Minn.*	.282	125	394	40	111	158	12	7	7	57	7	2	3	1	.401	40	3	1	44	7
Dade, Paul, Clev.	.254	93	307	37	78	101	12	1	3	20	5	1	12	9	.329	34	1	2	45	3
Dauer, Rich, Balt.	.264	133	459	57	121	162	23	0	6	46	3	3	0	4	.353	26	0	0	22	16
Davis, Dick, Milw.	.248	69	218	28	54	81	10	1	5	26	4	4	2	5	.372	7	0	2	23	5
DeCinces, Doug, Balt.	.286	142	511	72	146	269	37	1	28	80	0	2	8	7	.526	47	2	2	82	12
Dempsey, Rick, Balt.	.259	136	441	41	114	157	25	0	6	32	3	6	7	3	.356	48	2	0	54	11
Dent, Bucky, N.Y.	.243	123	379	40	92	120	11	1	5	40	6	5	3	1	.317	23	1	2	24	10
Diaz, Bo, Clev.	.236	44	127	12	30	40	4	0	2	11	2	0	0	0	.315	4	0	0	17	2
Dillard, Steve, Det.	.223	56	130	21	29	38	5	2	0	7	7	0	1	2	.292	6	0	0	11	5
Dilone, Miguel, Oak.†	.228	135	259	34	59	70	8	0	1	14	9	0	50	23	.270	24	0	1	30	2
Dimmel, Mike, Balt.	.000	8	0	2	0	0	0	0	0	0	0	0	0	1	.000	0	0	0	0	0
Downing, Brian, Calif.	.255	133	412	42	105	141	15	0	7	46	4	2	3	2	.342	52	2	6	47	14
Doyle, Brian, N.Y.*	.192	39	52	6	10	10	0	0	0	0	2	0	0	3	.192	0	0	0	3	2
Duffy, Frank, Bos.	.206	64	104	12	27	32	5	0	0	4	6	0	1	1	.308	6	0	1	11	1
Duncan, Taylor, Oak.	.257	104	319	25	82	107	15	2	2	37	7	3	1	2	.335	18	0	0	38	5
Eden, Mike, Chgo.†	.118	10	17	1	2	2	0	0	0	0	0	0	0	0	.118	4	0	0	0	1
Edwards, Dave, Minn.	.250	15	44	7	11	17	3	0	1	3	0	0	1	1	.386	7	0	2	13	0
Edwards, Mike, Oak.	.274	142	413	48	113	136	16	2	1	23	14	0	27	21	.329	16	0	2	32	7
Ellis, John, Tex.	.245	34	94	7	23	36	4	0	3	17	1	3	0	1	.383	6	0	0	20	0
Essian, Jim, Oak.	.223	126	278	21	62	82	9	1	3	26	15	3	2	1	.295	44	1	0	22	12
Etchebarren, Andy, Milw.	.400	4	5	1	2	3	1	0	0	2	0	0	0	0	.600	1	0	0	2	0
Evans, Dwight, Bos.	.247	147	497	75	123	223	24	2	24	63	6	2	8	5	.449	65	2	2	119	15
Ewing, Sam, Tor.*	.179	40	56	3	10	16	0	0	2	9	0	1	0	0	.286	5	2	0	9	0
Fairly, Ron, Calif.*	.217	91	235	23	51	86	5	0	10	40	2	5	0	1	.366	25	2	1	31	7
Fisk, Carlton, Bos.	.284	157	571	94	162	271	39	5	20	88	3	6	7	2	.475	71	6	7	83	10
Foley, Marvis, Chgo.*	.353	11	34	3	12	12	0	0	0	6	0	0	0	1	.353	4	0	0	6	1
Ford, Dan, Minn.	.274	151	592	78	162	251	36	10	11	82	6	3	7	7	.424	48	6	5	88	15
Fuentes, Tito, Oak.†	.140	13	43	5	6	7	1	0	0	2	1	0	0	0	.163	1	0	0	6	0
Gantner, Jim, Milw.*	.216	43	97	14	21	25	1	0	1	8	1	0	2	0	.258	5	0	2	10	0

*Bats Lefthanded †Switch Hitter

Batter	PCT	G	AB	R	H	TB	2B	3B	HR	RBI	SH	SF	SB	CS	SLG PCT	TBB	IBB	HP	SO	GI DP
Garcia, Kiko, Balt.	.263	79	186	17	49	63	6	4	0	13	4	2	7	1	.339	7	0	0	43	5
Garcia, Damaso, N.Y.	.195	18	41	5	8	8	0	0	0	1	2	0	0	0	.195	2	1	0	6	1
Garr, Ralph, Chgo.*	.275	118	443	67	122	167	18	9	3	29	10	1	0	5	.377	24	1	0	41	9
Gates, Joe, Chgo.*	.250	8	24	6	6	6	0	0	0	1	1	0	7	0	.250	4	0	0	6	0
Gaudet, Jim, K.C.	.000	3	8	0	0	0	0	0	0	0	0	0	0	0	.000	0	-	0	1	0
Gomez, Luis, Tor.	.223	153	413	39	92	105	7	3	0	32	19	3	1	10	.254	34	1	0	41	10
Goodwin, Danny, Calif.*	.276	24	58	9	16	27	5	0	2	10	0	0	0	0	.466	10	1	0	13	1
Gray, Gary, Tex.	.240	17	50	4	12	19	1	0	2	6	0	1	0	0	.380	1	0	0	12	1
Grich, Bobby, Calif.	.251	144	487	68	122	160	16	2	6	42	19	3	4	0	.329	75	1	7	83	6
Griffin, Alfredo, Clev.†	.500	5	4	1	2	3	1	0	0	0	0	0	0	0	.750	2	0	0	0	0
Gross, Wayne, Oak.*	.200	118	285	18	57	92	10	2	7	23	4	1	2	6	.323	40	0	5	62	3
Grubb, Johnny, 113-Clev, 21-Tex.*	.275	134	411	62	113	189	19	6	15	67	8	2	6	2	.460	70	5	5	65	5
Guerrero, Mario, Oak.	.275	143	505	28	139	174	18	4	0	38	17	3	0	1	.345	15	2	0	35	13
Guidry, Ron, N.Y.*	.000	37													.000				0	
Hale, John, Sea.*	.171	107	211	24	36	56	8	0	4	22	4	0	2	3	.265	34	1	0	64	0
Hampton, Ike, Calif.	.214	19	14	2	3	8	0	0	1	4	0	0	0	2	.571	2	0	0	7	-
Hancock, Gary, Bos.*	.225	38	80	10	18	21	3	0	0	4	1	0	0	0	.263	1	0	0	12	-
Haney, Larry, Milw.	.200	4	5	0	1	1	0	0	0	0	0	0	0	0	.200	1	0	0	1	0
Hargrove, Mike, Tex.*	.251	146	494	63	124	171	24	1	7	40	2	2	5	2	.346	107	8	7	48	11
Harlow, Larry, Balt.*	.243	147	460	67	112	163	25	1	8	26	3	4	14	1	.354	55	3	1	72	9
Harrah, Toby, Tex.	.229	139	450	56	103	162	17	3	12	59	9	1	31	8	.360	83	3	2	66	8
Hassey, Ron, Clev.	.203	25	74	5	15	21	0	0	2	9	2	1	0	2	.284	5	0	1	7	1
Healy, Fran, N.Y.	.000														.000					
Heath, Mike, N.Y.	.228	33	92	4	21	26	3	1	0	8	1	0	2	0	.283	4	0	0	9	1
Hendricks, Elrod, Balt.*	.333	13	18	4	6	10	1	0	1	1	0	0	0	0	.556	3	2	0	5	0
Hisle, Larry, Milw.	.290	142	520	96	151	277	24	2	34	115	0	5	10	0	.533	67	3	5	90	14
Hobson, Butch, Bos.	.250	147	512	65	128	209	26	2	17	80	4	8	1	0	.408	50	3	3	122	15
Horton, Willie, 50-Clev, 32-Oak.,33-Tor.	.252	115	393	38	99	153	21	0	11	60	0	3	0	1	.389	27	6	1	69	14
Hosley, Tim, Oak.	.304	13	23	7	7	9	2	0	0	3	0	0	0	0	.391	4	0	0	6	0
Howell, Roy, Tor.*	.270	140	551	67	149	207	28	3	8	61	4	4	0	1	.376	44	3	0	78	10
Humphrey, Terry, Calif.	.219	53	114	11	25	34	4	1	1	9	4	1	0	2	.298	6	0	2	12	2
Hurdle, Clint, K.C.*	.264	133	417	48	110	166	25	5	7	56	1	6	1	1	.398	56	1	0	84	6
Hutton, Tommy, Tor.*	.254	64	173	19	44	59	9	0	2	19	5	2	1	2	.341	19	0	0	12	6
Iorg, Garth, Tor.	.163	19	49	3	8	8	0	0	0	3	0	0	0	0	.163	3	0	0	4	3
Jackson, Ron, Calif.	.297	105	387	49	115	163	18	6	6	57	0	2	2	3	.421	16	1	9	31	9
Jackson, Reggie, N.Y.*	.274	139	511	82	140	244	13	2	27	97	0	3	14	11	.477	58	9	2	133	8
Johnson, Lamar, Chgo	.273	148	498	52	136	187	23	2	8	72	1	6	6	5	.376	43	2	2	46	17
Johnson, Larry Doby, Chgo	.125	7																		

Player	Pct.	G	AB	R	H	TB	2B	3B	HR	RBI	SH	SF	HP	BB	IB	SO	SB	CS	SLG
Johnson, Tim, 3-Milw., 67-Tor.*	.232	70	82	10	19	21	2	0	0	2	0	3	1		1	16	3	0	.256
Johnstone, Jay, N.Y.*	.262	36	65	6	17	20	3	0	0	0	3	1	1		1	10	3	0	.308
Jones, Ruppert, Sea.*	.235	129	472	48	111	159	24	12	6	46	8	5	2		5	85	22	15	.337
Jorgensen, Mike, Tex.*	.196	96	97	20	19	25	3	0	1	11	9	4	1		1	18	1	3	.258
Kelly, Pat, Balt.*	.274	100	274	38	75	122	12	1	11	40	4	3	2		2	34	1	9	.445
Kemp, Steve, Det.*	.277	159	582	75	161	232	18	4	15	79	0	9	4		10	97	2	9	.399
Kendall, Fred, Bos.	.195	20	41	3	8	9	1	0	0	4	2	0	0		0	1	0	0	.220
Kern, Jim, Clev.	.000	58														2			.000
Kessinger, Don, Chgo.†	.255	131	431	35	110	133	18	3	0	31	12	0	0		4	36	1	1	.309
Klutts, Mickey, N.Y.	1.000	1	2	3	3	3	0	0	0	1	0	0	0		0				01.500
Kuiper, Duane, Clev.	.283	149	547	52	155	185	18	6	0	43	16	4	3		9	19	1	1	.338
Kusick, Craig, Minn.	.173	77	191	23	33	52	3	2	4	20	0	2	0		0	37	0	4	.272
Kusnyer, Art, K.C.	.231	9	13	1	3	7	1	0	1	1	0	0	0		3	4	0	0	.538
LaCock, Pete, K.C.	.295	118	322	44	95	135	21	2	5	48	3	3	0		0	21	0	2	.419
Lahoud, Joe, K.C.	.125	13	16	0	2	2	0	0	0	0	0	0	1		0	1	0	0	.125
Landreaux, Ken, Calif.*	.223	93	260	37	58	90	7	5	5	23	0	0	0		7	20	0	5	.346
Langford, Rick, Oak.	.000	40														0			.000
Lanford, Carney, Calif.	.294	121	453	63	133	184	23	2	8	52	5	7	2		7	31	2	4	.406
LeFlore, Ron, Det.	.297	155	666	126	198	270	30	3	12	62	1	4	1		20	65	7	11	.405
Lemon, Chet, Chgo.	.300	105	357	51	107	182	24	6	13	55	8	5	5		68	39	8	4	.510
Lezcano, Sixto, Milw.	.292	132	442	62	129	203	21	4	15	61	5	7	3		16	64	1	5	.459
Lintz, Larry, Clev.†	.000	3														0			.000
Lopez, Carlos, Balt.	.238	129	193	21	46	64	6	0	4	20	2	2	0		5	9	6	4	.332
Lowenstein, John, Tex.*	.222	77	176	28	39	68	8	3	5	21	4	0	1		7	29	2	2	.386
Lynn, Fred, Bos.*	.298	150	541	75	161	266	33	3	22	82	0	6	6		16	37	3	9	.492
Machemer, Dave, Calif.	.273	10	6	6	10	1	1	0	0	1	0	0	0		2	75	0	1	.455
Mahlberg, Greg, Tex.	.000															0			.000
Mankowski, Phil, Det.*	.275	88	222	28	61	81	8	0	4	20	3	1	0		2	22	3	0	.365
Manning, Rick, Clev.*	.263	148	566	65	149	191	27	3	3	50	3	3	2		12	38	1	10	.337
Martinez, Buck, Milw.	.219	89	256	26	56	71	10	1	1	20	12	2	4		12	14	1	2	.277
Mason, Jim, Tex.*	.190	55	105	10	20	24	4	0	0	12	6	0	0		0	17	0	4	.229
May, Lee, Balt.	.246	148	556	56	137	230	16	0	25	80	0	5	5		0	31	5	18	.414
May, Milt, Det.*	.250	105	352	24	88	127	9	0	10	37	4	2	0		0	27	1	13	.361
May, Dave, Milw.*	.195	39	77	9	15	25	2	1	2	11	0	3	0		2	10	1	3	.325
Mayberry, John, Tor.*	.250	52	515	51	129	214	15	4	22	70	1	7	1		4	57	1	3	.416
McKay, Dave, Tor.†	.238	145	504	59	120	177	20	8	7	45	10	2	4		4	90	6	17	.351
McRae, Hal, K.C.	.273	156	623	90	170	267	39	5	16	72	1	11	0		17	62	6	15	.429
Meyer, Scott, Oak.	.111	8				1	2	1	0	0	0	0	0		0	4	0	0	.222
Meyer, Dan, Sea.*	.227	123	444	38	101	145	18	2	8	56	8	5	0		1	39	6	7	.327
Milbourne, Larry, Sea.†	.226	93	234	31	53	69	6	2	2	20	3	1	1		5	9	0	7	.295

*Bats Lefthanded   †Switch Hitter

Batter	PCT	G	AB	R	H	TB	2B	3B	HR	RBI	SH	SF	SB	CS	SLG PCT	TBB	IBB	HP	SO	GI DP
Miller, Rick, Calif. *	.263	132	475	66	125	161	25	4	1	37	10	4	3	13	.339	54	1	4	70	14
Milner, Brian, Tor.	.444	2	9	3	4	6	0	1	0	2	0	0	0	0	.667	0	0	0	1	0
Molinaro, Bob, Chgo. *	.262	105	286	39	75	108	5	5	6	27	2	1	22	6	.378	19	0	2	12	5
Molitor, Paul, Milw.	.273	125	521	73	142	194	26	4	6	45	7	5	30	12	.372	19	2	4	54	6
Money, Don, Milw.	.293	137	518	88	152	228	30	2	14	54	4	7	3	0	.440	48	2	7	70	10
Montgomery, Bob, Bos.	.241	10	29	2	7	10	1	0	0	5	1	0	0	0	.345	2	0	0	12	1
Moore, Alvin, Chgo.	.292	24	65	8	19	21	1	0	0	7	0	1	2	3	.323	6	0	0	7	4
Moore, Charlie, Milw.	.269	96	268	30	72	96	7	1	5	31	5	1	2	1	.358	12	0	2	24	4
Mora, Andres, Balt.	.214	76	229	21	49	81	8	0	8	14	2	0	0	1	.354	13	1	1	47	5
Morales, Jose, Minn.	.314	101	242	22	76	97	13	1	2	38	6	4	0	1	.401	20	3	1	35	10
Mulliniks, Rance, Calif. *	.185	50	119	6	22	30	3	1	1	6	0	2	2	0	.252	8	0	0	23	3
Munson, Thurman, N.Y.	.297	154	617	73	183	230	27	1	6	71	1	7	2	1	.373	35	6	3	70	20
Murphy, Dwayne, Oak. *	.192	60	52	15	10	12	2	0	0	5	1	2	2	3	.231	7	0	1	14	0
Murray, Eddie, Balt. †	.285	161	610	85	174	293	32	3	27	95	1	8	6	5	.480	70	7	1	96	15
Murray, Larry, Oak. †	.083	11	12	1	1	1	0	0	0	0	2	0	0	0	.083	3	0	0	2	0
Muser, Tony, Milw. *	.133	15	30	0	4	7	1	1	0	5	0	0	0	0	.233	3	0	0	5	1
Nahorodny, Bill, Chgo.	.236	107	347	29	82	121	11	1	8	35	4	1	0	2	.349	23	0	2	52	5
Nettles, Graig, N.Y. *	.276	159	587	81	162	270	23	2	27	93	1	9	1	1	.460	59	6	6	69	20
Newman, Jeff, Oak.	.239	105	268	25	64	100	7	1	9	32	3	0	1	3	.373	18	2	1	40	4
Nordbrook, Tim, 7-Tor, 2-Milw.	.000	9	5	1	0	0	0	0	0	0	1	0	0	0	.000	1	0	0	1	0
Nordhagen, Wayne, Chgo.	.301	68	206	28	62	93	16	0	5	35	0	5	0	0	.451	5	0	0	18	6
Norman, Nelson, Tex.	.265	23	34	4	9	11	2	0	0	2	5	0	3	1	.324	5	0	0	4	1
Norris, Jim, Clev. *	.283	113	316	41	89	119	14	5	2	27	1	3	12	7	.378	42	4	0	20	6
North, Bill, Oak. †	.212	24	52	5	11	15	4	0	0	5	1	3	20	2	.288	9	0	2	20	1
Norwood, Willie, Minn.	.255	125	428	56	109	161	22	3	8	46	3	3	25	10	.376	28	0	3	64	15
Oglivie, Ben, Milw. *	.303	128	469	71	142	233	29	4	18	72	3	3	11	7	.497	52	10	0	69	10
Oliver, Al, Tex. *	.324	133	525	65	170	257	35	5	14	89	1	9	8	9	.490	31	6	2	40	7
Orta, Jorge, Chgo. *	.274	117	420	45	115	177	19	2	13	53	4	7	1	4	.421	42	2	3	53	9
Otis, Amos, K.C.	.298	141	486	74	145	255	30	7	22	96	1	10	32	8	.525	66	7	4	39	9
Paciorek, Tom, Sea.	.299	70	251	32	75	113	20	3	4	30	0	2	2	2	.450	15	0	4	54	10
Page, Mitchell, Oak. *	.285	147	516	62	147	237	25	7	17	70	4	2	23	19	.459	53	6	4	95	7
Parrish, Lance, Det.	.219	85	288	37	63	122	11	3	14	41	1	0	0	0	.424	11	0	3	71	8
Pasley, Kevin, Sea.	.241	25	54	3	13	21	5	1	0	1	5	2	0	0	.389	1	0	1	5	2
Patek, Fred, K.C.	.248	138	440	54	109	140	23	1	2	46	9	4	38	11	.318	42	1	0	56	6
Perez, Marty, Oak.	.000	16	12	1	0	0	0	0	0	0	3	0	1	0	.000	0	0	0	5	0
Picciolo, Rob, Oak.	.226	78	93	16	21	28	1	0	2	7	3	0	1	3	.301	2	0	2	13	2
Pinella, Lou, N.Y.	.314	130	472	67	148	210	34	5	6	69	4	1	3	1	.445	34	8	2	36	12

Player	AVG	G	AB	R	H	TB	2B	3B	HR	RBI	SH	SF	HP	SB	SLG	BB	IBB	SO	DP
Poquette, Tom, K.C.*	.216	80	204	16	44	69	9	2	4	30	2	6	2	0	.338	14	1	9	6
Porter, Darrell, K.C.*	.265	150	520	77	138	231	27	6	18	78	1	7	4	2	.444	75	14	75	13
Powell, Hosken, Minn.*	.247	121	381	55	94	127	20	3	2	17	11	1	3	7	.333	45	2	31	5
Pruitt, Ron, Clev.	.235	71	187	17	44	70	6	1	2	17	3	2	2	3	.374	16	3	11	3
Pryor, Greg, Chgo.	.261	82	222	27	58	75	11	0	2	15	4	1	1	1	.338	11	0	18	0
Putnam, Pat, Tex.*	.152	20	29	4	7	11	1	0	1	2	0	0	0	0	.239	2	1	5	0
Quirk, Jamie, K.C.*	.207	17	29	3	6	8	2	0	0	2	0	0	0	0	.276	4	0	4	0
Ramos, Domingo, N.Y.	.000	1	0	0	0	0	0	0	0	0	0	0	0	0	.000	0	0	0	0
Randall, Bob, Minn.	.270	119	330	36	89	106	11	3	0	21	13	2	4	6	.321	24	1	22	7
Randolph, Willie, N.Y.	.279	134	499	87	139	178	18	6	5	42	4	1	4	36	.357	95	1	51	12
Remy, Jerry, Bos.*	.278	148	583	87	162	204	24	6	2	44	14	4	2	14	.350	40	0	55	13
Rettenmund, Merv, Calif.	.269	50	108	16	29	39	5	1	1	14	1	0	0	4	.361	30	1	13	3
Revering, Dave, Oak.*	.271	152	521	48	141	216	21	3	16	46	2	4	1	4	.415	26	5	55	12
Reynolds, Craig, Sea.*	.301	148	548	87	162	205	16	7	5	44	11	6	0	9	.374	36	6	41	4
Rice, Jim, Bos.	.315	163	677	121	213	406	25	15	46	139	0	5	5	7	.600	58	7	126	15
Rivera, Bombo, Minn.	.271	101	251	35	68	89	8	2	3	23	5	3	1	5	.355	35	1	47	3
Rivers, Mickey, N.Y.*	.301	134	472	78	142	243	25	5	11	48	7	6	2	8	.515	41	2	51	8
Roberts, Leon, Sea.	.301	141	559	78	148	222	25	8	22	92	4	6	3	17	.397	29	3	52	7
Robertson, Bob, Sea.	.230	64	174	17	40	73	5	2	8	28	0	0	1	0	.420	24	9	39	6
Robinson, Bruce, Oak.*	.250	28	84	5	21	26	3	1	0	8	1	0	0	0	.310	3	1	8	2
Rodriguez, Aurelio, Det.	.265	134	385	40	102	152	15	2	7	43	7	2	0	1	.395	19	0	37	9
Roenicke, Gary, Balt.	.259	133	387	58	127	207	27	3	25	79	3	6	2	8	.466	82	4	83	10
Rudi, Joe, Calif.	.256	133	497	58	127	207	15	2	17	79	0	6	1	3	.416	28	4	43	11
Sakata, Lenn, Milw.	.192	30	78	15	15	19	2	1	0	7	1	0	0	4	.244	8	0	11	0
Sample, Bill, Tex.	.467	8	15	7	7	9	2	0	0	2	0	0	0	0	.600	2	0	0	0
Schueler, Ron, Chgo.	.000	31	0	0	0	0	0	0	0	0	0	0	0	0	.000	0	0	0	0
Scott, George, Bos.	.233	120	412	51	96	156	16	1	12	54	7	3	1	1	.379	44	3	86	19
Sherrill, Dennis, N.Y.	.000	8	11	1	0	0	0	0	0	0	0	0	0	0	.000	0	0	3	0
Silverio, Luis, K.C.	.545	11	11	7	6	10	2	1	0	3	0	0	0	3	.909	0	0	3	0
Singleton, Ken, Balt.†	.293	149	502	67	147	232	21	1	20	81	0	3	2	2	.462	97	14	94	14
Skaggs, Dave, Balt.	.151	36	86	6	13	16	1	0	0	3	2	3	0	0	.186	9	1	9	1
Smalley, Roy, Minn.†	.273	158	586	80	160	254	31	3	19	77	1	7	2	3	.433	85	3	70	16
Smith, Billy, Balt.†	.260	85	250	29	65	96	12	3	1	20	7	0	3	7	.384	27	1	40	2
Soderholm, Eric, Chgo.	.258	143	457	57	118	197	17	1	20	67	3	7	0	2	.431	39	3	44	13
Solaita, Tony, Calif.*	.223	60	94	10	21	27	3	0	1	14	0	0	0	0	.287	16	3	25	5
Speed, Horace, Clev.	.226	70	106	13	24	30	4	1	0	4	3	1	0	3	.283	14	1	31	1
Spencer, Tom, Chgo.	.185	29	65	3	12	13	1	0	0	1	2	0	0	2	.200	2	0	15	0
Spencer, Jim, N.Y.*	.227	71	150	12	34	66	7	1	7	24	0	1	0	0	.440	15	2	32	4
Spikes, Charlie, Det.	.250	10	28	1	7	8	1	0	0	2	0	0	0	0	.286	2	0	6	0
Squires, Mike, Chgo.*	.280	46	150	25	42	55	9	2	0	16	2	3	0	1	.367	16	0	21	1

*Bats Lefthanded †Switch Hitter

Batter	PCT	G	AB	R	H	TB	2B	3B	HR	RBI	SH	SF	SB	CS	SLG PCT	TBB	IBB	HP	SO	GI DP
Staggs, Steve, Oak.	.244	47	78	10	19	25	2	0	0	9	0	0	2	3	.321	19	0	0	17	0
Stanley, Mickey, Det.	.265	53	151	15	40	58	9	0	3	8	4	0	1	0	.384	9	0	0	19	3
Stanley, Fred, N.Y.	.219	80	160	14	35	45	7	0	1	9	4	1	0	0	.281	25	1	0	31	3
Stanton, Lee, Sea.	.182	93	302	24	55	75	11	0	3	24	3	2	1	0	.248	34	1	1	80	6
Staub, Rusty, Det.*	.273	162	642	75	175	279	30	1	24	121	0	11	0	0	.435	76	5	3	35	24
Stegman, Dave, Det.	.286	8	14	3	4	9	2	0	0	3	1	1	0	0	.643	1	0	0	2	1
Stein, Bill, Sea.	.261	114	403	41	105	149	24	4	4	37	2	2	2	1	.370	37	1	0	56	10
Stinson, Bob, Sea.†	.258	124	364	46	94	147	14	3	11	55	4	4	2	1	.404	45	6	3	42	10
Sundberg, Jim, Tex.	.278	149	518	54	144	197	23	6	6	58	4	4	2	5	.380	64	6	3	70	18
Tabb, Jerry, Oak.*	.111	12	9	0	1	1	0	0	0	0	0	0	0	0	.111	2	0	0	5	0
Terrell, Jerry, K.C.	.203	73	133	14	27	28	1	0	0	8	9	0	8	4	.211	4	0	0	13	6
Thomas, Gorman, Milw.	.246	137	452	70	111	233	24	1	32	86	6	3	4	3	.515	73	2	2	133	6
Thomasson, Gary, 47-Oak, 53-N.Y.*	.233	100	270	37	63	99	8	2	8	36	2	1	4	3	.367	28	4	2	66	3
Thompson, Jason, Det.*	.287	153	589	79	169	278	25	3	26	96	0	5	0	0	.472	74	11	0	96	11
Thompson, Bobby, Tex.†	.225	64	120	23	27	42	3	3	2	12	2	1	8	4	.350	9	0	4	26	0
Thornton, Andre, Clev.	.262	145	508	97	133	262	22	4	33	105	2	8	4	7	.516	93	4	6	72	17
Torres, Rusty, Chgo.†	.318	16	44	7	14	26	3	0	3	6	1	0	0	1	.591	6	0	0	9	0
Trammell, Alan, Det.	.268	139	448	49	120	152	14	6	2	34	6	3	3	1	.339	45	0	2	56	12
Upshaw, Willie, Tor.*	.237	95	224	26	53	68	8	2	1	17	2	3	6	6	.304	21	1	0	35	4
Vail, Mike, Clev.	.235	14	34	2	8	12	2	1	0	2	0	1	0	0	.353	1	0	1	9	0
Velez, Otto, Tor.	.266	91	248	29	66	111	14	2	9	38	3	3	2	1	.448	45	1	2	41	8
Veryzer, Tom, Clev.	.271	130	421	48	114	143	18	4	1	32	15	4	1	0	.340	13	0	5	36	7
Wagner, Mark, Det.	.239	39	109	10	26	31	5	0	0	6	4	0	0	0	.284	6	0	0	11	3
Wallis, Joe, Oak.†	.237	85	279	28	66	102	16	1	6	26	4	3	1	6	.366	26	1	1	42	3
Washington, Claudell, 12-Tex, 86-Chgo.*	.253	98	356	34	90	134	16	5	5	33	2	4	4	2	.376	13	2	1	69	8
Washington, U.L., K.C.†	.264	69	129	13	34	38	2	1	0	9	2	1	12	6	.295	10	0	0	20	2
Washington, LaRue, Tex.	.000	3	3	0	0	0	0	0	0	0	0	0	0	0	.000	0	0	0	1	0
Wathan, John, K.C.	.300	67	190	19	57	75	10	1	2	28	3	3	0	0	.395	12	1	0	12	5
Whitaker, Lou, Det.*	.285	139	484	71	138	173	12	7	3	58	13	8	7	7	.357	61	0	1	65	9
White, Frank, K.C.	.275	143	461	66	127	184	24	6	7	50	9	2	13	10	.399	26	2	4	59	9
White, Roy, N.Y.†	.269	103	346	44	93	136	13	3	8	43	2	3	10	4	.393	42	7	0	35	9
Whitt, Ernie, Tor.*	.000	3	4	0	0	0	0	0	0	0	0	0	0	0	.000	0	0	0	1	0
Wilfong, Rob, Minn.*	.266	92	199	23	53	64	8	1	1	11	15	0	2	1	.322	19	1	1	27	1
Wills, Bump, Tex.†	.250	157	539	78	135	187	17	4	9	57	9	4	52	14	.347	63	3	4	91	11
Wilson, Willie, K.C.†	.217	127	198	43	43	55	8	2	0	16	5	1	46	12	.278	16	0	2	33	2
Wockenfuss, John, Det.	.283	71	187	23	53	79	5	0	7	22	1	1	0	0	.422	21	0	1	14	7
Wohlford, Jim, Milw.	.269	46	118	16	35	49	7	1	2	19	1	2	3	2	.415	6	0	0	10	2
Wolfe, Larry, Minn.	.234	88	235	25	55	76	10	1	3	25	3	3	0	1	.323	36	0	0	27	8

Woodard, Darrell, Oak.	.000	33	9	10	0	0	0	0	0	0	3	4	.000	1	0	0	1	0	0
Woods, Al, Tor.*	.241	62	220	19	53	80	12	3	3	25	5	2	1	2	.364	11	1	23	5
Woods, Gary, Tor.	.158	8	19	2	3	4	1	0	0	3	0	1	0	1	.211	1	0	1	0
Wynegar, Butch, Minn.†	.229	135	454	36	104	140	22	1	4	45	11	4	1	8	.308	47	2	6	42	7
Yastrzemski, Carl, Bos.*	.277	144	523	70	145	221	21	2	17	81	1	4	5	.423	76	8	3	44	9
Yount, Robin, Milw.	.293	127	502	66	147	215	23	9	9	71	13	16	6	.428	24	1	0	43	5
Yurak, Jeff, Milw.†	.000	5	5	0	0	0	0	0	0	0	0	0	0	0	.000	1	0	0	0
Zdeb, Joe, K.C.	.252	60	127	18	32	40	2	3	0	11	0	5	2	0	.315	7	0	0	18	2
Zaber, George, N.Y.†	.000	3	6	0	0	0	0	0	0	0	0	0	2	0	.000	0	0	0	2	0
Zisk, Richie, Tex.	.262	140	511	68	134	221	19	1	22	85	4	5	3	.432	58	7	3	76	14

AWARDED FIRST BASE ON INTERFERENCE—Stinson, Sea., 6 (C. Moore 2, Diaz, Fisk, Foley, Wynegar); G. Adams, Minn., 3 (Kusnyer 2, Nahorodny); Lopez, Balt., 2 (Milner, C. Moore); Alexander, Clev. (Dempsey); Dade, Clev. (Heath); Rup. Jones, Sea. (Wynegar); D. Meyer, Sea. (Fisk); Munson, N.Y. (Dempsey); Soderholm, Chgo. (Fisk).

TOP FIFTEEN QUALIFIERS FOR EARNED RUN LEADERSHIP

Pitcher and Club	ERA	W	L	PCT	G	GS	CG	GF	SV	SHO	IP	H	BFP	R	ER	HR	SH	SF	TBB	IBB	HP	SO	WP	BK
Guidry, Ron, N.Y.*	1.74	25	3	.893	35	35	16	0	0	9	274	187	1057	61	53	13	13	2	72	1	1	248	7	1
Matlock, Jon, Tex.*	2.30	15	13	.536	35	33	18	2		2	270	252	1097	93	69	14	12	3	51	4	4	157	7	0
Caldwell, Mike, Milw.*	2.37	22	9	.710	37	34	23	1		1	293	258	1176	90	77	14	7	6	54	1	1	131	8	1
Palmer, Jim, Balt.	2.46	21	12	.636	38	38	19	0		0	296	246	1197	94	81	19	10	4	97	1	1	138	5	1
Goltz, Dave, Minn.	2.50	15	10	.600	29	29	13	0		0	220	209	913	72	61	12	10	8	67	1	1	116	4	1
Gura, Larry, K.C.*	2.72	16	4	.800	35	26	8	1	0		222	183	890	73	67	13	18	9	60	3	4	81	1	1
Figueroa, Ed, N.Y.	2.99	20	9	.690	35	35	12	2	0		253	233	1038	96	84	22	13	6	77	4	3	92	6	1
Eckersley, Dennis, Bos.	2.99	20	8	.714	35	35	16	0	0		268	258	1121	99	89	30	7	8	71	8	7	162	3	0
Zahn, Geoff, Minn.*	3.04	14	14	.500	35	35	12	0	0		252	260	1056	101	85	18	13	9	81	2	4	106	5	0
Jenkins, Ferguson, Tex.	3.04	18	8	.692	34	30	16	3	0		249	228	990	92	84	21	10	4	41	2	2	157	2	1
Gale, Rich, K.C.	3.09	14	8	.636	31	30	9	0	0		192	171	821	78	66	10	12	4	100	1	3	88	5	0
Rozema, Dave, Det.	3.14	9	12	.429	28	28	11	0	1		209	205	848	83	73	17	12	4	41	1	2	57	3	0
Sorensen, Larry, Milw.	3.20	18	12	.600	37	36	17	1	1		281	277	1150	111	100	14	11	13	50	4	5	78	3	2
Waits, Rick, Clev.*	3.21	13	15	.464	34	33	15	1	0		230	206	957	97	82	16	6	3	86	0	2	97	10	0
Keough, Matt, Oak.	3.24	8	15	.348	32	32	6	0	0		197	178	838	90	71	9	7	3	85	2	4	108	12	3

*Throws Lefthanded

INDIVIDUAL PITCHING
(All Pitchers Listed Alphabetically)

*Throws Lefthanded

Pitcher and Club	ERA	W	L	PCT	G	GS	CG	GF	SV	SHO	IP	H	BFP	R	ER	HR	SH	SF	TBB	IBB	HP	SO	WP	BK
Aase, Don, Calif.	4.02	11	8	.579	29	29	6	0	0	1	179	185	773	88	80	14	5	1	80	4	5	93	3	0
Abbott, Glenn, Sea.	5.28	7	15	.318	29	25	8	0	0	0	155	191	689	99	91	22	4	0	44	5	1	67	4	0
Alexander, Doyle, Tex.	3.86	9	10	.474	31	28	7	3	0	0	191	198	822	84	82	18	10	8	71	1	1	81	4	0
Arroyo, Fernando, Det.	9.00	0	0	.000	2	0	0	1	0	0	4	8	21	4	4	0	1	0	1	0	0	1	1	0
Augustine, Jerry, Milw.*	4.55	13	12	.520	35	30	9	2	0	2	188	204	810	100	95	14	8	4	61	2	2	59	2	2
Baker, Steve, Det.	4.57	2	4	.333	15	10	0	1	0	0	63	66	289	37	32	6	4	4	42	0	0	39	6	0
Barker, Len, Tex.	4.85	1	5	.167	29	10	0	15	4	0	52	63	243	31	28	6	5	0	29	2	0	33	6	0
Barlow, Mike, Calif.	4.50	0	0	.000	1	0	0	0	0	0	2	3	8	1	1	0	0	0	1	0	0	1	0	0
Barrios, Francisco, Chgo.	4.04	9	15	.375	33	32	9	1	0	2	196	180	843	93	88	13	11	9	85	2	7	79	3	1
Baumgarten, Ross, Chgo.*	5.87	2	2	.500	7	4	1	2	0	0	23	29	106	15	15	3	2	2	23	0	2	15	1	0
Beattie, Jim, N.Y.	3.73	6	9	.400	25	22	2	3	0	0	128	123	553	60	53	8	9	3	51	2	8	65	8	1
Billingham, Jack, Det.	3.88	15	8	.652	30	30	10	0	0	4	202	218	857	95	87	16	4	12	65	5	2	48	9	2
Bird, Doug, K.C.	5.27	6	6	.500	40	6	0	13	1	0	99	110	434	63	58	8	8	0	52	5	2	48	9	2
Bomback, Mark, Milw.	13.50	0	0	.000	2	1	0	0	0	0	2	5	11	3	3	1	0	0	3	0	1	1	0	0
Brett, Ken, Calif.*	4.95	3	5	.375	31	10	1	7	1	1	100	100	428	60	55	12	1	4	42	5	1	43	1	2
Briles, Nelson, Balt.	4.67	4	4	.500	16	8	1	4	0	0	54	58	236	31	28	6	1	2	21	2	3	30	2	0
Broberg, Pete, Oak.	4.61	10	12	.455	35	26	4	2	0	1	166	174	728	101	85	16	9	6	66	4	0	94	1	0
Brown, Tom, Sea.	4.15	0	0	.000	6	0	0	2	0	0	13	14	53	6	6	2	0	0	4	0	0	8	0	0
Burgmeier, Tom, Bos.*	4.43	2	1	.667	35	1	0	13	4	0	61	74	276	33	30	7	4	1	23	7	1	24	0	0
Burke, Steve, Sea.	3.49	0	0	.000	2	0	0	2	0	0	5	6	22	2	2	0	1	0	3	0	0	3	0	0
Burns, Britt, Chgo.*	12.38	0	0	.000	2	0	0	1	0	0	4	8	20	6	6	2	0	1	2	0	0	2	0	0
Burnside, Sheldon, Det.*	9.00	0	0	.000	8	0	0	6	1	0	13	14	59	14	13	3	1	0	5	0	1	7	0	0
Busby, Steve, K.C.	7.71	0	1	.000	5	5	0	0	0	0	21	24	104	18	18	2	1	2	15	4	1	10	0	0
Buskey, Tom, Tor.	3.46	7	5	.583	37	1	0	34	7	0	54	62	226	25	22	5	4	3	17	2	0	47	1	0
Caldwell, Mike, Milw.*	2.37	22	9	.710	37	34	23	1	1	6	293	258	1176	90	77	14	7	16	54	3	7	131	8	1
Campbell, Bill, Bos.	3.88	7	5	.583	29	0	0	19	4	0	51	43	211	25	22	6	2	0	14	6	1	38	3	0
Caneira, John, Calif.	6.75	0	2	.000	8	6	0	2	0	0	32	43	211	26	24	6	6	0	17	1	0	17	0	0
Castro, Bill, Milw.	1.80	5	4	.555	42	0	0	35	8	0	50	43	211	14	10	2	5	2	14	10	0	17	2	0
Clancy, Jim, Tor.	4.08	10	12	.455	31	30	7	0	0	0	194	199	846	96	88	10	8	10	91	1	5	106	10	0
Clay, Ken, N.Y.	4.26	3	4	.429	28	6	0	13	3	0	76	89	336	41	36	3	5	2	23	6	3	32	4	0
Cleveland, Reggie, 1-Bos, 53-Tex.	3.08	5	8	.385	54	1	0	41	12	0	76	66	318	34	26	5	7	7	23	6	3	46	2	0
Clyde, David, Clev.*	4.29	8	11	.421	28	25	5	1	0	0	153	166	670	80	73	4	7	8	60	3	0	83	11	1
Colborn, Jim, 8-K.C., 20-Sea.	5.26	4	12	.250	28	22	3	1	0	0	142	156	630	95	83	25	10	4	50	3	1	34	2	1
Coleman, Joe, 10-Oak, 31-Tor.	3.78	2	8	.200	41	0	0	26	2	0	81	79	344	37	34	7	4	3	34	3	1	32	5	0
Comer, Steve, Tex.	2.31	11	5	.688	30	11	3	14	1	2	117	107	479	36	30	5	9	3	37	3	1	65	2	0
Conroy, Tim, Oak.*	7.20	0	2	.000	2	2	0	0	0	0	5	3	28	6	4	0	3	0	9	0	0	3	1	0
Crawford, Jim, Det.*	4.38	2	3	.400	20	0	0	10	0	0	39	45	180	24	19	3	2	3	19	3	2	24	7	0

Pitcher	ERA	W	L	PCT	IP	SO
Cruz, Victor, Tor.	1.72	7	3	.700	47	51
Darwin, Danny, Tex.	4.00	1	0	1.000	28	8
Davis, Ron, N.Y.	13.50	0	0		3	3
Drago, Dick, Bos.	3.04	4	4	.500	77	42
Eastwick, Rawly, N.Y.	3.24	2	1	.667	22	13
Eckersley, Dennis, Bos.	2.99	20	8	.714	268	162
Ellis, Dock, Tex.	4.21	9	7	.563	131	45
Erickson, Roger, Minn.	3.96	14	13	.519	266	121
Farmer, Ed, Milw.	0.82	2	0	1.000	11	6
Fidrych, Mark, Det.	2.45	2	0	1.000	22	10
Figueroa, Ed, N.Y.	2.99	20	9	.690	253	92
Fitzmorris, Al, 7-Clev. 9-Calif.	3.13	1	1	.500	46	13
Flanagan, Mike, Balt.	4.04	19	15	.559	281	167
Flinn, John, Balt.	7.88	1	0	1.000	16	8
Ford, Dave, Balt.	0.00	1	1	.500	15	8
Foucault, Steve, 24-Det. 3-K.C.	3.46	1	4	.200	44	19
Freisleben, Dave, Clev.	7.16				39	18
Frost, Dave, Calif.	2.59	1	0	1.000	71	30
Gale, Rich, K.C.	3.09	14	8	.636	192	88
Garland, Wayne, Clev.	7.80				30	13
Garvin, Jerry, Tor.	5.65	4	12	.250	145	67
Glynn, Ed, Det.	3.00	0	0			4
Goltz, Dave, Minn.	2.50	15	10	.600	220	116
Gossage, Rich, N.Y.	2.01	10	11	.476	134	122
Griffin, Tom, Calif.	4.02	3	4	.429	56	35
Guidry, Ron, N.Y.*	1.74	25	3	.893	274	248
Gullett, Don, N.Y.*	3.60	4	2	.667	45	28
Gura, Larry, K.C.*	2.72	16	4	.800	222	81
Haas, Moose, Milw.	6.10	2	3	.400	31	32
Harlow, Larry, Balt.*	45.00	0	0	.000	2	0
Harrison, Roric, Minn.	7.50	0	1	.000	12	7
Hartzell, Paul, Calif.	3.44	6	10	.375	157	55
Hassler, Andy, 11-K.C. 13-Bos.*	3.89			.375	168	49
Heaverlo, David, Oak.	3.25	3	6	.333	130	71
Hendricks, Elrod, Balt.	0.00	0	0		2	0
Hiller, John, Det.*	2.35	9	4	.692	81	74
Hinton, Rich, Chgo.	4.00	2	6	.250		
Holly, Jeff, Minn.*	3.60			.500		48
Holtzman, Ken, N.Y.*	4.00	1	0	1.000	35	12
Honeycutt, Rick, Sea.*	4.90	5	11	.313	134	50
Hood, Don, Clev.*	4.47	5	6	.455	155	73
House, Tom, Sea.*	4.66	5	4	.556	116	29

*Throws Lefthanded

Pitcher and Club	ERA	W	L	PCT	G	GS	CG	GF	SV	SHO	IP	H	BFP	R	ER	HR	SH	SF	TBB	IBB	HP	SO	WP	BK
Hrabosky, Al, K.C.*	2.88	8	7	.533	58	0	0	47	20	0	75	52	308	24	24	6	5	7	35		2	60	2	1
Hunter, Catfish, N.Y.	3.58	12	6	.667	21	20	5	1	0	1	118	98	477	49	47	16	4	4	35	1	0	56	2	1
Jackson, Darrell, Minn.*	4.50	4	6	.400	19	15	1	1	0	0	92	89	404	46	45	9	4	3	48	2	1	54	3	4
Jefferson, Jesse, Tor.	4.37	7	16	.304	31	30	8	0	0	0	212	214	907	109	103	28	9	6	86	5	3	97	4	1
Jenkins, Ferguson, Tex.	3.04	18	8	.692	34	30	16	3	0	4	249	228	990	92	84	21	10	6	41	2	3	157	2	1
Johnson, Tom, Minn.	5.45	1	4	.200	18	0	0	14	3	0	33	42	155	22	20	2	2	2	17	4	0	21	2	1
Johnson, Dave, Minn.	7.50	0	2	.000	12					0	12	15	58	11	10	1			9	0		7	3	0
Johnson, John, Oak.*	3.39	11	10	.524	33	30	7	1	0	0	186	164	789	81	70	18	13	5	82	6	0	91	5	5
Jones, Rick, Sea.*	6.00	0	0	.000	3	2	0	0	0	0	12	17	61	8	8				9		0	11	0	0
Kammeyer, Bob, N.Y.	5.73	0	0	.000	7	0	0	6	0	0	22	24	98	15	14	1	0	0	6	0	2	11	0	0
Keough, Matt, Oak.	3.24	8	15	.348	32	32	8	0	0	3	197	178	838	90	71	9	7	3	85	2	3	108	12	3
Kern, Jim, Clev.	3.09	10	10	.500	58	0	0	43	13	0	99	77	423	36	34	4	15	4	58	5	2	95	5	5
Kerrigan, Joe, Balt.	4.75	3	1	.750	26	0	0	16	3	0	72	75	319	44	38	10	6	5	36	5	1	41	4	0
Kinney, Dennis, Clev.*	4.35	0	2	.000	18	0	0	12	5	0	39	37	164	21	19	3	2	4	14	1	1	19	1	0
Kirkwood, Don, Tor.	4.24	4	5	.444	16	9	2	3	0	0	68	76	293	36	32	6	3	2	25	1	0	29	3	0
Knapp, Chris, Calif.	4.21	14	8	.636	30	29	6	1	0	1	188	178	797	94	88	25	9	6	67	6	1	126	3	1
Kravec, Ken, Chgo.*	4.08	11	16	.407	30	30	7	0	0	2	203	188	890	104	92	22	14	4	95	1	10	154	7	1
Kreuger, Rick, Clev.*	4.00	0	0	.000	6	0	0	2	0	0	9	6	38	4	4	1			3		0	7	1	0
Kucek, Jack, Chgo.	3.29	2	3	.400	10	5	1	3	0	0	52	42	223	23	19	5	4	1	27	2	0	30	1	0
Lacey, Bob, Oak.*	3.00	8	9	.471	74	0	0	41	16	0	120	126	514	52	40	10	9	3	35	13	1	60	3	0
LaGrow, Lerrin, Chgo.	4.40	6	5	.545	62	0	0	41	16	0	88	85	374	47	43	9	3	9	38	8	3	42	1	0
Langford, Rick, Oak.	3.43	7	13	.350	37	24	4	5	0	0	176	169	740	77	67	15	7	7	56	8	3	92	2	2
LaRoche, Dave, Calif.*	2.81	10	9	.526	59	0	0	46	25	0	96	73	403	35	30	7	12	2	48	11	2	70	0	0
LaRose, John, Bos.*	22.50	0	0	.000	1	0	0	0	0	0	2	3	11	5	5	1	0	0	0	0	0	0	0	0
Lee, Bill, Bos.*	3.46	10	10	.500	28	24	8	3	0	1	177	198	768	89	68	20	6	7	59	2	4	44	0	0
Lemanczyk, Dave, Tor.	6.24	4	14	.222	29	29	3	0	5	0	137	170	620	97	95	16	6	0	65	7	9	62	6	1
Leonard, Dennis, K.C.	3.33	21	17	.553	40	40	20	0	0	2	295	283	1218	125	109	27	11	6	78	7	9	183	12	0
Lindblad, Paul, 18-Tex.-7-N.Y.*	3.88	1	1	.500	25	1	0	12	2	0	58	62	254	28	25	6	6	2	23	7	3	34	3	0
Lyle, Sparky, N.Y.*	3.46	9	3	.750	59	0	0	51	21	0	112	116	470	46	43	6	9	7	33	8	4	33	1	0
Marshall, Mike, Minn.	2.45	10	12	.455	54	0	0	42	16	0	99	80	404	31	27	3	10	2	37	1	1	56	2	0
Martinez, Tippy, Balt.*	4.83	3	3	.500	42	0	0	16	5	0	69	77	318	41	37	4	2	2	40	2	1	57	6	0
Martinez, Dennis, Balt.	3.52	16	11	.593	40	38	15	0	0	2	276	257	1140	121	108	20	8	7	93	4	3	142	6	1
Matlack, Jon, Tex.*	2.30	15	13	.536	35	33	18	2	0	1	270	252	1097	93	69	14	12	0	51	4	4	157	7	1
McCall, Larry, N.Y.	5.63	0	0	.000	3	1	0	0	0	0	16	20	71	10	10	2	0	0	6	1	0	10	1	0
McCatty, Steve, Oak.	4.50	2	2	.500	8					0	20	26	98	14	10	0			9		0	10	1	0
McClure, Bob, Milw.*	3.74	2	6	.250	44	0	0	29	9	0	65	53	283	30	27	8	7	1	30	4	6	47	1	0
McGiberry, Randy, K.C.	4.15	0	1	.000	2	1	0	0	0	0	26	27	120	16	12	2	4	0	18	1	0	12	0	3
McGregor, Scott, Balt.*	3.32	15	13	.536	35	32	13	2	1	2	233	217	936	98	86	19	9	5	39	3	1	94	3	3
McLaughlin, Byron, Sea.	4.37	4	8	.333	20	17	4	1	0	0	107	97	457	58	52	15	2	3	39	0	6	87	4	4

Pitcher	ERA	W	L	PCT	G	GS	CG	IP	BFP	H	R	ER	HR	BB	SO	ShO	SV
Medich, George, Tex.	3.68	9	8	.529	28	22	6	171	717	166	78	70	10	52	71	3	0
Messersmith, Andy, N.Y.	5.37	0	6	.000	6	6	0	22	106	24	21	14	7	15	16	0	0
Miller, Dyar, Calif.	2.65	6	2	.750	41	0	0	85	374	85	29	25	5	41	34	0	5
Minetto, Craig, Oak.	3.75	0	2	.000	4	1	0	12	55	13	10	5	1	7	1	0	0
Mingori, Steve, K.C.	2.74	1	4	.200	45	0	0	69	289	64	25	21	2	16	28	0	7
Mirabella, Paul, Tex.*	5.79	4	7	.364	29	17	0	28	125	30	18	18	2	79	23	0	0
Mitchell, Paul, Sea.	4.23	8	6	.571	48	29	4	168	735	173	86	79	21	51	75	0	0
Monge, Sid, Clev.*	2.75	1	3	.250	48	1	0	85	374	71	36	26	4	54	54	0	0
Montague, John, Sea.	6.14	2	3	.400	37	0	0	44	198	52	31	30	3	14	14	0	2
Moore, Balor, Tor.*	4.94	0	1	.000	7	1	0	15	60	19	8	8	1	7	3	0	0
Moret, Roger, Tex.*	4.80	0	3	.000	7	2	0	12	60	12	10	9	2	9	7	0	0
Morgan, Michael, Oak.	7.50	3	5	.375	28	5	0	107	469	107	51	51	8	49	48	0	0
Morris, Jack, Det.	4.33	0	7	.000	50	0	0	16	61	16	11	9	0	5	6	0	0
Mueller, Willie, Milw.	6.23	1	0	1.000	14	0	0	49	396	46	43	30	8	37	35	0	0
Murphy, Tom, Tor.	3.93	6	9	.400	50	0	0	94	396	87	46	41	11	35	36	0	10
Norris, Mike, Oak.	5.51	0	5	.000	27	14	0	6	230	49	34	30	10	97	138	0	0
Palmer, Jim, Balt.	2.46	21	12	.636	38	38	19	296	1197	246	94	81	19	97	138	3	0
Parrott, Mike, Sea.	5.16	1	5	.167	27	18	2	108	389	82	59	47	8	41	41	0	0
Paschall, Bill, K.C.	3.38	0	1	.000	7	0	0	3	31	3	3	1	0	3	1	0	0
Pattin, Marty, K.C.	3.30	3	3	.500	32	12	0	79	326	72	41	29	8	25	30	0	6
Paxton, Mike, Clev.	3.86	12	11	.522	33	27	5	191	807	179	89	82	13	63	96	0	0
Perzanowski, Stan, Minn	5.21	2	7	.222	13	4	1	57	252	59	33	33	6	26	31	0	0
Pole, Dick, Sea.	6.45	5	5	.267	14	11	1	99	451	122	82	71	16	41	41	0	0
Proly, Mike, Chgo.	2.73	5	2	.714	52	0	0	66	266	63	24	20	4	12	19	0	0
Rajsich, Dave, N.Y.*	4.15	0	1	.000	3	0	0	13	58	16	6	6	0	9	9	0	0
Rawley, Shane, Sea.	4.14	4	9	.308	32	2	0	111	483	114	57	51	5	66	51	0	4
Redfern, Pete, Minn.	6.30	0	2	.000	18	0	0	10	44	12	7	7	2	8	7	0	0
Renko, Steve, Oak.	4.29	6	12	.333	38	25	6	151	660	152	77	72	10	67	89	4	0
Replogle, Andy, Milw.	3.99	9	5	.643	32	18	6	149	642	177	75	66	14	47	41	3	1
Reuschel, Paul, Clev.	3.10	5	5	.333	56	0	0	90	381	95	33	31	5	22	24	1	4
Ripley, Allen, Bos.	5.55	2	5	.286	11	8	0	73	326	92	49	45	10	22	26	0	0
Rodriguez, Ed, Milw.	3.94	11	11	.500	56	0	0	105	448	105	49	46	7	51	51	0	9
Romo, Enrique, Sea.	3.70	11	7	.611	28	0	0	107	445	88	44	44	12	62	62	0	5
Rozema, Dave, Det.	3.14	9	12	.429	28	28	11	209	848	205	83	73	12	39	41	2	7
Ryan, Nolan, Calif.	3.71	10	13	.435	31	31	14	234	1008	183	106	97	11	148	260	3	0
Scarce, Mac, Minn.*	3.94	1	1	.500	17	0	0	32	143	35	19	14	3	15	17	0	2
Schueler, Ron, Chgo.	4.28	3	5	.375	30	7	0	82	361	76	50	39	9	39	44	0	4
Serum, Gary, Minn.	4.11	5	5	.500	34	11	2	184	774	188	84	84	14	44	80	3	0
Slaton, Jim, Det.	4.12	17	11	.607	35	34	11	234	1003	235	117	107	11	85	78	1	3
Sorensen, Lary, Milw.	3.20	18	12	.600	37	36	17	281	1150	277	111	100	13	50	78	5	2
Sosa, Elias, Oak.	2.64	8	2	.800	68	0	0	109	461	106	37	32	6	44	61	1	14
Spillner, Dan, Clev.	3.70	3	1	.750	36	0	0	56	241	54	26	23	0	21	48	0	1

*Throws Lefthanded

Pitcher and Club	ERA	W	L	PCT	G	GS	CG	GF	SV	SHO	IP	H	BFP	R	ER	HR	SH	SF	TBB	IBB	HP	SO	WP	BK
Splittorff, Paul, K.C.*	3.40	19	13	.594	39	38	13	0	2	2	262	244	1069	113	99	22	11	9	60	2	3	76	3	0
Sprowl, Bobby, Bos.*	6.23	0	2	.000	3	3	0	0	0	0	13	12	59	10	9	3	0	0	10	0	0	10	0	0
Stanhouse, Don, Balt.	2.88	6	9	.400	56	0	0	47	24	0	75	60	326	28	24	9	5	1	52	5	1	42	3	0
Stanley, Bob, Bos.	2.60	15	2	.882	52	3	0	35	10	1	142	142	578	50	41	5	4	6	34	6	4	38	3	0
Stein, Randy, Milw.	5.30	3	2	.600	31	1	0	8	1	0	73	78	329	51	43	3	0	1	39	1	4	42	3	1
Stephenson, Earl, Balt.*	2.70	0	0	.000	10	0	0	4	0	0	10	10	40	4	3	0	0	0	5	0	0	5	0	0
Stewart, Sammy, Balt.	3.27	1	1	.500	2	2	0	0	0	0	11	10	46	5	4	0	0	0	8	0	1	11	1	0
Stoddard, Tim, Balt.	6.00	0	1	.000	8	0	0	3	0	0	18	22	84	17	12	3	1	1	14	2	2	14	2	1
Stone, Steve, Chgo.	4.37	12	12	.500	30	30	6	0	0	0	212	196	898	110	103	19	11	5	84	1	3	118	2	1
Sutton, John, Minn.	3.48	0	0	.000	17	0	0	9	0	0	44	46	191	19	17	3	1	0	18	1	1	18	5	1
Sykes, Bob, Det.*	3.93	6	6	.500	22	10	3	6	2	0	94	99	400	43	41	14	3	2	34	5	1	58	1	1
Tanana, Frank, Calif.*	3.65	18	12	.600	33	33	10	0	0	4	239	239	1014	108	97	26	8	10	60	7	9	137	5	8
Taylor, Bruce, Det.	0.00	0	0	.000	1	0	0	1	0	0	0	0	3	0	0	0	0	0	0	0	0	0	0	1
Thayer, Greg, Minn.	3.80	1	1	.500	20	0	0	12	0	0	45	40	194	19	19	5	1	0	30	1	1	23	0	0
Thormodsgard, Paul, Minn.	5.05	1	4	.200	29	2	0	0	0	0	66	81	286	40	37	7	1	4	17	0	3	23	0	1
Throop, George, K.C.	0.00	1	0	1.000	1	0	0	1	0	0	3	2	13	0	0	0	0	1	0	0	0	0	0	0
Tiant, Luis, Bos.	3.31	13	8	.619	32	31	12	1	5	5	212	185	863	80	78	26	7	7	57	3	5	114	4	0
Tidrow, Dick, N.Y.	3.84	7	11	.389	31	25	4	1	1	1	185	191	787	87	79	13	9	4	53	3	3	73	5	0
Tosik, Dave, Det.	3.75	0	0	.000	5	0	0	4	0	0	12	12	49	5	5	1	0	0	3	0	0	11	0	0
Todd, Jim, Sea.*	4.29	4	2	.429	49	2	0	25	3	0	107	113	471	52	46	4	5	5	61	4	0	37	0	0
Torrealba, Pablo, Chgo.*	4.74	2	4	.333	36	3	1	7	1	0	57	69	275	37	30	6	6	2	39	5	3	23	0	0
Torrez, Mike, Bos.	3.96	16	13	.552	36	36	15	0	0	2	250	272	1091	122	110	19	12	8	99	10	6	120	7	1
Travers, Bill, Milw.*	4.40	12	11	.522	28	28	8	0	0	3	176	184	760	93	86	20	6	4	58	1	6	66	6	0
Trout, Steve, Chgo.*	4.09	3	0	1.000	4	3	1	1	0	0	22	19	97	10	10	3	0	1	11	0	0	11	0	0
Umbarger, Jim, Tex.*	4.87	5	8	.385	32	9	0	11	1	0	98	116	433	58	53	9	3	4	36	4	2	60	2	0
Underwood, Tom, Tor.*	4.09	6	14	.300	31	30	7	0	0	1	198	201	864	105	90	23	8	4	87	4	2	140	7	1
Waits, Rick, Clev.*	3.21	13	15	.464	34	33	15	1	2	1	230	206	957	97	82	16	6	3	86	0	2	97	10	0
Wallace, David, Tor.	3.86	0	0	.000	6	0	0	4	0	0	14	12	62	6	6	1	0	0	7	1	0	7	1	0
Wilcox, Milt, Det.	3.77	13	12	.520	29	27	16	0	0	2	215	208	907	94	90	22	11	0	68	2	8	132	6	0
Willis, Mike, Tor.*	6.00	0	3	.000	3	0	0	1	0	0	3	3	12	0	0	0	0	0	1	0	0	7	0	0
Willoughby, Jim, Chgo.	4.54	3	7	.300	44	2	0	22	7	0	101	104	434	55	51	11	8	1	39	2	6	52	2	1
Wirth, Alan, Oak.	3.87	1	6	.143	19	5	0	1	0	0	93	95	376	41	40	6	6	1	19	2	4	36	1	0
Wise, Rick, Clev.	3.44	5	6	.455	16	14	4	0	0	0	81	72	332	40	31	6	8	0	34	0	3	31	4	1
Wood, Wilbur, Chgo.*	4.33	9	9	.500	31	33	11	0	0	0	212	226	903	116	102	22	8	10	59	3	3	106	1	0
Wortham, Rich, Chgo.*	5.20	10	10	.500	28	27	4	1	0	0	168	187	753	103	97	23	14	7	74	1	9	69	9	0
Wright, Jim, Bos.	3.05	3	2	.600	8	8	2	0	0	0	59	59	248	24	20	1	2	2	23	0	7	25	8	0
Young, Kip, Det.	3.57	8	4	.667	24	16	5	3	0	0	116	122	480	51	46	8	4	3	24	2	7	56	0	0
Zahn, Geoff, Minn.*	3.04	14	14	.500	35	35	12	0	1	1	252	260	1056	101	85	18	13	9	81	2	4	106	7	0

Dennis Eckersley had his first 20-win season.

1978 Official National League Records

(Compiled by Elias Sports Bureau, New York)

STANDINGS AT CLOSE OF SEASON
EASTERN DIVISION

Club	WON	LOST	PCT	GB	PHIL	PITT	CHI	MTL	STL	N Y	L A	CIN	S F	S D	HOU	ATL	EAST W-L	WEST W-L
Philadelphia	90	72	.556	--		11	14	9	10	12	5	5	6	8	6	4	56-34	34-38
Pittsburgh	88	73	.547	1½	11		11	11	9	11	5	7	4	5	8	10	49-41	39-32
Chicago	79	83	.488	11	4	7		7	7	15	11	4	7	6	5	6	44-46	35-37
Montreal	76	86	.469	14	9	7	11		9	8	4	5	6	6	7		44-46	32-40
St. Louis	69	93	.426	21	8	9	3	9		11	7	3	3	5	7		40-50	29-43
New York	66	96	.407	24	6	7	7	10	7		5	5	3	5	6		37-53	29-43

WESTERN DIVISION

Club	WON	LOST	PCT	GB	L A	CIN	S F	S D	HOU	ATL	PHIL	PITT	CHI	MTL	STL	N Y	WEST W-L	EAST W-L
Los Angeles	95	67	.586	--		9	11	9	11	13	7	7	8	8	5	7	53-37	42-30
Cincinnati	92	69	.571	2½	9		12	9	11	12	7	4	5	8	5	7	53-37	39-32
San Francisco	89	73	.549	6	7	6		10	12	7	4	8	7	9	9		42-48	47-25
San Diego	84	78	.519	11	9	9	8		10	4	7	5	6	9	7		46-44	38-34
Houston	74	88	.457	21	7	7	6	8	--	10	4	6	6	7	7		38-52	36-36
Atlanta	69	93	.426	26	5	6	11	8	8		2	5	5	5	5		38-52	31-41

CHAMPIONSHIP SERIES: Los Angeles defeated Philadelphia 3 games to 1

Batting

INDIVIDUAL BATTING LEADERS

Percentage	:	.334	Parker, Pitt.
Games	:	162	Cabell, Hou. & Garvey, L.A.
			(only players in all of team's games)
At Bats	:	660	Cabell, Hou.
Runs	:	104	DeJesus, Chi.
Hits	:	202	Garvey, L.A.
Total Bases	:	340	Parker, Pitt.
Singles	:	153	Bowa, Phil.
Doubles	:	51	Rose, Cin.
Triples	:	13	Templeton, St.L.
Home Runs	:	40	Foster, Cin.
Runs Batted In	:	120	Foster, Cin.
Sacrifice Hits	:	28	Smith, S.D.
Sacrifice Flies	:	13	Smith, L.A.
Stolen Bases	:	71	Moreno, Pitt.
Caught Stealing	:	25	Taveras, Pitt.
Longest Batting Streak	:	44	Rose, Cin. June 14 - July 31

During the 1978 season 429 players participated in regular season games

INDIVIDUAL BATTING
TOP FIFTEEN QUALIFIERS FOR BATTING CHAMPIONSHIP
(*Bats Lefthanded #Switch Hitter)

Player & Club	PCT	G	AB	R	H	TB	2B	3B	HR	RBI	SH	SF	SB	CS
Parker, David, Pitt.*	.334	148	581	102	194	340	32	12	30	117	0	2	20	7
Garvey, Steven, L.A.	.316	162	639	89	202	319	36	9	21	113	1	8	10	5
Cruz, Jose, Hou.*	.315	153	565	79	178	260	34	9	10	83	2	3	37	9
Madlock, Bill, S.F.	.309	122	447	76	138	215	26	3	15	44	9	2	16	9
Winfield, David, S.D.	.308	158	587	88	181	293	30	5	24	97	0	5	21	9
Richards, Eugene, S.D.*	.308	154	555	90	171	233	26	12	4	45	2	4	37	17
Clark, Jack, S.F.	.306	156	592	90	181	318	46	8	25	98	3	9	15	11
Rose, Peter, Cin.#	.302	159	655	103	198	276	51	3	7	52	2	7	13	9
Burroughs, Jeffry, Atl.	.301	153	488	72	147	258	30	6	23	77	0	6	1	3
Concepcion, David, Cin.	.301	153	565	75	170	229	33	4	6	67	3	4	23	10
Cromartie, Warren, Mtl.*	.297	159	607	77	180	254	32	6	10	56	2	6	8	8
Smith, C. Reginald, L.A.#	.295	128	447	82	132	250	27	2	29	93	0	13	12	5
Cabell, Enos, Hou.	.295	162	660	92	195	263	31	8	7	71	3	4	33	15
Bowa, Lawrence, Phil.#	.294	156	654	78	192	242	31	5	3	43	11	2	27	5
Perez, Atanasio, Mtl.	.290	148	544	63	158	244	38	4	14	78	1	5	2	0

ALL PLAYERS LISTED ALPHABETICALLY

Player & Club	PCT	G	AB	R	H	TB	2B	3B	HR	RBI	SH	SF	SB	CS
lexander, Matthew, Pitt.#	----	7	0	2	0	0	0	0	0	0	0	0	4	1
mon, William, S.D.	.252	138	405	39	102	125	19	2	0	21	3	1	17	5
lou, Jesus, Hou.	.324	77	139	7	45	58	5	1	2	19	4	3	0	0
andrews, Robert, S.F.	.220	79	177	21	39	51	3	3	1	11	5	0	5	1
adujar, Joaquin, Hou.#	.130	36	23	0	3	4	1	0	0	3	4	0	0	0
shford, Thomas, S.D.	.245	75	155	11	38	58	11	0	3	26	1	4	1	0
sselstine, Brian, Atl.*	.272	39	103	11	28	43	3	3	2	13	1	5	2	1
ckinson, William, Mtl.*	.500	29	4	0	2	2	0	0	0	1	0	0	0	0
erbach, Frederick, Cin.	.327	63	55	17	18	30	6	0	2	5	2	0	1	0
hnsen, Stanley, Mtl.	.091	44	11	0	1	1	0	0	0	0	1	0	0	0
air, C. Douglas, Cin.	.143	70	14	1	2	2	0	0	0	1	1	0	0	0
aker, Charles, S.D.	.207	44	58	8	12	13	1	0	0	3	6	0	0	0
aker, Johnnie, L'A.	.262	149	522	62	137	196	24	1	11	66	4	3	12	3
aldwin, Reginald, Hou.	.254	38	67	5	17	25	5	0	1	11	0	0	0	0
annister, Floyd, Hou.*	.161	28	31	2	5	6	1	0	0	0	5	0	0	0
arr, James, S.F.	.100	34	50	1	5	5	0	0	0	2	5	0	0	0
zall, Robert, Atl.#	.243	108	185	29	45	56	8	0	1	16	2	1	4	5
elloir, Robert, Atl.	1.000	2	1	0	0	2	1	0	0	0	0	0	0	0
ench, Johnny, Cin.	.260	120	393	52	102	190	17	1	23	73	1	6	4	2
enedict, Bruce, Atl.	.250	22	52	3	13	15	2	0	0	1	0	0	0	0
enton, Alfred, N.Y.	.500	4	4	1	2	2	0	0	0	2	0	0	0	0
erenguer, Juan, N.Y.	.000	5	3	0	0	0	0	0	0	0	0	0	0	0
ergman, David, Hou.*	.231	104	186	15	43	50	5	1	0	12	1	2	2	0
ernard, Dwight, N.Y.	.200	30	5	0	1	1	0	0	0	0	0	0	0	0
erra, Dale, Pitt.	.207	56	135	16	28	48	2	0	6	14	0	1	3	1

Expos' Warren Cromartie finished 11th in NL batting at .297.

Player & Club	PCT	G	AB	R	H	TB	2B	3B	HR	RBI	SH	SF	SB	C
Beswick, James, S.D.#	.050	17	20	2	1	1	0	0	0	0	0	0	0	
Bibby, James, Pitt.	.129	34	31	1	4	7	0	0	1	2	0	0	0	
Blittner, Larry, Chi.*	.257	120	343	32	88	117	15	1	4	50	1	6	0	
Blackwell, Timothy, Chi.#	.223	49	103	8	23	26	3	0	0	7	4	1	0	
Blue, Vida, S.F.#	.076	35	79	8	6	10	1	0	1	2	5	0	0	
Blyleven, Rikalbert, Pitt.	.129	37	85	4	11	13	2	0	0	11	7	0	0	
Bochy, Bruce, Hou.	.266	54	154	8	41	58	8	0	3	15	0	2	0	
Boggs, Thomas, Atl.	.167	16	18	1	3	6	0	0	1	1	1	0	0	
Boisclair, Bruce, N.Y.*	.224	107	214	24	48	69	7	1	4	15	2	5	3	
Boitano, Danny, Phil.	---	4	0	0	0	0	0	0	0	0	0	0	0	
Bonham, William, Cin.	.186	23	43	2	8	11	3	0	0	5	8	0	0	
Bonnell, R. Barry, Atl.	.240	117	304	36	73	93	11	3	1	16	2	0	12	
Boone, Robert, Phil.	.283	132	435	48	123	185	18	4	12	62	5	8	2	
Borbon, Pedro, Cin.	.182	62	11	0	2	2	0	0	0	1	1	0	0	
Bouton, James, Atl.	.000	5	7	0	0	0	0	0	0	0	0	0	0	
Bowa, Lawrence, Phil.#	.294	156	654	78	192	242	31	5	3	43	11	2	27	
Boyland, Dorian, Pitt.*	.250	6	1	2	2	2	0	0	0	1	0	0	0	
Brock, Louis, St.L.*	.221	92	298	31	66	75	9	0	0	12	1	1	17	
Bruhert, Michael, N.Y.	.075	27	40	0	3	3	0	0	0	1	1	1	0	
Bruno, Thomas, St.L.	.083	18	12	0	1	1	0	0	0	0	2	0	0	
Bruestar, Warren, Phil.	.143	38	7	0	1	2	1	0	0	0	0	0	0	
Brye, Stephen, Pitt.	.235	66	115	16	27	37	7	0	1	9	2	1	2	
Buckner, William, Chi.*	.323	117	446	47	144	187	26	1	5	74	1	5	7	
Burke, Glenn, L.A.	.211	16	19	2	4	4	0	0	0	2	0	0	1	
Burris, B. Ray, Chi.	.115	41	61	3	7	12	1	2	0	2	7	0	0	
Burroughs, Jeffrey, Atl.	.301	153	488	72	147	258	30	6	23	77	0	6	1	
Cabell, Enos, Hou.	.295	162	660	92	195	263	31	8	7	71	3	4	33	15
Camp, Rick, Atl.	.000	42	8	1	0	0	0	0	0	0	0	1	0	
Campbell, David, Atl.	---	53	0	0	0	0	0	0	0	0	0	0	0	
Candelaria, John, Pitt.*	.173	31	52	6	9	12	3	0	0	1	7	0	0	
Cannon, Joseph, Hou.*	.222	8	18	1	4	4	0	0	0	1	0	0	1	
Capilla, Douglas, Cin.*	.000	7	2	0	0	0	0	0	0	0	0	0	0	
Cardenal, Jose, Phil.	.249	87	201	27	50	74	12	0	4	33	0	2	2	
Carlton, Steven, Phil.*	.291	34	86	7	25	30	3	1	0	13	3	1	0	
Carroll, Clay, Pitt.	---	2	0	0	0	0	0	0	0	0	0	0	0	
Carter, Gary, Mtl.	.255	157	533	76	136	225	27	1	20	72	2	5	10	
Cash, David, Mtl.	.252	159	658	66	166	207	26	3	3	43	5	3	12	
Castillo, Anthony, S.D.	.125	5	8	0	1	1	0	0	0	1	1	0	0	
Castillo, Robert, L.A.	.000	18	7	0	0	0	0	0	0	0	0	0	0	
Cedeno, Cesar, Hou.	.281	50	192	31	54	87	8	2	7	23	0	0	23	
Cey, Ronald, L.A.	.270	159	555	84	150	251	32	0	23	84	2	7	2	
Champion, R. Michael, S.D.	.226	32	53	3	12	16	0	2	0	4	1	0	0	
Chaney, Darrell, Atl.#	.224	89	245	27	55	75	9	1	3	20	3	1	1	
Christenson, Larry, Phil.	.075	33	67	3	5	9	1	0	1	4	7	0	0	
Clark, Jack, S.F.	.306	156	592	90	181	318	46	8	25	98	3	9	15	
Clines, Eugene, Chi.	.258	109	229	31	59	73	10	2	2	17	2	1	4	
Collins, David, Cin.#	.216	102	102	13	22	23	1	0	0	7	1	2	7	
Coluccio, Robert, St.L.	.000	5	3	0	0	0	0	0	0	0	1	0	0	
Concepcion, David, Cin.	.301	153	565	75	170	229	33	4	6	67	3	4	23	10
Cornejo, N. Mardie, N.Y.	---	25	0	0	0	0	0	0	0	0	0	0	0	
Cornutt, Terry, S.F.	---	1	0	0	0	0	0	0	0	0	0	0	0	
Correll, Victor, Cin.	.238	52	105	9	25	35	7	0	1	6	2	0	0	
Cox, Larry, Chi.	.281	59	121	10	34	45	5	0	2	18	0	0	0	
Cromartie, Warren, Mtl.*	.297	159	607	77	180	254	32	6	10	56	2	6	8	
Cruz, Hector, Chi.-S.F.	.227	109	273	27	62	101	13	1	8	33	2	0	2	
Cruz, Jose, Hou.*	.315	153	565	79	178	260	34	9	10	83	2	3	37	
Cruz, Todd, Phil.	.500	3	4	0	2	2	0	0	0	0	0	0	1	
Curtis, John, S.F.*	.000	46	2	0	0	0	0	0	0	0	0	0	0	
D'Acquisto, John, S.D.	.190	45	21	1	4	5	1	0	0	0	1	0	0	
Davalillo, Victor, L.A.*	.312	75	77	15	24	30	1	1	1	11	0	1	2	
Davey, Michael, Atl.	---	3	0	0	0	0	0	0	0	0	0	0	0	
Davis, Robert, S.D.	.200	19	40	3	8	9	1	0	0	2	4	0	0	
Dawson, Andre, Mtl.	.253	157	609	84	154	269	24	8	25	72	4	5	28	
DeFreites, Arturo, Cin.	.211	9	19	1	4	8	1	0	1	2	1	0	0	
DeJesus, Ivan, Chi.	.278	160	619	104	172	219	24	7	3	35	15	2	41	
Denny, John, St.L.	.178	33	73	10	13	18	3	1	0	3	7	1	0	
Devine, P. Adrian, Atl.	.091	31	11	0	1	1	0	0	0	1	0	0	0	
Dineen, Kerry, Phil.*	.250	5	8	0	2	3	1	0	0	0	0	0	0	
Dixon, Thomas, Hou.	.100	30	40	0	4	4	0	0	0	0	6	0	0	
Dressler, Robert, St.L.	.000	3	3	0	0	0	0	0	0	0	0	0	0	
Driessen, Daniel, Cin.*	.250	153	524	68	131	208	23	3	16	70	3	6	28	
Drumright, Keith, Hou.*	.164	17	55	5	9	9	0	0	0	2	1	0	1	
Dues, Hal, Mtl.	.194	25	31	3	6	6	0	0	0	1	6	0	0	
Dumoulin, Daniel, Cin.	---	3	0	0	0	0	0	0	0	0	0	0	0	
Dwyer, James, St.L.-S.F.*	.223	107	238	30	53	87	12	2	6	26	3	2	7	
Dyer, Don, Pitt.	.211	58	175	7	37	47	8	1	0	13	2	1	2	
Easterly, James, Atl.*	.211	37	19	1	4	5	1	0	0	1	1	0	0	
Eastwick, Rawlins, Phil.	.000	22	3	0	0	0	0	0	0	0	0	0	0	
Eichelberger, Juan, S.D.	---	3	0	0	0	0	0	0	0	0	0	0	0	
Espinosa, Arnulfo, N.Y.	.209	32	67	6	14	17	3	0	0	4	7	0	0	
Evans, Barry, S.D.	.267	24	90	7	24	27	1	1	0	6	0	0	0	
Evans, Darrell, S.F.*	.243	159	547	82	133	221	24	0	20	78	6	10	4	
Falcone, Peter, St.L.*	.238	19	21	3	5	6	1	0	0	2	0	0	0	
Ferguson, Joe, Hou.-L.A.	.224	118	348	40	78	136	16	0	14	50	2	3	1	
Ferrer, Sergio, N.Y.#	.212	37	33	8	7	9	0	1	0	1	2	0	2	
Fingers, Roland, S.D.	.167	67	12	0	2	2	0	0	0	0	3	0	0	
Fischlin, Michael, Hou.	.276	11	29	8	8	10	0	1	0	1	0	0	0	
Flores, Gilberto, N.Y.	.272	86	261	30	71	90	9	0	3	27	5	3	3	
Flynn, R. Douglas, N.Y.	.237	156	532	37	126	154	12	8	0	36	6	3	3	
Foli, Timothy, N.Y.	.257	113	413	37	106	132	21	1	2	27	12	2	5	
Foote, Barry, Phil.	.158	39	57	4	9	12	0	0	1	4	0	0	0	
Forsch, Kenneth, Hou.	.185	52	27	1	5	5	0	0	0	3	3	0	0	
Forsch, Robert, St.L.	.181	34	83	2	15	25	7	0	1	8	5	0	0	
Forster, Terry, L.A.*	.500	47	8	1	4	5	1	0	0	2	1	0	0	
Foster, George, Cin.	.281	158	604	97	170	330	26	7	40	120	0	6	4	
Frazier, George, St.L.	.333	14	3	0	1	1	0	0	0	0	0	0	0	
Freed, Roger, St.L.	.239	52	92	3	22	34	6	0	0	20	0	1	1	
Fregosi, James, Pitt.	.200	20	20	3	4	5	1	0	0	2	0	0	0	
Fraislieben, David, S.D.	.000	12	6	0	0	0	0	0	0	0	0	0	0	
Frias, Jesus, Mtl.#	.267	73	15	5	4	8	2	1	0	1	0	0	0	
Fry, Jerry, Mtl.	.000	4	9	0	0	0	0	0	0	0	0	0	0	

Player & Club	PCT	G	AB	R	H	TB	2B	3B	HR	RBI	SH	SF	SB	CS
Fryman, Woodrow, Chi.-Mtl.	.060	32	50	1	3	5	2	0	0	2	5	1	0	0
Gamble, Oscar, S.D.*	.275	126	375	46	103	145	15	3	7	47	0	5	1	2
Garber, H. Eugene, Phil.-Atl.	.071	66	14	1	1	1	0	0	0	0	4	0	0	0
Gardner, Arthur, S.F.*	.000	7	3	2	0	0	0	0	0	0	0	0	0	0
Garman, Michael, L.A.-Mtl.	.000	57	5	0	0	0	0	0	0	0	1	0	0	0
Garner, Philip, Pitt.	.261	154	528	66	138	211	25	9	10	66	3	7	27	14
Garrett, R. Wayne, Mtl.-St.L.*	.250	82	132	17	33	43	4	0	2	12	0	0	1	0
Garvey, Steven, L.A.	.316	162	639	89	202	319	36	9	21	113	1	8	10	5
Gaston, Clarence, Atl.-Pitt.	.233	62	120	6	28	32	1	0	1	9	1	2	0	0
Geisel, J. David, Chi.*	.000	18	3	0	0	0	0	0	0	0	0	0	0	0
Geronimo, Cesar, Cin.*	.226	122	296	28	67	99	15	1	5	27	8	1	8	3
Gilbreath, Rodney, Atl.	.245	116	326	22	80	108	13	3	3	31	3	1	7	6
Gonzales, J. Fernando, Pitt.-S.D.	.246	110	341	29	84	105	11	2	2	29	7	5	4	4
Gonzales, Julio, Hou.	.233	78	223	24	52	60	3	1	1	16	7	0	6	1
Gonzalez, Orlando, Phil.*	.192	26	26	1	5	5	0	0	0	0	0	0	0	0
Gordon, Michael, Chi.#	.200	4	5	0	1	1	0	0	0	0	0	0	0	0
Grace, Michael, Cin.	.000	4	3	0	0	0	0	0	0	0	0	0	0	0
Grieve, Thomas, N.Y.	.208	54	101	5	21	30	3	0	2	8	0	0	0	1
Griffey, G. Kenneth, Cin.*	.288	158	614	90	177	256	33	8	10	63	9	3	23	5
Grimsley, Ross, Mtl.*	.144	36	90	5	13	14	1	0	0	4	11	1	0	0
Gross, Gregory, Chi.*	.265	124	347	34	92	121	12	7	1	39	3	7	3	1
Grote, Gerald, L.A.	.271	41	70	5	19	24	5	0	0	9	1	2	0	0
Guerrero, Pedro, L.A.*	.625	5	8	1	5	7	0	1	0	1	0	0	0	0
Gulden, Bradley, L.A.*	.000	3	4	0	0	0	0	0	0	0	0	0	0	0
Halicki, Edward, S.F.	.136	29	66	2	9	9	0	0	0	3	8	0	0	0
Hamilton, David, St.L.-Pitt.*	.000	29	7	0	0	0	0	0	0	0	1	0	0	0
Hanna, Preston, Atl.	.184	29	49	4	9	14	0	1	1	2	0	0	0	0
Hannahs, Gerald, L.A.*	—	1	0	0	0	0	0	0	0	0	0	0	0	0
Harrelson, Derrel, Phil.#	.214	71	103	16	22	23	1	0	0	9	6	0	5	2
Harris, Victor, S.F.#	.150	53	100	8	15	22	4	0	1	3	2	0	6	0
Hausman, Thomas, N.Y.	.176	10	17	1	3	4	1	0	0	1	3	0	0	0
Hebner, Richard, Phil.*	.283	137	435	61	123	202	22	3	17	71	4	4	4	7
Heintzelman, Thomas, S.F.#	.229	27	35	2	8	15	1	0	2	6	0	0	0	0
Henderson, Kenneth, N.Y.-Cin.#	.175	71	166	12	29	51	8	1	4	23	0	2	0	0
Henderson, Stephen, N.Y.	.266	157	587	83	156	234	30	9	10	65	0	5	13	7
Hendrick, George, S.D.-St.L.	.278	138	493	64	137	230	31	1	20	75	1	4	2	4
Hernandez, Enzo, L.A.	.000	4	3	0	0	0	0	0	0	0	0	0	0	0
Hernandez, Guillermo, Chi.*	.000	55	1	0	0	0	0	0	0	0	0	0	0	0
Hernandez, Keith, St.L.*	.255	159	542	90	138	211	32	4	11	64	1	6	13	5
Herndon, Larry, S.F.	.259	151	471	52	122	158	15	9	1	32	13	1	13	8
Herrmann, Hou.-Mtl.*	.143	35	76	2	11	13	2	0	0	3	1	0	0	0
Hill, Marc, S.F.	.243	117	358	20	87	113	15	1	3	36	2	0	1	2
Hodges, Ronald, N.Y.*	.255	47	102	4	26	32	4	1	0	7	0	2	1	2
Holdsworth, Fredrick, Mtl.	—	6	0	0	0	0	0	0	0	0	0	0	0	0
Holtzman, Kenneth, Chi.	.200	23	10	2	2	3	1	0	0	0	1	0	0	0
Hooton, Burt, L.A.	.149	32	67	4	10	11	1	0	0	2	18	0	0	0
Horner, J. Robert, Atl.	.266	89	323	50	86	174	17	1	23	63	1	9	0	0
Hough, Charles, L.A.	.333	55	12	1	4	5	1	0	0	2	3	0	0	0
Howard, Wilbur, Hou.#	.230	84	148	17	34	43	4	1	1	13	1	1	6	2
Howe, Arthur, Hou.	.293	119	420	46	123	183	33	3	7	55	1	5	2	3
Hubbard, Glenn, Atl.	.258	44	163	15	42	52	4	0	2	13	6	0	2	1
Hume, Thomas, Cin.	.067	43	45	2	3	3	0	0	0	3	5	0	0	0
Hutton, Thomas, Mtl.*	.203	39	59	4	12	15	3	0	0	5	0	0	0	0
Iorg, Dane, St.L.*	.271	35	85	6	23	29	4	1	0	4	0	1	0	0
Ivie, Michael, S.D.	.308	117	318	34	98	151	14	3	11	55	2	3	3	0
Jackson, Grant, Pitt.*	.250	60	12	0	3	5	1	0	0	0	0	0	0	0
Jackson, Roy, N.Y.	.667	4	3	0	2	2	0	0	0	0	0	0	0	0
James, Philip, S.F.*	.095	41	21	5	2	3	1	0	0	0	3	1	0	1
James, Robert, Mtl.	—	4	0	0	0	0	0	0	0	0	0	0	0	0
John, Thomas, L.A.*	.121	33	66	2	8	10	1	0	0	6	12	0	0	0
Johnson, David, Phil.-Chi.	.232	68	138	19	32	49	3	1	4	20	0	1	0	0
Johnstone, John, Phil.*	.179	35	56	3	10	12	2	0	0	4	0	0	0	2
Jones, Odell, Pitt.	.000	3	1	0	0	0	0	0	0	0	0	0	0	0
Jones, Randall, S.D.	.183	38	82	6	15	16	1	0	0	4	6	1	0	0
Kaat, James, Phil.*	.146	26	48	4	7	8	1	0	0	4	6	1	0	0
Kelleher, Michael, Chi.	.253	68	95	8	24	25	1	0	0	6	4	1	1	0
Kennedy, Junior, Cin.	.255	89	157	22	40	46	2	2	0	11	1	0	4	1
Kennedy, Terrence, St.L.*	.172	10	29	0	5	5	0	0	0	2	0	0	0	0
Kingman, David, Chi.	.266	119	395	65	105	214	17	4	28	79	2	6	3	4
Kinney, Dennis, S.D.*	.000	7	1	0	0	0	0	0	0	0	0	0	0	0
Kison, Bruce, Pitt.	.138	28	29	2	4	10	0	0	2	1	1	0	0	0
Knepper, Robert, S.F.*	.063	36	79	2	5	7	2	0	0	5	8	0	0	0
Knight, C. Ray, Cin.	.200	83	65	7	13	19	3	0	1	4	0	0	0	0
Knowles, Darold, Mtl.*	.167	60	6	1	1	1	0	0	0	0	4	0	0	0
Kobel, Kevin, N.Y.	.160	32	25	3	4	5	1	0	0	2	4	0	0	0
Koosman, Jerry, N.Y.	.086	38	70	1	6	9	3	0	0	2	5	0	0	0
Kranepool, Edward, N.Y.*	.210	66	81	7	17	28	2	0	3	19	0	3	0	0
Krukow, Michael, Chi.	.244	27	45	4	11	16	5	0	0	3	3	1	0	0
LaCorte, Frank, Atl.	.000	2	4	0	0	0	0	0	0	0	1	0	0	0
LaCoss, Michael, Cin.	.067	17	30	3	2	3	1	0	0	1	6	0	0	0
Lacy, Leondaus, L.A.	.261	103	245	29	64	127	16	4	13	40	1	2	7	4
Lamp, Dennis, Chi.	.205	37	73	1	15	17	2	0	0	3	2	0	0	0
Landestoy, Rafael, Hou.#	.266	59	218	18	58	65	5	1	0	7	4	4	7	4
Larson, Daniel, Phil.	—	1	0	0	0	0	0	0	0	0	0	0	0	0
Lavelle, Gary, S.F.#	.067	67	15	1	1	1	0	0	0	1	3	0	0	0
Law, Rudy, L.A.*	.250	11	12	2	3	3	0	0	0	1	0	0	3	1
Lee, Mark, S.D.	.000	56	5	0	0	0	0	0	0	0	0	0	0	0
LeMaster, Johnnie, S.F.	.235	101	272	23	64	91	18	3	1	14	14	0	6	6
Lemongello, Mark, Hou.	.172	33	64	3	11	12	1	0	0	3	4	0	0	0
Lentine, James, St.L.	.182	8	11	1	2	2	0	0	0	2	0	0	0	0
Leon, Maximino, Atl.	—	6	0	0	0	0	0	0	0	0	0	0	0	0
Leonard, Jeffrey, Hou.	.385	8	26	2	10	12	0	1	0	4	0	0	1	0
Lerch, Randy, Phil.*	.250	36	60	11	15	27	3	0	3	8	3	0	0	0
Llewallyn, Dennis, L.A.	—	1	0	0	0	0	0	0	0	0	0	0	0	0
Littell, Mark, St.L.#	.000	72	7	0	0	0	0	0	0	0	0	0	0	0
Littlejohn, Dennis, S.F.*	.000	2	0	0	0	0	0	0	0	0	0	0	0	0
Lockwood, Claude, N.Y.	.182	57	11	1	2	5	0	0	1	1	1	0	0	0
Lois, Alberto, Pitt.	.250	3	4	0	1	1	0	0	0	0	0	0	0	0
Lolich, Michael, S.D.	.000	20	3	0	0	0	0	0	0	0	0	0	0	0
Lonborg, James, Phil.	.176	22	34	2	6	8	2	0	0	3	3	4	0	0
Lopes, David, L.A.	.278	151	587	93	163	247	25	4	17	58	6	1	45	4

Player & Club	PCT	G	AB	R	H	TB	2B	3B	HR	RBI	SH	SF	SB	CS
Lopes, Aurelio, St.L.	.214	25	14	0	3	3	0	0	0	0	2	0	0	0
Lum, Michael, Cin.*	.267	86	146	15	39	66	7	1	6	23	0	1	0	0
Luzinski, Gregory, Phil.	.265	155	540	85	143	284	32	2	35	101	0	4	8	7
Macha, Kenneth, Pitt.*	.212	29	52	5	11	14	1	1	0	5	0	1	0	0
Mackanin, Peter, Phil.	.250	9	8	0	2	2	0	0	0	1	0	0	0	0
Maddox, Elliott, N.Y.	.257	119	389	43	100	128	18	2	2	39	2	5	1	6
Maddox, Garry, Phil.	.288	155	598	62	172	245	34	3	11	68	3	3	33	9
Maddox, Jerry, Atl.	.214	7	14	1	3	3	0	0	0	1	0	0	0	0
Madlock, Bill, S.F.	.309	122	447	76	138	215	26	3	15	44	9	2	16	5
Mahler, Michael, Atl.*	.098	34	41	4	4	4	0	0	0	1	5	0	0	0
Martin, Jerry, Phil.	.271	128	266	40	72	120	13	4	9	36	0	3	9	5
Martinez, Silvio, St.L.	.170	22	47	4	8	10	2	0	0	5	6	0	0	0
Martinez, Teodoro, L.A.	.255	54	55	13	14	18	1	0	1	5	1	0	3	2
Matthews, Gary, Atl.	.285	129	474	75	135	219	20	5	18	62	1	4	8	7
May, David, Pitt.*	.000	5	4	0	0	0	0	0	0	0	0	0	0	0
May, Rudolph, Mtl.*	.143	27	42	2	6	8	2	0	0	3	7	0	0	0
Mazzilli, Lee, N.Y.#	.273	148	542	78	148	234	28	5	16	61	2	5	20	13
McBride, Arnold, Phil.*	.269	122	472	68	127	185	20	4	10	49	2	3	28	3
McCarver, J. Timothy, Phil.*	.247	90	146	18	36	50	9	1	1	14	0	4	2	2
McCovey, Willie, S.F.	.228	108	351	32	80	139	19	2	12	64	0	2	1	0
McEnaney, William, Pitt.*	—	6	0	0	0	0	0	0	0	0	0	0	0	0
McGlothen, Lynn, S.F.-Chi.*	.188	54	16	1	3	4	1	0	0	0	2	0	0	0
McGraw, Frank, Phil.	.000	55	4	0	0	0	0	0	0	0	0	0	0	0
McLaughlin, Michael, Hou.	.000	12	3	0	0	0	0	0	0	0	2	0	0	0
McWilliams, Larry, Atl.*	.063	15	32	1	2	4	0	1	0	1	4	0	0	0
Mejias, Samuel, Mtl.	.232	67	56	9	13	14	1	0	0	6	0	0	3	0
Mendoza, Mario, Pitt.	.218	57	55	5	12	16	1	0	1	3	2	0	3	1
Meoli, Rudolph, Chi.	.103	47	29	10	3	5	0	0	0	2	2	0	2	0
Metzger, Clarence, N.Y.	—	25	0	0	0	0	0	0	0	0	0	0	0	0
Metzger, Roger, Hou.-S.F.#	.246	120	358	28	88	102	10	2	0	23	9	2	8	1
Miller, Edward, Atl.*	.143	6	21	5	3	4	1	0	0	2	0	0	3	0
Miller, Randall, Mtl.	.000	5	1	0	0	0	0	0	0	0	0	0	0	0
Milner, John, Pitt.*	.271	108	295	39	80	115	17	0	6	38	0	4	5	0
Minton, Gregory, S.F.#	.000	11	1	0	0	0	0	0	0	0	2	0	0	0
Moffitt, Randall, S.F.	.143	70	7	0	1	1	0	0	0	0	1	0	0	0
Monday, Robert, L.A.*	.254	119	342	54	87	160	14	1	19	57	3	2	2	4
Montanez, Guillermo, N.Y.*	.256	159	609	66	156	239	32	0	17	96	0	9	9	4
Montefusco, John, S.F.	.057	37	70	2	4	5	1	0	0	9	0	0	1	0
Moore, Donnie, Chi.*	.267	71	15	2	4	5	1	0	0	4	1	0	0	0
Morales, Julio, St.L.	.239	130	457	44	109	156	19	8	4	46	2	6	4	4
Moreland, B. Keith, Phil.	.000	1	0	0	0	0	0	0	0	0	0	0	0	0
Moreno, Omar, Pitt.*	.235	155	515	95	121	156	15	7	2	33	17	5	71	22
Morgan, Joe, Cin.*	.236	132	441	68	104	170	27	0	13	75	0	11	19	5
Morrison, James, Phil.	.157	53	108	12	17	29	1	1	3	10	4	0	1	3
Moskau, Paul, Cin.	.204	29	49	6	10	16	3	0	1	11	2	0	0	0
Mota, Manuel, L.A.	.303	37	33	2	10	11	1	0	0	6	1	0	0	0
Humphrey, Jerry, St.L.#	.262	125	367	41	96	123	13	4	2	37	2	3	14	10
Mura, Stephen, S.D.	.000	5	1	0	0	0	0	0	0	0	2	0	0	0
Murcer, Bobby, Chi.	.281	146	499	66	140	201	22	0	9	64	0	6	14	5
Murphy, Dale, Atl.	.226	151	530	66	120	209	14	3	23	79	3	5	11	7
Murray, Dale, Cin.-N.Y.	.000	68	10	1	0	0	0	0	0	0	2	0	0	0
Myrick, Robert, N.Y.	.000	17	2	0	0	0	0	0	0	0	0	0	0	0
Nastu, Philip, S.F.*	.000	3	1	0	0	0	0	0	0	0	1	0	0	0
Nicosia, Steven, Pitt.	.000	3	5	0	0	0	0	0	0	0	0	0	0	0
Niekro, Joseph, Hou.	.138	36	65	6	9	9	0	0	0	5	9	0	0	0
Niekro, Philip, Atl.	.225	45	120	5	27	31	4	0	0	10	4	1	0	2
Nolan, Joseph, Atl.*	.230	95	213	22	49	74	7	3	4	22	1	0	3	2
Norman, Daniel, N.Y.	.266	19	64	7	17	31	0	1	4	10	0	1	1	0
Norman, Fredie, Cin.#	.140	36	50	3	7	7	0	0	0	3	6	0	0	0
North, William, L.A.#	.234	110	304	54	71	81	10	0	0	10	5	1	27	8
Oates, Johnny, L.A.*	.307	40	75	5	23	24	1	0	0	6	0	0	1	1
Oberkfell, Kenneth, St.L.*	.120	24	50	7	6	7	1	0	0	2	1	0	0	0
Obradovich, James, Hou.*	.176	10	17	3	3	5	0	1	0	2	0	0	0	0
O'Brien, Daniel, St.L.	.000	7	4	0	0	0	0	0	0	0	0	0	0	0
Oester, Ronald, Cin.#	.375	8	8	1	3	3	0	0	0	1	1	0	0	0
Office, Rowland, Atl.*	.250	146	404	40	101	143	13	1	9	40	6	3	8	6
Ontiveros, Steven, Chi.#	.243	82	276	34	67	92	14	4	1	22	1	5	0	2
Ott, N. Edward, Pitt.*	.269	112	379	49	102	155	18	4	9	38	1	3	4	1
Owchinko, Robert, S.D.*	.175	36	63	3	11	13	2	0	0	4	6	0	0	0
Paciorek, Thomas, Atl.	.333	5	9	2	3	3	0	0	0	0	0	0	0	0
Pagel, Karl, Chi.*	.000	2	2	0	0	0	0	0	0	0	0	0	0	0
Palmer, David, Mtl.	.000	5	1	0	0	0	0	0	0	0	0	0	0	0
Papi, Stanley, Mtl.	.230	67	152	15	35	46	11	0	0	11	2	1	0	0
Parker, David, Pitt.*	.334	148	581	102	194	340	32	12	30	117	0	2	20	7
Parrish, Larry, Mtl.	.277	144	520	68	144	236	39	4	15	70	5	1	2	3
Pentz, Eugene, Hou.	.000	10	1	0	0	0	0	0	0	0	0	0	0	0
Perez, Atanasio, Mtl.	.290	148	544	63	158	244	38	3	14	78	1	5	2	0
Perkins, Broderick, S.D.#	.240	62	217	14	52	74	14	1	2	33	2	3	4	0
Perry, Gaylord, S.D.	.092	37	87	5	8	12	1	0	0	3	13	0	0	0
Phillips, Michael, St.L.*	.268	76	164	14	44	57	8	1	1	28	0	7	0	0
Pina, Horacio, Phil.	.000	2	1	0	0	0	0	0	0	0	0	0	0	0
Pittle, Gerald, Mtl.	—	19	0	0	0	0	0	0	0	0	0	0	0	0
Plank, Edward, S.F.	—	5	0	0	0	0	0	0	0	0	0	0	0	0
Pocoroba, Biff, Atl.#	.242	92	289	21	70	96	8	0	6	34	3	4	0	3
Puhl, Terry, Hou.*	.289	149	585	87	169	215	25	6	3	35	3	7	32	14
Pujols, Luis, Hou.	.131	56	153	11	20	33	8	1	1	11	2	1	0	0
Putman, Eddy, Chi.	.200	17	25	2	5	9	0	0	0	5	0	0	0	0
Rader, David, Chi.*	.203	116	305	29	62	90	13	3	3	36	3	5	1	1
Ramos, Roberto, Mtl.	.000	2	4	0	0	0	0	0	0	0	0	0	0	0
Ramsey, Michael, St.L.#	.200	12	5	4	1	1	0	0	0	0	0	0	3	0
Randle, Leonard, N.Y.#	.233	132	437	53	102	140	16	8	2	35	2	4	14	11
Rasmussen, Eric, St.L.-S.D.	.141	37	64	1	9	10	1	0	0	2	10	0	0	0
Rau, Douglas, L.A.*	.143	30	63	3	9	10	1	0	0	5	13	0	0	0
Rautzhan, Clarence, L.A.	.000	43	4	0	0	0	0	0	0	0	3	0	0	0
Reece, Robert, Mtl.	.182	9	11	2	2	3	1	0	0	1	0	0	0	0
Reed, Ronald, Phil.	.000	64	6	0	0	0	0	0	0	0	0	0	0	0
Reitz, Kenneth, St.L.	.246	150	540	41	133	193	26	2	10	75	3	7	1	0
Reuschel, Paul, Chi.	.000	16	4	0	0	0	0	0	0	0	0	0	0	0
Reuschel, Ricky, Chi.	.137	35	73	5	10	12	2	0	0	4	10	1	1	0
Reuss, Jerry, Pitt.*	.185	23	27	1	5	7	2	0	0	2	4	0	0	0
Reynolds, Donald, S.D.	.253	57	87	8	22	24	2	0	0	10	0	1	0	1

Player & Club	PCT	G	AB	R	H	TB	2B	3B	HR	RBI	SH	SF	SB	CS
Rhoden, Richard, L.A.	.135	30	52	5	7	8	1	0	0	4	6	1	0	0
Riccelli, Frank, Hou.*	---	2	0	0	0	0	0	0	0	0	0	0	0	0
Richard, James, Hou.	.178	37	101	8	18	21	0	0	1	10	5	0	1	1
Richards, Eugene, S.D.*	.308	154	555	90	171	233	26	12	4	45	4	4	37	17
Roberts, David A., Chi.*	.327	37	52	4	17	26	3	0	2	7	3	0	0	0
Roberts, David V., S.D.	.216	54	97	7	21	30	4	1	1	7	2	0	0	0
Robinson, Don, Pitt.	.235	35	85	2	20	22	2	0	0	3	6	0	0	0
Robinson, William, Pitt.	.246	136	499	70	123	205	36	2	14	80	2	11	14	11
Rockett, Patrick, Atl.	.141	55	142	6	20	22	2	0	0	4	1	1	1	2
Rogers, Stephen, Mtl.	.113	30	71	2	8	8	0	0	0	3	8	0	0	0
Rooker, James, Pitt.	.161	32	56	2	9	13	2	1	0	5	1	1	2	0
Rose, Peter, Cin.#	.302	159	655	103	198	276	51	3	7	52	2	7	13	9
Royster, Jeron, Atl.	.259	140	529	67	137	176	17	8	2	35	8	4	27	17
Ruhle, Vernon, Hou.	.056	13	18	0	1	1	0	0	0	1	1	0	0	0
Ruiz, Manuel, Atl.	.283	18	46	3	13	16	3	0	0	2	0	0	0	0
Russell, William, L.A.	.286	155	625	72	179	228	32	4	3	46	12	3	10	6
Ruthven, Richard, Atl.-Phil.	.221	34	77	7	17	21	0	2	0	4	6	0	0	0
Sadek, Michael, S.F.	.239	40	109	15	26	35	3	0	2	9	1	0	1	0
Sambito, Joseph, Hou.*	.167	62	6	1	1	1	0	0	0	0	9	0	0	0
Sanderson, Scott, Mtl.	.105	10	19	0	2	2	0	0	0	0	2	0	0	0
Sanguillen, Manuel, Pitt.	.264	85	220	15	58	74	5	1	3	36	2	2	2	2
Sarmiento, Manuel, Cin.	.000	64	16	0	0	0	0	0	0	0	1	0	0	0
Saucier, Kevin, Phil.*	---	1	0	0	0	0	0	0	0	0	0	0	0	0
Schatzeder, Daniel, Mtl.*	.222	32	45	3	10	15	2	0	1	7	2	0	1	1
Schmidt, Michael, Phil.	.251	145	513	93	129	223	27	2	21	78	0	8	19	6
Schultz, C. Budd, St.L.	.200	62	5	1	1	3	1	0	0	2	0	0	0	0
Scott, Anthony, St.L.#	.228	96	219	28	50	62	5	2	1	14	0	2	5	6
Scott, Rodney, Chi.#	.282	78	227	41	64	71	5	1	0	15	7	0	27	10
Seaver, G. Thomas, Cin.	.122	36	74	5	9	10	1	0	0	4	13	0	0	0
Sember, Michael, Chi.	.333	9	3	2	1	1	0	0	0	0	0	0	0	0
Seoane, Manuel, Chi.	---	7	0	0	0	0	0	0	0	0	0	0	0	0
Sexton, Jimmy, Hou.	.206	88	141	17	29	42	3	2	2	6	1	0	16	2
Shirley, Robert, S.D.	.125	50	40	4	5	5	0	0	0	2	7	0	0	0
Siebert, Paul, N.Y.*	.000	27	1	0	0	0	0	0	0	0	1	0	0	0
Simmons, Ted, St.L.#	.287	152	516	71	148	264	40	5	22	80	0	8	1	1
Simpson, Joe, L.A.*	.400	11	5	1	2	2	0	0	0	1	0	0	0	0
Sizemore, Ted, Phil.	.219	108	351	38	77	89	12	0	0	25	4	5	8	1
Skok, Craig, Atl.	.250	43	8	1	2	3	1	0	0	0	0	0	0	0
Small, G. Henry, Atl.	.000	5	1	0	0	0	0	0	0	0	0	0	0	0
Smith, C. Reginald, L.A.#	.295	128	447	82	132	250	27	2	29	93	0	13	12	5
Smith, Lonnie, Phil.	.000	17	4	6	0	0	0	0	0	0	0	0	0	0
Smith, Osborne, S.D.#	.258	159	590	69	152	184	17	6	1	46	28	3	40	12
Solomon, Eddie, Atl.	.138	38	29	2	4	4	0	0	0	1	0	0	0	0
Soto, Mario, Cin.	.000	5	1	0	0	0	0	0	0	0	0	0	0	0
Speier, Chris, Mtl.	.251	150	501	47	126	165	18	3	5	51	2	6	1	1
Spillner, Daniel, S.D.	---	17	0	0	0	0	0	0	0	0	2	0	0	0
Spilman, W. Harry, Cin.*	.250	4	4	1	1	1	0	0	0	0	0	0	0	0
Stargell, Wilver, Pitt.*	.295	122	390	60	115	221	18	2	28	97	0	3	3	2
Stearns, John, N.Y.	.264	143	477	65	126	197	24	1	15	73	2	6	25	13
Stennett, Renaldo, Pitt.	.243	106	333	30	81	103	9	2	3	35	1	2	1	1
Stewart, David, L.A.	---	1	0	0	0	0	0	0	0	0	0	0	0	0
Summers, John, Cin.*	.257	13	35	4	9	14	2	0	1	3	0	0	1	0
Sutcliffe, Richard, L.A.*	---	2	0	0	0	0	0	0	0	0	0	0	0	0
Sutherland, Gary, St.L.	.167	10	6	1	1	1	0	0	0	0	0	0	0	0
Sutter, H. Bruce, Chi.	.077	64	13	1	1	1	0	0	0	0	4	0	0	0
Sutton, Donald, L.A.	.083	34	72	1	6	6	0	0	0	3	14	0	0	0
Swan, Craig, N.Y.	.154	29	65	2	10	10	0	0	0	8	0	0	0	0
Sweet, Richard, S.D.#	.221	88	226	15	50	61	8	0	1	11	4	1	1	4
Swisher, Steven, St.L.	.278	45	115	11	32	42	5	1	1	10	0	0	1	0
Tamargo, John, St.L.-S.F.#	.224	42	98	6	22	31	4	1	1	8	2	1	1	1
Taveras, Franklin, Pitt.	.278	157	654	81	182	231	31	9	0	38	12	2	46	25
Tekulve, Kenton, Pitt.	.095	91	21	1	2	2	0	0	0	0	8	0	0	0
Templeton, Garry, St.L.#	.280	155	647	82	181	244	31	3	2	47	2	3	34	11
Tenace, F. Gene, S.D.	.224	142	401	60	90	164	18	4	16	61	0	2	6	5
Theiss, Duane, Atl.	.000	3	1	0	0	0	0	0	0	0	0	0	0	0
Thomas, Derrel, S.D.#	.227	128	352	36	80	103	10	2	3	26	9	2	11	6
Thomas, Roy, St.L.	.250	16	4	0	1	1	0	0	0	1	0	0	0	0
Thompson, V. Scott, Chi.*	.417	19	36	7	15	18	3	0	0	2	0	0	1	0
Tomlin, David, Cin.*	.200	57	5	0	1	1	0	0	0	0	0	0	0	0
Trevino, Alejandro, N.Y.	.250	6	12	3	3	3	0	0	0	0	0	0	0	0
Trillo, J. Manuel, Chi.	.261	152	552	53	144	183	17	5	4	55	3	8	0	7
Turner, John, S.D.*	.280	106	225	28	63	98	9	1	8	37	0	1	6	4
Twitchell, Wayne, Mtl.	.083	33	24	0	2	2	0	0	0	1	5	0	0	0
Tyson, Michael, St.L.	.233	125	377	26	88	113	16	0	3	26	1	3	2	0
Unser, Delbert, Mtl.*	.196	120	179	16	35	46	5	0	2	15	1	1	2	0
Urrea, John, St.L.	.125	27	24	0	3	3	0	0	0	2	2	1	0	0
Vail, Michael, Chi.	.333	74	180	15	60	82	6	2	4	33	0	2	0	1
Valentine, Ellis, Mtl.	.289	151	570	75	165	279	35	2	25	76	0	5	13	8
Valentine, Robert, N.Y.	.269	69	160	17	43	53	7	0	1	18	6	2	1	1
Vuckovich, Peter, St.L.	.138	65	58	6	8	9	1	0	0	3	7	0	0	0
Walling, Dennis, Hou.*	.251	120	247	30	62	88	11	3	3	36	0	2	2	2
Wallis, H. Joe, Chi.#	.309	28	55	7	17	24	2	1	1	6	0	0	2	0
Warthen, Daniel, Hou.*	.400	4	5	1	2	2	0	0	0	0	0	0	0	0
Watson, Robert, Hou.	.289	139	461	51	133	208	25	4	14	79	0	11	3	1
Wehrmeister, David, S.D.	---	4	0	0	0	0	0	0	0	0	0	0	0	0
Welch, Robert, L.A.	.172	23	29	3	5	6	1	0	0	1	10	0	0	0
Werner, Donald, Cin.	.150	30	113	7	17	22	2	1	0	11	0	4	1	0
Whisenton, Larry, Atl.*	.188	6	16	1	3	4	1	0	0	2	0	0	1	0
White, Jerome, Mtl.-Chi.#	.267	77	146	24	39	48	6	0	1	10	1	2	5	5
White, Myron, L.A.*	.500	7	4	1	2	2	0	0	0	0	0	0	1	0
Whitfield, Terry, S.F.*	.289	149	488	70	141	195	20	2	10	32	17	3	5	11
Whitson, Eddie, Pitt.	.182	43	11	0	2	2	0	0	0	0	0	0	0	0
Wiley, Mark, S.D.	.000	4	2	0	0	0	0	0	0	0	0	0	0	0
Wilhelm, H. Joe, Chi.*	.368	10	19	2	7	9	2	0	0	4	1	0	0	0
Williams, Charles, S.F.	.000	25	5	1	0	0	0	0	0	0	0	0	0	0
Williams, Richard, Hou.	.000	5	1	0	0	0	0	0	0	0	0	0	0	0
Winfield, David, S.D.	.308	158	587	88	181	293	30	5	24	97	0	5	21	9
Yeager, Stephen, L.A.	.193	94	228	19	44	63	7	0	4	23	0	2	0	0
Youngblood, Joel, N.Y.	.252	113	266	40	67	116	12	8	7	30	1	3	6	0
Zachry, Patrick, N.Y.	.070	21	43	1	3	3	0	0	0	1	10	0	0	0
Zamora, Oscar, Hou.	.000	10	2	0	0	0	0	0	0	0	0	0	0	0

Pitching

INDIVIDUAL PITCHING LEADERS

Earned Run Average	:	2.43 Swan, N.Y.
Won & Lost Percentage	:	.778 Perry, S.D. (21-6)
Games Won	:	21 Perry, S.D.
Games Lost	:	18 Niekro, Atl.
Games	:	91 Tekulve, Pitt.
Games Started	:	42 Niekro, Atl.
Complete Games	:	22 Niekro, Atl.
Games Finished	:	65 Tekulve, Pitt.
Saves	:	37 Fingers, S.D.
Shutouts	:	6 Knepper, S.F.
Innings	:	334 Niekro, Atl.
Hits	:	295 Niekro, Atl.
Batsmen Faced	:	1391 Niekro, Atl.
Runs	:	129 Niekro, Atl.
Earned Runs	:	107 Niekro, Atl. & Espinosa, N.Y.
Home Runs	:	30 Carlton, Phil.
Sacrifice Hits	:	19 Ruthven, Atl.-Phil.
Sacrifice Flies	:	13 Lemongello, Hou.
Bases on Balls	:	141 Richard, Hou.
Intentional Bases on Balls	:	23 Murray, Cin.-N.Y.
Hit Batsmen	:	13 Niekro, Atl.
Strikeouts	:	303 Richard, Hou.
Wild Pitches	:	16 Richard, Hou.
Balks	:	7 Carlton, Christenson, Phil. & Moskau, Cin.
Games Won, Consecutive	:	10 Blue, S.F. June 10 - August 4
Games Lost, Consecutive	:	9 Hume, Cin. April 19 - July 4
		Forsch, St.L. July 5 - August 19
		Lockwood, N.Y. June 16 - September 4 (1g)

During the 1978 season 177 pitchers participated in regular season games.

Vida Blue made Giants pennant contenders with 18 victories.

PITCHERS' RECORDS

NATIONAL LEAGUE PITCHING AVERAGES
(Top Fifteen Qualifiers for Earned Run Leadership)

* Throws Lefthanded

Pitcher & Club	ERA	W	L	PCT	G	GS	CG	GF	SV	SHO	IP	H	BFP	R	ER	HR	SH	SF	TBB	IBB	HB	SO	WP	BK
Swan, Craig, N.Y.	2.43	9	6	.600	29	28	5	0	0	1	207	164	819	62	56	12	5	4	58	8	2	125	1	0
Rogers, Stephen, Mtl.	2.47	13	10	.565	30	29	11	1	1	1	219	186	871	64	60	12	11	3	64	5	2	126	1	1
Vuckovich, Peter, St.L.	2.55	12	12	.500	45	23	6	15	1	2	198	187	819	65	56	9	13	6	59	5	2	149	7	2
Knepper, Robert, S.F.*	2.63	17	11	.607	36	35	16	1	0	6	260	218	1062	85	76	10	11	9	85	11	4	147	6	0
Hooton, Burt, L.A.*	2.71	19	10	.655	32	32	10	0	0	6	236	196	942	74	71	17	9	9	61	4	0	104	3	0
Perry, Gaylord, S.D.	2.72	21	6	.778	37	37	5	0	0	4	261	241	1055	96	79	9	8	9	66	8	2	154	4	3
Blue, Vida, S.F.*	2.79	18	10	.643	35	35	9	0	0	0	258	233	1042	87	80	12	16	8	70	4	1	171	5	0
Carlton, Steven, Phil.*	2.84	16	13	.552	34	34	12	0	0	3	247	228	1006	91	78	30	10	3	63	7	3	161	3	7
Halicki, Edward, S.F.	2.85	9	10	.474	28	28	9	1	1	4	199	166	823	74	63	11	12	5	45	9	7	105	1	3
Seaver, G. Thomas, Cin.	2.87	16	14	.533	36	36	8	0	0	1	260	218	1075	97	83	26	13	12	89	11	6	226	6	1
Jones, Randall, S.D.*	2.88	13	14	.481	37	36	7	0	0	2	253	263	1058	104	81	6	17	9	64	20	1	71	4	2
Niekro, Philip, Atl.	2.88	19	18	.514	44	42	22	1	0	4	334	295	1391	129	107	16	13	6	102	5	13	248	11	3
Denny, John, St.L.	2.96	14	11	.560	33	33	11	0	0	2	234	200	936	81	77	17	8	3	74	4	10	103	8	4
Blyleven, Rikalbert, Pitt.	3.02	14	10	.583	34	34	11	0	0	3	244	217	1011	94	82	17	13	2	66	5	6	182	6	2
Grimsley, Ross, Mtl.*	3.05	20	11	.645	36	36	19	0	0	3	263	237	1068	103	89	17	16	8	67	6	2	84	4	2

ALL PITCHERS LISTED ALPHABETICALLY

Pitcher & Club	ERA	W	L	PCT	G	GS	CG	GF	SV	SHO	IP	H	BFP	R	ER	HR	SH	SF	TBB	IBB	HB	SO	WP	BK
Andujar, Joaquin, Hou.	3.41	5	7	.417	35	13	2	11	1	0	111	88	470	45	42	3	11	5	58	6	4	55	3	5
Atkinson, William, Mtl.	4.40	2	2	.500	29	0	0	14	3	0	45	45	204	23	22	5	4	2	28	4	2	32	0	0
Bahnsen, Stanley, Mtl.	3.84	2	5	.167	44	1	0	22	7	0	75	74	317	35	32	9	2	1	31	2	0	44	2	0
Bair, C. Douglas, Cin.	1.98	7	6	.538	70	0	0	56	28	0	100	87	416	23	22	6	6	3	38	8	0	91	7	2
Bannister, Floyd, Hou.*	4.83	3	9	.250	28	16	2	3	0	0	110	120	503	59	59	13	7	1	63	3	0	94	0	2
Barr, James, S.F.	3.53	8	11	.421	32	25	5	1	2	0	163	180	690	69	64	7	8	7	35	6	1	44	0	0
Berenguer, Juan, N.Y.	8.31	0	3	.000	5	3	0	1	0	0	13	17	65	12	12	1	2	0	11	0	1	8	0	2
Bernard, Dwight, N.Y.	4.31	1	4	.200	30	1	0	10	0	0	48	54	213	25	23	4	3	1	27	3	0	26	2	0

Pitcher & Club	ERA	W	L	PCT	G	GS	CG	GF	SV	SHO	IP	H	BFP	R	ER	HR	SH	SF	TBB	IBB	HB	SO	WP	BK
Bibby, James, Pitt.	3.53	8	7	.533	34	14	3	10	1	2	107	100	460	52	42	10	11	4	39	7	2	72	5	0
Blue, Vida, S.F.*	2.79	18	10	.643	35	35	9	0	0	4	258	233	1042	87	80	12	16	8	70	4	5	171	5	0
Blyleven, Rikalbert, Pitt.	3.02	14	10	.583	34	34	11	0	0	4	244	217	1011	94	82	17	13	2	66	5	6	182	6	1
Boggs, Thomas, Atl.	6.71	2	8	.200	16	12	0	2	0	0	59	80	283	46	44	8	6	2	26	5	3	21	3	1
Boitano, Danny, Phil.	0.00	0	0	---	1	0	0	1	0	0	1	0	4	0	0	0	0	0	1	0	0	0	0	0
Bonham, William, Cin.	3.54	11	5	.688	28	23	3	0	0	0	140	151	610	59	55	9	5	0	50	8	3	83	8	0
Borbon, Pedro, Cin.	5.00	8	2	.800	62	0	0	22	0	0	99	102	420	56	55	6	10	3	27	8	3	35	2	2
Bouton, James, Atl.	4.97	1	3	.250	5	5	0	0	0	0	29	25	129	18	16	4	0	1	21	1	5	10	0	2
Bruhert, Michael, N.Y.	4.77	4	11	.267	27	22	1	0	0	1	134	171	585	83	71	6	8	1	34	5	1	56	10	2
Bruno, Thomas, St.L.	1.98	4	3	.571	18	0	0	8	1	0	50	38	201	12	11	3	6	1	17	1	3	33	0	2
Brusstar, Warren, Phil.	2.33	3	6	.667	58	0	0	17	1	0	89	74	348	25	23	0	3	2	30	7	7	60	6	1
Burris, B. Ray, Chi.	4.75	7	13	.350	40	32	4	0	0	1	199	210	870	112	105	15	7	2	79	11	10	94	3	3
Camp, Rick, Atl.	3.77	7	4	.333	42	0	0	9	0	0	74	99	344	42	31	5	6	2	32	3	3	23	3	2
Campbell, David, Atl.	4.83	4	4	.500	53	0	0	35	1	0	69	67	321	39	37	10	6	2	11	12	3	45	3	3
Candelaria, John, Pitt.*	3.24	12	11	.522	34	34	12	1	0	1	189	191	796	73	68	15	8	2	49	6	5	94	0	3
Capilla, Douglas, Cin.*	9.82	0	1	.000	6	0	0	0	0	0	11	14	57	12	12	1	0	0	11	7	3	9	0	0
Carlton, Steven, Phil.*	2.84	16	13	.552	34	34	12	0	0	3	247	228	1006	91	78	30	10	5	63	7	3	161	7	7
Carroll, Clay, Pitt.	2.25	0	4	.000	2	0	0	0	0	0	4	2	17	1	1	2	0	0	3	0	0	0	0	1
Castillo, Robert, L.A.	3.97	0	0	---	18	0	0	7	0	0	34	28	159	19	15	1	2	3	33	7	0	30	0	0
Christenson, Larry, Phil.	3.24	13	14	.481	33	33	9	0	0	0	228	209	925	90	82	16	15	5	47	7	1	131	6	7
Cornejo, N. Mardie, N.Y.	2.43	4	2	.667	25	0	0	10	3	0	37	37	155	12	10	1	4	5	14	5	3	17	3	0
Cornutt, Terry, S.F.	0.00	0	3	.000	2	0	0	0	0	0	3	1	10	1	0	0	0	0	0	0	0	0	0	0
Curtis, John, S.F.*	3.71	4	3	.571	46	0	0	0	1	0	63	60	270	31	26	5	5	7	29	8	2	38	6	0
D'Acquisto, John, S.D.	2.13	4	11	.267	45	3	0	24	10	0	93	60	390	24	22	2	2	2	56	2	7	104	5	1
Davey, Michael, Atl.*	0.00	0	1	.000	3	0	0	0	0	0	3	1	13	0	0	0	0	0	1	0	0	0	4	0
Denny, John, St.L.	2.96	14	11	.560	33	33	11	0	0	0	234	200	936	81	77	13	9	7	74	4	6	103	8	4
Devine, P. Adrian, Atl.	5.95	5	4	.556	31	6	0	11	2	0	65	84	294	45	43	3	7	2	25	5	1	26	4	2
Dixon, Thomas, Hou.	3.99	7	11	.389	30	19	3	4	0	0	140	140	592	70	62	3	11	1	40	3	1	66	0	4
Dressler, Robert, St.L.	2.08	0	1	.000	13	0	0	5	2	0	13	12	49	3	3	0	0	0	4	1	0	4	0	0
Dues, Hal, Mtl.	2.36	5	6	.455	25	12	1	0	0	0	99	85	407	29	26	5	5	2	42	4	4	36	7	2
Dumoulin, Daniel, Cin.	1.80	1	0	1.000	3	0	0	1	0	0	5	7	23	1	1	2	0	0	3	1	1	2	2	0
Easterly, James, Atl.*	5.65	3	6	.333	37	6	0	8	0	0	78	91	356	52	49	9	2	2	45	6	2	42	1	0
Eastwick, Rawlins, Phil.	4.05	2	1	.667	22	0	0	10	0	0	40	31	170	21	18	5	2	2	18	2	0	14	0	0

Eichelberger, Juan, S.D.	12.00	0	0	---	3	0	0	1	0	0	3	4	17	4	4	0	0	0	2	0	0	2	0	1
Espinosa, Arnulfo, N.Y.	4.72	11	15	.423	32	32	6	0	0	1	204	230	888	117	107	24	13	8	75	10	3	76	0	3
Falcone, Peter, St.L.*	5.76	2	7	.222	19	14	0	2	0	0	75	94	352	52	48	9	4	3	48	2	2	28	8	0
Fingers, Roland, S.D.	2.52	6	13	.316	67	0	0	62	37	0	107	84	434	33	30	4	4	3	29	12	1	72	2	0
Forsch, Kenneth, Hou.	2.71	10	6	.625	52	6	4	28	7	2	133	136	562	44	40	2	11	5	37	13	1	71	2	0
Forsch, Robert, St.L.	3.69	11	17	.393	34	34	7	0	0	3	234	205	981	110	96	15	9	8	97	9	5	114	8	3
Forster, Terry, L.A.*	1.94	5	4	.556	47	0	0	40	22	0	65	56	266	19	14	2	3	0	23	4	0	46	2	1
Frazier, George, St.L.	4.09	0	3	.000	14	0	0	3	0	0	22	22	96	14	10	2	0	2	6	2	0	8	1	0
Freisleben, David, S.D.	6.00	0	3	.000	12	4	0	2	0	0	27	41	131	22	18	3	0	3	15	3	0	16	2	0
Fryman, Woodrow, Chi.-Mtl.*	4.20	7	11	.389	32	26	4	2	1	3	150	157	657	76	70	10	11	4	74	6	3	81	5	2
Garber, H. Eugene, Phil.-Atl. ..	2.15	6	5	.545	65	0	0	50	25	0	117	84	453	32	28	12	5	0	24	6	5	85	3	4
Garman, Michael, L.A.-Mtl.	4.38	4	7	.364	57	0	0	35	13	0	78	69	326	40	38	8	5	2	34	8	0	28	2	2
Geisel, J. David, Chi.*	4.30	1	0	1.000	18	1	0	4	0	0	23	27	109	12	11	0	1	0	11	4	0	15	1	0
Grimsley, Ross, Mtl.*	3.05	20	11	.645	36	36	19	0	0	3	263	237	1068	103	89	17	16	8	67	6	2	84	4	2
Halicki, Edward, S.F.	2.85	9	10	.474	29	28	9	1	1	4	199	166	819	74	63	11	12	3	45	9	7	105	1	3
Hamilton, David, St.L.-Pitt.* ..	4.50	0	2	.000	29	0	0	8	1	0	40	39	180	29	20	7	4	0	18	2	0	23	1	0
Hanna, Preston, Atl.	5.14	7	13	.350	29	28	0	1	0	0	140	132	637	89	80	10	8	7	93	5	3	90	11	2
Hannahs, Gerald, L.A.*	9.00	0	0	---	1	0	0	0	0	0	2	3	9	2	2	0	0	0	0	0	0	5	2	0
Hausman, Thomas, N.Y.	4.67	3	3	.500	10	10	0	0	0	0	52	58	216	28	27	6	2	2	9	1	1	16	0	2
Hernandez, Guillermo, Chi.*	3.75	8	2	.800	54	0	0	21	3	0	60	57	265	26	25	6	8	3	35	7	1	38	3	0
Holdsworth, Fredrick, Mtl.	7.00	0	0	---	6	0	0	2	0	0	9	16	50	10	7	3	0	0	8	3	0	3	0	0
Holtzman, Kenneth, Chi.*	6.11	0	3	.000	23	6	0	9	2	0	53	61	250	40	36	10	0	1	35	3	1	36	3	0
Hooton, Burt, L.A.	2.71	19	10	.655	32	32	10	0	0	3	236	196	942	74	71	17	9	4	61	4	0	104	3	0
Hough, Charles, L.A.	3.29	5	5	.500	55	0	0	31	7	0	93	69	390	38	34	6	0	0	48	4	5	66	6	0
Hume, Thomas, Cin.	4.14	8	11	.421	42	23	3	8	1	0	174	198	750	89	80	12	7	5	50	9	4	90	6	1
Jackson, Grant, Pitt.*	3.27	7	5	.583	60	0	0	25	5	0	77	89	346	32	28	5	9	5	32	9	1	45	2	1
Jackson, Roy, N.Y.	9.00	0	0	---	4	2	0	0	0	0	13	21	61	13	13	2	3	1	6	0	2	6	0	0
James, Robert, Mtl.	9.00	0	1	.000	4	1	0	2	0	0	4	4	19	4	4	1	0	0	4	0	0	3	1	0
John, Thomas, L.A.*	3.30	17	10	.630	33	30	7	3	1	0	213	230	912	95	78	11	4	2	53	7	5	124	6	1
Jones, Odell, Pitt.	2.00	2	0	1.000	3	1	0	1	0	0	9	7	38	3	2	0	0	0	4	0	0	10	0	0
Jones, Randall, S.D.*	2.88	13	14	.481	37	36	7	0	0	2	253	263	1058	104	81	6	17	9	64	20	0	71	4	2
Kaat, James, Phil.*	4.11	8	5	.615	26	24	2	0	0	1	140	150	586	67	64	9	6	7	32	6	5	48	5	0
Kinney, Dennis, S.D.*	6.43	0	1	.000	7	0	0	4	0	0	7	6	31	5	5	3	0	0	4	0	0	2	0	0
Kison, Bruce, Pitt.	3.19	6	6	.500	28	11	0	4	0	0	96	81	407	40	34	3	5	4	39	0	5	62	4	1
Knepper, Robert, S.F.*	2.63	17	11	.607	36	35	16	1	0	6	260	218	1062	85	76	10	11	9	85	11	4	147	6	0

Pitcher & Club	ERA	W	L	PCT	G	GS	CG	GF	SV	SHO	IP	H	BFP	R	ER	HR	SH	SF	TBB	IBB	HB	SO	WP	BK
Knowles, Darold, Mtl.*	2.38	3	3	.500	60	0	0	27	6	0	72	63	294	20	19	5	6	6	30	9	2	34	0	0
Kobel, Kevin, N.Y.*	2.92	5	6	.455	32	11	1	12	0	0	108	95	442	42	35	9	6	6	30	9	1	51	1	0
Koosman, Jerry, N.Y.*	3.75	3	15	.167	38	32	3	6	2	0	235	221	986	110	98	17	17	11	84	11	8	160	5	1
Krukow, Michael, Chi.	3.91	9	3	.750	38	20	3	3	0	0	138	125	582	62	60	11	6	4	53	4	6	81	1	0
LaCorte, Frank, Atl.	3.60	0	4	.000	2	2	0	0	0	0	15	9	56	6	6	1	0	1	4	1	0	7	1	0
LaCoss, Michael, Cin.	4.50	4	8	.333	16	15	2	0	0	1	96	104	420	56	48	5	9	1	46	8	0	31	2	1
Lamp, Dennis, Chi.	3.29	7	15	.318	37	36	6	0	0	3	224	221	928	96	82	16	3	6	56	8	1	73	2	1
Larson, Daniel, Phil.	9.00	0	0	---	1	0	0	1	0	0	1	1	5	1	1	0	0	0	0	0	0	2	0	0
Lavelle, Gary, S.F.*	3.31	13	10	.565	67	0	0	39	14	0	98	96	424	41	36	3	8	5	44	11	2	63	2	2
Lee, Mark, S.D.	3.28	5	1	.833	56	0	0	21	2	0	85	74	357	34	31	2	8	3	36	13	2	31	3	4
Lemongello, Mark, Hou.	3.94	9	14	.391	33	30	9	2	1	0	210	204	893	100	92	20	16	6	66	5	9	77	0	3
Leon, Maximino, Atl.	6.00	0	0	---	5	0	0	1	0	0	6	6	29	4	4	1	1	1	4	0	1	1	0	0
Lerch, Randy, Phil.*	3.96	11	8	.579	33	28	5	3	0	0	184	183	784	89	81	15	11	7	70	3	0	96	5	0
Lewallyn, Dennis, L.A.	0.00	0	0	---	1	0	0	0	0	0	2	2	8	0	0	0	0	0	0	0	0	0	0	0
Littell, Mark, St.L.	2.80	4	8	.333	72	0	0	51	11	0	106	80	447	38	33	8	6	5	59	16	4	130	9	1
Lockwood, Claude, N.Y.	3.56	7	13	.350	57	0	0	40	15	0	91	78	370	36	36	10	5	1	31	5	3	73	2	1
Lolich, Michael, S.D.*	1.54	2	1	.667	20	2	0	7	1	0	35	30	140	6	6	2	1	0	11	3	1	13	2	1
Lonborg, James, Phil.	5.21	4	10	.444	22	22	1	0	0	0	114	132	505	69	66	16	7	4	45	1	2	48	4	1
Lopez, Aurelio, St.L.	4.29	4	2	.667	25	4	1	4	0	0	65	52	279	35	31	7	6	3	32	6	1	46	5	0
Mahler, Michael, Atl.*	4.67	4	11	.267	34	21	3	0	0	0	135	130	596	82	70	16	9	6	66	6	7	92	12	2
Martinez, Silvio, St.L.	3.65	9	8	.529	22	22	5	0	0	0	138	114	586	65	56	11	5	7	71	7	5	45	3	0
May, Rudolph, Mtl.*	3.88	8	10	.444	27	23	4	1	0	0	144	141	613	73	62	15	9	4	42	6	1	87	1	5
McEnaney, William, Pitt.*	10.00	0	0	---	6	0	0	3	0	0	9	15	42	11	10	0	0	2	6	0	0	6	1	0
McGlothen, Lynn, S.F.-Chi.	3.29	5	7	.625	54	2	0	14	0	0	93	92	399	42	34	7	6	2	43	5	0	69	0	0
McGraw, Frank, Phil.*	3.20	3	5	.533	55	1	0	39	9	0	90	82	363	39	32	6	4	1	23	7	2	63	1	0
McLaughlin, Michael, Hou.	5.09	0	1	.000	12	1	0	0	0	0	23	30	116	17	13	2	1	0	16	2	2	10	1	0
McWilliams, Larry, Atl.*	2.82	9	3	.750	15	15	3	0	0	0	99	84	417	38	31	11	5	0	35	4	0	42	0	0
Mejias, Samuel, Mtl.		0	0	---																				
Metzger, Clarence, N.Y.	6.57	1	3	.250	25	0	0	11	0	0	37	48	180	28	27	4	5	3	22	7	0	21	1	0
Miller, Randall, Mtl.	10.29	0	1	.000	5	0	0	0	0	0	7	11	36	9	8	1	3	2	3	1	0	6	0	1
Minton, Gregory, S.F.	7.88	0	0	---	7	0	0	0	0	0	16	22	76	14	14	3	4	1	8	1	3	6	0	0
Moffitt, Randall, S.F.	3.29	2	1	.667	70	0	0	38	0	0	82	79	355	35	30	5	8	3	33	13	1	52	3	4
Montefusco, John, S.F.	3.80	11	9	.550	36	36	0	0	0	0	239	233	1003	110	101	25	12	6	68	6	4	177	3	3

Pitcher	ERA	W	L	PCT	G	IP	H	R	ER	BB	SO	TBF
Moore, Donnie, Chi.	4.11	9	7	.563	71	103	117	55	47	31	50	450
Moskau, Paul, Cin.	3.97	6	4	.600	25	145	139	65	64	57	88	611
Mura, Stephen, S.D.	11.25	0	2	.000	2	15	8	10	10	5	5	40
Murray, Dale, Cin.-N.Y.	3.78	9	6	.600	68	119	119	59	50	53	62	520
Myrick, Robert, N.Y.*	3.24	0	3	.000	17	25	18	5	9	5	13	102
Nastu, Philip, S.F.*	5.63	0	0	.000	3	8	8	5	5	5	5	33
Niekro, Joseph, Hou.	3.86	14	14	.500	35	203	190	97	87	73	97	861
Niekro, Philip, Atl.	2.88	19	18	.514	44	334	295	129	107	102	248	1391
Norman, Fredie, Cin.*	3.71	11	9	.550	36	177	173	86	73	82	111	777
O'Brien, Daniel, St.L.	4.50	0	2	.000	7	18	22	12	9	6	2	86
Owchinko, Robert, S.D.*	3.56	10	13	.435	36	202	198	87	80	78	94	851
Palmer, David, Mtl.	2.70	0	0	.000	10	10	12	4	3	2	7	39
Pentz, Eugene, Hou.	6.00	0	0	—		15	12	13	10	8	8	73
Perry, Gaylord, S.D.	2.72	21	6	.778	37	261	241	104	79	66	154	1055
Pina, Horacio, Phil.	0.00	0	0	.000		2	2			8	4	5
Pirtle, Gerald, Mtl.	5.88	0	0	—	19	26	33	24	17	23	14	134
Plank, Edward, S.F.	3.86	0	0	.000		7	7	3	3	2	1	25
Rasmussen, Eric, St.L.-S.D.	4.09	14	15	.483	37	207	215	104	94	63	91	868
Rau, Douglas, L.A.*	3.26	15	9	.625	30	199	219	82	72	68	95	859
Rautzhan, Clarence, L.A.*	2.95	2	1	.667	43	61	61	27	20	19	25	258
Reed, Ronald, Phil.	2.23	3	4	.429	66	109	87	32	27	23	85	425
Reuschel, Paul, Chi.	5.14	2	2	1.000	35	28	29	16	16	13	13	122
Reuschel, Ricky, Chi.	3.41	14	15	.483	35	243	235	98	92	54	115	1006
Reuss, Jerry, Pitt.*	4.88	3	2	.600	23	83	97	48	45	23	42	361
Rhoden, Richard, L.A.	3.65	10	8	.556	30	165	160	77	67	51	79	698
Riccelli, Frank, Hou.*	0.00	0	0	—		3	1				2	10
Richard, James, Hou.	3.11	18	11	.621	36	275	192	104	95	141	303	1139
Roberts, David, Chi.*	5.26	6	8	.429	35	142	159	87	83	56	54	627
Robinson, Don, Pitt.	3.47	14	6	.700	35	228	203	98	88	57	135	937
Rogers, Stephen, Mtl.	2.47	13	10	.565	29	219	186	64	60	64	126	871
Rooker, James, Pitt.*	4.25	9	11	.450	28	163	160	94	77	81	76	717
Ruhle, Vernon, Hou.	2.12	3	3	.500	13	68	57	17	16	20	27	279
Ruthven, Richard, Atl.-Phil.	3.38	15	11	.577	33	232	214	95	87	56	120	937
Sambito, Joseph, Hou.*	3.07	4	9	.308	62	88	85	32	32	32	96	371
Sanderson, Scott, Mtl.	2.51	4	2	.667	10	61	52	20	17	21	50	251

Pitcher & Club	ERA	W	L	PCT	G	GS	CG	GF	SV	SHO	IP	H	BFP	R	ER	HR	SH	SF	TBB	IBB	HB	SO	WP	BK
Sarmiento, Manuel, Cin.	4.39	9	7	.563	63	4	0	27	5	0	127	109	538	65	62	16	9	8	54	10	1	72	1	1
Saucier, Kevin, Phil.*	18.00	0	0	.000	2	0	0	1	0	0	2	4	12	4	4	0	0	0	2	1	0	2	0	1
Schatzeder, Daniel, Mtl.*	3.06	7	7	.500	29	18	2	2	1	0	144	108	586	54	49	10	5	4	68	5	2	69	4	3
Schultz, C. Budd, St.L.*	3.80	2	4	.333	62	0	0	32	6	0	83	68	343	36	35	6	2	4	36	6	0	70	2	0
Seaver, G. Thomas, Cin.	2.87	16	14	.533	36	36	8	0	0	1	260	218	1075	97	83	26	13	12	89	11	2	226	6	1
Seoane, Manuel, Chi.	5.63	1	0	1.000	7	1	0	2	0	0	8	11	43	6	5	0	0	0	6	2	0	5	1	0
Shirley, Robert, S.D.*	3.69	8	11	.421	50	20	2	10	5	0	166	164	708	75	68	10	12	5	61	11	3	102	3	1
Siebert, Paul, N.Y.*	5.14	0	2	.000	27	0	0	5	1	0	28	30	130	18	16	2	2	1	21	5	1	12	2	1
Skok, Craig, Atl.*	4.35	3	2	.600	43	0	0	11	2	0	62	64	273	38	30	8	4	2	27	8	1	28	4	1
Solomon, Eddie, Atl.	4.08	4	6	.400	37	8	0	13	0	0	106	98	459	52	48	12	12	1	50	11	2	64	5	1
Soto, Mario, Cin.	2.50	1	0	1.000	5	1	0	1	0	0	18	13	79	5	5	1	2	0	13	3	1	13	0	0
Spillner, Daniel, S.D.	4.50	0	1	.000	17	0	0	4	0	0	26	32	110	15	13	0	1	1	7	1	0	16	0	0
Stewart, David, L.A.	0.00	0	0	---	2	0	0	1	0	0	2	2	6	0	0	0	0	0	0	0	0	1	0	0
Sutcliffe, Richard, L.A.	0.00	0	0	---	2	0	0	0	0	0	2	2	9	4	0	0	1	0	1	0	0	0	0	0
Sutter, H. Bruce, Chi.	3.18	8	10	.444	64	0	0	47	27	0	99	82	414	44	35	10	3	4	34	7	1	106	8	1
Sutton, Donald, L.A.	3.55	15	11	.577	34	34	12	0	0	2	238	228	990	109	94	29	14	4	54	7	5	154	6	0
Swan, Craig, N.Y.	2.43	9	6	.600	29	28	5	0	0	1	207	164	819	62	56	12	5	8	58	8	2	125	4	0
Tekulve, Kenton, Pitt.	2.33	8	7	.533	91	0	0	65	31	0	135	115	573	44	35	7	7	4	55	18	2	77	5	0
Theiss, Duane, Atl.	1.50	0	1	.000	3	0	0	2	0	0	6	6	24	1	1	0	1	0	4	0	0	3	0	0
Thomas, Roy, St.L.	3.86	1	1	.500	16	0	0	7	3	0	28	21	120	14	12	0	0	1	16	3	0	16	3	2
Tomlin, David, Cin.*	5.81	9	1	.900	57	0	0	23	4	0	62	88	309	54	40	3	4	6	30	7	1	32	1	1
Twitchell, Wayne, Mtl	5.38	4	12	.250	31	15	0	3	0	0	112	121	510	67	67	16	4	2	71	5	4	69	11	1
Urrea, John, St.L.	5.36	4	9	.308	27	12	1	6	0	0	99	108	445	75	59	9	6	1	47	4	7	61	5	1
Vuckovich, Peter, St.L.	2.55	12	12	.500	45	23	6	15	1	2	198	187	819	65	56	13	6	6	59	5	2	149	7	2
Warthen, Daniel, Hou.*	4.09	0	0	---	5	0	0	3	0	0	11	10	43	5	5	0	0	0	5	0	0	2	0	0
Wehrmeister, David, S.D.	6.43	1	0	1.000	23	0	0	6	0	0	7	8	35	5	5	3	0	0	5	0	1	2	2	0
Welch, Robert, L.A.	2.03	7	4	.636	23	13	0	4	0	3	111	92	439	28	25	6	6	6	26	2	1	66	2	0
Whitson, Eddie, Pitt.	3.28	5	6	.455	43	0	0	14	6	0	74	66	318	31	27	5	3	1	37	11	1	64	2	0
Wiley, Mark, S.D.	5.63	1	0	1.000	6	0	0	3	0	0	8	11	35	5	5	0	3	0	6	1	0	1	0	0
Williams, Charles, S.F.	5.44	1	3	.250	25	1	0	9	0	0	48	60	225	31	29	5	5	1	28	6	2	22	3	2
Williams, Richard, Hou.	4.63	1	2	.333	17	1	0	5	0	0	35	43	159	19	18	9	6	0	10	2	1	17	2	3
Zachry, Patrick, N.Y.	3.33	10	6	.625	21	21	5	0	0	2	138	120	580	57	51	9	4	6	57	3	1	78	3	1
Zamora, Oscar, Hou.	7.20	0	0	---	10	0	0	1	0	0	15	20	69	12	12	2	2	0	7	1	0	6	0	1

Kent Tekulve kept Bucs in pennant race with 31 saves.

SCORERS continued from page 45

cause a ground ball Darwin had punched down the third base line had been ruled a hit rather than an error.

"I want to talk to you about that ball Darwin hit," Jenkins began angrily.

"Which one?" inquired official scorer Bob Fowler.

"The one hit down the third base line," replied Jenkins.

"Well," said Fowler, who knew he would soon have to write a story about that day's game for his newspaper, "while I've got you on the phone, I'd like to talk about the one that landed in the left field seats."

When all else fails, players have been known to blame their own teammates rather than admit they may have made a mistake.

Back in the days when the Braves called Milwaukee their home, pitcher Denny Lemaster phoned the official scorer and ripped his own third baseman, future Hall of Famer Eddie Mathews, because Mathews had booted a ball Lemaster thought should have been caught. Bristled Lemaster, "A good third baseman makes that play."

The abuse official scorers are forced to endure doesn't always come from players, though. Visiting writers and radio broadcasters have been known to scream and curse when a close call goes against their club. A throng of angry Boston fans, upset because Ted Williams wasn't given a hit on a fly ball, once invaded the Fenway Park press box and assaulted the first sportswriter they encountered.

More recently, the Red Sox were playing in Minnesota one day when good-field, no-hit Doug Griffin, who had knocked out four hits in his first four at-bats, hit a ground ball to second that the fielder booted.

"It was a 50-50 call," recalled the scorer, Bob Fowler. "It could have gone either way. I ruled it E-4, error on the second baseman.

"Immediately the whole Boston press corps jumped up, pencils flying, and began screaming, 'How could you give him an error on that?'

" 'It was a 50-50 call,' I explained.

" 'Well, then give him a hit!' they screamed.

" 'Why?' I asked.

" 'Because,' they replied, 'it makes a better story if he's 5-for-5 than if he's 4-for-5.' "

One of the oddest official scorer's controversies involved Ty Cobb in August, 1922. During a game played in the rain between the Tigers and Yankees at the Polo Grounds (the Yanks' last year on Coogan's Bluff), Cobb hit a grounder to Yankee shortstop Everett Scott. Scott kicked and fumbled the ball, then had trouble picking it up off the wet field.

Most of the sportswriters, including official scorer Jack Kieran, had left the open-air press box to take cover in the grandstand. But Fred Lieb of the *New York Press* stayed behind because he was handling the play-by-play for his paper and the box score for the Associated Press.

Had Kieran stayed behind, Lieb would have asked him how he scored the play. But with Kieran gone, Lieb decided to give the speedy Cobb a hit. That showed up in the box score. But in the official report Kieran charged Scott with an error.

No one was aware of the discrepancy until the end of the season when the Associated Press listed Cobb's average at .401 and the league's official scorer, Irwin Howe, showed Cobb batting at .399.

After it was determined what had happened, Howe decided that since Lieb was more experienced, his judgment of the play should overrule the decision of official scorer Kieran. American League president Ben Johnson sided with Howe, arguing that a Cobb at .400 for the third time would prove the American League superior to the National League.

In the book, "No Cheering in the Press Box," Lieb recalled: "I was president of the baseball writers that year. We voted in favor of Cobb's .399 and in favor of Kieran's decision. We said if Cobb was listed at .401 in the record books, then they should place an asterisk after it saying 'Not recognized by the Baseball Writers Association.'"

But to this day, Ty Cobb batted .401 in 1922.

Scorers are more vulnerable to second-guessing and criticism when their decisions affect a no-hitter. Johnny Vander Meer can thank Fred Lieb for his place in baseball history. On Sept. 11, 1923, the Boston Red Sox' Howard Ehmke took the mound against the Yankees in the Stadium after pitching a no-hitter against the Philadelphia Athletics in his previous start. First man up, Whitey Witt, hit a sharp grounder at third baseman Howard Shanks. The ball seemed to bounce just right, but it hit Shanks in the chest and rolled toward second base. Before Shanks could get to the ball, Witt had reached first base.

Lieb ruled a hit on the play. "I took into consideration that Shanks, an outfielder by trade, had played the ball clumsily, but also that Witt, a left-handed batsman, was a streak of lightning going down to first," Lieb said afterwards.

Ehmke turned away the rest of the strong Yankee lineup without a hit. The fans mobbed him after the game, assuming they had seen Ehmke's second straight no-hitter. Then they discovered that Lieb had credited Witt with a hit.

An appeal to American League president Johnson to reverse Lieb's ruling was turned down even though umpire Tommy Connally said, "I saw it perfectly and it was an error."

Virgil Trucks of the Detroit Tigers earned his second no-hitter of the 1952 season against the Yankees in the Stadium, but he did it with the help of a rare, late-inning reversal by official scorer John Drebinger of *The New York Times*.

In the third inning, the Yankees' Phil Rizzuto sent a bouncer down to shortstop Johnny Pesky, who fielded it but juggled the ball. He made a late, low throw. Drebinger ruled error, but quickly changed it to "hit," saying the ball had struck in the webbing of Pesky's glove.

Other writers in the press box disagreed. Drebinger received so much heat from his colleagues that in the seventh inning he put a call through to Pesky in the dugout.

"I messed it up," Pesky told the scorer.

So Drebinger reversed his decision. And Trucks set down Billy Martin, Johnny Mize and Irv Noren in the eighth, and Mickey Mantle, Joe Collins and Hank Bauer in the ninth to complete his no-hitter.

Such is the life of the official scorers, practitioners of what is truly one of the world's oldest professions.

With one exception, major league baseball's official scorers are all sportswriters, assigned by their newspapers to cover the very teams on which they must pass judgment. The one exception, in Milwaukee, is a retired sportswriter.

To be eligible, a writer must have covered big league baseball on a regular basis (100 games a year) for at least three years —although that rule is frequently ignored because a growing number of newspapers do not allow their baseball writers to moonlight as official scorers, claiming it is a conflict of interest.

Since the scorers are paid by the two leagues, newspaper executives argue that their writers may be reluctant to criticize the sport. And because the writers will inevitably wrangle with players who object to their decisions, it is thought by some that they jeopardize their ability to thoroughly and objectively cover their assignments.

After all, New York writers score only in New York. Los Angeles writers score only in Los Angeles. Boston writers score only in Boston. So obviously a scorer's decisions, right or wrong, most often affect those players he is expected to cover every day.

With that in mind, all the major dailies in Atlanta, Milwau-